Oceans
OF US

VANESSA LUISA

Oceans of Us: A Novel
Copyright © 2021-2022 by Vanessa Luisa
Published by VL Publishing.

Oceans of Us:
Cover Design: ©Bailey Cover Boutique
Editor: Emily A. Lawrence, www.lawrenceediting.com
Proofreader: Emily A. Lawrence, Gemma Woolley
Formatter: Champagne Book Design

ISBN: 978-0-6450535-2-4

He's Italian, older, a gorgeous tattooed Harley lover... and the one man I can never have.

From the moment Saint Lisconti moved in next door and recklessly stepped all over my favorite rare tiger lilies, it's been war between us. Now, three years after our first encounter, hate simmers down, giving way to heated stolen glances that leave me drowning in his piercing ocean blue eyes.

Our attraction blooms. Sparks I crave to unravel fly. Everything changes.

Saint becomes my savior. The reason I find poetic beauty in life. He's thirty-six, burdened by the scars from his past I so desperately want to heal. I'm eighteen, a good girl, but no matter how many times Saint warns me away, I find myself breaking all the rules for a taste of the forbidden.

Because Saint isn't just a guarded bad boy... he's also my father's best friend.

And when he agrees to wanting more, all bets are off.

But as I fall deeper, our love may be the very thing that breaks us when fate twists with our plans...

Or will it?

This one is for everyone who has been strong for too long.
Who just need somebody to wrap you in the solace of their arms when
the world feels like it's caving in. Who need them to hold you tight,
brush your hair behind your ear, and softly murmur, "I've got you
and everything is going to be okay... I promise." Let this be hope...
hope that one day soon your agony will turn into beautiful poetic
warmth... just like it did for Paisley and Saint.

And to Mamma, Nonna, and Nonno,
My love for you all is infinite.

"He was her dark fairytale, she was his twisted fantasy and together they made magic."

F. SCOTT FITZGERALD

"Here's looking at you, kid."

HUMPHREY BOGART
(*Casablanca*)

Playlist

"Luz"—Rubio, Carlos Cabezas
"Unholy"—Santino Le Saint
"Love Me"—Adrian Daniel
"Are You With Me"—nilu
"Untitled (How Does It Feel)"—Matt Bomer
"WHO"—BRIDGE
"Everyone Changes"—Kodaline, Gabrielle Aplin
"In The Dark"—Matt Woods
"Oceans"—Seafret
"Him. Her."—James Gillespie
"Holy Ghost (feat. Jon Harvey [Monster Truck])"—The Picturebooks, Jon Harvey, Monster Truck
"The War"—SYML
"Saint"—Izan Denver
"Bold"—Faith Richards
"Et Tu?"—Aaryan Shah
"Devil Knows"—Armen Paul
"Shallow"—Lady Gaga, Bradley Cooper
"Alibi"—Bradley Cooper
"Take it eazy"—Tom Harmon
"I WANNA BE YOUR SLAVE"—Måneskin
"Saints"—Echos
"Dressed in White"—TS Graye
"Always Remember Us This Way"—Lady Gaga
"Sex and Candy"—Alexander Jean
"Rebels & Outlaws"—Everybody Loves an Outlaw
"Wonderful Life"—Smith & Burrows
"Mirror"—SoMo
"Red Desert"—5 Seconds of Summer
"Wicked Little Monster"—Veda
"Forever In My Mind"—LiLucifer
"Wait For You (feat. Zoe Wees)"—Tom Walker, Zoe Wees
"Your Song"—Elton John
"With or Without You"—U2

Oceans
OF US

Preface

Paisley

PRESENT DAY…

I N A PERFECT WORLD, IT COULD BE HIM AND ME UNTIL THE VERY END. But this isn't a perfect world…

It's far from it.

After all, he's whiskey, tobacco, and speeding Harleys. I'm green tea, poetry, and twirling flowers. To the naked eye, we would be beautifully incomplete if up until this point life had gone our way. But we were never that—*beautifully incomplete*—we're the opposite.

Saint Lisconti is wholeheartedly the best thing that ever happened to me.

Our newfound spark…

Our emotional connection…

The heated stolen glances we share…

It's all like a fairy tale and he's my very own forbidden desire

But Saint isn't a prince. He could never be. And although I'm a good girl, one to follow the rules, he's always enticed me. Halfway through hate, I fell in love, and now we're two broken souls mending each other's flaws, but love isn't supposed to hurt this deep.

Saint was never supposed to be anything more than the bad boy next door. My father's best friend. A man eighteen years older than me. Someone I can *never* have. Instead, as the years progressed, he's become my entire life...

My every single thought.

My every single second.

My every single breath.

They are his. *All his.*

Until I'm drowning in the oceans of us...

Chapter
ONE

Paisley

PAST

Three Years Prior…
Paisley is 15. Saint is 33.

"Hᴇ ᴅɪᴅ ɪᴛ ᴀɢᴀɪɴ! Hᴇ ᴘᴜᴛ ʜɪs ʙɪɢ ᴏʟ' ꜰᴇᴇᴛ ᴀʟʟ ᴏᴠᴇʀ ᴍʏ ʟɪʟɪᴇs!" I grit, stepping closer to my house's front-facing window to witness the devil at work. My fists clench until my nails threaten to puncture the thick skin. *Damn him!*

"Just let it go, Paisley." My father sighs from the couch. He's typing away on his phone with zero to no interest in my preoccupation. "Besides, you can barely see that the lilies are there."

"But they're in bloom! They'll never grow now!"

"Let it go, sweetheart."

Let it go.

Let it go.

Let it go.

No, I can't *let it* go! I can't just stand here and do nothing! I need to do something. Run out and tell him to be a little more careful at least. *Nana would want me to say something...*

Yes, that's it.

Nana. I'm going to go outside and do this for her.

I stare through the shutters a little longer, observing the three men unloading various furniture items from a white hire truck. Due to the shiny black metal Harley Davidson parked in front of the new house next door, the truck is parked in front of mine.

The men bypass one another with little conversation, each effortlessly carrying items diagonally across the parking strip into the house on my left. My heart thumps to the untuned rhythm of their leather boots violently stomping all over my rare blue tiger lilies, crushing them to get through.

How RUDE!

Two of the men work around the delicate flowers, but not this one particular guy. He's the tallest and most handsomely mysterious of them all. It's almost as if he's doing it on purpose. *Darn it!* My gaze stays on his six-foot-two frame, taking in his beautifully tousled dark hair and perfectly chiseled jaw. He's easily the most attractive man I've seen in my fifteen years of living. But there's something about him—almost a glowing dangerous aura—that has me staring longer, deeper, harder. And that lethal crooked smirk he flashes one of the men he bypasses after saying something only confirms it.

He sports a leather jacket, except he's shirtless underneath, wearing nothing but black jeans and a fancy chestnut belt. As he pulls a walnut bookshelf from the truck—not that he looks like someone who would read—the hot summer Californian sun illumines his naturally tanned olive skin, bronzing his glistering washboard abdominal muscles and vaunted V-line. I'm almost certain that leather jacket is hiding some ink.

I'm so blinded by the godly sight, my cheeks flush, and for

a moment I forget about the lilies… until he sets the bookshelf right on top of them and finishes massacring them all!

It's as if he doesn't notice or care. I hear shouting from a blind spot to the left and he looks up, nods, and proceeds to leave the bookshelf right there on the parking strip. Then, he jogs out of sight.

"Oh my God! Dad, come look at this!"

"It's your summer break, sweetie, enjoy it instead of stalking the new neighbors!"

"It's not stalking if it's looking out for what's mine."

"Yeah, that's what Ted Bundy said, and we all know how that ended up."

Dramatically rolling my eyes, I ignore my father completely and hurry to the hallway. I don't bother announcing my plans or kicking off my fluffy pink slippers before I rush to unlock the front door.

I'm out of the house in seconds, bolting to the parking strip in an attempt to pull the bookshelf away. But after countless efforts, it's no use. I don't have muscles, not like *him*.

"Hands off what's not yours, kiddo."

My body tenses at the harsh voice and I glance up, raising a hand to my brow to shield the sun's glare, but find myself squinting just the same. There's a man standing beside the truck with his arms crossed over his chest. Cocking his head to the side, his brows rise in challenge at my lack of response.

While the other two men looked in their early to mid-thirties, this man seems older but intimidating just the same with a lethal stare, perfectly styled hair, and a white scar just above his upper lip.

"Lost something, kiddo?"

"No." I gulp, taking a step back when the corners of his lips rise in a cold, sly smirk.

"Then get outta here. This ain't the place for little kids."

"But I live right next door and saw that my lilies are getting ruined!"

The man scoffs and gestures toward the house to my left—*the new house.* "From now on, that's where my good friend lives. Don't like something he does? Learn to live with it."

And then, just like that, the man rounds the truck, gets in the driver's side, and takes off down the street. My mouth remains hung open, left to simply witness the truck get smaller and smaller until it transforms into a distant shape of white nothingness.

"So rude!" I utter under my breath, glaring at the ultra-modern home beside mine. Its exterior slaughters every chance of brightness with its dark color palettes of black, Pietra gray, and midnight blue… the devil's colors.

That's it. I'm not giving up.

I'm doing this.

The house was only listed for a few weeks before it was sold. Mr. and Mrs. Jenkins were the best kind of neighbors. Always remembering birthdays with apple pies, treating the lilies with kindness, and after Nana June passed always looked out for me while my father worked shifts at the hospital as a doctor.

My mom left my dad and me when I was one. It's crazy… the fact that I haven't seen her since and don't even know what she looks like. My father ripped up every single photograph of her in a fit of rage one night when I was too young to comprehend what was happening. He doesn't like to talk about her, so I never push it. I know he's been hurt by her—*deeply*—and I don't want to cause any more pain. My mother wasn't happy with us—that's what she apparently told him. She hated routine. Hated Sacramento. Hated the prospect of revolving her entire life around me, especially because my parents were only twenty-two when I was born.

There's a gaping hole in my heart, an unfilled void from missing out on what most people are too fortunate to realize. I don't blame my mother for leaving. I blame her for the cracks she left behind. I blame her for my inability to contact her because it's as if she's vanished without a trace. I blame her for the darkness clouding me, that same darkness that remains with me no matter where I go after my father spilled what exactly she thought of me.

My mom doesn't care for me. I'm convinced she never will,

and I'll never know her face. I can be the perfect daughter for however long I like. She isn't coming back to Sacramento. Her story with my father and me is done. It was a long time ago when I was too young to both remember and understand what it felt like to be held by her. I've come to accept it, but it still hurts to comprehend I've seen Mr. and Mrs. Jenkins more times than my actual mother.

Mr. and Mrs. Jenkins' house has always comforted me... *Now it's home to hell.*

My Nana always used to say, *those who fear the devil's home fear freedom itself.* The words are a metaphor to life, a testament to follow your gut, no matter how daunting or risky, which is why I'm going to go ahead with my plan.

Gravel crushes loudly underneath my feet as I power walk past the neighbor's gate and through the short maze of vibrant green short hedges, before climbing up the wooden porch steps. Two knocks on the black heritage door—the only vintage element—and it swings open ajar on its own.

"Hello?" My voice lowers, giving up on me as the whisper escapes my lips.

No answer.

"Hello?"

Nothing.

Curiosity gets the better of me as I peer my head through the large gap between the door and the doorframe but see nobody.

Do it.

As I step inside, a mixture of leather, tobacco, and musky sandalwood flood my lungs. Massaging the nape of my neck, I step through the gap and glance down the never-ending hallway. While the plain entryway in my house is straight and leads to the living room—so you can see exactly who's stepping in—this one is different. It has a huge floor-to-ceiling mirrored wall on the right-hand side, which ends just before the hallway curls to the right, leading to the kitchen, living room and beyond.

The silence accompanying my every step has me thinking

that perhaps the men are in the backyard. It would be the only logical answer as to why they haven't heard me. And then I hear it, the sound of the backyard door sliding open, followed by a few heavy foot thuds before the crashing of glass. Men exchange streams of curse words.

"I said they're *fragile*, you bastard!"

"Do you think I *meant* to break them? Plates are the least of your problems now, Saint."

Saint?

I halt in my position in the hall, my back pressed against the wall. *Maybe this isn't the best idea.* I don't know who these men are, but I've come too far to back out now.

Think of Nana. Save her lilies.

"You walked straight into the fucking glass door. I was right behind you," Saint grits.

"Yeah, okay, fine, I wasn't thinking. That any better?"

"Much better."

"*Jesus.* Focus on your final fight tonight instead, will you?"

Fight?

"Already am." Saint chuckles, his voice a hot, gravelly tone.

"Yeah, you'll have the fucker knocked out in the first round for a three-time streak, you watch. I've learned that from… well, let's say *experience.*"

"Didn't mean to knock you out that time, man."

"Bullshit."

The previous bickering turns into full-blown laughter.

The back of the house. They're in the back of the house near the kitchen. Slowly, I walk closer along the hall to hear them clearer, my hands pressing against the cold wall to steady myself from making a sound. My heart pounds wildly at every step. I have no game plan from here. I didn't think any of this through, *but I can't leave now…*

I settle by the edge of the hallway, inches from where the wall curves, and listen on.

"All right, I'm going to head out and see if Nico is still there or went for another load."

Oh no.

Just like a moth drawn to a flame, my mind begins to burn at how my curiosity triumphed over any minimal thought of an escape plan before I stepped inside. Because now as heavy footsteps speed toward me, my body freezes up when I finally process what Saint said; *I'm going to head out and see if Nico is still there.*

Crap.

He's going to see me!

All of a sudden, my confidence from a few moments ago falls down a never-ending rabbit hole. I glance toward the front door to my left, knowing that if I make a run for it down the hallway now, someone is bound to hear me. My only option is to crouch down into a little ball and pray Saint changes his mind or passes without seeing me.

What false hope considering I'm adjacent to a mirrored wall... but I do it anyway.

The thumps get louder.

My palms begin to sweat.

My heart rate exceeds normality.

I shove my head into my knees and hug them to my chest. *Please don't see me.*

Please don't see me.

Please don't see me.

Please. Please. Please.

Black leather boots round the hallway and the supply of air to my lungs cuts short.

He hasn't seen me yet. Thank God.

I've never held my breath for this long before and while I may die in this very spot from it, at least it's better to go out this way rather than him seeing me first. Yes, I'll still be their problem, sure, but at least I'll already be their *dead* problem. And besides, they can't bring me back to life just to kill me again... *right?*

Oh, God. Where did my young woman pride go?

"Owww, my feet!" I scream out as the man's heavy boots step on me, crushing my toes in my flimsy slippers. "Ow! Ow! Ow!"

"Shit. Where the fuck did you come from, kid?"

Oh no!

I squeeze my eyes shut and let out a frustrated breath at myself for getting caught so easily. It was going so well until I stuffed it all up for myself and screamed. Now it's all going to blow up in my face. *Just great.*

I remain quiet, not glancing up a single inch as I clutch my throbbing feet in agony.

"Kid, I asked you a damn question."

"Don't you ever look *down?*" I murmur to myself.

"If you're going to act all smart and talk into your knees, you and I are going to have a problem, not that we don't already."

Slowly, I lift my gaze up and my eyes widen in shock. *Him.* My lips part to no words. It all just stockpiles in my brain. *It's him*—the mystery man I saw outside who crushed all my lilies. I also recognized the man's voice as… *Saint.* How ironic that the most devilish man on my street has a name that kisses the gates of heaven.

Damn this guy and his habit of stepping on every damn thing in his way without looking down for one split second. *First my lilies and now ME.*

Saint stares down at me, his piercing ocean blue eyes narrowing at my every breath. He's even more attractive up close, but it all doesn't matter after everything he's done today.

"I said, don't *you* ever *look down?*" I hiss, balling my fists as I rise to my aching feet.

Saint's extended stare is beyond intimidating, but I give in to the fading sensation in my heart and stare right back. My five-foot-three frame beside his tall one gives him the upper hand. *Well… it's not just that.* He's taller, sure, but he's perfectly built with just the right amount of toned muscle, and not only do his broad shoulders and narrow waist reveal God's unexpected favoritism in sweet sin, but I'm one thousand percent sure he's strong enough to throw me out of his house with his pinkie finger.

Not today.

Yes, I'm fearful, but I'm not leaving without an apology from him.

"What did you just say to me?" he growls.

Sure, let me repeat this to you for the third time, why don't I...

"I said don't *you* ever *look down?*"

"What on earth are you on about, kid?" Saint hisses, stepping so close into my personal space that my back hits the wall. My jaw ticks at the whiff of his masculine, musky cologne. *So hot.*

"The flowers!" I explain. "You stepped on my *flowers* outside and then proceeded to put a bookshelf on top of them! There's even a sign I made out there that clearly says, '*no walking*' for a reason!"

"Rules suck, kid."

My nose scrunches up in fury. "No, *you* suck! They were rare. My nana gave them to me to grow before she passed away last year."

"Still don't know what you're talking about, kid, and guess what? I don't *want* to know." Saint confidently snarls. He continues to look at me for the longest time, so long those light eyes burn deep into my soul, destined to steal anything he likes. He dusts off his leather jacket before crouching down to my level and wags his pointer finger at me. "Get the hell out of here, kid. Don't know how your parents raised you, but entering a stranger's house unannounced is a big no in my book."

My eyes narrow. "But my lilies—"

"Forget the damn flowers, kid. Nobody cares."

"*I* care!"

"And who exactly are you?" He smirks, rising to his full height, and begins to take smooth, long strides toward the front door. He oozes dominance in his fierce walk, as if he's some type of supermodel with that head held up so high and those relaxed shoulders pulled down and back at every step.

"I bet if my father were the one to tell you all this, you'd listen!"

Saint pauses in his stance and I witness those shoulders tense up, a tall devil ready for the burning flames.

"No, kid. That's where you're wrong," he says without turning back. "I don't listen to anybody. I do everything on my own terms."

"Fine, but how'd you feel if somebody ripped out your flowers?"

"Never ask that to a man whose heart has been ripped out of their fuckin' chest."

"Makes sense. No wonder I couldn't find it."

That has Saint turning around and lowering his gaze on me. Although I take a step back, I keep my head high and poised just like his moments ago. This man... he scares and frustrates me all at the same time. He's wrapped in fury, a fury begging to be unraveled and challenged, and that's exactly what I plan to do whether he likes it or not.

"Say that again," Saint deadpans. "I. Dare. You."

My lips press shut.

"No, don't lose that mouth of yours now." He clicks his tongue with a mocking chuckle, his dimples the most perfect I've ever seen. So deep and long, even under all his stubble. "You definitely said something. Spill it. I don't like being lied to."

"I alluded you have no heart."

"*No heart?*" Saint scoffs at my comment, shaking his head as his hands rest by his waist. It draws my attention there for a little too long. I've never seen a man so perfectly up close like this before, but the scarlet flush on my cheeks and pitter-patter of my heart don't come close to my disdain for him. *Such a coldhearted, cruel, rebellious outlaw.*

"Yeah, *no heart,*" I confidently nod.

Ha!

"Get the fuck out of my house!" he roars. "And while you're at it, that sign of yours—wherever it may be—I want it removed too. Never wanna see your face again, kid. If I do, so God help you for what will happen, got it?"

"But the lilies—"

"I said fucking run, kid." Saint widens his hands on his waist to reveal a red Swiss Army Knife tucked into the right side of his waistband. "This isn't the place for you. Wanna know why?"

I bolt past Saint, darting out of the house before getting to know the reason. Outside his gate, I give in to my blurry vision and tears burn down my cheeks. Standing up for myself has never burned this badly. Any second now and my heart will beat out of my chest, never to be found.

I hate him.

Hate him.

Hate him.

Crouching down beside the patch of my damaged lilies, in all my anger, I manage to finally push the bookshelf away. The damage is already done. The flowers are flattened, dead.

My nana wouldn't want this.

More tears fall as I work to get rid of the sign, trying my best to repatch all the dirt, but again it's no use. *They're all gone. Just like Nana June.*

I feel a presence beside me and turn to my left to find Saint feet away, leaning against a sidewalk tree. His soul-piercing stare remains on me all while he locks his ankles, pulls out a cigarette from his back pocket, and lights it. The burning orange tip distracts me for a second before the toxic nicotine smell has me scrunching up my nose.

"Smoking is bad for you," I whisper under my breath and wipe away my tears with the back of my hand. But this man must have some super-hearing because he seems to hear my every breath.

Saint smirks, pulling out the death stick for a moment to blow out a large cloud of white smoke. It obstructs his entire face before clearing up again. "Concerned about me, kid?"

"No. Just saying it kills over eight million people each year. That's one every five seconds and equals just under five hundred thousand people here in America."

Saint looks at me as if I've lost my mind. "Where'd you come up with that statistic?"

"The news."

"The fuckin' *news*. Doesn't faze me that you watch that shit."

The second he continues smoking with that big smug smirk, something inside me snaps. My young woman pride can't have it any longer. I stand up, brush the dirt from my knees, and storm up to him. It takes rising on my tippy toes to reach for the death stick and crush it underneath my slippers to finally feel satisfied.

I don't think I'll ever forget the switch to coldness in Saint's expression or how his narrowed eyes darken in havoc as he towers over me like roaring thunder. His jaw clenches so tightly I think it may explode right here on our tree-lined street, Portola Way.

"Why did you do that, kid?" Saint growls.

"I gave you five extra seconds." I smirk for the first time today. "You should be thanking me."

"*Thanking you?*" he spits. "One day you'll grow up, kid, and you'll learn that life isn't always about listening to the statistics or following the fixed rules all the damn time—it's about *surviving*. It's about constantly getting knocked down and instead of getting back up on your feet again, crawling your way to the finish line. We all need little releases in life, and you, kid, you just slaughtered mine."

And then he's off, collecting the bookshelf so effortlessly before storming toward his house.

My smirk drops.

Oh.

I stand there frozen, unsure of everything around me. *What just happened?*

I stare at the back of Saint's head, at the speckles of allusive flames wrapped around the man next door, all the while he climbs up his porch steps. I gulp down as he glances over his shoulder just as he reaches his front door. Saint's blue-eyed gaze meets mine and narrows. It's as if there's this unspoken havoc between us, a vow that this is unfinished business.

Rushed footsteps come from behind me. It's my father. I just feel it.

"You okay, Paisley?"

I turn to him. "I will be."

Silence laces the air for a moment as my father's dark brown eyes travel beyond me. "Who is he? Our new neighbor?"

I don't even have to ask who he's talking about. I just *know*.

"He's the devil of Sacramento… and he's just getting started."

And just like that, Saint's front door slams shut, confirming he heard every single word.

Great. Just great.

My heart thumps wildly in my chest.

Game on, neighbor dearest.

Chapter
TWO

Paisley

PAST

Two Years Prior...
Paisley is 16. Saint is 34.

I TOLD MY FATHER NOT TO APOLOGIZE TO SAINT ON MY BEHALF AFTER the flower incident a year ago... *Because I wasn't sorry!* People like Saint never learn. Besides, what was I even apologizing for? Apart from a minor privacy breach, I did nothing wrong. *He's the* one who crushed my lilies and young woman pride!

Saint could have simply apologized, and we could have moved on. Instead, now, a year later, I'm still thinking about the heat of the fire that rumbled inside me when his gorgeous blue eyes landed on me in his fateful hallway.

That one conversation between my father and Saint, one I wasn't involved in, was all it took for my life to become ten thousand times worse. Ever since that day, they've become close friends and it's an instant *boom* backfiring in my face. I knew it was a possibility with my father only being four years older than Saint, but I guess I just didn't expect it to happen so soon...

After being a professional boxer for the past ten years, Saint Lisconti retired at the end of last year. Now at thirty-four, Saint is a personal trainer at Fearless Fitness. It's a respected and successful fitness studio he cofounded with his close friend and ex-coach, Nico Quivez. Nico's also the man who was by the moving truck and told me to mind my own business when Saint moved in last summer.

For the better half of a year, there hasn't been a week where I didn't see the Devil of Sacramento at my house with my father... *okay,* the *hot devil,* but *still,* looks are nothing when you have the attitude of a fly on the wall. So, no matter how attractively beautiful Saint may be, *and gosh how much he is,* it doesn't change the way I feel about him—utter hatred.

Whenever I see him, I rush into my room to study or out the door to attend to my flowers. Saint always has that conniving smirk on his face that I'd love to wipe off with my bare hands. It's as if he's winning this invisible race between us, but there isn't any and even if there were and Saint was my prize at the end of the race, I'd start running backward.

So, okay, perhaps I shouldn't be doing this right now, but somebody has to be a good citizen and look out for danger in the neighborhood, *right*? I swear that's all I was ever doing. I didn't intend to witness a scene between Saint and two other men out of *The Godfather.*

Because I adore the warm, sultry breeze, I usually do my homework on the balcony outside my bedroom and while today should be just like any other afternoon after school while my father is at work, it isn't because of one single aspect...

Saint.

My balcony partially overlooks some of his backyard and I was in the middle of a math equation when a shout had my eyes wander there. My pen fell from my grip, and I sat up on my heels to see better, and now five minutes later my gaze still hasn't been able to return to my page. In fact, the math book is long forgotten, spread out on the terracotta-tiled ground.

Saint and Leo—the other man I saw moving a few furniture items the day Saint moved in—have another man cornered in the backyard, a few feet away from the crystal clear in-ground pool. From where I'm standing, I can't see the victim's face, but his hands rise in surrender as pleas escape him.

"You don't have to do this! I'll make sure it doesn't happen again! Please!"

"It isn't the first time you've said that, Anderson," Saint hisses, crossing his toned arms over his black short-sleeved V-neck. "And to be fair, I'm getting a little sick and tired of all the running around to make sure you have your head in the fucking game. It ain't my job, understand?"

"I know, Saint, I know it's not your job. But lately my whole life has gone to shit. My job is the only thing I have, and yes, I slipped up, more than once, but there won't be a third."

"I don't know, Nico told me to finish you off good, and seeing as I own half of the business…" Saint shakes his head, veering his gaze off to the distance before glancing toward Leo. "What do you say, Leo? Should we believe a word that comes out of his mouth, because I already have my answer."

Leo laughs mockingly and begins shaking his head. In a domineering stance, Leo rakes a hand through his dirty-blond hair and slowly rubs his clean-shaven jaw as if in thought. "I say do what Nico asked and what you called him over to do."

Anderson's hands lower and he makes a run for it, rushing past Saint and around the pool in a flash, but he doesn't get far. Leo bolts after him and the thuds of his feet over the grass section by the shed violently echo in my chest. Anderson is seconds from reaching the pocket doors before Leo takes him down from behind and slams him to the ground.

Still stationed by the perimeter fence dividing our homes, Saint slowly shakes his head. "You know not to run from us, Anderson," he says, striding toward them. "When are you going to listen, huh?"

Leo has Anderson pinned down and that seems to be the only security Saint needs before his big fist collides with the poor man's jaw. He doesn't stop there. He keeps going and going until the man's light skin turns all bloody and crimson stains Saint's hand. Loud groans come from the man, who attempts to fight back, only for Leo to restrict his hands from moving.

Anderson's body weakens as he spits out blood into the grass, his eyes still widening in fear as Saint seems to settle down... *for now.* "Please, please don't do this. I have a son."

Saint lets out a cold chuckle while pulling out something from inside his jacket. I cover my mouth, desperate to mute my gasp as the shiny blades of his Swiss Army Knife catch the sun, blinding me for a split moment.

Oh no! Holy sunflowers!

He's going to kill him!

Saint's going to kill this man. Right here, right now.

"You have a son? And what did you think that was going to change after you fucked with my business, huh? Thinking you can do some dirty work under the table and steal money and then pledge my name like you want to drag me down with you. Sorry to break it, man, but that's fucking low."

"Saint, please."

"I SAID WHAT IS THAT GOING TO CHANGE?" Saint roars, lifting the knife for a beat, but when Anderson does nothing but thrash his arms in Leo's grip, he lunges the knife down toward him and my heart aches in disbelief.

"NO! DON'T DO IT!" I scream, my throat burning, just in time for the tip of the knife to halt an inch from Anderson's chest.

It takes one breath, two at the maximum, for Saint's head to snap over his shoulder in the direction of the scream... *my* scream. *Holy...* Saint eyes my house and his gaze quickly lands on me, widening for a split second before darkening back to his signature style.

Heated fear rushes around my heart.

Oh no.

Trembling, I let go of my sweaty grip on the metal railing and feel my body begin to shake. I don't like the look in Saint's eyes. The look of death. It's lethal and sickening. As if he was actually capable of digging that knife into that man's heart with no regrets or second thoughts.

I know Saint and I are from completely different worlds. I understand from the conversation that Anderson was stealing money from Fearless Fitness, but what Anderson did... could it really merit death?

Saint hands Leo the knife and stands to his feet. Leo glances toward me, narrowing his gaze before Saint screams at Anderson to run, which he does, bolting through the side gate and down the street, away from the property.

I want to move. I want to go back inside and lock the door, but a devious numbness has overtaken my entire body, immobilizing me from taking a single step. My eyes snap from Saint's clenched jaw to the speckles of blood on his face and clothes as he walks toward me.

I stare down at him from the balcony, nervous about what exactly Saint is capable of. And just like that... I *learn.* He climbs the dividing fence between us, despite my pleas to stay away. But he doesn't care. It's as if this is our own version of Romeo and Juliet, except we are not fateful lovers and the poison comes from his stare, not a little toxic bottle.

From the fence, Saint latches onto the metal railing of the balcony and pulls himself up with his toned arms. It's there where adrenalin kicks in and I rush backward, only to trip on my math book and fall on my ass. Meanwhile, Saint casually perches himself on the edge, swings his legs over, and jumps into the balcony, always with those same speckles of chaos clouding his big blue eyes.

He brings a finger to the center of his lips, signaling *silence.*

I scurry to get myself up, using the outdoor wooden chair to steady myself, but there's barely enough space between us on this tiny balcony. Saint inches away, ready to pounce... I'm in trouble.

Locking his jaw, Saint gestures toward the door behind me. "You go inside. I go back down."

"You let him run... Were you going to kill him?"

"Get. Inside. *Now.*"

I shake my head at the sensory overload of the metallic smell of blood. It's even worse up close, worse to see the fresh crimson sprayed and smeared all over his beautiful face like he's some wolf disturbed while going in for the kill.

"Were you going to kill him or was it a warning?"

"Inside, kid."

"I—"

Saint cuts me off. "Paisley, I'm going to say it one more time."

"I don't trust my back to you. I don't know if you have any other weapons on you... like a gun."

Saint lets out a frustrated breath. "I don't own a gun."

"Prove it."

Saint glances off to the side and lets out a deeply irritated sigh. His chest must be pounding, beating so fast because it rises and falls beneath his top out of control. I'm so caught up in the moment that I don't realize the blood-stained T-shirt gets closer until a hand covers my mouth and the other lifts me up against his chest.

I let out a muted scream, kicking and screaming for him to let me go, but he doesn't. My cheek grazes against his stubble as he whispers in my ear to calm down.

Calm down?

How can I *calm down?*

No matter how many times or how hard I slam my fists into his chest, it doesn't faze him. The only thing it does is transfer some of the blood to my hands. Tears burn down my cheeks as Saint walks us inside from the balcony, through my bedroom, and out into the hallway.

Another hallway.

Saint's eyes meet mine and my whimpers soften, but my throat already begins to ache from my restricted screams. "If I set you down here, promise me you won't scream. Nod if you won't scream, kid."

It takes a full moment, but I eventually slowly nod.

Saint continues staring for what feels like years before he must see something in my eyes he's willing to surrender to and puts me down. *Finally.* His hands instantly move inside the pockets of his jeans, while mine rub my tender cheeks from just how tight his grip was.

"You didn't have to do that," I grumble, staring at the smeared blood on my hands.

"You saw nothing, Paisley, understood? You saw *nothing*."

"But I did! I saw you and Leo—"

"You saw NOTHING."

"Okay." I blink away the harshness of his tone, my voice a bare whisper when I say, "Just promise me you won't kill him."

Saint's eyes roll and he blows out another impatient sigh. "Yeah, yeah, I won't kill him. Promise."

"No, you're just saying that!"

"No, I'm not. I promise we were just giving him a warning."

"Really?"

"Yes. I made a promise to you, kid. A promise is a promise."

"Except I don't know you and it seems as though you hate rules."

"Fuck." Saint pinches the bridge of his nose. "Okay, fine, listen to this. You don't say a word to your father about what you saw, even though it was just a warning, and I'll pay for some new lilies out the front, deal?"

"Mmmm…" I ponder the thought.

This could be a good deal… Maybe.

"And you won't step on them this time?" I ask out of curiosity.

Clenching his jaw, Saint shakes his head. "No, I won't step

on them this time. One hundred dollars. I'll give it to you right now, deal?"

"And I can put my sign back up too?"

"Yes, kid. That too. You can put that damn sign of yours back up too. Now, is there anything else?"

"Yes."

"God help me…"

"You have to promise to be nicer."

"I don't do nice, kid. If you really knew me, you would know that."

My brows furrow. "But you're nice to my dad and I met you first!"

"Look, kid, I'm busy. One hundred dollars for the damn lilies and we'll both go back to our lives as we know them. The altercation outside and this deal right here never happened."

"One hundred and fifty dollars and we'll be even."

"One hundred."

"One fifty."

Saint's jaw ticks. "One hundred."

I cross my arms over my chest and narrow my gaze up at him. "Okay, two hundred."

"One-*fucking*-hundred."

"Two-*freaking*-hundred."

"One fifty."

"Two fifty."

"Two hundred. Shit, I mean—"

"SOLD!" I grin as Saint recoils, raking a hand through his hair as a curse word spills.

Eventually, Saint reaches inside his back pocket, pulls out his wallet, and fishes through his bills. *All hundreds.* I eye a photo of him and an adorable little girl who can't be more than three or four in the photograph section. It seems like the photo was taken a few years back as he seems younger and she's cutely kissing his cheek and hugging him, while he's grinning at the camera with his piercing ocean eyes and hugging her back. I step closer to see it better, but he notices and slams his wallet shut with a grunt before I can take in anything else.

"Who is she?"

Ignoring the question completely, Saint hands me the money and I take it. "This never happened, okay?"

"Okay."

And then just like Saint entered, he leaves, walking through my room and smoothly maneuvering himself down from the balcony like it's an Olympic sport. Only when I know he's truly gone, do I step into the bathroom and almost lose my footing at the brush of blood on my face from where he held me.

As I wipe it away and stare down at the red blotches on my damn face towel, I can't help but cringe and whisper to myself, "But it did. It did all happen."

Chapter
THREE

Saint

PAST

One Year Prior...
Paisley is 17. Saint is 35.

"**M**Y DAD'S NOT HOME," PAISLEY SOFTLY MURMURS BY THE FRONT door, her small fists gripping the doorframe so tightly, blotches of white smooth over her creamy skin. "He should be back any minute, though. He just went to the store."

My brows furrow down at Alaric's seventeen-year-old daughter, the same woman who thought she could rip a fucking cigarette out of my mouth and I'd just let it go. The same one who had the audacity to stop me while I was showing Anderson what happens when you mess with my business. But in this case, I'm forced to freaking let go. Paisley's my best friend's daughter. *Innocent to this world of mine.*

"I'll wait inside then."

"No," she squeals when I proceed to take a step forward, shutting the door slightly ajar. Fortunately for me, my Italian leather biker boots are caught in the door. "No, you can't come in."

"Why?"

"Because Dad said I can't allow anybody in unless he's home. I know he said you're an exception, but…"

"Don't you remember what I always say about rules, kid?" I ask, taking this as the perfect moment to pull out my stash. I slip a cigarette into the center of my lips and pull out my lighter to get it going. "Rules fuckin' suck. They're illusions."

Paisley seems almost mesmerized by the burning orange light whenever I take a drag. It's as if her dark eyes glitter with rebellion, at the same time the flame brings her intrigue to life.

"Rules don't suck, they are placed for a reason," she says after the longest pause.

"Finally found your voice again, huh?" I smirk, a low rumble echoing in my throat when she crosses her arms over her chest as if *that's* going to intimidate me. *Nice try, kid. I'm gonna need a little more than that.* "Took you a while, didn't it?"

"Stop mocking me."

"All right, all right. Listen, I'll stop pissing you the fuck off if you let me in. I'll wait for him inside. I gotta talk to him."

"But Dad said—"

"Rules suck, kid."

Paisley lets out a huff, glaring up at me before she opens the door to reveal her entire face. Sun-kissed skin, light freckles on her cheeks, dark waves wrapped in a messy bun like she doesn't give a shit and I like it better that way. Paisley's not a girl to swear. At least her hair can do it for her. She's grown up so much in these past couple of years but is still the freaking strictest person I know.

I tell myself I better start freaking concentrating because all of a sudden Paisley has a notebook and a pen in her hands and is busy scribbling something down. My brows uptick in amusement as she bites her tongue, head down in concentration until she halts, pulls back the page to see it clearer, and nods to herself. Then, she thrusts the notepad up, inches to my chest. "Please sign at the bottom."

Yep, this one's going to be a Harvard fucking scholarship graduate.

"Sign at the bottom?" I ask.

"Mhmm."

"What the hell am I signing?"

"A contract that states if you want to come inside, you need to promise you'll be on your best behavior first. That means no smoking, no cursing and... no saying rules suck."

"So basically, you want my three signature traits to fuck off, yeah?" My gaze flickers between the paper with her large cursive handwriting to her *I'm not-backing-down* expression between my drags. "Can't sign something I don't agree with, kid."

"Then you can't come inside."

"Aren't you supposed to be at school anyway?"

"No, student-free day. Aren't you supposed to be at work?"

A slow, crooked smirk rises on my lips. "I *am* working. I'm just currently on break."

Paisley rolls her eyes. "Going around on your Harley all day with a death stick and beating people up is your *job*?"

"No. Fitness, maintaining both grit and resilience, and training people to be their best self is my job. Cigarettes, my Harley, and whiskey are just added bonuses... alongside iron fists. Sure, I'm suited to fight in the ring, but I can also protect people like you. Seeing you all in one piece has me thinking I'm doing a pretty good job of keeping people like you safe from a city full of corruption, guns, and false alibies. Which has me thinking, I haven't heard one thank you."

Paisley huffs and pushes the notebook into my chest. I chuckle and for a split second decide to give her the benefit of the doubt. Even though that doesn't relate to nor define the kind of man I am at all. I don't forgive. I don't forget. And I certainly don't give in to seventeen-year-old women.

I hand the notebook back to her. "Said I ain't gonna sign it.

Take it and draw on the back instead. Save the trees, help climate change, or wherever the fuck the world is heading toward nowadays."

"*Please.*" Her deep-set gaze follows mine, a silent plea alongside her parted plump lips.

Paisley Reign's a different type of girl from the rest. For some reason, she isn't afraid to speak her mind with me, yet at the same time I get the feeling she recognizes when she oversteps. It's evident in the way the paper shakes in her grip, and yet she attempts to have a poised, composed face. Tight jaw. Steady eyes. And now pierced-shut mouth...

But Paisley isn't fooling me. I've been around people like her for too long not to call them out on their shit. Every single time I see Paisley, she evokes the devil in me, pissing me off beyond repair. This time is no different and this little contract she wrote up, it can go right back where she found it... *hell.*

In the midst of my thoughts, I flicker on my cigarette lighter and catch the edge of the paper with the allusive orange flame. Paisley's eyes widen and she gasps out a large breath, covering her mouth as we witness the contact burning into a charcoal mess.

I can't wipe the smirk off my face when she grumbles something under her breath and swings the door entirely open. I follow her in, but she bolts away down the hallway and stomps up the stairs in fury.

"Pointless rules get you nowhere, kid. Running doesn't get you anywhere either. Remember that—" The thud of her bedroom door slamming shut cuts me off. I shake my head with a soft chuckle and settle onto the living room couch. "Remember that for next time."

"What are we gonna do about this girl next door?" Nico asks beside me on my porch steps, blowing out a cloud of smoke. "What's her name again? Ainsley?"

"No, Paisley." I take a drag of my cigarette, burning my vision into the house next door and Paisley, who's been by the parking strip digging up dirt with a pink shovel and planting seeds for the past half hour. "Paisley Reign. And I don't fuckin' know. All I do know is I don't trust her to stay tight-lipped about last year. She's already seen too much. Alaric would kill me if he knew his daughter witnessed me beating the shit out of Anderson last year."

"Exactly. I'm not placing my fate in the hands of some sixteen-year-old who's already got her own hands three feet into soil."

Of course Nico Quivez—my ex-boxing-coach and co-partner at Fearless Fitness—is getting hotheaded about it. That's the type of guy a man training boxing beasts like myself and MMA fighters in a thirty-square cage for the past twenty years becomes. One wrong word out of someone's mouth and he's ready to ruthlessly pounce. A man whose mind never stops ticking. A man whose good judgment and coaching were a major asset in my fighting career years ago.

"Paisley's seventeen, Nico."

"Sixteen, seventeen, same shit. She has no reason not to run to the police because you listened to me and warned Anderson of what happens when you fuck around with business. Who knows if she opens her mouth to her father, or worse, the police. We don't need that shit."

"She's got a reason to stay quiet, trust me."

"What is it?"

Alaric's dark Jeep turns into the drive next door and Paisley glances up, waving at him.

Grinning, I crush the cigarette under my foot and nod toward the car. "We're looking at it."

"Gonna talk to Alaric about his daughter? Yeah, good fuckin' luck."

"None needed, Nico."

On my way to her, my hands slide into my jean pockets. Paisley glances up when I pass her by the parking strip. The way her jaw ticks has me halting. I guess I can spend a couple of minutes with *Miss Door-slammer.*

Crouching down over Paisley's array of garden tools, I pull out a light pink frilly blossom from the flower cluster already in bloom and twirl it between my thumb and pointer. Drawing it to my nose, I take in its sweet floral scent of... well, I have no freaking clue. I'm not a flower guy. Never have been, never can be, never will be. *Fucking sue me.*

"Great, just great!" Paisley glares up at me and lets out an agitated groan. "You've really done it this time!"

"What? I thought the whole thing about planting flowers was to pick them, no?"

"If you want them to die, yes. If you want to preserve their beauty, you stand back and *watch*."

I smirk, continuing to swirl the pinkish flower around. "What are these flowers called?"

"Geraniums. Why?"

"Was gonna say they look like a pain in the ass to maintain to me."

"You're terrible, you know that, right?"

"Sure do."

"Good," Paisley grumbles and goes back to planting new seeds.

I nod over her work. "Yeah, keep digging, kid."

I turn around and look over at Nico, who nods toward the girl with knitted brows. I raise my hands up with a shrug before jogging up Alaric's driveway and throw the flower I've already forgotten the name of aside.

Sporting a white polo shirt and dark slacks, Alaric's in the midst of taking out two bags of groceries from his car's trunk when he glances my way. Smirking, his brows rise in amusement. "What you looking at, Sainty boy?"

"Nothing." I laugh, shrugging casually. "I just love how you switch from doctor to '*let's go to Vegas*' in two-point-five seconds."

My best friend grins. "It's called Clark Kent-ing the shit out of life. Don't worry, I don't expect you to understand."

"Oh, I'm already there, man. Guess you just gotta catch up to be in the race."

"Fucker." Alaric shakes his head in laughter. "God, I love how you're acting all smart now, but we'll just forget last year after the Sawyer versus Jenson match in Vegas where you drank the whole liquor store and I had to freaking carry you home like you were a newborn. The way I was running to prevent my back from breaking and you know—dying—*that's* being in the race."

"Thanks for having my back and *not* reopening the Vegas vault."

"Welcome. We say the same shit every year, and then right about this time, fly back to Vegas to get our asses kicked. Have I mentioned that I *love* being your best friend?"

"Many times." I laugh. "Good thing we actually don't live in Vegas."

"Yeah, I thank God every day for that one."

"Sure you do."

"I really do." Alaric chuckles as he gets the last of the grocery bags and sets them down on the concrete garage floor. "Oh, while you're here, I was going to ask if you wanted to stick around for dinner. Paisley's making her signature chicken and rice. I know how much you like it. What do you say?"

"Would love to, but I have Nico back at mine. Promised the fucker I'll go to one of the matches he's coaching tonight. Somebody had the audacity to say MMA is for the big dogs, while boxing is for the Chihuahuas."

"Did you tell him to fuck off?"

"*Fuck off?* I was going to show him the mark *chihuahuas* make."

"Why didn't you?"

"His niece is watching the game. That was his defense. Didn't want her to worry about a black eye."

"Shit. Where the fuck did Nico's balls go?"

I smirk. "Was wondering the same thing. Apparently big dogs get neutered first."

Alaric throws his head back in laugher, resting a hand on his chest. "Fuck, that was a good one. I love it, man."

My own chuckle rumbles up my throat. "Shame I didn't tell him that one yet."

"Real shame. Anyway, I'll catch you later then. When you pass by Paisley, can you tell her to come in soon so we can start dinner 'cause I'm getting a beer the second I walk in, yeah?"

"Sure thing." Glancing over my shoulder, I don't expect Paisley to be staring at me. She's a good ten feet away and I mockingly wave at her. She rolls her eyes at my smirk and turns back to the flowers unamused, yet I keep on staring. "So, what college degree is she interested in? Journalism? Landscape architect? Flower arranging? Professional eye roller?"

Alaric bursts out in laughter. "I have no clue, but she still fucking hates you, man."

"Well aware of that fact. I learned today that you're apparently not supposed to pull out flowers. They're purely there for *observation*. Who knew?"

"God, I think my daughter's going to be the death of you."

"She already is."

"Trust me when I say it's better this way. She doesn't need to be around guys like you. God forbid she wants to be when she's older. I'd kill any guy who looks at her for a second too long."

Nico's voice comes ringing in my ear. I need to make sure what Paisley witnessed last year wasn't repeated to anyone. If she's spreading any word that I'm exacting my own type of revenge to men who double-cross me... well, I'm fucked.

"Does Paisley talk to you much?" I ask.

"Rarely."

Good.

"Nothing out of the ordinary lately?"

Alaric shakes his head with a slight shrug. "No, she's not the type of girl who speaks a lot. She keeps to herself and out of trouble. Total opposite to me, right?"

"She doesn't keep to herself around me."

"True. She speaks her mind with you. I think her mom not being around a lot affects her. Paisley never vocalizes it, but I see it. You know how it is. Everybody at school probably talks about theirs, whether it be good or bad memories... and instead, she doesn't have any of those stories of her own. After the divorce, Faye told me she was fucking off to Spain to be with some rich bastard and hasn't contacted Paisley and me since."

"Shit, I didn't know that part. I'm sorry, man."

"Yeah, it's fucked up. I mean, I don't give a shit about it, but it's not fair on Paisley. She never hears from her mother. No birthday messages. No Christmas cards. No nothing. It's as if she doesn't exist, and I know that's bound to hurt at some point. But what can I do? Paisley was close to my mom, her nana June, so when she passed three years ago, she really needed family to rely on. There wasn't any. Her mother, Faye, was long gone, and I was busy working overtime to distract myself."

"Does she have a couple friends at least?"

"No, doesn't have any close cousins or friends. So Paisley started with these flowers and poetry and hasn't spent a single day without them. It's a good habit, but I can't help but think she's wasting available time where she could be out socializing, you know."

I knew about Alaric's dramas with his former girlfriend and Paisley's mom in the past, but never to this depth, especially never spoken about the long-term effects it has on Paisley. From the day we met, Alaric and I have been super tight. I'm an only child, so he's like the brother I've never had. I can tell him anything and he'll keep it safe, just like all the shit I've told him about my past. I know he has a lot on his plate and that being a single father isn't easy. I just think sometimes he doesn't give himself enough credit. He's doing incredible. Far much more incredible than I would be in his position.

Glancing back over at Paisley, I watch as she drops a few seeds into another dug-up hole. But then I look at her, like *really* look at her, and notice the frown on her lips. How she reaches up with her dirty glove and sweeps underneath her eye, almost as if she's stopping tears from flowing.

Swallowing down, I pull Alaric into a brief side hug. "You've both been through a lot, man. But at least Paisley has you. You're taking care of her and you're *here* for her. Continue being there for her. Even when she says she doesn't need you and pushes you away, be there."

"I will, but I just feel at times what I do is not enough," he admits, his voice breaking at the last word. "I feel like Paisley suffers in silence and doesn't let me in. I'm the closest person to her and yet... I can't help her. You get what I mean?"

Alaric doesn't know how close he's hit home. I massage the lump in my throat and nod. We're silent for a few moments and I shift my eyes to the sky outside the garage on this clear, sunny day.

I clear my throat. "I don't know how it would help, seeing as Paisley hates my guts, but anything I can do to help, you know I'm just one house away."

"That means more than you know, Saint. Thank you for that and for listening."

"Anytime. I better go now, or else Nico will bust my balls. See you tomorrow, yeah?"

Alaric smiles softly, playfully slapping my back. "Yeah, see you then, man."

I squeeze his shoulders and smile back. "You've got this, brother. Be brave for her."

"I will."

I give him a curt nod and jog down his driveway, knowing that somewhere deep inside me I'll remember the words he told me. Those of himself. Those of Paisley. They came from a place of raw emotion and hurt, and who am I to challenge Paisley now that I know the truth about why she's so uptight, yet vulnerably timid?

Who the fuck am I to do that?

Paisley doesn't have anybody, and on the outside looking in, it could appear like I'm losing my damn mind and someone's unscrewed my balls, but I... *I feel sorry for her.* I really do. I need to leave her the fuck alone. The bickering and constant back and forth tension-filled conversation—it needs to stop. It's not fair for us to venture any deeper into spiraling hate.

We're neighbors, I'm her father's best friend, she's eighteen years younger. I need to tone this shit down. Because now that I know Paisley's hurting, I won't be able to deal with myself if she got caught in the crossfire of the scorching war in my mind. I can't let anything happen to innocent people who deserve more than the path life has callously given them.

Paisley catches my gaze as I pass her by the parking strip. "Dad said dinner's soon."

"Okay, thanks. What were you and my dad talking about?"

"Nothing you haven't heard before."

"You seem pensive. What are you thinking about?"

"Just that if you get stuck on the past too much, you drown in a pit of burning flames."

Paisley's gaze narrows and she places her hand by her brows, blocking the sunlight as those honey-brown eyes dive deep into my soul. "Thought you didn't have a heart to begin with..."

"True. I don't." Slowly, my smirk turns into a frown. "But the heat hurts just the same."

I should leave.

I should continue walking back to my house, but I don't. Something stops me. Something beyond my control. I turn toward Paisley's father's garage just as it begins to close. I catch a glimpse of Alaric stepping into the house through the garage access, head in his hands.

Glancing at my own home, it seems as though Nico has ventured back inside. My gaze flickers down to Paisley on the ground, who's working her magic with the flowers, but I don't need to make my presence further known as Paisley's eyes haven't left me once.

"Are you coming over for dinner again?"

"Not tonight, no." I nod toward the pink flowers again, avoiding her stare because I know it's bound to unlock another question if I don't change the topic soon. "What are those flowers called again?"

"Geraniums."

"Right, geraniums. Well, I didn't mean to pull it out, kid. Those flowers must mean something special to you. Didn't mean to disrespect what you stand for."

Paisley's brows rise a fraction. "Are you... are you *apologizing?*"

Her comment draws a smile to my lips. "Maybe."

"Wow." She genuinely gasps. "And to respond to your previous comment about maintaining geraniums being a pain in the... well, *you know*, geraniums are perfectly easy to maintain. You just need to water them accordantly, speak to them, and not *unnecessarily rip them out.*"

"What the fuck, did you just say speak to them?"

"Yes, speak to them. Stop swearing."

I can't help but chuckle. "Do you *read* to your flowers too?"

Paisley rolls her eyes and turns back to her work, but not before a small hint of a smile crawls its way up her lips. She may never admit it, perhaps didn't even notice she did it at all or that I would pick up on it, but I did. I've seen it all, but this is something I thought I'd never see. Witnessing a smile come out of Paisley Reign, the one girl in this city I was beginning to think was born with the defect to smile. I mean, yeah, I'm one to talk, but Paisley smiling because of me? So fuckin' rare that if I hadn't seen it, I would have pinned the world ending before I saw a fraction of her upturned lips.

"Hold up. You actually do read to them, don't you?" I smirk.

"No... well, not novels anyway."

"What do you read to them then?"

She's silent for a second before she says, "Poetry."

"Don't worry," I murmur. "Your secret's safe with me, kid."

Paisley looks up at me with flushed cheeks. "What secret?" She bites down on her lip, squinting as the sun moves into her eyeline, illuminating her honey browns. "I don't have any secrets."

"Yeah, you do. You're a flower nerd and you know it."

Paisley laughs brightly, a cute snort escaping her, and I can't help but smile. "Am not!"

"Don't get so defensive, the government hasn't made it illegal... *yet.*"

"Go away, Saint," she says with the biggest grin I've ever seen on her lips.

I smile. "Not until you read me a stanza from your favorite poem."

"Never."

"Come on, Pais. One stanza and I'll leave you to keep on diggin'."

Paisley looks away and begins to shake her head before halting. The beautiful smile on her lips transforms into a slight frown as she pulls off her grimy, vibrant pink gloves and sets them to the side, one on top of the other. If it were me, I would have thrown them to the side, but not Paisley—she's precise, organized, and my greatest nightmare living right next door.

Paisley dusts down her floral print yellow sundress and muddy knees before standing up before me. The distant sounds of rumbling car engines and children laughing in nearby front yards drown out at the look in her eyes. At how they're such perfect almonds and look into mine so deeply she has me gripped. It's like I'm the only one who can save her from a stare so potently rich of tales nobody ever dared to unravel or hear from her.

Standing before me isn't Paisley Reign the cigarette snatcher, crime stopper, or wildflower... it's simply *her.*

The depths of her pain will be laid out in the next word she speaks, in the poetic rhythm of her voice, in the very poet she chooses. You learn a lot about a person by their favorite line of poetry... and Paisley has unraveled me from the first day. How she shifts from timid to sweet to fierce. How she's so mature for her age. How she managed to seep through all the cracks in my soul and somehow, we've gone from flowers to poetry.

Nobody knows this. The boys would give me shit about it and to be honest, I've never needed to bring it up, but I know a thing or two about poets. The best of them turn madly insane by the time they reach thirty, with every stain of ink a representation of all the tears burning inside them like a lethal flame.

They keep their agony inside.

Slow river their anger across the page until they're drowning in a sea of nothingness.

Some of them don't make it to publish their work. The audience—the protagonists of their own destiny—seeps in the pain of the words and translates them to relate in their life. It's funny how people collect poetry like little pockets of hope and have faith in pulling somebody up from the deep end, but little do they know they've been refusing the anchor the entire time.

"Do you want me to..." Paisley swallows thickly in a fit of nerves. *Nerves.* This is what I don't understand about her, the push and pull of who she really is. "Do you want me to tell you who it's by first?"

"No, let me guess who after you say it."

"You know poetry?"

"I know a thing or two."

"Oh... I didn't know that." She clears her throat as if she's preparing herself for the performance of her life. Her eyes are all over the place, from my boots to her hands to my eyes. "Okay. Ready?"

"Ready."

Paisley nods softly, keeping her head on my worn-out bikie boots, her voice even lower as she begins. "I've... I've looked for..." She shakes her head and turns away from me, her long, rich chocolate waves covering her face. "I'm sorry," she chokes out, her voice so low I barely catch her words. "I can't say it. Not today."

I furrow my brows. "Everything okay?"

"Mmhmmm."

"You know when somebody responds *mmhmmm*, it usually means yes, but I don't think that's the case here."

"Promise I'm okay, Saint," she whispers, but her tone gives it all away.

She's *not* okay.

"Paisley?"

"You can go. I'll be okay."

Go, Lisconti. She told you to go.

Turn the fuck around and get inside your house.

NOW.

I shake my head with a sigh and curse at the small fucking part of me that wants to help her. I don't know why. I don't know how. But I feel like I owe her something. I was the one to bring up the poetry and it seems as though it's exactly what set her off... *but why?*

Reaching out my hand, my fingers wrap around the soft cotton of her left wrist that's covered by her long-sleeved sundress. Paisley jerks her head to my hand at the action and just as I anticipated, I fall witness to the big tears rolling down her cheeks. It's crazy how the stiff tension between us for two years straight breaks away right in this moment.

I don't know for how long, or even the true reason why it does, but I know it's the right thing to do. It's as if our past fights, our past misunderstandings, our past troubles don't matter anymore.

Nothing else matters when my hand slips from her wrist.

Nothing else matters as my thumb slowly wipes her tears away.

Nothing else matters but those anguished doe eyes that find their way back up to mine.

Paisley isn't my opponent. She's a seventeen-year-old with nowhere to go and no one to call home.

"Geraniums!" she blurts out suddenly, her glassy eyes snapping to mine as my thumb falls from her face. "Geraniums are one of the most popular greenhouse plants. They were first discovered in 1576 in Southern Europe. Versatile. They're a very versatile flower and can be utilized for cakes, teas, and other things like compresses. They love the sun and prefer damp but well-draining soil."

I arch a brow at the outburst of information. *Huh?*

"Something tells me that wasn't the poem."

"No, not the poem. Whenever I'm stressed, I say as much as I know about a flower. You... probably think it's weird."

"No, not weird at all," I assure with a genuine smile. "Just wasn't expecting it, that's all."

"Why are you being nice?"

"I'm being nice?"

Paisley gives me a side-eye and shoots me a small grin. "Yeah, nice."

"Guess I woke up on the right side of the bed, kid."

"You didn't. You pulled out one of the flowers from the root. That's definitely not waking up on the right side of the bed."

"Ah, *right*. All right, I just feel like it then."

"Well, it feels... strange."

I can't help but laugh. "Thanks for having faith in me, kid."

"Is your real name Saint?" she asks after the longest time.

A warm smile breaks on my lips because out of all the things she could have asked me, *this* is what she aspires to unravel. "No, well, technically yes, but my real name... it's..." I clear my throat, yet the burning knot remains. "It's Santo."

"Why Saint then?"

"Fighters are typically susceptible to nicknames. Mine was Saint, and it just stuck. Santo is also Saint in Italian."

Paisley nods twice as if she gets it. Sniffling, she wipes away her tears. "But you're no saint."

Anyone else who said that to me would already be six feet under, but with her, I find myself laughing. "Ironic, isn't it? Don't want to get into too much, but they call me that because I'm the opposite. But it's better the devil you know than the devil you don't, right?"

Again, Paisley nods. But this time, I'm not too sure she understands it.

"Sorry I couldn't say the poem. Tomorrow just isn't a good day for me and so today... it's hard. The poem... it's mine and I wrote it about somebody I loved." She shakes her head to herself with a deep sigh. *"Still* love. Tomorrow… it'll be three years since my nana died."

And just like that I find out my why.

Fuck. Paisley has it freaking hard.

"Sorry to hear that. I know what it feels like to lose somebody you love. Keep that poem to yourself, kid. Maybe one day I'll be mad enough to want to hear it."

"I don't think it's any good. Haven't performed it to anybody, not even my father."

"The flowers listened."

"And what good does that do?" She shrugs, as if it all doesn't matter, *but it does.*

"Well, they're still alive, aren't they?" I chuckle and when silence greets me, my expression falls. I turn to leave but just like before, something stops me in my tracks. I come back, rubbing my stubbled jaw twice over. "You know, Paisley, sometimes it's not about having a lot of people around. Sometimes it's just having that one person who makes everything feel okay and them filling the void of what a hundred people would."

"I like that, but there's only one problem."

"Go on."

"What do you do when that one person goes away?"

I know what she means and what she's opposing, but I give her another response anyway. "They'll come back eventually."

Paisley shakes her head adamantly. "No," she whispers and gestures up to the clouds up above. "What do you do when the only person you have leaves you?"

"I think it's about keeping their memory alive in all that you do."

"Yes, but there must be more than that."

I frown and look down. "Don't know, Pais. Haven't figured that part out yet myself."

"Neither have I."

I smile softly at those sad eyes and turn around, prepared to return home, when I hear the faintest call.

"Santo?"

I spin around, acknowledging how Paisley called me by my first name, but don't dare show what it does to me. I smooth my clenched jaw and let go of the tension in my broad shoulders, as well as my fists that have balled in my pockets.

After everything that happened, only two people call me by my real name.

Two.

"Yeah?"

Paisley looks up at me and a painfully hopeful smile rises on her lips. "Just let me know when you've figured it out, okay? I could really use the answer."

I stare at her for the longest time, wondering when the hell we got on civil ground. Something tells me it won't be like this again, always this peaceful, that soon we'll return to the fighting, but for now, right in this moment, understanding paves its way to acceptance.

I give Paisley a curt nod, keeping my eyes on her five-foot-three frame as I walk backward. At my gate, I shoot her the faintest smile before turning around into my front porch and losing sight of her, but never of the promise I vow to make her.

I will, I tell myself. *At whatever costs, I'll find it out for the both of us, kid.*

Chapter
FOUR

Paisley

PRESENT DAY
Paisley is 18. Saint is 35.

G REAT. JUST GREAT.
I can't believe I locked myself out of the house on a night like tonight. Not only is it my eighteenth birthday—not that I care much about it—but my father hasn't showed up yet, even though he should have finished work at the hospital by now… *this isn't like him.*

After all, he was the one to book dinner reservations at this new rustic Italian restaurant in the heart of Sacramento to encourage us to do something different when it comes to celebrations. But now, as I glance down at my watch and it veers onto seven o'clock, hope fades. I've been sitting on my wooden porch steps for an hour in this sweltering humidity of a day with no luck of getting the door unlocked as I left my phone, my purse, and house key inside.

Yeah, today is definitely not my day.

Earlier on, I thought I heard my father hoot his car horn and so I rushed outside in my floral satin robe to tell him I need a few more minutes as I was having trouble picking an outfit, only to find it was just a passing car and I had locked myself out in the hurry.

My only hope is that my dad returns home soon, but as time goes on, I'm not so sure. I can't even get up and render assistance in my half-naked state. With all limited options exhausted, I run my hands over my face and through my wavy, dark hair.

How can you do this to yourself, Paisley?

I shake my head at just how unlucky one person can be. *This could only happen to me.*

Just when I think I may die in here... I hear *it*, the engine roar of road thunder. I know that sound. I've heard it during all hours of the day and night for the past three years... a Harley's rumble. It's loud and clear in the middle of my despair.

A dark, shiny Harley Davidson turns into my street here on Portola Way, alongside three other similar bikes that follow close behind in a V-type formation. The vibrating engines grip at my chest, trembling my entire soul. *I can only hope it's Saint.*

Although I'm not too sure what Saint can do to help seeing as he gave me back the only spare key he had for my house at the start of the year when I began working part-time at Maralyn's Florist. It's senior year and I needed a key to enter after walking home from my shifts. My father said he was going to copy another spare for Saint because it's always good for him to have in case of an emergency, but with work being so hectic he hasn't had the chance to do it yet.

But... maybe just maybe Saint can help me out of this mess.

Or, maybe he can tell me what's keeping Dad seeing as my phone is inside my house.

The four motorbikes kill their engines in front of Saint's

house, striking down their kickstands almost synchronously. It almost seems like a scene out of an outlaw movie, a gang of tattered-up men, leather jackets their tough uniform, three with full-face helmets and another younger-looking man I don't recognize with a black bandana with skulls and crossbones and a buzz cut.

I lower my legs and cross them over the porch steps, well aware I only have hipster panties on and a bra that's too small for me underneath this satin robe. The frilly white lace bra exposes way more cleavage than I would ever show, and the robe doesn't do too good of a job hiding it.

I gulp down hard at the sight of Saint pulling off his full-face helmet. *Whoa.* After resting his black helmet on the handlebars of his Harley, Saint rakes a hand through his beautiful dark hair, giving it that sexy bad boy tousled look. His vibrant blue eyes entice me from feet away and he isn't even looking my way. Just then, he laughs at something inaudible Leo says, and those deep, long dimples come to play over his short, stubbled beard.

Aside from Leo, Nico's also present, but as they all swing off their sleek bikes, Saint speaks to the unfamiliar younger-looking man.

I don't know what to do. Don't know if I should approach him or let it go and wait it out a little longer for my father. My decision chooses for itself when the four men begin to approach the gate of Saint's house and I launch up from the wooden porch, unexpectedly catching the attention of the younger man.

He nudges Leo and nods toward me with a sly smirk. "Look at that fuckin' hot babe," he says, his voice booming. "Hey, baby! I'm sure there's a spot open at the new strip joint that just opened downtown if you want to give your incredible tits a run for their money."

Oh.

My.

God.

My eyes widen in shock. *What the hell?*

The nerve of this guy!

The man roars in laugher, capturing the attention of all the other men... including Saint, but he isn't laughing, he's livid. I've never seen eyes like his turn to stone-cold black so quickly as his attention snaps to the younger man.

Loud thuds in my chest trail up my body like burning waves of electricity. Lethal electricity. I simply stand here on my porch steps, gaping and incapable of saying a single word.

"Saint, I didn't know Alaric's little girl grew up that fast. Oh, she's looking at me now. Hey, baby, want me to put that gorgeous mouth of yours to work?" The young man winks, a full-blown smirk on his lips as he suggestively clutches his crotch. "Time of your fuckin' life. Believe me."

I cringe. *For the love of God, can I just punch this guy in the nose already?*

Just as I'm about to tell him to shove his comment up his ass, Saint has him in a headlock faster than I can blink. Saint's muscular, toned right arm wraps around the guy's neck, restricting him firmly. *Whoa.*

"Shut the fuck up and listen to me, you bastard," Saint grits near the man's ear. "Don't you dare fuckin' speak to Paisley or any damn woman like that. She's not yours to fucking comment on, so keep your damn hands and eyes off her before I mess you the hell up. Understood?"

Oh my God.

The young man simply chuckles, redness crawling up his face. "Come on, man, I was just teasing. She's hot, that's all." His hands grip onto Saint's muscles to loosen the strain, but Saint doesn't allow it and instead tightens it. It takes seconds for the man to gulp down and begin coughing, slapping on Saint's arms to let go, but he doesn't do a thing. "Okay, okay, okay, I understand. This won't happen again. Promise."

"She's Alaric's daughter. She doesn't need to hear the shit that comes out of your mouth, got it?"

"Yes, got it. You can let go of me."

"I let go of you whenever I fucking feel like it, got it, Jason?"

"Yes, got it." Jason nods, gasping for air.

Saint's jaw tightens when his eyes meet mine in a lingering gaze. It's as if he's staring straight through me. Jason struggles in Saint's grip, tensing in the chokehold. Nico and Leo simply watch on as if this is a normal Friday night. Leo even pulls out a cigarette to his lips and leans against the fence, his leather boot up against it. *Normal.*

But it isn't to me.

This isn't *normal.*

Not even in the slightest.

Scarlet blotches rise on Jason's face as his hands fall away from Saint's bicep when Saint lets go. Jason falls to his knees, massaging his neck in a fit of coughs. "Fuck. *Fuck!*"

"Talk to Paisley like that again and you'll wake up in a hospital or perhaps not even at all, you piece of shit." Saint kicks him hard in the groin and Jason lets out a howl, gripping his crotch with a hand, his head to the concrete ground. My neighbor dusts off his leather jacket and turns to the other men. "Get him inside. All of you."

Oh my…

What the hell just happened?

My eyes lock with Saint until it's just us around. The back of my throat has never felt this dry, and it only worsens as Saint walks up to me, his jaw clenched. I see tension in every single part of him, and yet he's still the most beautiful man I have ever laid eyes on. Yes, he's a little older than me, well, *a lot* older… eighteen years older to be exact—but that never stopped a woman from looking before… *or ahem, gawking.*

I can't peel my eyes away from how damn sexy and reckless Saint looks. He's getting closer and I love the way his white T-shirt hugs his solid pecs and biceps and how his jeans are that perfect shade of worn-out baby blue. His light outfit complements his beautiful Italian olive skin and the stunning dark ink that laces down his left sleeves, stopping short of his wrist.

For the first time since we met, Saint stood up for me.

He was there for me.

Protected me.

The first thing Saint does when he's in front of me is grip the edges of my robe and inch them closer together, hiding away my breasts. My eyes shut at the warmth of his calloused knuckles brushing against my cleavage. I know it's by accident. A quick accidental motion as he closes my robe up and pulls away, but I still feel sparks I know I shouldn't feel about him.

We live in completely different worlds. He's the bad boy. I'm the good girl. He shouldn't come to my rescue like this. I shouldn't have these sparks spreading across my entire body. It's the same odd sensation that grips me when I reopen my eyes to his ocean eyes and instantly shut them again.

Stop feeling like this.

Stop making something out of nothing, Paisley.

Saint's touch lingers and he raises his hand to softly caress my jaw. In one sweep motion, he pushes back a loose wave behind my ear and rests his thumb against my chin to lift my head to him. Every inch of his warm touch electrifies me. "You okay, kid?"

I meet his eyes and manage to nod. "I am now. Do you know where my father is?"

"Work emergency at the hospital. He told me to let you know he's going to be a little late as he couldn't get through to you."

Makes sense.

"Oh," I whisper, gulping down.

Fumbling with my hands, my gaze meets my shoes and I let out a heavy breath.

At least Dad's okay.

The air crackles as silence takes over between us. I try to concentrate on the warm Sacramento breeze... on the sidewalk trees as they rustle in the air, leaves swaying... on anything, but with my wildly beating heart, it isn't so easy.

"Paisley, what's going on?" Saint raises my chin higher until his eyes are all I see. "Why were you out here when I arrived?"

"Well... I kind of locked myself out."

"Then let me help you get back in." He pauses for a moment. "Let me also apologize on behalf of Jason for what happened. He's a newbie Nico is training. What he said was beyond unacceptable and disrespectful. Don't know why Nico didn't say anything. But don't worry, it won't happen again. You can trust me on that."

I smile. "Thank you, Saint. I really appreciate it."

Inside, my eyes are widening in pure shock because this is such a different man from when we first met. I don't expect Saint to be here for me, protecting me. We don't matter to each other like that. For the past three years, it's been tense conversation and glares, but for some reason, that isn't tonight.

In the past year, my disdain for Saint turned into having a crush on my father's best friend. I don't know when exactly *everything* changed but I feel as though *something* changed the day I attempted to perform to him the lines of poetry I've kept buried inside me.

Now, I feel my walls slowly coming down and that the dynamic between us is shifting.

I'm not sure into what, but it's *shifting*.

"Also, thanks for standing up for me." I casually wrap my arms around my waist. "It means a lot."

"Anytime." Saint's eyes flicker down to my cleavage, and he instantly snaps his attention away from me, pinching the bridge of his nose. "Jesus Christ, Paisley," he groans.

I glance down and gasp. "Shit! I knew I shouldn't have put this bra on. I freaking hate it!"

"Yeah, I didn't need to hear that." Clearing his throat, Saint grips the back collar of his white T-shirt and peels it over his body. *Oh, wow.* He simply hands it to me to wear while he stands there looking like some shirtless sex god. "Here, put this on."

I'm left gaping and not so subtly eyeing Saint's beautifully sculpted abs, narrow waist, and that vaunted V-cut for a little too long… *but I can't help it.* It's hot and tempting and laced in undeniable desire. Arousal heats my blood as I fixate a little too long on the sexy, short trail of dark hair beneath his navel that runs down the center of his V-cut and disappears into the waistband of his jeans. *Oh my good God… so sexy.*

Being a former professional boxer and current personal trainer, there's no denying how much Saint's body screams grit and endless resilience from maintained fitness. I love all the ridges, grooves, divots along his body. Love the devotion and thrill that must come from not only *being* your best self, but *feeling* your best and also putting that into a career.

I've admired the tattoos across Saint's body too many times to count in this past year alone. I've been in his pool countless times, subtly absorbing every detail of his left arm sleeve and astonishing back tattoos whenever he and my dad are working the barbeque and not looking.

God, get yourself together, girl.

Gulping down, I know I need to snap myself out of it… *for now.*

Thanking Saint, I pull his shirt over my robe, his warmth and that alluring, masculine scent of musky sandalwood flooding my every breath. The T-shirt is extremely oversized on me and reaches my mid-thigh, but I guess it's better than flashing unwanted cleavage at my father's best friend… *a man so off-limits.*

"All right, come with me, I have some tools in my shed to get this door opened up."

I follow suit behind Saint, entering his front yard and turning left alongside the side of his house. As we enter the already open side gate that leads to his backyard, my eyes snap to the huge epic work of art on his back. A thick, black-gray outlined cross runs down his spine, stopping at his mid-back, almost as if it's 3D. Vines of shadowed roses, thorns, and leaves wrap around the cross. It's beautiful, almost as if it's a tribute to somebody special as breathtakingly rendered wide angel wings lace underneath the top half of the cross, expanding up his back and broad shoulders. Then, at the bottom of the cross, a few inches above the two perfect dimples of Venus on his lower back, is a name written in a thin cursive script…

Lea.

It's as if his back tattoo tells a story of its own. Such beautiful ink.

Who's Lea?

Saint enters the shed, a little far from the pool, while I wait by the grass. Staring into the glass pocket doors on the adjacent side of his backyard that open to his living room, I eye his friends inside. The three men are all huddled in the living room; Nico cracks open beers, while Leo is deep into a conversation with him on the leather couch. Jason, on the other hand, is limping toward them. My gaze narrows on him, softening as I turn back to Saint.

"Where did you all come from?" I ask.

"The fitness studio." Saint's voice comes from inside the shed.

"Oh."

"Why? What did you think I was gonna say? Church?"

My eyes widen. "*Church?*"

Saint emerges from the shed chuckling as he holds up a black leather tool bag. "Good reaction. You won't see me in there. I wouldn't be allowed into the Jesus type of church, only the devil's kind."

A few moments pass.

"Just wondering, why don't you fight anymore? I asked my father once, but he didn't give me much. What secrets are you hiding?"

"No secrets." Saint clears his throat, avoiding my gaze. "There comes a stage when you need to let go and not overdo it after your peak."

"That's true. I can imagine that personal training is incredible, don't get me wrong, but I guess with you being so much in the industry you could have ventured into being a boxing coach instead, no?"

"Yeah, I could've but… let's just say at times life fucks with you and you can't always obtain what you love. So, I switched careers and focused on personal training. I teach self-defense, boot camps, and all that shit instead. It's better for my headspace."

"Were any of your fights televised?"

"All." Saint arches a playful brow. "Why? What are you scheming against me, Paisley Reign?"

"Nothing at all."

"I don't believe you..."

"I promise!" I find myself laughing, softly biting down on my lip when he shoots me a slow, beautiful smile. "I just... want to see one of the boxing fights you were in, but I guess it just feels weird searching you up online when I know you personally, you know?"

Saint's smile instantly falls.

Oh...

His eyes fall away from mine. "Don't look me up. I don't want you to see that side of me, Paisley."

"Why not? Want to keep the reputation of being my knight in shining armor for five minutes out of the three years I've known you?" I tease.

"You know I'm anything but that."

"Okay, I'm sorry. I just wanted to see you in your element. Understand you more."

That has his ocean eyes snap to mine. "There's nothing more to understand about me, Paisley. I shouldn't..." He shakes his head, blowing out a sigh. "I shouldn't intrigue you or be somebody you want to know. You're my best friend's daughter. We live next door. We're amicable now. That's it. Don't try and find me, or watch me, or anything. Just concentrate on senior year. On yourself. On your future. You shouldn't give a fuck about me."

It feels as though my heart has taken a hit and I don't even know why. Yes, I have feelings for him, a big, reckless crush, but I'm curious. I want to know more, everything there is to know about Saint Lisconti if that's possible. But he doesn't want me in. He doesn't want me to see that side of him. He leaves me no choice but to just accept it.

"I'm sorry. I just thought..." Not even knowing what point I wanted to make, I remain tight-lipped. Glancing down at the grass beneath my feet, I feel Saint's hot gaze on me. "I just thought we could get to know each other better if we want to be amicable like you said."

"There's nothing good about me, Paisley."

"Well, a part of me is inclined to believe that, but what I really feel like saying is *yeah, right,*" I murmur and clasp my hands together. "I'm sure your girlfriend wouldn't say that."

"I don't have a girlfriend. I'm not seeing anybody."

"I know... I'm just saying in the future. Your future girlfriend or fiancée or wife will love you for you, with all the bad parts included. That doesn't mean there's nothing good about you. Just that you have faults and flaws, just like every other human on this planet."

"But that's just the thing, Paisley, I don't do love or real relationships in that case. Not now. Not in the future. It isn't me, so you can forget about the lovin' part."

"Why only casual relationships?"

Yes, you really did just say that out loud, Paisley.

Saint stares at me long and hard. "Because in a world like mine, love isn't forever, and in my case, not even for a flash of a second."

It takes a split second to fully grasp what he said. A question brews in my mind, one I wanted to know ever since I set eyes on him returning home tonight. I'm eighteen now, and to be honest, ever since last year something changed for me whenever he looked my way. When he asked me about saying a line of poetry and wiped away my tears, his touch was electric. I wanted more of him, just like I crave more of him now, even though I know I'm nothing to him. *Nothing.*

"Does that mean you've *fucked* but have never actually *made love* before?" I blurt out.

Oh. My. God.

Holy sunflowers, does my mouth not know when to just shut it?

You're a fool, Paisley. Fool. Fool. Fool.

Saint's shoulders tense, but he gives me nothing more. Absolutely nothing. Not a hint of a smile. Nothing in his eyes.

He remains completely motionless as the bright sun casts over his face.

I groan, feeling my cheeks flush. "I'm so sorry. I didn't mean to overstep by asking—"

"I don't deserve love. I haven't deserved it for a long time. Does that answer your question?"

Why doesn't he deserve it?

Does it have to do with Lea?

"Yes," I whisper, gulping down. "Yes, it does."

It's just like I suspected it to be. Saint is the type of man to fuck hard and fast, not sensually slow and passionate with somebody he truly loves and would go to the end of the earth for... *but why?* It shouldn't concern me so much. I know it shouldn't, especially considering I've never had either and he's eighteen years older, so forbidden... and yet right now it's *just us* and that has me thinking wild things. *Very* bad, wild things.

What is Saint hiding?

He doesn't want me to see his past fights.

Doesn't do love.

Doesn't want me to call him by his real first name.

He's hurting. But from what?

Does my father know? *They're super close. He must know.* But asking my father about his close friend... I can't do it. It's too risky. My father can't know the slightest bit about this fascination I have with his friend. How I just want Saint to see me as something more than the little girl with lilies.

I'm not little anymore. I'm a woman and I know what I want. And that something is Saint. I want to feel his strong arms wrapped around me, his warm lips pressed on mine. I want to feel his rough stubble graze my inner thighs as he takes me to pure ecstasy, pure bliss.

Hmmm. A woman can dream. Just like I did last night when I imagined my vibrator was his tongue and came so damn intensely at the mere thought of that alone. *God. So incredible.*

"Stay in the house while I get your door open."

I snap out of my thoughts at Saint's call as he ventures past me. *Huh?* I'm breathing heavy and only register what he said moments later. Getting his attention, I gesture toward the glass pocket doors. "You mean you want me to go in there with your friends?"

"That's what I said, didn't I?"

"Honestly, I…" I swallow the lump in my throat. "I don't really feel comfortable going in there with them after what Jason said."

"He'll behave himself this time, trust me. Just knock on the pocket doors and one of the guys will open it for you. I'll come around when I'm done with your front door, all right?"

Saint doesn't even give me a chance to answer before he strolls away from me, rolling his shoulders back. *Damn. Is he pissed at me? Have I ruined everything?*

I'm left standing in the middle of his yard, numb and completely frozen as I eye the pocket doors. *I don't want to go in there.* I've never been in a room with men like those before and I don't want today to be the day I find out. I want to follow Saint. *Wow, 'follow Saint'… how the tables have turned.*

And yet it's exactly what I do as my slippers crush the fresh green grass with every jog toward him. I catch up to Saint, only for him to stop in his tracks, and I crash right into his hard, muscular back. *Shit.* I stumble back with a squeal and land right on my ass in the gravel.

Ouch!

Saint turns to me, arching an amused brow as he eyes me on the ground. "You losing it, kid?"

"You still call me that. I'm not a kid anymore. I prefer Paisley."

Saint stares at my breasts through the T-shirt and I feel my nipples harden. My heart is pounding, my entire body throbbing in anticipation of the thoughts clouding my mind. But Saint doesn't give me much. He simply nods and rubs his stubbled jaw with his free hand, as if he's relieving some tension. "Yeah…" He clears his throat. "Clearly not a kid anymore."

The air crackles between us.

Say something, Paisley.

ANYTHING!

"I'd rather stay with you and wait by my porch while you open my front door, Saint."

Saint glances at me for the longest time, as if he's considering it, then at the last minute averts his gaze to the tool bag he's holding. "But I may take a little while as I have to go through this shit and figure out how to unlock the door. You and I both know I'm not calling a locksmith. You'll probably be waiting on your porch with me for a little while..."

"Yeah, that's fine with me."

"Well, it's not with me. I'm not giving into you, Paisley." Saint sighs, pinching the bridge of his nose before slightly crouching down to take my hand in his. His grip is strong, electric, confident... everything I'm not as he helps me back to my feet.

His hand slips away from mine the second we turn back to his backyard, and he knocks on the pocket glass doors. Leo slides them open, smiling kindly at the both of us as we peek our heads inside. I bite my lip and offer a shy smile back while brushing myself off. The other two men snap their attention our way and Jason instantly rolls his eyes at me.

"As you're all aware by now, this is Paisley. She's Alaric's daughter," Saint announces, so tall and confident. "Paisley will be here for a few moments until I unlock her front door. Leave her the fuck alone or you'll deal with me, got it?"

All the men nod.

Saint turns to me. "Feeling okay?"

I swallow thickly and let go of a heavy breath. "Sure."

Yet deep down I feel uncomfortable, and somehow, Saint must manage to see that because next thing I know he curses and says, "Fine, come with me, Paisley."

Back at my front porch steps, I watch him work his magic on my front door. The grin hasn't left my lips since we walked back. I love how he was able to understand me.

"I thought a guy like you could kick front doors open." I smirk.

Saint chuckles. "If I did that, I'd break it off the hinges. You and your father would both kill me if that happened."

We share a brief warm smile before he turns back to the door in silence, unscrewing a part and jiggling a few things around. It's as if he's an expert at this, as if everything he touches turns to gold.

Biting my lip, I lean back against the wooden railing, eyeing the gorgeous beast in front of me. This definitely feels like one of those moments where I should have my phone to film him in his element on YouTube or TikTok and the video goes viral with millions of views. Saint lets out a rough groan as the screwdriver slips from his grip and he picks it back up, but the groan comes out all breathy. So damn sexy.

Yeah, this is definitely one of those viral moments.

I try to concentrate on something else.

The tense silence.

Birds chirping in the distance.

Cars rushing down our street.

An instant replay in my mind of the 'making love' question I asked him.

I shake my head to myself. *Oh God. I can't believe I actually said that to him.*

"Saint?"

"Mhmmm."

"I'm sorry if I made things awkward back then. I didn't mean to mak—"

"It's already forgotten."

"Thank you," I whisper in relief. "Also, thank you for before. For making me feel comfortable."

"It's all right."

More silence, and then…

"Where were you heading tonight?" he asks.

"Out to dinner with Dad, but as I now know he'll be a little late… it's my eighteenth."

"Nothing from your mom again this year?"

"Nothing."

"So, for now you'll be alon—"

"Alone? Yep," I sniffle, unshed tears coating my eyes. "I'm sorry. I don't mean to get this emotional about it or play the role of the victim. That's not what this is at all. I'm just thinking about my mom and how different life would have been if I had known her."

"But you *are* the victim, Paisley. There's constantly victimizing, but then there's also not seeing ourselves as the victim enough, so we eventually cave from the inside in, and the latter is what you are doing and it's going to end up killing you inside if you don't feel those emotions. If you feel hurt, allow yourself to feel it. Don't make excuses for it when you're the unfortunate victim in this story with your mom." Saint jerks his head over his shoulder but never completes the full turn to actually look at me. A sob escapes my mouth and I cover it just as his sharp jaw clenches. "Maybe it's not my place to talk, Paisley... but you deserve so much more than how she treated you by abandoning you and your father. You really do."

His words engrave deep into my soul.

You deserve so much more.

"Thank you. In a way it's all I know, seeing as she left before I could even remember, but it still hurts."

"You have every right to be hurt. Every single fucking one."

Something crosses my mind. "Any leads in figuring out what to do when the only person you have leaves you?"

"Working on it, Pais."

"Okay," I whisper, just as he unlocks the door and swings it open. "Oh, thank you!"

A desperate relief rushes over me as we stand up. Saint has his head down, hands in his jean pockets as I pull off his T-shirt and wordlessly hand it to him. He takes it with a soft nod and slides it back on. For a moment, I ruminate over the idea of my jasmine scent now mixed with his.

"You can come in if you like..." I offer.

The corner of Saint's mouth twitches into a smirk. "No

permission this time from your father or with your signed paper and contract?"

"Oh my God, no!" I laugh. "None of that. Plus, that was ages ago!"

Saint grins, dimples and all, and it's one of the first times I've seen one last more than a few seconds. He shakes his head softly. "I should get back to the boys. I'm heading out to a fight soon but seeing as your father will be late... if you need me for whatever reason, I'll come back for you."

My heart squeezes. All I feel is warmth. "Oh, you don't have to do that!"

Saint smiles sadly, "Yeah, I do. Nobody deserves to be alone on their birthday. Even girls who are overprotective over lilies."

Fresh tears well in my eyes and without thinking, I run up to him at full speed. Saint responds instantly, catching me as my legs wrap around his waist and he laces his big arms around me in a bear hug. Arms around his neck, I bury my head in his collar, taking in his cologne as he simply holds me through the trembling tears.

He doesn't know how much this moment means to me.

Saint's fingers softly lace through my hair, relaxing me with every touch as he massages the back of my head. I never imagined a man like Saint could hug so well, so tight with no roughness, to be so responsive to me, to witness my vulnerability without judgment.

We don't have to say a word. It just feels right. *He* makes me feel right. It's as if he understands it all and I've never had that. Never had somebody I could silently vent to. Not even my father. He would cut me off, tell me to think of other things, but the insecurity and pain remain, burning me deep, and that's something nobody else seems to understand... *except Saint.*

"I'm sorry," I sniffle after a while. "I don't know why I'm crying."

Still wrapped in him, Saint lifts my chin higher, so his eyes are the anchors to my rising tides. "Don't you ever apologize for feeling emotion, Paisley. *Ever.*"

Our embrace turns so much more intimate. We're so close as I rest my forehead against his. I feel the sparks envelop my entire body as his hot breath lands on my lips, our eyes shutting as he holds me even tighter to him. I swear if Saint were to rest his hand by my chest right this minute, he'd feel just how crazily it beats... *for him.*

"Promise me," he murmurs against my lips. "Promise me you'll never apologize for it."

"I promise," I whisper back, giving into temptation and blindly cupping his stubbled jaw. "I promise I won't, Saint."

"Good."

My cheeks heat as he sets me down and my feet hit the ground. I leave the door open and step inside, shaking my head to myself at my phone and purse that are right there by the hall table. When I step back out onto the porch, I hand Saint my phone to write his number in my contacts. I don't know why we haven't done this sooner, perhaps because he's just one house away, but it's good to have his number, especially in a case of an emergency with my father.

Excuses, excuses, excuses.

Saint saves his number, calls himself so he has mine too, and once he's done slips his phone back inside his pocket. Smiling, he hands me my phone. "Anything you need, just call me, okay?"

"Okay. Thank you, Saint. I really appreciate it."

"No trouble. Even if you need a ride to work after school or on the weekends, I'm here."

"Why are you helping me?"

Saint parts his lips, pausing for a moment. "Because maybe I got you all wrong, Pais."

Maybe I got you all wrong.

I blink up at him, astonished. "What's that supposed to mean?"

Saint simply shrugs, but there's so much in his clouded eyes he doesn't allow me time to analyze as he says, "Nothing." And then he's gone.

Once inside my house, I shut the door and head to my bedroom. Stripping down, I put on my favorite floral pajamas and make my own dinner—chicken and rice. Just when I'm about to strain the rice, my phone buzzes, and I rush to it, thinking that perhaps it could be Saint, but my thoughts come crashing down when I read the text.

It isn't Saint, it's from my father.

DAD: Sorry, sweetheart, I have to cancel our plans for tonight. Work emergency. Don't think I'll finish until 10 p.m. or so. I'll make it up to you, Paisley. Promise.

I spend the rest of my night browsing the net for new flowers and writing poetry. At a quarter to ten, just as I'm about to slip into bed, the doorbell buzzes. I hurry downstairs and swing the front door open, only to find there's nobody there.

Weird.

I'm just about to shut the door when something on the faded 'welcome' mat catches my attention. A white box with a yellow satin bow.

What's this?

Collecting it, I step inside and press my back against the oak front door. There's a little envelope attached to the bow, but my curiosity has me opening the box first. A gasp escapes me at what's inside. A huge cupcake with buttercream frosting shaped in a flawless pink rose. It's the most beautiful design I've ever seen in my entire life!

Ecstatic, I pull out the card and my jaw drops right there and then.

Finally, a flower I won't step on...
Happy Birthday, wildflower.

There's no sign-off, but there doesn't have to be. Not after a night like tonight and not for a man like him. *Saint. This is from*

Saint. He was so raw and compassionate with me tonight, it was like a dream the way he defended me, clasped my hand, held me through my tears.

Maybe he was right…

Maybe I've gotten you all wrong too, Saint.

My mind can't stop racing. *He called me wildflower.*

Back inside my bedroom, I devour the sweet red velvet cupcake in a flash and send him a text.

Paisley: Wow, what a surprise! Thanks for making everything better, Saint. xx

My heart clenches as I hold my breath and await his response. I feel all these butterflies in the pit of my stomach, threatening to unravel and let go.

The *'delivered'* under my text message instantly changes to *'read'*.

Saint sees my text within seconds but never replies.

Chapter
FIVE

Paisley

EVER SINCE MY EIGHTEENTH BIRTHDAY ALMOST A MONTH AGO, THE dynamic between Saint and me has changed. I don't know how to quite describe it, but there's a warmth whenever he's around. What used to be filled with animosity is now laced in stolen glances and short embraces whenever we meet. It's as if it's normal—*the expected*—as if he isn't the man I despised for three years straight for slaughtering my flowers.

Every time I look at Saint Lisconti now, my chest erupts in violent butterflies. It never stops. Especially not right now as Saint dives into the ocean water seconds after my father.

It's the start of May and although not summer, it certainly feels like it with how warm and sultry Sacramento currently is. I wouldn't be lying if I said the combination of my father's best friend and a little eye candy never hurt anybody. *That* and a huge pair of sunglasses to hide the fact that I haven't taken my eyes off Saint since the start of our day trip to Stinson Beach this morning.

For a few weeks now, Saint's been talking about this stunning beach being one of Northern California's best hidden gems. My father has always been adamant to go, and the timing was perfect with a freed-up weekend and a belated birthday getaway.

It was a two-hour drive from Sacramento to Stinson Beach, one that was filled with writing my own poetry, impromptu karaoke tunes from my father, and Saint driving his sleek Maserati. Two hours filled with stealing glances at Saint. There's this burning fire inside of me, this heat whenever he's near, and being confined in a car with this man and not being able to talk to him like I do because my father was in the front seat was a challenge.

I found it impossible to zone out of the conversations he was having with my father about work, boxing, UFC, and solid guy talk because I was so intrigued to hear his wise opinions and thoughts. There were times during the drive up here where I was pretending to go through my poetry book, but instead was listening to the conversation. To Saint's sexy gravelly voice, which I swear I could listen to forever. *On and on and on.*

We haven't messaged since he sent me that cupcake. I didn't mention it to my father and Saint never did either. So, the gift became our little secret. There wasn't any harm in it. It was simply a treat.

During the hour and a half mark, just when I thought Saint wasn't looking, I glanced up at the rearview mirror, only to find his deep ocean eyes lift and find mine at the exact same moment.

At. The. Exact. Same. Second.

It was so synchronized, as if we planned it. My father was too busy looking out the window at the scenic route to notice. The warm Californian heat through my opened car window blew through my hair as I flashed Saint a bright smile, and he returned it. And although moments after he slid his black aviator sunglasses on, that smile didn't fall from his lips the rest of the drive.

Saint's hype for this beach is paying off. It's gorgeous. *This is my place,* he said as we stepped out of his car. But right now, I so desperately want this to be *our* place.

The refreshing scent of the ocean… Willow trees that make up some of the green hills behind me that work to seclude some of the long expanse of the beach to the quaint little town… The sandy, clean coastline surrounding some rocky cliffs farther east… The endless channels of water swiftly moving strong waves from the shore out to the North Pacific Ocean…

So beautiful.

For the past few hours here, I haven't been able to take my eyes off Saint. Lying down on my front, my breasts squeeze against the yellow and white striped beach towel and warm sand surrounds me as I set my poetry book beside me, letting go of the words hammering my brain. *Those can wait.* What's unfolding in front of me can't.

Saint resurfaces from the water looking like a god and says something to my father before both men throw their heads back in laugher. Despite all the people crowded around at the beach, I can't seem to look away from Saint and at just how perfectly his toned biceps tense as he rakes his hands through his wet dark hair, effortlessly slicking it back as if he's on a shoot for *Men's Health* magazine and they need a sexy slow motion of him exiting the water.

Saint's definitely a walking (or in this case, *swimming*) sex god. Like a twisted fantasy I can't get out of my mind. The longer I let my eyes take in the way his beautiful European olive skin becomes bronzed in the hot Californian sun, the more I want to trace my fingertips over every one of his tattoos as he explains the meaning behind them all.

The more I want to put my mouth to work and kiss every inch of his skin.

The more I want his hands to slide across every single part of my body and recklessly ease the current throbbing between my thighs as I squeeze my legs together.

Truthfully… I just want him. *All of him.*

But I know Saint can never be mine or want me in the way I so desperately need him.

I haven't taken a dip in the water yet and although today's plan was to act normal, that all changed when Saint stepped through my front door with just a pair of white swim shorts and a white T-shirt. The moment we embraced to say hello, a few seconds were enough to feel every single inch of him through his clothes and my white embroidered sundress. The hardness of his abdominal muscles. The strength of his board chest and shoulders. The heat in the hand that rested on my lower back.

I almost melted right there and then, which *definitely* wouldn't have been a good look, especially with my father finalizing his beach bag upstairs. Saint and I pulled away and the second those blue eyes met mine, my blush deepened. In a bid to break the ice, I flopped my hands about like a pigeon under attack and smiled, muttering something stupid about our clothes matching color, then proceeded to accidentally brush my hand over his crotch through his swim shorts when I clasped my hands in front of me.

Yeah… I almost died right there and then.

I think I said I was sorry about five times in a row and was expecting some sly smartass comment from him, but there weren't any. I don't know if it was because of my father's soft footsteps approaching down the stairs and Saint didn't want him involved in our conversation, but Saint just continued gazing down at me. The sexy flame in his eyes persisted in rupturing with awe as he smirked, then spun to meet my father by the stairs as if nothing had happened.

That incident is the reason why I haven't left this spot on the sand all day. I told them it was because I wanted to get some poetry down, when in reality even after the two-hour car ride, I'm still reeling from being so close to Saint's cock… *his semi-hard cock.*

I rub a hand over my face just thinking about it. *God, I'm such a mess.*

Not even a hot mess. Just a mess.

Biting my lower lip, I stretch out my legs as I attempt to stop myself from writing the lines of poetry that haven't stopped playing in my mind for the past hour…

Sometimes I see you and it's as if I'm floating,
Into another world, with or without you

I shake my head to myself. *No. I'm not going there.* Writing poetry about Saint is the definition of forbidden. He's off-limits. He's older. He's the complete opposite of me.

Don't go there.

Saint and my father are talking amongst themselves, throwing a football to each other in the shallow area of the water *as if I didn't need to see more of his gorgeous arms flexing at every move.*

With his back to me, my father is closest to the shore, while Saint is on the other side, practically forcing me to watch them play a mixed game of water polo meets tennis.

Okay, maybe not forcing... more like tempting.

Pulling off my sunglasses, my eyes squint at just how bright it is. *Jesus, so this is what Damon Salvatore feels like during the day.* I slip them back on. Where I'm lying is close to the water, so I can see them well.

For a split second, Saint's eyes find mine and I swear it's all in my head until it happens for a second time. This time, longer... *much longer.* My entire body feels like it's on fire and it's torture the way I can feel my heartbeat in my ears, thump after thump after thump.

Do something, Paisley.

Don't just stare.

Grinning, I raise my hand and wave to him. *Great. Now you seem obvious. And desperate.*

Saint shoots me a lopsided smirk and it lingers on, even when he focuses back on my father.

Sometimes I see you and it's as if I'm floating,
Into another world, with or without you

With your ocean eyes
My flowers will never die

Just as I'm about to pick up my poetry notebook, a loud bang has me rushing a hand to my heart and glancing over at my father and Saint. My father bursts out in laughter, and Saint joins along as he shouts, "Oops! My bad!"

"What happened?" I call out, my heart beginning to calm.

Saint gestures behind me and I turn, finding the football by the bottom of the huge green hill, a little farther away. "Guess my aim was off. Wasn't concentrating and threw too far."

I glance between the football, Saint, and my dad numerous times before returning his ocean blue gaze. "Want me to get it?"

"Nah, I'll come over. Wouldn't want to disturb the poet." The Devil of Sacramento grins, jogging out of the water. My pulse rises when he turns to walk my way and... *holy fuck.*

Someone hand me a fan. Right. Now.

Gulping down, I can't help but roam my eyes down the length of Saint's body and take in every. Single. Inch. Of. Him. He's dripping in water, his entire body this dreamy glistening wonderland as I eye his defined V-line, alongside the sexy trail of short dark hair below his navel that disappears into the waistband of his swim shorts and the dark tattoos that lace certain areas of his skin... and that's not even the start of it.

Those white swim shorts cling to his toned thighs, almost transparent and taunting me with the slightest outline of his cock, which leaves nothing to the imagination. *Ohmygod.* This moment is so freaking hot. I feel my nipples harden and poke through the material of my bikini top. Biting my lower lip, the smile on my lips doesn't fade as I ask myself why the most mysterious man I've ever met has to be the most blessed.

Almost nearing me, Saint catches me red-handed checking him out, and that damn cocky grin rises, killing me a little more with those gorgeous dimples and the quick wink he shoots my way when all my father can see is his back.

It's then—when Saint is moments from passing me—I feel my father's eyes switch to me and I automatically grab my notebook the most subtle I can, alongside my pen.

Shit. Shit. Shit. That was too close. *Too close.*

I continue writing the piece of poetry about Saint, adding God knows what to it as long as it seems I wasn't just ogling a man I shouldn't be.

Sometimes I see you and it's as if I'm floating,
Into another world, with or without you
With your ocean eyes
My flowers will never die

Oh my good God.
Oh my good God.
You, Paisley Reign, you're going to hell after this.

"Writing about me, huh?" Saint's sexy, raspy voice so close has me gasping and sitting up quickly. I turn to find him crouching down beside me, those amused eyes on me.

Of course that smirk is still there. At this stage, it's his trademark. *Breathe.*

"Oh, please." I laugh nervously, rolling my eyes as I nonchalantly set the notebook on my lap facing down. "I've got better things to do than to lose my mind over you."

"Oh yeah?"

"Oh yeah."

"Hmmm, interesting," he murmurs, rubbing a hand over his stubbled jaw, the other holding the football. "Thought I saw ocean eyes on there…"

Shit.

I shrug casually. "I could have been writing about anybody."

"Who else do you know with blue eyes?"

Only you.

I almost laugh. "God, Saint, it's not like you're the only person in the world who has blue eyes!"

"Oh, I know." He chuckles. "But I'm just intrigued to know who else you know with blue eyes. It's pretty rare to come across."

"Personally?"

"Mhmmm."

Literally nobody but you.

"Why do you want to know?" I tease, arching a playful brow. "Jealous or something?"

Saint rolls his eyes, that smirk still on his lips as he casts a glance at my father. Dad's completely oblivious to the conversation, talking to two enthusiastic male surfers who just jogged down the shore.

Oh, thank God. He won't let them go now for ages. My father's always been fascinated by riding the waves. I remember he once told me that when I was a few months old, he brought me to a beach with my mother. With them both being such young parents at twenty-two, any zest for adventure in their lives had to be put on hold. Yet, that summer day pro surfers were teaching surfing lessons and my father was so adamant to join. He would have if it wasn't for my mom, who practically swore to never forgive him if something tragic happened while he was riding a wave and she was left with me on her own. A lump still forms in my throat at the words she spoke about me to him.

Saint's eyes turn back to me. "I'm not jealous, just want to know who the bastard is so your father and I can kick his ass."

Every single inch of me craves his touch so badly. Boldness takes over as I lean forward, my lips brushing the shell of his ear. "Okay, I'll stop playing," I whisper softly. "It *is* about you. Now what?"

When I pull back, I ignore my rapidly beating heart and graze my tongue across my lower lip, wetting it in the California heat. That's when Saint's piercing gaze lingers on my lips. I certainly don't anticipate the soft moan that escapes his throat. It's so unexpected and… *sexy.*

"Got a little crush, Pais?" Saint teases with a chuckle.

"As if!" I laugh and playfully shove his chest, feeling his warmth transfer through me. But Saint's an intelligent man and I swear sees straight through my lie as my cheeks burn up.

As our laughter fades, this thick tension between us reemerges. A hot, angsty tension that's so sexually driven, for me anyway. It only gets worse as Saint sets the football down on the sand and takes a seat beside me on the beach towel, his long legs sprawled out in front of him, and hands effortlessly pressed behind him on the sand to hold him up.

Slipping off my sunglasses, I set them on my notebook and sit up to match his pose, crossing my legs over each other. I sneak a glance at my father, who's still engrossed with the surfers as they talk while gesturing to their boards and to the sea. But when I turn back to Saint, I find his hot gaze never left mine. Yet, the second I catch him, he glances in the distance behind me, as if it's been where he's been looking all along.

The biggest smirk sprawls on my lips. *Yeah, I totally saw that, Saint.*

"You're not going back in the water?" I ask.

Saint shakes his head. "Nah, not for now. Going to take a breather. Your father doesn't seem like he's missing me too much."

"*The* Saint Lisconti just got replaced. How does that feel?" I tease.

"I'll pretend I didn't hear that."

"You're good at this game of avoidance."

"Thank you. Just call me Ocean Eyes from this point forth," he jokes, rising his right hand and motioning it in a horizontal line in the air as if he's reading a headline. "Ocean Eyes, the face of the man troubled by avoidance, replacement and stepping on flowers seven days a week. Any inquiries, just call Paisley Reign. Actually don't, she'll lock herself out of her house getting to you."

I practically roll my eyes as Saint looks back at me with the sexiest, naughty grin. "Gee, thanks. You *really* know how to make a woman feel special."

His grin fades and he gets all serious with a clenched jaw. "No, I really don't."

"Bullshit. Let's face it, you're hot and you work in a fitness studio. I'm sure women go crazy for you."

"Did you just swear? And, hold the fucking phone, did you just call me hot?" Saint laughs, snapping out of his gloom in two seconds. "'Cause that's when I stopped listening."

"How did I know you were going to say that?"

"I don't know, am I that predicable?"

It's ironic how a group of four guys around my age walk past us at that exact moment. One catches my eye and throws me a wink, a sly smirk on his lips as he nods toward me.

"She's with me, fuckers. Keep. Fucking. Walking." Saint growls and the guys take one look at the man beside me before apologizing and practically speed walking away.

That's when I finally roll my eyes, but I can't help the smile on my lips as I turn to Saint. It takes a full moment for his narrowed gaze and clenched jaw to ease and move off the guys who are now well away from us and return to me.

"*So* predictable." I nod, all flustered, nibbling on my lower lip, and his eyes drop there for the second time today. His gaze darkens and I squeeze my thighs closer together, the need to have his hands all over my body reaching its peak. I want that thrill. That desire. That escape.

But I'm forced to let it go. Nothing can happen. Not with this.

Just then, a thought crosses my mind.

"Who's Lea?" I ask softly.

Saint's eyes widen a fraction, and his body freezes up at the question, but he recovers well, stabilizing himself with a thick gulp. "Somebody I knew... I'd prefer not to talk about her."

"Oh, I'm sorry. I shouldn't have asked. I didn't know that—"

"It's okay. You didn't know. Don't apologize."

Silence falls between us. I can't look away from him, or just how cloudy his gaze on the water becomes. It's almost as if they've been laced in coldness, a coldness I feel so guilty of because I was the one to bring up Lea. Now I know it's a sensitive topic for him.

She means something to him.

It doesn't matter how much I love the sound of the waves crashing against the shore, the birds chirping in the distance, and the way people's voices travel so smoothly across the beach, in this moment they all fade away. Nothing matters to me but how bad I feel that I'm the reason his defenses are back up, like I've prolonged the shattering of something inside him when it was already so irretrievably broken to begin with.

"Saint?" I whisper, hoping to get his attention.

Nothing.

Reaching out a hand, the air becomes thick as I cup the back of his neck. I feel my pulse in my fingertips as my digits glide up over his warm skin and softly run through his damp, dark hair. His eyes shut at the action, a low hum escaping his lips as he lowers his head, allowing me to take over.

"You're quiet," I murmur, a small smile rising at the way his body relaxes in my touch. "I'm not used to you being quiet."

"Just thinkin'."

"Okay."

I hate how I need to look away from Saint to glance over at my father. *Still in the clear.* As much as I don't want it to, my left hand slips away from him and returns to my lap. Saint's eyes remain shut, so I look out at the water instead, prepared to tell him my truth and hoping it will bring us even closer.

"I used to go to a beach just like this when I was younger. My nana June and I practically lived there. When she passed, I was so torn, I used to swim out so far into the ocean, trying to find an escape from the world. I thought if I swam far enough, everything would just fade away and be better. I felt so lost, I just wanted to find a reason to breathe again without her."

"Did you find a reason?"

You're my reason.

"I didn't then." I turn to him and smile. "I might have now."

Those piercing blue eyes stare at me for the longest time. He doesn't give me anything, not a smile, not a light in his eyes, no indication of how little or how deep my words have hit. Instead, Saint is somber and looks at me as if he has an ache in his chest he doesn't know how to alleviate.

"Before I started up boxing…" he begins, his voice so intimately low. "I hit this dark period in my life. I remember one night, I came to this beach past closing time and I just started swimming out to sea, not caring where I'd go. I guess looking back, I was looking for that escape too, just like you. That sense of just feeling nothing. *Numb.* I wanted to be numb."

"Why?"

Saint lets out a sigh. "You really care?"

"You know I do."

"Because… I didn't feel capable enough. I still don't. I still don't feel like I'm enough when it comes to certain aspects of my life. It's like I've failed. Another version of me would have been married, with a family by now. Instead, I have no fucking idea where I am, how I got here, or what I want."

"You're enough," I whisper, reaching out to clasp his right hand, and it's then I notice the long white scar that runs from the center of his hand to the pad of his thumb. "I know you may not always feel it, but believe me when I say you have a heart of gold underneath. You're always here for me. Let me be here for you."

Saint shakes his head and lets go of our intertwined hands. "You don't understand the brunt of my life, Paisley."

"Then help me understand."

"No, you shouldn't give a shit about me. You should just be concentrating on school, on your future. You're far too beautiful and intelligent to care about me. If your father were right here beside us—"

"I don't care about what he thinks. I'm not letting go of my truth."

"What is your truth?"

I can't back down from a stare so intense. This is it. *The moment.*

I swallow my pride and say, "That I can't stop thinking about you. You're my escape… my *reason.*"

Once more, Saint shakes his head adamantly and a piece inside me breaks. "I'm on your team, Paisley, but that doesn't mean

I'm your escape or your reason. I'm not your reason. I can't be that for you."

I'm on your team, Paisley.

"I can't help the way I feel."

"Please," Saint whispers, his pained eyes never leaving mine as he lifts my left hand to his soft lips, holding only the fingertips. Starting with my pinkie, he softly kisses my every knuckle anti-clockwise with each staccato word he says...

"Please." *Kiss.*

"Stop." *Kiss.*

"Thinking." *Kiss.*

"About." *Kiss.*

Saint tilts his head, finding my thumb's knuckle, and whispers, "Me." *Kiss.*

Oh. My. God.

And then, Saint lets go and it feels like the air has ripped out of me. Like I can't breathe. Like I can't... I don't think I'll ever be able to forget the guilt that flashes across his eyes as he shifts them from me to my father, who's still with the surfers.

Before I can say anything, Saint stands and jogs back toward the water with tense shoulders. He never turns back. He simply rushes away, as if nothing happened. As if my heart isn't destined to burst out of my chest any minute now... *because of him.*

Gulping down, I flash my father a fake smile as he parts from the surfers and begins to walk back up to shore to me. "Oh, Paisley, wait until I tell you everything I just learned from those two legends. What do you say I finally take up surfing in a couple of years?"

"If anybody can do it, it's you, Dad."

"See, I know I can always rely on you, sweetheart." He grins, jogging backward toward the water again. "Are you coming in the water with Saint and me?"

"I think I'll stay by the sand today. This scenery is good for poetry... very inspiring."

My father simply nods and gestures toward the water. "All

right, I'll be here. Happy writing, sweetheart." And then he's off, diving into the water and swimming toward Saint.

I shouldn't be thinking about his best friend in his moment. About the man eighteen years older than me. About the bad boy neighbor who's swimming in the clear waters several feet away. *Yet I can't help it. He's all I can think about.*

My gaze stays on Saint and it all crumbles away. It's as if my heart ricochets, exploding bullets of both heartache and thrill. And it's enough to confirm it all for me.

It's not going to be that easy to forget you, Saint.

The thoughts of Saint and the words he spoke linger in my mind all night and the following morning. At school, studying for my upcoming finals is the best distraction. But as the bell rings for lunch and I make my way to the library, the thoughts of him come back in waves.

Please. Stop. Thinking. About. Me.

I shake away the echoes of Saint's words and enter the library. *The library.* I love it here and it feels safe from the world in these four walls, especially after Erik Sanders—the senior year jock—gave me the stink eye in English class this morning just because I was the only one who could recite an entire piece of Sylvia Plath's poetry.

Erik hasn't spoken a word to me during high school, but as the weeks shorten until finals and graduation, lately I feel his eyes on me whenever I cross him in the hall. In fact, during lunch last week, I had to pass his group to get to the library and heard him call out my name. I turned and saw Erik smirking at me, his arm wrapped around his girlfriend's waist. My entire body felt numb as he nodded toward the books in my hands and shouted, *"Trying to make yourself disappear into those books, Loser?"*

Erik's entire group erupted out into mocking laughter, while I simply squeezed my lips shut. I wanted to tell him where exactly to go, but I didn't want to cause any trouble or drama in my last weeks of high school, so I continued my walk toward the library as if nothing ever happened, yet my heart darkened at his words, which dug into the back of my head.

Trying to make yourself disappear into those books, Loser?

As I step into the library now, I love how much it is my haven. The place I go to during lunch when I want to escape the madness of senior year and get lost in poets and complete solitary. I've never been one to be fortunate enough to find loyal friends and God knows I'm not the type of person to be a part of the popular crowd or attend parties every Saturday night as if life depends on it. Nothing makes me happier than some warm green tea, poetry, and flowers. I don't really need anything or *anybody* else. Honestly.

Being friends with the nerd turned cocky quarterback jock? *No, thank you.*

The catty cheerleader who puts you on her hit list if you glance at her current boyfriend of the week for two seconds? *Yeah, I'll pass.*

The class clown who's always getting suspended? *Don't think so. I'm actually dedicated to studying for finals until my eyes bleed. Yeah, I wish that were an exaggeration.*

The mean girl who blows her college scholarship because of a DUI? *Goodbyeeee.*

Times like these, I'm almost glad it's just me, myself, and I just like that G-Eazy song says. I don't exactly have many friends… well, *none* to be honest. I guess it's a combination of something inside me holding me back from being completely myself in front of others and trusting them to have my back. It's hard to get close to somebody when you know that you're either going to end up strangers or are one day going to suffer through the pain of losing them.

Until he came along and changed all the rules… Saint.

His words don't stop echoing in my head.

Please stop thinking about me.

A thought comes alive in my mind. *Look up one of his fights, Paisley.* I shake my head to myself. No, no, I couldn't possibly do it. Saint told me himself that he didn't want me to see that side of him. As curious as I am, I need to respect his wishes. It's only right.

But is it really? The devil on my shoulder taunts me. *The whole world has seen his fights. Why can't you?*

I sit down on the plush carpet in the corner of the library and press my back against the wall, my fingers tracing against the smooth edges of my laptop, adamant not to open it up and type in his name. The entire thing is so crazy to me. The thought alone of typing up Saint's name and pressing *enter* feels borderline stalkerish seeing as I know him personally.

"You're going to hell, Paisley," I murmur to myself as I flip up my laptop's lid and start typing up his name on Google. My heart is beating out of my chest as I glide my pointer finger across the mouse pad, hovering the mouse right on top of *search*.

Click it.

Click it.

Click it.

Shutting my eyes, I slam my laptop shut and let out a suffocating sigh.

I can't.

That devil on my shoulder resurfaces and the raging fire of curiosity in the pit of my stomach grows.

Do it.

Opening my laptop, I click *search* and halt my breath as I wait for the information to load. I don't know what I'm about to uncover. All I do know is there's something Saint's hiding. Something he doesn't want me to know.

Oh. My jaw drops at the gorgeous blue-eyed man grinning back at me on the screen. *God, he's so beautiful.* Saint's definitely been downplaying just how successful he truly is because as I click through his Google pages of images, videos, and news updates, each section is flooded with thousands of photographs, post-fight interviews, and current updates of him.

My God...

Pulling my laptop closer to me, I return to the first page and begin reading.

Santo "Saint" Lisconti is an American former professional boxer who competed at an elite level from 2004 to 2014. Lisconti was born on June 3, 1981, in Santa Rosa, California. Aged 35, Lisconti was nicknamed "Saint" in his early career, an infamous ironic nickname due to his reckless, relentless, yet flawless boxing technique. In July 2014, Lisconti retired from boxing, winning his final match with style in an epic Vegas battle.

Lisconti is an only child and is of Italian descent, in which he is fluent, alongside Spanish. After graduating from Stanford University studying business, Lisconti undertook short education as a personal trainer before embarking on his boxing career at the end of 2004.

Noted for his piercing blue eyes, irresistible dimples, and tattoos, Lisconti has appeared in several magazines such as GQ, Men's Vogue, *and* Men's Health *magazine, and is an ex-Olympic contender of boxing in London 2012 Summer Olympic Games. Despite his winning streak, unfortunately Lisconti needed to withdraw from the Olympics due to the sudden passing of his father. Alongside the successes in his life, tragedy has also blanketed Lisconti's life. While he maintains an extremely confidential private life, in several interviews when asked of the motivation behind his passion for boxing, Lisconti stated the loss of somebody close to him following a tragedy that occurred in 2004 before his impeccable boxing career began. Lisconti has made no other comment on the details of the tragedy, despite rumors from numerous sources claiming the white scar on his right hand was sustained from it. Lisconti has neither addressed nor confirmed these rumors.*

He currently resides in Sacramento and works as a personal trainer at his Sacramento based exclusive fitness studio, Fearless Fitness. Fearless Fitness was cofounded in 2015 by Lisconti and his ex-trainer, Nico Quivez, who is also an ex-boxer and MMA fighter.

In 2015, Lisconti also founded a charity—Silent Hearts—in which he has donated twenty percent of his prize winnings to assist sufferers of mental health, homelessness, and domestic violence. In December

2016, Lisconti's net worth was assessed as $152 million, from prize winnings and endorsements.

My jaw drops at the words I read. *Holy shit... Stanford? The Olympics? A charity?*

Wow.

My heart expands at every single sentence. The fact that Saint was able to pick himself up after what seemed to be two terrible tragedies in his life is inspiring. Most recently, his father, and then thirteen years ago a tragedy I believe has to do with... *Lea.*

I may not always understand him, and we may come from two completely different worlds... but after reading what I did, I feel closer to him than ever before. My chest aches at all the heartache Saint's had to endure, heartache I'm sure he's told my father about. Truthfully, I know there's only so much Saint and I have shared with each other, but I just don't understand why he didn't want me to discover this side of him, this sweet, generous side of him.

It's as if all Saint wants me to see is the reckless side to him—not all the broken, generous pieces inside of him. Because after today, I know he has them. He's just afraid to show them to me. A part of me wants to think he's doing this to protect me, so I don't grow too close, but it's too late for that.

I open a new tab in Google and search up *Lea and Saint Lisconti.* Nothing. Nothing comes up at all. It's almost as if Saint's hidden Lea from ever being searched up or spoken about. Like he doesn't want whatever happened shared with anybody but himself, which is understandable, yet leads to so much curiosity.

I shut my computer lid with this burning desire inside of me. And as I glance around the library to ease my mind, I realize I can't tell Saint I searched him. He was adamant for me not to. There are only two ways I can go about this... let go of the way I feel for him or step into his world.

And as much as I know the answer that would save me from heartache and a friendship between him and my father, I've never been more enticed by that musky oak scent, the built-up vulnerability behind his tough exterior... from *him*.

As much as I want to step away, the second I step into my house later that afternoon and Saint is training my father with boxing drills in the backyard, all hope fades away. As our eyes meet, one single glance at his ocean eyes is all it takes for the throb between my thighs to intensify. One single glance and my heart tells me this has only just begun and the crazy thing about the heart is... it wants what it wants.

No matter how forbidden it may be, the heart always wins. *Always*.

Chapter
SIX

Saint

"Come on, Reign, is that all you got?" I chuckle, holding up my boxing pads as my best friend delivers jab after jab after jab. Each hit more aggressive at my every shout of encouragement.

I had a rare opening in my schedule and was able to fit Alaric in, seeing as he got off work at the hospital and wanted to train a little before he rested up. Being a doctor keeps him busy, and it's difficult for him to catch a moment for himself, let alone consistent workouts, which is why me being his best friend is a win-win.

We've been out here in his backward training for a good forty-five minutes now. The hot California sun shines down on us, tingling my bare chest, arms, and back.

"How long do we have to go?" Alaric says as I alternate between moving the boxing pads higher and lower, heightening the intensity.

"Give me thirty seconds of hardcore punching and we'll call it a day."

"Thank fucking God, because I only have thirty-one seconds left in me."

"What happened to, '*I can do this all day, man. All dayyy'!*'"

"It fucked off, just like my ego."

"True!" I throw my head back in laughter. "You said it, not me."

Alaric rolls his eyes with a smug smirk. "You sly, fit motherfucker."

And just like that, Alaric gives me another thirty seconds of his best punches as the familiar adrenaline courses through my veins, the same ones I used to get every time I stepped in the boxing ring. Grit. Determination. Sacrifice. That's how you grasp sweet victory.

With ten seconds to go, I catch someone in my peripheral vision and inhale a deep breath at the sight of Paisley. She's *here*, standing by the opened sliding doors that lead into the backyard where her father and I are. Leaning against the steel doorframe, Paisley crosses her arms over her chest and her eyes find mine.

I gulp down and continue staring, as much as I know I shouldn't. But there's something about her, this magnetic allurement pulls me back to her, like she's my fucking gravity. Paisley chews on her bottom lip, a slight grin rising on her lips as she waves at me.

I throw my best friend's daughter a smile and turn back to her father before I'm caught. He has his back to her and hasn't seen her yet.

"Okay, I quit, I can't do any more," Alaric groans, stepping back and dramatically lying down on the grass. I pull the boxing gloves off my best friend as he just lies there, gasping for air. At one point, he turns his head and smiles when he sees his daughter. "Hey, you're back!"

"Yeah, it's been a busy day studying for finals. How was work, Dad?"

"Good, good, daydreaming about Nevada whenever I was in the doctor's lounge as always…"

A sweet chuckle escapes her. "I bet you were. It seems so stunning there!"

"It is." I nod. "I had several boxing matches there during my time and it's so beautiful, especially the sunsets and sunrises over the desert."

"So beautiful. You just made me so jealous." Those honey-brown eyes flicker to mine and her smug smile grows as she nods toward the boxing gloves I'm holding. "And I didn't realize you were taking house calls?"

I smirk. "I usually don't, but your father threatened my life if I didn't train him here."

"Bullshit." Alaric laughs, still on the grass. "It's just more convenient here at my house, seeing as I can't daydream about Nevada in the fitness studio like I can here. Don't even need to drive back home, can just roll into bed and sleep for a thousand years after my long shift and dream about Nevada... about Vegas... about the weather... Nevada, Nevada, Nevada."

"All right, man, we get it you love *Nevada*. You said it like five times in the past thirty seconds alone."

Gesturing toward me, my best friend turns to Paisley. "You see what I've had to put up with, sweetheart? You see this sarcasm? That's what I get for having a friendship with this guy for the past three years. Saint's trouble."

"Oh, don't tell me about that." She laughs. "I knew Saint was trouble from the moment he stepped on my lilies."

"*Wowww*, thanks, guys, for *having my back*. I see what this is. The Reigns are ganging up on me. Nice, nice," I playfully tease. "I should go. I think I've just outstayed my welcome."

"You have. Don't let the door hit you on your way out."

My eyes fall to Paisley at her smug comment, and I love just how brightly she's grinning. I feel my eyes darken as the smirk carved on my lips deepens. "It never does."

"Sometimes luck runs out."

"Sometimes," I say, my voice soft. "But today is definitely not that day. Isn't it, Pais?"

A scarlet flush graces Paisley's cheeks as we continue staring at each other with a playfully raised brow for what seems like hours. In reality, it can't be more than a few seconds as I cross my arms over my broad chest and Alaric rises to his feet.

I tear my gaze from her and turn back to my best friend. "All jokes aside, I need to get back to the studio."

"Cool, thanks for the workout, man. I'm sure I'll feel it tomorrow morning the second I step out of bed."

"You're forty, man, not eighty."

"Yeah, okay, Mr. *I'm-an-athlete-and-feel-no-pain*." Alaric laughs and flips me off in front of Paisley. "I'll see you later, man. We still on for going downtown for drinks tomorrow tonight?"

"Yeah, still on. I'll be here around nine."

"Perfect." He turns to Paisley next and smiles. "I'm going to have a quick shower now but was wondering if we should head out to dinner tonight? We have no groceries and all we do have in the fridge is leftover stir-fry and I'm kind of sick of that crap."

She shrugs. "Sure, anything works for me, Dad. I just have to do a little studying for my finals, but that shouldn't take me too long."

"Perfect!"

And then Alaric's jogging back in the house, kicking off his runners as he makes his way upstairs. The second he's gone, I feel Paisley's hot gaze on mine and turn to her, finding I was right. She smiles, brushing a hand through her gorgeous wavy dark hair before that same hand pats down her tight-fitting jeans. *She looks so good in them.*

"I didn't know you had a charity," Paisley suddenly says.

My heart clenches. *Fuck.*

How the hell does she know about that?

I gulp down thickly and Paisley groans at my reaction, shutting her eyes as if she regrets her words. "Oh shit... I... I really shouldn't have said that."

"You looked me up..." I say, but it's neither a question nor a statement. It's something in between the two because I already know the answer.

Of course she did. She wouldn't be asking me if she didn't.

Paisley nods softly, guilt in her eyes. "I did. I'm sorry. I know you told me not to, but I... I wanted to know."

Despite all the carnage in my mind, my eyes drop to her lips. She's no longer Alaric's little girl. She's a beautiful, intelligent woman who last time I saw her told me I was *her reason*. I can't shake the memories out of my head, like those at the beach when Paisley told me she can't stop thinking about me. It isn't right. I shouldn't cross her mind. And as much as she's trying to play it cool in front of me, I see the sparkle in her eyes, her changing complexion, the way she's still blushing whenever our eyes lock.

It's so wrong... wrong that I *like* it. Wrong that there's a side of me that's so tempted to rub my thumb over her lips. They're so pink and seem so soft to touch, to suck, to kiss...

Fuck.

I shake my head, more pissed off that I'm seeing my best friend's daughter in this way than I am that Paisley broke our promise of not searching anything about me.

Taking my eyes off Paisley, I turn my back to her and drop the boxing gloves and pads into my leather duffle bag on the ground.

"Saint, I'm sorry. I really didn't mean to probe. I'm just... curious, that's all."

"Curious about what?"

"Curious about you. About who you really are."

I sigh, my back still to her. "Paisley, I've told you this before. You should stop thinking about me."

"And I've told you I can't."

All of a sudden, her soft hands are on my bare lower back, caressing the glistening skin there before her fingertips spread out and trace my back tattoo ever so slowly. The action is so sensual, so bold for Paisley. There's this intimacy to her touch, one that feels like she's opening me up and all my hurt is at the tip of my tongue, ready to confide in her.

I shut my eyes and tip my head back, a soft groan escaping my lips when her fingers pave their way up and across my broad shoulders, where the inked angel's wings expand out.

"It's beautiful," Paisley murmurs and I squeeze my eyes tighter, refusing to give into how good the sensation of her hands on my body feels. I've never let anybody touch the tribute tattoo, not in the way she is—so damn sensually. I'm not proud of Paisley being the exception, or the fact my hardening cock just twitched in my workout shorts, but I'm too far gone to change it. "I'm sure Lea was a lucky woman. Did you love her?"

My jaw remains tense as Paisley's words drill into my mind.

Did you love her?

Did you love her?

Did you love her?

Lea's voice circulates through my mind, the first time in years. It may have been thirteen years, but the last words she ever said to me will be forever be engraved in me.

This is all your fault. I hate you, Santo. I'll hate you forever. Remember that.

Our love story didn't start that way. It was genuine. Raw. The purest thing I've ever seen... until everything changed.

I'm so trapped in my own mind that at first, I don't even notice Paisley's in front of me. Yet the second she reaches out for my right hand and her fingers inch to caress the scar, I roughly grip her wrist with my left hand to stop her.

"Don't," I growl, my heart beating crazy wild. "Don't touch it."

My raged eyes soften at the shock in hers. My grip is tight, so tight that I swear I can feel her every pulse. *Fuck.*

Calm down, Lisconti.

I let go of Paisley's hand and she's quick to mumble an apology and I feel worse for it—as much as I shouldn't—I *do.*

"Fuck, I'm sorry." I sigh, rubbing my face. "I didn't mean to... didn't mean to do that, I..."

My words fall blank because truthfully, I don't know how to

express exactly what I'm feeling. Luckily, Paisley's good enough to accept it and goes on to bring some light into the conversation because after moments of silence, a smile lifts up her lips and it soon transforms into a smirk as she says, "So… Stanford, huh?"

It feels like a weight lifting off me as laughter rumbles through my body. The tension between us of only moments eases and is comfortable again as Paisley joins in, giggling.

"You didn't expect that, did you?" I chuckle.

"Definitely not…" And then her voice drops lower, and it's the sexiest thing I've ever heard as she looks up at me through her lashes and murmurs, "Who the hell are you, Saint Lisconti?"

I simply smile because that's all I can manage. I maintain my expression, all while I nod her goodbye, grab my duffle bag, and shoulder out of the house with the distant running of the upstairs shower taunting my mind.

The second I shut the front door behind me and my sneakers slap against the wooden porch, my smile crumbles into a pit of nothingness. With my fist balling around the duffle strap, a frown takes over my lips; one with unbreakable strings of guilt and an agonizing knot at the back of my throat.

I can't breathe.

I can't feel.

I can't be.

Who the hell are you, Saint Lisconti?

Who the hell *am I*?

Well, that's exactly what I'd like to know too…

Chapter
SEVEN

Saint
13 Years Ago

"ARE YOU SURE YOU WANT ME TO LEAVE? YOU KNOW I CAN STAY A couple more days…"

That typical '*Are you kidding me?*' expression takes over my father's face as we step out to his front porch. "Yes, for the hundredth time, I swear I'm going to be just fine. You deserve to go out there and live your life too, Son. You've taken care of me enough. You haven't been home in three weeks."

I push the strap of my duffle bag higher up my shoulder. "It's been two weeks, Dad."

"Same thing." He chuckles. "I know you want to take care of me, but I'll be fine. Your mother is right here with me. I've defeated it before, I'll do it again. Believe me, Santo."

It's back.

Cancer. Thyroid cancer.

My gaze falls to that thin fine line across the base of my

father's neck... the surgery he underwent years ago was successful, but nothing in life is certain. Fate can fuck with you. It can
fuck with you hard until you're left with nothing but fragments
of the man you were before.

I need to stare into his light blue eyes a little longer, just to
tell myself I'm still alive. That he'll make it through this. That
I need to trust God. There are so many thoughts circling my
mind, those of losing him, those of what it will do to my mother,
Nonna, and me.

I can't lose him.

My heart spasms at the sorrow in my father's eyes when he
reaches out and squeezes my shoulders. He's compressed the fear
for so long, not wanting us to see he's suffering, but right now
when it's just me, the façade is stripped, and I see it. He's a man
of a few words, but the ones he does say... they mean the world.

My father has taught me a lot in my twenty-three years, the
most important being no matter how tough and strong you may
be, don't let vulnerability hold you back and love until you can no
more. I'm so in tune with my fucking emotions because of him.
He wears his heart on his sleeve, and if I can be a fraction of the
man he is, I'll be happy.

Despite staying with my parents for the past two weeks while
my father began his treatment, I was ready to prolong my stay.
Anything my father needs, he knows I'm right there for him. But
as much as he's a loveable man, he's stubborn. He doesn't like
being treated special and he doesn't like saying something twice.
Which is why I know he'll decline every single loophole if I tell
him I'm more than happy to stay another week and help him
around while my mother goes between work, taking care of him
and his mother—my nonna.

Pulling my father into a tight embrace, I hold on to him as if
this is the last time. The doctors said the chances are on his side,
but with the universe... you never truly know.

"Don't worry, son, I'm not going anywhere," my father whispers, his voice breaking at the last words. "Why don't you bring

over this girl you've been seeing to Sunday roast this weekend? I think it's time for her to meet the family."

I chuckle as we step away from each other. "God, you're the third person who told me that today. Mom and Nonna want to meet her and introduce her to the family too."

"Well, now you have to..." My father throws me a wink. "You can't upset Nonna, not unless you want her to hit you with a broom again like she did when you ate half of the meatballs she made one Christmas before the guests arrived. How the fuck did you eat half of them anyway?"

"I was eight! To be honest, I would do it all over again."

"I'm sure your girl would love to hear all those stories."

I smile, my heart warming at the thought of spending Sunday roast together as one big family. "I'll be sure to ask Lea."

"No, us Liscontis don't *ask*, we *do*. I want to meet this Lea and want to know how exactly she handles you. It'll make me happy to finally meet the mystery woman after all these months, you secretive son of a bitch. Okay?"

Smirking, I throw my head back in laughter. "Oh, so are you the bitch then?"

"For fuck's sake, Santo!" Warm laughter escapes my father, and it makes me so happy to see him so content with those long dimples and deepening crow's feet. He hasn't laughed this hard in weeks. Not since the diagnosis. As he settles down, he wipes away happy tears and smiles. "Just promise me I'll meet Lea before..."

He stops himself because I know exactly what's on the tip of his tongue.

Before it's too late.

I swallow thickly.

Just promise me I'll meet Lea before... it's too late.

I glance away, easing my blurring vision as I take in the warm Santa Rosa breeze and the long green leaves on the street trees that softly sway in harmony. *Breathe.* Turning back to my father, I flash him my bravest smile, but the sigh that follows is a dead giveaway to how I'm really feeling. I'm breaking inside and he knows it.

"I promise, *papà*." I nod, ready to do everything if it means making him proud.

❄

"SANTO!!!" Alexis grins, her cute little feet rushing up to me across the park. She's wearing the pretty pink polka-dot dress I bought her last month and I can't get over how adorable she looks with those pigtails and white ribbons.

As she nears, I pick her up, loving her cute squeals as I spin her around mid-embrace. I can't believe she's three and I've known her for almost a full year now.

"There's my favorite girl!" I smile, softly kissing her forehead.

"That's me!" Alexis giggles, her big brown eyes forming small slits as she smiles even wider. Wrapping her arms around my neck, she pulls me in tighter and plants a big, sloppy kiss on my cheek before screaming in my ear, "I MISSED YOU!"

The laughter that escapes purifies me. It has me forgetting all the shit in my life and my father's diagnosis. It has me just focusing on the present and everything I *do* have versus all that I don't.

"I missed you too, but I'm here now, *gioia!*"

"Yay!"

I set Alexis on my hip, my heart skipping a beat at Lea, who's finally caught up to her daughter. Setting down her bag on the wooden park bench, Lea flashes me her brightest smile. Her silky blonde hair is up in a high ponytail, and she sports that denim romper she knows I adore. I haven't seen my girlfriend and her baby girl in a couple of weeks because I wanted to be by my father's side in case he needed anything. But seeing them right now refuels me with *life*. It's as if they're my very breath. Exactly what I need to put me back together.

"Welcome home, baby," Lea murmurs, her hand running up my white button-up shirt. "Two weeks feels like a year without you."

My lips meet hers in a quick peck and a smirk floods my lips when I cup her jaw with my free hand. "You're telling me…"

Lea grins and her light green eyes meet mine, but before she can say anything, Alexis cuts in. "Am I going to have a baby sister or brother now?"

Lea laughs, covering her flustered face.

"Someone's blushing." I wink before glancing to meet Alexis's eyes as she starts bouncing up and down in excitement in my hold. Taking Alexis's hands in mine, I smile. "A baby sister or brother? What are you talking about, *gioia*?"

"Well, Mommy said that if you really love somebody, you give them a special hug and kiss at the same time, and then"— she points her finger to Lea's flat stomach—"then there's a baby sister in there."

I glance up at Lea, amused, trying my best to conceal my smirk when my brows rise. "*Oh*. Is that so, *Mamacita*?"

Lea can't even scowl at me for a full five seconds, *that's* how hard she's laughing. Some parents at the park we're at even glance toward us, but hell if we care. "Well, Alexis asked me the other day how babies are made and that's what I explained to her…" Lea says and cutely taps her daughter's nose. "No, baby. Mommy didn't give Santo that special kiss right now."

"But it looked special to me!"

"Because your mommy is one special woman," I say.

"Awww! You gotta marry my mommy."

Before I can say anything, Lea lets out a nervous laugh. "Okay, I think that's enough with the questions, sweetheart."

Alexis pouts and turns to me. "But I want a baby sister! Pleaseee!"

Lea seems as though she'd rather be talking about anything else but this, and as amusing as this is to me, I know I need to save her sweet ass. Smiling, I crouch down and set Alexis on the ground. She instantly clasps her hand in mine, squeezing it tightly in comfort, and it makes me so happy that she trusts and accepts me so much.

Lea and I may have only been together for the past few months since the start of the year, but it feels like an entire lifetime. I'm not Alexis Goldberg's biological father, but it's been so special being able to give her every opportunity there is to at least be a friend and for her to know I'll always be there for her, whenever she needs me, unlike her deadbeat father.

Michael Goldberg told Lea he wanted nothing to do with the baby when she announced she was pregnant. Lea was crushed and left him. She's been so brave setting up this new life with her now three-year-old. I feel fortunate that I met Lea when I did. It was my final month of college at Stanford and one single conversation in line at a local Santa Rosa coffee shop was all it took for a spark to catch alight between us, and it hasn't been doused since.

I love how wild Lea is, how she's a little edgy like me and a true rock chic at heart. I thought my reckless heart wouldn't be able to be tamed enough to actually dive into a relationship that wasn't simply casual, but with Lea it's different. This isn't only about her, it's about her daughter Alexis too. She's the most important thing.

Growing up, I've never wanted kids, but the second I met Alexis for the first time and Lea placed her in my arms, I fucking melted right there and then. Alexis was the cutest little thing—still is—and all I wanted to do from that moment forth was to protect her from this bittersweet world.

"Santooo! I want a baby sister! Pleaseee!" Alexis's squeal brings me back to reality. She lets out a giggle, her hands resting on my cheeks, over my dark stubble, and pulls on my tight skin to make all these funny faces. "Say *yesss!*"

"How about a baby kitten or puppy instead?"

"Noooooo!"

"Yesssss!" I chuckle. I pull her closer and she bursts out in historical laughter as I tickle her sides. "I'll buy you any pet you want, and we can make it live in our house."

Mid-laughter, Alexis shakes her head before she freezes and lets out a big gasp. "A BUNNY! Yes, I wanna bunnyyyyyy!"

"Okay, I'll buy you a bunny and you can name it *baby sister.*" I bite my lip to stop the laughter.

"NOOOO!" She giggles. "I wanna baby sister *and* a bunny, pleaseee!"

"See what you did, Santo…" Lea smirks down at us, a sassy hand on her hip. "Now she wants both."

"Well, I guess it's up to Mommy to decide." I wink.

Alexis starts jumping up and down. "Please, Mommy! A bunny!"

Lea smiles. "Maybe in a couple of years when you're bigger and are old enough to actually take care of a pet."

Alexis pouts with puppy eyes and hugs me. "But Santo said he'll buy me one!"

"He will, but when you're older."

"Fine." She sighs.

I lighten up Alexis's mood with an offer to buy her some ice cream as a treat after she spends some time on the playground. Her face instantly brightens to pure joy again and she agrees.

"Want me to push you on the swing? Or will you play on the playground first?" I ask.

"Playground first and then the swing!"

"Okay, *bella*. And remember, if any child comes up to you and causes trouble, you show them your knuckles."

Lea gasps, shaking her head with a soft smile. "No, Lexi, no knuckles."

"Yes, knuckles!" A mischievous smile works up Alexis's lips as she shows me her knuckles and we fist pump before she's skipping away.

"You're a bad influence, mister," Lea purrs as I stand to my full six-foot-two frame again.

"For you I am."

"Nah, ah. You're bad."

Smirking, I wrap my arms around her waist and flush our bodies together. "Ooo, is that so, *Ms. Special Kiss?*"

"It wasn't supposed to backfire like that."

I wink and kiss her forehead. "Don't worry, I'll make up for it tonight." I trail my lips down to her ear. "My specialties are *special hugs and kisses.*"

Lea laughs. "Shut up, Santo."

"That's not what you'll tell me tonight."

"We're in a playground!"

"I love it when you're nervous."

Lea cups my jaw and whispers, "You're so bad for my ego."

I take her hand and we sit down on the wooden bench. It's the perfect spot to supervise Alexis at the playground as she plays with the other kids at the slide and all the little obstacle courses. Further on, a few families are having picnics on the perfectly green grass, evergreen trees aligning the perimeter of the park.

It's a five-minute walk from my beach house near Stinson Beach and a place we usually come to. It was fortunate enough that Stinson Beach—where I was already currently living prior to meeting Lea—is such a diverse and beautiful community with easy living and friendly reputation that attracts many young families with kids. Even though we were our own kind of little family, I knew Alexis would love it here.

"How's your father doing?" Lea asks.

"As good as he can be. I offered to stay a few more days, but he practically forced me to leave. He's a strong man. A fighter. I only hope he'll pull through."

"He will. I honestly believe it, Santo."

"I hope so too. Sometimes I just wonder how I'd feel if I were in his shoes. It's already hard enough for me and my family as it is. I just can't imagine what's going through his head."

"I know but thinking those thoughts won't do you any good. The doctors said his chances are high and they wouldn't give you that hope if they didn't believe it. All you need is a little faith."

"Faith came to me the day I met you, Lea."

Lea shoots me a sad smile, resting her head on my shoulder as I pull her closer to me on the bench. The gloom of the reality of my world lightens up at the sight of Alexis on the playground. She's at the top of the bright red slide and pulls a funny face when she catches us looking. We wave at her, and she grins back. She's such a happy girl.

"I'd love for you and Lexi to come to Sunday roast this week," I say after a while. "My family is going to be there, and they'd really love to finally meet you both. Plus, the fact that they haven't met you yet has them thinking I'm making you up."

"I'd like that." Lea nods into my neck. "I'd also like to start a family with you one day."

The thought warms my heart. *My own family.*

"We're already a little family."

"I know, but I'd love for Alexis to be a big sister one day."

"Ohhh." I smirk down at her. "So, all of that *baby sister or brother* thing wasn't total bull on your part, hmm?"

Lea playfully shoves my chest. "I'm not pregnant. if that's what you're thinking. I just think in a couple years when Alexis is a little older… maybe we could open up the conversation."

"I'd love that," I tell her truthfully, threading my fingers through hers.

We rest our foreheads together and Lea grins as I hold her tighter. "Me too."

Nothing feels better than having my entire world in my arms. I never expected to feel this much so soon with Lea. I never expected to want to live this crazy life by somebody's side. But the moment Lea and Alexis stepped into my life… everything changed for the better.

Everything is better right now, so much fucking better, which is why I never expected our love to turn so bittersweet so soon after that day at the park…

Chapter
EIGHT

Paisley

T HIS IS THE SECOND TIME IN THE PAST HOUR THAT I WISH I COULD just throw myself to the wolves. It's one thing craving any sort of a touch from an older man, and it's another having to pay witness to another woman doing everything you wish you could do to him.

God help me...

My father thought it was a good idea to invite Saint over for dinner tonight. It's a usual thing for us, seeing as there are two of us and Saint lives by himself. Unless my father has a shift at the hospital or Saint is training late, we have most dinners as a three. It's become one of my favorite things. It's what I live for because honestly at this point, I'll take anything I can get. And if that means seeing Saint for a few extra hours every day, I'll take it.

When I opened the front door tonight, my heart skipped a beat just like it always does. Saint's such a beautiful man, so ruggedly handsome and masculine. The way his dimples deepen at every smile... it's enough to have a woman come undone right there and then. Tonight, I was feeling a little risky and decided to put on a white halter-neck bodysuit and denim shorts. I say risky because I couldn't wear a bra with the halter-neck without it ruining the whole look, so I didn't. And although the shorts aren't booty cut... if I were to bend over to pick something up, a little cheeky skin would show.

But I don't care. It's a warm Sacramento evening, I'm horny as hell, and quite frankly... I really want to see Saint's reaction.

When I came down the stairs to the mouth-watering smell of lasagna that my father just took out of the oven, he almost had a heart attack at what I'm wearing. It took about zero point zero-one seconds for him to tell me to change, and while I knew it was a bit much, I told him it already took me long enough to choose this outfit. It's a total lie seeing as I was thinking about this exact outfit the entire lunchtime at school.

To be honest, he didn't have much to protest about when Saint step through the front door and revealed the Manhattan-Barbie behind him, who had close to nothing on. *Seriously.* A tight, short, pink minidress and a pair of silver strappy heels. *That's all.*

My jaw almost dropped when I saw her, not because I was blind to the casual relationships and one-night stands Saint has, but because he's always kept them so private and low-key, so it was odd seeing them in person, especially during one of our dinners.

Saint introduced Manhattan-Barbie as Mercedes Blaqwel. Mercedes is an international model from Manhattan and after being an angel on the Victoria's Secret runway for several years, now has her own lingerie line. When she mentioned it when we sat at the dinner table about to eat, it was hard not to imagine the blonde bombshell with the gorgeous blue eyes and perfect figure in her own lacy lingerie rolling around the sheets with an achingly aroused Saint.

This undesirable jealously stayed in the pit of my stomach the entire dinner, intensifying after Mercedes mentioned she didn't eat carbs, so Saint whipped up this epic vegetable stir-fry for her

like he's an Italian Gordon Ramsay and I'm the idiot sandwich…
because I truly am.

I know I have no right to be jealous. Saint has his own life
and I'm not a part of it, not sexually anyway—that I know. *But
it still hurts.*

Hurts to pretend my feelings for him are at bay.

Hurts to pretend I'm completely fine because I need to be
with my father here.

Hurts to pretend I didn't wish it were me Saint was laughing
with, not Mercedes, even if it was only a one or two-night thing
between them. I mean, how could I even *compare* to her? Her name
was a damn luxury car brand for starters—*she's already freaking won!*

So now, as we settle into dessert—Lavender Crème Brûlée I
made earlier on—I'm breaking through the top layer of hardened
lavender and caramelized sugar harsher than I should at the sight
of Mercedes dipping her spoon into Saint's creamy portion while
she laughs at some story my father just told.

*I don't get it. She skipped the pasta for carbs, but now she can have
the dessert?*

Ugh. I'm not even going to bother.

It's a good thing Saint's sitting directly opposite me at the dining table and is naturally where my eyes fall because my father
would definitely catch on to how I haven't been able to take my
eyes off him all night if he wasn't.

"That's sensational that you're a doctor!" Mercedes grins over
at my father, stealing another bite of Saint's dessert. I didn't know
she was coming, so I only made three. But that doesn't seem like
an issue for her as she turns to me and adds, "Great brûlée, Paisley.
I personally would have turned it into a keto version, but to each
their own, you know."

I flash her my fakest-authentically-genuine smile. "Aww, thank
you very much." I turn to Saint. "If I knew Mercedes was coming, I would have made a fourth."

There's a glimmer of guilt in Saint's eyes as he swallows down his own piece of the dessert. "Mercedes actually surprised me. I didn't know she would be joining us either."

"Yeah, I totally sprang it on him." She giggles, turning to Saint with a wink. "But you can't blame me, babe. I know how much you liked those new pieces I added to my new collection. So much so you ripped one."

Oh my...

As I said before, just feed me to the wolves already because I totally don't need to hear that Saint's a rough and wild beast when it comes to sex. Not when it's the sexiest thing I could ever hear as I squeeze my thighs together to ease my throbbing sex. Not that it does much.

My father starts laughing at just how uncomfortable his best friend looks. And while Saint also joins the laughter, it's a nervous one. I see past the false façade as he gulps down. Rubbing the back of his neck, he soon glances toward Mercedes with a tight smile. "Did you really have to say that? At *dinner?*"

"What? It's not like Alaric and Paisley seem to mind."

"I know, but it's a little TMI, don't you think?"

"What is? That you like ripping my clothes off and cooking me stir-fry for a weekend only?" Mercedes smirks, cupping Saint's stubbled jaw. "Admit it, you like it too."

My father throws his head back in laughter. "God! Look at his face, Mercedes! I think you officially broke him!"

"I'm not broken, just shocked." Saint chuckles softly, his eyes surprisingly meeting mine, and the smile on his lips drops, but his gaze doesn't. It's so hot and intense, darkening even as my father and Mercedes continue talking.

There are so many things I wish I could communicate with him, but it all comes to a crashing halt when butterflies flutter in my caged chest when Saint gestures to the Lavender Crème Brûlée and then back at me with a grin. He completely snaps out of the pit of gloom from before in seconds as he asks, "This is so beautiful, Pais. Do you follow your own recipe?"

Both my father and Mercedes end their conversation and turn to me.

"Uh, yes. It's one that my nana used to make all the time. I've always cherished it."

"Well, it's perfect. She would be proud of you."

Aww.

I offer him a small smile and hope it communicates how much his words touched me.

"It's freaking heaven." Dad nods. "My mother used to make them religiously once a week and Paisley always helped her out. Everything you touch turns to gold, sweetheart."

Saint nods, and something lights up inside me. "All right. I have a story about crème brûlée, but I kind of need everybody at this table to sign an NDA before I share it."

We all burst out in laughter, and I love the dimples that carve Saint's cheeks.

I set down my spoon and lean back in the leather dining chair. "I'm sure it can't be that bad."

"You have too much faith in me." Saint chuckles.

I hold up two fingers as if I'm a Girl Scout. "Secret's safe with me. I promise."

My father nods. "You know I won't say shit."

"Me neither, babe," Mercedes purrs, her hand trailing up Saint's T-shirts, her bold pink nails softly running down his chest. His eyes never leave mine as she kisses his cheek, the hot red lipstick stain ruining me whole. "Promise I won't tell."

I swallow thickly.

Saint nods, clearing his throat, and glances between us all. "Okay, so one night two years ago I wanted to feel… Frenchie. So earlier on in the day, I bought the ingredients for a crème brûlée and my cousin, Enrico, was visiting for the weekend. It was pretty late, and Enrico was just flipping through the channels and landed on *Magic Mike*…"

I'm already laughing.

"I haven't seen that shit," my father says. "But I can't wait to hear what happened."

Mercedes gulps down her wine. "The first or second *Magic Mike?*"

"The second," Saint confirms and continues, "Anyway, so *Magic Mike*'s on and I was like, *change the damn channel.* Enrico said and I quote, '*Wait, let me see two seconds of this shit and see what I'm lacking.*' So, naturally I acted like a piece of shit and started groaning about it. In that moment, I got out the blowtorch and was using it to golden the top of the crème brûlée. I glanced up for two seconds and Matt Bomer was doing that scene where he sings that song, "Untitled (How Does It Feel)", and then he strips down to barely anything while continuing singing like a fucking legend. Part of me was like, '*all right, that's actually pretty impressive*' and I just kept on watching. All of a sudden, Enrico turned around and said, '*What's that smell?*' I looked down and not only did I burn the desserts, but my hand was all red from the heat of the blowtorch. The motherfucker couldn't stop laughing as he drove me to the ER and luckily it was only a first-degree burn, but the doctor wrapped it up and I had to make up some shit as to why it happened to not only him but *everybody* else. I think I told you, Alaric, that I hurt myself while training a client at my fitness studio."

I bite my lip to prevent myself from bursting out into laughter once more.

Saint Lisconti watching Magic Mike XXL? *Now that's a sight...*

"Oh shit, yes! YES! I remember that!" My father chuckles. "God, I remember thinking, *he's an ex-professional boxer and he hurt himself when training a client?*"

"That was me creating total bullshit to keep my guilty pleasure under wraps."

"Oh my God!" Mercedes speaks over everybody as she turns to Saint. "I love that film!" And then she starts talking about God knows what. All I know is that my father is listening to her every word like the curious host he is, while I... well, I just want to close my eyes without seeing that face... or hearing that high-pitched voice. I mean, it's great to spark a conversation, but this girl doesn't shut up. *Seriously.* Shouldn't her mouth be dry by now?

I manage to catch, "A few friends and I were actually invited to the premiere of *Magic Mike XXL* and it was just wow. It was *wow*. Like I looked around and it was just like *wow, wow, wow*." And that's where I zone out.

Forget trying to impress Saint. Stabbing my eyes with a fork sounds good right about now.

"God help me." I sigh under my breath and gulp down the rest of my water.

Great, just great. She even met Matt freaking Bomer.

Maybe I should change my name to Maserati. Actually no, Toyota is more accurate.

My eyes travel to Saint, who smiles at me, and I return the action as I set down my glass. Rolling my tongue across my lower lip to collect the stray drops of water, I lick it away and can't help but smirk when I catch Saint steal a glance at my plump lips, his eyes darkening as his stare extends. Saint gulps down moments I catch him watching, and he pulls out his phone instead. Seconds later, my phone vibrates in my jean shorts pocket and my heart beats out of my chest at the sender.

Him.

SAINT: You okay?

I glance up at Saint through my lashes, but he's still facing down toward his phone.

SAINT: If you look at me, it's obvious I'm texting you...

PAISLEY: Promise I'm okay... I liked your little story there about Magic Mike. I watched the movie on Netflix one night when my father was working a shift... The second I saw Joe Manganiello going around that leather swing, I almost choked on my popcorn.

SAINT: Oh, you've got a thing for Italian men do you...?

I bite my lip, my sex heating even more.

PAISLEY: Just a little... ;)

SAINT: I'm glad we can relate over Magic Mike.

PAISLEY: Yeah, alpha men in silver G-strings are totally my kryptonite...

SAINT: But are they really?

PAISLEY: In movies? Yes. In real life? I don't know, but for now I'll say no thanks.

SAINT: Don't knock it until you've tried it, Pais.

My heart speeds up as my mind wanders to places I know it shouldn't with him.

SAINT: Hahaha, I'm kidding. Stay away from men. We're fucked.

PAISLEY: Very encouraging... ;)

SAINT: Very... Anyway, maybe one day you can teach me how to properly make crème brûlée from scratch? I liked the lavender touch you added to it... very you.

PAISLEY: I'd love that. No Magic Mike this time? ;)

SAINT: Definitely not. I learned my lesson the first time... ;)

My gaze flickers to Mercedes for a moment, shocked to find her staring directly at me while she continuously talks to my father. I don't miss the way her nose flares. I'm sure if she glanced over now, she'd see my name in Saint's contact info, unless...I'm not saved as *Paisley*.

PAISLEY: What am I saved as on your phone?

SAINT: You're saved as Paisley... Why? Are there any other names you've failed to tell me about?

I've never shut my phone fast enough as my father nudges my side. "Who are you texting?"

"Maralyn from work at the florist," I lie. "She wants me to fill in a spot for her next week as she just booked an appointment that she can't schedule on any other date."

I hold my breath as my father nods. "All right but keep it short. You shouldn't text at the table or in company."

"Got it."

He turns back to Mercedes as she tells him about her adventures of meeting a handful of Formula One racers that my father is obsessed with when traveling the world as a grid girl.

I unlock my phone and bite my lip as I walk the line of no return.

PAISLEY: No, no other names as of yet, but right now I'm thinking of changing it to Toyota. What do you think?

I hoped Saint would get some sort of kick out of it, but what I didn't expect was for Saint to burst out in laughter. Huffing, Mercedes snaps her head his way. "What are you laughing at? I'm trying to tell your friend, Alaric, about the Formula One. Can you not interrupt me?"

Saint raises his hands in surrender. "Sorry. My nonna just sent me a text and she's just so witty. I'll only be a second."

Mercedes and my father resume their chat.

SAINT: I think I just died and went to heaven with that comment. I can't even look you in the eyes right now. I think I'll just keep laughing. You're such a smartass, Paisley Reign... :) P.S I like the name Paisley better.

PAISLEY: You like it better than Toyota?

SAINT: I like it better than Toyota, Mercedes, fucking Audi... I like Paisley better than anything. It's a beautiful name for a beautiful woman... like you.

Warmness fills my heart. *Is he flirting with me?*
Yeah, right. He definitely isn't flirting with you, Paisley.

The devil on my shoulder taunts me, *Then why does it feel like he is?*

PAISLEY: Oh yeah?

SAINT: Mhmmm.

PAISLEY: My father tells me my mother chose it... I searched it up once and apparently Paisley is of Scottish origin and means 'church or cemetery' ... Can you tell my mom hated me?

SAINT: Think of it this way, my name is Santo. It means Saint, but also

'Holy'. Church and Holy... seems like you and I have more in common than at first glance.

PAISLEY: Whoa, that's so interesting. Well... it seems like our sins will always be with us.

SAINT: Pfttt, speak for yourself, baby. I'm pure. So damn pure.

Baby.

PAISLEY: Hmmm, I'm sure you are... ;)

SAINT: Don't doubt me, believe me ;)

I feel my cheeks heat as I glance up at him and at the exact time those ocean eyes land on mine. Saint casts a glance my father's way and when the coast is clear, turns back to me and gives me a slow, sexy smirk. With an arched brow, he mouths, *"Believe me."*

"I will," I mouth back, a smirk almost growing on my lips, but it's all cut short when Mercedes says my name, forcing everyone to glance my way as I shut my phone.

"Sorry, what did you say?" I ask.

"I said, have you started thinking about college? Your father tells me you're into... flowers." Her nose scrunches up. "Flowers give me hayfever. Plus, they steal all the oxygen and are honestly such a waste. You just end up throwing them away anyway or they simply die. I feel as though you can like flowers if you don't really have much to do. I split my time between Europe, California, and New York during the year for work, so I'm definitely too busy to take care of flowers."

From the corner of my eye, I notice Saint clench his jaw.

Breathe, Paisley. Breathe.

Oh fuck it. What do I owe her? Nothing.

Grinding my teeth, I can't bite my tongue quick enough as I say with a sly smile, "Well, it's called *balance.*"

"Oh, *sweetie*, if you only knew how balanced my life is!" She laughs, mocking me. "I just think going to college for... *flowers...* is a waste. I was in Law School when I was scouted."

"Well, I was actually accepted into The University of Washington for a bachelor of Landscape Architecture. Although I would have preferred to stay in California, Seattle will allow me to step out of my comfort zone and meet new people. Plus, there's this epic award-winning architecture and interior design company, Notti Designs, with its headquarters there. It's owned by Giulio Giannotti, and they just opened a new landscape architecture department exclusive to their Seattle office. It's my dream to work there one day!"

Mercedes's eyes slightly widen. "Wow. Big move."

"*Brave* move." My father nods, offering me a warm smile. "It's going to be so strange not seeing your face around, but you made the right decision, Paisley. I truly believe Washington State is your calling and that you'll have the best time there."

"Even if that means somebody else stepping on your flowers." Saint winks, causing my father and me to chuckle.

Mercedes looks around all confused. "Umm... I think I'm missing something."

"It's an inside joke," Saint says, brushing her off as his gaze never leaves mine. "Alaric's right, this is definitely going to be a brave, bold move, but if it's anybody who can do it, it's you, Paisley. You're much stronger than you know. Seattle is going to show you that."

"Thank you, Saint. I appreciate it." My vision becomes all glassy. Nobody has ever said something as sweet as that to me before. Nobody has made me feel this emotional before. Only *him*.

Only Saint.

One of the hardest things come August will be not only saying goodbye to my father and Maralyn—my boss at the florist I work at—but saying goodbye to Saint. As much as I would have liked to attend a college based in Sacramento, I know deep down it would have been the easy option. Up until this point, my entire life has been a disaster. I think I just need a fresh start, one where nobody will know my name.

I need something new, something different, an opportunity to soak in all that life has to offer.

I need to move forward in my life, not get stuck in a rut like

I am here. And as much as it breaks my heart that I'm not going to be close to my father, Maralyn, or Saint, I just need to do this for me.

Saint was actually the one to convince my dad this was a good thing for me because my dad was devastated I've chosen to spend my college years two states north. I'm surprised with how supportive Saint has been about Seattle these past months. He was right there with me when I filled out my application and even amazed both my father and me when he hired a private jet to send us to Washington State to check out The University of Washington, speak to an advisor and discover the city a little so I could get a feel for not only the college but also Seattle itself before my application deadline. While Saint didn't attend the three-day trip with us, it felt as though a part of him was there with me. It was hard not to fall for a man like Saint when he's so attentive and... *beautiful.*

Mercedes gives me the cattiest look; a glare submerging into the fakest grin I've ever seen. "You'll love Seattle. They have really good *hairdressers* there, *sweetie.*"

My brows knit. *Hairdressers?* Why did she say that so... directly? And who does she think she's calling *sweetie?*

"Hairdressers?"

"Yes. Maybe they can fix your hair up, *sweetie.* Humidity is a killer. I have a few friends in the industry. Maybe I can link you up and you'll find a way to tame it."

I'm fuming. *Tame it? Seriously?* I've never had an insecurity with my hair, *but thank you so much, Manhattan-Barbie, now I do!*

I turn to my father, who simply smiles at me, missing the entire point. He nods softly, hovering his wine glass over his lips. "Is that something you're interested in, sweetheart?"

"Thank you for the offer, but my hair is okay." I turn back to Mercedes and do my best to maintain a smile as I rake a hand through my dark waves. "I'd prefer not to ruin my hair with chemicals. Natural all the way!"

"Oh, just like me then!" She grins with her pearly whites and it's so freaking annoying. My eyes not so subtly shift to her cleavage. Her perky, large breasts that are so obviously fake make my C-cups seem like babies. While there's absolutely nothing wrong with women who decide to have breast augmentations, at least own it.

"Yeah, *au naturel*," I say under my breath.

Mercedes cocks her head to the side with attitude. "Did you say something, *sweetie?*"

Bloods bursts up my veins.

"Look," I snap. "Firstly, I'm not your sweetie—"

"Paisley..." my father warns.

She holds up a hand to halt him and says, "*Oh*, I'm sorry, what should I call you? The *girl next door?*"

"How about *Paisley?*"

She scoffs. *Scoffs!* "No, *sweetie* works fine with me."

"Mercedes." Saint rises from the table, clenching his jaw as he gestures to her. "A word, please."

"Anything you want to say to me in private you can say to me right here."

"Back off Paisley's case."

Time stops. *Whoa.*

My jaw drops because I certainly wasn't expecting him to say that. While my father attempts to defuse the situation, Mercedes refuses to leave the table with Saint. There aren't enough nerve endings inside me to calm down and I don't trust myself to not say something I'll probably regret tomorrow morning. So, with a fake smile, I stand up from the dining table, feeling my heart in my throat.

"Kindly excuse me. I just need to touch up."

In reality I should just say, '*I'm going to be busy doing hot girl shit*', but that will never pass. It hurts to feel Saint's hot gaze on me, but I need to look away for my own sanity. I didn't mean to get into a semi-cat-fight with his new flame, but it happened, and I have no right to tell him what to do. So, it's better I remove myself for the situation to cool down, and that's exactly what I do as I turn my back to them and begin walking out of the open-plan dining room.

"You sure you're okay, Paisley?" my father asks from behind.

All I do is nod.

The second I'm in the downstairs bathroom, my fists wrap around the vanity, and I shut my eyes. *Forget about her. She isn't worth it.*

Breathing out a deep breath, I shake my head. *Who am I kidding? While it may not be the personality Saint went for with her, it's definitely the beauty. She's gorgeous, talented, much more than I could ever be.*

I force this calmness to eventually work over me and relax not only my tense body but spiraling state of mind. When I hear the bathroom door click open, I half expect it to be my father, no matter how deeply I wish it were Saint. Yet when I open my eyes and perfectly styled blonde curls are all I see, I wish I had locked the damn door.

Mercedes mockingly laughs and rests her back against the door, pushing out her chest as she watches me. "Paisley... Paisley... Paisley."

"What do you want, Mercedes?"

She cocks her head to the side, her eyes raking down my body as I turn around. Feeling self-conscious, I wrap my arms around my waist as she meets my eyes and says, "You really think you have a chance, don't you?"

Holy shit.

I know *exactly* what she's talking about but play dumb anyway. "Huh?"

"Saint. You really want to fuck the man, don't you?"

My heart drops. *Was I that obvious?*

Shaking my head, my mouth dries up. "I don't know what you're talking about—"

"You're a bad liar." Mercedes smirks, striding to the vanity with that killer supermodel body of hers. Pulling out a gold packaged lipstick from the side of her bra, she leans forward toward the mirror and starts aligning her lips. Once she's done, she rubs her Ruby Red lips together, slips her lipstick back inside her bra, and turns around to face me, blocking my view of the mirror as she towers a few inches taller than me in those heels.

It takes a while for my gaze to move from her mouth to her gorgeous light eyes. I can't help but think of her lips on his. Of what happened before they came over. Of what exactly Saint was doing the moment he allegedly *ripped* her lingerie.

"Let's cut out the bullshit," Mercedes starts, narrowing her gaze. "I'm a woman. You're a woman. We both have needs... *desires.* So, I know exactly what was crossing your mind throughout dinner. You couldn't take your eyes off him at every opportunity your father wasn't looking. You're playing it smart, Paisley, probably don't want your father to know your dark and dirty secret."

"There's nothing going on between Saint and me."

"Oh, I know there isn't. I know because I was moaning his name last night. And, just from woman to woman..." Her devilish eyes glance beyond me. "He's. So. Fucking. *Good.*"

"That's enough, Mercedes." I jump at Saint's hiss behind me because it shocks me to the core. "Leave Paisley alone."

"Oh please, Saint. Can't you see it? Can't you see that—"

"I said that's enough. An Uber's waiting outside for you. Kindly leave."

Mercedes' jaw drops. *"What?"*

I spin around and catch Saint's ocean eyes on me by the doorframe. Taking two strides inside, he settles by my side. "You okay?" he whispers, and it's the gentlest and purest thing.

I nod, my heart rate through the roof.

Saint turns back to her. "Mercedes, please leave."

She confidently stays in her place. "Why?"

"Because you're disrespecting my friend and to be honest, you're just not getting how much it's hurting her."

Friend.

"Seriously?" Mercedes screeches. "You're defending *her?"*

"Yes. Any day of the goddamn week I'd defend Paisley." Saint nods, gesturing toward the bathroom door. "Go. I don't ever want to see you again, Mercedes. *Ever.*"

Mercedes gulps down, giving me the stink eye before glancing up at him through her fake lashes. "Well, if you change your mind—"

"I won't," Saint snaps, matter-of-fact. He's fuming, his eyes so ice-cold as he stares her down. "I want nothing to do with you. Kindly leave Paisley's house."

Whoa.

With one last glare my way, Mercedes struts out the doors, swaying those hips with every step like this is some sort of runway. Saint and I continue staring at each other until there's soft murmuring of goodbye between my father and Mercedes, and the front door slams shut.

Saint's sexy, masculine cologne overpowers Mercedes's Coco Chanel perfume that lingered only moments ago. It purifies me, integrating with my jasmine scent as he pulls me into a tight embrace, our arms tangling around each other, and the tension inside me eases.

I feel his heartbeat against mine and everything gets better. *Every single thing.*

"I love your hair, for the record," Saint murmurs into my ear and the sweet words alone have me coming undone. My heart thumps wildly against his. "You sure you're okay, Pais?"

"I am now."

"I'm sorry about what transpired. I shouldn't have brought Mercedes along."

"This isn't your fault. I could have possibly handled myself better. In fact, I'm sorry I acted like an idio—"

Saint cuts me off. "Don't even think about it. You did nothing wrong."

Cupping his stubbled jaw, I caress my thumb over his spikey hairs before rising on my toes and softly kissing his cheek. "Thank you for always having my back."

"You know I always will, *wildflower.*"

I gulp down. "Why did you let Mercedes leave so quickly?"

"Because she isn't who I want."

"Why?"

Saint answers my question with another question. "Why do you think I brought Mercedes tonight?"

I shake my head, stumbled by the question. "I don't know…" I admit honestly. "Convenience."

"No, not convenience. She was a distraction, but it didn't fucking help in the slightest bit because lately I… because lately I can't stop…" Saint whispers as we pull away, his eyes sparkling in a heated passion. "Can't stop thinking about you. No matter how badly I wish I could, I can't stop, Paisley. It's driving me fucking crazy."

Oh my…

I can't stop thinking about you.

No matter how badly I wish I could, I can't stop, Paisley.

My expression softens and the warmest smile takes over. *He feels something. He feels something too.* Even if it's a fraction of what I feel for him, it's enough to have hope.

"I can't stop thinking about you either, Saint," I murmur. "I know I've already told you, but… nothing's changed for me. Nothing at all. You mean everything to me."

Saint parts his lips, and just as he's about to speak, my father's footsteps coming down the hall are all it takes for the echoing reminder of Saint's words to fade away and for our invisible, forbidden line to divide us; swallowing us whole in ocean waves deeper than the Atlantic.

Because the second my father steps inside of the bathroom, I feel like I'm drowning in a world of reality meets temptation. A world so tangible, yet so out of reach. One so dark, yet vibrant with fields of holistic flowers. One I'm convinced just collided the second my father's eyes meet mine and says, "What the hell, Paisley?"

Chapter
NINE

Paisley

"WHAT THE HELL, PAISLEY?" MY FATHER SNAPS, SETTING HIS HANDS on his hips. "I know she went a little too far, but you have no right making Saint's girl so uncomfortable she had to leave."

Holy cow.

I internally blow out a sigh of relief. *He didn't notice anything between Saint and me.*

Shit. My heart is still pounding recklessly at the close call. *That was close.*

Too close.

Saint shakes his head at my father, seeming even more pissed than he was when Mercedes was in here. "Mercedes wasn't my girl, and I was the one to tell her to leave. Didn't you see the way she was talking to Paisley? You can't fucking defend that, man."

"I know, but Mercedes was a guest and Paisley didn't help the situation when—"

"There's no fucking excuse, Alaric. You, of all people, should know it. I don't give a shit who Mercedes is. I don't feel comfortable her attacking your daughter about her education, career, and appearance and neither should you. Fuck her being a guest, that shit isn't cool."

"You're right." My father gulps down, sighing when his eyes land my way. "I'm sorry, Paisley. I just don't like guests leaving abruptly. But I get it. The things she was saying... I should have acknowledged it hurt you and backed you up. I'm sorry."

"It's okay." I offer him a tight smile. "I could have acted better, like I was telling Saint."

"And like I said, you did the right thing," Saint promises. "Believe me."

My father pulls me into a warm hug. It's the first in weeks, but it feels so good to know the only blood I know is right here.

Back in the dining room, we clean up the table before Saint convinces us he wants to wash the dishes. So that's how it goes. Saint washes. My father dries them. I put them away. The night feels easier, and that tension that brewed at the table is over. It's as if a cloud is lifted, like I can breathe again, and I don't have to feel smaller than I already am.

I can't stop thinking of the conversation Saint and I were having before it was put on hold when my father stepped inside the bathroom. There was so much paranoia in my head earlier that I was convinced my father heard what I said to Saint, even though I *murmured* it. But I don't have to think about that now because he didn't hear us. I know our worlds are bound to collide at some point, but right now I just really want to enjoy the warm thrill and sparks I'm wrapped in.

After the dishes are washed and we've tidied up, it's just after eight. We decide to watch a movie in the lounge, not before my father makes his signature popcorn. Truthfully, it's simply the store-bought kernels that he pops in a pan with store-bought caramel that he salts and mixes with the popcorn, but I let him get away with it because it's delicious. Movie nights with Saint after dinners are something he and my father have been doing for years. Usually, I would move upstairs and do my own thing, but tonight after everything that happened, I feel like staying.

Saint takes his shotgun seat at the corner of the studded cream three-seater couch, while my father sits on the nearby armchair. I sit down on the left side of the couch where Saint's sitting. The opening credits of *Casablanca* flash across the television and I smile. I can't believe my father caved and gave into my request to re-watch it tonight for what feels like the millionth time. But I love this film so much, I could watch it forever. I know my father and Saint had some hardcore action blockbusters in the mix, but a black and white classic Hollywood film, especially starring Humphrey Bogart and Ingrid Burman is something truly special.

"If I fall asleep, it isn't because I'm getting old," my father announces, leaning back in the chair as he downs his beer. His eyes are glued to the screen. "It's because I had a twelve-hour shift today and only slept five hours after."

"Excuses, excuses," Saint teases, laughing at my father's glare. Saint lifts his bottle of pineapple vodka and nods toward his best friend. "*Salute*, man."

"Fuck off."

"Don't worry. He loves you." I grin over at Saint.

Saint turns to me and subtly winks. "Tell me about it."

"Shut up, I might not see you, but I can still hear you perfectly."

"Oh shit, now I can't gift you the hearing aids I ordered for your birthday."

We all burst out in laughter at Saint's comment. My father turns his head to him and flips him off mid-chuckle. "Yeah, because I'm totally not forty and we're totally not four years apart. You're such a shit stirrer, Saint Lisconti."

The smile remains on my lips all during the opening scene of *Casablanca*. I spend the first half hour watching the film, but after a little while, my gaze travels to Saint when soft snores escape my father. My heart skips a beat as I find Saint's hot gaze already on mine. The second I catch him, he swallows thickly and his gaze trails back to the film, but mine doesn't.

I can't stop thinking about you...

The words he spoke an hour ago linger in my mind now that my father is asleep. I take the time to analyze the way the television light casts a beautiful silver outline across Saint's profile. How masculine his defined stubbled jawline, nose, and soft lips are. I wish I could reach out and caress his short, spikey beard, wish we could just lie here on this couch while he tells me about his passions, his dreams, the reason boxing aided that vigorous beating in his chest.

I've uncovered so many versions of Saint Lisconti already. The protector. The intelligent, mysterious man. The intimidating alpha. I wish I could unravel more, every single piece of him before the end of summer when I move to Seattle, Washington, for college.

"You're missing out on the film," Saint murmurs, flickers of white flashing across his face as the scene transforms into a flashback.

Shit.

I scoot a little closer to him on the couch, our thighs brushing as I whisper, "I've seen it so many times I think I can recite the lines. It's that striking."

Saint doesn't give me anything, and so I turn back to the scene and set my bowl of popcorn on the couch with my tongue between my teeth. *The silent treatment. That's what you get for staring at him, girl!*

It's not long before I feel Saint's eyes on me again while a montage of scenes plays between Rick and Ilsa of their time in Paris when they were madly in love. The scenes have my heart clenching every single time I watch this film—especially when Bogart says that iconic line for the first time; *Here's looking at you, kid*—but this time is an exception. No matter how beautiful their love is unraveling in the scenes, I can't get the heat of Saint's thigh pressed against mine out of my head.

The fact that I know he's watching me changes something for me.

What is he thinking about?

"Paisley," Saint says softly and I'm ashamed of how quickly I snap my head toward him. It wasn't even in a breath. *So much for being subtle.*

I wonder if he's going to say something about our conversation in the bathroom before my father walked in. Now that my tired father is asleep in the armchair, part of me hopes Saint will mention something because this could be an opening.

"I have a confession…" he trails off.

I turn my body toward him, my smooth thigh grazing higher up the denim of his jean-covered thigh. The anticipation has me biting my lower lip. "Mhmmm?"

Saint's gaze lowers to my lips and I swear they darken. It takes a full five seconds before those gorgeous blue eyes are on mine. "This is my favorite film."

"No way! I didn't know that. Why did I think it was *Rocky*?"

"*Rocky*? Fuck no!" His stunning smile breaks out on his lips and my heart backflips at the dimples. "My father used to always have this on. I guess over the years it became a remedy after all my boxing fights. I used to hide away and watch it. It used to calm me post-match."

Here's another version of Saint—*the sentimentalist.*

"Aww, that's so beautiful. It's touching that your father inspired your love for *Casablanca*. It must be nostalgic for you… comforting." A thought crosses my mind. "Wait, is that why you used to call me 'kid'? Because that's what Bogart calls Bergman in the film?"

"You caught me red-handed, huh?" The most beautiful grin sprawls across Saint's lips. "Yes, I guess I've heard it so many times it just stuck. I used to call you it not because you were an actual little kid at the time, but because it means something to me."

"You're quite the romantic."

"No, I wouldn't call myself that." Saint frowns, his eyes

wandering to his sleeping best friend and then back to the film. "My father was, though, a romantic. At least one Lisconti got it right. My father was the type of man who would help anybody, no questions asked. During the day, he was a hard worker—tough and direct—but the second he stepped inside the house at night, he was the biggest family man. So wise and genuine, *so* fucking genuine. He loved my mom so damn much it hurt."

Saint's words touch me so deeply because I hear the haunting emotion stripping his low voice. He may not be the type of man to so easily open up, so the fact that he is right now means a lot to me. "I'm so sorry for your loss, Saint. Your father seems like he was an incredible man. The type of man who wore his heart on his sleeve."

"He did. He always used to tell me to fight hard for what I love with integrity. The way he used to look at my mother, even after they were married for thirty-one years. So much pure love. I just wanted to be like him."

"What happened?"

Silence falls between us as my father stirs in his armchair, but after a few moments, his soft snores take over. *Poor thing,* I feel bad for him. He's had such a long shift at the hospital.

Turning back to Saint, I find his eyes are closed, and his defined jaw is shut so damn tightly. It's as if he's fighting something within himself, something so potently alarming that seems to intensify the moment I gulp down and cup his face with both hands. He gives in with resistance, and with guidance faces me. I love the feeling of his stubble grazing my hands, of how those blue eyes turn cloudy as if they're lost waves crashing out to the shore. *Pain.* Pain is all I see.

"Who hurt you, Saint?" I whisper, gulping down the agony I feel in my chest for him. "Who did this to you?"

"Life. Life fucked me over. Love didn't seem worth it. Everything changed."

"I'm so sorry."

"There's nothing to be sorry about, *wildflower.*"

"You went from *kid* to *wildflower*..."

"*Wildflower* seems more iconic. Because iconic is what you are."

My heart swells when Saint's hand hovers over my waist. It's almost as if he wants to pull me closer but is afraid of the repercussions. I part my lips, longing to ease his ache as his hot breath trickles over my lips. It taunts me, teases me, yearns for me to lean forward and kiss our flaws away. He's so close I breathe in his musky college and can taste his peppermint breath with a touch of late-night liquor. So close that if I kissed him right now, with my father feet away, I wouldn't know what would happen.

"You can touch me." The words escape me so low I barely hear them myself. "You don't need permission to pull me closer to you. Saint... you know how I feel about you."

"Fuck, Paisley. You're honest," he whispers, resting his forehead against mine. "You're so damn honest and it's refreshing. You're just so damn mature."

"I am because I've been through a lot for my age. Grieving my nana changed me. It swallowed me in this deep void and forced me to grow up faster than you would like. Grief... it's such a fucked up roller-coaster that never stops, no matter how many years have passed. As much as we'd like to think we're the creators of our own destiny, we're not, but I'm certain my path was bound to cross with yours because I know exactly how you feel about your father. I know you. I know you hold onto your past like it's your shield. But it's okay to surrender from time to time, Saint."

I smile sadly and wrap my arms around his neck as I continue, "It's okay to talk about how you feel and to be vulnerable, as long as you come out braver. I know me saying this may make me a hypocrite because I'm so in touch with my emotions yet braveness sometimes still falls short, but I'm trying my best to see the other side of the dark, even if it takes longer than I hoped. You miss your father and this film... it brings back all those emotions you've kept hidden because the world told you to. Well, forget about the world right now. Forget about the world and just listen to that beating in your heart because only it knows how far you've come and what you represent. Your father would be so proud of you. Of the man you've become. Of the man you are. Don't let anybody tell you otherwise, not even yourself."

Within seconds Saint's hands are on my waist, and it's as if they're scorching forbidden fire as he pulls me into a tight embrace. I feel his warmth all over me, across every single inch, and as much as the sexual tension lingers between us during this hold, it's also filled with emotion and hope and rapidly breathing hearts.

I take in the way our bodies respond to each other, how my erect nipples stab through the material of my halter neck and beg to be touched. How I feel his arms around me, destined to never let go. How we let the soft piano playing in the film become the background melody to something greater than us.

I know it's risky. I know my father could wake up any second and catch us because this isn't a simple embrace between a woman and an older man; it's an embrace of two broken souls trying to mend each other. And although we may be from completely different worlds, and our flaws turn to sacrifice, I'm convinced Saint came into my life for a reason. I may not believe in coincidences, but I believe in this.

Saint doesn't respond to the words I've spoken, but he doesn't need to. That fact that he holds me even tighter communicates everything I've ever needed to know. As we pull away, I lean my head on Saint's shoulder while his hand remains around my waist. We stay like this, watching the film like two lovers following their usual Saturday night routine.

We don't talk about what's going on between us. We don't overthink the fact my dad is in the room. We simply spend the entire film wrapped in each other. We don't speak another word all night, but occasionally Saint kisses the side of my head and holds me closer. It has me wondering if I'm making the biggest mistake of my life by moving to Seattle when August ends.

I thought four years away would be enough to simmer my attraction for Saint, but as he holds me to him now and I'm wrapped in that sensual sandalwood scent after he stated he can't stop thinking of me either earlier, something tells me those years won't do anything but intensify my feelings.

They will only make me want him more.

It's crazy because four years is both an extremely long and achingly short period of time, depending on how one looks at it. I'll be twenty-two. He'll be forty. *What if everything changes?*

What if the woman of his dreams walks into his life?

What if in four years' time he's married?

Deep down, I know it's more than just infatuation for me, but this is life, and anything can happen. *Anything.* And that's the most terrifying part.

It's scary.

Daunting.

Surreal.

I glance up at Saint now and find his eyes already on mine. He smiles warmly and I return it, but I'm breaking inside.

Three months to go…

Three months and it could all be over, just like *that.* It'll be over before it even started. Everything I could ever hope for could vanish and no matter how desperately I try to find the people we are tonight on this couch, I fear I'll never find Saint again. That this moment between us will just be a distant memory in a few months' time, something I'll think of when I'm 761 miles away and lying in bed watching the Seattle rain glide down my window with a blurred vision, all broken, frazzled, and confused.

Oh my God…

A thick lump clogs my throat; the first one in my twenty-minute walk home from school. I should be ecstatic, considering it's Friday and one day closer to both finals in two weeks and officially being done with high school. It's mid-May and the green leaves in the tree-lined street softly sway in the wind, calling my name with every step home… until…

He followed me home.

Erik followed me home.

"Hey, Paisley, nice house," Erik Sanders mocks, leaning against my house's oak front door with a sly smirk and crossed arms. "What are your plans for tonight?"

Great. Just great.

I don't have time for this, especially not today. It's final weeks and while some losers are using it to finalize their plans for the summer and tick off the final things on their senior year to-do list, I actually plan to study.

Gulping down, I take my eyes off the most popular guy in senior year and refocus on fishing out my keys from my backpack. *Just breathe, Paisley.* I do just that, completely ignoring his dark-eyed stare, yet feel the back of my neck bundle with tension. Erik has barely spoken a word to me the entire four years of high school and I don't plan on starting now.

Breathe.

"Oh, I see what this is." Erik chuckles coldly. "This is you trying to ignore me until I finally cave in and leave. Good try, loser, I can be here all night."

That nickname taunts me, swirling me into a pit of darkness. It's a place I don't want to be. But every time I attempt to crawl out and see a glimpse of the light, I'm blinded again.

I take in the scar on the base of his neck and scoff because it's probably from some street fight. *When are these guys going to learn?*

"What do you want, Erik?"

He doesn't respond.

"Please, just leave me alone," I mumble, finding my keys. "Please."

"Leave you alone? Why? Do I scare you that much?"

"No, you don't scare me."

"Then look at me, baby."

I grind my jaw. "Don't call me that."

"I can call you whatever I freaking like. I'm just trying to have a friendly chat, *baby*."

Opening the front door, I step in, set down my backpack on the hardwood floors, and prepare to slam it right in his damn face. "No, I know you want something from me."

"Yeah. Your attention." Erik reaches out his hand, preventing the door from shutting when I attempt to close it. Those dark eyes finally find mine and he chuckles as if to mock me once again. "I asked you a question, Reign. I think you should answer it."

Raising my chin, I narrow my eyes. "I don't think my plans are any of your business!"

"Oh, really now?" He arches a brow and steps closer, closing the gap between us. So close I'm forced to breathe in that spicy, over-exaggerated cologne and almost die because of it.

"Yes, *really*."

Cold shivers run across my exposed back as it meets the cold wall of my hallway. Erik presses his body close to mine, that permanent smirk on his lips deepening. I want to slap it away so badly. I hate myself for ever having the smallest crush on him back in freshman year.

Erik's eyes settle on my lips and then back on mine. "Wrong answer, loser."

"If you call me what one more time, I'll—"

"You'll *what*? Scream? Slap me? Get me suspended?" he taunts, inches from my lips. His cold fingertips slip under my skirt, brushing against my mid-thigh, and I panic. Heart racing, I slap his hand away and all he does is chuckle. "Not going to happen, baby, you're forgetting who runs our school—my *uncle*. I can do whatever I want, whenever I want, and nobody will believe shit over me." My eyes snap shut as his nose trails up my cheek, his mouth settling by my right ear in a lethal whisper. "Especially won't believe the girl who hasn't made one single ally in eighteen years. How fucking sad. They should give you an award for that shit, you freak."

"Get the hell out of my house," I grit, feeling my heartbeat in my ears as I shove his chest back.

Erik mustn't have been expecting it, because he stumbles back by the doorframe, yet that infamous smirk remains as he begins laughing. "Why? Is your mom home? *Oh*, that's right, she fucked off because she doesn't give a shit about you. Wow, your own mother."

My mom. That strikes a chord.

I swallow down the lump in my throat, forcing myself not to blink, no matter how impossible it is with tears brimming in my eyes. But there's no way in hell I'm going to let this asshole see how I really feel.

This is what his group does, taunt the students who don't speak up, the ones who seem weak and vulnerable and lonely. Erik's laughter heightens, and a chorus of taunting chuckles follows. I didn't notice it before, but three of Erik's closest friends are leaning on my fence, including his girlfriend, Sofie, who simply watches on.

I attempt to drown the inner turmoil in my mind. That same turmoil that toys with my every breath. I don't have time for this, time for their crap. For this pointless cat-and-mouse game. But it doesn't surprise me with Erik because he's nothing but a bully. He has been ever since the first day of freshman year when he mocked a girl with Lupus and gave another freshman a black eye because he bashfully glanced at his former girlfriend.

Stepping closer to Erik now, I lift my head to meet his gaze and forget his little cheerleader posse. "Want to know something?" I grit with a soft hiss. "People in glass houses shouldn't throw stones. You may seem invincible. You may seem strong and powerful and capable of crushing people who are already running on low self-esteem, but I see right through you. You *don't* intimidate *me*."

Erik grinds his jaw, darkness clouding his eyes as he steps forward. I hate the way a wicked half smile rises on his lips. "Did you hear that, guys?" he hisses, directing his questions to his friends, yet his gaze never leaves mine. "I don't intimidate Paisley Reign. *Ouch*."

"Oooo, better do something about that, baby," his friend Ryder taunts.

"Read my mind, man." Erik nods.

Shit. Get out of this, Paisley.

Get out of this.

I take a step backward into my hallway in an attempt to reach for my phone in my backpack, but I'm too late. All it takes is two strides for Erik to be inside the house again. He slams the front door shut beside me and grips my waist when I attempt to run. Erik holds me back, pressing my body against his for a moment before his strength takes over, overpowering mine, and in a split second my back is pinned against my hallway.

Oh my God!

Eyes widening, my attempt to scream is muted by his large left hand that slaps over my mouth. His taunting, evil chuckle ruins me whole. *What the hell is happening?* Numbness takes over my entire body and I feel all the little hairs on the back of my neck rise in fear. The beats inside my chest rush across my body. I can feel those deafening thumps everywhere. In my heart. My throat. The pit of my stomach.

With my father at work, there's no other way I see myself getting out of his hold but fighting with everything I have. But as Erik traps my body against his own and his free hand wraps around my neck, I lose all hope. No matter how hard or fast I attempt to shove Erik away, he doesn't budge, as if he were a fixed statue. He's taller. Broader. Stronger.

I never stood a chance.

Those dark eyes find mine and instantly I feel like I'm drowning in a fateful game of Russian roulette. *I shouldn't have said anything. I shouldn't have opened my big mouth and defended myself.*

"See what happens when you question my intimidation, *baby*," Erik grits. He's all up in my face, so deadly close as he tightens the hand over my mouth. "I'm going to have to teach you a lesson…"

The second he applies pressure to my neck, I slam my fists harder against his shoulders, my fingernails digging into his skin through his T-shirt. *No avail.* My muted screams lodge straight back down my throat, acting as silenced squeals upon deaf ears as he squeezes my neck even tighter.

No. No. No.

I don't know what his intentions are—to scare me, to break my neck, to choke me to death. All I know is that it hurts just the same. The pain in my heart aches because I don't deserve this. I didn't do anything to deserve this.

My eyes burn as they brim with tears and widen in a silent plea. *Please don't do this.* The cords in my neck feel as though they're going to explode. I feel them throb against him as tears torrent down my cheeks and come to a halt on his hand by my mouth. The top of his hand is so tightly pressed against my mouth, it virtually covers my nostrils and strangles my every shallow breath.

It feels as though my body is suffocating itself. The harder he chokes me, the darker Erik's eyes grow and the more I struggle for air. My lungs ache. My chest recklessly rises and falls, desperate for another breath, to hold on for another second as his body works to crush mine. There's only so much I can take. I'm trapped inside my own game of fate, feeling the world closing in on me while I'm forced to accept through the burning sensation across my chest and tightness in my throat.

I don't have another breath to take.

Erik's eyes. His eyes are going to be the last thing I see.

Breathe. Push on, Paisley. He doesn't get to break you.

A cunning smirk lifts his lips.

He wants this. He wants to see me struggle to hold onto life.

Just as it feels like I'm caving in, he lets go and steps away from me. My knees instantly give in and I stumble to the floor, face-first in uncontrollable coughs. Gasping for fresh air, the tightness in my throat remains as if his imprint is still there. My body is so numb, I can't even feel my hands, not enough to push myself up. It's as if I'm paralyzed from the neck down and I'm forced to lie crouched in a little ball with my cheek against the walnut hardwood floors.

Oh my God.

Erik's navy All Star Converses are all I see as my fingernails scratch against the floor, desperate to get on my feet again and run for help, but I can't. I watch hopelessly as the Converses stride away from me, each heavy thump vibrating through my ringing ear.

And then... he comes to a halt inches from the front door and my heart drops.

No.

"I hope you learned your lesson. Talk back to me again and I'll finish you off," Erik threatens. "And *oh*, tell anybody about this and I'll be seeing you way earlier than Monday. You better understand what that means. And don't worry, I'll lock the door on my way out."

With a click of the lock, the door slams shut behind him and he's gone. Except nothing changes for me as panic overtakes my body and the agonizing pain in my neck continues. A terrible metal taste of blood laces my tongue and my breaths all rush into one. I can't inhale without feeling as though I'm being choked all over again.

My backpack is inches away and as much as I want to clasp it to pull out my phone and call somebody—*anybody*—it all starts to fade away. My heavy eyes shut amongst struggled breaths as I feel myself being swallowed up in a pit of unconsciousness here on the hallway floor with fleeting distant thoughts.

I can't leave my father. Not like this.

I'm not going to make it.

Saint.

His words... 'I'm on your team, Paisley...'

Yet as darkness greets me, I accept that perhaps life won't give me a chance to be a part of *his* team.

Not now.

Not for any longer.

Not in this lifetime... *maybe I won't.*

Chapter
TEN

Saint

ALARIC: Are you still home?

SAINT: Yeah, just about to head to the UFC prelims with Nico. Why?

ALARIC: Paisley hasn't been picking up for the past three hours. It's not like her. I'm worried, but can't leave work... Would you mind just knocking on the door to make sure she's okay? I have this feeling something happened and it's fucking with me.

Reading the text twice over, my heart drops at the last sentence.

Shit.

"Saint!" Nico violently claps his hands together, averting my attention to him. He's standing by his Star motorbike in my driveway, dressed in his signature Harley T-shirt, dark jeans, and faded biker boots. "Hurry up, man!"

Nico and I made a pit stop at my house after work before we're set to go to watch the UFC prelims, before the main card event that is set to be one of the most anticipated UFC fights on the calendar. Alaric was supposed to tag along, but he had a work shift to cover at the hospital. But right now, after this text from him, I couldn't care less about who's playing who.

"Give me a second," I call back to Nico, locking my front door and jogging down the porch steps with tense shoulders. The key of my Maserati grows warm in my tight grip as I furiously reply to my best friend.

SAINT: On it, man.

"Who the fuck are you texting?"

Grinding my jaw, I don't even look up from my phone. "Wait, Nico."

ALARIC: Shit, thank you, Saint. I owe you big time. Let me know if she's okay.

SAINT: Will do.

"We're going to miss the damn fight, Saint. Come on and—"

"One second, Nico!"

I pull up Paisley's contact and send her a short text.

SAINT: Hey. Everything okay?

No response.

Just 'delivered'. Fucking *'delivered'*.

"Saint! Come on, man. Let's gooooo! We're going to be fucking late!"

"I don't give a fuck! I said WAIT A SECOND!" I growl, meeting his chaotic gaze in frustration.

Nico's glare may have the power to kill, but it doesn't work on me. Not now. In this moment, I don't give a shit about his impatience, or that we may miss the first round of the fight he's been anticipating for months or the fact he's fuming with flared nostrils, I need to make sure Paisley's okay.

Sliding my phone into the back pocket of my jeans, I storm toward Alaric's house.

Nico ticks his jaw. "What the hell are you going there for?"

"Need to check on Paisley. Alaric's worried. She hasn't been returning his calls all evening."

"*Paisley?*" he mocks, bursting into laughter behind me. "You fucking losing it or something? You're telling me we're going to be late because of some chick not answering her phone?"

"I don't give a shit about missing the fight. I need to make sure Paisley's okay. Don't like it?" I taunt, turning around to face Nico's clearly pissed off expression. "Too fucking bad."

"You fucking bastard! It took me months to get these tickets!"

I halt by my best friend's front door and glare back at Nico, who's just a few steps behind me. Pinching the bridge of my nose, I let out a deep breath. "Nico, do not test me today."

My fists vigorously knock on the wood oak. "Paisley? Paisley, it's me. Saint."

Nico scoffs, shaking his head to himself. "Why do you care about her so much? She ain't our responsibility. She's Alaric's. You've sacrificed a whole fucking lot to still be breathing. Don't fuck it up now for a woman who doesn't want to be saved. Screw your fucking balls on, man up, and let's forget about this girl."

I stare straight through Nico, through his complexities and that little dark place in his heart I know so well and it's pissing me off. Every time I hear Paisley's name from another man's mouth that isn't her father's, I want to pounce. I don't know why, but she doesn't merit the way she's being talked about. They don't know her like I do. They don't understand her like I do.

Dio mio.

The fact I just admitted that… well, it shows that maybe Nico is right. *I do care.*

Snarling, I grip the collar of his T-shirt and shove him back. "My balls are perfectly screwed on, *thank you*. It's your heart I'm worried about and just how ruthless you can be toward a woman who has lost it all. She's Alaric's daughter, have a little respect."

Nico rubs his chin, our eyes burning straight through each other as he adjusts his T-shirt. "Fine, get it over with then. We've got shit to do. Can't wait all night for a woman who doesn't want to be saved."

My eyes narrow down on the front door. "Maybe she's... stressed."

"Good, she should be. Teach her a fucking lesson for making me late to a fight. I don't want to miss the damn prelims."

Selfish fucker.

"Easy now. The aim isn't to scare her."

"Bullshit."

I glare at Nico.

"Fine, if you understand her as much as you say you do, get her to open up the door."

I will.

I turn back to the front door and slide my hand up the door again. *I care about her.* When the hell did that happen? *A long time ago, Lisconti, you confirmed it the night you told Paisley you couldn't stop thinking about her and meant every single world.*

Dio... I'm so done if Alaric finds out about all this.

"Paisley?" Inhaling a deep breath, my fingers form a fist and I knock on the door. "Paisley... I know you're in there. I'm not going to hurt you. I just... I just want to make sure you're okay. Your father's worried and so am I. Please, Paisley. I never say fuckin' *please*, but I *need* to know you're okay. I know you're listening."

Once again, silence greets me on the other side of the door, yet a visual invades my mind. One where Paisley is on the other side of the door, her forehead pressed against it and fingers brushing against the door handle, too frazzled to twist it open.

That's just it... she's stressed.

Stressed.

"*Wildflower*, it's just me," I murmur against the door, pressing my hand against it this time and imagining her synchronizing and doing the same. A small smile pulls on my lips, one I'm not proud of, but push through nonetheless at what I'm about to do... or rather *say*. "Okay. *Marigolds*. Go ahead, tell me, Paisley. Tell me everything you know about marigolds. I want to know."

It's nearing 6:00 p.m. and as glowing orange and red smear the sunset sky and birds chirping in the distance fill the white noise, I glance over my shoulder at Nico's pressed lips. My head snaps back to the door when I swear I hear something... a bump or scratch against the door. It's silent for the longest time and I'm about to pull out my phone to call Alaric when that soft, trembling voice douses my soul in relief.

"*Marigolds*," Paisley murmurs through the door. "Marigolds ca-can be either orange or gold in color. They thrive in full sun and heat. My grandmother... she used to call them the devil's flower. They symbolize a lust for success and prosperity and can be used in textiles. Commonly, they are used when... when grieving somebody you love dies, or... celebrating those who have passed."

At her last couple words, the door clicks unlocked and opens wide. Everything inside me comes to a screeching halt the second Paisley steps forward from behind the door and faces me.

Slowly, her gaze moves up until those anxious honey-brown eyes meet mine and her hair falls away from her beautiful face, revealing pinkish-red blotches around her neck. The sides of her neck are even more concerning, with thicker and taller purplish blotches, as if they were thumb imprints. It's almost as if her neck has been... as if somebody tried to... *FUCK*.

"Who the fuck did this to you, Paisley?" Despite my flared nostrils, clenched jaw, and anger bubbling inside my blood, I manage to speak softly and stay calm for her. "Who the fuck hurt you because I swear to God I'll kill 'em with my bare hands."

The way she's looking at me, the hope in her stare, I don't know what to do with it.

"Paisley," I breathe, taking a step forward, but she takes one back.

Shit.

"You're staring," she sniffles, her voice a touch huskier than usual as if it's been strained. Her eyes thin as tears brim in them. "I know I look hideous."

"No, *wildflower*," I whisper, gulping down thickly. "No, I'm not staring... I'm..."

Paisley shakes her head and slaps a hand to her mouth to hide her sob. The second she turns to leave, I pull my head out of my ass and gently wrap my fingers around her wrist. The action draws her back to me. Her glassy eyes lift to mine and despite all my rage for whoever did this to her, I manage to shoot her a soft smile.

I don't wait for Paisley's reaction or permission. Instead, I tug her to my chest, no questions asked, and pull her into a warm embrace. I guide her arms around my neck as if it's automatic and she holds onto me so damn tightly. It breaks me to see her sobbing into my chest as I pull her closer to me in a bear hug. My arms wrap around her, one by her petite waist and the other across her shoulder blades as I lower my head into the crook of her neck, keeping a little distance from her soft, blemished skin in case she's feeling any pain.

"You're safe now, Paisley. You're safe. Whatever did happen, I'm going to make sure it never happens again and be there for you. I'm going to fucking be there for you and if they want to get to you again, they need to get through me first. You're not alone in this. Not anymore," I whisper softly in her ear, preventing Nico from hearing a word. "I promise."

I've never held somebody this damn intimately before. It isn't just a comforting hug; it's clinging onto each other for dear life. A guilty fucking hug with both her father and Nico circling my mind. But I don't care what Nico may be thinking right now. It's the same reason I shut my eyes and ignore everything else but her... I *don't* want to know.

This embrace changes me. As I breathe in Paisley's sweet jasmine scent it should bother me after everything in my life, but it's the only thing that calms me down and relaxes my body, like a devil embracing the gates of hell. Right now, I want to break away from Lucifer and be the saint my mother intended me to be.

I want Paisley to know I'll never hurt her like the person who attacked her did. In this moment, I want to be everything Paisley Reign needs, but I don't know how.

"You're beautiful, Paisley," I murmur, meaning every single word. "So fucking beautiful. And nobody can take that away from you, not mentally, not physically, not in your heart. You hear me? You're beautiful."

"You really mean that?"

"You know me, Pais, I don't say anything I don't mean."

She cries harder, which only prompts me to hug her tighter.

As his boots slap down beside us on the wooden porch, I hear the scoff in Nico's judgmental voice without even having to see it as he rounds me and whispers in my ear, "Hug all your best friend's daughters like that, Saint? Alaric would have you in the fucking gutter."

I blink my eyes open and flip him off with the hand around Paisley's shoulder blades.

"*Fuck off*," I mouth, and he throws his head back in mocking laughter before disappearing down the hall.

Breathe. Just breathe, Lisconti.

Nico isn't going to tell Alaric anything.

Alaric asked you to be here for her. This isn't wrong.

For a second, I concentrate on the frantic beating inside my chest. It's beating this hard because of her. Because of the slightest touch from her. *Fuckkk. This is so wrong.*

I remain outside with Paisley until she settles down. When I attempt to step back, she's the one holding me closer this time.

"Wait," she whispers, "I like it like this. I feel... safe."

I feel safe.

It dawns on me that I shouldn't be the one allowing her to feel this type of way. It shouldn't be *me*, it should be some other guy who's able to gift her the entire world and the stars while he's at it—I can't give her that. I can't give her half the things she thinks I can.

But I can't help myself from wanting to be that guy so badly right now.

"Can I ask you something, Saint?"

"Mhmmm."

Paisley pauses for a moment before saying, "How do you know about marigolds?"

Her question brings a small chuckle to my lips, one I haven't let out in a long time. "Yeah, I'm definitely not telling you that."

Still wrapped in each other, we pull our heads back until our eyes meet. I look into her reddened eyes from crying and draw my lips closer to her cheeks and kiss her tears away. I can't control it, can't help but cherish her warm skin against my lips, knowing she's going to be all right.

When I'm done, my lips move down to her neck and brush over the blotches on her soft, delicate skin. Her breath hitches, turning into a soft moan as I shut my eyes and trail my lips over every area of blemished skin and blotches, knowing very well that if whoever did this to her isn't dead by now, they will be very soon.

I kiss away the pain, slowly pressing my lips over every inch of her skin as if my touch has the ability to repair her. Heal her. Mend her. I wish it did. I wish this never happened. I wish she had called me.

"I thought you weren't the kind of man to kiss and tell."

That has me pulling away and smirking down at her "And I thought big girls don't cry."

A slight smile cracks on her lips and I'm happy I'm the one who brought it there. Even if it's small, it's something. "Oh my God, shut up!"

Yeah, she's definitely feeling like her old self now.

"Come on, let's get inside and talk this through."

"Okay."

As I step in behind her and shut the front door, I shoot Alaric a quick message that she's home and that he needs to get home ASAP. I know I should tell him about the blotches on her neck via text, but it's better to hold off until he gets here to prevent him from getting into a pile-up on the way home. Besides, he's a doctor and can assess her here, seeing as she's okay now.

As selfish as it is and as fucked up as it sounds, I want to be the one Paisley confides in first. I want to take the pain away. I want to be the one to hold her again tightly, as if the world is ending and all that is left is one single touch and a lifetime of memories in the forms of poetry and flowers.

Nico awaits our arrival in the living room, already helping himself to a glass of whiskey. He's already taken a seat on the left side of the studded cream three-seater couch. Although it's a similar layout to mine and the design is flipped, I've always loved the extra touches in Alaric and Paisley's house. Stepping inside it feels like home. It's cozy and contemporary filled with natural woods, light colors, and vibrant art pieces.

I take a seat beside Nico on the couch, while Paisley settles into a matching studded linen blend armchair.

"I thought this could help me feel better," Paisley mumbles shyly, almost more to herself than to anyone else as she picks up a floral tea mug from the coffee table. She does so as if she needs to explain herself, but she doesn't. Paisley could do anything and it would be perfect.

My eyes stay on her plump, heart-shaped lips as she takes a sip. I swallow thickly the second she draws the mug to rest on her crossed legs as her pink, glistening tongue runs over her lower lip to collect a stray tea drop. *Fuck.* The visual drives me wild and takes me to another dimension. One I know I shouldn't be in because of how forbidden we would be. And yet, I can't take my eyes away from that gorgeous mouth of hers.

This is what it must feel like to be between both heaven and hell.

What the hell? *What the fuck am I saying?*

Paisley's too fucking good for me. She's completely off-limits, too young for me and most importantly, I don't do love. Yet these thoughts... *Dio.*

"You want to feel better? Well, you should ask Saint for some remedies." Nico coldly smirks, leaning back on the couch. "He'll happily supply."

My eyes practically budge out of my sockets. For. The. Love. Of. God. Nico.

"Shut it down, Nico," I grit.

"Oh, come on. You used to sell them, don't shy away now."

"You know I don't sell them anymore."

"But you *did*. Sure you don't have a few stashes hidden away?"

I grind my jaw, remaining silent as Paisley turns to me and says, "What are remedies?"

I know I need to answer honestly. She isn't a kid anymore. She's eighteen, a woman, and I can't sugarcoat this shit, no matter how badly I want to. This is a side of me not even Alaric knows about, and I wanted to keep it that way, especially around Paisley, but of course Nico's enjoying busting my balls a little too much and has pushed me to tell her the truth.

"Pills I used to produce... during a low time in my life, before boxing," I explain, rubbing my hands together. "Increased energy pills."

"*Oh*," she whispers innocently, "That's... not too bad."

"They were coated with Molly," Nico smugly interjects.

Fuck me.

"What's that?" Paisley's question has me side-eyeing Nico, who grins.

Letting out a controlled sigh, I lay it all out on the table for her. "It's also known as Ecstasy." She continues to stare at me blankly and so I clarify even more, rubbing the nape of my neck with how ashamed I am at this. This is a part of my past I've buried and forgotten. "MDMA. It's a psychoactive drug. Remedies for people craving an escape... until you're arrested for taking or possessing an illegal substance. Never happened to me, but..."

"Oh." Paisley's mouth drops open in a wide 'O' and she shakes her head. "No, thanks."

"*No, thanks*, what's that?" Nico mocks with a scoff. "Shit, didn't know Alaric's girl was so damn gullible. Told you we should have just gone to the fight tonight, man. We're going to be late!"

"Oh, are you talking about that UFC fight that my dad was supposed to come along with too?" Paisley asks in confusion.

"Hey!" Nico growls, unexpectedly slamming his fist on the coffee table, and Paisley jumps in her seat. As good as my reflexes are, the bang scared the shit out of me too. My heart's in my fucking throat. *Fuck, man.* "No questions. Understand?" he continues in an uncalled-for grit. "If we ask you something, you open that pretty mouth of yours. If not, it remains chained shut, got it?"

Frightful eyes snap my way. Paisley clenches her fists and looks down at her tea, blinking away tears. I glance toward Nico with narrowed brows and raise my arms out to the side as if to say, *'What the hell happened to not scaring the shit out of her?'*

I see the redness on her neck, see the petrified fear in her eyes, the insecurities, and instead of saying what I would have said to anybody else that wasn't her—which would have been, *'answer him'*—I find myself taking it out on him.

"Nico, tone it down."

Paisley's eyes widen as she looks up at me. "No, it's okay. I got it, sorry."

"Don't apologize for his behavior. If your father were here, they would be at it."

"What?" Nico scoffs at me. "You my dad now or something, Saint?"

He hits a sensitive wound and he freaking knows it. *My father.* Yet right here in front of Paisley, I'm forced to just shut my mouth with a tense jaw. Nico and I have the stare down of the century before I turn back to Paisley.

Pushing forward on the couch, I lean closer to her with my hands clasped. "Can you tell us what happened? Why didn't you answer your dad's calls? He was going batshit crazy."

Paisley's gorgeous eyes drop to my hands. "Because I didn't want to cause any trouble. I'm fine."

"No, you're not."

"I promise I am."

"You're a bad liar."

"I can't tell anybody about it. If I do, then…"

"You can tell me. I'm not leaving until you tell me what happened."

Nico groans beside me. "For fuck's sake. We'll never make it now."

Paisley sucks in a deep breath, her gaze flickering between Nico and me before it lands on me. "Okay, fine. I was walking home from school and didn't notice a group from school walking behind me. One of the guys followed me to the front door and made a comment. At first, I ignored him, but he made it impossible for me not to retaliate with some of the things he was saying…"

"Who's the guy?"

She swallows hard. "Remember that Erik guy I was talking about a few days ago?"

"Mhmmm."

I feel Nico's eyes on me.

"Well, it was him and a few of his friends… and his girlfriend. But Erik was the instigator. In fact, the others just watched on."

Fucker. He'll get what's coming his way.

Paisley clears her throat and continues the story and when she gets to the part regarding Erik choking her and her blacking out when he left, my heart practically falls out of my chest. I feel bad. *So fucking bad.* Because while Paisley was clinging to life, I was at my work training a new group in self-defense; completely oblivious to everything and it's so fucking ironic now. She explains how she only came to about five minutes after blacking out, all paranoid and beaded in sweat. She didn't go to the hospital out of fear Erik would find her first, and too nervous to pick up her father's latest calls because she could barely speak, and even if she could, didn't know what to say. I know Paisley. I know she wants the minimal attention her way. It's why she didn't reach out for help.

The entire thing makes me sick to my stomach.

Fuck.

"I'm sorry this happened to you. I really am," I admit. "After you update your father, we should go to the police with this. I don't give a fuck who this Erik thinks he is. He can't taunt you and treat you like this."

"No," she pleads, shaking her head adamantly. "No. I don't want to go to the police."

"It's one of the few options here."

Paisley opens her mouth to say something, but then her eyes land on Nico and she shuts it again.

Falling back onto the couch, I nod. "Ask it."

"If you help me, what's in it for you?"

"A good deed. It's what your father would want too. I know a guy down at a nearby precinct. It'll be quick and easy. I promise."

Paisley gulps down but doesn't say a word. The second those honey-brown eyes meet mine, I have an idea of what's running through them to make her so skeptical. She's scared. Conflicted. Doesn't want to reach out to the police, fearing Erik will strike again.

"Okay, we can go about this another way," I say after moments of dead silence between us and lean forward, my forearms pressing against my thighs. "You can let me deal with it personally. No police or reports need to be involved."

"What do you mean by you *dealing* with it…?"

"You don't want to know, Pais. Just know I'll make sure Erik doesn't fuck with you again. It'll just stay between you, Nico, and me… and your father as well, of course. I'm sure he'll be more than willing to teach this dick a lesson."

Paisley's eyes widen a fraction and I feel as though everything I'm saying is beginning to click for her. She shakes her head softly, setting down her tea mug on the coffee table, and leans forward, closer to me. "No, no. I don't want anybody to get hurt. I know what you're capable of, Saint, I've seen it. I don't want that to happen. I don't want any more violence. I just don't want Erik to glance my way ever again. That's all."

My lips twist. "So, then what happens when the same shit happens again but inside a classroom after class? Or in a secluded area next week during finals week? What happens when the fucker attacks somebody who's defenseless or somebody who doesn't have a support system? Erik needs to be taught a lesson, Paisley. You don't need to be worrying about the *next time*. Trust me when I say your dad, Nico, and I will help you. I *want* to help you and if I were you, I would take it, no questions asked."

"I want to know how far you'll go."

Till the freaking death.

"Enough with the fuckin' questions," Nico hisses. "Just let us help you and that's it."

Paisley has bottled up her frustration well until now but explodes at Nico's comment. I witness her fists balling tighter as she snaps her attention to him. Her small peeks of confidence are coming back, burning up like a firecracker awaiting to explode… only it just did, all over Nico's fucking face. *Ha!*

"If you don't like it, get out of my property!"

Nico scoffs. "What did you say to me? Think you can snap orders and I'll just do it?"

"Yes," Paisley grits back.

Nico lets out a cold chuckle and rises to his feet. "Well, then you don't know me at all."

"Good, because I don't want to." Paisley stands up and struts up to him. Jaw tight, she glares up at him. "There's a little thing called respect and I think you should learn it, Nico."

I know Paisley, but I know Nico just the same. Just because he's mutual friends with her father doesn't mean he'll lighten up for her. The moment Nico grinds his jaw and steps closer to her until not even a gap can save him, I launch up from my seat.

"Nico, back off," I warn.

Nico doesn't take his eyes off her as he sneers, "Or *what*?"

Paisley huffs and walks past him, strutting down the hallway to open the front door. Then she turns to face us again and gestures toward him. "I want you to leave, Nico."

"Good luck getting me out, *sweetheart*."

"You heard her, get the fuck out, man!" I growl, my jaw tense. "Just because Alaric isn't here doesn't mean you treat her with disrespect, you asshole. Especially not after what she just bravely told us."

Nico's eyes meet mine and his jaw ticks when all I do is glare. Eventually, he raises his hands and strides toward Paisley, who steps back against the hallway. I launch forward, prepared to show the motherfucker out myself, when he holds up a hand, signaling something in the lines of *'it's all good'*... But it isn't. Not as he snarls the following words to her, "You're lucky I'm a considerate man."

What the fuck is wrong with him?

Nico then glances at me. "I'm fucking leaving and heading to the match. Coming?"

I shake my head, too fired up to say anything because it will end up with Nico sporting a black eye, and he isn't who I'm here for.

"Your loss," he mumbles under his breath and leaves.

Paisley continues holding the door open, her pained eyes all glassy, and yet she stands in victory, head up strong with her mouth pierced shut. She's trying to keep it together. Trying to stay strong. She snapped, and when Paisley Reign snaps, she stands her ground and means exactly what she says. This much I know.

We stay like this for what seems like forever; she watches me, and I watch her.

I fall into the armchair she was just sitting in moments ago and watch as she pivots to face the front door, her back to me. My gaze lingers on her vintage red sundress that cuts off at her mid-thigh and then lower to her long, lean legs for more than it should.

God, she's so fucking beautiful.

I shake my head, numbing away the guilt. *Stop. This is Paisley. Alaric's daughter. Stop.*

With my eyes never leaving her, I draw her floral mug to my lips and take a small sip of her tea and instantly regret it. *Fucking hell, it's green tea.* I scrunch up my nose at the bitterness. *Some honey anyone?*

"Leave, Saint," her soft voice pleads, the raspiness easing, but her back is still to me.

I set the mug down on the coffee table and sit back in the armchair. "Not yet."

"Please, just go. *Please.*"

"I'm not leaving you alone. Not now."

"*Please*, Saint. I need to be alone."

"I'm not—"

"Is this how it's going to be? *Huh?*" Paisley hisses in frustration, her boldness shining through as she turns to face me. She's burning up, cheeks tinged in a flustered shade of scarlet. The front door remains wide-open, bringing in a brush of the warm wind as she holds her fierce defense, standing tall with her head up high. "My father's friends order me instructions and I'm meant to accept it with no questions asked? Do you want me submissive? Is that what you call *helping* me?"

Paisley's getting her nerve back. That tension we used to have years ago comes back in waves, only now this thick tension coats it. It's as if we didn't even embrace each other tightly by the doorstep before. Like she didn't smile at me. Like she didn't unlock a piece of her in me.

"Paisley—"

"No, answer me, Saint! For once be the good guy! I suffered through enough today, and perhaps I deserve what happened for speaking up to Erik, but I refuse to tolerate an ex-MMA fighter like Nico screaming in my face and thinking he owns me!"

"I agree and understand perfectly what you're saying, but that's just Nico's style. But you need to understand Nico's life and mine are very different from yours. It's ruthless and direct. My normal is—"

She cuts me off. "Your *normal?* Are you seriously defending him? Do you condone screaming in a woman's face, belittling them like they are nothing? Do you?"

"Fuck no, Paisley. Please just close the door so we can talk without—"

"NO!" Paisley screams. "I am sick of it! Sick of myself! Sick of my past! Sick of this fucking life! Sick of people constantly putting me down and of myself for not having enough courage to fight back! Sick of everything because the only thing I have in this life is my shadow!" She painfully pants out the words in fury, her voice breaking as she finishes with a broken whisper, "I'm sick and I'm tired, Saint. I'm sick of it *all!*"

I am sick of it all.

I swallow thickly.

I understand Paisley completely. She's sick of the world as she knows it and she has every right to be after the way people treat her. But there's something I need to know.

"Are you sick of *me* too?" I murmur after a few passing moments.

After a long, agonizing pause Paisley shakes her head and presses her forehead against the wall. It's there—as agony and frustration tangle into one—where her hands spread out above her head, trembling in their pursuit to be perfect. But I don't like perfection... or normality. It isn't me. It isn't what I do. It's too complicated. And it isn't Paisley either and that's what I like about her. Because that's all I've ever known life to be too—*complicated.*

"Paisley, come here."

Eventually she does, but first she shuts the front door and leans her back against it for a split moment. Her chest is frantically rising up and down and I don't like it one bit. It hurts me to see her like this and I don't know why. I shouldn't care about her, but Paisley Reign has this way of sneaking inside my mind, and I never seem to want to get her out.

Avoiding my gaze, Paisley begins her stride to me with her arms wrapped around her waist and wavy dark hair sweeping over her left shoulder. Then... she stops inches from me. She's hesitant at first, chewing on her lower lip before her eyes meet mine. I make the move for her, standing up and meeting her halfway.

We're at the end of the hallway, start of the living room, when I step closer to her, and we share a long, intense stare with no words attached. It's by far the most emotionally intimate we've ever been.

Pushing a strand of hair behind her ear, I cup her smooth neck and caress my thumb against the blotches, which seem a little lighter now. She trembles against my touch, so I pause and pull away.

Maybe this is all too much for her.

What I don't anticipate is for Paisley's warm hand to slide over mine, for her to place it back on her neck, or the way her touch paralyzes my speech for a moment.

"Paisley," I whisper sincerely, gazing into those honey browns. "Our lives may be different. I may be a former professional boxer. I may be sin in your eyes. I may step all over your damn flowers. But I would never, *ever*, condone any type of abuse toward women, and I will back that until the very end. I want you to speak your truth. I want you to defend yourself without the fear of others crushing you down. You're much stronger and braver than you know. You deserve so much, Paisley. So much more than this."

Paisley lowers her head, and my thumb trails against her soft lower lip, caressing her beauty. I raise my hand higher, wiping away her falling hot tears. "I believe you, Saint. I believe you," she croaks. "I'm sorry I said that and blew up. I know you would never... I'm just so scared."

"And you have every right to be after what happened, but when you feel that way, don't shut me out. I want to be there for you, Paisley. I'm on your team, *remember?*"

She glances back up at me and flickers of the violently glowing flames borrowed from my soul are in her eyes. There's a world to unlock in them. A world to unlock that doesn't belong to me. Perhaps may never. I don't even need a good enough reason for why. It just can't.

That's good enough.

"I remember." Paisley reaches up and cups my own stubbled

jaw, trailing her fingers through the spikey hairs. "I could never forget that. Whenever I'm with you, I feel so seen."

"Because you're so fucking beautiful. Inside and out. Those people who overlook you will never see how golden you are, but that's their loss, not yours. You don't owe them a damn thing. You deserve to be loved, cherished, and adored. You know your worth, so never ever be afraid to speak out when it means protecting your heart from a web of lies. Always choose truth, Pais. I'll talk with Nico and see what's up his ass. You'll be getting an apology out of him."

The warmest smile I've seen all day grows on Paisley's lips. "Thank you, I needed that. That's the sweetest thing anybody has ever said to me."

Once again, we get lost in each other's eyes. Ocean blue on honey brown. I can't stop gazing, staring, craving the way she bites her lower lip, and my eyes darken a fraction. There's a desire in her eyes too, a sudden spark that has my cock throbbing in ways it shouldn't for her.

I can't take my eyes off Paisley. Off those gorgeous lips. Whenever she's around, I find myself letting go of the past and the reasons I've been so caged up about my feelings. There's something about her that makes me want to help her in any way, no matter the cost.

I hate that I'm drawn to her. Hate that I care, because I know I can never be more than her father's close friend and neighbor. But the way she's looking at me, with so much allure, it questions everything inside me.

Paisley steps forward, her fingers brushing her hair back behind her shoulders, and that has my gaze dropping to her dress and the slight dip at the front, displaying the beautiful curves of her breasts… those clearly hard nipples that stab through the fabric, begging to be touched. *God.* A quick visual of running my warm tongue down her cleavage and swirling it over her pebbled nipples before sucking on them with just the right amount of suction crosses my mind.

Christ. Get it out of your head.

Needing to deflect where my mind is going, I say, "So... how about you give me this Erik's last name and a description of what he looks like so I can go out and kill him myself before your father arrives and starts stressing out about it all?"

A soft, unexpected giggle rumbles through her. *It warms me.* "Oh my gosh, no, you're not going that far!"

"I know, I just like firing you up." I smile. "But I wasn't entirely kidding. I'm going to go after him. You don't think your father and I will?" My hands come to rest on her waist as I remember what she said moments ago. "Please don't ever say you feel worthless or that all you have is your shadow. It's not true. You deserve love, a whole fuck load of it, from somebody who will respectfully see you as the best thing that happened to them. And don't think you won't get that. I mean, look at you, you're so fucking selfless."

"Saint?"

"Yes?"

Paisley grins and rises to press a soft, passionate kiss on my cheek. Her voice is a sweet tremble when her eyes find mine. "Thank you. Truthfully. For *everything.*"

"Anytime. I'm on your team. I'm on your fucking team, Paisley. I hope you know that."

"I know you are, and I'm just really glad I know you."

"So am I." I nod. "You're beautiful, Paisley. Don't you ever think otherwise."

Paisley's cheeks flush as she sniffles away her remaining tears.

"Tell me it. I want to hear the words come out of your mouth. Tell me you're beautiful."

Paisley parts her heart-shaped lips, her eyes dimming as no words fall. A part of me wants to know the exact thoughts running through her mind. The other part wants to scoop her into my arms and never let go.

Just as I'm about to speak, there's a rattling at the front door of metal keys clashing and it startles her. Closing her mouth, she glances away from me, and I know exactly why.

Alaric.

Her father's home.

Fuck.

But I don't care. I need to say this to her right now.

Paisley's sweet jasmine scent fills my lungs as I take a step forward. Cupping her soft jaw, my thumb trails over her rosy lower lip. Those honey brows watch me with a warmth I haven't felt in a long while. It turns me on and makes me want to walk away all at the same time.

Alaric curses loudly on the other side of the front door, and being so close to it, I vaguely understand it. Something about never being able to get the right key and so I use every extra second to my advantage.

I grasp Paisley's hand in my free one, weaving our fingers together before raising up our intertwined hands to my lips and kissing her soft skin. Only then, with my right hand gently holding her jaw, do I lean forward and shut my eyes, pressing my lips against her cheek. It's a soft, sensual kiss to the skin, but it communicates everything we've spoken about this evening.

I inhale a deep breath as I pull away because I don't do this. I don't let women get this close to me. Not emotionally. Not this physically deep. Not for a long time. But when it comes to Paisley... I find myself unraveling and I can't control it, no matter how badly I wish I could.

"Then let me say it for you," I whisper, meeting her eyes. "Paisley Reign, you're beautiful. So fucking beautiful. If I were another man, a better man, and we didn't have any history between us, I'd do everything to show you just how special life can be and just how much more it blooms with you in it."

Through the emotions, Paisley flashes me the deepest smile, tears streaming down her cheeks, and it's everything for me. *Everything.* I feel something change inside me, like a flick of a switch, but I don't know if it's for better or if it's for worse. All I know is that it changes me. *Paisley* changes me.

For reasons beyond me, a smile curls on my lips too, just as the door clicks unlocked and just like that, I step away from her. I pull out my phone from my jeans pocket and pretend to be engrossed in it, feeling Paisley's hot gaze leave mine as Alaric steps inside.

Murmuring he's sorry, her father pulls her into a tight embrace and shuts his eyes. Paisley's head rests against his chest, yet those honey browns never leave mine. And we go back to being passing ghosts. Now that her father's here, it changes everything. I can't look at her the way I do. I can't tell her how beautiful she is or fantasize about what it would be like to kiss those gorgeous lips of hers.

It's like we don't exist.

Like this connection between us becomes oceans apart when other people are around.

Like we're living two entirely different worlds; forbidden to touch but tempted to hold.

Because maybe we are.

Chapter
ELEVEN

Paisley

FOUR YEARS. FOUR YEARS AGO TODAY AND THE HEAVINESS WEIGHING in the pit of my stomach is just as horrific as the first day. Sitting crossed-legged by Nana's tombstone, my fingers brush over the dark marble headstone with thin white veins, my heart tearing more and more with every touch.

To many, cemeteries are eerie, but to me, they're the only place where I feel free and able to breathe. Perhaps because I can talk to Nana here without being questioned, cry without being judged, and grip flowers without it being known that they follow me wherever I go.

This is my safe place… it's where I always come to feel closer to my nana June.

It's just after 10:00 p.m. now and darkness laces the sky with peeks of glittery stars and the growing full moon. It was only a couple of hours ago the sun kissed the horizon, and an alluring orange-pink sky overtook like a real-life masterpiece.

Somedays during lunch at school, I stare up, wondering how far high up it goes. When I was younger, Nana and I used to play that game with the clouds—lying down on the fresh grass and letting my young, creative mind run wild, imagining shapes from moving marshmallow clouds up above. Now, as I lay my head beside Nana's grave and stare at the sky with my fingers clasped over my chest, I control my breathing and try to imagine just like I used to when I was little.

I try and try and try... but nothing. No shapes. No letters. No animals. Just dark gray night clouds of nothingness. It has me fisting my hands, shutting my eyes, inhaling a deep breath, and starting again.

I'm a mess. *A complete and utter mess.*

Earlier, just as I was about to walk here, Nico showed up at my front door. I said Dad wasn't home, but he wasn't there for my father, he was there for me. He apologized for acting like a dick last night, and part of me knows Saint had something to do with his apology. I didn't want any further drama, so I forgave Nico and appreciated the genuine smile on his lips before he walked back to his car and left.

After counting to sixty, I reopen my eyes and stare up, only to let out a blood-curdling scream at who I see. This time I don't see any shapes. I see a person hidden by the darkness, but not up in the clouds, staring down at me.

Pressing my palms to the grass, I push myself back to create some distance and launch up on my feet. "Get away from me! Get a-away!" I say, my lip trembling as the figure takes a step closer to me. "Don't step any closer! I'll, I'll..." I pull out my phone and wave it around, continuing to step back. "I'll call the police! Don't think that I won't!"

I stumble back and let out another scream as I hit a tree trunk. "I'll call the police right now if you don't step away right now—ORCHIDS! There are over thirty thousand types of flowers, including the cattleya and vanilla orchid. Each variety of orchid has—*Stay away!*—its own color and—*Don't move!*—its own meaning. Dendrobium orchids represent beauty and—*that it! I'm calling the police!*" I threaten, dialing 911 and turning on my flash to point it at the person for reference in the police report.

And that's when everything explodes in my face.

Oh. NO!

My jaw drops at who's staring back at me with an expression that screams '*seriously?*'. I'd know those ocean eyes anywhere. Arms casually crossed over his chest, Saint raises an amused brow, seemingly unaffected by the whole *bright-light-in-your-face* look.

"Orchids?" Saint smirks. "*Really?*"

I clutch a hand to my chest. "Oh my God!"

Just then, a woman's voice on my phone says, "*Nine-one-one, what's your emergency?*"

"Hi, sorry, I accidentally called. It's a false alarm," I mumble, cringing to myself.

"Oh, okay. Are you sure you don't need any assistance?" the dispatcher asks.

"Yes, I'm okay. I'm so sorry about that."

"It's perfectly okay. Have a safe night."

"You too," I say as I hang up but keep the light on Saint.

His eyes widen a fraction. "You actually called nine-one-one? Shit, you've got more guts than I originally thought, Pais."

"I didn't know it was you! Where did you even come from?"

"I was smoking a cigarette on my porch when I literally saw you get in your dad's car. I followed because I wanted to make sure you were okay and that the late-night drive didn't have anything to do with Erik. I didn't mean to scare you." Smiling, he playfully teases me with his next words. "Or for you to tell me everything you know about orchids. That can't be helpful if it was an actual attack."

"You know I do that when I'm stressed." I laugh, stepping away from the tree and dusting myself off. "Besides, I… totally knew it was you, that's why I—"

Saint cuts me off with a chuckle. "Bullshit."

I playfully roll my eyes at him but can't help the grin shining through. "Well, thanks."

A slow, sexy smirk rises on his lips. "I can't even see you but I just know you rolled your eyes at me."

"Am I really that predictable?"

"Take the light off my face and I'll tell you."

I switch it off and just like that, we're surrounded by darkness except for a little brightness in the light the silvery moon reflects. "Well... this isn't ideal."

"Fucking hell."

"What?"

"Nothing, I'm just seeing fucking dots of light everywhere."

Laugher rumbles up my throat. "Oops, sorry."

"You're really not sorry, are you?"

"Not really."

"Thought so. What were you doing here at this cemetery so late?"

"My nana... Today is four years since she passed. Lying down there at night is therapeutic for me. Creepy, I know, but somehow it calms me."

"I know your dad's working late. But did your mom contact you at all to say she's thinking about you today?"

"She... No, no, she didn't—" I cut myself off as the knot at the back of my throat tightens. It's fitting, really, how the darkness disguises the tears streaming down my face. But Saint has this type of radar to notice. It's been there since the first day I met him and I'm not too sure it'll ever go away.

Saint steps forward, a flash of the moon illuminating his blue eyes, and for a split second I see something in them I've never seen before... *sadness.* He walks past me and sits down, his back resting against the tree trunk and long legs spread out. In the sleek silvery glow of his silhouette, his fingers brush against mine, effortlessly lacing his hand in mine and tugging me so I stumble down into him.

Saint breaks my fall by gently gripping my hips and I

unexpectedly straddle him. My hands crash against his hard chest, and I let out a soft gasp at just how close we are. Warmth floods my body, pure desperation to kiss him as his long lashes lift and finally meet me.

Oh my... yes.

As secure as I feel right here and as much as I love this, I want to make sure this is okay for him. As I part my lips and wet them in anticipation, I expect him to tell me to get off him. Instead, Saint wordlessly wraps his arms around my waist and pulls me closer to him.

My lips part as I rest my head on his chest and focus on my heavy breaths instead of the speeding of my heart. Of how his touch warms that inner part of me that doesn't come alive for anybody else. I'm so attracted to it. He's the only man who both electrifies and warms me from the coldness of not only the night but the depth of my soul.

"I've got you, *wildflower*," Saint murmurs. "Seeing somebody like your nana lose grip of their life right in front of you... it changes everything, so I can relate to how you're feeling."

Wildflower...

"Exactly. It's like I have the bad visions constantly engraved in my mind instead of the good ones. Instead, all the good memories... well, they hurt too much to resurface."

"I get that. Grief is so fucked up, just like you said a couple of weeks ago. But you're strong, Paisley."

"I wouldn't say that."

"I would. It's true. You're one fuckin' strong woman."

A sad smile rises on my lips. "Thank you, Saint."

He glances between my eyes and gulps down. "It's okay."

"It's crazy," I say after a while of us just sitting here in the silence, watching the stars wink down at us with his arms wrapped around me.

"What is?"

"How much I trust you. You understand me more than anybody else in this world."

Saint sighs. "Your father knows you..."

I shake my head. "I don't open up to him like I do to you."

It's the truth. There are things I've told Saint that I'll never tell my father. I know my mother struggled through a lot after she had me and it's not that I'm angry about it. I understand that part and just how bittersweet it must be. The anger festering inside comes from another place. It's that she abandoned me. It's that she gave up on me by restarting her life. It's that she told my father things about me... things somebody should never say about their daughter. It's that she never reached out, changed her number after she left my father, leaving no trace to contact her.

I've never voiced all these things to my father because I don't want him to feel guilty or responsible for the pain deep inside my veins, because he isn't. My father's done so much for me, sacrificed his entire life to put me first. I love him so much, I don't want him to hurt more.

Saint pushes strands of my hair away from my right cheek and tucks them behind my ear, then he replaces the warmth of my tears with that of his hot lips brushing against my cheeks.

"Hurts me when you cry, *wildflower*," he whispers. "Hurts to see you like this."

Sparks cross my entire body at the way his spikey stubble grazes against my soft skin when he cranes his neck to me and kisses away my tears.

"You're the only one I trust, Saint," I murmur. "Truthfully, the only one."

"Then don't hide your demons from me," he says. "If you're hurting, don't you dare hide them away from me. You understand me?"

I nod, the stinging in my throat too strong to speak as a sob escapes me.

"And for the record, I trust you too." Saint holds me closer to him, his dark musky scent purified by my jasmine one. "Paisley, talk to me. What's going through your mind?"

"I just feel... so alone."

"You're not alone. You have your father. You have me."

"For how long?"

"For however long you need. I'm here."

"Why?" I sniffle, resting my head against his shoulder to stop further tears from falling. "Why are you helping me?"

Saint takes it as an opportunity to kiss the side of my head softly. He doesn't pull back straight away, not until his hands find mine and he squeezes tightly. His voluntary presence is destined to protect me from any tempest with his warmth alone. "Because that's what reckless saints do."

My heart explodes into little, tiny rose petals. I can't ignore the butterflies in the pit of my stomach. I've never felt this way about anybody else in my life. *Nobody but him.*

"I'm sorry, Saint. I'm sorry for always being a mess whenever I'm around you."

"You once promised me you'll never apologize for feeling emotion. Remember?"

When his words fall in a silent response, Saint releases one hand and cups my jaw, turning my head to face his until our eyes meet. In the softness of the moonlight, his eyes shine in the silvery gray glow. When his lips part, my gaze drops to them and I wonder just what it would be like to taste the other side of purgatory on his lips.

This is all new to me.

These feelings…

This side of Saint…

All so new… and enticing.

"Paisley?"

"Hmm?" I murmur.

"Promise me. Promise me you won't hide from me when you need somebody the most."

"A couple of weeks ago you told me not to think about you," I say, all choked up. "You can't be the person I don't hide from and the person I don't think about. The two can't coexist with each other. When you told me to stop thinking about you... did you mean it?"

Our shared gaze is so intense, so passionately motivated by both grief and hope. I try to find something in them, *anything*, anything that tells me he doesn't want me to let go... and then, just like that, *I find it.*

Saint smiles and holds me tighter. "Yes, yes, I meant every word, *wildflower.*"

He meant it.

I let out a breath, my heart squeezing because he feels this too—whatever *this* may be.

A weight feels as though it's being lifted off me when I say, "Then I promise you. I promise I won't hide when I need *you* the most."

Saint smiles and softly comes to rest his forehead against mine, yet he makes no comment of how I said *you* instead of *somebody.*

"Why do bad things happen to good people?" I ask, knowing the answer so damn well.

"Because the world can be a cruel life sentence," Saint murmurs against my lips.

"My heart hurts me. It feels as though there's a piece missing, like somebody ran up to me and pulled it out of my chest."

"There is. Your grandmother's piece. I feel it too with my father... and other people I've lost."

"I'm so sorry for your losses. So sorry you feel it too," I whisper into the darkness, slipping my arms around his neck. "I'm just so scared. Of this. Of living. Of dying. Of what comes next."

Saint nods against my forehead. "I know, *wildflower*, I know, but sometimes you've got to walk into fear and forget all else. I feel the most alive when I'm in the fire, when I'm burning, when the flames rise and swallow me whole."

"How do you get out?"

His smile saddens. There's no hesitation from Saint as I reel him closer. In fact, his hands slowly caress the patch of skin exposed between my top and jeans.

"I haven't gotten out," Saint eventually admits. "I'm still in that fire, slowly fading."

"Don't say that."

"Say what?"

"That you're fading."

Saint chuckles. "Why? Scared I'll disappear on you, Pais?"

"No," I lie. "That has never been my problem with you."

"Then what is it?"

"You're unpredictable. Reckless. Destructive. I never know what I'm going to get. But when you give, you don't back down. You follow through."

"You learned all that by staring out of your bedroom balcony?" Saint playfully chuckles.

Blushing, a grin takes over, no matter how hard I bite my lip. "Oh my God! Shut up!"

A calmness seems to come over Saint as he reaches out his right thumb and brushes it against the soft skin of my flushed cheek, slowly drifting to my lips. He smirks for the first time tonight, complete with his dimples, and it's the sexiest, most beautiful yet devilish one I've ever seen.

"Made you smile," he whispers so damn low. "You're so different, Paisley. So different to anybody else I've known."

"Is that a good or bad thing?"

"With the kind of life I live, I don't know. A little bit of both, I guess. Truth is… even though I know I shouldn't see you like this… I would be lying if I said I don't find you so damn fucking beautiful inside and out," Saint admits inches from my lips. "You're a mystery to me, Paisley Reign, one I'm craving to unravel."

Saint's confession awakens something inside me, partly because I wasn't expecting it. Although I knew he isn't blind to this strong spark and emotional connection between us, I didn't know he felt this forbidden temptation. Didn't know he wants this as much as I do.

"So do it," I reply, cupping his stubbled jaw. "*Please*. Unravel me, Saint Lisconti."

"I can't." Saint squeezes his eyes shut, breathing heavily. "It's too complicated. You know I don't do love. You're supposed to be my best friend's daughter. We shouldn't be... we shouldn't even be talking about this."

"I know, but we are. We *are*, Saint, and I'm not ashamed of it because you mean too much to let go of. The thing is, I don't do or know love either. Love is a fragile, delicate thing and I hate fragile because it's all that I am."

Saint's brows knit as he opens his eyes. "Who said that to you?"

"Nobody did. Just me."

"Bullshit. Alaric must have told you your mom once said it about you, didn't he?"

Crap.

I feel Saint's eyes on me and know better than to lie in his face. He has a way of knowing me more than myself with these things. Staring down at my hands, I swallow down the thickness clogging my throat and nod slowly. "Yes."

I await Saint's response for the longest time, so long the night begins to change before our very eyes as darker skies cover the night with brighter winking stars and city lights from far away California hills. I don't know what to say or do. All I know is Saint's clenched jaw doesn't mean anything good. He's thinking everything through. I know he is. I can see the clockwork in his mind reiterating what I admitted as his body tenses up around me until all tension seems to ease away when he whispers, "You're not fragile, Paisley. You're beautiful."

And that's when it all stops for me. *Fragile.*

I hate it.

Hate how a single word can cut so deep.

Saint leans further back against the tree stump, his ocean blues never leaving mine.

"Why, Paisley?" he murmurs, his hands coming to a halt by my waist again. The warmth the single action provides sends me to heaven. "Why believe her false words?"

"Because after a while, I start looking around and realize the world isn't as bright as I once thought it was. Nobody ever saw me for me. Never stood up for me. Loved me enough to stay. I know I don't put myself out there, so perhaps it's partly my fault, but it's only because I'm protecting myself from the torment I know is going to occur," I admit with a frown, my vision glossy. "So, when my father told me of the words she spoke... I believed in them because she's right. I can be fragile, I can be fragile because I'm scared of the world."

"That's not true."

"It is." I nod. "I'm fragile because I'm scared, and because of that... I've never felt affection or learned what it feels like to really love somebody outside of a father's love. I ask too many questions because I have a fear of misunderstanding rendering me weak. I work up the courage to stand up for myself in small peeks of certainty, only to shut myself down again from fear of my own self-consciousness. I feel out of place every single day, as if the world doesn't know me and I don't know it. It's like we don't sync, and I'm just an outcast wasting life's time. Life has always thrown either grief or chaos my way. So, when that happens, I close myself up, hoping nobody else ever finds the key that unlocks all my vulnerability. Because I'm always just my father's daughter, or the crazy girl with the damn flowers, or the little baby her mother left behind. I'm never simply Paisley Reign."

"But you *are* to me." Saint's eyes dive into my soul and I cling to his every word with all I have. "You're Paisley Reign, the flower obsessed poet who hides her stanzas. The listener with the brightest questions. The woman with the kindest heart. You know what you want, but you're so damn scared to take it. You think you need to ask for it, wildflower, but you *don't*—when something is yours, learn to steal it without permission. You're the type of woman who doesn't give your heart away to people who don't earn your respect, and I appreciate that. But you're so blinded by your fears you've covered up all the mirrors. You don't know just how fucking beautiful you are, inside and out. *That*, that's who Paisley Reign is. You're more than the woman next door, or somebody's daughter, you're a person. A fucking good person, and I care for you more than I should. And you're not fragile, you never could be, you're simply blooming."

Tears stream down my face at the sweetness of his words and of just how much they speak from the heart. This is the Saint Lisconti I know and appreciate. This is *him*.

Saint clears his throat, clearly concealing his emotion as he looks away from me for a split moment. "And I wouldn't be able to live with myself if something happened to you, *wildflower*. I don't know what I would do without you. You're the only good thing in my life. I need you in it—a part of it—not just some woman I used to know that Heaven took too early." With that, his eyes move back to mine, rimmed with unshed tears. "I don't know what's going through your head, but if you think ending it all is the answer because there's no reason to live it, then let me be your reason. Know that doing it for me is doing it for yourself. Because as fucked up and forbidden as it may be, I want us to both know what it feels like to grasp the thorns of a rose and smile while doing so. I want you to forget everything you think you are because you are everything you think you are not. You're so special, Paisley Reign, so special in the best goddamn fucking way, and I just want you to see it."

Saint takes a breath and continues, "And you deserve happiness, and life, and love. So much love. And you deserve to *live it*. So, if you feel like an outcast, then I'm an outcast too right with you. Because I'm scared of lovin' just as much as you're scared of livin'. You're not alone. No matter how much you think you are. Your father loves you to bits. He may not always show it, but I know it. And while your life now may be a version without somebody who should truly be here for you, you're better without her. Trust me on that. And while it may also be a version without your nana, never forget she's alive right there in your heart. So, let that love grow into wildflowers that you cherish and hold close to you because your heart... it will never grow old because Paisley Reign doesn't let anyone trample over her damn flowers—*nobody*—and the same should apply to her life. Because it's irreplaceable. And it's beautiful. And it's yours."

Wow. That was beautiful.

All I can do is stare at Saint, teary-eyed, with the biggest smile I can manage. Because he's beautiful. And he's compassionate. And he said everything I needed to hear without me knowing it. My heart has never felt this complete or this beautifully raw before. Saint took my vulnerabilities and reassured me in ways nobody ever has before, in ways I know nobody ever will again.

As wrong as it may be behind my father's back, it feels so right. *So good.* So poetically rhythmic. Saint and I understand each other on this interpersonal deep level, one I never thought could be realistic, better yet, *possible.* But it is and God, how beautiful it is with him. Saint knows me more than I know myself and un-locks me in ways nobody has ever dared to before.

"That means more to me than you know. Thank you. You always have been my reason, Saint," I murmur as a mixture of happy and emotional tears doesn't stop flowing. "Even when I didn't know it at first, you always have been the reason I kept on going. Because you believed in me and cared about me even when nobody else does except for my father. You still do."

"Of course I do, *wildflower,*" Saint smiles sweetly, wiping away my tears with his thumb while his own run down his cheeks with vengeance. "That's what neighbors are for, right?"

It feels so nice to share a chuckle as my nose scrunches up mid-laugh.

Swallowing down the lump in my throat, I nod. "That's what neighbors are for."

"And I will always be here for you." Saint cups my cheeks, reas-suring me with trusting eyes. "*Always.* In the middle of the night. Ten years from now. Even when you hate me the most, you call my name, and I'm yours in a heartbeat. I'm *yours.*"

I press my lips to his right cheek and kiss it in a way I hope communicates every single emotion I'm currently feeling. Desire. Grief. Hope. Fear. Devotion. Saint smoothed my heartache in more ways than just one tonight. It places a much needed temporary hold on my mourning—and even if it's for a single moment—it's enough.

When the time comes, I pull away from his cheek and lay my face on his chest, shutting my eyes to drown out any other sound but his vigorously beating heart. His chin rests on top of my head, protecting me from the world itself with his warmth and alluring masculine cologne that transports me into a world of him.

Tonight, I feel all of Saint, want all of him as his hand pulls me closer to him—*tighter*—as if our time is running out. Like there's no better remedy to heal our aching chests from this destructive world around us. Like there's no better place to be than right here with him. Like there's nothing else that truly matters but him and me and the rest of the air around us.

I love it and desperately don't want to let go of this feeling. But as my father crosses my mind, it's hard not to imagine the consequences of falling for a man I can never truly have, because I've already fallen for Saint Lisconti and now that I know how sweet hell can really be, I don't want to be an angel anymore.

I want to be unholy if it means having a single opportunity to be with the man who means the most to me.

If only I knew how.

<hr>

"Let me know when you've finished with that one. I have something to tell you." Maralyn grins with her bold red lips, her thick Brooklyn accent shining through just as I finish arranging yet another bouquet and set it on the flower arranging table.

I love how the calmingly sweet floral scent takes me away from reality, even for a few seconds. The flowers are a gorgeous mix of dusty pink, lilac, and white flowers. Azaleas. Lavenders. Daisies. The perfect mid-May combination.

"All done." I smile, turning to my boss and closest friend here at Maralyn's Florist.

Maralyn nods, pulling back her long, dark waves in a large

tortoiseshell hair claw clip. Hands planted on her hips, her denim apron—the same one I'm wearing—hides her khaki-colored linen jumpsuit with neon pink roses printed all over it.

I've been working here for the past few months since the start of senior year and every shift Maralyn's bold enthusiasm and wild stories never cease to amaze me. She's in her late forties, says it as it is, and is easily one of the nicest people I've ever met. At times, like the mother I never had.

"All right." Maralyn claps her hands together, scaring our final customer, whose head snaps back at us before she continues browsing the florist we're about to close for the day. "You'll never believe what happened on Friday night. When I closed the florist, my husband, Maxwell, called to say his brother and sister-in-law want to meet up. I was planning to have a nice Friday night at home, watching *Judge Judy* while being fed grapes while lying down on the couch."

I smile. "I have a feeling that didn't happen."

"Yep, that *definitely* didn't happen. Anyway, we all went out and had one too many drinks, mainly because of my brother-in-law, who's younger. We got home at around two o'clock in the morning and while I was half decent, Maxwell was far gone. As we slipped into bed, I somehow remembered he had a doctor's appointment in the morning and started stressing. Maxwell told me we'll sober up in time and all that shit men say that makes you feel okay at the time but later you wish you never listened. *So*, Maxwell managed to put on the alarm, and we fell asleep."

"What time was the appointment in the morning?"

"It was at eleven," she clarifies and continues. "Anyway, I woke up the next morning and the sun was blaring through the window. The idiot was still out cold beside me. The first thought that came to mind was, *I need coffee and something to get rid of the head pounding.* Close behind that thought was, *Maralyn, the sun shouldn't be this bright for eight-fifteen in the morning.* Then… I checked his phone and saw it was two o'clock in the damn afternoon. Instead of setting on the alarm, the idiot set the calculator for eight dollars and fifteen freaking cents."

I cover my mouth to prevent myself from bursting out laughing in the vicinity of customers. The grin burns up my lips as I step closer to her, eyes wide. "No!"

"Yes! It was so embarrassing calling up the medical clinic and canceling three hours late. Oh, Paisley, you should have seen me take him up like the house was on fire."

"Whoa, I swear you two should have your comedy show. You're both like Lucy and Ricky!"

"Ahhh," Maralyn groans. "I *wish* my husband looked like Desi Arnaz! The closest thing Maxwell has to him is that he usually burst out in song at six o'clock in the morning."

I smile. "You know he loves you, Lyn."

Maralyn sighs, but eventually starts nodding. "I know. I know. I just like teasing the guy." Then, her eyes light up as she gestures toward me. "Speaking of men, you're graduating in a couple of weeks and this whole new chapter is opening up. Any men you have your eye on, hmm?"

My mind wanders to Saint and that gorgeous, dimpled smile. To the way his deep, ocean eyes take me on a journey I never want to come back from. The way his sexy, sandalwood scent remains in the air long after he's gone. The way he held me so damn tightly and reassured me days ago at the cemetery. The words he spoke to me that night... I'll never forget them.

Let me be your reason.

I don't know what I would do without you.

You're not fragile, you never could be, you're simply blooming.

Our bond has only tightened since then. During the past week, he and my father have been going downtown for drinks with a few of their friends and the stolen glances Saint and I share just before my father hugs me goodbye... *wow.*

Saint means everything to me... and the fact that he openly admitted to caring for me in ways he knows he shouldn't... it changes *everything*. During these past few days, the desire has only heightened. Not that I thought it was possible. It's as if my heart has punctured and I bleed bittersweet crimson rivers for him.

There have been so many times where I die in his embraces because we hug tighter and longer than before.

So many times where I wish he could just kiss me whenever my father isn't looking.

So many times where I want to tell Saint, *I'm yours too.*

I focus back on Maralyn and simply smile. "Nope, nobody."

Maralyn smirks and shoots me a knowing look. "Nah, ah, ah. You're definitely crushing on somebody. You had to think about that question *way* too long, girlfriend. Okay, that's it, spill. Who's the guy?"

"Nobody!" I lie, yet the darn grin isn't wiping off my lips. "I swear, he's nobody."

And just then I realized I addressed that there is in fact somebody. *Greattt.*

"*Sure* he's not, that's why you're blushing scarlet red."

I cup my hot cheeks. *Oh shit, I am!* "It's really nothing, trust me."

"Does this guy have a name?"

"Maralyn, stop!" I laugh.

"Okay, fine. Keep mystery man all to yourself, but just know I will crack the mystery. I always do." She winks, leaning against the oak table beside us. "I think you're just nervous."

"Of course I'm nervous about it. I mean, when am I not? I'm just... a constant mess."

"Around the guy?"

"Yes, but also in general. I'm always afraid I'll mess up and make things worse."

That has Maralyn frowning. "Where did those feelings come from?"

"My past... Let's just say I didn't have the best childhood. I feel like the one to blame. It's as if I did something wrong to my mother, even though I know it's not the case."

"Have you been to a therapist to talk the issues through? I think it could really help."

I shake my head softly at Maralyn, feeling the weight of the world settling at the back of my throat. I don't know why this emotion has overcome me right now at work. *Shit.*

"You know, sometimes I look back at life and wish I'd done things differently, Paisley, but there comes a stage where you need to let go of all fear and dive deep into the unknown." Her emerald eyes stay on the assortment of flowers I placed down moments ago before slowly turning back to me. "So, I opened up this florist only a few years ago. It's always been a dream of mine, but I put it on hold because I was scared and nervous of the outcome, if it would pay the bills, if I would even break even."

"How did you push yourself to take the next step?" I ask, craving the answer more than she'll ever know.

"Well, it took time, but ultimately one day I had enough of the old life I was living. I shook myself, looked in the mirror, and said to myself: *This is my dream. This is where I want to be. I can do this. I don't have to be successful, just successful enough. Trying is enough. Trying is doing.* And I haven't looked back since. So, do the same, Paisley. Live the life you want to live, not by the rules. Tell yourself you're worth it. Tell yourself your past doesn't need to define you. Free your soul of blaming yourself for not being good enough. You *are* good enough. It's on her if she doesn't want to be a witness to your greatness. So don't let her hold you back from unlocking that greatness. Thrive in doing what you love and fall in love recklessly instead. Because when you thrive, you get so much purpose and ahead in life that the people who matter will show up. Those who don't just aren't meant to be as important in our lives as life originally planned them to be."

"I've never thought of it like that. God, I needed that so much. Thank you, Maralyn."

"Anytime, lovely. You know I'm always here. Also… whoever *this man* is and whatever he truly means to you—just *try.* Because one day you'll look around and realize life went by like *this.*"

Maralyn snaps her fingers with a frown. "And regrets may mean nothing now, but one day you'll bank them all up and realize it's an entire life of regrets, and if you were bold enough, you could have taken a different path. So be bold. Be brave. Be Paisley fucking Reign."

Our final customer interrupts us with a vase of flowers she wants to purchase and Maralyn smiles softly, squeezing my shoulder before guiding her to the cash register.

Maralyn's right. She's so damn right... and so is Saint. The parallels in the words they've both spoken to me spiral in my head, echoing so violently fierce.

Maralyn. *Live the life you want to live, not by the rules.*

Saint. *You deserve happiness, and life, and love. So much love. And you deserve to live it.*

Maralyn. *Free your soul of blaming yourself for not being good enough. You are good enough. Be bold. Be brave. Be Paisley fucking Reign.*

Saint. *Paisley Reign doesn't let anyone trample over her damn flowers—nobody—and the same should apply to your life. Because it's irreplaceable. And it's beautiful. And it's yours.*

Tears blur my vision as my eyes flicker down to my trembling hands. Both Maralyn's and Saint's words dig deep into my soul. There's so much truth laced in every sentence that I value more than they'll ever know.

I need to start living my life according to me.

Saint floats in my mind and my heart clenches and shatters into a thousand tiny pieces. It does because I know I haven't felt so safe in anybody else's arms but his. He's my support. My security. My safe place. A man so different to me on the outside looking in, but on the inside, we couldn't be more connected.

Saint's voice repeats in my mind until the words he spoke turn into something so beautifully poetic, yet so painstakingly bittersweet.

Forget everything you think you are because you are everything you think you are not.

A smile rises on my lips.

I am. I tell myself. *I am everything I think I'm not.*

I vow to myself that today is going to be the first day of the rest of my life. Because not only did that night at the cemetery with Saint change for me for the better, it drew a line in the sand and put our differences aside and made me realize how similar we truly are. How much we need each other. How desperately I want to try... try to be something more to him.

Because we're no longer the good girl and the bad boy.

We're no longer light and dark.

It's just Paisley.

It's just Saint.

It's just *us*.

Chapter
TWELVE

Saint

I'VE ALWAYS BELIEVED THERE ARE CERTAIN ASPECTS IN LIFE WE'RE destined to never wash away. No matter how deeply I suppress the past and choose to let it stay in the back of my mind, the memories come back in waves. It's as if there is a burning piece inside me and each day it festers. The flames get warmer and warmer until I feel uncontrollable guilt lace in my chest, wrap around my soul, and blanket the spark to my once fulfilled life.

No matter how desperately I want to douse the fire, I can't. I can't because it turns into an inferno. Raging with heated darkness that intensifies and becomes even harder to let go of…

At times I find small remedies to numb the pain, like visiting my beach house in Stinson Beach. But I haven't been there in a long while. Not because I don't want to, but because I honestly don't have it in me to face it. I've spent the past thirteen years tearing myself down, stripping myself from the man I once knew, using any excuse to blame myself for what happened. During this time, there have only been two escapes to the pain…

Late night Harley rides and boxing.

Boxing.

For ten years, since twenty-three to thirty-three, boxing at a professional level was my entire life. It was my only way to express all my built-up anger, hurt, and guilt without being labeled reckless. Every jab, every uppercut, every victory won… meant everything to me. Every match felt like a home away from home. The ring was the only place I felt like myself. Uninhibitedly myself. No filters. No facades. Just *me*. With boxing, I didn't have to deal with all the shit in the world during those rounds.

Training and conditioning, pre-match rock tunes, the roar of the audience chanting my name whenever I stepped into the ring… it edged this thrill inside of me, one I thought was forever tainted when fate came knocking the year before I was a professional boxer.

Now, as Alaric and I watch on as students flood out the gates of Paisley's high school at the end of the day, a sense of fury mixed with peace ripples through me. That same exact feeling that used to cross my body before every match. The nickname *Santo 'The Saint' Lisconti* was pegged on me on my fifth fight, when relentless training, high stamina, agility, and perfecting every single aspect of my newfound career had me knock out the former champion of the world in the first ten seconds.

A saint on the feet, a devil in the eyes… that's what they all used to say.

My life hasn't been anything far from both heartache and unexpected success. When I hit rock bottom, I never would have anticipated months later the boxing world would open new doors for me and pin me as one of the greatest fighters of all time. Or, the amount of craze, and paparazzi, and private jets to all over the world. Or this numbness inside me during every single postfight. It's been three years since I retired from professional boxing, and I still feel it.

As Paisley jogs up to us, I snap out of my past and focus on the now. She's carrying a white leather backpack and I love how her dark waves sway from side to side with every step.

Shit. Did I just say... love?

There's a small smile on Paisley's lips as she sets a hand on her sundresses covered waist. "Erik's still at his locker with his friends. He didn't see me. You know you don't need to do this."

"Of course I'm doing this." Alaric clenches his jaw. Rolling up the sleeves of his button-down shirt, he pushes his tense shoulders back. "I want to see the guy who touched my girl."

"Dad, I don't know if this is a good idea. Erik's uncle is the principal and—"

"He and his fucking uncle can kiss my ass."

Alaric's fuming, tense ever since we constructed a plan last night to intercept Erik at Paisley's high school at the end of the school day and teach him a lesson he'll never forget. Alaric has the mouth. I have the fist. If Erik so much as tries to say anything about Paisley, I'm ready to give him my definition of a fucking *warning*.

But I know Paisley. I know she would have preferred to go through this civilly, but it seems as though her father and I forgot the definition of being civil years ago.

As Alaric storms off, his leather boots stomping on the gravel schoolyard, Paisley shoots me a frazzled look. "I'm sorry my father dragged you along for backup. Just know it's okay if you want to leave and head back to work. I completely understand."

"Are you kiddin' me?" I almost laugh as I cross my arms over my black Henley shirt. "I wouldn't miss this for the world. Plus, I'm not going to pass this opportunity to put the motherfucker who hurt you in his place."

And with that, we're off and catching up to Alaric, who's already closing in on the school doors. Paisley hesitantly leads the way, passing empty classrooms and the few dozen students rushing out into the hall; reaching for their schoolbags in their lockers and loudly talking with their friends. Shit. There's so much chaos happening you can't even freaking think in here.

As we round the corner to another hallway with lockers aligning both walls, Paisley slows in her tracks. I know exactly what's she thinking without even asking, and my senses tell me so does Alaric. A good ten feet away, a group of three guys and two girls are by the left side of the lockers. They're laughing at something one of them said. One glance and I can already tell what these motherfucking bullies are—*trouble.*

"Which one's Erik?" Alaric grits, his eyes darting around.

Paisley swallows down and whispers anxiously, "Dad, please don't do this."

"Answer my damn question."

"The one with the white T-shirt."

"Stay here, sweetheart," is all Alaric says before he's off, storming toward the group with this heated vengeance in his stride. I follow right beside him, not caring if we seem like two damn bodyguards ready to cause carnage... because that's exactly my plan.

"Hey, Erik! You think putting your hands on a woman is a joke?" Alaric growls and the group's eyes trail to us as we approach. "Don't seem so smart now, do you?"

Erik steps forward with a cocky smirk and the chickenshit thinks he's some type of god, the way he crosses his arms over his chest. "You talking to me?"

"Yeah, you," I grit. "So quit the fucking De Niro act."

He glances between Alaric and me, despite him being a good five inches shorter, and scoffs. "Do you know who my uncle is?"

"Do you know who the fuck I am?"

One of his friend's eyes widen. "Shit. Are you Lisconti?"

"You bet your sweet life I am." I turn back to Erik. "Tell your friends to leave."

Chickenshit stares at me for a solid moment before glancing over his shoulders at his friends. With a clenched jaw, he nods toward the end of the hall. "You guys start walking to the diner. I'll catch up when I'm done here."

Erik's friends don't seem too eager to leave, but when he tells them for a second time, they all swing their backpacks over their shoulders and start to scramble out. Oh, but not before the death glares they give both Alaric and me, as if *that's* enough to make us run.

Yeah, give me a break.

The hallway clears out and some of the remaining students must get the memo that shit is about to go down because one look at me and they all begin charging out of the hall until it's just chickenshit, my best friend, Paisley, and I.

Erik's eyes dart to her and mockingly says, "Hey, loser, those fading marks look good on you. Probably the first time a man's ever come close to touching you, am I right?"

Alaric steps forward, blocking Erik's view of Paisley with his broad shoulders. "Apologize to my daughter before I take this up with the principal."

"Oh, I'm *so* scared, Mr. Reign. I'm shaking." Erik smirks.

What a fucking cocky bastard.

"I said apologize to her *now*. I want to know why the hell you targeted my daughter. Paisley doesn't deserve to be bullied by people like you anywhere, especially at *school*. This is supposed to be a safe place and considering you're in senior year and practically an adult. I just don't understand it. Do you have no human decency?"

Erik scoffs. "Please, you're just pissed because you're a single dad and have had to bring up a fucking loser all on your own. Should have gotten her into therapy a long time ago, because she's fucked in the head. Hasn't made a friend since the day she got here." His eyes flicker to Paisley. "Isn't that right, loner? You probably haven't even had your first kiss, right?"

That's all it takes for me to snap. I know in hindsight I shouldn't probably say anything. After all, this is Alaric's daughter and he should be the one to control the situation, but I can't take the way Erik's speaking anymore. It's as if he has authority over everybody. As if Paisley is worth nothing.

"Say that again," I growl and step forward, getting all up in his cocky face. I violently punch the locker vents beside his head twice, ignoring the slight sting of the cuts it leaves. "Go on. Say it. I. Fucking. Dare. *You*."

"Paisley's fucked in the head."

That does it.

In one swift motion, my fist collides with his nose and metal crashes as he slams against a locker. An agonizing groan escapes his lips, his cheap overdone cologne flooding the air I breathe. It pisses me off more, knowing I smelled it on Paisley. *Fucker.* Gripping his collar to stabilize him, I throw another punch and another and a-fucking-nother; my pent-up anger only growing.

Alaric grips my bicep in an attempt to pull me back, but I'm too in the zone to justify the words he's saying, let alone stop. "Saint, I get you're angry and, trust me, so am I, but this is too far."

"You should have seen the look on Paisley's face when she opened the door, Alaric. I don't give a shit if this is going too far. He's going to get what he deserves."

"I understand that, but I don't want the police to be called or—"

"I've got it, trust me." I confirm, putting an end to his concerns. I ignore his further bids to calm me down. Ignore Paisley's gasps. Ignore every single thing but my objective to show Erik what happens when you play with fire.

I lose it because I hated how broken Paisley was. Tidal waves of reminders of how badly he hurt her and my guilt for my past twirl and come undone in the form of rage. I give no mercy throwing strong punches at the fucker like I'm back in the ring until I see fit to pull back.

"Call her that again. I fucking dare you. Call. Paisley. *That*," I say through gritted teeth, smiling devilishly as crimson pours from Erik's nostrils.

I've hit him so hard blood is smeared all across his cheeks, mouth, T-shirt, and my right fist. But I don't fucking care. I'll go all afternoon if I have to. The beast within has taken over and there's this fire that burns deep inside me, one that used to fuel me every single match.

Erik doesn't answer, instead grunts and pleads with me that

he gets it. *He's getting cold feet fast.* His left eye is twitching—halfway open—and the smugness on his lips from only moments ago is now replaced with a grimace.

"*Oh*, you want me to *stop*? Ding ding, motherfucker, this is just round fucking one and the odds are in my favor. It doesn't get any prettier from here." Tightening my grip on his blood-stained T-shirt collar, I pull him even closer and press my lips by his ear. Then whispering so chilling low, I say, "I've come close to putting men to sleep, understand what I'm sayin'? I've come within seconds of it, so I have no trouble perfecting my record with you. Remember that. You come after Paisley again, I'll make sure your family never finds your body, got it?"

Erik's knees buckle and he falls to the white vinyl tile floor by his backpack and my leather boots. *Oh no, you don't.* Scoffing, I drag his entire body back up with one hand alone and spin him around. I slam his front against the lockers, his blood smearing all over the navy metal. With his left cheek pressed against it, I take hold of his wrists behind his back and roughly squeeze them before letting go.

"Okay, okay, okay," Erik breathes, squeezing his eyes shut. "I'm sorry. Please, don't hurt me."

"Think that's going to stop me? When the fuck did *you* stop when Paisley was begging you, huh? When the fuck did you stop, you piece of shit? You're lucky I don't put you six feet under me right now. You ask that dickhead friend of yours. He knows the shit I'm capable of."

"I'm sorry, I swear, I'm sorry."

"Don't tell that to me, tell that to Paisley Reign."

Gripping his copper-colored hair, I tug on the strands and guide his head until his gaze is on her. I take this as a chance to glance her way too, and a single glance at her is enough to compose my tense shoulders and soften my heavy breaths.

"Oh my…" Paisley gasps, her eyes widening at the sight of Erik's bloodied face.

"Tell Paisley Reign you're sorry and that you won't mess with her again," I say to him. "And just remember, if you call the police or don't come up with an excuse to who did this to you when your uncle or parents ask, I will hunt you down. I'll find you and rip you to shreds and you can kiss your ass goodbye to college football or whatever the hell it is you're chasing. Do you know what reign means? It means to rule with sovereign power, and it couldn't be truer because Paisley isn't a loner or a loser or on her own, she has a fucking reign and you better believe she's the most powerful fucking queen out there when idiots like you don't drag her down. Understood?"

"Yes." Erik coughs out blood. "I'm sorry. I swear to God this won't happen again."

"Tell Paisley, not me."

"I know you probably won't accept it, but I'm sorry, Paisley."

Paisley's eyes narrow. "I don't believe you, nor should I."

"Look, I know that—"

"Oh, do you?" Paisley explodes, and I couldn't be any more freaking prouder. "Because there's nothing you can say that can fix this. *Nothing.* I'm not the same girl I was on Friday. I'm done with people like you mistreating others when they're already crumbling. I'm not taking your shit anymore, Erik. I'm. Not. Taking. It. I know my worth and I'm not going to be lowering it anymore to idiots like you."

A proud smile works its way up my lips. *That's my girl.*

"Paisley... I'm sorry. I... I shouldn't have done what I did. I just wanted to... Criticizing somebody else felt better than confronting my own issues and I didn't mean to hurt you. I just..." Erik's voice breaks as his eyes turn glassy. *What the hell?* My brows actually knit up because I swear to God he's... *crying?* "I just have a lot going on and I decided to take it out on you, Paisley."

Paisley gulps down, those beautiful honey-brown eyes shifting between her father, me, and then back to Erik. Wrapping her arms around her waist, she whispers, "Just promise me this won't happen again."

"I promise. I really do," he sniffles and after a few lost seconds adds, "I know you probably don't care, but you know how I've been absent a lot during some of the year...?"

"Yeah?"

I cautiously step back as Erik turns around and reaches for the collar of his shirt. Slowly and with his brown eyes on Paisley's, he pulls down the collar of his shirt, revealing a thick, flat scar on the base of his neck. My heart drops. Fucking *drops*. Because I know exactly what it means... precisely.

Shit.

"At the start of the year, I told people a gang did this to me. But in reality, in January I was diagnosed with..." He gulps down, almost as if he's summoning the courage to say the next words. "Cancer. Thyroid cancer. Stage one. I had surgery to remove my thyroid and fortunately the cancer is gone for now, but it's been recovery and a daily pill ever since. None of my friends know and I wanted to keep it that way... I haven't been the same since. I'm not happy with myself, so I hurt other people, and I know it's wrong, but I just... I just feel so lost. I can't help but want to escape, so I do it through other people's problems. But I promise after today, I won't. I'm sorry for hurting you, Paisley, I'm sorry for everything."

Silence unfolds between us as Erik breaks out into a full-on sob. I never expected this from a guy like him. Erik may be a shit stirrer, but I know just how genuine his words were. He isn't bullshitting about this because I... *Fuck.*

My heart is in my throat because I've never gone from wanting to destroy somebody to wanting to still destroy them but with this strange sense of sympathy laced around my body.

Swiping some blood off my face, I turn to Paisley and Alaric and tell them I'll meet them in the car. I should be better than this, stronger than this. That's what I tell myself when I peel my gaze off their concerned ones and stride down the high school hallway with a blurred vision.

This can't be happening. *Not fucking now.*

My stride turns into a full-on jog as I rush out of the school gates and head to my Maserati, not caring about the wide eyes of people as I pass them. I know what they're staring at—the blood— but they can think whatever they like. I need to get inside my car right now. Once I'm in the passenger seat, I rub my face and leave my hands there for a few moments as I concentrate on my breaths.

Thyroid cancer.

Breathe.

Remission.

Breathe.

Recurrence.

Breathe.

Moments later, the driver's and back seat doors click open, jolting me back up as I slide my hands away. Alaric and Paisley step inside, with my best friend opposite me in the driver's seat, yet my eyes can't help but trail to her.

"I forgave him," Paisley says as if she can read the question lingering in my eyes. "Thank you for protecting me back there. I appreciate it more than you know, Saint."

I stare back, expecting to find a drop of fear in her gaze, but there's none.

"No trouble," I manage to whisper, despite this sudden gloom that's taken over me.

My heart is numb. My pain is numb. My entire body is numb.

Alaric's eyes knit in concern. "Hey, man. Everything okay?"

Clenching my jaw, I nod and hand him my car key. "I don't think I can drive. Do you mind?"

"Of course not." He gives me a double look and shoots me a soft smile. "Thanks for everything back there. I didn't expect him to say what he did… but I appreciate you made him realize there are consequences to every action in life."

I nod as Alaric turns the engine on and pulls out of the parking lot. He has no idea how much his words spoke to me. *Consequences.* Because if there's anybody that knows the true impacts of con- sequences in this world more than me, it's him. Especially when it comes to love.

Just then, as my eyes lock with Paisley's through the side-view mirror of the car, this gravitational pull from inside me drags me back down to reality. The kindness in her gaze, the gratitude in her comforting smile... I just need to know she's okay. I want to hold her. Have her tell me everything is going to be all right. Because right now, I'm not so sure myself anymore.

It scares me. Scares me that I'd do anything for Paisley, today being a clear example... and that's dangerous for a man like me. Dangerous because for the first time in years, I feel this abundance in my chest threatening to explode.

I vowed myself to stay the fuck away from Paisley Reign because not only is she forbidden, she doesn't deserve a man who still doesn't have his shit together. But God knows I can't walk away from the warmth she holds, from the security she gives, from the beauty she is. Because maybe... *maybe*, I'm already in far too deep and Lord knows there's no saving me.

Not now...

Not from the Devil himself...

Not from *me*.

Once Alaric turns into Portola Way, my pulse speeds up as he suggests I spend the evening at his house to clean myself up and simply relax. He even offers to order some pizza and as much as I want to be alone with my own thoughts, I've had my fair share of solitary overpowering my ability to confront situations over the years, so with a heavy heart, I accept.

Paisley's quick to unlock her front door and Alaric helps me inside, the doctor in him concerned about the small bloody cuts on my right knuckles. I make a joke about them forgetting I'm a former professional boxer, which brings on echoing laughter, and while it lightens the mood between us all, there's still this fog overtaking my frame of mind.

It's been there ever since Erik dropped the bombshell about his cancer. While it wasn't an excuse for his bullying ways, I related when he said picking on other people's issues made him escape from the fucked up life he had. Because although I didn't find my escapism in hurting innocent people, I found it in the boxing ring.

Every match was exerting my pain.

My grief.

My anger.

Fighting has always been my release, and while a part of me isn't proud of the way I went wild with Erik in front of my best friend and Paisley, another part is just happy he'll finally leave her alone.

It hasn't even been five seconds since we stepped inside and Paisley's already brought down a first aid kit from the upstairs bathroom. I thank her and disappear into the ground-level bathroom to fix up the mess I've made.

Wetting a couple of Kleenexes, I squeeze out the moisture before stepping toward the vanity mirror. As I glide them over my cheeks and stubble, wiping away Erik's blood that has inevitably transferred onto me, it's hard not to stop a couple of times and pause at the look in my eyes... such sadness pools in my ocean blues.

What is going on with me?

For a moment, I stare deep into my eyes in the mirror, feeling my soul reach out and touch the surface of the mirrored glass, banging for an escape before coming back to me. It's within that second where my father's face flashes across my mind. I blink and it's gone. Only tainted fragments of the light eyes, soft crow's feet, and smile lines that bind us together remain.

Cancer.

Remission.

Recurrence.

I'm tempted to slam my fist against the granite bathroom counter to crush the thoughts circulating in my brain. But I refrain because firstly, enough damage has been done. Secondly, this is Alaric's house. Although he didn't say anything further about the way I responded to Erik, I don't want my luck to run dry and know any future acting out will warrant an explanation from my best friend when it's the last thing I wanna do right now.

I find my eyes in the mirror. "Calm down, Lisconti. You're okay."

Skipping the damn antiseptic cream, I run my right fist under the faucet. I clench my jaw at the slight sting of the small cuts as clear water turns red for a few seconds before I splash some on my face to wake me the hell up. Scanning through the first aid kit, I take out some gauze and unwrap a small amount before ripping it with my teeth and wrapping the dressing around my right fist. It takes me back to my boxing days.

It doesn't even take a second before blood begins seeping through the gauze tape and I let out a frustrated groan, just as a knock comes from the other side of the bathroom.

"Saint? Is everything okay?"

It's her.

Paisley.

"Yeah, just fucked up this damn gauze tape."

"Can I come in?" her soft voice asks after a few seconds.

Without hesitation, I pull on the door handle and lower my heavy eyes to meet hers. There's a moment of silence that passes between us, just lingering smiles until her gaze moves to my right hand and softens.

"Shit," Paisley murmurs, brushing her hair behind her ear and taking my hand to examine further. The action exposes that beautiful long neck of hers and I bite my cheek for staring. "Why don't you sit at the edge of the bath and I'll fix up the gauze?"

Wordlessly, I nod. A part of me wonders where the hell Alaric is. The other part doesn't give a shit. It's as if my words transcribe to her mind when Paisley lets me know a former work colleague just called him.

I take a seat at the edge of the free-standing tub, gulping down at the sight of Paisley as she gets a cotton ball and wets it with water before stepping closer to me. She sets the first aid kit nearby on the floor tiles and kneels in front of me. The pretty angel knows exactly what she's doing as she settles between my parted legs and retakes my right hand, not before sexily wetting her lower lip with her glistering pink tongue. Paisley glances up at me through her eyelashes, her breasts grazing against my thigh as she turns to take the antiseptic cream out of the kit, and my damn cock throbs through my jeans.

We share this deep, intense stare as Paisley passes the cotton ball over the bloodied small cuts on my fist. *I can't stop looking at her.* When she's done cleaning the blood away, she opens the antiseptic cream and her soft fingertips smear the cold white substance across my knocked-up knuckles, smoothing my skin with her touch.

"Was this how it was at the end of every match?"

I nod softly, unsure of where this conversation is going, but there's this rawness between us, this stripped façade of all the make-believe. *It's just us.* Us and our wildly beating hearts and the deep, intimate lingering gazes both of us can't seem to drop.

I suck in a deeper breath, feeling her touch slowing as my hand begins to shake. I wish I could make it stop. Wish it would all fucking go away, but my past doesn't let it.

"Your hand... you're trembling," Paisley murmurs, softly tracing my trembling right hand with resistance. She flips it over, my hand so big against hers, and I hold out my palm wider, watching Paisley's brows knit. *I know the exact moment she sees it again.*

Paisley glides her pointer over my palm, her deep-set eyes flickering to mine in a bid of permission to continue. I don't say anything. I simply watch her with tense shoulders and a heavy heart. *Fuck.* A jolt crosses through my entire body as her finger slowly runs up the sensitive spot of the long white scar that runs from the center of my palm to the pad of my thumb.

The memory attached to it swallows me whole.

Tell her to stop...

"Who did this to you?" Paisley asks, her voice pleading for me to let her in.

There hasn't been another woman I've been more comfortable

around but the one right in front of me, but I can't let her into my fucked-up world, not any more than she already is.

"Saint..."

Standing, I tighten my jaw and her hand slips away as I maneuver around her. Picking up some fresh gauze from the kit, I stroll to the vanity and once again measure up a length for the gauze before cutting it with my teeth.

"Let me do it," Paisley's sweet voice comes from behind in a whisper.

No.

I swallow thickly and am on the brink of saying it when I lift my gaze to meet the mirror. I find those brown eyes already on mine. There's this somberness to the air as she stands in front of me, her back pressed against the vanity as she wraps up my knuckles, even though I would have been perfectly fine without it.

"Why haven't you said a word?"

"Didn't like your questions."

"I'm sorry." She sighs. "I don't mean to impose."

"You aren't imposing. Tonight's just not the night to unload."

"Okay."

The air crackles between us.

"Also," Paisley says. "Thank you for always knowing what to do."

"I just wanted to protect you, nothing special."

"Well, it's special to me, Saint. I appreciate it more than you know."

"Anytime. You know I'm here for you."

She smiles. "Were you okay back there? It's like Erik said something touchy." She must see the apprehension on my face because a couple seconds later she adds, "Of course, you don't have to tell me. You're probably more inclined to tell my father, but just want to say I'm here if you want to talk about it—"

I surprise myself when I blurt out, "Five years ago when I was thirty-one... my father died of thyroid cancer. I guess hearing Erik talk about his own battle... it... it fucked me up."

OF US | 187

Paisley's eyes widen in sympathy. "Shit, Saint... I'm so sorry. I didn't know your father had... if I'd known, I wouldn't have asked."

"You have nothing to apologize for. This is just life."

I hate the way I fucking adore how smooth Paisley's hands are against my scruff as she cups my jaw. Hate it even more that it instantly makes me feel calmer, instead of tensing me up.

"The bad boy lost his touch," Paisley whispers, her warmth electrifying me. "The more we talk, the more I realize you're not the bad guy you wanted me to believe you were when we first met. You're a good guy. The world just fucked you over and so you created this rough, invincible exterior. You want others to see you as intimidating so you don't have to open up to them... but not with me. I have a feeling you don't talk to many people like you talk with me and sometimes you push me away because you feel better if there's a barrier between us. That's why while I may know your favorite movie, I rarely know anything else. Your passions, your dreams, your desires, why you left Santa Rosa, why you started boxing, what makes you laugh, what a Saturday night with you would look like if love was what you chased. I don't know any of that—"

"Because it's better that way, Paisl—"

"But is it really? Or are you just scared of the beauty life may give you?"

I gulp down because she's spot-on and I'm ashamed she's able to read me so well. It means I'm lowering my walls for her and I've spent so many years reinforcing them, only for her to knock them down with the slightest touch. I'm vulnerable to her. I can be myself around her and that scares me and thrills me all at the same time.

"Every single time I've attempted to see the beauty, life strips a piece of my soul away. I know you, Paisley. You want to see the good in everything, but my life isn't structured that way. That's why you and I should stop trying to..."

"Trying to *what?*" Paisley cocks her head to the side, her thumb brushing against my lower lip, and my cock feels it as if her mouth is there instead. Her honey browns drop to my lips and my gaze darkens. Desire swirls in her eyes. It's as if she wants to kiss me. I'm sure if she did right now, I'd have no resistance to back away because I'm so damn responsive to this woman it hurts. "Tell me, Saint. Trying to *what?*"

"We should stop trying to dance around the fire when we're bound to get hurt. Look, I know we have this emotional connection and it's so fucking intense. I *know*. Believe me when I say I do. I've never had this type of connection with anybody else in my life. But this can't develop into any more… not a physical relationship, not any kind of relationship. It isn't right."

"Is that why you told me you *can't stop thinking about me?* Is that why you said you wanted to *unravel me?*"

Fuck.

When I attempt to step away from her, the hand by my jaw tightens, forcing me to stay in place and face Paisley. She offers me a weak smile. "I know what you're trying to do, Saint. You're trying to have the best intentions at heart and while I appreciate it, I know that what's going on between us isn't purely derived from emotion. There's something more and we both know it. Sometimes best intentions don't allow you to clasp that beauty in life. I just… I just want to see the type of man you can be without the strings hardwiring you to never feel content in life. I know you've had a hard life, and while the pain in mine may not come close, I just want to see us come out on the other side and *live*."

"And how do we do that?"

"By allowing me to see the full extent of who Saint Lisconti is."

Maybe I've gone fucking insane, but every breath feels like thunder swallowing me up as I say, "On one condition."

"Anything."

"You allow me to see the full extent of who Paisley Reign is."

Her eyes light up. "In a heartbeat."

In a heartbeat…

"After your graduation."

"Okay, after my graduation."

The air crackles between us.

"Well, I think we're both in need of some two-wheel therapy after this."

Paisley's brows knit. "Did you say... *two-wheel therapy?* What does that consist of?"

"You. Me. My Harley. A long, breathtaking ride across California to escape reality."

Her eyes light up in awe. "In your dreams, Lisconti."

I shoot her a slow, sexy smile. "Oh, that's totally happening."

"I'm not going on your Harley," she says, but her bright grin contradicts her every word.

"We'll see about that." I wink.

Paisley's warm laugh centers my entire soul.

God, this woman has me wrapped around her finger, destined to never let go.

I thank Paisley for wrapping my gauze and step out of the bathroom and down the hall to the living room. This warm anticipation of what's about to come crosses my entire body. Alaric, who's still on the phone, waves me over by his seat on the couch. As he talks into the phone, he analyzes my wrapped-up fists before nodding. I can't help but chuckle. It's the fucking doctor in him, always wanting to overlook everything.

A few moments later, he gets off the phone and lets out a long, exaggerated sigh when he throws his phone on the couch. "Fucking hell, when this friend calls, he doesn't know how to shut up. Sorry I couldn't help you out, man. If I don't answer, he won't stop ringing until I pick up. Seems like you managed fine without me."

"Yeah, I'll live."

"Did Paisley help you? I saw her walk down the hall when I got the call."

Don't. Slip. Up. Lisconti.

I shake my head. "No, she went past the bathroom. Think she was in the library."

"Typical Paisley move. That's all right."

What a freaking save.

My throat dries up. "Got anything to drink? That thing with Erik fired me up. I need something to ease me."

That's apparently all it takes for Alaric to jump off the couch and clap his hands together with a grin. "Don't tell anybody, but my father used to say the best medicine is liquor, so you'll definitely live." He chuckles, slapping my back as he passes me to get to the kitchen. Once there, he raids his alcohol section before showing me a Highland Park Whiskey bottle. "This okay?"

I smirk and cross my arms over my broad chest. "Doctor my ass."

"Smartass. You should know I take care of my patients with maximum attention. It just so happens that you're *not* my patient, and so..." He laughs, setting down the whiskey bottle to raise his hands up in defense. "I can't control what the heart wants after hours."

"I'm only pulling your strings and yes to the whiskey. Thanks, man."

Alaric pours us two fingers and I thank him again as he slides my glass across the kitchen island. As I swallow down the cool amber liquid, thoughts of Paisley cross my mind. The more I think, the harder it is to meet my best friend's gaze as we talk.

"I can't thank you enough with how you handled it back there, Saint. I'm not going to lie, you went a little far, but that Erik definitely received a lesson."

"You don't need to thank me. I know Paisley's your everything. She doesn't deserve to be treated like that."

"I know." Alaric nods and rubs a hand over his cleanly shaven jaw. "What did you think about Erik opening up like that? I mean, about the cancer. It certainly made me see the whole situation from a different perspective. Your dad also had thyroid cancer... didn't he?"

"Yeah." I sigh. "Erik's fortunate they caught it in the earlier stages. My father's was much more aggressive... as you know. When Erik said that... I didn't know what to think. I'm just glad we put him back in his place, so don't worry, he won't tell the principal shit."

"After what you did to him, he definitely won't. Erik may be a fucker, but he certainly doesn't have the balls to tell his uncle a former professional boxer destroyed him. I just hope it'll be the last of him trying to come after my daughter."

His daughter.

Paisley.

Can two broken souls really come together and make something special? I don't fucking know. But what I do know is that I'm sick of all this uncertainty in my life. Ever since Paisley turned eighteen and she wrapped her arms around me, I've been a goner.

Paisley Reign is the one thing in my life I'm certain of, and while genuine and so damn beautiful, I admire her for more than that. I admire her intelligence. Her strength. Her courage. Despite this unspoken rule between Alaric and me about Paisley... I feel myself letting go of the promise because for once in my life I feel safe. Secure. *Understood.*

When Paisley emerges from down the hall, her eyes glued to her phone, I still feel her hands lingering across my skin. She glances up, her eyes meeting her father with a soft smile and so I look down at my glass, my finger slowly tracing the rim as they speak.

"Have you decided what we should do for dinner, Dad? I'm searching up this new sushi place that opened downtown just the other week. My boss, Maralyn, can't stop raving about it. They deliver. Maybe we could try it?"

"Sounds good to me. What do you think, Saint?"

I look up at my best friend, pretending my entire body isn't on fire as I feel his daughter's hot gaze on the back of my head. "Yeah, sushi's perfect."

"Cool. Oh, how did you go with fixing up your fist?" Paisley asks.

I turn to her and it's as if she's in sync with my cover-up. "Yeah, good. I'm all wrapped up. Thanks for asking."

"It's okay." She smiles and turns back to her father. "So, how was the call?"

I zone out after that, returning my gaze to my glass. *Can I really do this? Go behind Alaric's back like this?* My questions seem to answer themselves. *It's not up to me anymore. It's forbidden temptation and the devil controlling this fate.*

Somebody once said miracles happen every single day and that it's just up to us to find them. As much as I want to deny it, something tells me my miracle is right across the room. *Paisley.* She's changed me in these three years. She's making me a better man. And although I'm not perfect—I'm far from it—I'll always be here for her.

Always.

Just like she is for me.

Thirteen years ago, when everything crumbled around me, I promised myself I'd never put myself in that situation again. After what happened, I was convinced I didn't deserve any other woman's heart. But now that I've accepted that whatever is going on between Paisley and me—whatever it truly is—is much more than emotionally driven... I'm *terrified.*

Terrified I will jeopardize everything we have and fuck it up beyond repair.

Terrified Paisley won't be able to handle the full extent of the flaws that cage me.

Terrified I'll become chained to guilt. Because I know that feeling too well... *guilt.*

Chapter

THIRTEEN

Saint

13 Years Ago

"Are you sure you can't come, Santo? Not even for a little while?" My mother sighs through the phone. "You know how much we all wanted to meet Lea and Alexis."

It's finally Sunday; the day I've been looking forward to this entire week. Today *was* supposed to be a good day. My family was supposed to meet Lea and Alexis for the first time. I was nervous as hell, mainly because I've never introduced a woman to my parents or Nonna. Everything was set until I woke up at 2:00 a.m. to heavy sobbing. The light in the kitchen on. Dozens of pills in Lea's trembling hand, moments away from…

"I know, Ma. But as I said, Lea's not feeling well. It's probably just a cold, but I don't want to leave her alone. Tell Dad and Nonna I'm sorry. I'm sure there'll be another time."

"Could it be that perhaps… perhaps she doesn't want to meet us?"

I glance down at Lea, my fingers threading through her blonde waves as she sleeps with her head against my bare chest. "Of course she wants to meet you, Ma," I whisper, not wanting to wake her up since she only dozed off moments ago. "I promise we'll come visit soon. *Ti prometto.*"

"Okay, well, sending all my love and hope Lea feels better soon."

"Me too. *Ti amo, mamma.*"

"*Ti amo,* Santo."

I hang up with a heavy heart and slowly reach over to place my phone on my nightstand. I hate that I had to lie to my mother about what really happened, but Lea deserves her privacy.

Lea stirs against me in the bed and I freeze, hoping she'll adjust and fall back asleep. It's the first time she rested her eyes after we were up for three hours talking in the kitchen after she freaking scared me to death. I've never been in a situation like that before. Never had to coax somebody out of life or death, especially somebody so close to me. My heart aches from the aftershocks... the aftershocks of what could have happened if I didn't wake up in time.

I hate the eerie feeling rushing up my spine. Hate how Lea glances up at me, her light green eyes red from crying, and she crumbles right here wrapped in me. Hate that no matter how many times I kiss her forehead, hold her tighter to me, and tell her everything is going to be okay, it's as if it doesn't help.

"I'm sorry, Santo," she sobs, her breath laced with alcohol. The same alcohol she consumed last night while I was sleeping. My heart broke when I found her like that in the kitchen and even more so the way she looked at me, so completely done with the world.

"It's okay, Lea," I reassure, kissing her forehead once more. "It's okay."

"No, it's not okay."

She's right. *It isn't.*

"You scared me so much, Lea," I whisper against her soft skin, sucking in a sharp breath as if it's my remedy. "I thought… *fuck.* I didn't know what to think."

"I know. I'm sorry. I'm just so tired." Lea's silent for a few moments. "I feel like nothing makes me happy anymore, Santo. *Nothing.*"

Her words break my fuckin' heart.

"You need to talk to somebody. Somebody that isn't me." I swallow thickly. "A professional who can help you through this. I'm going to be right here, okay? I'm not going anywhere, Lea."

Lea nods, sniffling away her tears.

We're quiet for a few moments, and I just hold her to me like we're stranded and drifting off to sea. Lea shifts her head on my bare chest, her cheek pressing against me so that she can gaze out the window and down to our backyard and the beautiful private long stretch of beach beyond it, only a gate dividing the two. My eyes follow hers past our backyard and to shimmery dark ocean waves, glazed with a silvery shadow of the moon and winking stars above.

"What would you have done if you were too late?"

"Jesus, Lea. Don't even ask me that."

"I want to know. Would you have taken care of Alexis?"

"You already know the answer to that, baby." I meet her light eyes. "In a heartbeat I would."

In a heartbeat…

Emotion overtakes Lea. She cups my stubbled jaw and rests her forehead against my cheek. I can't do anything but wrap my arms tighter around her and lift us up until I'm sitting up and leaning against the headboard with her straddling my waist. Her head falls into the crook of my neck as she trembles in my hold, her sobs faint at first before shaking me to my core.

"Breathe, Lea." I thread my fingers through her blonde waves, rubbing small circles on her bare lower back. "Breathe."

Her hot tears drip, stinging my cold neck and ruining me whole. "Why don't I feel happy? I want to love you so much,

Santo... *so* much, but it's as if the entire world is in black and white. Like I'm falling apart."

The knot in my throat tightens. "Do you trust me?"

"With all my heart."

"Then trust me when I say we're going to get through this. *Together.* Okay, baby?"

It takes a few seconds before she whispers back, "I hope so."

Those three little words haunt me the entire night. As Lea falls asleep in my arms, all I can imagine is how we left the kitchen... shattered hope, near-miss dreams, and fateful pills scattered on the hardwood floors.

Would Lea really have done it?

As Alexis's bright face flashes through my mind, my heart pinches hard because I know the answer. I don't sleep a wink, too worried that something could go wrong if I shut my eyes for a second. At around 5:00 a.m., I slip out of the bed and take a cigarette and my lighter from my nightstand. *I need a release.*

Stepping out on my bedroom's balcony, a light warm breeze kisses my skin. My gaze averts from Lea asleep in our bed and to the glittering ocean water as I light my cigarette. The view of the beach under the backdrop of the midnight-blue night sky always used to calm my soul... *until right now.*

Rolling my tense shoulders back, I press my back against the white shiplap wall and lean my head against it. White smoke hazes my thoughts with every drag I take. My heart is overthinking everything, spiraling.

Nothing clears my state of mind. Nothing at all.

I could have lost her tonight.

My eyes squeeze shut as my breath hitches.

I could have lost everything.

Three months have gone by since *that* night and Lea is slowly getting back on track. She started seeing a psychiatrist. She seems happier. Brighter. Like a fraction of *Lea* again. The psychiatrist recommended that now that Alexis is in preschool, perhaps finding a job would free up her time, so for the past few weeks job hunting has been on Lea's mind.

It took a while for my body to ease when we would fall asleep at night. The tragic near miss turned me into a light sleeper. My eyes snap open at the slightest sound and heart drops whenever I reach out across the crisp bedsheets and Lea isn't inches from me. It isn't the way to live, *this I know*, but fear remains when bad things happen.

It took me a while to feel like my old self again, but that's the crazy thing about life... As soon as your body calms, something out of the corner of your eye makes you jump. *Like tonight.* Lea's been tossing and turning all night, suffering from nausea. I've just come back from reassuring Alexis everything is going to be okay and tucking her back into bed after she ran into our bedroom scared after a nightmare. I returned to our bedroom moments later, only to find Lea in the bathroom throwing up in the toilet. I hate seeing her in pain like this. Now, as we slip back into the sheets, I pull her to me and pray she doesn't get any worse.

My fingertips slowly trace over her flat stomach. "Could it be that..."

"That I'm pregnant?" Lea faintly smiles. "I already thought of that. I took a test this morning while you were at work... *negative.* I think it's just my body telling me to slow down after doing so much readjusting. It's probably also just stress from trying to find a job."

"You know I could ask around and—"

Lea cuts me off. "No. I told you from the beginning that I put myself in this mess and I'll be the one to get myself out."

"I just want to help."

"Baby, you are. The fact that you're allowing Alexis and me to stay here without paying you anything is—"

I brush my lips against hers. "It's what family does."

Because that's exactly what we are... a family. *The three of us.*

Lea found a job. The moment she sat me down for a chat on a Friday night a month ago, I knew there was something she was hiding by the look on her face. She found a job at this bar downtown to work Thursday to Saturday nights from 9:00 p.m. to 2 a.m. As much as I loathed the idea of her being out at all hours serving wasted asshole men who weren't blind to her beauty killed me, but I needed to support Lea's decision. She was excited about this work and all I wanted was for her to be happy, even though I was ready to kill any motherfucker who got too close.

In these past few weeks, we buckled down a schedule. From Thursday through to Saturday Lea would spend time with Alexis after preschool while I work. Then, we would have dinner at the beach house, or occasionally try a new restaurant and spend time together. Whenever we do go out, there's almost a guarantee we end up at a dessert bar at least once a week because ice cream with sprinkles is Alexis's favorite.

Lea insisted she could drive back and forth on her own to work, but I wasn't allowing that. I felt bad having to wake Alexis up to put her in my car, but she slept the entire drive to pick her mom up.

Tonight… the second I pulled out of my driveway, I felt something different. Call it a figment of my imagination or something in the air, but something just felt different. Now, it's just past 2:00 a.m. and Lea is yet to meet me outside of the club where I always park.

Is she okay?

My eyes flicker to Alexis in the rearview mirror, who sleeps so peacefully in her car seat, and I smile at the little fluffy plush giraffe toy that's still in her hands. *She's such a happy girl.* She loves that giraffe so much. I bought it for her last weekend when I had a day off and Lea and I went with her to Safari West Zoo. She hasn't separated from it since.

Turning back to the front of the bar Lea works at, I attempt to get a peek inside through the windows from inside the car, but they're too tinted. *What the hell?* I pull out my phone and put it on silent so I don't wake Alexis, then text Lea.

SANTO: Hey baby, I'm out front. Everything okay?

My phone vibrates in my hand moments later.

LEA: Mhmmm. Be out in 1 seccc!!!

My brows knit at the extra letters, but I let it slide.

Calm down, Lisconti. It could just be a slip of the thumb.

Hope fades the second I lock my phone and Lea stumbles out of the bar, landing face-first on the sidewalk. *Dear God.* My eyes widen. *She's drunk!* I jump out of the driver's side and help her up, only for Lea to start giggling uncontrollably the second she's back up on her feet.

Lea suggestively bats her lashes, and her drunk-laced eyes meet mine. "Hiiiii, baby!"

Concern takes over my entire body. "Lea, are you okay? What happened?"

"Nothinggg! Gee, lighten up, Santo."

"Lea." I sigh, shutting my eyes for a second. "You can't be like this. I thought you weren't even allowed to drink while you were working."

Lea winks. "I didn't."

"Liar."

"What happened to Mr. Bad Boy?" she scoffs.

"He's concerned. Alexis is in the car and I don't want her to see you like this if she wakes up."

Lea laughs, and before I know it, her lips are on mine. I can taste the liquor on her as she deepens it in a reckless fury, as if she's been craving me all night. I don't kiss back. My hands snake around her waist, holding her to me to stop her from swaying as I pull her away.

Lea's lips press against my neck, her hot breath fanning my stubble with every peck she places. When she reaches my ear, she whispers with a hiccup, "Want to know a secret?" She answers her own question before I can say anything, "You turn me on *so much*."

Dear God.

I completely dismiss the words she just spoke. "Stop, Lea. Come on, let me help you into the car."

"No." Lea's hand moves down to cup my crotch through my jeans. Her green eyes darken as they lift to mine, dripping in desire. "Fuck me, Santo," she purrs. "Come on, I know you want to."

I shake my head with a clenched jaw. "Let's get you home, Lea."

"No, I want you to fuck me. Right *here*. Right *now*."

I roll my eyes and take her hand away from my jeans. "I'm not fucking you when you're drunk and in the middle of a sidewalk," I say with a slight smirk. "Jesus Christ, Lea. How much did you drink?"

"Not enough. Come onnnn! Be a little wild with me, baby."

"Not happening. Let's go, Lea. Alexis is in the car."

Lea throws her head back in drunken laughter, her blonde hair softly blowing in the slight breeze. Her hands grab my jeans again and attempt to undo the button. "I know you want me."

"Stop, Lea." I sigh, growing a little impatient as I gently push her away. "Please, stop."

She pouts, drunken tears in her eyes. "Why? You don't want to fuck me?"

A group of men passing by glance over their shoulders at us. I swear to God they heard Lea's every word. A smirk rises on their lips as they ogle her body, and my jaw tightens in fury.

Motherfuckers.

"Come on, Santo, I know you want to…"

"*Oh Dio.* Stop it, Lea! You're drunk, and there are people looking!"

"Let them look!" She turns around to face the men and in a split second she pulls her black camisole down, flashing them her breasts. "Wooohooo!" she cheers. "It's the motherfucking weekend, guyssss!"

What the fuck, Lea?

Eyes wide, I launch forward and pull the damn camisole back up. My blood is boiling when I turn to the men, who haven't stopped gawking at her. "What the fuck are you all looking at?" I growl, fuming to the point I feel a vein pop out on my forehead. "Keep fucking walking unless you want me to place every single one of you six feet under."

Eventually, the group starts walking away, laughing to each other as they go.

I turn back to Lea just as she bends over and throws up on the sidewalk. Cursing, I make sure she's okay before carrying her to the passenger seat. Thank God Alexis is still asleep.

"Jesus, what possessed you to get this drunk? You know this isn't good for you." I fist the steering wheel when I'm in the driver's seat. "I can't fucking believe this…"

Lea drunkenly giggles and leans her head against the headrest. "I can and it's AMAZING!"

"Lea," I hiss, nodding toward her daughter in the back seat. "Please, she's sleeping."

Lea rolls her eyes and all she does is press her lips shut as I pull out of the parking lot, hitting the accelerator through downtown. "Why would you even put yourself in these conditions, Lea?"

She scoffs. "Are you saying I'm a bad mom?"

"God, no, that's not what I meant at all. All I'm saying is I think it's time to find a job more suitable, maybe something during the day."

"Nope. I like finishing late and you fucking me all night long." Her hand cups my cock for the third time tonight, this time quickly unbuttoning my jeans and scrambling to unzip my fly, but I stop her before she can complete the action. "Pull over, baby."

I bat her hand away and redo my button. "I'm not pulling over, Lea. Please stop acting like this."

"Come on. Don't you want me?"

"Not when you're like this."

"Like what?"

"Intoxicated."

"I don't have to feel anything when I'm like this."

My voice comes out softer now. "What are you hiding?"

Lea gulps down and puts her hand on the wheel. "Come on, pull over, Santo."

"Baby, please stop." I nudge her hand off.

She reaches for it again and this time steers it into the outbound lane. A blinding flash of white lights has me aggressively tugging the wheel back into my lane, missing the nearing car by seconds.

My heart jumps. *Fuck.* That was too fucking close.

"Are you fucking insane?" I growl, shoving her hand away from the wheel. "Are you trying to get us fucking killed or some shit?"

Lea's eyes narrow, lacking any sort of sympathy or responsibility. "D-Don't you fucking swear at me," she stutters through hiccups.

"Maybe if you had some fucking control, you'd stop acting so damn selfish and I wouldn't have to."

Lea gasps, her bottom lip trembling. "Fuck you!"

"That all you got for me?" I scoff and shake my head, wondering how the hell we got here. "You're a mess, Lea. A mess I don't know how to fucking help."

She launches for the door handle. "That's it. I'm getting out."

"Lea, stop."

"Let. Me. Out."

"I'm not stopping the goddamn car."

"Fine." Lea opens the glove box and rummages through it until she finds my lighter. Her eyes glow in a dark shade of sin as she flickers on the taunting orange flame. "Then I'll burn this damn car and us in it if you don't stop the car."

My heart picks up speed.

I glance between her and the road. "You wouldn't do that."

"Try me," she snarls.

"What the hell is wrong with you tonight?"

"Let me show you?" Lea grinds her jaw, fucking with my head as she lowers the lighter, the flame inches from licking her skinny jeans. I practically rip the lighter from her grip, un-flicker the flame, and throw it back in the glove box.

"What the fuck was that?"

Silence greets me.

"Grow the fuck up, Lea."

Her green eyes turn all glassy, sobs taking over. Instantly I know it isn't from my words alone, it's a combination of everything. *I'm so sick of this back and forth. I can't do it.* I let out a strangled breath and hit the brakes as the lights turn red.

"I can't do this, Santo," she cries.

Fuck.

My heart aches at her every strangled breath.

Reaching out my right hand, I cup her knee and bear witness to the tears streaming down her face. Long moments pass between us as comfort fills the tense void between us.

"I'm sorry, Lea." I sigh, swallowing thickly. "I just… I just don't like seeing you like this."

"I know," she whispers. "I know you don't. Neither do I."

I feel so bad. I know she's having such a hard time; I just didn't put two and two together.

"I thought therapy was helping."

"It's not that easy…" Lea shakes her head. "I still feel so alone. So alone and small and I don't know why."

"You have me, baby."

"Not forever, I don't. I'm not dumb, Santo. I know what we have isn't a forever thing. I mean, look at me, I'm a mess raising a three-year-old. I know the type of man you are. Kids are not in your plans. We'll be okay for a while, then I know we'll fizzle out and when that happens—"

"Don't think like that because it isn't true," I say as the light turns green and I turn into our street. "Yes, I admit at the start this wasn't for the long haul. I thought it was better that way because you're right, kids were never in my plans. I didn't want to hurt Alexis. She's still so young and I didn't want to give her false hope that I'll be around, just to disappear like her damn father. But then something changed when you told me you want to start a family with me. *Everything* changed," I murmur, slipping my fingers through hers. "*You* changed me."

Lea smiles softly through the tears, clenching our intertwined hands tighter. "I'm sorry, Santo. I'm just so scared to lose you. Alexis loves you so much. I just... I just don't know what I'd do without you."

I lean over and kiss her cheek before whispering, "I'm not going anywhere, baby."

"Promise?"

"Promise."

Lea smiles sadly. "I love you, Santo. I really do. God, you probably think I'm a mess."

"We're all messes." I wink, smiling through the havoc. "But you just happen to be a pretty mess."

I pull into the driveway of my beach house and park.

"You're too good for me." She rests her forehead against my shoulder. Our hands loosely intertwine in front of us, my fingertips caressing all the lengths and curves of her left hand. After a while, my fingers smooth down to the butterfly-like beauty spot on her arm that she always says she hates. Our gazes stay there, as I trace my love in patterns, loving the calmness in her smile when she finally turns my way with heavy eyes I'm bound to never forget.

"You're saving me, Santo," she whispers to the background of my rapidly beating heart.

You're saving me, Santo.

There's this deep tug in my chest, one I know will break any second now as I help Lea out of the car before unbuckling Alexis's car seat. A tug I know won't go away anytime soon.

Alexis slowly blinks her eyes open, rubbing them with her cute little fists as I set her on my hip. She smiles softly at me. "Where are we, Santo?"

"Home, *tesoro*."

I kiss Alexis's forehead and her tired eyes close once more as she slowly drifts off to sleep with her arms around my neck. My heart squeezes as I take her giraffe toy in my free hand and catch Lea's gaze as I shut the car door. There's so much utter love laced in them as they warm, and regret takes a back seat. It has me smiling and drawing her closer with a one-handed hug while I'm still holding her little girl.

"I'm so sorry, Santo. Forgive me."

"Already forgiven."

Lea closes her eyes as I kiss her forehead.

"I'm sorry too."

"No," she hiccups, "it's my fault. You… you deserve somebody better."

"Let's forget about tonight, okay? Let's just focus on moving forward."

Lea smiles. "I love the sound of that."

"Me too."

I hold her tighter to me as we walk up the steps of the white wooden front porch. But the words Lea spoke only moments ago never leave my mind. They circle around and grip my heart like a vise.

You're saving me, Santo.

You're saving me.

Little did I know in the end I was the one who needed saving from this game we call life. Because as much as I didn't expect it, soon everything changed… *for the worst.*

Chapter
FOURTEEN

Saint

Ever since Nico told me he apologized to Paisley after being so damn rude to her the day Erik attacked her, the tension between us has eased. I prefer it this way. I mean, who wouldn't. Nico Quivez isn't just a friend I can pull to the side and pep talk whenever shit goes down, he's my business partner here at Fearless Fitness and so it's important to create a good work-life balance with him that doesn't affect business. While Nico can be a pain in the ass, I'm glad he had the balls to acknowledge his faults, and we can all move forward.

I mean, I did threaten Nico's life if he didn't, but according to Paisley, it was a genuine apology and that's all I ever wanted. I know Paisley well enough to know she won't tell her father about the way Nico acted toward her, but it still isn't fair. She sent me a text earlier on this week thanking me regarding Nico's apology. It made me smile because Paisley's such an intelligent woman… she totally sensed I had some involvement in putting Nico straight.

Ever since her text, we haven't stopped messaging. It's been four days. *Four.* And my heart still spasms whenever my phone buzzes with her name. We talk about everything and anything.

It's been hard having to act as if she doesn't mean a single thing to me whenever Alaric's around. Paisley and I vowed to explore each other's lives more after she graduates soon, but we never determined the limits. As guilty as I feel regarding Alaric, the thrill of the chase fuels me with adrenaline I only used to feel before a boxing game or riding my Harley. This untamed desire bursting at the seams, destined to come undone and clasp what I truly desire. *And crashing my mouth against Paisley's gorgeous plump pink lips is what I truly desire lately.*

I wanted it like crazy bad, wanted to taunt and suck on those beautiful lips for every time she teased me whenever she bit them, and I felt my hardening cock pulse. What's going on between Paisley and me is something I can barely describe. We're walking that fine line between friends and wanting more. God knows I've been close to making a move and kissing her already. Like the night at the cemetery when I was holding her so close, or when I brought Mercedes over to dinner, or when she was dressing my wounds the other day. I'm hanging on by a bare fucking thread.

Thirteen years ago, I would have given her the world, but demons of my past fuck with my subconscious and scar my reality with flaws deeper than the Atlantic. I'm not a man to love. That I know. But fuck, whatever Paisley has in mind... *I want to know.* I don't know what this promise we made after her graduation entails, but I'm so fucking curious and desperate. Desperate to unravel just how far this can go... because I care for her more than she knows.

She's made it clear to me more than once how she feels about me, but Paisley is a romantic. She deserves all the happiness and a happily ever after. I can't give her that, so starting something I'm not going to finish isn't fair, not for her. But right now, I don't give a fuck about fair.

All I know is that she's taken over every inch of my mind.

I can't stop thinking about her.

"LISCONTI!"

My attention snaps toward Nico, who's staring at me with a raised brow in the middle of our Fitness Studio. An amused smirk grows on his lips when he crosses his boxing-pad-covered hands over his chest and gives me a *'what took you so fucking long?'* look.

My brows knit. *Huh?*

It's only when I glance around that I realize why Nico's looking at me. *Oh shit.* Two dozen pairs of eyes stare back at me, and it all comes back to me. Bootcamp, 5:30 a.m. I literally fucking zoned out in the middle of demonstrating with Nico the next set of drills.

That's what Paisley does to me.

Here at Fearless Fitness, not only can members come in and work out, but we train clients one-on-one, offer a diverse range of fitness classes, HIIT, and boot camps. We have a fast-growing, successful community, and I'm just fortunate to have sensational members who simply laugh off what just happened and Nico, who only encourages them.

Rubbing my stubbled jaw, I let out a breath between and chuckle. "Jesus. Did I just blank out?"

Nico can't stop nodding. "I was calling you for a solid five minutes, wasn't I, guys?"

Laughter heightens in our industrial-styled fitness studio, and I shoot them all an apologetic smile. "Sorry, guys. That won't happen again. Let's continue where we left off."

We all retake our positions and I deliver alternative jabs, explaining the technique of each precise movement as I go. After the demonstration, Nico and I watch on as members split up in pairs of two and begin their drills. The gym is thriving, super busy this time of morning, as usual with people all over.

Concentrate this time, Lisconti.

I cross my arms over my fitness uniform T-shirt and stay focused.

Fearless Fitness is located on 21st St. in Sacramento midtown.

Tall, tinted doors open to a lobby that leads to a massive industrial open area gym with distressed white painted exposed brick walls, steel finishes, gym mirrors, televisions, black rubber gym flooring, and elite fitness equipment like rowing machines, treadmills, weights, and battle ropes to say the least. The classic white alongside moody grays and dark color pallets with beautiful architectural features and three rows of twelve thirty-two-inch metallic LED triangular chandelier lighting in black that screams luxury.

One of my favorite touches is the inspirational affirmations and quotes on certain sections of the walls in cursive white neon signs. My personal favorite…

'Rise and grind'.

The right side of the fitness studio is specifically assigned to boxing and MMA training, as it's a passion both Nico and I share and envisioned here. Punching bags, boxing balls, gloves, kick pads, and skipping stations fill the space. My favorite section is the boxing ring where I get down and dirty professionally training clients to build their strength and endurance and be their fiercest, best selves.

Seven large private fitness rooms with floor-to-ceiling frosted glass walls align the left wall. Each holds allocated fitness classes such as spin class, yoga, self-defense, Pilates, cardio dance, aerial silks, and pole dancing with dedicated certified trainers. By the last room is a hall that leads to a staff room and kitchen on the left and on the right high-end wood tiled shower rooms with matte black accents, saunas, and ice baths to recover after a hardcore workout.

I wonder what Paisley's doing right now seeing as finals week is over.

I shake my head to myself. *So much for not thinking about her. Stop thinking.*

I attempt to get Paisley out of my mind, but it isn't so easy. I get caught in a song pumping from our music sound system and furrow my brows. *What the hell? How did this get into the playlist?*

It's some song by John Mayer that was a hot hit at the start of the year, "Moving On and Getting Over". It's definitely NOT the type of song we usually have pumping in the gym. It's nothing against Mayer, but slower songs don't match the fast momentum while working out. Music is important to me; it was my way of keeping level-headed when I used to train and box professionally. There was nothing like listening to an upbeat tune like something from Bon Jovi moments before stepping in the ring. I want to create the same experience with clients in this gym. Music and rhythm, that's my thing.

Not only isn't it a typical song of ours, but the lyrics taunt me, reminding me exactly of what's going on between Paisley and me. My jaw grinds as John Mayer sings about two people who can't be together and are not the friends they once were, yet still are unable to not think about each other. Even when they want to move on, aspects of the other person remain.

I'm grateful when the song ends and "Life of an outlaw" by Tupac comes on.

Yeah, that's what I'm talking about.

I step behind one of the women I'm training, Liz, and straighten the tension from her shoulders to ease her jabs with more precision. She smiles over her shoulder at me, fluttering her lashes, and continues punching away.

Nico arches a smug brow when I'm back beside him. We talk lowly, making sure nobody else hears as he leans over and says, "I'm not going to say anything, but I'm also not *not* going to say anything. She's into you."

"This is a fitness studio, man, not some speed dating bar. Plus, I'm not interested."

"Saint Lisconti *not interested*? Okay. Fine. You've already got a girl then, huh?"

Paisley's face flashes in my mind.

Swallowing thickly, I shake my head. "No girl, just want to keep things professional at work. My priorities have changed. They're not what they used to be."

Correction: There's only one woman I care about. A woman I can never truly have.

"What changed?"

Paisley. That's what changed.

I shrug. "Life."

"Bullshit."

"Look, can we not talk about this now? We're kind of in the middle of something." I gesture around the fitness studio. "If you don't remember…"

"Oh, I remember. Don't worry about me." Nico smirks and rubs a slow hand over his chin as if in thought. "Okay. Fine. Let's say you have *changed*. That only means one thing… who's the girl who changed your mind? You haven't been having any casual relationships lately. It must be because there's a woman you can't stop thinking about and you're trying to polish up your character to impress her."

Holy shit. *Who is this guy? Bond?*

I feel my heartbeat in my ears as I glance away from Nico, a little freaked out he hit the target. Liz meets my eyes and shoots me her pearly whites in a bright grin. She doesn't stop staring until I give her a small smile and a courteous thumbs-up. It's only then that she returns to hitting the pads another woman is holding.

I turn back to Nico and the motherfucker's smirk has grown wider. "I'm right, aren't I?"

My eyes narrow. "No, you're not, you piece of shit."

"Oooo, I'm *so* right! Who is it? That Mercedes chick?"

"God, no. That ended weeks ago. Besides, it was only for a weekend with her."

"Who's the woman you can't get out of your mind then?"

I sigh and look at him. "There honestly isn't anybody. Trust me, man. You know I wouldn't lie to you."

Nico stares at me long and hard before eventually nodding. "All right, I'll stop pushing your buttons now." He smiles and slaps my back. "I trust you. You're many things, but you're not a liar."

He walks off to help a member who's struggling to keep up with the group and I remain standing here with a strangled breath, completely taken aback at what just happened.

It's crazy... crazy because Nico trusts me enough to just dismiss it after being so persistent. Crazy because there *is* a woman I can't get out of my head, and no amount of John Mayer can fix my *wildflower* clouded mind. Crazy because Nico believed I would never lie to him, and yet...

I just did.

PAISLEY: Do you also have a blackout, or does the world just hate me tonight?

I smile at Paisley's text. Neither of us can stop these late-night texts. It's exactly two weeks since we promised each other to be more open, and now that her graduation is tomorrow, the smoke behind our heated tension is on the verge of clearing.

Paisley knows what she wants, and she isn't afraid to tempt the beast within me. Paisley's becoming bolder. I'm becoming a more stripped-down version of the man I used to be. But being that type of man feels so damn natural and pure and *right*.

So far, I've been *almost* caught by Alaric... *once*. It was when I was over at his house the other night and I caught a glance of Paisley's gorgeous ass bent over as she sorted through the kitchen cupboards, adamant to bake some sweets. I almost choked on my whiskey at the fucking sight of her and had to pretend my cock wasn't pulsing in my jeans when I returned my gaze to the movie and Alaric's eyes snapped from the television to me.

When it was safe, I subtly glanced her way, only to find Paisley smirking my way in the kitchen. *Caught.* Now, the thoughts keep on circling as I stare at her text, well aware it's 2:33 a.m. and her dad left just over half an hour ago for his hospital shift. It's the first time Paisley has texted me this late. Right now... it's just her and me and the unfiltered white noise.

SAINT: World just hates you, wildflower.

PAISLEY: Gee, wow, thank you. That's one way to get a woman's confidence back...

SAINT: Kiddin'. I've got no power either... It's after 2, shouldn't you be asleep?

PAISLEY: Shouldn't you? ;)

I smirk.

SAINT: Who says your text didn't wake me up?

Those three dots dance and dance and fucking dance and then they drop.

Nothing.

I pull down the bedsheets and swing my legs to the edge of the bed. Stretching my neck from side to side, I decide she probably doesn't know how to respond. Cute.

Cute?

What the fuck was that and since when did such a word enter my vocabulary?

Raking a hand through my hair, I lie back down on the edge of the bed. It's the first week of summer in June and already it's freaking boiling here in Sacramento. While I usually love the warm weather, this heatwave is beyond uncomfortable for sleep. To add to the shit, the electricity is out, and the only source of fresh, breezy air is slaughtered.

SAINT: For the record, it didn't wake me up, Scaredy Cat.

PAISLEY: Oh. Were you preoccupied?

A second text comes through.

PAISLEY: A woman?

SAINT: No, not a woman, you creep. Can't sleep. Too fucking hot. What's keeping you up?

PAISLEY: Well, you know how I'm graduating from high school tomorrow?

SAINT: Mhmmm.

PAISLEY: Well, I'm just stressed about my high school diploma. So, when I can't sleep, I need to listen to some calming sounds like rainforests and birds chirping like I told you. But the app I use doesn't work without the internet and my data isn't working, so... here I am.

Smirking harder, I bite back a laugh.

SAINT: And you thought the most logical solution was to message the guy next door?

PAISLEY: I can feel you smirking, asshole.

Fuck. I can't help but let out a chuckle.

SAINT: I am. Love how your brain works, Pais. Why don't you try reciting some of those flowers?

PAISLEY: I have, but it hasn't helped.

SAINT: Impossible. Come on, you've got this. Also, don't stress about tomorrow, it'll be smooth sailing, I promise. I'm sure you've been preparing yourself for it since you learned how to tie shoelaces. If I ask Alaric, he'll probably second that.

PAISLEY: Ha. Ha. Very funny.

SAINT: It's true. Don't sweat it or overthink it. I believe in you, you know that.

PAISLEY: Aww, thank you, I really appreciate it! It'll only be my father at the Commencement Ceremony tomorrow... so I guess that will be a bit less pressure without my mom in a way. It sounds odd... but I always imagined she'd be back for it, you know?

SAINT: It's her loss, Pais. She doesn't know what she's missing seeing such a beautiful, intelligent, and brave woman grip life by the horns and still win. She's not worth it, Pais, not after all the shit she caused you.

PAISLEY: You're so right... I couldn't have said it better myself. It's just crazy knowing she's worlds away. Sometimes you can grieve for somebody while they're still alive... How fucked up is that!

Paisley's words drag an invisible knife down my throat, the tip digging and digging until the skin is punctured beyond repair. *Fuck.* Her words shouldn't affect me as much as they do, this much I know, but as for the rest… I have no fuckin' clue of the reason why I can't put my thoughts together and remain composed.

I clutch at my chest, at that little spot just above my heart, and shut my eyes. Letting go of my phone, the other hand rests by my core, my fingers spreading against the grooves of my abs as I inhale and exhale rapidly. *Too* rapidly. Slowing my breath, I let out a curse and re-grip my phone.

Get it together, Lisconti.

SAINT: I learned a long time ago that you can't change people. Sure, you can attempt to sway their actions, but changing somebody to suit your needs only paralyzes your own desires.

PAISLEY: Wow, I've never thought about it that way. Powerful words, Santo.

Santo.

My heart pounds recklessly.

SAINT: It's Saint.

PAISLEY: Sorry, yes… Saint.

She sends another text.

PAISLEY: Can I ask you something?

SAINT: Why do you need permission to ask me something now when it's what we've been doing?

PAISLEY: Because… it may be too personal.

SAINT: Then call me.

My heart beats wildly as I hit send.

It's past two in the morning.

I should be asleep.

She should be asleep.

We shouldn't have even noticed the blackout. *Yet we did*, and we're *talking*. It's like our minds are synced and it's fucked up, but that doesn't stop me from answering her call on the first freaking ring.

"It's weirder like this." Are Paisley's first words.

I chuckle. "What is?"

"Asking you what I'm about to ask you."

"Preferred it without hearing my voice? Did it make it less real?"

"Mhmmm."

"Too bad, this is how we're gonna do it, Paisley... and no, don't roll your eyes at me."

She gasps, her voice a soft daydream. "How did you know I did that?"

"Just did." I laugh softly, resting my left hand behind my head on the pillow. "All right, ask me."

"Okayyy." Paisley sighs. "Why don't you like being called by your real name? Did something happen?"

Dio.

My eyes fall shut and I feel my throat closing up, only a deep sigh easing it. "Yes, something happened."

"Oh, okay, you don't need to tell me what. I was just curious and maybe should have never asked. Sorry, it just slipped, and you know me, once I'm thinking something I can't help but ask. I won't call you it again."

"Thank you."

White noise invades the line before Paisley's soft voice shines through. "Whatever it is that made you close up to the world around you, just know that you're entitled to happiness too. I've only seen you smile a handful of times and I just... well, I want to know if you're okay."

Whatever it is that made you close up to the world around you, just know that you're entitled to happiness too.

"Yeah, I'm all right, Pais."

A sad smile breaks through as I come to terms with how much the warmth of her voice resonates in my chest. Sure, we started off on the wrong foot—*literally, I stepped on her damn flowers*—but then on her eighteenth birthday she ran into my arms, and everything changed.

"Saint? You still there?"

"Still here."

A lifetime passes before she murmurs, "Who hurt you?"

"Nobody hurt me." I suck in a deep, uncontrolled breath. "I hurt myself... I hurt myself loving her... Loving Lea."

"You loved her?" Paisley asks, her voice so breathy it kills me physically.

It's crazy how natural it feels to talk to Paisley about Lea if I just allow myself to.

"I did, with everything I had, enough that I wanted to spend the rest of my life with her. I loved her until she gave me reasons not to and I don't need to be deceived twice to step away. She was mentally unwell and..." My throat swells as I swallow thickly. "It just hurts, you know?"

"I know. I don't want you hurting. Do you think you could ever move on from her?"

"I have moved on from Lea. I did a long time ago when boxing took over my life. It's why I started, to escape reality. I've moved on from her, but it's the feelings I took away from the relation-ship that have stayed with me and molded me to be... scared of seeing the beauty of the world, just like you said."

"That makes so much sense now. Thank you for talking to me about her. I know it isn't easy, but I find the more we talk about hardships, the easier it gets in the long term."

"I agree. I'm sorry to be unloading all this shit on you. I really don't feel like talking any more about her now. I know you should be sleeping for your graduation tomorrow and—"

"Don't be silly," Paisley says, but it comes out so damn sexy. "You know everything about me and my fucked up life and strug-gles. I want to support you like you support me."

She's so curious.

So determined.

So *beautiful*.

"Paisley, do you know who I am?"

"Yes, of course I do. You're a former champion professional

boxer in one of the most notoriously dangerous sports. Now, you're a fitness trainer. You're my father's best friend. The mysterious guy next door. A man I'm supposed to know nothing about, but in these past months that's changed, and I know you feel it too. You hide yourself away from how you truly feel. You walk around with intimating blue eyes, rarely smile, used to knock men out cold. Yet, at the same time, you know the most delicate of flowers and are always here to support me. I'm not scared of you, Saint. You're always here for me and I know you won't hurt me."

"You've got some confidence, Pais."

"No, I really don't. I'm sinking in a world that's swimming."

"You're not alone in that feeling."

"Maybe that's why I'm not scared."

"And maybe that's exactly why *I* am scared. You understand me so fucking perfectly and I've… I've never had something like that before, you know. Maybe we're just crazy…"

"Maybe… Or maybe we're two broken souls trying to find a way to perfect our flaws together, while ocean waves crash against our bodies and cleanse our hearts. Maybe we were supposed to meet, and you were supposed to step on my lilies that day. Maybe we were supposed to have this crazy connection and at the same time, be complete opposites."

"Maybe." I smile softly. "Now, I'm going to let you go because it's late. This conversation stays between us, as always. Good night, Paisley."

"Night, Saint," she whispers, and I hear the hint of a grin in her voice too.

Just as I'm about to hang up, I murmur, "Enjoy every single moment of tomorrow."

And maybe, just maybe, if Paisley reads between the lines, she'll realize that's all she'll ever need to know and understand about me.

I'm not the type of man to crave connection or love.

I don't deserve it.

Not in this lifetime.

SAINT: Happy graduation in advance, wildflower. Don't make a fool out of yourself with your father watching up on that stage... unlike I did at mine. ;)

PAISLEY: Aww, thank you so much! Oh, you definitely need to tell me about that story one day... ;) Dad has a work emergency at the hospital. A patient is critical and wants him to stay on, so he's going to be there for a couple more hours and pull a double.

What?

I come to a halt across the street to my fitness studio.

Alaric's missing her graduation?

My brows draw close together as I slip my black duffle bag from my shoulder and reread the text.

SAINT: What do you mean? He's going to miss your graduation?

PAISLEY: Inevitably, yes. But it's okay. He says he feels bad, but I completely understand. His patients need him, you know.

It's a fucking double-edged sword, because as true as it is that Alaric's patients rely on him... this is Paisley's *graduation*. It only happens *once* in a lifetime. Today is supposed to be a special day surrounded by the people who support and care for you. My heart breaks that she's not going to have anybody there.

SAINT: Where are you now?

PAISLEY: About half an hour early to my graduation... I'm so nervous!!!

SAINT: No need to be nervous, Pais. You've got this!

PAISLEY: I hope so. Fingers crossed.

SAINT: They're crossed... toes too. HAHA!

PAISLEY: LOL! Thank you. I'll talk to you soon. xx

SAINT: Talk then, *tesoro*. x

An idea crosses my mind.

Sliding my phone into my back shorts pocket, I glance across 21st St. at my fitness studio doors. Nico is walking up the other side of the road and hasn't seen me yet. He heads toward Fearless Fitness's tinted doors, pulls out his phone, and comes to a halt.

Come on, man. Walk in!

But of course with Nico being Nico, he doesn't. At least his back is to me. If he stays where he is and doesn't see me... maybe I can actually pull this shit off.

I'm meant to host a mixed boxing and MMA training boot camp with him this morning. While last week we alternated between training boxing and jiujitsu drills, low and high intensity cardio, weights and conditioning, this week we're focusing on wrestling, kickboxing, pad intervals, strength, and live situation. I know I can't bail on him or my clients now. There are a good twenty minutes until our boot camp begins... *and yet...*

Slinging the duffle bag strap over my shoulder, I pivot in my Nikes and jog toward my Maserati's parking spot. Just as I reach for the car handle, Nico's damn voice booms from across the street.

Well, shit.

"Hey, Lisconti! Where the hell are you going? Left your pride in the car or something?"

I turn to Nico and rub a hand over my stubbled jaw. *I was so damn close.*

"No, man." I nervously chuckle. "I, uh, I just need this morning off."

"*Seriously?* Bootcamp's going to start in twenty. What the hell am I going to tell our clients? Nobody else can fill in for you. There needs to be another trainer with me."

"Tell them it's a personal emergency. Promise I'll make it up to you."

"Is something wrong with family?"

I shake my head softly. "No, man. It's just personal."

Nico's eyes narrow down on me, but whatever he's searching for, he won't find.

I've got nothing to hide. *Except for the fucking reason I'm going to skip work this morning, even though I'm the co-owner.*

I know Nico. He would give me shit if I told him the real reason. He'd tell me to get my priorities straight. But he also knows how focused and dedicated I am to my work. Hell, I founded the damn place with him. It's the same reason Nico seems to trust my word and begins walking backward toward our fitness studio with a curt nod.

"All right." Nico gestures toward me. "But you fucking owe me, *Chihuahua*."

I flip him off with a chuckle. "You're the best, man."

"Go already, you sneaky shit!"

Chapter
FIFTEEN

Paisley

TEN MINUTES.

Ten minutes until my graduation and I'm nervous as hell. My heels slap against the gravel as I pace up and down outside my school, where it's inundated with students, parents, and teachers. Crowds of burgundy graduation gowns walk down, eager graduation day is finally here and for the ceremony to begin. It shouldn't make me feel this type of way, but seeing the wide, joyous smiles on parents' faces… squeezes my heart for all the wrong reasons.

Tucking my graduation cap under my arm, I pull up my father's last text.

DAD: Once again, I'm so sorry. I feel so bad. I know what this means to you, and I should be there. I promise I'll make this up to you and be there for you more. Just know that I love you so much and kill it up on that stage! I'm so proud of you and so glad to call you my daughter, Paisley. I really am.

I'll make it up to you. I've heard that before, one too many times. But I need to give my father the benefit of the doubt. His job is strenuous and although rewarding, he sacrifices a lot too, working hard and exhaustingly long hours not only saving lives, but to keep our little family afloat for eighteen years as a single dad. I love him so much and he's the only family I truly have too. And even though it breaks my heart, of course I forgive him. This is his job. His patients need him.

Slipping my phone into my purse, I cast a glance and freeze at the sight of Erik about to step through the gates. While the black eye Saint gave him has faded and some cuts to his face have healed, others are still here... scars. Erik slows in his step the second he sees me and gulps down thickly as his parents slow behind him too. They're looking at him all confused, probably wondering why he stopped. But unlike other times I've seen Erik, the smugness in his stare is gone, replaced with something more genuine and emotive.

I flash him a small, encouraging smile, and relief ripples through me when he slowly smiles back and nods before continuing his walk into the hall with his head low. *God.* I'm proud of myself. I've never been that calm and strong in my life. Never looked a former bully in the eye without my heart beating wildly in my chest. But that all changes today. I'm a different woman. A better woman. One who doesn't let people drag them down.

Graduation is getting closer.

Sucking in a deep breath, I tell myself I can do this.

You've got this, Paisley.

I spin on my heels with the intention of stepping through the gates when I come to a sudden halt at what I see, or rather *who* I see.

Oh.

My.

Dear.

God.

My jaw drops at the sight of the man striding toward me.

Dressed in an elegant suit… a black luxurious blazer, a crisp white dress shirt with a dark gray *paisley* pattern tie, slacks, and shiny dark Italian leather shoes… Saint's potent ocean eyes burn straight through me in the best kind of way.

Saint looks so different but equally handsome and beautiful with his sexy suit and all his tattoos covered up. I can't help but tear up at his slow, sexy smile as he rakes his fingers through his perfectly tousled hair and stands in front of me. It's as if this sight is part of the outtakes of a *GQ* magazine shoot, only I don't feel worthy of being the lens.

I can't believe it!

He's here. Saint's *here.*

Out of all the people in the world, *Saint* showed up.

"What a surprise! How did you get here?"

"By car." He smirks mid-grin; long dimples and all. "You know I wouldn't miss this for the world!"

"Oh my. I honestly cannot believe it! You don't know how happy I am right now!"

Saint is definitely the type of alpha male people notice and double take whenever they walk by, and that's exactly what a few of the students (*and their mothers*) do right now. I love the feeling of knowing he's all mine as his musky sandalwood cologne engulfs me in a world of him when he closes in and pulls me into a tight, secure embrace.

Shutting my eyes, I wrap my arms around Saint and rest my head by his chest, letting my body enjoy every single second. His warmth restores that missing piece inside me. With one action alone, Saint finds a way to make everything right. It has me letting go of the tension in my shoulders, of my rapidly beating heart, of the preoccupation floating in my mind. I feel so calm wrapped in him. I feel… *free.*

The widest smile grows on my lips when he kisses my cheek and whispers in my ear, "You look beautiful."

"Thank you." I feel my cheeks heat. "You look pretty

handsome yourself. I didn't think you even owned a suit with all the leather jackets you have."

Saint smirks. "I'm Italian. Of course I own a suit. Besides, I don't wear a lot of leather anyway."

"*Ha!* Is that supposed to be a joke? You own a Harley Davidson. You wear leather, Saint. You should sponsor Saint Laurent. How does it feel like having your initials on a jacket when it doesn't even stand for your name?"

"Well, shittt, when did this become a Saint Lisconti roast and why didn't I get the memo?"

We laugh.

"Congratulations in advance, *wildflower*," Saint murmurs, still holding on to me. "I'm so proud of you."

"Thank you, Saint. I couldn't have done it without your encouragement and support."

"Bullshit, this is all you. Own your success, *bella*."

"Thank you. Does my father know you're here?"

Saint shakes his head.

I nod. "Don't worry, I won't tell him anything."

My father wouldn't understand. He wouldn't see it like Saint supporting me. He would see straight through my flushed cheeks.

"By the way," I add, slowly gliding my finger up his tie. "I like this. Very clever."

Saint chuckles. We're so close it vibrates through his chest and into me. "Ohhh, you noticed, huh?"

"Mhmm, it's a *paisley* tie."

"Wore it for you."

The smile on my lips extends. "That makes me feel special."

"You should. You are."

I cannot describe the full extent to how much hearing his heart synchronize with my beats comforts me. Once again, Saint has found a way to rescue me. I want to freeze in time the idyllic feeling of his warm touch being so close forever and the beautiful scent of him with a hint of tobacco I've grown to love.

Glancing to my side, a few people are staring over at us with unreadable expressions.

"Umm, Saint, everybody is watching us…"

"Let them fucking watch. I'm proud of my girl."

"*Your girl?*" I tease, welcoming the warmth that spreads across my chest. "I'm *your girl* now, hmm?"

Saint's eyes darken as they lower, meeting mine, and he grins. "Do you prefer my crazy next-door neighbor?"

"Definitely not." I laugh.

"Thought so." A sexy, lopsided smirk appears. "Now, you don't worry about a thing. Don't worry about who's here and who isn't. Right now, it's your time to shine. This is *your* time. So, be proud of yourself for how far you've come. You've got this, Paisley."

I pull back from the embrace, grinning. "Thank you, Saint. You're coming in, right?"

"Of course. Seeing you in your nerdy element with a graduation gown and cap that make you look like you're ready to defeat and conquer whatever the hell you like? Fuck yeah. Wouldn't miss this for the world."

Smirking, I narrow my gaze. "You went to *Stanford* and you're calling me nerdy?"

"Shh, don't rat me out. Come on, let's get this cap on you."

Saint takes my graduation cap, and we never break eye contact as he fits it on top of my head, the golden tassel on the right side of the cap. Once he's satisfied, he steps back to observe his work with a curt nod, obviously impressed with himself.

"Perfect, now get your ass in there."

I nod, flashing him my brightest smile, and turn to the hall. Just as I'm about to step toward it, I turn back to Saint—the tall, mysterious tattooed bad boy who could be anywhere he'd like to be right now—instead, he's *here*… with *me*.

"Saint?"

He slips his hands into his slacks pockets. "Yeah?"

"Thank you for being here. It really means a lot to me."

Saint steps closer and presses his lips to just above the corner of my mouth, only inches away from my lips, and gives me a soft, warm peck. My entire body bursts with sparks. The second he pulls back, those deep dimples come to play, curved beneath his stubble. He winks at me and that's all it takes for the blush to deepen on my cheeks.

I spin on my heels, feeling the first hot tear roll down my cheek, but it's a mixture of sadness that my family isn't sharing this memory with me and relief that Saint is here. He's forbidden. Older. Sexy. He's the one man I can never have, but right now I can't help but imagine what it would feel like to be loved by him. If being wrapped in his arms feels like heaven, what would it feel like to have his lips on mine and to never let go?

Whatever that feeling may be... I want it.

I want *him.*

Since Nana June passed, I never knew what this day would look like for me. Deep down, I was convinced my dad would be here. That my mom would magically show even though I wouldn't even recognize her considering my father deleted and ripped every single photo he ever had with her in a fit of rage when I was little.

But it's okay. It's okay because my heart feels full with my nana—my guardian angel—looking down on me from above and with the incredible Italian man behind me, who makes me feel so strong.

Saint Lisconti may never know how much him being here today truly means to me, but I'll never forget this day or the reason my heart skips an extra beat whenever he's around...

Never.

"Okay... it wasn't *that* funny!"

"Wasn't *that* funny?" Saint laughs, throwing back his head against the leather headrest of his stunning Maserati. "You basically tripped *up* the stairs to get your diploma and then stared down at your principal's hand when he wanted to shake yours as if he had an electric buzzer in it."

I groan, yet I can't help the smile crawling up my lips. "Well, I did say I wanted to go out with a bang... I just didn't anticipate it being banging my ass on the stage."

When graduation ended, Saint offered to take me home. I didn't want to cause any inconveniences for him, knowing he must have skipped some work to attend, especially because I was more than happy to go home with an UBER, just like how I arrived here, but he insisted.

This car smells like him.

Everything smells like him.

"Ahhh, high school, the good old days."

"Anything happen at your graduation that I can make you not live down too? You said there was in your text earlier today. It's a shame my father didn't know you back then. For sure a story or two would have spilled out if he had."

Saint shakes his head, just one hand on the wheel as he glances at me. Grinning, he chuckles at my statement. "Nah, ah, ah, those days are locked down in the vault. Never coming out, Pais."

Oh, I see how this is.

I arch a playful brow. "Hmmm, so something *did* happen?"

"Maybe..." His dimples deepen as he turns back to the road. "All right, fine, you win. So, I was up there on stage and my principal was about to say my name. Weeks before, my nonna said to me I had to wear her Italian flag broch on my graduation gown. She wears it everywhere and it brings her good luck, so she wanted me to pin it to the gown and wear it so I was blessed or some shit."

"Don't tell me you forget to wear it."

"You're damn right I forgot and all of a sudden I see my nonna running up the stage stairs in the middle of the ceremony, get it from my pocket under my gown, and put it on me. The whole school was laughing at me because she was slicking back my hair, making sure I looked even more presentable in her eyes before proceeding to say the Hail Mary in Italian. Then, she gave me a wrapped meatball sandwich she had in her pocket and told me to eat it after I got my diploma and was waiting for everybody else's names to get called. She said it would calm all the nerves… but all it did was embarrass the shit out of me, but I love her for it."

"Saint! That's gold!" I can't stop laughing as I slide a hand through my wavy hair. "Did you eat the sandwich your nonna gave you?"

"No, I didn't eat it up there." Saint chuckles. "My nonna went back to her seat, but when she saw I wasn't eating, she stood up from her chair and yelled, '*Mangialo! Nonna l'ha fatto per te con amore. Non ti piace più la mia cucina, Santo? Non far piangere tua Nonna. Dai, mangialo! Non farmi venire di nuovo lassù!*' Which ultimately translates to, '*Eat it. Nonna made it for you with love. You don't like my cooking anymore, Santo? Don't make your nonna cry. Come on, eat it! Don't make me come up there again!*'… And oh, did I mention my father was recording the entire thing?"

Hearing Saint speak Italian has me melting. *So damn sexy.*

It feels nice to listen to this side of him today—the *real* him.

"Your nonna sounds amazing and quite the character, although I would have died up there if that were me."

"Oh, I *definitely* did. I couldn't help but smile through the entire ordeal, but inside I was dying. Just when I thought Nonna was going to settle down, she began yelling at me in Italian about making our home country proud and how bad luck would follow me now because I didn't put the brooch on before the ceremony. Security almost ushered her out."

"Did she eventually forgive you?"

Saint nods, a smile still lingering on his lips. "An hour later when we got back home. She makes the best meatballs. I got them all."

I giggle, shaking my head. "That sounds like the ultimate forgiveness."

"It sure was." Saint grins. "I have a soft spot for my nonna and her cooking. When I used to box professionally, she would create this huge table the next day with the best Italian food. I kind of regret retiring just because of that."

"That sounds delicious."

Saint nods and turns back to me. There's happiness flooding his ocean eyes, an abundance of warmth that I want to never look away from. This little crush I started having on him years ago has magnified into a huge swell in my heart. The more we stare at each other with no words spoken and this heated gaze, the more it does something to me. I look at him, this time *really* look at him, and the second he gives me that slow, sexy smile, nothing can compare to the double backflip my heart does.

He's so loving and compassionate... so sentimental.

Saint clears his throat and breaks our long stare when he returns his gaze to the road and takes a right turn. He frowns slightly. "I'm sorry I'm talking about family when..."

"No, don't apologize. I love hearing about it. Please, unlock that vault more often."

Saint smiles, turning to me as he slows down and comes to a perfect halt by the set of red lights. "There was this other time in Santa Rosa. I was really into tennis growing up. I used to spend the summer break with my nonna as my parents worked. One day, she drove me to this tennis court because I wanted her to play a few games with me. Anyway, we're on the very first game. I served and she returned the serve strong but let go of the racket. It flew down two courts and hit this man in the head, and he blacked out. When he came to, we had to go to the ER with him because this huge bump appeared, and he was threatening to sue. My nonna was saying so many prayers, it was like she was performing her own rosary. Come to think of it, she *did* have rosary beads. The poor guy ended up being treated for a concussion. Three weeks later, I start freshman year and guess who my sports teacher was..."

Eyes wide, I burst out into laughter. "No way!"

"Yes way. He held this grudge against me for the entire year. Made me always be the one to pack away all the sports equipment. He was lucky I loved sports or else I would have fucking complained."

"I think that was the best story anybody's ever told me."

"Not for the guy, it wasn't." Saint chuckles. "But I agree, it was pretty intense."

"True." I smile. "Thank you for sharing a piece of yourself with me. I love learning all these things about you... I like being with you, Saint."

We share an extended stare and Saint parts his lips, about to say something, when a loud, persistent car beep from behind breaks our trance. I fly up in my seat and am about to clutch my heart in shock when Saint thrusts a protective hand over my chest, even though I have my seat belt on. I have no idea what's happening, yet I brace for an impact that never comes. Instead, Saint's hand slips away when he looks up at his rearview mirror and his eyes narrow at the driver behind us.

The lights are green. That's why they beeped.

"Jesus." I gasp. "God, that scared me."

"Fuck. Are you okay?"

"Yes, I just wasn't expecting it."

"Motherfuckers," Saint whispers under his breath. He presses his foot down on the accelerator and speeds up the street, building momentum.

My fingers clutch the door handle. *Whoa, so fast. We're flying. No wonder these cars go for hundreds of thousands of dollars.* I never thought I had motion sickness until this very moment as houses zoom past us in fast motion and flashes of evergreen trees and people on the sidewalks go by too quickly. I can't even make out any of the faces.

I guess now I know the difference between Saint and UBERs.

Moments later as we come to a stop by another set of red lights, I sigh as a young mom slowly walks across the road with a cute little boy. He can't be any older than two and is the sweetest little thing. I may only be eighteen, but the baby fever is so damn high. I think after growing up with a lost sense of security in family after grief, all I want to do is to be a mom one day and feel secure surrounded by little bare feet and pure love.

"You okay, Paisley?"

I clear my throat. "Yeah."

Loosening his tie, Saint turns his shoulders to me with only his left hand by the leather wheel. "You know I can tell when you're not okay, right? Don't feel like you need to fool me. It's just us in this car. Just Paisley and Saint."

I smile. "Just Paisley and Saint."

Saint smirks, his perfect dimples deepening. "Glad you know our names now, *wildflower*."

"Shut up." I giggle and glance back down at my hands, rubbing them together slowly. "God, my cheeks hurt from laughing and smiling so much."

"I'll take that as a compliment."

"It is."

"Oh, really now?"

The air crackles between us as Saint and I share an extended stare. It's so heated and playful. So intimate, as if he's staring right into my soul and I'm staring back into his.

"Mhmmm," I murmur, the vibration getting caught in my throat.

Saint sighs and reaches out to push back my waves behind my left ear. His knuckles then softly caress down my smooth jaw, igniting me. "You're going to be okay, beautiful. You're going to be okay. I promise."

"I know I am," I whisper. "I always am when I'm with you."

Saint smiles, his breath thick and mine non-existent as I bite my cheek and anticipate what comes next. My heart skips a beat the lower Saint's touch falls... from my jaw to my neck and exposed collarbone now that the graduation gown is in the back seat and I'm just wearing a dress. It rouses my entire body to feel his touch on me, so much so I feel my nipples harden and stab through my cherry red bodycon midi dress, seeing as I'm not wearing a bra.

And then... just like that, it all falls apart as Saint's hand backs away from my skin and that smile dissolves from his beautiful face. Mine follows suit. I don't have to ask why. I know why... *my father.*

Even though Saint's warm touch is stripped from me, I still feel him. I still feel the warmth in my heart. The abundance of joy in my lungs as I breathe in his scent, one I never want to leave behind.

"I'm always going to be here for you, Paisley, you know that. But..." Saint sighs and runs a hand over his stubbled jaw. Those irresistible toned biceps tense at the action, so perfect in that luxurious white dress shirt. He placed his blazer on the backseat before the drive. Taking his eyes off me, he gains momentum of the car as the lights flash an emerald green. "Please don't get used to me being everything you always need, because I'm not always going to be that."

"You don't know that."

"I do. I've shown you what you want to see, not the ugly. I can't promise you won't see the bad side of me, just like you did when I hit Erik... and I don't expect you to understand that in reality I only have one side... the *ugly*... but that's the truth."

"But that's not what you're showing me right now. That's why we agreed to stripping down the walls and showing each other the full extent of who we really are."

"I know, but I should scare you. You should see me and want to run."

I look at him and feel those butterflies in the pit of my stomach the second I meet his dreamy, blue gaze. "I once told you I'm not scared of you. I still feel the same."

"But why?" he murmurs in such a hot kind of way.

"You *know* why."

Saint's eyes hold mine and darken.

The thought of telling him how I *really* feel about him... it thrills me. I can't deny the sparks in my chest anymore. Not when they only grow stronger even more at the way he's looking at me.

This is such a surreal feeling, so intimately new, full of such expressive emotion in those ocean eyes I get lost in.

I want Saint.

I want him in ways I've never wanted anybody else before.

Saint pulls into our street and parks in front of our houses. I reach for my seat belt buckle and the cool tips of my fingers brush against the metal, but I don't tug it loose.

Not yet.

I make a split decision and listen to my heart. The tension between us thick, the air heavy with need. My breaths quicken as my left hand rises to rest on top of Saint's right hand, on the wheel. His blue eyes don't leave mine as warmth meets coldness. My cold fingers fan out over his big hand, tingling as they brush against his calloused knuckles. I love everything about it. Everything about his skin on mine and the lustful gaze we share.

Saint is so masculine, so wise, so strong—the type that only comes from experience.

Then, it happens in a split moment. Saint's hand slips from under mine and he turns mine over. The back of my hand falls to the wheel and his comes over mine, lacing his fingers through mine.

My God...

I'm certain my heart can't race any faster. Not as Saint draws our hands to his mouth and softly kisses my every knuckle with his warm lips. When he rests our clasped hands on my lap and squeezes tight... I *melt*. My body is so responsive to him and craves him even more as Saint continues to look at me as if nothing else matters. I want a little taste of sin. Fuck it, I want it all. The more time I spend with him, the more I want the Devil of Sacramento in his full wild and beastly ways.

Saint's hand slips from mine and it kills me. He stares ahead at our street with pursed lips for the longest time and in a flash of a second, he's transformed from charismatic to all serious. Just when I think it's all over, Saint turns his head to me, and I forget how to breathe.

His piercing gaze shifts from my own eyes down to my lips and stays there. It's as if he's fighting an urge within himself to look away. I bite my lip. *God.* The extended stare lingers for so long and my blood heats as I clench my thighs together.

Oh my...

Saint runs his tongue over his lower lip, and I can't help but imagine all the things that tongue could do to me. *Dear God. Stop looking at me like that, Saint, or I will kiss you...*

At this rate, I don't know how my heart hasn't burst out of my chest, because while I hold back the words threatening to fall, I feel myself throbbing in arousal. This sensual stare-off also doesn't help. It's almost as if he can read all my dirty secrets. As if he knows exactly what I do when I'm aroused and aching to take the edge off.

Parting my lips, I decide to poke the beast and murmur, "I want more, Saint."

There, I said it.

Saint's eyes darken even deeper, dripping with a desire only women who've never kissed can comprehend. I suck in a breath after a pause that lasts several seconds.

One second.

Two seconds.

Three seconds.

And then...

"Fuck it," Saint breathes. "I want more too, *wildflower.*"

Biting my lip mid-smile, I do a terrible job at pretending my soul didn't just explode into deep red rose petals. "You do?"

"Yes. More than you know."

My heart spasms in big waves of happiness. "I feel the same way."

"Mhmmm," Saint murmurs, the pad of his thumb softly grazing over my lower lip. The slow and teasing touch electrifies me. "I wish I could see you tonight, but I'm working."

"You're seeing me tomorrow night."

It's Saint's thirty-sixth birthday tomorrow and we're planning to celebrate it at a Downtown Sacramento restaurant to coincide with my little graduation dinner.

"I know." Saint nods. "But I meant just you and me. Alone. What time does your father start work on Saturday?"

"Three p.m."

"I'll meet you on your porch at three thirty p.m. on Saturday. Dress for the beach, with a change of clothes too."

"Oh, I have an afternoon shift on Saturday and am meant to be closing the—"

Saint cuts me off with a sexually frustrated growl. "Change it."

"Done."

"*Brava.*"

I grin. "What do you have planned, Mr. Lisconti?"

"Want to take you on a ride on my Harley to my favorite places in California." A slow, sexy smirk breaks on his lips as he adds, "And then some…"

It's just after 4:00 p.m when my father steps into the kitchen. I didn't even notice he came back home as I've been on a quick call with Maralyn. She wanted the full rundown of how my graduation went and couldn't stop squealing that high school is now a thing of the past for me. It's what I love about her most—her enthusiasm and bubbly personality.

As much as I would have loved Maralyn to come along to dinner tomorrow night, it's her sister's birthday, and she couldn't get out of it. I haven't told her a thing about Saint, but I hope soon that can change.

I don't know what that Harley ride on Saturday will entail, but now that we're on the same page, I can't rule anything out… *and that's a good thing.* Being emotionally connected and sexually attracted to such a beautiful Italian older man is one thing, but him admitting he wants more too… it's something else, something *beyond.*

I've been feeling giddy ever since. *I can't wait to see him.* Saint makes me a better woman. I'm bolder. Freer. Respect myself more than I ever have. And that's all because I met Saint and he showed me how.

Now, as my father pulls me into a tight embrace and I breathe in his familiar firewood scent, all the built-up guilt I've had in the back of my mind these past months washes away. *Is it bad that I'm so drawn to Saint that I don't even feel guilty?* I know my father will kill both Saint and me if he finds out that there's something beyond simply being amicable, which is why I'm determined for him not to suspect a thing.

Sorrow laces my father's eyes as we pull away from our embrace.

"Paisley... I don't even know where to begin. I'm so damn sorry. You don't know how bad I feel that I..." He sighs, rubbing a hand over his face. "Jesus, I can't believe I missed your graduation. I didn't expect to work overtime and couldn't say no."

"Dad." I smile, retaking my seat on one of the metal kitchen barstools. "You don't need to apologize. I know how demanding your job is and would never want to jeopardize that. Your patients need you."

"But I need you more. You're the only family I have left, Paisley. I want to be there for you, and I just feel like... I never am. I'm never there when you need me the most and I want to cherish these final months before you head to Seattle for college, but I always seem to screw it up. Like today. I..." My father pauses with another sigh. He runs a hand through his salt-and pepper hair, tugging hard at the ends. "I... I feel like the worst father in the world. Such a failure."

"You know that's not true."

Dad swallows thickly. "Isn't it, though?"

I don't like that he's feeling this way because it isn't true.

I shake my head at his words. "No, it's not. Yes, you've missed out on certain aspects of my life, but you make it up to me when you're here."

"You give me too much credit, sweetheart."

"You don't give yourself enough. You're not a failure. You could never be."

"You mean that?"

"You know I do."

My father shakes his head, taking a seat on the barstool beside me. His Adam's apple bops up and down as he gulps down again. His brown eyes stay level with the glossy white backsplash, unable to meet mine as they turn all glassy. "It isn't fair, Paisley. This isn't the life I wanted for us."

"Your job is physically and mentally demanding, it's—"

"I meant a life without your mom."

Oh.

As I tuck a strand of my hair behind my ear, my heart thumps in loud pitter-patters at the mention of her. My dad rarely talks about her, but when he does it's deep.

Squeezing his left shoulder, I offer him a soft smile when his eyes land on mine and say, "Dad, I love you and everything that you do. I wouldn't change a single thing in the world. You inspire me more than you know. Schedules can get in the way, but I know you always have the best intentions at heart. We don't have to be together to be together, you know what I mean?"

"I know exactly what you mean. You're so right." My father smiles back, and it's the happiest I've seen him in a while. "God, I'm so proud of you, Paisley. You've grown up into such a beautiful woman. So wise and intelligent. Your mom doesn't know what she's missing."

"I have you. That's all that matters now."

"That's all that matters to me too. When I started med school, everything was different. Faye... your mother. She was still in the picture back then. I was a twenty-two-year-old father to such a beautiful newborn baby girl, and I was the happiest I'd ever been. I thought I had it all, the perfect little family with the woman of my dreams standing right beside me. I loved your mother so much, Paisley. So damn much. I mean, I was ready to propose to her, you know? But the world was black and white to her. She wasn't happy. She hadn't been for a long time. As much as I wanted to be the one to change her, I couldn't. So, when Faye told me she couldn't handle it anymore and left, I didn't know what life would look like for you and me. I never chased her. Not for a second chance. Not for anything. I didn't because I wanted whatever happiness she was attempting to seek to set her free."

"And because you're a good person. Not many people would have done what you did."

"I know, but I just didn't want drama either. Sometimes you've got to know when to fight for it and keep the butterfly caged. Other times, you simply have to rid it of suffering and watch it flutter away... and that's what I did."

Warm tears stream down my cheeks at just how touching my father's words are. It means a lot to me that he's chosen to open up about something so sensitive to both of us. The salty tears slide down and baptize my lips. I lick them away as I scoot closer to my father.

"Hey," I whisper and squeeze his left shoulder tighter. "You did everything for her. You couldn't have done anything else, Dad. I know it hurts that she left us both because it all got too much, but you also need to know it isn't on you. It never was. I don't blame you for a single thing and neither should you. We're in this together and I'm so happy it's you. You know I love you more than anything."

My father's reddened eyes meet me moments from breaking. He pulls me into a tight embrace, and I let my head rest on his shoulder. My eyes close as I wrap my arms around him.

This feels like home.

I've never seen my father like this. He just needs to get all the built-up, emotion-filled rage out. He's kept it all trapped inside him since I was a little girl. Now it's time to let it go.

I don't know who's supporting who in this moment, but whatever it may be, it's such a bittersweet moment between us, filled with emotion, history, and hope. My heart is beating so fast because all my life I've been so concentrated on how my mom leaving impacted me. Sometimes it's easy to forget the scars it left my dad with too.

As my father holds me tighter and it's just his heartbeat against mine, flashes of his best friend cross my mind... *Saint*. I try to put on a brave face and smile when we pull away, but it isn't so easy. My father smiles back with pure love as he wipes away his tears and leans to softly kiss my forehead. The guilt that had left me before crashes back to shore in heavy waves.

I'm betraying my father with his closest best friend.

Yet Saint is the best thing that ever happened to me, and I'll never be able to forgive myself if I don't explore the strong feelings I have for him and where it may take us.

It's as if there are veins of roses wrapped around mine, their thorns seeping deep inside and forming dints.

And I know exactly what happens to the heart when those little dints become major...

It *breaks*.

Chapter
SIXTEEN

Saint

"PAISLEYYY!" ALARIC HOLLERS AT THE BOTTOM OF THE STAIRCASE, his hands on either side of his mouth like he's a boxing coach going into the last round. "It's going to be tomorrow morning in a minute if you don't come down!"

"Okay, one second!" Paisley calls back from somewhere upstairs.

"You said that for the past twenty minutes! We're going to miss the reservation!"

"One second!"

Alaric dramatically rolls his eyes in defeat and plops down on the couch beside me when he rejoins me in his open plan living room. He smiles, gesturing to the whiskey glass I'm holding. "Yeah, I'm going to need that in a second."

I chuckle. "Patience, brother."

"I'm trying. I love her, but I swear I'm always late whenever we go out."

I just smile.

Paisley could make us thirty minutes late or miss my birthday dinner/her graduation celebration and I wouldn't mind. Just seeing her... it'll make up for it. Whenever those honey eyes meet mine, it takes every fiber of my being not to dive into her tempting touch.

I want more, Saint.

God, how badly I wanted to put this agonizing angst to bed and kiss her right there and then in my Maserati yesterday. *Paisley.* I can't stop thinking about her and that Harley getaway we have planned for tomorrow. *I'm counting down the seconds.*

"Saint?"

I rub a hand over my stubbled jaw and nod toward my friend. "Yeah?"

"Everything okay, man? It seems as though you've got something on your mind... no?"

Yes, your daughter.

"Yeah, I'm okay."

Alaric smirks. "Bullshit. You were smiling to yourself. So, tell me, who's the woman?"

I can't help but laugh, heat rising up my neck because this is the second time this week one of my friends has asked me this exact question. First Nico. Now Alaric.

"Why does it immediately have to be about a woman?"

"Because you're not denying the fact that it could be."

Shit.

I need to deflect where this conversation is going ASAP. When I stepped into Alaric's house half an hour ago, I could sense something wasn't right with him. He let me in the loop about how his mind has been a little clouded with thoughts of Faye, Paisley's mother. I've been trying to get his mind off it ever since with a man-to-man pep talk and liquor.

I shrug nonchalantly. "I was just thinking about life, you know, in general."

Alaric shakes his head, unconvinced, grinning as if he knows something I don't. "Nah-ah, man. It's some woman, I'm telling you. If you don't give me a name, I will turn into Maxwell Smart and solve this shit myself. I thought we didn't keep *secrets*."

So much for deflecting, Lisconti.

I can't even look him straight in the eyes anymore. Clasping my hands over my lap, I breathe out a long breath.

Think of something, chickenshit.

Anything.

"Okay," I say after a while. "I was... thinking of Lea."

The name burns my throat and instantly the pounding in my chest intensifies. The pit of guilt I've been spiraling in for the past thirteen years deepens.

I still can't believe what happened.

Still can't comprehend how one single second can change your life for good.

Still blame myself.

"Oh shit, man. I'm sorry, I didn't mean to push it."

"No, it's okay. It's just tough, you know?"

"I completely understand. It's crazy how quickly life can change. So fucked up." Alaric squeezes my right shoulder as I glance over at him. "I can't begin to imagine what's going on in your head, Saint, but you know I'm always here, right? You know we can talk about it whenever you like. Even if it's just needing me to listen, I'm here."

I feel bad at the way his light brown eyes soften into a space of comfort. I know I shouldn't have said her name, but it was the only legitimate answer Alaric will believe.

"Thank you, man, it really means a hell of a lot."

He smiles and pulls me into a half hug, playfully slapping my back. "You've got this, Saint. Make her proud tonight, all right?"

"Mhmmm."

As we pull back from the embrace, the loud thuds of Paisley's heels slapping against the oak stairs pull both our attention behind us and my heart feels like it stops beating.

Holy fuck.

Paisley's hot gaze flickers to mine for a fraction of a second and that's all I need for the past thoughts of deceiving Alaric to dissolve. The moment she grins at me from the landing and I mirror the action, she turns her concentration on her father and I'm done for.

Those perfect heart-shaped lips are a glossy delight this Friday evening, painted with the most gorgeous shade of red I've ever seen. Her silky dark brown hair is tied back in a perfect high ponytail, perfect to wrap my hand around and sexily tug. *Definitely perfect for that.*

Dio...

Paisley is already a natural beauty, so seeing her like this has my hard cock throbbing in my slacks. I don't trust myself to say a word out loud, because right now my brain and mouth don't have the best line of communication. It's more like my mouth and cock are on the same team, while my brain is a couple of miles behind, alongside my fucking sanity. And so, in a bid to calm my sexually frustrated mind, I reach out for my whiskey and drink.

But... it's no fucking use because that stunning, dark red dress she has on—I'm pretty sure it belongs to the *'How to kill Saint Lisconti in five seconds'* collection. It's as if this dress was made for her.

So fuckin' beautiful.

The mini cocktail dress barely reaches Paisley's mid-thigh, and that's not even the most daring aspect. With thin spaghetti straps, the neckline is low with a deep V, displaying the most cleavage I've seen from her since the day of her eighteenth birthday where she was locked out with a robe that barely covered anything.

God.

I can't look away from the luminous shine of the satin dress.

As I finish off my liquor, I keep my heated gaze on her over the glass, lowering my eyes down her beautiful body, taking my time with those gorgeous hips, killer legs, and gold strappy heels that have me feeling an insatiable hunger. Like I'm the big bad wolf in this twisted fantasy. Paisley has gone daring tonight. She seems the happiest she's ever been and I fuckin' love it.

Alaric, on the other hand...

"Jesus, Paisley! You forgot to put pants on and a jumper on top."

Paisley cocks her head to the side and gestures down her body. I don't miss the death grip she has on the chain of her gold purse bag. "I'm wearing a *dress*. Why would I need either?"

"Because you're not *wearing a dress*, you're wearing a small scrap of fabric. Where the hell did you buy it anyway? I'm going to call the manufacturers and tell them we're missing the other half of the dress. You're going to be surrounded by guys tonight. I don't exactly want to spend my night kicking all of their asses."

"Trust me, Dad, they won't look."

"*Won't look?*" Alaric screeches in full protective mode. "Ah, hello, Paisley. Have you *ever* met a man in your life?" He then turns to me, and my eyes instantly snap away from his daughter and to him instead. "Saint, we're going to be spending the night kicking their asses, aren't we?"

More like kicking my ass.

Paisley playfully rolls her eyes at her father, and I chuckle. Little does Alaric know *I'm* the *asshole friend* he should be worrying about. The one who wants to accept the challenge in his daughter's eyes, that look of growing desire.

I lift my hands in surrender. "Oh no, I ain't getting into this. This is between you and Paisley."

My best friend gasps in disbelief and it's the most hilarious thing. "Did you just say you're *'not getting into this'*? Man, help a guy out. I don't want freaking idiots gawking at her all night."

"She's eighteen, Alaric. She can wear whatever she likes, just like we can wear whatever we want. Fair call?"

"*See!* Even Saint's on my side!" Paisley grins over at us, giving me a secret wink when Alaric rubs his hand over his face. "I'll be fine, Dad. Let me enjoy being free for one night. You know I never go out," Paisley adds with a sigh and proceeds to cross her arms over her chest.

I tell myself not to go there, not to let my eyes lower to her even more exposed cleavage, but it's a fucking magnet. *I'm definitely the fucking asshole friend for sure.*

"Plus, I never wear things like this. I'm not trying to be Carrie Bradshaw in college, but something close would be nice."

"Carrie *who?*"

Paisley grins. "Forget it."

"God, help me." It takes a few moments before her father eventually groans in defeat. "Okay, fine. You're right, you should wear it if it makes you happy. But just bring a jacket in case you get cold later in the night."

"No, thanks, Mom."

Laughter echoes through the room before Alaric's phone starts blaring Will Smith's "Gettin' Jiggy Wit It" and I can't help but shake my head with a smile.

He pulls out his phone from his jeans pocket and groans, "Shit. It's Nico. He's probably there already. Give me your keys, Saint, I'll wait for you both in your car."

I throw Alaric the keys of my car and he catches them so damn smoothly with his non-dominant hand as if it were nothing.

Grinning, I gesture to the keys. "Don't get used to them."

"Sorry, can't hear ya, I'm a Maserati guy now," he mocks with a smirk before walking toward the front door.

The second I hear him on the phone and the sound of the door slamming shut, I look at Paisley. She's smiling, her honey browns already on me as she takes a step closer, her heels slapping on the hardwood floor. "Thanks for having my back earlier."

"It's nothing."

"It's something to me, so thank you."

Paisley approaches, my crisp white button-down shirt and charcoal slacks inches from her. Her lingering jasmine perfume drives me wild because it has me getting lost in a world full of her.

"You look so damn beautiful," I murmur, my voice low. It's

so obvious how aroused I am by the sexy growl at the end. "You *are* so damn beautiful, *wildflower*."

Paisley grins, her smokey eyeshadow bringing out her sparkling honey eyes. It's crazy how quickly her warmth transfers through me the second my arms wrap around her petite waist, and I pull her into a tight, prolonged embrace. She completes the hug by resting her head in the crook of my neck. My forbidden embrace tightens, kissing the side of her head before my nose buries in her ponytail. *Hmm, she smells so good.*

Paisley is pinned against me, yet with the current sexual tension between us… it's as if she's right underneath me. There's a look in her eyes, one of passionate challenge, and it sends shock waves across my entire body. I imagine carrying her upstairs right now and burying myself between her thighs. Her gorgeous red lip-gloss wrapped around my cock. Her screaming out my name as I give her what we both so desperately crave deep down inside.

Yeah, Paisley fucking Reign has destroyed me badly.

"Happy early Birthday, Saint," she whispers seductively by my ear as if it's a secret—*our* secret. Her lips brush against my spikey stubble as she kisses my cheek. Her touch leaves a permanent throb. *A permanent reminder of her.*

"Grazie, *amore*."

"I have a birthday gift for you… It's a surprise."

My brows perk up at this. "What kind of surprise?"

"A *surprise*. Something I… want to give to you tomorrow when it's just us."

I grin. "Give me a clue."

Paisley smirks with a cute laugh that has my eyes darkening in pure heat. "Do you know what a *surprise* is, Lisconti?"

"Apparently not. Oh, come on. Just one clue. I want in."

"Nah-ah."

"Fine, have it your way." The chuckle vibrates my throat. I lean to brush my warm lips against her ear and hold her closer to me. "I'm looking forward to it being just us again."

Desire burns in her eyes.

So beautiful.

"Me too." A devilish smirk works its way up her lips as her hands trail up my dress shirt like scorching fire destined to set me free. The first button of my shirt is already undone, but I swear to God she can feel my cock jolt against her lower stomach when she unbuttons the second. "That's better..." Her sensual eyes find mine. "Oh, *wow...*"

"Wow, what?"

"Your eyes," Paisley says, glancing between them. "I've never seen them so dark *and sexy.*"

Holy shit.

The last part has me sucking in a breath as I tower over her. I lose control and lower my hands down to her ass. My gaze settles on those glossy lips that part open, so goddamn ready for me.

Kiss her, my mind taunts me. *Kiss her right now.*

I wrap my left hand around her ponytail in a sexy kind of way and tug. It's the hottest thing witnessing her initial gasp turn into a sensual grin as her head tilts back to me. It feels as though an entire lifetime passes between us as I get caught in her gaze. Caught in watching her watching me with such lust. Caught in a world of her, on the other side of the flowers and sassy comebacks. A side I desperately want to explore.

Right fucking now.

"What the hell are you doing to me, Paisley Reign?" I sexily growl.

"I don't know..." she purrs. "But whatever it is you're feeling, just know I feel it too."

Just know I feel it too.

The need to simply kiss Paisley and end this agonizing angst between us couldn't be any stronger. Just as the resistance comes undone inside me, I'm too late because she steps back, and I let go of her ponytail.

Paisley gives me one last naughty grin before walking out the door, leaving me with a million forbidden thoughts, a heavy head, and an even harder cock.

"Sorry about that," I announce, setting my phone back down on the restaurant's polished chestnut table. "It was just my nonna checking in on me and wondering when I'm coming back to Santa Rosa because she wants to cook me—"

"Meatballs?" Paisley smiles, finishing off my sentence from across the table.

"Yeah." My grin lights up in awe. "Exactly."

Alaric's brows knit beside her. "You psychic or something, sweetheart?"

Paisley rolls her eyes. "No, that's his favorite food. You should have known that!"

He turns back to me, confused. "I thought your favorite food was falafel, no?"

"Fuck no. I've never touched that a day in my life."

Alaric sits back in the booth, scratching the side of his head. He stares at me with furrowed brows as if he's lost it. "Shit. Why did I say falafel then?"

My throat is seconds from closing as I down the rest of my Jack Daniel's.

For the past two hours since we arrived at this exclusive contemporary restaurant, we've had a good time. It's been a good distraction from all the shit in my life as stress fades away and I simply concentrate on the people around me instead.

Alaric.

Paisley.

Nico, beside me on my right. And Leo, at the head of the table on my left.

But I would be lying to myself if I didn't admit that some of those moments were filled with long, stolen glances with Paisley throughout dinner whenever nobody was looking. Or the fact that I wish I could knock out our eyeballing server when he returns because his gaze always lingers on Paisley for a second too long. *Not that I can do anything about it.*

"What the fuck? Why the hell did I think you liked falafel?" My best friend continues.

Setting my bottle on the table, my gaze flickers from Paisley to her father before murmuring, "Because it was Lea's favorite. I must have told you once."

Running a hand over his clean-shaven jaw, Alaric groans in regret as if he's just remembered the fact. "Ah, yes, that's right. Fuck. I'm sorry, man."

"It's okay."

But it's not. Because I have no fucking idea how a single name of food can affect me so much. But it does. And I feel the complete impact of it with Paisley's hot gaze. I haven't turned to look at her, but seeing her from my peripheral vision is enough. I know she's curious. I've never shared anything about Lea with her except for the fact of how burned I was. I've never gotten into the details with her. Not because I didn't want to, it just never seemed right.

Nico's the one to break the stiff silence. "You ever visit Lea's parents?"

"No, they were never in the picture to begin with," I gulp, picking the empty beer bottle once again as I turn to Nico. "Let's just cool down on the subject, all right?"

He raises his hands, shrugging smugly. "Cooled down."

We return to devouring the chocolate lava cakes we've improvised on as my birthday cake and Paisley's graduation celebration. I eat as if I didn't just freak the hell out and go into a mental block.

"Saint?" Paisley's soft, sweet voice asks.

My heart is pounding out of my chest, knowing exactly what she's going to ask next.

Who exactly is Lea?

It wouldn't be the first time she asked it. I don't even remember the shit I said to Paisley at the beach weeks ago when she asked, only that I wasn't in the mood to talk about it.

Now, as my eyes lift to see Paisley's intense gaze on me, it's confirmed. It's as if we have a silent conversation through our eyes. She's asking me something, wants me to allow her in. She's the only person who doesn't know my story with Lea at this table, yet deep down, I know she's the only person aside from Alaric who would truly understand losing somebody you love.

I clear my throat. "Mhmmm?"

"Can you kindly pass me the water jug?"

Huh?

My brows furrow. "The water jug?"

Paisley innocently nods. "Yes, water jug, please. Sorry, I can't reach it."

Ohhh right.

Well, I wasn't expecting her to ask about the water jug.

Collecting the jug, I swallow thickly and hand it to her with a soft smile. My mind is in pieces as she smiles back warmly, and I appreciate in this moment that she's letting it be.

Paisley's fingers brush with mine as we exchange the jug. I cast a glance around the table, ensuring all the men are heads down eating before I latch to her fingers. It's just for a split moment, but all I need to feel like myself again as I mouth, *"Thank you."*

Paisley nods, her cheeks flushing a deep shade of scarlet. The second Alaric's head snaps up from his dessert, I let go of Paisley and go back to eating mine.

My best friend claps his hands together, grinning. It instantly brightens the mood. "All right! What do we say we drop Paisley home and the rest of us can head to Vegas?"

"*Vegas?*" Paisley's the first to laugh as she turns to her father. "As if!"

"What?" He chuckles in defense, glancing between Leo, Nico, and me for some sort of backup. "Well, I was considerate, wasn't I? Said to *drop Paisley home* and everything."

I smile. "We're not going to Vegas. Why are you so obsessed with it?"

Alaric groans, dramatically slamming his head against the table. "Okay, fine, just know I'm unfriending all of you in real life."

"Yeah, good luck with that." Leo laughs.

Alaric shakes his head with a mocking smile as he turns to

me and points his thumb at Paisley. "Bro, help a man out. Defend me. Tell her Vegas is my happy place, and she should be happy her dad actually wants to go out and live life."

"All right. Let me tell you what you want to hear, Pais." I smirk, crossing my arms on the table and turning to her. Paisley's eyes light up and so does my damn fucking chest. "Vegas is your father's happy place. *Literally*. He arrives there a decent guy, returns home stumbling in Dorothy's red shoes."

The table roars in laughter, my best friend included.

"You're so full of shit, man!" Alaric chuckles, shaking his head.

I smirk. "Truth hurts, huh?"

"That place ruins me and this idiot over here laughs, just because he never gets drunk anymore."

I raise my beer, smirking smugly once again. "It's called drinking responsibly."

"Bull-fucking-shit."

"You see, the thing you may not know about Saint is while the guy doesn't get ruined on vino, you piss him the fuck off and he'll knock you out cold." Nico chuckles coldly, turning to Paisley. "Why do you think he went from boxer to personal trainer?"

Paisley's eyes widen a fraction as she glances at me. Those gorgeous heart-shaped lips gape open in disbelief. "Really?"

I shake my head.

"No." Clenching my jaw, I turn back to Nico and hiss, "Don't bring shit like that up again, got it?"

Nico laughs mockingly as he draws his glass to his lips and nods toward Leo. "Hey, wanna remind our guy Saint over here about that match six years ago?"

"You mean when Saint knocked the guy out cold and then his opponent's coach got into it, and so Saint knocked him out too?"

I meet Paisley's eyes no matter how badly I want to avoid it... and I hate it. Hate she's forced to see the monster in me. The one she claims she isn't afraid of.

"I meant that one, yes." Nico nods. "But you weren't there for the fifth fight he did thirteen years ago now. You remember that,

Saint? You knocked out the champion in the first ten seconds and then proceeded to—"

"Nico, stop."

"What? Just sharing a little of your history. It'll prevent Paisley from all the questions later, seeing as she's the only one who doesn't know about it." He turns to her. "Right…?"

The beats in my chest are beyond fucking normal. *Calm down, Saint.* I can't do anything to Nico. I can't do anything with her bearing witness. No matter how much I fucking want to.

I grind my jaw with flared nostrils. "You always take it too fucking far, don't you?"

"Oh, come on, Saint." Alaric smiles. "We're just messing around."

"You know I don't want to talk about that period of my life. This one over here," I say, gesturing toward Nico, "needs two seconds of encouragement before he goes off on a tangent."

Nico scoffs at my words. "Oh, loosen up, Saint. What? Want to be seen as a hero in front of a woman's eyes?"

"This isn't about Paisley."

"Yeah, leave my fucking daughter out of it, man," Alaric scolds.

"You both need to calm the fuck down," Nico suddenly hisses. "God, Saint, it's like I can't mention anything to you anymore. First Lea and now your figh—"

"Don't you fucking say her name again. *Understood?*" I growl, rising from my seat and walking toward the back of the restaurant before I lose all resistance and all hell breaks loose.

"Man, come back! Where are you going?" Alaric calls out from the table.

"I'll be back. I need some space."

Storming through the black-framed steel glass doors, I don't dare to glance behind me. A few diners in the outdoor patio section glance my way, yet I continue walking past the laughing and joyous couples at tables. Past the fairy lights hanging off the stunning oak tree, its branches filled with circular lights. Past everything I once believed to be true—*happiness.*

By the steel balcony outlooking Sacramento's skyline and darkening night sky, I pull out a cigarette and furiously light it.

I can't fucking believe it.

Can't believe Nico would take it this far when he knows how I feel about the subject.

As smoke fades into the winking stars and my heavy breaths are canceled out by people's chatter, I notice my right hand trembling. It's a habit I thought I lost years ago, yet now, in the midst of the war in my head, I can't seem to let it go.

My lungs feel tight with every breath I take. *I can't do this.* Thoughts of Lea circle my mind and I hate it. Hate that Nico has to dig up my past. I was fine going into today. Completely fine. Then he says her name and like a damn trigger, I react.

And then I hear the thick heel clicks of the only person who can save me from it all.

"Is this spot taken?" that soft voice I know so damn well asks from behind.

Paisley.

Paisley's here.

It's going to be okay.

I spin around, finding those sweet honey-brown eyes staring back at me. There's a placid smile on her lips and she doesn't wait for my permission before coming to stand beside me on the balcony. For a split moment staring out into the world is all we do, city lights and red-and-white car lights blanketing the view for miles on end.

"I told my father I would come out and check on you… simmer the situation if I could."

"Thank you." Shaking my head to myself, I blow out another drag. "After everything you heard, you probably think I'm a fucking monster."

"I don't."

I scoff, not daring to look at her. "You should, Paisley. You really should."

When she says nothing more, I drop the damn cigarette and crush it underneath my Italian leather derby shoes. Her jasmine scent taunts me, reminding me that I'm not alone out here. *She came.* Out of everybody at the table and after everything she heard, she still came.

"You can ask me…" I sigh after moments of deafening silence trickling between us. "I know you want to know."

"Want to know what?"

Swallowing thickly, I turn to her, watching her eyes sparkle. "Who Lea is."

"I would be lying if I said it isn't eating away at me, but I also respect you enough to know that if it's something you're not comfortable with sharing right now, then that's okay. When you're ready, *if* you're ready, then you'll let me into the loop."

I simply stare at Paisley, a warm smile forming at the words she just spoke. "More people should be like you."

"How's that?"

"Considerate."

Paisley lets out a small laugh. "With the number of things I've said to you when I was younger… I don't think you would call that considerate, beginning with how I ambushed you on your first day of moving in next door because you stepped on my flowers. I could have approached the situation differently, not thinking I was the tough guy and all."

"True. But you know what I mean. You don't judge me, even though you should."

"I trust and respect you too much to judge you. All the crap you know about me and my emotional baggage… you never judged me for it. So why should I judge you?"

"Because this is different." I sigh. "What Nico and Leo were saying… it's *true*. That should scare you. It should… I don't know, make you not want to be here with me right now."

"Nothing could ever make me not see you in the way I do."

The air crackles between us. Casting a quick glance over my shoulder toward the large steel Fleetwood doors that divide the indoor-outdoor restaurant, I make sure the coast is clear and neither her father, nor Nico or Leo have come out in search of us. When it's clear, I glance back at her.

"And how is it you see me?" I whisper, taking a step closer to her.

Paisley looks away, but I take her hands and lace them in mine. I don't care my right hand is still trembling. Tonight, I want her to see me for me. No more facades. Just *me*.

"Tell me, Pais. I need to know," I murmur, a knot at the back of my throat. "If I'm not a monster to you, then what am I? Is it worse than that?"

"No." She smiles sadly. "I see you as Saint Lisconti, the Maserati obsessed boxing personal trainer. The man who perhaps doesn't always get it his way, but when he does, he knows how to cherish it. The man who puts on this tough, dominant façade but has a heart of gold. You're intimating to people, and yet your nonna will give you your favorite food and you'll melt right there in her arms. You don't seek permission to go out and clasp what sets your soul on fire—I admire that. But most importantly, what I see the most, is a man I trust wholeheartedly with no hesitation whatsoever, because while you used to knock opponents out in the ring, I know you will never hurt me. Not physically. Not emotionally. Not mentally. And that means a lot to me, because I've been burned before… Whenever I glance at you and you look back, you feel like the very water replenishing me. Every time I think my bloom is over, you revive me."

Whoa.

I can't take my eyes off Paisley after the beauty of her words. There's this abundance in my chest, something I haven't felt in over a decade, and it scares and excites me all at the same time. I have never felt so deeply before, and something tells me I will never feel like this again.

Paisley's words speak to me, right to my soul, a place nobody else has dared to put one finger on before. Right now, watching her watch me… I can't get over how beautiful she is. Not only physically, but mentally. Her mind is something special. Intelligent. Generous. Thoughtful. *My type of special*, a part of me wants to add.

"That was beautiful, Paisley," I tell her, glancing between her eyes with a forming smile. "Nobody has ever told me anything like that before."

"I'm only speaking from the heart."

I never knew how much Paisley Reign would mean to me the day she accused me of stepping on her flowers, but now… three years later, I can't imagine a life without her in it.

It's as if she's my revival.

My very strength.

The very thing keeping me afloat.

Stepping back, I slowly rub my face as my vision blurs. "Why do I feel like you're the only person who truly understands me? Why?"

"It must be the flowers."

"Must be." I laugh through all the emotion I'm feeling. "I'm surprised you weren't reciting them before at the table."

"As I said, I wasn't scared."

That has me gulping down and admitting to her my greatest fear; one I've been carrying for a whole decade now. "But I am. I'm scared. That day at the cemetery when you told me your fears… I comforted you, but mine are the same. I'm so scared. Of this. Of living. Of dying. Of what comes next. Of loving. Of *you*…" I say, my voice cracking. "Because I'm scared of caring for you in the way that I do and as much as I do. I'm scared of it being too good to be true. I don't want to lose you, Paisley, but I don't see how… how this could ever be more than this because I can never *ever* be enough for you."

The second Paisley steps closer to pull my hands away from my face, she bears witness to the warm tears rolling down my cheeks. Her eyes search mine so emotively desperate as if it's her place to ease the pain inside me. Never in my fucking life has a woman enticed and confused me more. Never have I cried in front of anybody since I was a kid.

"Don't be scared, Saint, not of me," Paisley reassures me so lovingly it hurts. When she rubs my stubbled jaw, my eyes shut. "You're enough. You're not only enough for me, you're enough for yourself."

"No, I'm not—"

"Yes, you freaking are," she sniffles, drawing me closer by my jaw. Her hands are fucking velvet against my spiky beard as she caresses my tears away with her thumbs ever so slowly. "You always have been. Believe me when I say you *always* have been, Saint."

"Your father could come out and see—"

"*Shhh*," Paisley whispers so damn close, her right hand falling. Seconds later, it grips my trembling hand, and she draws my palm to her warm chest, her own hand lacing over mine. "Don't worry about anything else but *this*. Concentrate on my heartbeats, on my breaths."

I give in to Paisley's comfort and in to the fact that despite everything, *she* is the one to relax my shoulders and ease my shaking hand with the simple beats of her heart. She's the one to refill my lungs, pull me back into life and make me forget about everything else.

The sensation is new to me. As my hand rests on top of her cleavage, tranquility takes over me. Knowing that this is Paisley, it fucking calms me, when deep down I know it should be the opposite.

Snapping my eyes open, I see hers are peacefully closed and realize that perhaps she needs this as much as I do. Leaning my head into her left hand, I kiss her wrist. This has Paisley fluttering her eyes open, and without a second thought, I wrap her in my arms. Burying my head into her neck, I allow myself to feel everything I've been hiding away for the past years... *Vulnerability*. I have never felt this damn vulnerable, and this damn content at the same time.

I appreciate the way Paisley tangles her free hand through my tousled hair, the other running circles on my back. Appreciate the way my rapid breaths soothe in her hold. Appreciate that in this moment I'm being greedy and need her comfort a fraction more than she needs mine.

Nobody has ever comforted me like this before.

Nobody has made me feel this calm.

"You okay, Saint?"

"Mmhmm," I murmur against her neck. "I'm sorry for breaking down like that."

"Emotions don't make us fragile, they set us free. It just took me this long to realize it too... Should we head back in?"

"Yeah, you can. I'll be there in a second."

We pull away from the embrace and Paisley frowns, giving me a warm look that I simply want to capture and never want to look away from again. A forbidden look that says the opposite to everything that is right, but exactly how I'm feeling. A comfortable silence fills the space between us, even after she squeezes my shoulder one last time before walking back inside the restaurant.

It's crazy how the rumbling commotion of the diners behind me fizzled out in the moments before. I didn't hear a single thing when I confessed to her how I feel or when she cupped my jaw or when I held her. Not a single thing. *Just Paisley.*

Paisley's jaw drops at the sight of my Harley stationed in my driveway and I can't help but smirk. It's a FXDB model, sleek phantom black with classic dark chrome trimmings and just the right number of custom aspects to suit a man like me—like the outlined angel wings on the side of my motorbike near the Harley Davidson logo.

It's the kind of angelic beast that turns heads whenever I ride past. She's a looker. Therapy. A piece of me I'll never part from. I've been riding for so long the engine's rumble has synchronized with the beats in my chest. The Harley and whiskey-infused pitter-patters never let go. When it does, so will my soul.

It's finally Saturday and just over a week since Paisley and I vowed we'd let each other step into our worlds on a deeper level. It's also the day after I completely broke down in front of her and she was there for me. When I stepped back inside that restaurant last night, I felt much more cooled off and apologized to my friends for lashing out. I know they were only trying to help me out. It's also two days since she graduated and I'm so goddamn proud of her, and although I couldn't celebrate her success with her alone because Alaric was in the way, today I could.

Paisley and I planned this meet-up without her father knowing and he's currently beginning a twelve-hour shift at the hospital. Despite breaking bro code, I thought it would be a good way to end the week by introducing Paisley to my world with one of the things I adore most—therapeutic Harley rides in the warm summer breeze with breathtaking California views. It means having some time away from Sacramento... *time alone with her.*

"You mean we're actually going to ride around on this beauty?" Paisley gasps.

I tug on my sand-colored leather gloves with my teeth, wiggling my fingers in place. "Mhmmm."

"Uh, yeah, that's not happening. I'm not getting on your Harley. I mean, what if I fall off?"

I smugly roll my eyes, a smirk creeping up the corner of my lips. "You're not gonna fall off. I promise. You don't trust me?"

"Of course I trust you. It's just that... well, I..."

I arch a playful brow. "Making up excuses now, huh?"

"Me? No, no, of course not. I'm just concerned, you know, for my *life!*" Paisley laughs.

"Don't need to be. I wouldn't hurt you, *wildflower.* Would hurt myself before I hurt you. You know that. My father was a Harley fanatic. That's where I get it from. While other kids dreamed of being racecar drivers, I used to imagine riding around California on a metal beast. I used to work restoring and maintaining Harleys back in Santa Rosa for a good five years before boxing. I've been riding them for twenty years now and—"

"*Wait...*" Paisley cuts me off with wide eyes. "Did you just say *twenty* years?"

"I started in 1997... so yeah, twenty."

"Gosh, I wasn't even born until two years later."

A chuckle rumbles between us. "Just realized that..."

"Also, did you just admit you started riding when you were sixteen?"

I smirk. "Keeping tabs on my age, huh?"

"Maybe... okay, yes." She laughs. "What I meant to say is sixteen seems really young to have responsibility for a motorbike like that on the road."

"To some, yeah."

"*Uh*, I think to most, Saint."

"True." I tuck my helmet under my arm and hand her the other helmet. "I guess one just has to not fuck shit up and know what they're doing at that age."

"Which you obviously knew."

"Exactly." I wink. "But my point is... If there's anybody who'll keep you safe around the rolling hills, switchbacks, and speed, it's me. You said you wanted to get the full extent of who I am. This is who I am, Paisley. Harleys. Whiskey. Late nights. If you want to know my world, you need to experience the things I love most. *So*, are you in?"

Goddamn how beautiful Paisley is as she sexily bites her lower lip in apprehension. Her naturally plump lips are heart-shaped and so damn kissable, coated with a glossy cherry-red I so desperately want to suck on and taste. I love it because Paisley knows exactly what she's doing to both my mind and semi-hard cock when she bites her lip like that, but she decides to do it anyway. It's so evident in the slight smirk she makes whenever she catches me staring for too long... she knows she's unlocking the beast in me, not that it takes much to come out whenever I'm with her.

Yeah, this woman is going to be the death of me.

Adventurous deep-set eyes. Sun-kissed olive skin with gorgeous soft freckles that come to light whenever she's out in the sun for too long. Silky hair pulled back in a low bun with two wavy strands framing her face. *So damn beautiful.* Paisley takes my breath away.

She's wearing a black fitted top with a deep V-neck and frilly short sleeves, cropped white leather jacket and sexy denim shorts that continue to drive me crazy from the second she stepped outside of her house. It's not healthy for a man like me to see those gorgeous long legs. Even the floral pattern on her white Converse shoes fills my chest with indescribable warmth. Don't get me started about how well that white biker leather jacket suits her. There's something about seeing Paisley in leather that turns me the fuck on even more. I love the edgy style she's put together today.

"Yes!" Paisley begins bouncing on the spot. "I'm in!"

Her words make me grin. I've been fuckin' stoked for this ride. She's never been on a Harley before, or motorcycles in general, so I know just how nervous she must be feeling. But the fact that she trusts me enough to keep her safe while we're flying across Sacramento feels so damn good.

At first, I admit I was hesitant about today because I've never intended to let somebody into my world this intensely after Lea. It was a no-go zone. The same reason I've only been in casual relationships since because I was destined to ruin anything else. But Paisley… She has this way of looking at me that has me wanting to strip down my every flaw and give her everything she desires.

It's in her presence alone. In her warmth. In the deep connection and bond between us. She's been the only woman in thirteen years who makes me want to lower the walls I've placed between myself and the world. Paisley makes me want to break out of the cold exterior shell I wrapped around myself to protect myself from getting hurt. She is chipping away at the vulnerable man beneath, a fixer to my every fault… *And that means a lot to me.*

I smile. "All right, let's get you all safe and shit."

I set my dark helmet on my driveway near my biker boots and take hers from her. It's the same high-end full-face helmet as mine, only white. Paisley dramatically does the sign of the cross twice before I slip on her helmet and all I can do is tip my head back in laughter.

Christ. She seriously thinks I'm gonna kill her.

I lift up her helmet visor and our eyes meet, unobstructed. We share a heated stare, an extended one that doesn't break for a single second as I blindly fasten her helmet strap.

"Just so you know, I *do* trust you..." Paisley reassures me, her eyes forming small slits that let me know she's grinning. "But sometimes you've just got to let God do his job, you know?"

"You're still nervous, huh?"

"Very," she breathes, all raspy and... *sexy.*

God, Lisconti, get a grip.

Swallowing thickly, I glance between her eyes and say, "Let's change that, okay?"

"Okay."

A soft gasp escapes when I zip up her leather jacket, slowing by her breasts before I step away and place her small beach duffle bag into my motorcycle's side leather saddlebag. My phone is in my handlebar bag, alongside my set of keys, wallet, and a half-full packet of cigarettes, just in case I need a breather because today's an important day for me. I'll be taking Paisley to a place close to my heart, a place I've never let any other woman see in a long, long time.

This is all a part of showing Paisley Reign more of who I am.

Finally, I zip up my leather vest and handle bag. Raking a hand through my dark, tousled hair, I turn to her and flick down her helmet visor. "No need to be nervous. I promise."

"Mmhmmm. I trust you, Saint."

"Good. When we get on, I want your hands around me at all times. No need to crush my lungs, but I do need some tension in those arms whenever I make a turn. Trust the bike. Trust me. In saying so, if you need me to slow down or stop for any reason, tell me. There's a Bluetooth intercom system between rider and passenger in these helmets. They'll sync up the second I put mine on, so I'll be able to hear all the curse words, or in your case, I'll probably become an expert in flowers by the end of this. Lucky me. Got it?"

"Got it. An intercom system? So cool! I didn't know they made helmets like this."

After I zip up my black leather vest and handlebar bag, I slip on my helmet and the usual soft chime alerts me our helmets are now synced. Gripping the handlebars, I swing my leg over the bike from the kickstand side and mount it, my feet firm on the ground.

I turn to Paisley and grin through the helmet. "Welcome to my world, *wildflower.*"

Welcome to my world.

Chapter
SEVENTEEN

Saint

"READY TO HEAR THIS BABY PURR?" I say over the intercom with a smirk.

"Yes! Ready as I'll ever be!" Paisley laughs. The helmet prevents me from seeing, but I can just imagine the bright grin on her face and her nose scrunching up in that beautiful kind of way.

A natural beauty. That's what she is. An intelligent woman standing by my Harley in the middle of our side by side driveways as if it's purgatory.

Alaric.

I swallow down the potent taste of guilt. *How can something so wrong feel so right?*

Fuck it. All I want right now is her.

"That's what I like. A decisive woman."

"I don't think I have much of a choice."

"You always got a choice with me, *wildflower*. We don't have to do this if you don't want to."

"You know I want to. If there's a moment between us that I love the most, it would have to be this moment right here with you. As nervous as I am, there's this thrill inside me. It's anticipation of what happens next, and I wouldn't change this feeling for the world. Especially when it means I'm stepping into your world."

My eyes darken. *Wow.*

Air crackles between us. I feel my heartbeat at the base of my throat, beating so damn fast, and I don't even know how I'm still breathing.

"I'm glad we're doing this too."

"Me too, Saint. More than you know."

Oh, baby, I know.

I start the Harley, loving its purr, and fold down the foot pegs on both sides. "Ready to roll?"

"Yes! Where are we heading again? A beach?"

"Yes, a beach, but that's all I'm going to tell you for now." I smile. "All right, hop on!"

Paisley squeals as she climbs on the left side peg and carefully settles into the passenger seat behind me. "I can't believe this!"

Paisley's arms quickly wrap around my chest, *tight*, and I feel her firm breasts press up against my back. I stand the bike upright, straighten up, and grin while folding the kickstand back. Her warmth does something to me beyond describing, but it's eclectic, euphoric, such a contagious feeling of pure joy, that much I know.

Hold on to me, darlin'.

I rev the engine and we're off with her contagious laughter brightening my soul. It has me chuckling too as we speed down our street, Portola Way, out of Curtis Park, and fly past sand-colored city buildings and tall palm trees in Downtown Sacramento. The afternoon reddish-light blue sky is an incredible masterpiece, so mesmerizing as we cross onto Highway 80, over the Sacramento River into West Sacramento and farther down. I want the location of where we're heading today for a little wanderlust to be a surprise to her, even though we've already been there before together, but this time will be different.

"This is sensational!" Paisley gasps. "Now I know why you love it so much. It feels like we're gliding! You should feel my heart right now!"

"Pretty sure mine feels the same!"

"You don't know how much this means to me."

"Anything for you, *wildflower*," I murmur as I slow at the set of red lights. I move my leather-covered left hand back and playfully slap her smooth bare thigh before slowly caressing the skin. "*Anything.*"

Paisley softly moans through the intercom. "Turns out the Devil of Sacramento does have a heart after all... and he's no devil either."

I smirk. "You rebranded me for the better, huh?"

"Mmhmmm, sure did." I can hear the smirk in her voice. "Damaged good. That's what we are."

"I like that." I laugh, returning my hand to the handlebar as the lights turn green and I take off. Revving my engine, I speed down the street with the therapeutic rumbles seeping deep into my bones, and her hold gets even firmer.

"You know... you should have worn jeans, not shorts."

"Why do you say that?" Paisley teases, and I can hear the sexual undertone in her voice from a mile away. "Because you're getting distracted?"

Mmhmmm.

"You want the honest truth?"

"Nothing but it."

"I said it because I can't get your damn legs out of my mind. Also," I add, "because jeans are better protection, you know, just in case..."

"Don't need protection. You promised you'll take care of me, remember?"

That makes me chuckle because I can hear the smirk in her voice. "True. I love the way you think."

"I love the way you ride Harleys."

"Sure, Miss University of Washington. Give yourself a few years. You'll be flying past me in a hot pink Ferrari with a successful landscape architectural company, published poetry books, and Forbes articles under your belt. You'll probably flip me off and continue driving."

Paisley laughs. "As if I would ever do that, Mr. Stanford. I'll never forget about you."

A cloud dampens over me at the thought of her leaving in a couple of months' time.

How the fuck am I going to go on every day not seeing her?

"Four years is a long time, Pais. With you moving to Seattle, I may never see you again after this summer. You know that, right?"

"I know," she whispers after a little while. "That's why we're doing *this*, learning everything about each other before the summer ends. I want to understand the world behind your ocean eyes."

My heart clenches.

"Nobody has ever said that to me before."

"They have now." Paisley squeezes her arms around me tighter, but it isn't a hold of wanting to be securer behind me. It's one of utter warmth and appreciation and affection. "I don't know what will happen during these next four years while I'm at college, but what I do know is that I've never met somebody like you before and I don't think I ever will again."

I gulp down. "You will."

"I won't, and I'm almost glad because nobody compares to you. Nobody."

My heart races in reckless beats. I've never felt this goddamn complete.

"Ditto, *wildflower*," I whisper into the warm summer breeze and smile.

I feel the solidness of her helmet against my shoulder and quickly glance behind to see Paisley snuggling into me. I laugh because it's easier than ripping off our helmets and pressing my lips to hers at seventy miles per hour. *No matter how tempting the feeling is.*

I turn back to the road and my cold stone grief-stricken heart that I've been carrying around for so long begins to soften. It started long before today, months ago when we embraced for the very first time. But every day I see Paisley, every second I spend with her, I feel the coldness slowly warming and melting away. Today it's happening at double the speed.

It's my first time riding my Harley with a woman, and I never imagined it could feel this good having Paisley hold on to me. I don't want her to let go. I don't know what this all means for us, but I do know one thing: after today the dynamics between us will be forever changed.

'Cause Paisley's right… There's no other place I'd rather be than right here with her too. I mean that from the bottom of my melting heart.

Nowhere else I'd rather be.

🌊

Less than two hours later, the biggest grin works up Paisley's lips as I park my Harley in the driveway of my Stinson Beach summer house. It's a beach house I bought almost fifteen years ago when I was living in Santa Rosa. Even though I sold my house in Santa Rosa when I moved to Sacramento, I kept this beach house. It's the place I go to whenever I want to escape Sac.

Although I love The City of Trees with all my heart, there's something about having Stinson Beach as my little sanctuary. Plus, it's so convenient seeing as Santa Rosa is such a short distance away. I usually spend most of August in Marin County on the west coast of California on vacation every year. Stinson Beach in Marin County. *It's my favorite place.* Less than two hours away from Sacramento by motorbike. The peaceful North Pacific Ocean breeze, beautiful crashing waves, the taste of freedom. This is the type of place one goes to escape the reality of the world and create moments that become memories.

Paisley gasps, glancing around my Hampton-style two-story beach house in complete astonishment the second we step inside. "I would have never pegged you for having a beach house. Oh my gosh. You just keep on surprising me, Saint Lisconti."

"I hope that's a good thing."

Paisley glances over her shoulder at me and winks. "Definitely a good thing."

I smirk. "*Oh*, you're so confident about it, aren't you?"

"Mhmmm." The sexiest scarlet blush suffuses her cheeks. "You make me this bold and confident."

Grinning, I pull her into a half-hug and brush my lips against her ear. "First you text me in the middle of the night when the electricity's out, then you ride my Harley with me. What's next?"

"Showing me a sunflower field."

"Is that the dream?"

"That's the dream."

"I think that'll be a cool fucking adventure," I murmur. "I also think you've always had that little boldness in you."

Paisley flutters her lashes up at me and bites her lip. "Well, you help bring it out."

"That's why I call you *wildflower*," I whisper with a wink.

Paisley playfully shoves me away from her and I can't stop laughing.

She practically begs me for a tour of the house, and I happily comply. Last summer I completely upgraded and renovated my beach house, giving it upscaled rustic meets sophisticated casual beach vibes. Paneled walls. White hardwood floors. Three large bedrooms each with their own bathroom and walk-in closet. Every room of the house is luxuriously resort-like, with massive picture windows outlooking the scenic ocean views. Outlooking those mesmerizing turquoise waves at night with the moonlight and winking stars while sitting on the patio with the firepit burning or walking along the wooden private pier is beyond stunning.

Paisley adores every room and can't stop telling me how she can't believe I haven't talked about this house before. It's a part of showing her beyond a simple glimpse of myself and instead showing her all of me. *She's the first woman I've had in this house in thirteen years.*

A day trip to Stinson Beach to soak up the sun is exactly what Paisley needs after all the shit she's been through. Besides, it's also a perfect place for her to relax after her graduating and celebrating this next chapter of her life.

It makes me so happy that she loves the idea too.

Paisley can't stop grinning the entire house tour. Once we're back in the kitchen, she takes off her leather jacket and I tell her she can just leave it on the living room couch. Then I excuse myself and walk upstairs to my primary bedroom to change out of my clothes and into a white linen button-down and black swim trunks since we want to walk up to the beach. Since Paisley only came with her beach duffle bag and apparently already came with bikinis underneath her clothes, she doesn't need to change.

When I'm dressed, I step out of the bedroom and jog downstairs only to find Paisley looking out the white French doors that lead to the outdoor patio and gate to the private access to the large stretch of beach, simply staring out in awe at the scenic views above the gate.

It takes everything within me not to wrap my arms around her from behind and glance out with her. Instead, we share a warm smile as she glances around, her eyes hungrily falling to what I'm wearing, yet she doesn't say a word. My gaze darkens and I make no effort to hide the way my eyes fall upon her body now that her jacket's off.

So freaking beautiful.

I don't know how on God's earth I thought I could survive a beach day with her with the way we're looking at each other. Guess I'm about to find out.

"Ready to go?"

Paisley nods, slipping the strap of her small duffle bag higher up her shoulder. I must surprise her when I take the duffle from her because she says, "Oh, you don't need to carry it."

"You said you want to know the real me. The real me doesn't let women hold their bags."

Paisley smiles warmly. "Aww, thank you!"

"Anything for you, *wildflower*."

"You're a sweetheart, Saint."

"You'll say how much of an asshole I am in three seconds."

She laughs.

"It's about a ten-minute walk to Stinson Beach. Let's do it!"

"Looking forward to it."

After putting her duffle bag in the bigger beach bag I'm holding that has two towels, a baseball cap and my phone, wallet, and house keys, we're off to the beach. We've been to Stinson Beach before months ago, but today will be different... *Her father isn't here.*

It'll be just *us.*

Only us.

As if it's our little secret... because it is.

I almost die right here on the sandy beach when we find a vacant spot on the sand and while I roll out our towels, Paisley begins stripping down. She kicks off her shoes and shimmies out of her clothes and when I see what's underneath... *Fuck.*

A stunning red triangle tie-up bikini top and matching thong-style bikini bottoms. *Red.* God, I fucking love red on her. *Dio.* Her almost naked body is so smooth and goddamn beautiful. I'm *barely* surviving it. *Barely.*

Paisley's eyes are on me as I peel my T-shirt from my back collar. I rake a hand through my dark hair first before slipping on my baseball cap, backward, some hair peeking out on the sides and bottom. Flicking my gaze to the ocean, I subtly adjust my hard cock through my dark swim trunks and take a seat beside Paisley, enjoying the sunny skies and refreshing ocean breeze... while getting harder and harder by the fucking second until it's unbearable.

We watch the clear waves slowly crash to shore and it's so peaceful, exactly what I need.

"I can't believe how beautiful it is here." Paisley grins beside me on the warm sand. "It's so mesmerizing. No wonder it's your favorite place."

I smile. "Tell me your favorite place."

"It's not necessarily a place, but I would have to say sunflower fields in general. However, to be honest, this beach is coming in close second. I love it!"

Hearing her admit she loves Stinson Beach as much as I do... it does something to me.

Paisley turns to me, intrigue infusing her beautiful, brown-eyed gaze. That same gaze that flickers down to my tattooed sleeve on my left arm, and she gestures toward it. "Every ink of tattoo tells a story, hmm?"

I smile. "Just like every poetic stanza tells a story."

"I like that."

"What's our story, *wildflower*?"

Paisley grins. "Well, it's simple. Girl meets boy. Girl goes from despising him to understanding that their opposites create beauty. Girl runs away with boy to West California and *dot, dot dot...*"

"What happens next?"

"Don't know." She smirks. "It's unwritten."

I chuckle. "The classic cliffhangers, huh?"

"Yeah, that's right." Paisley nods, tracing her finger along the ink on my arm, her touch forming sparks along my skin. "They always happen around now. Unless you're the writer, you can make anything happen." Her eyes lift to mine and passion floods them as her smile transforms into a beautiful grin. "Can you tell me a little bit about your tattoos?"

My heart clenches.

My tattoos. Nobody has ever wanted to know that before.

For the next few minutes, I explain to her the meaning behind every black and white tattoo on my full sleeve. Tattoos like the black and white Holy Madonna's face on my shoulder blade for my nonna, representing faith, believing, and my adoration for her.

The deck of cards with the facing card being the ace of hearts with a tinge of red inside the heart for my mom, representing all my love for her and always staying true to myself.

For my dad, alongside my inner bicep I have *'Here's to looking at you, kid'* in cursive as a nod toward my father and his favorite film, which is also mine, *Casablanca*. I also have a shaded tattoo of Humphry Bogart's face on my forearm, a tipped hat covering some of his face, a cigar in his mouth with the smoke turning into a dove.

I also have a little stuffed giraffe toy to remember somebody special by. That's all I have in me to say to Paisley about that one. All kinds of other tattoos like roman numerals, words in both Italian and English, an eagle, and other objects fill the spaces between the tattoos that hold the most significance to my heart, creating an epic full sleeve tattoo. Then, of course I also have the large, shaded cross on my back, along my spine, with thorns wrapped around it and angel wings behind it, as well as the small cursive name, *Lea,* written on my lower back.

All my tattoos have a purpose, a significance, and a meaning that touches me deeply. It's as if it's a collection of art, a collection of everywhere I've been and everything that I am. Paisley's in awe when we finish, stating that she loves every one and that means a lot to me.

Something I've been meaning to tell Paisley for a couple of days now crosses my mind. "Remember that day last year where you were planting flowers on the sidewalk, and you asked me what to do when the only person you truly have leaves you? Remember how I said I'll get back to you?"

"Yeah?"

"Well, I think I have the answer now. I think it's to have faith."

"I don't know how to have faith."

"By giving in to every last desire, even if it's wrong."

"I like the sound of that. I'll remember that, thank you. I can't believe you remembered it!"

"I remember everything."

Laughter escapes Paisley. "Obviously."

I chuckle. An abundance of warmth rushes across my body. I simply watch her beautiful profile in awe, loving how her eyes observe the busy beach for a second longer before her long lashes flutter closed. Paisley tips her head back to take in the glorious warm sun, her beautiful grin never falling.

God. Paisley Reign just continues to take my breath away. Again and again and again. I can't believe how lucky I am to be here with such beauty.

"Let's play nine questions!"

My brows knit in amusement. "Isn't it twenty-one questions?"

Paisley laughs. "Yeah, but we should do a rapid-fire round instead."

"That's good with me. You start!"

She nods without hesitation. "Films say a lot about who we are as people. Why is *Casablanca* your favorite film?"

"Because sometimes it's not always about getting the girl in the end. Sometimes it's just about spending a brief period of time with the greatest thing that ever happened to you. Even if it's an instant in your life. Even if it's bittersweet."

"That's such a beautiful way to look at it!"

I gulp down. "What's your favorite film and why?"

"*A Patch of Blue.* It's way before my time, but I love the movie because it shows there's more to life than what we see. The emotions that love evokes are a powerful sensation, a powerful thing that can turn gray skies into patches of vivid blue."

Paisley's words touch my soul.

"I've definitely watched my fair share of that movie too. It's so powerful, isn't it?"

"It truly is. What motivated you to start boxing?"

Swallowing thickly, I glance toward the ocean waves for a moment. "Escapism. What are you most passionate about?"

"One day becoming a mom. Having my own family to cherish. How about you?"

"I love that. You'll be an amazing mom one day." I smile. "What am *I* most passionate about? Hmm, I don't know, I think at this stage in my life it's just to continue making my mom and Nonna proud. My late father too, because he's still watching."

"That's so warming and true. Your dad is still watching down. I feel it."

I nod. "So is your nana, Pais. I feel it too."

Her eyes shut as she takes in a breath and nods. "Tell me something I don't know about your life."

"Well, I'm left-handed, but that's not necessarily life-changing, so I'll answer your question by admitting I used to be in a cover band." I laugh when her eyes widen to something between pure shock and awe. "And no, I'm not joking. I actually was... for like two years. My cousin, Enrico, is four years younger than me. His mother and mine are sisters. Enrico's this piano mastermind and while it's just a hobby of his, I swear that guy could be the next Beethoven. When he was ten and I was fourteen, we started this cover band just for the fun of it. We alternated between my parents' garage and his. Naturally, Enrico was on the piano, and I was on the guitar, and we shared the singing. We made it a hobby for four years, practicing and writing songs as if we were going to make it to the Staples Center one day with the lamest shit. We got better in time, but when I headed to college it kind of fizzled out, you know..."

Paisley smiles. "Whoa, that's amazing. I didn't know you play guitar and sing a little. You're a man of many talents! Do you still have a jam session with your cousin sometimes?"

"I wish. Enrico moved to Seattle when he was sixteen but now resides in New York. I don't see him as much as I used to, but we keep in touch a lot and when we do meet up, it's as if nothing's changed.

"Care to sing me a line of something you and Enrico wrote?"

I tip my head back in laughter, loving how her smile transforms into a grin too. "Is that one of your questions?"

"Sure is."

"All right, here it goes. This is *Betty* and would have been our EP... imagining me singing this at fourteen years old." Smirking, I clear my throat and crack my neck before pretending to strum an invisible guitar. I give her those dramatically intense eyes all great love songs talk about, like this is an audition at *America's Got Talent* and just go for it. "Okay, get ready for this... *Betty, I think about you all the time. I can't get you out of my mind. It's like you look at me and I get hypnotized... like when you kissed me on the Fourth of July. Now I missed the school bus and you're going out with Chad. But I can do your math homework and that's pretty rad. So you left him and now you're going out with me. Yet you're playing this game of chance, but oh, Betty, all I wanna do is dance... oh, oh, yeahhh.*"

Paisley can't stop laughing and I can't help but rumble in chuckles too. I've never in my life sung that chickenshit song out loud since Enrico and I were kids. It feels so good just letting loose and laughing with her so warmly.

Feels so good that I can be myself.

Feels so good I'm *here* with her.

"Oh my gosh!" Paisley wipes away happy tears, grinning, and she can't even look at me for a straight second before we burst back into laughter. "Excuse me for laughing, but I didn't expect that! That's just too good. Betty seems like she was a pretty special girl."

"I highly doubt it. Enrico and I didn't have girlfriends, so we wrote that song to feel better about ourselves. We got the name Betty from the Archie comics because she was hot, but agreed that if we ever produced the song with a record label and it went viral to the point where an exclusive documentary was made, we would say the song was inspired by this girl called Betty who played us both and this was our rebellious heartbreak song. Mike-drop moment."

"That's the best thing I've heard in my life! I'm sure you and Enrico would have lived it up."

"I'm sure we would have too. I mean, between *Betty, The Heart Is a Fragile Planet, Italian Brown-Eyed Girl* and *When I Take a Plane To Switzerland, Don't Take One There Too,* we would have been stars. Timberlake? Pfft, who knows him. We would have ruled the world," I joke with a grin before breaking out to the rhythm of the latter of the song and pretend to play the piano. "*Da-ra, dun dun dun, da, dun dun, da, da-ra, dun dun dun, da, da-rah… One, two, one, two, three… When I take a plane to Switzerland, don't take one there too. You had your chance to get to me, now you need an 'I owe you', 'cause you owe me… oh, yes, you do… you owe me… oh, yes, you do.*"

Paisley slaps a hand over her mouth to soften the laughter, but a few people at the beach sneak glances our way anyway, but I don't give a fuck. As long as I see my girl happy, that's all that matters.

My girl…

"My God, Saint. I think I need an album! I didn't know you were that good!"

"*Good?* Don't be so kind, they were shit songs written by two teenage cousins in the late nineties."

"Okay, but you have a really beautiful voice, so it compensates for it."

"Yeah, yeah." I wink. "Now, less about me embarrassing the hell out of myself and more about you. Biggest dream?"

"The small dream is to own an original 1940s Olivetti typewriter. I just love the idea of typing my poetry down on it. The biggest dream is to work at Seattle's Notti Design firm as a landscape architect after I graduate from college. It's a goal I've had for a long while. Just the thought of working for such a prestigious company and doing what I love brings me so much happiness. I know it's complex work, but I'm ready for the challenge."

"How did I know you would say that? That's incredible, Paisley, I really think you'll love it too. Come to think of it, my cousin, Enrico, is good friends with the owner of Notti Designs, Giulio Giannotti."

Paisley's jaw practically drops. "You mean you have *connections* to Giulio Giannotti, the *owner* of Notti Designs?"

"Mhmm. Met Giulio a couple of times too through Enrico at some birthdays and business parties. He's a real nice guy. A dedicated businessman but a diehard family guy too. Tailored suits. Italian leather shoes. Three cute kids. Beautiful wife. The two of them seem like something out of a Golden Age of Hollywood film. A modern-day Bogart and Bacall, except with brunette hair. Perhaps I could talk to him about introducing you and Giulio so you could have a deeper insight into what it would be like to work there."

"That would be incredible! I know you have a busy schedule, so if you don't really want to I completely understa—"

"Don't even think about it. Of course I want to. Enrico's just a phone call away and I know how special this is to you, *wildflower*."

Paisley's eyes get a little teary. "That's so sweet, thank you so much!"

"No need to thank me." I smile. "You're there for me, I'm there for you."

She nods before gasping. "Oh, gosh! I can't believe I forgot the other big dream I have. Llamas."

Llamas?

"Hold up." My eyes widen. "Did you just say *llamas*, or have I just become hard of hearing?"

Mid-laugh, Paisley runs a hand through her damp beach waves. "Yes, I did say llamas. They're my favorite animal!"

"Well, that's definitely not what I was expecting. Now I'm curious, why llamas?"

"Is that even a question? They're so cute and such intelligent animals too! I guess it's always been a dream to someday own one."

"Are they even legal to have as pets here in California?"

"Yeah, some ungulate species are. Believe it or not, even

though llamas are exotic, they're domesticated. They're like three to five grand or something like that, let's say four."

"*Ohhh.*" I smirk, crossing my arms over my bare chest, my toned biceps tensing. "So just to set the record straight, you'd allow a llama to eat your flowers because they're *cute*, but lost your shit that one time I accidentally stepped on your lilies three years ago? Nice. Nice. I see how it is. Seems like I totally missed that '*cute*' requirement."

Paisley can't stop giggling. "My cheeks ache from laughing so hard! Somebody's jealous, huh?"

"Yeah," I playfully huff. "Never thought I'd be jealous of a freaking llama."

"I'll make it up to you, Mr. Lisconti."

"Hmm, yeah," I murmur with a smile. "You better."

I don't want this day to end…

Not when we're closer than we've ever been.

Not now as Paisley glances at me, her head still tipped back, with such happiness as she reties her silky long dark hair in a high ponytail and it softly blows with the ocean breeze.

Not when she pulls out a small bottle of tanning oil from her duffle bag and applies it to her front before asking me to lather her back in the shimmery tanning oil. I agree without hesitation.

"Any hidden talents I don't know about?" Paisley asks as I squeeze the oil into the palm of my hand.

I try to think for a minute. "Hmmm, no. *Oh*, wait. I can knot a cherry stem using my tongue. Don't know if that's classified as a talent, though."

"Sure it is! I'm pretty sure they even have a whole Guinness World Record for that." She pauses for a moment before her eyes darken, and she sensually bites her lower lip. "That's kind of hot, Saint."

I'll show you hot, baby.

I feel the damn purr of her voice right on the tip of my cock. *Dear God.*

It doesn't help that she's practically naked in front of me. Our stare extends until she smirks and takes her eyes off me. Paisley lies down on her taut stomach and ample breasts, which her bikini barely covers, and it feels so good roaming my oil-laced hands over the backs of her toned arms and legs. I continue to run my hands over her beautiful body, craving running my tongue over her every curve.

The next words just slip out of my mouth. "Next question. Who was your first kiss?"

Paisley's quiet for a split moment. "I… I kind of haven't done anything intimate with anybody else before… including kissing."

"Nothing?"

"*Nothing.*"

"Not even—"

"Nope. Nothing at all." Paisley sighs. "It's sad, I know."

"It's not sad, it's perfectly okay. It's better to wait than to regret it, yeah?"

"Yeah, I know, it's just that… Can I admit something?"

"Of course."

Paisley hums, a sultry smirk on her lips as she turns her head to me, and her hooded eyes meet mine. "Sometimes… sometimes I just really crave to be touched… to have an orgasm that doesn't include my vibrator. I just crave that release, to let go of all that built-up tension."

Holy fuck.

My hard cock throbs in my swim trunks at her words. *God.*

That definitely isn't what I need to hear as I spread the tanning oil over her back, underneath the tiny tie-up string holding her bikini together and lower down to her gorgeous round ass. *I need to distract myself, but I can't.* My mind goes wild at how her ass is practically bare because while her bikini bottoms cover her front, the back is exposed aside from a thin strip of fabric that disappears between her cheeks.

So hot.

"Jesus Christ, Paisley," I groan, all worked up. "You have a vibrator?"

The smirk is still on her lips as she turns back to the towel. "Mhmmm."

"Fuck, *that's* hot," I rasp, all breathy. "*Dio*, you can be such a bad girl when you want to be, Paisley. So fucking bad."

A visual of Paisley pleasuring herself has me losing my mind, so much so my breaths deepen as arousal takes over me. I've never had a need to satisfy a woman so badly. Never like I do with Paisley right now. Another vision crosses my mind of her lying on my Harley Davidson and me fucking her so hard on it until her throat aches from moaning out my name so goddamn loud.

"Want to know something else?" Paisley murmurs. "Something I probably wouldn't have the courage to say if you weren't touching my body like you are right now...?"

I smooth over her ass, my breath completely lost while I slowly massage in the oil. The second I can hear my frantic heartbeats over the crashing waves, I know I'm in trouble. Lust turns to reckless desperation because my fingers are inches from her pussy through the bikini bottoms, yet I can feel its heat.

I want her so fucking badly.

"Yes."

"It's pretty dirty," Paisley teases.

Dio.

I'm well aware of how sexual this game has turned, but I have no intentions of stopping. Every part of me aches for her. Aches for us to rush back to my beach house so I can bury my tongue into her heat and give her that orgasm she so desperately craves.

"Tell me, *wildflower*." My hands linger on her ass for an extended moment. "Tell me all of your dirty secrets."

Crossing her arms in front of her over the towel, Paisley glances over her left shoulder at me, eyes dripping with dark desire. I part my lips, feeling the exact same, but I need to snap out of this because we're in public with tons of beachgoers.

Ah, what am I talking about? Fuck the public.

I know how detrimental whatever she's about to say is for us. It could change everything. *Not that it's not already changed.* But this is a bold step for her, so fucking bold and confident, and all I want to do is reward her with orgasm after orgasm after orgasm.

"Okay," Paisley murmurs, gazing between my eyes. "Every time I make myself come, I think of *you*."

Oh God.

I said it once and I'll say it again. *This woman is going to be the death of me.*

The sexual tension between Paisley and me does anything but simmer when I spank her ass to signal that I've finished with massaging in the tanning lotion. Paisley sits back up beside me and thanks me with a naughty smile.

I can't do anything but smirk back. *More than welcome, babydoll.*

Seeing Paisley like this... her olive skin all oiled up and glistering under the glowing sunshine, her sultry complexion so beautifully tempting, her hard nipples saluting me through the thin fabric of her bikini... it's almost too much for me to handle.

Almost.

It has me wishing there was nobody else on this beach so we can put an end to this erotic madness. My cock is so damn hard, throbbing against the confines of my swim trunks at how Paisley's looking at me with eyes that beg me to take her right here. So much need is in them, so much forbidden desperation I'm eager to taste with my tongue.

I breathe in her sweet vanilla jasmine scent with a hint of the beach, and it drives me absolutely crazy. This woman understands me on such a deep level. It's as if we're connected by fate, connected by destiny. My eyes flicker to her plump lips and *dear God*... all I want to do is kiss her like I mean it.

"Last question..." Paisley whispers. "What are you currently thinking?"

"Things I know I shouldn't."

"Tell me."

"Trust me, you don't want to know, Pais."

"I do."

I rest my forehead against hers, my free hand rising to cup

her jaw. "You've made me feel this kind of way ever since you rushed into my arms on your eighteenth. Every time I see you now, it amplifies, but seeing you today with this stunning bikini on... *Fuck*. You know how to drive a man wild. You know how to make his heart race."

"Not any man... *you*."

"Me," I murmur against her lips, loving the way it sounds. "I know you wore it on purpose. To taunt me. To tease me. To make me go out of my fucking mind, and guess what?"

Paisley grins, knowing exactly what she's doing to me. "What?"

"It's fucking working. But you could be wearing *anything*, and I still wouldn't be able to stop thinking about you. Even when I know I shouldn't, I can't stop, Paisley."

"Then don't."

"I shouldn't feel this way about you. *You* shouldn't feel this way about me."

"I can't help it, Saint," she breathes. "You once told me to never hide the way I feel and I... I really care about you. I've never felt like this before."

"I care about you too. Much more than I should. You know that."

Paisley grins, slowly slipping the baseball cap off me, and rests it on the sand behind us. A wild breath escapes my throat when her fingers thread through my tousled hair. I moan in satisfaction. *It feels so good.*

Everything about Paisley so beautifully entices me—*everything*. The way her breaths synchronize with mine. The fact that she's so open about what she wants. The loud thumps I imagine in her chest and how mine madly beat for her too.

"You're going to get me in so much trouble, Paisley Reign." My warm lips trail against her left cheek and tenderly kiss her warm skin. "So. Much. Trouble," I whisper in staccato before moving back up so we're face-to-face. The pure sight of her has me smiling in awe. *"Dio mio.* Look how beautiful you are, *wildflower.*"

"Saint," she murmurs. "Saint, I need you."

"Tell me where."

"On my lips."

"No, babydoll."

She bites her lip. "Why not?"

Why not?

Despite how badly I want to kiss Paisley, there's so much logic behind it that tells me I shouldn't. So many barriers in the way. Our age gap. The forbidden nature that comes with her being the daughter of my good friend. *Alaric.*

"I'm too old for you. An eighteen-year difference. That's a lot, Paisley."

"Age is only a number when it comes to what truly matters. Plus, it's hot. *Really* hot."

"Alaric would kill us."

"My father doesn't need to know. It can be our secret. Between us only."

Tempting.

"We shouldn't be doing this," I say, but I don't know who the hell I'm trying to convince, her or myself. I clench my jaw twice before I forget about all else and ease into a slow, sexy smile. "I kiss you and I won't be able to stop."

"That's exactly what I want," Paisley admits in desperation, her eyes achingly searching mine. "Whatever happens can stay between us. Nobody else needs to know. I just need you. Badly. More than I've ever needed anything else."

I'm freaking losing my mind. Seeing the way we're both so worked up and flustered. Restraint never burned this deep. I can't think of anybody else but the two of us. Right now, I don't care that she's forbidden. I don't care that she's my best friend's daughter. I want her more than I've wanted any other woman in my life.

God, I need her too.

"You intrigue me so much, Paisley. You're an angel I want to unravel, and that's not a good thing for a man like me. I'll get addicted to heaven when I don't deserve it."

"You deserve it, Saint. You deserve it more than you know."

The air crackles between us, thickening, and even though we're at the beach, all I see is her. I swear to God I'm about to die from the way I'm feeling toward Paisley.

I never stood a chance against the angel that she is.

Paisley's eyes drop down to my swim trunks and pool in hunger as she sexily bites her bottom lip. I know without a doubt exactly what she's looking at. My raging erection confined inside my trunks that's pulsing even more intensely at the way she's looking at me.

"No white swim trunks today?" she teases.

I smirk, remembering the exact moment I caught her staring at my cock through the fabric that day at this exact beach a few weeks ago. "Nope. I learned my lesson there. Don't go around in white swim trunks when you have your best friend's daughter gawking at you and telling you she can't stop thinking about you *after* she was writing a poetry piece about you."

Paisley laughs. "I didn't gawk!"

"This isn't two truths and a lie, baby. You and I both know you're guilty as charged."

"Okay, you're right. I *was* checking you out. I give you full permission to gawk at me all you like today, so we'll be even. *Unless…*" She glides her tongue over her bottom lip and my eyes instantly drop there, my cock feeling the stroke instead. *God, how I'd love that tongue circling around me.* "Unless… you plan to do a lot more than gawking, to which I would say…"

"To which you would say *what?*" I breathe.

"Guess."

Smoldering, my heart beats wildly at her words and the scorching heated stare we share only makes me harder. *Jesus Christ. I'm so goddamn aroused.*

"Tell me," I say. It comes out all sexy and breathy. "Come on, baby."

"Guess, Saint."

"Tell me, babydoll," I growl this time, my sexual frustration hitting its peak as I cup her cheek and draw her closer to me. The pad of my thumb brushes over her soft pink lips. "Tell me," I repeat, my voice a desperate murmur, inches from her lips. "I want to hear it from your lips. What would you say if I told you I wanted to do more than gawk? Tell me what you truly desire, *wildflower*. I want to hear the exact moment my good girl turns bad. Do you want it, babydoll? Don't you want to be bad for me?"

Her breathing quickens and I don't miss the way she not so subtly squeezes her thighs together with a grin. Smirking, I trail my lips up Paisley's cheekbones, my hot breath against her skin, and her sweet jasmine scent consumes me whole.

Yes, I know you feel it too, baby.

My lips roughly meet her ear as I sexily whisper, "Do you want to be my bad girl, babydoll?

"Yes, yes, I do." Paisley seductively whispers with a straggled moan. "I want to be bad for you, Saint."

"*Dimmelo di nuovo. Dimmi che lo vuoi anche tu.*"

Tell me it again. Tell me that you want it too.

"Oh *God*."

I've never seen Paisley's honey browns so dark in desire. I cup her face so tenderly with both hands. There's a fraction of a gap between our lips and a moan escapes my throat when she murmurs my name so erotically sweet. Her hands trail down my bare abs and we share the kind of grin lovers do.

Dear God, forgive me because I'm about to fucking sin.

Forgive me, Alaric, too.

Forgive. Me.

"What would you say if I told you gawking isn't enough?" I glance between Paisley's eyes. "What if I told you all I want to do right now is kiss you until you don't know whose air you're breathing? What if I told you that you can be my bad girl for the entire summer?"

"I would say, '*what took you so long*'?"

"You're such a bad girl, Paisley Reign," I say, completely losing it. "*My* bad girl."

"Yes. Yours," she whispers, slowly closing her eyes. "Always *yours.*"

Mine.

Inhaling a heavy breath, I shut my eyes.

"Fuck it," I growl, and then I do what we've both been craving for way too long. I lean forward and crash my lips onto hers, recklessly kissing her like all we have is right now.

Like she's the very waves keeping my caged heart afloat.

Like I need Paisley more than my very next breath. *Because I do.*

Chapter
EIGHTEEN

Paisley

S AINT KISSES ME WILDLY AS IF THE WORLD IS BURNING AROUND US AND I'm the only desire he craves, because I know he's mine and God does it feel *so good*. Our kiss is hot. Breathtaking. Intimate. Everything I've ever imagined and more. We're kissing with so much force it's as if my air is running out and he's my only supply.

I love the dominance that comes with kissing Saint so seductively. Cupping my face tighter, his tongue runs over the center of my lips and I gladly part them, our dancing tongues colliding, hungry for a taste of sin. Saint tastes like peppermint with a hint of smoky tobacco. I love it so much. *I love it.*

The intensity of our kiss turns even more passionate as Saint's left-hand cups the nape of my neck to kiss me even deeper, with possession. *Ohmygod. Yes.* My lips are tingling in desire and the pitter-patter of my heart beats ferociously. This doesn't only feel like the first kiss in my life, this feels like the first real breath I've ever taken.

It consumes me whole as I kiss Saint harder. Deeper. With everything I have and follow the rhythm and movements with those of his.

I don't care we're at the damn beach…

I don't care he's older and is forbidden to me…

I don't want this moment to end.

Our bodies couldn't be any more pressed together as I straddle his lap. My sex throbs faster through my bikini thong. They're drenched in arousal, and I'm convinced he can feel it too. His hard cock pulses under his swim trunks as my hips impulsively grind against him, getting lost in the moment and aching for a release.

Wow, this feels amazing.

We both moan mid-kiss at the exact same moment. When we pull back, my chest continues to flutter at the sight of the sweet desire in his bright blue eyes. Saint grins sexily and my heart returns to beating like crazy. In fact, it never stopped. I love I can feel his heartbeat against mine, and it's beating just the same.

Saint doesn't regret it.

I grin back, a soft giggle escaping through our intimate, extended stare. We're both panting for our next breaths. Panting into heaven. I run my tongue over my lower lip, the heat of my pussy throbbing to the beats of my heart.

"I never knew a kiss could be that beautiful and *wow*."

Saint rests his forehead against mine, our lips brushing as he whispers, "Did I take your breath away, *wildflower*?"

"Completely."

"Good, because you take my breath away every single day too."

Aww.

I can't stop smiling. Can't stop believing he's *right here* with me.

"And you told me you weren't a romantic." I smirk.

Saint chuckles and I feel the vibrations in my chest. "I'm not a romantic."

"Liar," I murmur, inches from his lips. "You're a romantic for sure. You've just been hiding it away for so long in fear of letting the world truly see the type of man you were born to be. So, you've caged your heart in an endless tunnel of darkness. You've thrown away the key. You think all falling in love again will do is unlock it and leave you bleeding out cold. It's why you don't let people in. Why you don't allow others to see the beauty inside. But I see it..." My gaze flickers between his eyes. "I *see* it, Saint."

I cup his jaw, loving the sensation of my fingertips caressing his spiky, dark stubble. "I see who you truly are underneath. A fiercely beautiful Italian romantic. I want you to be *my* fiercely beautiful Italian romantic."

"*Non posso resisterti,*" Saint whispers, and I love that he's speaking his mother tongue. "I can't resist you, *wildflower.*"

"Then don't."

Saint takes one good look at me, the warmth in his gaze so insatiable, and then with the backdrop of the ocean waves crashing to the shore, he presses his lips on mine again. I *melt*. This kiss is slower, more tender than the last, but addictively intimate just the same. It's beyond anything I've ever fantasied. It's sensual and hot, yet at the same time angsty, emotional, and erotic.

This is what it feels like to be kissed by Saint Lisconti.

This is what it feels like to be destroyed by him.

Saint's strong arms snake around my waist, drawing me even closer to him, and I wrap my legs around his waist. *Tight.* I feel so secure with him. So safe. So *seen.* His warmth ignites this fire inside me, burning my every flaw. It's a crazy thing—how Saint becomes both my fuel and the only thing that can douse me.

I inhale a breath of air, smiling through the kiss because his alluring musky sandalwood cologne mixed with the ocean breeze are now my only air.

I could do this forever.

Not just for an entire summer.

Forever.

Saint threads his fingers through mine and our hands blindly intertwine on the warm sand. It's such an intimate moment with a different kind of affection. So pure and holy. I love how our fingers lace together perfectly as if our hands were created for the sole purpose of staying like this forever.

Our kiss slows and speeds up in accordance with our synced heartbeats. We can't get enough of each other, and I can't help but want Saint even more in other ways when I let out a chorus of throaty moans and he groans against my lips. The sexy sound runs straight through my body and to where I need him the most.

Every single part of me bursts into happy sparks. It's as if I'm spinning in a field of sunflowers. Instead, I'm spinning in a world of Saint Lisconti. One I never want to escape. Ever.

"*Sei incredibile,*" Saint pants when we pull away. A slow, sexy smile rises on his lips, his dimples deepening as the sunshine continues to kiss our skin. "You're incredible, Paisley."

Before I can say anything, I'm squealing as Saint scoops me up into his strong arms, bridal style, and stands up. Laughter bubbles out of me as he starts running down the sand toward the clear water.

I wrap my arms around his neck to stabilize myself and notice a few people whose eyes are on us. "I think you better put me down. All these people are watching us."

"Let them watch and *correction*, they're watching *you*, beautiful. The little red bikini is enough to drive any man insane."

My lips meet his ear. "Well, you're lucky you're the only man who can get close to it."

"Mmhmm." Saint's smolder that follows is the sexiest thing I've ever seen as he steps into the water. "You don't know how badly I want to undo those bikini strings with my teeth. Every single one. Then, I'm going to show you what happens when you taunt the beast and have him craving more. How does that sound, babydoll?"

Oh God.

"I want that. I want that so badly."

"Beggars can't be choosers, Paisley."

I grin. "But they can *beg…*"

"Oh, they certainty can, babydoll." He smirks. "They certainly can."

Just as I'm about to peck Saint's lips, I let out an excited scream as he drops me into the ocean waves, the murmured underwater echoes of his beautiful laughter bringing me back to life.

We spend the next two hours at this beach until 8:00 p.m. Swimming, sunbathing, and talking while walking along the shore, before deciding to head back to the beach house with about half an hour until sunset, although the breathtaking summer evening sky is already a perfect shade of a burgundy red, orange, and soft yellow delight.

I'm enjoying creating these memories with Saint. I absolutely adore it here at Stinson Beach. Glorious sunny skies. This sense of escapism right in the palm of your hands. A sensational little getaway from the normal routine of Sacramento life. Plus, everything is a walking distance, and everybody is just so friendly.

The second we step inside his beach house, Saint walks toward the sleek cocktail bar cabinet that is integrated into a part of his spacious kitchen. His back is to me as he picks up a bottle of whiskey and a glass tumbler.

I grin. *Hmm.*

I slide onto a cream kitchen barstool, my eyes appreciating ogling Saint's body for a little too long, especially considering all he has on is a pair of swim trunks. That beautiful sun-kissed olive skin, all those toned muscles along his strong and athletic body... his beautiful broad shoulders... that back tattoo... his toned ass.

Saint's eyes catch mine when he turns around, a heated glimmer lacing them as he nods toward the whiskey bottle he's holding. "Want a drink?"

"Oh," I tease, clasping my hands over the oversized marble kitchen island. "Are you forgetting I'm eighteen not twenty-one, Mr. Lisconti?"

Saint smirks. "Haven't forgotten, Miss Reign." His eyes darken to such a stimulating hunger. "Just want to know who I'm with right now, my *good* girl… or my *bad* girl?"

My heart picks up speed.

Oh my…

I cross my legs, feeling my bikini thong so wet in arousal at Saint's words alone. There's so much allure in his gaze and seduction in his words. *I'm so damn horny.*

"Your bad girl," I purr through my lashes. "Always bad with you."

"Jesus Christ, Paisley." A moan escapes his lips and it's confirmation that we're in this too deep to let go now. "You know I would never give you a drink, especially not when all I want to do is bury my head between your thighs and taste you all night long right on this marble kitchen island—"

"I need a tequila, Saint. I need one *right now.*"

"Not happening."

"Fine." I smirk, getting up from the barstool and rounding the marble island. "I'll make one myself. As soon as I figure out how to make one."

The sexual tension between us couldn't be any thicker as we come face-to-face in a heated extended stare. The air crackles. Desire lingers. The way Saint's looking at me with so much starvation… I've never been this turned on.

"You really want a tequila?"

"Mmhmm."

Saint stares at me for the longest time before letting out a frustrated sexual growl, "I'm going to hell for this. Absolute hell." He puts away his whiskey arrangement and replaces it with two shot glasses, tall tequila bottle, and a saltshaker. I watch in awe as he pours tequila into the glasses and cuts two wedges of fresh lime in seconds.

So many firsts with Saint… and I love it.

"Thank you," I say when he hands me my shot glass.

Saint takes his own and steps closer to me until my bare hips are pressed against the cold oversized marble kitchen island. He's inches from pinning his body against mine. My ample breasts are heavy and my erect nipples are stabbing through the soft material of my red bikini, so sensitive and round, the only part of me that grazes against Saint's bare chest.

I don't know where to look. Those aroused blue eyes that take me on a journey I'm dying to explore. The dimples deepening on his stubbled cheeks as he smirks at me. How masculine and tall he is in front of me. Saint stands at six-two, towering over my five-three frame by almost a full foot. My gaze trails over his sexy lean physique with just the right amount of muscle... trim narrowed waist... breathtaking toned biceps with a few veins visible, ripped abs... that deep, vaunted V-line and trail of short dark hair just below his navel that leads beneath his swim trunks. That aching bulge in his shorts that's so hard to miss. *Wow.*

Saint is an absolute alpha male at his prime, a former professional boxer who still keeps his stoic form and knows how to take care of his body with discipline. He must have so much endurance, so much *stamina*, and there's something so erotic about that.

I'm so crazily physically attracted to him, but that's not all I'm drawn to. There are so many layers, versions, and aspects I adore about Saint...

His mindset.

His dedication.

His intelligence.

His maturity and experience.

His openness to talk vulnerability.

His endless encouragement and support.

His constant reliability and humorous one-liners.

His spontaneous recklessness and Harley-lover soul.

His compassion when it comes to family and those he loves.

His golden caged heart, the *Casablanca* addict, and the chivalrous side.

This is some of what I like about Saint.

This is what I love.

Saint motions to our shot glasses. "I can't believe I'm doing this with you."

"Oh, you better believe it." I grin. "Now, kindly help a woman out and teach me how to drink it."

"Watch me, beautiful."

Without ever losing my gaze, Saint uses his glistering tongue to lick and moisten the back of his hand between his thumb and index finger before sprinkling a pinch of salt over the skin.

My lips part in pure awe. *Holy hell.*

Saint's ocean eyes continue to stay on me as he takes my hand in his and smoothly licks the same spot, like he did his. The tip of his warm tongue so achingly slow in its pursuit. It's easily the hottest thing I've ever witnessed. When he's done, he sprinkles a pinch of salt on my hand too.

I don't know how a simple movement can be so sexual, but *my gosh… it is.*

Saint gives us both a lime wedge.

"All right. All you've got to remember is lick, drink, and suck."

Easy.

We bring our shot glasses together and clink them in *salute.* Saint raises his glass and I follow suit; ocean eyes are all I see.

"To new beginnings." He smiles.

I smile back. "To all the firsts."

After simultaneously licking the salt off our hands, we quickly down the strong tequila and slam the glasses on the marble island once we're done. *Oh God.* I immediately scrunch my nose at the awful burning sensation down my throat and chest.

Holy shit. What the hell is in this crap?

Saint's already laughing at me as he brings the lime to his lips and starts sucking on it. I follow suit, biting down on my juicy citric wedge. The smirk doesn't leave Saint's lips as he sets down his lime wedge on the island and leans forward, his hot breath hitting my skin as he murmurs, "Suck on the lime, baby. Suck on it. Don't bite, *suck.*"

Oh. My. God.

Our continued eye contact becomes such a wicked thing as I suck on the lime. I cross my legs, feeling desire pool at Saint's words alone. I know he was referencing the lime, but the innuendo was so evident in his sexual undertone. My heart picks up speed because I'm aching for what comes next. There's so much allure in his gaze, seduction in his words. I just want him already.

I know it's a big step for me. I've never been here before, but I'm so ready. I trust him so much. I know he's going to take care of me. I want this. Need it. Crave it right now.

"Better?" Saint asks, the whisper so low.

"Better."

"Give me a taste."

In a flustered daze, I offer him my lime.

"Babydoll, I don't mean the actual lime." Saint chuckles. "I mean I want to taste that sweet citric blend on your tongue."

My cheeks heat as I set the lime aside faster than my next breath. "*Oh*, right."

"I love it when you blush like you are right now." His warm lips trail across my right cheek, settling by my neck. "Makes me want you even more."

Oh God, I can't take this anymore. I need him.

"Please," I beg. "Please, Saint."

"Tell me what you want, babydoll."

"You," I breathe. "I need you. *All* of you."

"God," Saint breathes against my neck. "I need you so fucking bad too."

"Show me."

An uncontrollable moan escapes my throat at the sensation of his hard cock when Saint pins our bodies together against the kitchen island. I feel his erection press against my lower stomach through his swim shorts and go crazy.

"Feel *that*, baby?" he teases all breathy. "Do you feel how badly I want you too, hmm?"

"Yes, I feel it." My words transform into a gasp as sparks skitter up my neck for every kiss Saint places there. He starts softly before going wild with reckless and rough hot kisses that have me moaning out his name and my pussy throbbing harder. *"Oh, Saint. I need to feel you inside me so badly. Please. Please."*

"Such a bad girl, begging me to take you. I'm going to make you feel so fucking good, Paisley, going to make you come so damn hard with my tongue and then on my cock. I bet you taste so sweet. Bet your pretty pussy is so damn wet and tight for me." Saint goes wild, teasingly nibbling at my neck before circling his tongue over the erotic havoc he makes. "Are you wet for me, babydoll?"

I love that he dirty talks. *Dear God.*

I need a release. Friction. *Him.*

"Yes," I breathe.

"How wet?"

"So wet."

My hands loop around Saint's neck as he takes a hold of my hips and lifts me, setting me on the kitchen island. I wrap my legs around his waist, locking my ankles, loving how he holds the back of my knee so I can feel him deeper. A chill spreads across my entire body from the marble against my almost bare ass and thighs, but it all washes away when his warm hands roam my body, caressing every inch of my skin.

And then, Saint kisses me with so much possession, so much power it takes over me. The moment our sweet citric-laced tongues collide, a raging fire only he can ignite rumbles inside of me. Our tongues dance in smooth harmony as I cup the back of Saint's head and pull him even closer to me mid-kiss. So intimate. So raw.

Kissing him changes me.

Heals me.

I love that Saint's everywhere—his body so close it covers every inch of mine. I love that I feel his every groove. Every divot. Every muscle. Saint slowly strokes up my thighs, halting by my inner upper thighs. My pussy pulses faster. No amount of softly grinding against his hard cock over the fabric of his swim trunks makes it stop.

There's so much longing in our heated kiss, so much allure as Saint gets lost weaving his fingers through my wavy ponytail. He tugs on it softly and it has us smiling through the kiss for a moment, but we don't stop kissing, not even when his air becomes mine and vice versa.

Mid-kiss, Saint takes out my hair tie, letting my hair fall free behind my shoulder before he reaches around my back and blindly unties the spaghetti straps of my bikini top. The fabric falls and the heat between my thighs turns to a longing ache as Saint's big hands mold my bare ample breasts, squeezing them. *Oh yes.*

Saint detaches his lips from mine and lowers his eyes to my breasts. "You're so beautiful, Paisley. So fucking beautiful."

My heart practically melts right here in this kitchen. Saint watches on with a smolder as I lean back on my forearms, buckling my hips toward his cock for friction with only two layers of clothing separating us.

"Use me," he murmurs, continuing to caress my breasts as he grinds his hips with mine. "Fuckin' use me, Paisley."

The only other item of clothing I have on are my bikini thong bottoms. As exposed as my body is to Saint, I trust him so much. Yes, I'm hella nervous because this is a first, but he makes me feel so comfortable with the way he's looking at me, as if he's got me.

It feels so good having Saint's hands on my bare skin, like a scorching flame. Saint focuses on my left breast and I almost quiver when he slips his pointer and middle finger around my nipple before he teases me by sexily tugging the tip, elongating my nipple before circling it with his thumb.

"Saint," I gasp, tipping my head back in pleasure as he does the same to my right nipple. I roam my fingers through his hair, pulling him even closer. "That feels so good. Too good."

"Mmhmm."

The second Saint's warm tongue flicks over my nipples and he alternates sucking on them mercilessly with just the right amount of suction, even more arousal pools in my thong. His tongue is so soft. So quick. He knows exactly what he's doing, and it drives me into crazy ecstasy.

"Oh fuck," I moan, my mind exploding as my grip on his hair tightens. There comes a point where I crave his lips, so I pull Saint's head back up to me and we kiss frantically.

"Please. Touch me," I whisper when we pull away, my lips brushing against his as my hot breath escapes. "Destroy me."

Saint hisses. His hands move to my hips to halt how fast I'm gliding against his swim trunks. We were grinding so fast, so when I glance down at us now, I grin at the outline of his big hard cock through the fabric. It's so evident due to the wet patch of arousal my sex transferred through my thong.

We stare deep into each other's eyes and Saint's are hooded. A tender longing laces them as he murmurs, "Lie down."

My heart races in fast pitter-patters. I listen to him, bracing the coldness of the marble and I lie down on my back. With my legs straight I fit perfectly on the oversized kitchen island, just my hair sprawled out and hanging over the other edge.

"Spread your thighs."

I spread them wide.

A slow, sexy smirk deepens on his lips. "Good girl."

I grin.

My chest rises and falls breathlessly as Saint unties the sides of my bikini thong, watching intrigued as he undoes the final bow. *Breathe.* His piercing blue eyes hold mine as I suck in a deep breath.

"You with me, *wildflower?*" he whispers.

"Yes, I'm with you." I nod. "Keep going."

Saint slips off my bikini thong and blindly throws it aside. The wet fabric falls against the hardwood floors with a soft thump, my arousal so evident. I bite my lip, a cool breeze rushing across my bare sex as I lie naked on Saint's kitchen island. His eyes darken as they roam the length of my body, still glowing in tanning oil, before hungrily stopping at my throbbing heat.

"You're so goddamn beautiful, Paisley." Saint strums the pad of his thumb over my sensitive clit, creating soft patterns that have me slapping a hand over my mouth at the tangled moans that fall. I gasp, my eyes shutting as his fingers glide down my wet pussy, feeling my warmth ever so slowly as if to tease me to see my reaction. "You feel so good. So wet for me."

A gasp turned moan escapes me the moment Saint spanks my throbbing pussy, creating only waves of pleasure, then the intensity ramps up. *Oh. My God. Yes.* Saint spanks my sex a second time, the sound of my wetness making my hips buckle toward him in desire and clench down around nothing.

"Keep your eyes open, baby," he murmurs. "I want to see your face when you come soon."

I watch as Saint spreads all my glistering wetness around in several fast wide-handed rubs, before slipping two fingers inside me, and a breath escapes me as he begins to pump them hard inside me. "God, what a pretty hot pussy. So tight and wet for me, isn't that right, *amore?*"

"Yes, all for you."

"Mmhmm. I can't wait to feel you wrapped around my cock and clenching down on me like you're doing to my fingers right now. Can't fucking wait, Paisley."

I moan out again and again, and a second later he adds a third finger, working me so good and deep. My hips rock, desperate to meet the thrusts of his pumps, but he quickens the pace to an unbelievable rhythm. It's as if I'm flying in the middle of pure bliss and ecstasy as our eyes lock.

I'm not going to last long. Not with the way he's finger fucking my pussy.

I've never felt like this before. Never felt this addictive pleasure. My body is so responsive to Saint. Responsive to his every touch as his thumb returns to my clit and his three fingers continue to bring me closer and closer to the edge for several moments. His free hand squeezes my breasts together. *Yes.*

"I'm so close," I breathe, arching my back and feeling myself clench around his fingers tighter when he continuously hits my

G-spot. "Saint!" I scream out his name as his hand vibrates my entire body. "I'm going to... *oh, God*. I'm so close to..."

"Come for me, baby girl. Come on my hand like a good girl."

Saint and I share a lust-filled smile, and it's the most beautiful thing as my heavy eyes hold his blue-eyed gaze with such reverence. Saint's hand on my breast reaches out to tenderly clasp my left hand by the marble island. Such a wholesome touch to the moment.

"Oh, my good God."

"Feel it, baby. Feel yourself losing control."

Warmth rushes across my entire body and I orgasm hard around his hand, gushing as I come undone. "Wow, Saint," I pant, sucking in breaths after such high.

Saint smiles darkly as he sucks on the three fingers that were just inside me. They glisten with my orgasm and him licking off my taste is easily the most erotic thing I've ever seen. Humming in satisfaction, his eyes roll to the back of his head. "You're so sweet, Paisley. Want a taste?"

Grinning, I bite my lip and nod.

Saint gives me no mercy. He dominantly grips my ankles and uses them to roughly slide me closer to him on the marble kitchen island. I giggle as his strong arms hold my spread legs around his narrowed waist and he leans down to kiss me slowly. I taste myself on his tongue, so sweet with a hint of saltiness and tequila from earlier, and it's enough to rile me up all over again.

"Why are you so good?" I murmur against his lips, taking advantage of him being closer, and caress his stubbled jaw. "You seriously blew my mind."

"Oh, we're just getting started, babydoll."

Before I know it, Saint props my legs on his shoulders and our heavy eye contact never strays as he buries his head between my thighs with a sexy, smug smirk. His warm, wide tongue laps all over my pussy, and I curse in pleasure, gripping his hair to push him deeper into me as I fall back on the kitchen island. I'll never forget the raspy growl he makes when I do.

I don't think I'll ever be able to get enough of this man.

My heart is about to beat out of my chest with how crazy my pulse throbs when his warm tongue continuously swirls over my clit before sucking on it with just the right amount of suction. Perhaps it's the mixture of the lingering liquor, how turned on we both are, and the way I just screamed out his name and begged him not to stop, but Saint turns into a starved beast. He goes frantically wild, driving his tongue inside me before recklessly moving it up and down, side to side, diagonally, and swirling around over and over and over, until I'm breathless with the kind of pleasure I didn't know could ever exist.

I haven't even recovered from my last orgasm, and now I'm on the edge of my second.

Saint's entire face is pressed against my pussy, his eyes shut like he's enjoying every moment, and it turns me on even more that he wants this as much as I do. I throw my head back as he presses a hand over my taut stomach in possession to ease my quivering body as his tongue works magic.

It's too much, so intense. His shoulder muscles contract and tense as he holds on to my legs tighter. The visual of a thirty-six-year-old man between my eighteen-year-old thighs. His stubble scraping my inner thigh as he eats me out like it's an Olympic sport. *Whoa.*

I smile up at the ceiling, my knees buckling and legs trembling as waves of desire become more and more intense. I'm riveting in pleasure and after a few moments I reach my peak and come undone, squirting down his throat as I tug the ends of his hair through the moans. He rides out the orgasm with me and continues lapping his tongue over my pussy with a moan of his own until the wave eases and my breaths settle down.

When Saint finally looks up at me, still between my thighs, I grin down at him, and he gives me the most beautiful, dimpled grin back. He's looking at me with such allure in his eyes as his lips and stubble glisten with my orgasm. *So hot.* I watch in pure adoration as he runs his tongue along his lips, gently sets down my legs from his shoulders, and kisses my ankles before helping me off the marble island.

"I think I'm addicted to you," I whisper against his lips, all giddy. "I know earlier at the beach you said only a summer, but I don't think I'll be able to forget that for my entire life."

"That makes two of us."

"Yeah?" I smile, running my hand down his abdominal muscles, loving feeling all the ridges before teasing my finger over the band of his swim trunks. "You feel that way too?"

"Mhmmm." Saint rests his forehead against mine. "The way you screamed my name. The way you writhed beneath me. *You...* All I want to do is hear those moans again as I fill you with my cock."

"I want that so badly... I want *you.*"

"I know, but..."

"There's always a but, isn't there?"

A slow, sexy grin works up Saint's lips. "I promise it's for a good reason."

"Go on." I smile.

"As much as I want to devour you right this second, there's this place I want to show you first. Whenever I'm here in Marin County there isn't a time when I don't visit it. I love it and thought you'd really like it too. So, earlier on today I made reservations for dinner tonight, so we have to be there in like twenty minutes from now."

See, a romantic.

"Hmmm. I see what this is," I tease. "You're giving me a twelve-hour tour of Stinson Beach in Marin County. Trying to get as much in before my father finishes his shift, huh?"

Saint smirks. "Oooo. You're onto me, aren't you?"

"Always am. Anyway, go on..."

"Well, the place I want to take you to takes five minutes to get there by Harley. So, we kind of have to start getting ready now if you don't want me to ruin the surprise."

"Aww, that's so nice. I can't wait! But do you mean we need to get ready right *now*? Like *right now*, right now?"

"Yes, that's typically what somebody means when they say *right now*."

I groan, all while he can't stop laughing at my reaction. *I thought we had more time.*

"Soon, baby." Saint chuckles, his lips brushing against my ear. "When we return home, I'm *all* yours. I promise."

His words thrill me. *Home.*

The second Saint and I step inside the restaurant and bar, Martin's, I'm completely blown away. I'm surprised it isn't the typical beach-style restaurant, especially with it being beach-side. It's completely modern and on such a sophisticated level.

This place is spectacular, with moody darkish pallets mixed with creams and textured beiges throughout the entire bar and restaurant. I'm so in love with the black herringbone floor tiles in the bar section and that LED strip lighting beneath the granite bar counter. The front bar expands to a spacious restaurant section where Saint and I are currently sitting. Modern dark gray Venetian plaster aligns every wall. Opposite, an alternative band is performing on the sleek elevated stage. It's why reservations are essential. Some couples are already dancing around it.

But what honestly surprises me the most is the bouquet of yellow roses in a vase with water on the oak table. Apparently, Saint arranged it as he explains he wanted to give me flowers for my graduation but didn't want my father to question him and mistake the kind gesture for something odd. The roses right now, they're gorgeous alongside the thin long candlestick beside it. This is such a beautiful and intimate setup, and for the man who doesn't date, this feels like much more than showing me around Stinson Beach.

This felt like *more.*

When Saint told me to pack for the beach the other day, he

also mentioned a spare change of clothes. So, I'm currently wearing my favorite yellow sundress that cuts off around my thigh, and a black lace pair of bra and panties. When I walked down the stairs of his beach house and saw Saint in elegant dark slacks and a white button-up shirt that was slightly unbuttoned with perfectly slicked-back hair and leather derby shoes, my stomach flooded with butterflies. I'm always so used to seeing Saint dressed like a sexy biker alpha. Classic jeans. Harley tee. Leather jacket. But when I saw him dressed so damn elegantly like the Italian man he is… it was just another level of beautiful. I'll never forget the way Saint pulled me into him, kissed my cheek, and twirled me around to give my outfit even more justice before saying how much he loved it.

I swear I've blushed more times in these past seven hours with Saint than I have my entire life.

"I can see why this is your favorite place." I grin, glancing around the lively modern restaurant and bar. Diners are everywhere enjoying their meals. "You know, I've been thinking. Why did you move here to Marin County… Stinson Beach?"

"To be honest, it was to escape from reality. A breath of fresh air. I lived in Santa Rosa up until before the first year of college. I was working a decent job at a restoring garage fixing up Harleys and other high-end motorcycles. I was paid exceptionally well because I worked every day and continued to even when I moved here to Stinson Beach. Here… Stinson Beach was almost like middle ground for me because I rode a lot between going back to Santa Rosa for family and work, and then the opposite side across the Golden Gate and past San Fran and Palo Alto for college at Stanford. You probably don't want to hear all this, but…"

"No, of course I want to hear all of this. It interests me more than you know. It's part of the *full extent of Saint Lisconti*, remember?"

Saint smiles across the leather booth. "I remember."

"Good, so keep going."

"Let's go outside for a breather while I tell this long ass story."

I agree and Saint flags down our server, telling him to keep our table reserved as we'll come back in a bit. I follow Saint outside the front of the restaurant, thanking him when he holds the door out for me. The live music inside becomes mumbled as I take in a fresh breath of the ocean breeze once we're outside. *This is definitely the place to be.*

It's even a better view of the water and the long stretch of beach. *So beautiful.* There are a few diners outside, but Saint and I walk over to a little private section by the perimeter of the restaurant where we won't be disturbed by anybody. The violent crush of the rocks beneath my Converses eases when Saint and I sit next to each other in two wooden chairs that surround a gorgeous outdoor firepit with glowing specks of orange and the comforting scent of cedar and campfire. The air is chilly, and a little windy too with the beach so close, so it's nice to warm up a little with the soft orange hue of the flames our only light.

Saint gets comfortable in his seat and turns to me. "All right, as I was saying, I was making a sizable amount at work, so I bought the beach house."

"What's the story behind the beach house? Why a beach house?"

The question has been eating away at me ever since we first arrived.

"Why does there have to be a story behind it?"

"I just know you. Everything you do has a plan. The beach house must have been one of those plans."

"You're an intelligent woman." Saint gulps down and pulls a packet of cigarettes and a lighter out of his slacks pocket. Just before he lights the cigarette, his eyes meet mine in a slight hesitation that I've never seen before. "Mind if I smoke?"

"No, not at all. Why do you ask? You've never asked before."

"Well, you may smell like smoke when you get home. Wouldn't want Alaric to notice."

Oh.

"It's okay, I'll smell of the firepit anyway. I can just take a shower when I get home before my dad arrives."

"You sure?"

"Positive. Go for it."

Saint lights up his cigarette, settling the packet and lighter on the edge of the metal outdoor firepit. I keep my eyes on the glowing orange tip as he takes a drag, clouds of smoke circling his face. When he catches me staring, he offers the cigarette to me, a smirk rising on his lips because he most likely knows what my response is going to be.

I laugh, bringing my knees up to my chest on the chair with a shake of my head. "I can be your bad girl, but I'm not that adventurous when it comes to trying new things."

Saint's smirk deepens. "Fair enough. All right, where were we…oh yes, that's it. You're right. I did have a plan. A long time ago it wasn't just a beach house to me, it was simply a *home*."

"I'm sorry," I whisper. "I didn't know or else I wouldn't have asked."

"No, don't apologize, Paisley. It's good for me to get it out, I guess. Besides, you weren't the one who broke my heart. It's just… guilt can do a lot of things to you. Make you go fucking crazy."

My heart aches for everything Saint's been through.

Silence settles between us. I rub my hands together as sadness flashes across Saint's eyes when they travel to the smooth ocean waves, and he blows out another cloud of smoke. My gaze follows his, outlooking the water.

"It seems like you blame yourself for whatever happened in your past… with Lea."

"I blame myself for how it ended, not how she and I fell apart. Just like I've moved on from her, but not from the repercussions her actions still have."

It's as if I feel his pain right here next to him. I know what Saint's trying to do by not looking my way. He's hiding the emotion in his deep blue eyes, the same emotion I caught a peek of before he glances away toward the water. But I see right through him. I always do.

Saint's never spoken of Lea to me this openly. So, I appreciate everything he entrusts me with and don't take it lightly. Not in the slightest.

"Look at me, Saint."

He doesn't move.

"Saint?"

Nothing.

Caressing his back, my fingers fan out behind his neck and rub his warm skin.

Look at me, baby.

Gulping down, I smile sadly. "I can see how much pain you're in for your past and all I want to do is ease it. I just want you to know that whatever happened in your past isn't your fault."

"But it is," Saint chokes out, turning my way. The sadness in his eyes haunts me. "It's all my fault."

"Look, I understand the betrayal and hurt and loss you are feeling. You've been caged to these feelings for so long that it's all you believe and holding onto regret and punishing yourself for it, but it isn't the way to live."

"It may not be, but it's the only thing I seem to get right."

"You know that's not true, beautiful blue-eyed boy." I cup his stubbled jaw and he leans his head into my hand. "You love her, Saint. I see it in your eyes how much you do."

"*Loved*," he corrects. "I don't love her anymore. Love destroyed me."

"Will you talk to me about Lea?"

"One day. Not today."

"Is Lea why you're afraid to love again? Because you're afraid to be hurt again?"

"No, I'm afraid I'll fuck it up and break your heart. I don't want to do that. I don't want to hurt you. *Ever*. I don't want to hurt Alaric either."

"So, where does that leave us?"

I so desperately need to know.

The air crackles between us.

"One summer." Saint swallows thickly, his eyes softening. "It's all I can give you, Paisley. One summer filled with you."

My heart stops at the words he's just spoken because I already know how impossible it will be for me. *I need more. Crave more.* I look up at Saint through my lashes earnestly, honestly. It's without any added filters. *Just me.* Just an eighteen-year-old woman, looking at a thirty-six-year-old man who I've had close to my heart for three long years.

Saint Lisconti—the same man I've had sleepless nights rolling around in my bed fantasizing about—is sitting right beside me. He's the only man I feel understands me more than I do myself. A true angel, with the look of a devil, one I want to unravel and show him he's no sin. I want to do it badly. *So. Badly.* Right now.

I search his eyes. "What if I want more than just a summer with you?"

"You won't. Seattle will fill that gap. We explore everything there is to explore, and then we walk away."

Bittersweet. This is so damn bittersweet.

"I'm hoping to find an apartment in Seattle and move there at the start of August. So, I'll stay there a month before college begins to settle in and adjust to the new city."

"So then it won't be a summer. It'll be eight weeks then?"

"Eight weeks," I confirm, knowing I so desperately need more, but if this is all he can give me, I'll willingly take it without mercy.

"Two months."

"Sixty-one days of what specifically? Of… some sort of relationship?"

"Yes. Sixty-one days of each other uninhabited. Okay. We need rules."

I smirk. "I didn't think you were the rules kind of guy."

My comment brings out the warmest smile on his lips, a warm welcome from the gloom cast over us only moments ago. It feels so good to see him smiling again because it brightens every avenue inside me too.

"Me neither." Saint chuckles. "But if it's one thing I want, it's exclusivity."

I grin and press a kiss to his cheek. "Of course, and I think we can both agree that we need to hide what's going on from my father."

"Agreed. That's the most important aspect, *that* and having honest communication if anything should change between us, not that we're not honest already."

"Exactly, and the rest… I guess we can just make up the rest of the rules as we go, yeah?"

Saint grins back. "Mmhmm. I like the sound of that."

I'm surprised my heart's still okay because it's beating so fast it may just explode.

I bite my lip mid-smile, thrilled that this is actually happening.

"Me too," I say just as my stomach growls *so loudly*, and we burst out into laughter.

"Let's go inside. I didn't take you out to dinner only for us to starve out here."

"*Oh*, you *took me out to dinner*, did you?" I smirk with a playfully arched brow. "Is this a date, Mr. Lisconti?"

I love teasing Saint, especially because he's always so sly and humorous about it.

Saint throws his head back in laughter, his deep dimples even more beautiful against the shadowed carving of the firepit's flames. "Definitely not a date, Miss Reign."

Hmm.

"Sure, sure, Mr. *When-I-Take-A-Plane-To-Switzerland*."

"Oh, God. I shouldn't have ever sung those songs to you. Now you're going to embarrass me for an eternity."

"Not an eternity, just from time to time."

"Mhmmm that's better, good girl." Saint winks as he puts out his cigarette with his leather shoe and stretches as he stands up to his tall height. He's a truly charming Italian gentleman when he holds out his hand for me and helps me out of the wooden chair with that smolder on his lips that I love.

Our hands clasp as we walk toward the entry of the restaurant and bar we're at and it warms me completely. The sensation of feeling so seen whenever I'm with Saint doesn't ease, especially not when he lowers his lips to my ear and softly begins singing, *"When I take a plane to Switzerland, don't take one there too. You had your chance to get to me, now you need an 'I owe you', 'cause you owe—"* Saint doesn't get far before he breaks out in chuckles. "Hahaha!"

I can't stop laughing alongside him all the way back to our oak table because this is what life is all about... *feeling alive.*

Chapter
NINETEEN

Paisley

As I GULP DOWN MY FRESH WATERMELON JUICE, MY EYES FLICKER UP to those beautiful ocean blues above the glass. We've just finished dinner and are onto our last bites of dessert.

I set the glass down and smile. "So, you come to this place *every* time you're in town?"

"*Every* time, yeah."

"Can I ask a question?"

Saint nods, leaning back in the comfortable dark leather booth with a grin. "Hit me."

"I once read this article about a psychology study that found certain people rewatching the same TV show or movie because it creates a sense of safety and comfort. That consequently eases their anxiety levels and is kind of therapeutic. Would you say it's kind of the same for you too coming to this place?"

His grin drops.

The pitter-patters of my heart slow.

Oh.

Saint's gaze falls from mine for a second, focusing on anything but me. It's as if I've hit home a little too hard and now he doesn't want to face the music. *Shit.*

"I'm sorry," I say after a few seconds with nothing but the backdrop of chatty diners and the soft strum of the guitar and vocals who are performing live opposite us on the elevated stage. "I… shouldn't have said anything. I'm sorry, I didn't mean to pry. Obviously, this place is very special and personal to you. I'm just grateful you chose to bring me here. I know it means a lot to you."

Saint doesn't say a word. He simply swallows thickly, rubs a hand behind his neck, and focuses on the whiskey glass in front of him with a frown.

Shit, I didn't mean to hit a sensitive nerve.

I knew it. I just knew it.

Everything that's going on between us is just too good to be true. *Or… is it?*

Out of all the questions I've ever asked Saint, never has he responded like this. He'd either give me a legitimate answer and we'd get deep into conversation, or he'd give me a brief answer and I'd know not to mention it again, or he would let me know it's a no-go zone, but this time… he's shutting down and giving me nothing. *Nothing.*

I glance around at the large picture window outlooking the beautiful Pacific Ocean. The night sky has blanketed the midnight blue water with dazzling twinkling stars on the surface. It's the benefits of being in a beach-side restaurant. The views everywhere are breathtaking.

When I turn back to Saint and his eyes are shut, almost as if he's lost in thought, I clear my throat and chew down the final piece of my delicious iconic apple pie with my heartbeat in my ears. *Well, this is awkward.*

To be seated adjacent to Saint right now while he's all silent is concerning. It's concerning because Saint isn't like this. He's never shied away from a question. He's the most confident, dominant, and assertive man I've ever known. *So why is he acting like this now?*

I part my lips, but Saint beats me to it before I can say anything. Gulping down his glass of whiskey, those blue eyes lift and hold mine. There's a small improvement in his complexion with the soft smile he shoots my way, but I can see the sudden sadness beneath it. I can see that it isn't all that meets the eye with Saint tonight.

Leaning back against the leather booth, Saint runs a hand down his crisp button-down and settles his hands clasped in his lap. "I'm sorry," are the first words he speaks, and I know from the loaded emotion how hard it was to speak those words "I hate when... I hate when I get like this."

"It's okay." I nod with an encouraging smile. "Take your time. I don't have a knife to your throat."

I'm grateful for the light chuckle that escapes him at my little sarcasm. It makes me happy that even with all the thoughts that must be clouding his mind, I can still make him happy.

Diners' muffled conversations and bursts of laughter, alongside the live music, fade from my mind. There's nobody else more important than Saint and whatever he entrusts me with. We've come so far since that day three years ago when he stepped on my lilies and we declared war. So far from all the fights, the stare-offs, the angsty tension that's turned both sexual and emotional.

"You're right when you say rewatching the same show or going to the same place is almost like an anxiety cleanse. Like some sort of therapy. This place... Martin's, it was my father's favorite place to visit. When I used to live here, there wasn't a week where he wouldn't come down and we'd share some laughs here at this restaurant. It's changed a lot in the past five years, but the essence remains. In 2012 when my father's cancer returned after years in remission, he was receiving aggressive treatment, so I visited him and my family in Santa Rosa instead. Treatment made him extremely exhausted, and he didn't have the energy to come down to Stinson Beach. I hadn't come to this place for months because it meant nothing without my father. Treatment wasn't helping with the stage he was in. The doctor said that... that..."

The lump at the back of my throat aches at the emotion in his voice and how he broke at the last word. There's no doubt that Saint has been through so much. I cannot imagine where his mind must be at, but all I do know is that I feel so grateful that he's taking the time to share this personal story with me.

Stretching out my hand across the oak table, it takes a moment for Saint to snuffle away some emotion and reach up his hand to weave it through mine. I clasp our hands tightly together, like a cage unable to be unlocked without its key.

"I'm right here, Saint, I'm right here."

"I know..."

Saint's glassy eyes meet mine and a hot tear rolls down my cheek at the sad story.

"One breath at a time."

We both inhale a deep breath and the world around us seems to fade away. *Breathe.*

"My father... he was running out of time. I was due to head to London in the middle of July ahead of the London Olympics and wanted to pull out because I wouldn't be able to forgive myself if something happened while I was there. I'll never forget how fucking proud my father was of me. It was his dream to see me in the Olympics doing what I loved... boxing. He forced me not to pull out. He said if I did it would ruin him, so I decided to go ahead with it, even though my heart wasn't fully in it. The weeks before making the trip to London, I spent the most time I could with not only him but my entire family. The weekend before I left for London, my father practically begged me to meet here. Said he wanted to have one last drink with me before my residence for the next few weeks was the Olympic Village. I agreed, although I could see how sick he was. How much he was deteriorating. But I said yes because he's my father and I love the hell out of him and would have done anything for him."

"You're a good man, Saint. You really are."

Saint lets out a breath, squeezes my hand, and keeps going. "We had dinner and drinks, right at this booth, just my father and me. That night, he told me to get up on that stage." He gestures toward the very stage across the room. "He told me to get up and sing him a song. 'Our Song' by Elton John. It was his favorite song. He was adamant about it. So, I took one of the guys' guitars and started singing. He couldn't meet my eyes the entire song, just shut his eyes and listened to the song, to the melody, to my voice. At the final note, he opened his eyes, and I saw he was sobbing. Now, you've got to understand that I never saw my father cry in my entire life. He always wanted to be strong around his family, but that particular night he lost it. I was crying too, so damn hard, and when I got down off the stage, he held me so tight. It was like he *knew* because that was the last time I saw him alive. During my first week at the Olympics I was on a winning streak and one night my mom called me and... she told me that... that he had... and my entire world shattered right in front of me. I didn't want to believe it. Hell, I still can't fucking believe it. My mother told me not to leave, but mentally I was in such a fucked up space that I had to return back home and be there with my family. So now, even though I'm in Sacramento, this is the last place where I saw my father, so I come here to remember him, but also remember myself. I come here to escape. I come here because it helps with all of the anxious thoughts. Because it's familiar... because it's a sense of comfort. Just like you said."

Warm tears don't stop cascading down my cheeks as I slide around the booth with Saint's hand still in mine and pull him into a tight embrace, straddling his waist. I have no words. None. The emotion and tragedy of the words Saint just spoke have taken them right out of me. Even when I close my eyes, I can still see the agonizing pain in his ocean blues, the clouds of tears in his gaze from seconds ago... and it breaks my heart. Shatters me into a million tiny pieces because not only does he trust me enough to open up, but Saint's life has been so awfully bittersweet.

Saint and I hold on to each other like we're the last people on this earth. An embrace so warm and comforting and filled with emotion. His arms wrap around my waist, pulling me closer into him, while my head is buried into his neck, breathing in his familiar scent amid tears. The second Saint's chest begins to tremble, I lose it and hold on tighter.

Saint buries his head into my hair, his sobs silent as he completely lets go of the man he's been perceived to be for all these years, into the man he really is...

A man with such honesty, a heart of gold and sentiments that run so deep.

A man I'm so wholeheartedly in love with.

My heart aches to see Saint like this. So emotionally broken, which is so understandable after everything he's told me. It's as if he's kept all these emotions of grief and loss bundled up inside him for all these years and right now, they're completely letting loose. I know firsthand how terribly grief can fuck with somebody. Losing my nana like that... I can empathize with Saint perfectly.

"Let it out, baby, let it out," I murmur, slowly running my fingers through his hair, and sniffle away my tears, knowing I need to be strong for him. "I'm so sorry for everything you've battled through. Just know that your father is so proud of you and is still looking down at you with a smile. I feel it."

"Thank you."

"You've helped me understand who I really am during all these years, but all this time you've been carrying such a burden. A burden I so desperately want to heal."

Moments pass with me rubbing small circles across his skin through his shirt. When he finally settles down and those glassy eyes meet mine, I don't care about the new diners that are glancing our way as I wipe away his tears or the fact that we're both such emotional messes...

All I care about is the way his complexion warms the second I cup his stubbled jaw and whisper against his lips, "Even in a world where the lines between what we really mean to each other are blurred, even though I don't know what we are to each other, even if this little rendezvous stops the moment we're back in Sacramento or is just for the summer... I ask one thing from you... Let me heal you, my blue-eyed boy. Let me heal *you*."

"Don't you see it, *wildflower*?" Saint murmurs with the type of emotion that has waves crashing against my heart and seeping in, the water reviving me. "Don't you see that being with you makes me a better man? It heals me. No matter how much a part of me wants to let you go because you deserve better, I can't."

"Then don't."

Flicking his eyes between mine, Saint smiles. "I won't."

And then, his lips are on mine and at this stage I don't know which one of us needs the healing more. This kiss is a little bittersweet, so sensual, and all of what I need. All I know is that whenever I'm with him my flaws fade away and become strengths...

They become reminders of who I am.

Reminders of why my heart beats this fast.

Reminders of *us*, here tonight wrapped in each other at his favorite place... because right now, it's mine too. In fact, from this point forward, I know *it will always be.*

※

Saint

I've never been grocery shopping at a quarter to eleven before. So doing it with Paisley seems almost like a novelty. There's something about sharing a basket with her and strolling down every aisle, picking out items to buy and laughing at some of the ridiculous things we find that feels so intimate and pure. It's as if we're playing house. As if for just a little while I was her forever and she was mine.

To be honest, I didn't know how we would return to our bubbly selves after I completely broke down at Martin's just over half an hour ago, but there's just something about Paisley that instantly makes me calm down and feel better. She didn't manipulate me for feeling emotion or ignore the pain I was in when I opened up.

She told me everything was going to be all right.

She held on to me.

She rescued me.

After a little while, Paisley suggested we leave the restaurant and take a walk around the block before heading back to the beach house. The idea was to start heading back to Sacramento by midnight so that we could be back home around 2:00 a.m. with an hour to spare before Paisley's father finished his shift, but with the way things are going between us, I want nothing more than to spend the entire weekend here with Paisley.

I know it's risky. I know Alaric will blast his daughter's phone if he finds she's not home in the morning, but Paisley is a grown-ass woman and she's allowed to do whatever the hell she likes. It's why when she came to a halt in front of a small grocery store by my beach house and her eyes lit up as if she had an idea, I didn't protest about it with the excuse of us having to head back to Sacramento soon. Fuck going back. I'm staying here with her. Where I belong.

I'm a jealous man, a reckless jealous man who for some reason turns into a fucking cinnamon bun whenever I'm around the poetic flower queen, but *fuck*, how much I like melting into something so damn sweet around her.

Although it makes sense because since I only go to the beach house during the summer and all I have in the kitchen are basic items like honey, condiments, and liquor, I love how Paisley and I are placing items into the cart like fruit, bread, milk, and Napoleon ice cream as if we're some married couple and it's automatic.

Love that I don't even know how we're going to carry all of these items home.

Love it even more that she's still holding onto the bouquet of flowers I had ordered to our dinner table earlier because she didn't want to leave without them. The stems are pressed together, wrapped in a few napkins from Martin's because they're still a little damp from being submerged in water for so long.

I'm so happy she loved them.

"You planning on staying over at mine for a week?" I smirk when Paisley's fingers brush over a bottle of Italian pasta sauce.

Paisley glances over at me, her silky beach waves gliding over her shoulder as she shoots me a bright grin. I playfully arch my brow and she moves her hand away from the bottle. "I guess I got a little carried away, didn't I?"

"Not at all. All you've got to do is tell me."

"Tell you what?"

"That you want to do this Bonnie and Clyde style and let Stinson Beach be our hideaway." I laugh.

Although I said it jokingly, there's a part of me that wants this so much and I don't even know where it came from.

Paisley smiles and reaches up to brush her thumb over my stubble. It's become a habit, a thing she does to show she cares, and I love it so much. Her eyes meet mine in amusement. "Bonnie and Clyde, huh?"

"That's right."

"Oh my God." Paisley dramatically gasps, teasing me good as she plays along with my joke. "You're asking me to move in with you? Already? But what am I going to tell Joe Manganiello when he comes looking and confesses he loves me?"

"Tell him to back off."

"Tempting…"

"Move in with me and it'll be Harley rides whenever you like."

"The offer's getting better now, but… *Joe*, he's just…"

"All right, I got it now. Move in with me and I'll buy you all the fuckin' llamas in the world."

Paisley bursts out in hysterical laughter and a couple people in the aisle glance over at us with wide eyes, but I don't give a fuck about them and turn back to her. Paisley has a hand slapped over her mouth, but her eyes tell me she's grinning and still dying inside.

I wink at Paisley as I get a bottle of the Italian pasta sauce she was eyeing moments ago and place it in the cart I'm holding. "It may have been a joke, but I win over Joe Manganiello any day of the week."

"Glad you're feeling like your old self again," Paisley murmurs all serious when we walk out of the aisle and down the next.

I glance over at her and smile. "Me too, *wildflower*. Me too."

During the next few minutes, we finish up our shopping, my brows knitting in amusement when Paisley walks into the floral section of the store. There are only a few flowers remaining from the early morning and she takes them all and places them on top of the grocery basket. I'm even more lost when she grabs a packet of little electric candles.

"What are you going to do with those?"

"You'll see," Paisley says all secretly, like I'm missing something.

I can't help but chuckle. "You have something planned?"

She grins. "Maybe."

Hmmm, I wonder what it could be…

It gets even stranger when she walks into the baby section aisle and tells me to shut my eyes.

"I'm so confused."

"Just close your eyes. It'll all make sense when we get to your beach house."

My lips pull up into a smile as I comply. "Whatever you say, Pais."

What feels like half a second passes before Paisley instructs me I can open them again. There's this smirk on her lips as she stands before me with something behind her back, like she's hiding something from me. "When this item gets scanned, don't look."

"Why? You going to pacify me or something?"

Paisley giggles and I laugh with her. "Not quite. It'll all make sense very, very soon."

After we've paid (well, after we had a solid five-minute debate over who should pay as she wanted to and I wasn't hearing it because I wanted to pay, and I finally won), we take a quick walk back to the beach house and start putting the items away in the fridge and cupboards. Once we're done, we wash our hands with the new lavender handwash Paisley convinced me to buy to make this house seem more lively compared to my old basic handwash. I don't even know how she thought about it, but God was she right. The lavender smells so damn good and smooth against my skin.

Then, it's a waiting game because Paisley tells me to wait downstairs in the kitchen until she calls me. The *'okay'* is barely all out of my mouth before she's mounting the stairs two steps at a time with the packet of candles, flowers, and that mystery item I haven't managed to catch a glimpse of, no matter how hard I tried. All I can do is laugh because I have no idea what she is planning. Her eagerness for whatever it is she's hiding has me so intrigued and amused.

What is she scheming?

So, I sit on one of the kitchen barstools and wait. I smolder as my hand brushes over the oversized marble kitchen island, memories of earlier today running through my mind of when Paisley was lying down on it while I drove her to ecstasy.

So. Fucking. Hot.

My cock throbs in my slacks at the mere memory of her sweet moans and how her body reacted so naturally to my tongue and fingers. I love the intensity of us. I love how we can be so passion-filled and full of lust and temptation, and that we can also be so tender, raw, and sensual. I enjoy the mix, the dynamics, all the in-betweens. I love that we feel all this, even without sex yet.

Opening up to Paisley earlier tonight wasn't easy for me. It took trust and *fuck* how much I trust this woman. I could go my whole life and never meet a woman like Paisley again. I know I only said a summer but… could I really let her go at the end of August? Or in reality the end of July before she heads to Seattle at the start of August to settle in before college?

It takes a lot for me to connect with somebody, but with Paisley Reign it's on another level. The way she was looking at me after I told her the depth of where some of my past traumas lay really spoke to me. She was looking at me with such emotion and grief in her eyes as if she empathized with me on this completely other level.

No other woman has ever connected that deep with me before.

No other woman has ever wanted to make sure I was truly okay.

No other woman has ever assumed that just because I present this tough exterior, that I don't need a little healing too.

Nobody. *Nobody.* Nobody but *Paisley.*

"YOU CAN COME UP NOW!"

I take the stairs three at a time, beyond eager to uncover what Paisley's been hiding. I stop at the top of the stairs, turning on the recessed lights, and my gaze drops to the single yellow rose petals leading up the hallway like breadcrumbs through my primary bedroom and to my bathroom. Smiling, my Italian leather shoes slap against the hardwood floors as I inch closer and closer to the closed bathroom barn door.

Whoa, what is going on?

As I slide open the barn door, my jaw literally drops at the sight in front of me.

Dio mio.

Wow.

Scattered yellow rose petals create a curved pathway to the free-standing oversized bathtub, a few of those electric candles outlining the path. The warm glow the candles create is so moody and romantic, mostly because they brighten the bathroom without having to switch on any other light. Paisley's sundress and black lingerie are scattered on the floor beside the candles and *holy shit.* I've never closed that barn door behind me so fast.

I don't know what to look at first, the filled-up bubble bath full of beautiful light pink, orange, red, and white flower heads floating around, or the huge picture window behind the free-standing tub that outlooks beautiful scenic views of the nearby ocean waves and full moon and twinkling stars that reflect upon it in the dark midnight sky, or Paisley who's sitting by the edge of the bathtub completely naked. I go with the latter because I can't take my eyes off the beauty that she is. Her stunning soft cream skin. Those beautiful, ample breasts and light pink nipples. Striking long legs and perfect curves. Her dark hair pulled up in a top bun. That bright grin. Paisley is such a natural beauty, so genuine and real.

Boldness.

Confidence.

A newfound spirit.

This is what I see when I look at her.

I can feel my heartbeat in my ears. In my throat. In my pulsing hard cock. Everywhere especially my heart because it's capsized at sea. I've never been surprised in my life, not until right now. Paisley is special. So damn fucking special it hurts.

"Wow, *wildflower*. I could spend my entire life telling you how beautiful you are."

"And you said you're not a romantic." Paisley grins wider, her honey-brown eyes twinkling as she steps closer to me. "I really appreciated the courage you had to share so much about yourself, so I want to be a little brave too. I want to show you you're not the only one who seeks comfort from anxious thoughts and the world itself by going to your favorite place to find yourself. So, this is *my* thing..." She steps even closer, and I wrap my arms around her petite waist, loving the feel of her bare body against my shirt and slacks as she gestures behind to the bathtub. "I want it to be ours. I want it to be *yours*. When the world gets too much, when you just want some quiet, when you want to remember me... escape into a world of me here."

I'm in awe.

Complete awe.

A relaxing little mind escape with a bubble bath filled with a bed of pretty flowers.

Whoa.

I lower my head to kiss her, but Paisley presses a finger on the center of my lips to stop me and smirks. "Not yet, baby."

The way she calls me baby, that smirk, the way her hips softly sway as she picks up a black envelope from the bathroom counter... *God*, I want to devour her.

Paisley shakes the envelope in her hand. "*Voilà!*"

I laugh.

"Remember that day I was planting the flowers and you asked me to recite a poem?"

"Yes."

"Well, over a year on and I finally have the courage to share my work. But this isn't the one I was going to recite that day. This is another one I wrote for you. The one you peeked at that day at the beach weeks ago."

This warmness rushes across me. *Whoa.*

She did this... *for me.*

"Paisley... I don't know what to say. I feel honored. Thank you."

"You're more than welcome."

Our fingers brush at the action, causing my eyes to snap back to hers. *She's so damn gorgeous.* My eyes darken as Paisley's arms wrap around my neck, and her hard nipples graze my chest through my button-down shirt, making me go crazy.

Paisley's soft lips brush against my cheek in an extended kiss before she pulls back and whispers, "I know it was yesterday, but Happy Birthday, Saint. From me to you."

"Thank you, *wildflower.*"

Grinning, Paisley nods down to the envelope. "Open it!"

Open it, Lisconti.

Why are you so nervous?

I gulp down, knowing the words I'm about to read will be like none other. The depth in them... I know is going to destroy me, more than I already am. My gaze continues flickering between Paisley and opening the envelope, always with a smile on my face because this moment means a lot to me.

Setting the envelope back on the bathroom counter, I unfold the piece of paper inside and clasp Paisley's hand in mine with my free hand. The second my eyes land on the paper and I read the title, my heart… it fucking stops. It stops because everything about this piece of poetry is *everything that we are*.

Oceans of Us

Sometimes I see you and it's as if I'm floating
into another world, with or without you.
With your ocean eyes
My flowers will never die

There's nothing more that knows me, than the daisies lying next to me
They know my song
Have seen my story
Yet all along, can never breathe in glory

And then, there was you
The only man that understood
That sometimes in life, there's much more to the heart than 'I love you too'

Sometimes it's a glance
Or a single gentle touch
Sometimes it's your voice, saying that 'you're enough'

Either way, and whatever it may be,
even forbidden shadows dance in the wind
With the waves beside us, that crash us back to shore
Just know this feeling of being entirely gripped,
like whenever I'm with you and the ocean flowers sing, stripped
Is so new and gold, that I never want it to grow old

Because in your hold, I feel things that could make flowers cry
But my love for you… I know for certain, it will never die.

All I know is whenever I'm with you,
In these fateful waters...

I'm found.
I've loved.
I'll drown.
In these Oceans of Us

I forget how to breathe.

Words fail me.

I've never read anything this powerful before in my entire life, let alone it being written for me. I'm speechless. I literally have no words because I'm so taken aback by her compassion, so grateful for her existence, in awe of her newfound confidence.

When I glance back up at Paisley with a heavy knot in my throat, I'm surprised to find she's not in front of me anymore. I became so lost in that poetic gold that I didn't even notice her hand slip from mine. I didn't notice a single thing but the intensity of my heartbeat as emotion laces every beat.

Paisley steps into the bathtub, the water lapping by her breasts and glistening her skin as she sits up against the left side. Her warm eyes meet mine... and there's something inside me that explodes, something so fragile yet gold. So warm. So insatiable.

"Come join me and tell me what you think." Paisley smiles.

I catch the kids' bubble bath bottle on the bathroom counter, and as much as I feel like laughing, it makes me want to cry because nobody has ever made me feel this special before. Nobody has gone out of their way to surprise me with words beyond all the moon and all the stars in the galaxy. Nobody has moved me this deeply, nobody but my *wildflower*.

I'm found.
I've loved.
I'll drown.
In these Oceans of Us.

As I set the paper on the vanity counter, my eyes darken as I quickly work the buttons of my dress shirt with one hand while stepping out of my shoes and socks. Once I strip out of my button-down, it falls to the tiled floor with a soft thump, all while my hands quickly work to undo my belt and slip it off alongside my slacks. Gaze never leaving hers, I find myself smirking at how Paisley crosses her arms over the edge of the bath, simply waiting for me with a sexy lip bite.

My thumbs brush against the side waistbands of my boxer briefs, and my hard cock that's straining against the soft material is aching to be freed. My heart has never raced this fast before and without a doubt it's because I know the second I step into the bathtub with Paisley, nothing will ever be the same between us… *and fuck, I'm so ready for it.*

Ready to give Paisley Reign every single part of me.

Ready to show her the type of man she makes me become.

Ready for whatever tonight will bring as long as I'm with her. Only her…

Always her…

My *wildflower*.

Chapter
TWENTY

Paisley

M Y HEAVY EYES LINGER ON MY BEAUTIFUL ITALIAN BEAST AS HE HOOKS his thumbs into the side waistbands of his black boxer briefs and teases me by holding an agonizing pause. There's just something so sexy about watching Saint—a man so masculine and alpha-like—undress in front of me. I chew on my lower lip, wondering how the hell I'm going to let go of him at the end of the summer and we haven't even fucked yet.

Saint's gaze roams across my entire body, half of it submerged in the relaxing flower bubble bath, desire pooling when those ocean eyes finally meet my honey browns. I'm so ready for this. Ready for him. Ready to let my heart flutter free.

One Californian summer.

One beautifully forbidden older man.

One flower-addicted eighteen-year-old woman.

What could go wrong?

I could fall.

I could fall deeply in love with this man. Who am I kidding? I already have.

Saint slips off his boxer briefs and my gaze darkens as his gorgeous, hard, thick cock slaps against his stomach. He's so beautiful, *so big.* Precum glistens over his velvety tip, gliding down the length of his shaft that pulses the second I rub my thighs together in the bath.

Oh. My. God.

I grin as Saint steps forward and into the free-standing oversized bathtub. The warm water that blankets my skin laps as he sits up with his back resting on the adjacent side of the tub. Saint holds his hand out and I clasp it, using it to push me forward and lay my front on top of his naked torso and between his legs. The feeling of his erection against my stomach is new and thrilling.

We're skin to skin, face to face, heartbeat against heartbeat, laced in bubbles and blossom-filled waters. A large window beside us outlooks the beautiful ocean and midnight sky. *I never want this to end.*

I'm inches from Saint's lips, loving how vibrant flower heads of all kinds float around us in the bathtub and the sweet holistic scent of them and us. Roses. Lilies. Marigolds. Geraniums. Brushing my hands up his warm torso, I wrap my arms around Saint's neck and my breasts press harder against his chest, loving how his right hand slowly glides down my spine and rests on my lower back. His left hand rests between us, his thumb softly caressing my jaw before it settles beneath my chin and tilts it up, guiding me closer to him.

"I can't begin to tell you how much those words touched me. I will never forget how much that piece of poetry means to me. To us," Saint whispers, glancing between my eyes. "Thank you, *wildflower.*"

"You don't need to thank me. It came from my heart."

Saint grins. "You have a heart of gold, baby. You know that?"

I smile, not remembering another time where I was this happy. We stay like this for what feels like forever, in our own kind of warm embrace that allows stress to fade away and hope to fill its absence. We're so calm here soaking in the bath like this. It's the perfect escape. The perfect calm. The perfect reset as I breathe in his sandalwood scent alongside the flowers and my heart feels content.

This is what it's all about.

Butterflies are still fluttering in the pit of my stomach at the piece of poetry I gifted Saint. I felt so vulnerable handing him over the '*Oceans of Us*' poetry piece, but vulnerable in the best way because now he can see exactly what I'm feeling. Every word I wrote, I meant.

Saint brushes his soft lips against mine. "Nobody has ever done something like this for me before."

"Then let me be the exception."

Saint smiles so damn beautifully, as if he's baring all his secrets within the confines of the space between us. "I think you already are."

"You *think* or *know*?" I breathe.

"*Know*. I've known for a long time but was just too scared to admit it."

"Admit what?"

"That I've drowned… that I've drowned in the oceans of us too."

Our lips collide and it's the most tender kiss I've ever experienced with Saint before. Our tongues explore each other so passionate and slow, so breathtaking and raw. This isn't a frantic lust-sick kiss. This is the type of kiss memories are made out of.

Saint's hands glide down to my hips, and he pushes me up to straddle his waist. The action has me smiling through the kiss because I'm so goddamn aroused and so desperately know what I want to happen next. With the way we both groan when his thick length slowly glides over my lower stomach and throbbing pussy, never entering, I know he wants this too.

When we pull away and our foreheads rest together, I shut my eyes and whisper, "I want you, Saint. All of you. Limitless."

"Are you sure you want this, Paisley? Are you sure it's with *me* you want to lose this part of yourself with? Lord knows I'm not strong enough to stop now, but I will if this is too much. At any point if it's too much, tell me and I will stop."

"Yes, I want this with you. I've never been more certain in my life. I trust you so much. I want you to make love to me."

Saint's stubble grazes against my cheek as he kisses my neck. "You know I don't make love."

Cupping his jaw, I open my eyes and pull him back, so we're face to face again. *That's better.* My lips part, brushing against his and hot breath escapes. "Make the exception."

Saint's eyes are hooded when he looks at me again. A tender longing laces them.

The slow, sexy smirk deepens on his lips. "Okay."

My heart squeezes as I smile back.

See, a romantic.

We kiss and a soft moan escapes my throat when he slips one hand from my waist and slowly traces down underwater to between my spread thighs. I'm so sensitive and eager for him that my hips buck forward the second he circles his thumb over my clit. The warmth of the water, his smooth skin, and the flowers I feel hitting my skin make this moment even more of an oasis from the world.

My breath begins to escape me as he continues swirling before driving three fingers into my sex, just like earlier today but much calmer. It's as if he's making love to my pussy first with his talented fingers, making love with every inch of me like this before he becomes the first man to explore me uninhibited.

Saint slowly rocks his fingers in and out of my pussy for a few minutes, our kiss deepening with every wave of losing control that ripples through me. The desire intensifies. The orgasm builds. I'm on the brink of coming undone for the third time in a few hours.

"Saint," I breathe, my lips parting from his when I know I'm close. "Oh, God."

"That's it, babydoll. Give in to it. Give in to me," Saint

murmurs. "Come for me because I want to make love to you right here while you're still falling down from heaven."

His words have me absolutely losing it. My sex tightens around his fingers and then I'm falling, falling into a world full of Saint as I whisper his name again and again as I let go with my nails raking down the back of his neck.

"Baby, you're so ready for me," Saint moans against my lips as I begin to recover. His hand wraps around the base of his hard cock, half of it submerged in the bathwater, while some of his length and his glistening head are above it, covered in precum. I so badly want to wrap my lips around it and suck him. I'm completely mesmerized as he gives himself a solid stroke up his length before brushing his thumb over the head, spreading his precum around.

Well, fuck. This is so hot.

I'm such a desperate hot mess as I continue to watch in awe as my pussy's throbs turn more intense. I feel even more turned on than a second ago and that can't be possible because I'm so wet it's unreal.

Saint's darkened eyes meet mine with a half smirk as he halts touching himself. "God, I want to feel your tongue swirl over the head of my cock so badly. Go on, I know you want to, my bad girl. Just for a little while, 'cause I'm about three seconds away from making love to you and want to feel that tongue on me first."

Mind reader.

As much as I want to bring him pleasure, this sudden panic halts me. *My inexperience.* What if I do something wrong with my mouth against his cock? What if I don't satisfy his needs?

"I want that more than anything, but as you know I've never... What if I don't do it as good as you want and—"

My words turn into a gasp when Saint possessively unwraps my right hand from around his neck and instead guides it down to grip his thick cock. His hand that covers mine squeezes down, which has me replicating the action on his length and my jaw drops in desire at the loud moan that escapes Saint, all while his piercing blue eyes never leave mine.

Fuck. He's so big and thick, so beautifully smooth, so hard like steel.

"Do you feel how hard I am, Paisley? Hmmm, do you?" Saint sexily growls. "I've never been this fucking hard in my entire life and it's all because of you. All because of how damn crazy both you and your body make me, and you think you can't *satisfy me?* That's the most ridiculous thing I've ever heard. I may be the first man who's ever seen you like this, but you're such a fucking natural it makes me want to spank you."

"Do it."

I squeal, letting out a chorus of giggles when Saint slaps my ass underwater before whispering in my lips, "Suck me, Paisley. Lick and suck me before I make this gorgeous ass of yours turn red, and trust me, I won't be making love to you after that. Instead, I'll be fucking you so damn hard you'll be screaming out my name and lose your voice as I fill you with come all fucking night. I'll fill you until you're overflowing, and our mixed orgasms are running down your thighs."

Oh YES.

"You're such a dirty boy."

Saint winks and shoots me the most boyish cheeky smirk. "You like it. I know you do."

I grin. "I do."

Saint pulls the hand over mine away. I slightly push back from him and instead of straddling his waist, scoot a little back in the bathtub so I'm in child's pose with my mouth positioned by his cock and my ass slightly in the air underwater. The water sloshes around. Our gazes lock as my tongue glides around his velvety head, loving the smoothness of it and the sexy breath that escapes Saint. "Jesus fucking Christ, Paisley. Oh fuck, yes, *yes*, keep doing that. Keep moving your pretty tongue on my cock like that. It's as if you're a fucking goddess mixed with the devil right now, sending me to both heaven and hell. Do you like it, babydoll? Do you like driving me this wild?"

"Mmhmmm."

"Me too. *Fuuuuck*. This is where good girl meets bad girl, isn't that right, babydoll?"

Smirking, I eagerly glide my hand up and down his length, like I watched him do moments before, and nod. I widen my tongue and lick up his precum, softly sucking on his sensitive head for a brief moment as I swallow his warm and slightly salty precum.

"Mmmm, so good, Saint."

"Suck me, baby. Good girl. Just like that, just like... *oh*." Saint's eyes almost roll to the back of his head in pleasure, and it makes me happy that I can give this to him. It makes me happy that although he's such a dominant man, right now he's allowing me to control him.

I need to squeeze my legs together to ease the throbbing between my thighs, but it only intensifies when I pick up a floating red rose petal and slowly let it run up and down Saint's full length, even through the bubbles and beneath the water, so the sensation deepens. Using flowers on Saint in this kind of way... I can't even describe the thrill it gives me.

It's so hot.

"Oh, fuck me," Saint groans, tipping his head back, his Adam's apple bopping up and down as he starts swearing in Italian. I giggle as I let go of the petal and his hard cock pulses in my grip. Even more precum beads and leaks down his length in such a sexy kind of way that has my mouth watering at the pure sight. Adamant to taste him before it hits the water, I lean closer and lick him all the way up to his tip that's pooling even more arousal.

He's so responsive to me.

"That's it, I need to feel you on my cock *right now*." That's all Saint can seem to take before he reels me back to him and water splashes everywhere from the sudden movement as I straddle his waist again, this time our sexes grazing even more against each other so teasingly.

I laugh, looking deep into his deep blue eyes, and bite my lip. "So eager, hmm?"

"Very." Saint smiles warmly. "Are you on the pill?"

I nod. Just under a year ago I was put on them due to menstrual irregularity issues.

Hands still on my hips, Saint's thumbs slowly caress the junction between my hips and start of my thighs. It's so relaxing and I really enjoy how slow we're easing into sex, like we have all the time in the world and Saint is making sure everything is perfect for me. *For us.*

"I'm clean, but if you'd prefer me to get a condom first, I will."

"No, I trust you. I want to feel you with no barriers in between."

"Okay." Saint pecks my lips. "Guess this will be a first for both of us. I've never not used one before."

Grinning, my eyes widen. "Really?"

"Mhmmm." He chuckles. "So don't worry, it's not just you with a first tonight."

"*Oh*, so in a way I'm one of your firsts too, Saint Lisconti?"

"That's exactly right, Paisley Reign."

Giggling, I gulp down the little jitters at the back of my throat because this is such a big moment for me. I never thought my greatest fantasies could come true with Saint, like they are tonight.

What if I completely freeze up?

What if I do or say something that ruins everything?

What if I orgasm in like five seconds, or worse, I'm too tight he can't even fit?

Saint must notice I'm getting a little frazzled because he says, "You okay, Pais?"

"Of course. I'm just… I'm just a little nervous that I'll ruin the moment, that's all."

"Hey, look at me, baby," Saint murmurs, slowly rubbing his thumb over my lower lip, and he smiles affectionately at me. "You don't need to worry about a single thing. You're not going to ruin anything. I promise. Be comfortable and confident and don't be intimidated by the fact that this is your first time. Let it come to you naturally, just like it did when you were teasing my cock with your tongue seconds ago and I almost came. I'm going to take care of you, Paisley. I'm going to take care of you so well and make sure your first time is perfect and everything you've ever hoped for. It's going to be beautiful and I'm going to be right here with you, right *here*... But if it isn't about that and you now think this isn't what you want, then that's okay too. You know I would never force or blame you. If this isn't what you truly want, we can stop and pretend nothing ever happened. Anything to make sure you feel safe and—"

I cut him off with a smile. "I always feel safe when I'm with you. This is what I want and it warms me so much how respectful and attentive you are. I trust you so much. I want this, Saint. I want *you*. I've wanted you for such a long time now, and although I know we've left a lot of questions unanswered, this feels so right. It feels so right giving it to you."

Saint breathes out a sigh of relief and rests his forehead against mine. "You want me to make love to you, Paisley?"

"More than anything in the world. Make love to me, baby."

Saint grins. "With pleasure, *wildflower*."

And then he crashes his lips on mine, easing my every worry. He lifts my hips above the water, and I press my hands against his solid chest, breaking away from the kiss as we share a smile, and he glides his hard cock to my pussy. *It feels so good. Too good.* But the second Saint begins lowering me onto him, my nails almost dig into his chest at the slight pain.

Oh shit.

"Holy shit, you're so tight, Pais."

I wince, shutting my eyes to ease the slight ache because his head is not even fully inside me. *Fuck.*

Saint stops for a moment. "Paisley, look at me."

I find his ocean blues swirling with concern. "You okay?"

"Yes, keep going."

"Relax yourself for me, babydoll. Okay?"

"Okay. Just perhaps go a little slower on me, yeah?"

Saint bites his lower lip and nods. "Noted. Sorry, I got a little carried away." His thumb softly rubs my sensitive clit and I smile, grateful it helps the pain subside as he pulls out of me and once again continues to slowly slip inside me.

My. God.

Is he... is he even going to fully fit?!

This is not the time to be shy, Paisley!

Saint gives me a slow, sexy smirk. "Don't worry, Pais, I'm going to fit."

My eyes widen. "How did you know what I was thinking?"

"Because you said it out loud."

I freeze up, my cheeks burning in embarrassment.

Oh NO.

My jaw drops, but instead of any awkwardness, laughter fills the space between us as he thrusts into me slowly and I'm filled with all of him, so deep and... oh *wow*.

This feeling is beyond... so beautiful.

Saint readjusts us slightly in the bathtub, so that although I'm straddling him, he'll also be in control in a few seconds when my life will change forever with his hands on the side of my hips and ass like that. But for now, he pauses for a second and lets me get used to the sensation of him inside me.

The laughter is contagious.

This is what I love about Saint Lisconti most. He never makes me feel like a fool.

He never makes me feel broken or manipulates our deep connection.

Instead, he makes me feel seen. *And that's all I've ever needed.*

I'm still giggling as I wrap my arms around his neck once more and the bath bubbles caress our skin, flowers floating on the warm water around our bodies and making this feel even more special. I love it.

Love how our reckless passion from earlier has melted into such deep tenderness and intimacy. Love the adoration in his eyes.

Love how ready I am to give him all of me. Love all the different versions and layers and oceans of him and me.

Saint cups my jaw, his thumbs softly brushing over my flustered cheeks as he looks at me as if there's nothing else in the world that matters.

"Don't be shy, *wildflower*," he whispers. "Don't be shy, because I'm about to turn into the Saint of Sacramento for you."

Saint

I've never felt this way in my entire life. Never felt this rush. This need. This desire to completely and utterly be in this moment with Paisley as I make love to her, our hips thrusting together in pure bliss in the midst of sex, perspiration, and water lapping around us as if we're reaching heaven.

The emotions I'm feeling right now with Paisley are beyond anything I've ever felt before. As my lips trail across the warmth of her neck and collarbone, kissing and nipping the skin there, I groan as her hot pussy squeezes around my cock. I grip her hips tighter and pump into her deeper. At this stage I can't even keep my eyes open from the building pleasure as my face falls between the junction of her neck and shoulders and I breathe in her sweet jasmine scent.

"*Oh, Saint,*" Paisley murmurs against my lips, tugging my hair as the erotic sound of our skin slapping together beneath the bathwater drives me even wilder. "This is... *wow.*"

"You're such a good girl. Such a fucking good girl."

My head tips back against the edge of the bathtub for a moment. I'm so lost in the tenderness and passion in each upward thrust, that for a second I lose it and increase my pace, my ass tensing with every moment as I slip in and out of her so quickly and frantically. I'm pounding into her like there's no tomorrow.

Paisley Reign may have been a virgin just a few minutes ago, but when I'm done with her, she'll be a goddamn sinner.

Her moans urge me on and on. Deeper and deeper. Harder and faster. Squeezing her bouncing breasts together, I play around with her hard nipples with the pad of my thumbs, loving the way Paisley leans back and it allows me to drive into her deeper. *Holy fuck, that feels so good.* My cock is pulsing like crazy inside her, knowing it's not long before I lose all control. Feeling her bare against me with no barriers only makes me want her to come right fucking now. I can't wait to feel her quivers. I can't wait to feel everything else that comes with it.

Fuck, I'm so damn close.

Paisley slides her hands through her hair and then over her mouth to muffle the sounds that escape her. The same sounds that have my cock pulsing even harder in her as I slow down my pace and my abs tense to control the growing waves of desire that only increase when she squeezes around my cock again.

"I'm so close, Saint."

"I know you are, baby. Hold on a little longer," I whisper against her lips when her arms wrap around my neck again, her gorgeous tits against my chest. "When we come, I want us to come together. At the… *Oh, fuuuuck.* I want us to come at the… Exact. Same. Moment. Okay?"

"Mmhmmm."

The pace of my thrusts slows right down to a rhythm so tender because I want to preserve this moment. I want to continue making love to her tonight, just like she asked me to and just like we both crave. I have such an urgency to take her to my bedroom, lay her on my bed and fuck her from behind so hard the bed strings snap. But there's plenty of time for soul-destroying fucking. Tonight I just want to feel her body against mine and be intimate with reminders of the people we are. I want to make love to her for all that we are. Right now all I want to do is stay wrapped around her and bring her the type of pleasure she never knew existed.

"Look at us, *wildflower*, look at how perfectly we connect."

Our gazes fall between us to how beautifully her bare pussy rides my cock while I thrust up in and out of her. I'm coated in both of our arousal and the fact that we're having sex in a bathtub filled with flowers is so fucking hot that I can feel my precum go crazy inside her.

"God," Paisley moans, mesmerized by how well we connect. "It's as if we were made for each other. You feel so good. *Oh, yes.* Just like that, baby. Just like that."

I'm making love for the first time in my life to an eighteen-year-old woman who's so goddamn young and responsive. It's so addictive. Her stamina is incredible and she's meeting my every thrust with so much ease. She's a fucking goodness destroying my cock and mind, one second at a time.

I can't believe how intimate this moment truly is between us. How we go from holding each other strongly for life, to soft caresses and lingering touches. It's so sensual between us that when Paisley grins and I grin back, there's this warmth in my chest I can barely describe. All I know is that it's there.

I kiss her neck again before looking back up at those honey-brown eyes. "You feel so good against me. So bare. So beautiful."

Paisley grins so beautifully, I take my hands off her hips and instead cup her face. My fingers crave tracing every detail of her grin. The soft smile lines that surface at the highest point of her lips... those soft plump lips... the way infectious laughter falls from them when she kisses my finger. It has me chuckling with her. My joyous soul that's already so full intensifies to a limit I never deemed possible. Full of true happiness. Passion. *Trust.*

Laughter is one of my turn-ons, and with Paisley it always comes from a place so pure and genuine.

"*Come puoi essere così bella?*" I whisper, every single part of me on fire and addicted to feeling so damn insatiable with her. "How can you be this beautiful, hmm? Tell me, baby."

"Stop it." Paisley laughs, the soft warm glow of the candles flickering across her face. "You sure know how to make a girl feel special."

"Not just any girl. Only *you*," I whisper, speeding up my thrusts a little when Paisley starts to moan uncontrollably and her body begins to quiver in my hold. Seeing Paisley like this, so close to losing control with all the flowers around us... it makes me want this more than I've ever wanted. "How are you feeling, babydoll?"

"Like I'm in heaven," she pants, pressing her cheek up against mine, and we turn to face the picture window and midnight scenic views. Dark ocean waves crash back to shore, replicating the heartbeat in my chest as I edge us closer and closer to complete bliss.

"Then let me take you there, baby girl. Let me take you to heaven."

And then I press my lips on hers and kiss Paisley with everything I have inside me. The passion intensifies as I grind my hips harder and pound into her deeper and deeper until I'm swallowing her loud moans and her entire body is trembling in my grip, on the edge of her orgasm. The second I begin to vigorously circle her clit with my thumb while I make love to her like the world depends on it, Paisley pulls away from my lips and her mouth forms a huge O.

Those darkened eyes meet mine in so much lust and pleasure, I can barely think straight through my own moans. "I can't hold on any longer, Saint. I'm going to come all over your pretty cock. Yesss. Saint... Saint... *Saint!*"

My heavy balls tighten hearing her say my name like that... with so much seduction, and I cup her face, our gazes never falling as moans fill my throat too and I fuck her harder than I ever have before. "I'm right here with you, Paisley. Right fucking here."

The bathwater and flowers splash around us like crazy and it only prompts me to thrust even deeper and my hips swiveling in half circles as I drive into her mercilessly. Paisley can't stop making all these sexy sounds that I feel right around my pulsing cock, even more so when I recklessly rub her clit and our air turns into short lust-filled breaths as we continue to make love so sensually—our firsts colliding into one first together.

Eyes locked, Paisley screams out my name and just like that her throbbing pussy clenches down around my cock and she's orgasming hard. Quivering, she comes violently and the way she gushes around me has me moaning out her name and before I know it, I'm coming apart right here with her and explode, ropes of my warm cum filling her good and long. I continue thrusting until she squeezes my cock so hard, she's milking me clean. We're both sated and lost in each other and I can't stop telling her how beautiful she is.

Fuck, that was something else.

Holding on to each other with grins, pants fill the space between us as we slowly come down from our highs. "Fuck. That was incredible, Paisley. *You're* incredible."

"Most beautiful moment of my life. I'll never forget the people we are tonight."

"Good, because I won't either, *wildflower.*"

Once we've settled down, the first thing I do is kiss Paisley slowly, showing her just how grateful I am for how intimate we've become and how much I fucking appreciate her in my life. We pull away grinning and I kiss her cheek slowly, noticing how glassy her eyes are.

"Happy tears. I'm just so glad it was you, Saint," she murmurs, glancing between my eyes. "So, so glad."

I hold on to Paisley tighter, feeling her words right to the core, and it warms my entire heart. I kiss her tears away and when I slowly pull out of her, Paisley spins around and the water sloshes. It brings me solace as she lays her back against my front and my arms protectively wrap around her waist, her own covering mine. Our gazes flicker to the ocean views outside the window and as I look out at the world, a feeling that I haven't felt in forever emerges...

Hope.

Paisley holds up my right hand and after a slight pause traces her pointer finger over my white scar. This time I don't pull away. I allow her to feel the full depths of me, without the heavy breaths or tensed-up body. I feel completely at ease with her caressing the mark of my past. Completely free to show her all of me as she brings my hand to her mouth and slowly kisses every inch of the scar.

My heart has never felt this warm. *Ever.*

"Thank you for allowing me in," Paisley whispers against my scar. "Thank you for showing me all of you. Thank you for being Saint Lisconti, the greatest man I know."

I trail my fingers over Paisley's soft skin, loving just how much this embrace speaks volumes. It fills the void of the comfortable silence between us... sensual intimacy... trust... devotion. Everything I thought I never wanted I have right here in my arms.

Paisley's changing me.

Changing me for the better.

"Anything for you, *tesoro.*" I kiss the side of her head and smile into her hair, breathing in that jasmine scent I don't see myself living without. Not now. "Anything for you."

Chapter

TWENTY-ONE

Saint

AFTER SOAKING IN THE BATHTUB FOR A LITTLE WHILE LONGER, PAISLEY and I decided to have an actual shower to wash the day away. *Not that anything needed to be washed away.* We were all smiles, hands gliding over each other's body with lathered soap and with all our strength had a legitimate shower.

I think one of the things I love most is now that we've been intimate, there's this glimmer in Paisley's eyes whenever she glances my way, and I'm sure as hell there's that same glimmer in my gaze too. It's as if we understand each other on another level. Are more connected. There's not a part of my life I don't feel comfortable sharing with Paisley Reign right now as we step back into the kitchen at 1:32 a.m.

I love that I'm scooping Neapolitan ice cream into two bowls while the rest of California is sound asleep. Okay, that was probably a long shot considering Los Angeles is 408 miles away and between Hollywood and high-end parties at multimillion-dollar residences, but I know what I meant.

It isn't lost on me that there's no time for us to make it back to Sacramento before the end of her father's hospital shift at 3:00 a.m. The fact that Paisley hasn't said anything… the fact that she wants to stay with me here in Stinson Beach—such an important place for me—means a lot to me.

Paisley's sitting on the marble kitchen island, watching on as I place the ice cream tub back in the freezer and open the cutlery drawer in search of two spoons. She's wearing nothing but her black lace panties and my faded dark gray Harley T-shirt that reaches her mid-thighs, her long legs and hard nipples that stab through the fabric stealing my attention.

God, I'd love to push those panties to the side and fuck her into tomorrow.

My karma comes when I blindly reach for the utensils and end up placing two knives into each ice cream bowl instead of spoons. *Great. Just great.* Swearing, I correct myself and grab the two spoons instead, all while my cock doesn't get the memo because I'm already semi-hard again after that breathtaking sex.

Paisley grins over at me. "Concentrate, Lisconti."

"Yeah, *concentrate.* That's easy for you to say when there's another part of me that has a mind of its own."

She looks at me genuinely confused, so I gesture down to my *very* obvious erection straining against my gray sweatpants, and her jaw drops. "Holy hell, *again?*"

I smile bashfully because this is actually so fucking irritating. All I want to do is enjoy some post-sex quiet time with Paisley, but apparently my dick has other plans. "Goddamn, I need the opposite of fucking Viagra right now."

She bursts out laughing. "Just stop thinking whatever it is you're thinking."

"Uh, kind of hard to do when you're right in front of me."

Paisley bites her lip to hide her smirk, but I still see it. She thanks me as I hand her an ice cream bowl, and I watch with a smile as she tastes the creamy strawberry, chocolate, and vanilla delight, and her eyes almost bulge out of their sockets. "This is so delicious!"

"Don't tell me you haven't had this flavor before…"

"I totally haven't. Now I know what I've been missing out on."

"Definitely been missing out. It's my favorite."

"Oh, really? Why this one?"

"Hmmm, I think I have to be a little biased because I'm half Neapolitan on my mom's side."

"Aww. That's amazing. I hope you don't mind, but I'm going to be stealing all your favorites."

"Don't mind at all. What's your favorite ice cream? Well, I mean after this one now."

Paisley's cheeks flush. "Vanilla…"

Vanilla.

I smirk. "Vanilla? Not on my watch. Nothing will be vanilla from this point forth, babydoll." I wink, and she bursts out in laughter at my innuendo. *Of course my damn cock twitches.* "Jesus Christ, not even deflecting is helping me."

"Okay, how about I recite some flowers? I'm sure that'll bore you."

"I doubt it, but sure, that could work."

"All right, let me think. Oh, *asters.* Perennial flowering plants that encompass around one hundred eighty species. Colors range from white, purple, blue, or pink. Monarch butterflies love asters and usually feast on them during the late blooms throughout their fall migration. Is this helping at all?"

I scratch the back of my head. "Not really, your knowledge of all these flowers is kind of turning me on even more."

Paisley rolls her eyes, and I don't blame her. I'm a fucking mess. "God help me."

"No, babydoll, I don't need any more helping right now."

Paisley grins, crossing her legs as she runs a hand through her damp beach waves. My eyes linger on her gorgeous long neck and the mark I left at the base of it.

God, I want to suck on her skin again so badly.

Wait… a hickey? A *hickey*!

Alaric.

ALARIC.

My erection softens in seconds. Alaric is going to fucking *kill me* if he puts two and two together. He knew I was going to be here for the weekend and that Paisley and I don't exactly what to kill each other anymore like we once used to. Yes, I've always been careful around him and have never once alluded to what's happening between Paisley and me, but… what are the chances that I'm out of town and all of a sudden, his daughter isn't home in the early hours of the morning?

Paisley's hand blindly rushes up to her neck and she smiles softly as she caresses her skin. "Stop stressing, it's fine. My father won't see a thing. I'll cover it up."

"With what? You can't exactly wear a scarf. We're in California and it's summer!" Raking a hand through my hair, I start pacing up and down the kitchen with my ice cream bowl in hand. "God, what are you going to say if your father sees and asks? We should think of something, right? *Dio.* I should have been more careful and kept in mind that he… *shit,* I fucked up, didn't I?"

Yes, Lisconti, you royally fucked up.

It should have been the first rule. Don't leave hickeys on your best friend's daughter!

Don't make it obvious.

Don't create complications on the first night.

Paisley's so damn calm as she arches a brow in amusement. "Okay, firstly… How did you go from worrying about your erection to stressing about my father possibly seeing a hickey you left on me in two-point-five seconds?"

"I don't know, but I kind of wish I were still worrying about flower knowledge turning me on."

She laughs. "Secondly, come here."

I let go of the weight draping my shoulders and stride closer to her. Setting my ice cream bowl on the kitchen island beside her thigh, where hers is also placed, I settle my body between her legs and allow this deep breath to escape me. I don't know why I'm stressing about it so much. I guess it's just because now Paisley needs to create an excuse for her father because of me. I don't want to place her in that position. I don't want to lie to Alaric more than we already need to.

"And thirdly," Paisley whispers against my lips as she cups my stubbled jaw and lifts it so I'm focused to look at her. She smiles so placid and sweet, so tranquil that for a second I forget why I'm stressing. "Stop being in your head so much. I know you, Saint, you're thinking about a thousand possible scenarios my father could conclude to when he discovers I didn't sleep the night at my house. Let those thoughts go because he isn't going to suspect a thing. When I was getting dressed after the shower, I sent him a text saying I went out with Maralyn to celebrate my graduation and spend time downtown and she didn't want me going home to an empty house, so I stayed over and would see him later on tomorrow."

"Okay, that's the best save I've ever heard in my life. Does Maralyn know?"

"Not yet, but I'll tell her first thing tomorrow when I go in for my shift, so there's nothing to worry about. I've got all bases covered."

Sighing in relief, I can't help but rest my forehead against Paisley's and shut my eyes. "Shit, I made something out of nothing, didn't I?"

"No, not at all. You were just worried and that's understandable. I just don't want these worries to come between us during the little time we have this summer, you know?"

"I know. I just don't want you to be making excuses because of me, that's all. I don't want any feathers to be ruffled between you and your father because of me. I know how important he is to you, and I could never forgive myself if... you know... this doesn't turn out right and it causes a rift between you two."

"I think you're forgetting something here..."

I open my eyes and meet her gaze. "What's that?"

Paisley grins as if I'm being clueless to it all. She kisses my forehead, her beach waves brushing against my face. "You're forgetting that all these possibilities and challenges that could come with this summer don't depend on just *you*, Saint, they depend on *us*. What I'm trying to say is, if something goes wrong or I need to make an excuse to my father or some feathers are ruffled, it isn't solely because of you, it's because of *us*. We're attracted to each other and when two people who aren't supposed to be together feel this heated passion for one another, lust is unstoppable. That's what's happening to us, so we've agreed to spend this summer together before I move to college. We made a joint decision; I want this as badly as you do. So, if there are consequences, it's because I wanted this too. The battles we'll face, we'll face them together, just like we always have."

My heart spasms because Paisley's so right. All along I've been thinking that all this weight with her father finding out would be because of me, but she couldn't have explained it more perfectly. Whatever happens, it's on us. Neither one of us is at fault, because we both want this. *And fuck, how much I want this with Paisley until the end of the summer.*

All that comes to me is to pull her close and kiss her passionately, tasting the sweetness of the ice cream on her tongue as she kisses me back with no regrets.

The second we pull away, Paisley glances at me in awe. "Hmm, what was *that* for?"

"For being you." I smile. "For always knowing what to say. For calming me down with your smile alone and being so wise. I'm sorry for freaking the fuck out."

"No need to apologize. Look, let's forget about the whole thing. Besides, this isn't something a little concealer can't fix."

The pad of my thumb brushes over her hickey, a smile on my lips when I glance up and find those honey browns filled with so much warmth. I groan, slipping my hand away, and slap her thigh.

"Come on, let's eat this Neapolitan ice cream before it melts, and I bend you over the kitchen island and fuck you instead."

"Gee, what a *gentleman*," Paisley sarcastically teases, her snicker turning into a squeal the second I pick her up from the island and carry her over my shoulder—fireman style. She slaps my bare back mid-laughter. "I'm joking, I'm joking! You really are a good guy! The greatest! Put me down!"

I laugh and set her down on her feet, not before I spank her peachy ass through the Harley T-shirt.

"What was it that you said about me being a good guy?" I tease.

Grinning, Paisley pokes out her tongue and collects her ice cream bowl, walking backward toward the large French doors that open to the patio, pool, and gate to the private access to the large stretch of Stinson Beach. "Um, I have no idea what you're talking about."

I smirk. "Oh, I see how you want to play this."

Paisley winks and nods toward the French doors. "Can we eat ice cream on the beach outside? The view is too beautiful to pass on."

The smirk vanishes on my lips, and I swallow down the forming knot in my throat. It's been thirteen years since I opened that gate that leads to the private stretch of beach. *Thirteen years.* I know Paisley notices just how tense her question has made me, but she doesn't push it. She simply stands tall by the doors, waiting for my next move.

I brought Paisley to Stinson Beach because I wanted her to see the full extent of the type of man I truly am. Beyond those backyard gates and onto the beach... that's who I *really* am, or perhaps... that's the person I left behind. Either way, I know that tonight is the night I need to let go of all the masks confining me. I need to step up. Be a man. Fucking face the reality of things. And it's exactly what I do as I roll my shoulders back and replace my motionless expression with a soft smile.

Taking a hold of the ice cream bowl in one hand, I walk up to

Paisley and clasp her hand in mine. "All right, let's go out there. It's a warm night anyway, and you're right... the views are incredible."

But Paisley can see past the front I'm putting on. She always does. That's what I like most about her. The fact that she doesn't try to be something she isn't around me, and she doesn't let me either.

Her eyes glance between mine. "Are you sure that's okay?"

I gulp down and nod.

"I don't... I don't know what happened, but I don't want to cause you any pain if you don't want to go out. We can stay in, eat, talk."

I shake my head and kiss Paisley's forehead, a smile rising on my lips. "No, let's go out there. There's no pain I feel when I'm with you, babydoll, only pleasure."

Paisley's grin is so bright as she squeezes my hand and we walk together through the French doors and across my patio. It's dark out here, with the only light being that of the stars and moon shining above. The ocean breeze that comes through my backyard is just so refreshing and calming, as the early morning warm wind wraps around my skin.

Once I unlock the gate dividing my beach house from the beach, I suck in a breath while Paisley's jaw drops at the sight of the sand that starts from my back gate. We're right on the beach—a private beach that's farther east from Stinson Beach. There's about just under a hundred yards of the sandy beach shore before the ocean. It's literally my backyard and that's one of the things that attracted me the most to this beach house.

We kick off our shoes by the gate and begin walking down the long expanse of beach barefoot, the sand warming my every step.

Paisley gasps. "This is *incredible*! I've never seen anything like this!"

"Well, it can be our hideaway for the summer. Whenever you need an escape, this can be it."

"I seriously don't even feel worthy of stepping on this sand."

"Bullshit. You're the worthiest person I know, Paisley."

She glances up at me, the stars twinkling in her eyes. "You really mean that?"

"You know I do. You're worthy of the entire world and universe too while we're at it. Never forget that. Never forget how important you are in this world of ours."

Paisley smiles, emotion written all over her face. "I won't."

I smile back. *"Brava."*

After a couple of minutes, we're closer to the beach and are sitting by the shore, eating our melted ice cream and watching as the waves crash back to shore. This was the view from the upstairs bathroom that we saw in the bathtub while we were making love and just something about that makes me so relieved. Relieved I can replace bad memories with the good.

Paisley's hair is softly blowing in the beach wind as she smiles out at the water and that has me setting my empty ice cream bowl down on the sand beside me and turning to her. "You really do love the ocean, don't you?"

"Mhmmm. When I was little, I used to think I was the Mother of the Sea." She turns to me and grins. "Crazy, right?"

"A little." I chuckle, appreciating the way our gazes never drop. "Don't worry, I was the same. The beach was always a part of me too growing up. It's why everything you wrote in that piece of poetry spoke to me so much. Because it's everything that we are."

"Everything that we are and everything I hope we continue to be… even after the summer."

I nod but don't answer as I return my eyes to the beautiful ocean. It feels like paradise when Paisley's fingers lace up my neck and into my short tousled dark hair, her nails slowly bringing me so much ease. I remember when she did this the first time we came to Stinson Beach a couple of months ago and how far we've come since then.

My heart is beating so fast, thundering like lightning because of the way Paisley touches me. I swear it can convert any devil into an angel because that's exactly what it does to me. She purifies me, purifies me until there aren't many fragments remaining of the coldhearted man I was before, only of the different man I am right now. It's because of her I'm changing into a better me. All because of Paisley. *All because of her.*

"Saint?" Paisley murmurs beside me.

"Mhmmm."

I already feel it. Feel what she's going to ask me next.

A breath.

A heartbeat.

A crash of the ocean waves... and *then...*

"Will you tell me about Lea?"

I gulp down the burning pit at the bottom of my stomach and glance at Paisley over my shoulder. Our stares extend and the way she's looking at me with such softness and grace... it's as if she's the only thing that can revive me from the guilt still rippling on my skin.

I'm quiet for a long moment before I eventually nod, knowing I owe Paisley this much. She's been so patient with me. I bet the whole mystery of Lea has been eating her up inside. She deserves to know the full story of why I've caged myself off from the world to protect my heart, body, and soul.

Paisley smiles. "Whenever you're ready. Take your time."

I nod.

Moments pass where all I feel are my own heartbeats, the sting alongside every breath and the warmth that eases it all thanks to the woman sitting next to me.

"I met Lea thirteen years ago. I was twenty-three and had just finished college. Was working restoring Harleys and other motorbikes like that. I was living at this beach house. As I said earlier at the restaurant, this place was just a home back then. Anyway..." My gaze returns to the ocean, and I continue. "We met at a café by chance... a few months later she moved in with me here at this beach house. It wasn't just her. Lea had a three-year-old daughter, Alexis. She was the cutest thing. Always carried around this giraffe toy I bought her when we went to the zoo one day. Lea told me that Alexis's father didn't want anything to do with her when she found out she was pregnant with his child, so she had been raising Alexis on her own."

"Oh, I bet you loved Alexis as if she were your own daughter."

"Yeah, I did." I smile softly. "At that stage of my life, I never thought I wanted children. Then Lea and Alexis came into my life, and everything changed. It's crazy how life works. Lea had been trying to find a job for the longest time. She really only had experience as a bartender and club DJ, but that wasn't really ideal because she had Alexis. At the start, it was perfect. It was perfect until it wasn't. From the inside looking in, we looked like the perfect little family, but on the inside, cracks started to form. Lea... she wasn't happy with the world. Depression. One night I woke up... and..."

My voice cracks on the final words and Paisley squeezes my shoulders. It feels like I'm suffocating from the inside out.

I turn to Paisley, emotion clouding her eyes so deeply. She offers me a small smile, and after a few breaths, I'm about to offer her a weak one back and continue. "Lea was clutching onto these pills in the kitchen. If I had been a minute too late... Lea fell asleep in my arms that night sobbing. I wouldn't sleep the full night for weeks after that. All I kept on thinking about was Alexis. What would happen if she grew up without a mother? What would have happened if I wasn't in the picture, and it was just Lea and Alexis living in some place and I wasn't there to stop her?"

"That must have been a lot to carry on your shoulders... all of the *what-ifs*."

"It was. Those *what-ifs* were eating me alive. The thoughts didn't stop, not even after Lea started therapy. The therapist recommended Lea find a job, so she bartended for a few nights a week, but that only lasted a little while before it all went to shit. One night, I picked her up to take her home and Lea was drunk, telling me the most absurd things while her daughter was sleeping in the back seat. She threatened to start a fire in the car if I didn't pull over and let her out. I talked her out of it and we got home safely, adamant she'd find another job, but ever since that night... I just had this bad feeling. I even stopped work for a period of time because I was scared Lea would try something while I wasn't at home and Alexis was at preschool. It wasn't a way to live. Constant paranoia... constant worrying about something that hadn't even happened but could."

"I'm so sorry, Saint. It seems as though being with Lea was... bittersweet."

"That's exactly the word... *bittersweet*. Falling in love with Lea was the easy part. It was all that happened next that made me realize that the heart is more fragile than I thought... It was that constant feeling of fear, of something going wrong at any minute and I wouldn't be able to stop it... that I would be too late... that I would carry this guilt for the rest of my life. It was a feeling that I wouldn't have wished upon my worst enemy. A feeling so cruel and tragic."

Silence falls between us for a moment.

"What happened next?" her soft voice asks.

Swallowing down thickly, I take Paisley's hand in mine and hold our clasped fingers to my rapidly beating heart, ready to give her every single piece of me.

"Then..." I whisper, my voice breaking at the words that follow. "Then that feeling became reality..."

Chapter
TWENTY-TWO

Saint
Thirteen Years Prior

L EA FOUND ANOTHER JOB. A BARISTA AT THE SAME LITTLE CAFÉ WHERE we met. Call it fate, but the café was looking for a casual role Monday through to Friday from 9:00 a.m. to 1:00 p.m. and it fit Lea's schedule perfectly with Alexis at preschool. What I love most about it is that once I return from work at the motorbike garage, I return home to both Lea and Alexis, and it makes my day.

During the past eleven months since Lea and I met, there has been so much purpose in my life. But with that purpose comes the bittersweet aftertaste of all the *what-ifs*. Even though Lea has been seeing a therapist and is slowly progressing, it's as if there's this cloud of doubt over me that's destined to pull me under every time I close my eyes…

Lea.
The pills.
Alexis.

My mind is swirling in an endless pit of unease. All night. All day. Every breath.

Calm down, Lisconti. It's going to be okay.

My lips pull into a smile as I slow by the French doors and see Lea swimming laps in the pool. Her long blonde hair is slicked in a high bun, and she has a white one-piece bikini on. The same one she bought earlier on this week, despite it being December and the usual sultry, warm sunshine by the house is replaced with a cooler, ocean breeze. But that doesn't stop Lea. She swims all through the year whenever she feels like it. Summer. Winter. It makes no difference to her.

I'm here by the French doors for a solid five minutes, watching in awe at Lea's swift agility underwater. Her strong strokes. Her diehard passion.

Meravigliosa.

It brings me so much happiness to see her like this—content. It's been months of uncertainty, and seeing Lea being her best self makes me so proud.

Keeping my eyes on Lea, I reach into my leather jacket pocket and pull out the little red velvet box that will not only seal our fate, but everything Lea and I represent. I bought this diamond ring this morning when it caught my eye in a storefront as I was heading to work, and it's easily been the happiest and most nervous purchase I've ever made.

I know we've only been together for just under twelve months. I know Lea hasn't even met my family yet. I know I'm only twenty-three, but I'm ready. Ready to solidify this life adventure with her.

My gaze lowers to the velvet box and I flip it open, my heart swelling at the sparkling diamond ring as it catches a glimmer of the shining sun, despite some pockets of cloud in the sky. *I can't wait to propose.* The thrill of it all has me flickering my gaze to Lea as I shut the ring box. She's still swimming, so I decide not to disrupt her and step back inside the house.

The weight in my heart intensifies with every step away

from her. Shutting the French doors behind me, I place the ring box back inside my pocket.

Calm down, Lisconti.

When the time comes, she'll say yes. We love each other. Marriage is the next step.

I've been thinking about it for a long while. I know with Lea having Alexis, it isn't so easy to jump into a life that ensures Alexis is happy too. I never want to be that wedge in the way between Lea and Alexis, which is why I'm so fortunate it isn't the case for us. It brings me so much happiness that Alexis loves me so much and is comfortable around me.

Alexis has this thing where every day after preschool she begs her mom to play dolls with her. Often after work, I either find Lea playing with her up in Alexis's room, or swimming. When it's the latter, I always play dolls with Alexis instead, partly because she begs me and gives me those cute little puppy eyes and pouting lip that I can't say no to. Today is no exception.

Alexis is where she normally is in her bedroom upstairs today, cutely sitting cross-legged on the hardwood floors and playing with her dolls, some of which are Disney princesses. I love that her favorite toy giraffe is also in the mix. She's been obsessed with dolls ever since I bought her a little collection and dollhouse mansion that was so lifelike and straight up *huge*.

I was supposed to hold off until Christmas to gift it to Alexis, but I literally had no resistance and ended up giving it to her as an early Christmas gift four months ago. Now, she spends every single day playing here, and while it has Lea rolling her eyes and she says I spoil her too much, there's so much warmth in my chest for my cute little girl and I'd give her the entire world if she asked me to. I love Alexis as if she's my own daughter. I always will. I provide for both Lea and Alexis, so if I want to spoil them, I will, because they deserve all the love in the world.

During the summer that just passed, Alexis entered a pink phase, so I painted the entire room a dusty pink and installed a new rosy ceiling fixture to make her happy. Her cute little puppy eyes even made me buy a pink canopy above her bed to make her feel extra special, just like the beautiful princess she is.

Alexis's big brown eyes look up at me and a huge grin works up her lips. "Santo!" she beams, her entire face brightening. Standing, she practically throws her dolls to the side and bolts toward me. "Yay! I missed you, Santo!"

"I missed you too, *tesoro!*" Outstretching my arms, I pick her up and spin us around in circles, loving the way her giggles off-set my own chuckles. "How was preschool today?"

"I like my dolls better!"

"I bet you do, sweetheart."

As I put Alexis down, her eyes fall on the ring box in my leather jacket. Alexis is three and at this age, she has a million questions and needs to know every little thing. It's what I love most about her. Her curiosity.

"What's that, Santo?"

My heart is beating so damn fast as I fall to my knees and nervously smile at her. We're eye to eye, leveled, and all that's going through my mind is how much I need to get Alexis's blessing to marry her mommy. I may not be a fucking tradition-alist, but when it comes to this, it's only right seeing as Lea isn't in contact with any of her family at all, so Alexis is all that matters right now.

I slowly reach into my jacket pocket and wrap my hand around the box but don't pull it out yet. "There's something I need to show you, Lexi. But... you have to promise me you won't tell Mommy anything about it."

"Ooo, is it a secret?" Alexis asks, but it comes out more like *sea-ket.*

"You mean a *secret*, sweetheart." I smile, clasping her hands with my free hand. "Yes, it's a surprise for Mommy. You know I love you and your mommy so very much. You both came into my life and taught me the meaning of living with purpose. Gave me opportunities. Strengths. I can't imagine my life without you two in it—"

"Or pink!" Alexis cutely adds with a bright grin, her eyes becoming long slits with how hard she shut them. "I LOVE PINK! PINKKK!"

"Yes, Lexi. I certainly can't imagine my life without pink in it too!" I laugh, so much happiness in my heart. "Anyway, what I really want to say is although I'm not your real daddy and never want to take his place, you know we're the greatest friends and I love you very much. I'll always be here for you, Lexi. I'm not going anywhere. Just like I have up until this point, you know I will always protect you and keep you safe. I will always be here for you. I will always love you, sweet pea, no matter the cost. Your mommy makes me feel so special. She's pretty and kind and a little crazy like me, but don't tell her I said that."

Alexis bursts into a fit of giggles. "Funny, Santo!"

"Yes, funny, beautiful girl. But I need to know you understand what I just said. I need to know you know I love you so very much, not because I have to, but because I truly feel it from the warmth of my heart. You bring me so much happiness, Alexis. So much joy and grace and laughter."

"What's grace?"

"Somebody who is a good person... kind and nice."

"Yeah, that's me!"

I chuckle. "It sure is. You bring me so much of that, Alexis, so much happiness and so I wanted to ask you a very important question. You don't have to give me an answer right now. We can talk about it more or you can ask me any question you'd like. But I'd really love to ask you this..."

"Ask! Ask! Ask!"

Smiling, I pull out the velvet box and open it, revealing to her Lea's sparkly engagement ring. Gasping, Alexis's eyes go all wide in pure awe. "So pretty!"

"You like it?"

Alexis grins and rapidly nods her head. "Yes!" Her big brown eyes then lift to mine, so much happiness and glee in them as she whispers, "Marry Mommy?"

Warmth laces my heart.

I nod. "Yes, Lexi. I would love to marry your mommy and would like to get your permission to do so. Do you want me and Mommy to get married and then we can live happily ever after?"

Alexis squeals in happiness and starts jumping up and down. "Yes! Yes! Marry Mommy! I wanna daddy! I wanna daddy! Mommy gonna look like a princess!"

My throat closes up at the words that escape her because they come from a place of true rawness and joy.

I wanna daddy.

It breaks my heart because Alexis doesn't deserve her deadbeat father that she never sees. She deserves so much more than that. And although I don't want her calling me 'dad' because it isn't right, it makes me happy that Alexis sees me as something close to that. It has me honored.

"You want me to marry your mommy and be with you and her forever and ever?"

"YESSSSSSS!"

"And you promise to keep it a secret between us because I'm going to surprise Mommy with it next week."

Retaining her cheeky smile, Alexis is quiet for a moment before she leans in closer to me and whispers, "I won't tell if you buy me a puppy."

"Ah." I smirk, in awe of her ways of persuasion. "I see what this is. You really want a puppy, don't you, sweetheart?"

She nods like there's no tomorrow.

"Okay, I'll buy you a puppy, sweetheart, but first you have to promise to keep this secret safe. Mommy can't know about this ring, or that I'm going to ask her to marry me, okay?"

"Okay!" Alexis starts dancing on the spot. "I'm going to get a puppy! I'm going to get a puppy!"

I hold out my pinkie finger. "Pinky promise?"

Alexis curls her pinkie with mine. "Pinky promise, Santo!"

I smile warmly and kiss our intertwined pinkies before

364 | VANESSA LUISA

pulling away and bringing her into a tight embrace filled with warmth, hope, and dreams. Alexis's arms wrap around my neck so damn cutely as she presses her lips to my ear. "You're going to be the best prince and Mommy the best princess."

"And how about you?"

Alexis puts her hands in the air and does jazz hands. "I'm the pumpkin!"

I throw my head back in laughter and Alexis does the same, her fit of giggles making me hold her even closer to me, never wanting to let go of her adoration.

"You're much more special than that, *bella*."

"Okay." Alexis's big grin is on display as we pull away. Her cute little hands cup my face, her fingers continuously poking my stubbled jaw as those warm doe eyes lift to mine. "Then I'm Cinderella's glass slipper because I want all my shoes to sparkle like that!"

I don't think I've laughed this hard in my life. Alexis brings so much happiness, so much compassion, so much brightness into my world that if you asked me a year ago, I would never believe it felt so good. I'm not Alexis's biological father, but being with her brought so much love to my world that it's almost as if she were mine. That's exactly how I feel as she takes my big hand in her little one and guides me to the floor to play dolls with her. We play, laugh, and talk for what feels like hours, when in reality it can't be more than ten minutes.

I swear I could spend my entire life doing this. Being the father she never had because that's how much Alexis Goldberg means to me. She means everything. And it isn't because loving Lea means I'm forced to love Alexis. No, it could never be that. The love I have for her daughter is built from a substance so pure and special, it makes me crave marrying Lea even more and expanding our family.

I've never had the desire to have a family more than I do right now. Protecting them. Empowering them. Loving them until my very last breath.

It's all I want.

All I dream.

All I need.

"Can I have an apple, Santo?" Alexis asks just as our dolls sit down on the couch to watch a movie from a non-existent TV, seeing as she's somehow lost that piece.

I nod, also keeping a mental note to buy her another little toy TV because we definitely don't want Katie and Destiny to be staring at the wall like that. *God, you can totally tell I'm the type of guy that drives a Harley, right?*

Standing to my full height, I stretch and smile over at her. "You want the peel off as usual?"

"Mmhmmm. Can I also have some of that ice cream I like?"

I know exactly what she's talking about—Neapolitan ice cream. Alexis loves all the good shit, just like me.

"But it's winter, baby."

"I know, but I LOVE ice cream!"

"Perhaps after dinner, if you finish all of your vegetables and Mommy says yes, okay?"

Alexis rolls her eyes dramatically and huffs. "Okayyy."

I chuckle because that would totally be my reaction too as a kid. "Let me see those pearly whites. Come on, Lexi."

Alexis flashes me a grin, a little giggle escaping her, and it's all I need to know she's just pretend pissed off at me. We fist pump and then I step out of her bedroom and hurry down the stairs. Red apples are both Lea and Alexis's favorite fruit, so I manage to stockpile the juicy sweet fruit for them.

Once I'm in the kitchen, my heart skips a beat at the sight of Lea stepping back inside the house through the French doors. She has a white towel wrapped around her body and her wet blonde hair remains up in that slick high bun.

Lea winks over at me as I'm peeling the skin of the red apple with a knife and I smile back.

"Somebody's happy this afternoon," she purrs, rounding the kitchen island, and pressing a kiss to my cheek.

"Mmhmm. I came outside and saw you swimming laps. Thought it would be best if I left you to it and not scare the shit out of you. Worked out well as I played some dolls with Lexi instead."

"That apple for her?"

I nod.

Lea rolls her eyes, a frown on her lips.

Huh?

My brows knit. "What's wrong?"

"Nothing. It's just that Alexis shouldn't get used to asking for so many things."

"It's just an apple, Lea."

Lea crosses her arms over her chest, narrowing her eyes with a frown as if I just sinned. "Today an apple, tomorrow a Ferrari. She's asking too much of you because she knows you're the loophole. I say no to something, and you give it to her anyway."

Sighing, I set down the knife and turn so I fully face Lea. I can't help but notice the usual spark in her light green eyes has lost its touch, and it feels like I'm looking into a galaxy of uncertainly inside. It has me arching a conserved brow. "Wait, is this about the dollhouse?"

Lea never wanted me to get it. Thought I was wasting my money on something too expensive that Alexis would grow out of. But she's a three-year-old kid and deserves some elation. It's every little girl's dream to own a fancy dollhouse, and I wanted to give that to Alexis not because I could, but because I *wanted* to. Because I know it would *mean* something to her.

"I never said it was about the dollhouse."

"That's true, but you're alluding to it—"

"Okay," Lea huffs, cutting me off with a slight hiss. "It's about the dollhouse."

I groan, rubbing my hands over my face. "Lea, I wanted to give Alexis something I know she loved. Please let's not keep talking about this, because I'm not going back to that conversation. It's done now. Let Alexis be happy."

"You see, that's exactly it, *'Let Alexis be happy'*. Why don't you go and buy her the whole fucking world, Santo? Buy her every damn thing just because you went to Stanford and have a stable job, this gorgeous house and a good amount of money to your name, while all I have is a few clothes and cheap thrills to mine."

Gulping down, I shake my head and let out a sigh. My heart stings from this type of tension between us because I hate it when we're like this. I hate when we concentrate too much on particular topics and let them eat away at us.

I smile softly and attempt to thread my fingers through hers, but she slaps my hand away with glassy eyes. "Don't touch me, Santo."

What the hell?

Frowning, I step closer until she's inches away and finally her eyes land on mine. "Lea, don't do this," I murmur, swallowing down thickly. "Please don't start going on about the money. You know it's not an issue for me. We're practically a family now and it makes me happy that I can spend a little on our happiness too."

"Well, it's humiliating for me."

"Why?"

Lea shuts her eyes and it's as if her entire body depletes as she turns away from me and puts her head in her hands. I haven't seen her like this for a few months and it pains me to see her so vulnerable and broken, especially after everything we've been through. I don't know why she's feeling this way. Why she's choosing to pick a fight that doesn't need to be reopened.

"Baby," I whisper, going to wrap my arms around Lea's waist from behind when she slightly nudges me out of the way with her elbow.

"I said don't touch me, Santo."

"Lea, please. What's going on? Why are you feeling this way? Did something happen at work?"

"No, Santo. Just stop talking."

"I want to know if something happened, Lea. Did some fucker hurt you?"

"No, I'm okay."

"You don't look okay—"

"Fine. I missed a few therapy sessions and am not feeling like myself again. Is that good enough for you? Huh? Or will you just not understand because I need to *grow the fuck up* like you once told me, huh?"

My heart sinks. "Lea, why would you do that? You know we can talk about this. I'm always here to talk. You don't have to push me away or mock me like that based on a heated conversation when you were drunk. I would never shame you for skipping therapy, you know that. Your health means so much to me and I understand it more than anybody else in this worl—"

"Shut the fuck up, Santo!" Lea growls, her voice so tense before she shakes in a fit of tears. "All you do is make it worse."

What?

My mouth parts and for a second no words escape. I pull my hands back, right into the back of my jeans pockets and simply wait for her to make the next move. I don't want to push her, but I also have this urgency to get to the bottom of this. This isn't like Lea, isn't like her to swat away my touch, talk to me like this, and not want anything to do with me.

It's as if her personality changed in two-point-five seconds and I have no idea as to why. It hurts. Burns. Aches because my forever girl is standing right in front of me and I have that diamond ring in my leather jacket pocket, destined to seal our fate. But that's the thing about fate. It can never be too certain.

I can't take seeing Lea like this anymore and reach up my hand, my warm fingers tracing the skin of her cold back in a bid to calm her down, but it only seems to agitate her more. "I said don't touch me. What don't you understand about that?"

Fuck.

I instantly retract my hands behind my back. "I'm sorry," I say without hesitation and clench my jaw twice. "I just want to make sure you're okay, that's all. I'm just concerned with how you were okay a minute ago and now you're—"

"I'm okay," Lea snaps before my words are even out. She doesn't sound one bit okay.

We stay in silence like this for what feels like forever, but I'm a respectful kind of guy and listen to what Lea said. I don't touch her. I don't say a word. I don't do anything to jeopardize the likelihood of her opening up to me when she's ready. I simply wait for her to be ready.

Wordlessly, I finish peeling Alexis's apple and bring it up to her with a napkin and a little plate. She thanks me with bright eyes and asks me to continue playing with her, but I tell her I'm in the middle of a conversation with Mommy, but as soon as it's finished, I'll join her. That seems to content her and I slowly walk downstairs, sucking in a deep breath when I see Lea in the exact same position as before.

Her eyes are shut as it's as if she's thinking of something that's destroying her from somewhere deep inside with her face scrunched up like that.

"I saw you looking at it," Lea whispers lowly in the silence.

I halt by the oversized kitchen island on the opposite side of her. *I saw you looking at it.* My brows furrow deeper. My mind spirals, trying to figure out what she means.

"You saw me looking at what?"

"Earlier I looked up while I was swimming a lap. You didn't see me. I saw you looking into something small, like a box."

My heart drops. "Oh, fuck."

It wasn't supposed to happen this way. Lea wasn't supposed to find out like this. I wanted to be all romantic and all smiles. Not this. Not this dead silence in the heart of my home.

Lea turns to me, tears rolling down her cheeks. "What was it?"

Without hesitation, I ignore the heavy beating in my chest and blindly pull out the ring box and set it on the kitchen island. Slowly, Lea comes around the other side, her eyes never leaving the red velvet box. She sniffles away a few tears as she picks it up. I've never felt this nervous in my life because while before I was certain marriage was what we both wanted, now I'm not so sure.

Lea flips open the box, and a gasp escapes her lips.

"Why?" she whispers, her breath so low. "Why would you do this?"

"Because I love you, Lea. I love you and I so desperately want to call you my wife. Of course I wanted this to go differently. I wanted to make this moment romantic, would have gotten down on one knee, made Alexis involved in some way... but in essence, I know we've been through hell and back. I know this life isn't easy, but there isn't anybody else I would rather live it with than with you right here by my side..."

Lea studies the huge diamond ring and a part of me breaks when she slaps it shut and turns to me with eyes raged in fury. "I can't. No, I can't marry you, Santo. Not like this..."

My entire world stops and my heart shatters into billions of little, tiny pieces.

It feels like I can't fucking breathe. Can't think. Can't breathe.

I can't marry you, Santo.

"Lea, I..."

"How could you think this was a good idea? We aren't ready for this, Santo. We've barely known each other a year and Alexis is way too young to even think about a stepfather. This is just too much."

"I don't understand. I thought you wanted this," I mumble, stepping closer to her, not feeling the slightest bit better when she allows me to cup her jaw and gaze into those glassy eyes. "I thought you wanted this too. If this is about Alexis, then I get it, but I'm not going to fuck off like her father did. I would never do that to you both. I told you from the very first day that I respect that I'm not her father and that it'll never be like that between us, but I love Alexis so fucking much. I feel like... it's more than just Alexis. Fuck, Lea, you told me you wanted to start a family with me one day. Was it all just a lie?"

Lea gulps down and avoids my eyes as she sets the ring box on the kitchen island and shakes her head. "I can't do this, Santo."

"Do what?"

"Tell you how I really feel when you're looking at me like that."

"How am I looking at you?"

"Like I'm breaking your heart."

Because you are.

Swallowing thickly, I slap a hand over my chest as a vein pinches. Fuck, it feels like somebody's killing me from the inside out, like there's this toxin running across my whole body, and I don't know how to stop it. I feel like a fool. Such a fucking fool for reading this all wrong.

Lea doesn't want me.

Perhaps she never did. Perhaps this was all a game. A wicked fucking game.

My clenched jaw tightens. "Was this all just a lie, Lea? Shit, do you even love me?"

Lea's deafening silence is enough to confirm everything I've ever been afraid of, and it kills me that I didn't see this sooner. Didn't see the cracks in the way. I knew we were shifting, knew there were parts of our relationship that were trembling away and ripping at the seams, but these cracks... I never felt them before. Never felt so used and betrayed in my entire life.

"I love you with everything I fucking have, Lea, *everything.* There isn't a piece of me that isn't in love with you. We live together. You trust me with your daughter. We're in a damn relationship, and now this is all a freaking game to you? I don't understand. I don't understand the reasons behind it."

Lea's light green eyes soften at my words, and she shakes her head, her towel slipping and landing between our feet in a thud when she steps forward. "It isn't a game, Santo... believe me."

"That's not what you said a minute ago."

"Because I wasn't expecting it to actually be an engagement ring!" Lea says, all matter-of-fact. "Look, Santo, you're young. So young. At twenty-three, your life is just beginning. You should be living it, enjoying every second of it, not tied down to a wife and a child already, especially a child that isn't even yours."

Seriously? That sets me off.

"My age has nothing to do with this. Lea, you're only a few years older. That's nothing. Marriage doesn't equal being tied down, it equals unconditional love, passion, devotion. Understanding each other more than anybody else in the entire world. Having priorities, and you and Alexis are my priorities. I thought you of all people would know that."

"Alexis is *my* priority, she isn't *yours*. You don't owe her anything."

"Yes, I do, I fucking love that kid, Lea. You know that. Don't make this something it isn't. If you don't want to be with me, if you don't love me, then I'll accept it and as much as it pains me, we can go our separate ways. But if you're only saying this to try and change my mind, then stop. Don't put words in my mouth, especially when it comes to Alexis."

"You literally just finished college. You don't know what you want from your life."

"I think I fucking know what I want more than you," I growl. "I proposed. I'm ready to start my life. I may be young, yes, but I was built on resilience and passion. I come from a proud Italian family. I know how to love the fuck out of some-body... and that's exactly what I wanted to continue to do for-ever with you, Lea. I wanted to love the fuck out of you until I couldn't breathe no more and—"

"I met somebody."

Silence.

My mouth drops and it feels as though the air is being punctured from my lungs. *"What?"*

Lea's entire face crumbles as she shakes her head and covers her face. "I never meant to hurt you, Santo. I never meant for this to happen," she breathes, heavy emotions in her words for the first time this evening.

"Who?"

"Santo, I—"

"Who is he, Lea?"

"I wasn't going to tell you, but… Michael contacted me a couple of months ago."

"Alexis's father?"

Lea nods, bringing her hands away from her face to reveal just how broken she is. I want nothing more than to wrap her in my arms and kiss her and tell her everything is going to be okay, but not after tonight. Not after everything that's unfolding. Not now when there's a chance that she… *fuck.*

This doesn't feel real. Nothing feels real.

Taking a seat on one of the barstools, it takes everything within me not to just explode. Instead, I stay quiet, rubbing a hand over my mouth and stubble as I glance over at her with a look of complete heartache.

She cheated…?

Lea shakes her head to herself and begins to tremble as she picks up the towel from the hardwood floors and rewraps it around herself. The second her light eyes meet mine, she pierces her lips together and it's as if she's forcing herself to breathe. Like she'll miss a breath if she doesn't concentrate.

"Santo, please say something. I know I'm a mess and all over the place, I know, I just…" She squeezes her eyes shut. "I just want you to know that I never meant to hurt you like this."

My jaw tenses. "What happened?"

"Michael kept calling and eventually I agreed to meet with him. I knew you would have been cautious about it, so I decided not to tell you. He told me his mother passed. She and I

374 | VANESSA LUISA

used to get along, so it meant a lot to me that he let me know. I didn't go into the meeting with any other intentions. You have to believe me on that, Santo. Michael felt bad about how we left everything and I... I summoned the strength to forgive him. He said he regretted pushing me away when I needed him the most and it was so genuine... it reminded me of when he and I were together, before the bullshit. I told him I was with somebody, *you*. He made a point about wanting to see Alexis and I said we should take things slow with how we approach the matter. Alexis doesn't even remember him. Then... then remember when you went to Florida with your parents last month for two weeks and I had just gotten the job at the café, so I couldn't come, but you took Alexis?"

"Yes, I remember."

"Well... Michael asked me out to dinner and..."

I gulp down, my heart already palpitating at where this is going. "And?"

"Santo, I—"

"Continue. The. Story."

"I said yes." Letting out a breath, Lea slides onto the barstool beside me and lowers her gaze to her hands. "I went out with him. I continued to do so almost every night you and Alexis were away, and I realized the spark I had with him... came back. I've never felt that way before, not even with you. I... I cheated, Santo. We were intimate. Every time we met except for the first time. Things just got wild, and we weren't careful and... it... it just happened."

Dio.

She cheated.

I can't fucking breathe.

"What *just happened?*"

Lea's eyes meet mine and all I see is guilt.

"I'm pregnant." Her voice breaks on the final words. "Five weeks. It's... Michael's. The timeline just adds up with him, and besides, it's virtually impossible it's yours since we always use protection, but with Michael... I... I just got carried away."

"Jesus Christ, Lea..." My eyes shift to her flat stomach covered by the towel and swimsuit. "You're pregnant?"

Moments of silence pass.

"Yes. Santo, I'm so sorry. I should have confronted you when you came back from the trip, but I didn't have the strength." She takes a breath. "I can't marry you because it's not fair for you to live with the repercussions of my actions. I continued to stay here because... because I don't know why. Some hope that my guilt would wash away and things would get better, I guess..."

"I'll tell you why you continued to stay here," I hiss, feeling heat rise up my neck and face. A vein pulses in my forehead and I completely lose control. All I see is fucking red, because I'm breaking at the seams. "Because it's *convenient* for you. If I never proposed, I bet you would have manipulated me into believing that somehow luck was on our side and the baby was mine. Well, guess what, I finally get it, Lea. I finally get what you do. You use people for what you want until you get bored and move on to the next best thing. You play fucking mind games, make me feel sorry for you, make me have empathy, then you stab me in the back and cheat on me. I've never felt this fucking disgusted in my entire life."

Lea can't stop shaking her head. "No, no, that's not it at all—"

"No, that's exactly what you do. I fell in love with you, only for you to burn the world to my feet," I growl, standing up from the barstool. "You see this?" I grip the ring box and wave it around before angrily throwing it across the fucking kitchen and it slams into the stovetop with a loud bang. "That's how I fucking feel—useless and used."

"Santo, please stop. Let's just talk about it."

"There's nothing left to talk about, Lea. You said it all perfectly. I cannot believe you would deceive me like this. I never in a million years thought we'd end like this. I would have gone to the end of the freaking world for you, Lea. The end of the world… but apparently that isn't good enough for you. Have Michael. Have him. You know who I feel sorry for in this whole story? That little girl upstairs. Alexis. Because she doesn't deserve the fucked up life you're giving her by using people to get where you need before letting go."

"I don't want to let you go, Santo."

"Why? Because it felt good when you were playing me, huh?" I scoff. "You already made your choice, Lea. You made your choice the second you said 'yes' to that piece of shit and went behind my back. Congratulations. *Congratulations*, Alexis is finally going to get what she always wanted, to be a big sister… and this time it's happiness I didn't buy her. It's happiness you created in sacrifice of our relationship. Or should I say, lack thereof now…" I kick the barstool back under the kitchen island. The metallic scraping against the hardwood floors echoes in my mind, alongside the throbbing pain inside me. "I'm leaving. I need a breather."

"No, Santo!" Lea pleads, reaching out to grip my bicep when I attempt to walk away. "Please, I don't want it to end like this. Let's talk this out rationally."

"There's nothing to talk about. We're over, Lea. Don't know if you heard yourself straight, but I just learned that my partner had an affair with her ex-boyfriend and is now pregnant with his child. The same man who neglected her for over three years with another child. So, excuse me if I need some time to catch my fucking breath."

I can't believe this. *Can't fucking believe this.* Slipping out of her grip, I grab my wallet and phone from the counter and put them in my pockets.

Lea's eyes narrow. "You walk out of that door, and I will never let you in again!"

"It's *my* damn house, Lea."

"I'll burn it down to the ground!"

"God." I chuckle coldly, shaking my head to myself. "You

really need to check yourself out. One day you're going to look around and realize this is life, not some sick game you are playing."

"You did this to me, Santo. You made me this way. You're the devil that burned me. It could have been perfect, and you had to fuck it up with a ring."

"Are you *serious*?" I turn to her and take three strides until I'm right in front of her. She glances up at me all intimately and I scoff, shaking my head once again as I gaze between her eyes. Apart from all the anger, there's sadness that settles in my chest, sadness of what we could have been, and I feel it right this second. "The only person who ruined us is you, Lea," I whisper genuinely. "I don't say that to victim blame. I'm saying it because it's the truth. I hope you find what you want with Michael. I hope you're happy. I hope he can give you everything I apparently can't. I wish your baby boy or girl a beautiful life. I wish you the best in life too, Lea, but I can't be a part of it anymore. Not like this. Not when love is a one-sided feeling."

Tears roll down Lea's cheeks and she opens her mouth to speak, but nothing comes out. She's crumbling right here in front of me, and I can't do a single thing to help her.

I thought about saving her. I used to think love equals helping the person you love out of the burning flames. Now I know there's only so much you can do before you're bound to get burned too. It's up to that person to not enter the Devil's doors in the first place. Because once you're in, there's no coming out.

"I'm sorry, Santo," she cries.

"I want you out of this house by the end of this weekend. I'll stay at a hotel until then. Don't even think of calling. I won't answer." I gulp down and lean forward, letting my anger subside for a second because there's a part of me that wants her to know I've done all I can to save us. Now it's time to let go. Letting go of a heavy breath, I press a soft kiss to her wet cheek and whisper, "Please tell Alexis I love her, and that I'll never forget her.

Take the dollhouse. I want her to remember the Christmas that never came for us."

The prospect of never seeing Alexis again kills me. But I think it'll be worse if I need to say goodbye. I wouldn't know what to say, how to react. It's better this way. It's better this way if I just walk away now and when I return, there's nothing left of them.

Sucking in another brave face, I have to ignore the burning sensation across my chest and knot at the back of my throat as I turn my back and walk away from her. I don't think I'll ever forget the fear in Lea's eyes, one of complete and utter destruction. It saddens me that this is how I'll remember her... how I'll remember *us*.

I'm at the front door, my fingers clasping the handle, when scurried footsteps rush behind me. I turn around at the last minute to see Lea standing before me in just her one-piece swimsuit, all frazzled and in tears... and then I see it, the sharp shiny blade that catches the light of my eye. It's the same knife I used to cut Alexis's apple. The same one I never got to wash and put away in time.

Oh fuck.

"If you leave, it'll all be your fault!" Lea sobs, softly lowering the tip of the knife to her chest, which frantically rises up and down. "If you leave, I'll do something you'll never forget. I'll make you remember me for the rest of your life. I'll make you suffer, Santo. I'll make you hate me even more for haunting you from another world while you're still in this one."

My breaths slow. *Oh, God.*

No. No. No.

"Whoa, whoa, Lea. Put the knife down," I plead, raising my hands up in defense. "You're not thinking this straight. Please, put the knife down."

"I'll make your life a living hell, Santo. One you'll never believe existed, believe me."

"Lea, put the knife down. Think of Alexis and—"

"She's not going to save me," Lea hisses, her grip on the knife's handle tighter. "Don't you get it, Santo? Nobody in this entire world can save me but you. Please forgive me, Santo."

"I can't."

"Forgive me, *please*."

I launch forward toward the knife, desperate to throw it out of Lea's grip, but instead she's one step ahead and turns the knife toward me and it all happens too fast. Lea stabs the sharp blade into my right hand, puncturing the skin deep and my breath staggers.

Holy shit.

A groan escapes my lips at the instant sharp pain and throb as Lea pulls out the knife and warm blood gushes out, hindering my ability to even think. The stinging agony is nothing compared to the hysterical look on Lea's face as I glance at her, my mouth parted through the grunts as I press my bleeding hand against my jacket to compress it.

"Fuck," I hiss, panicking when I go to move my fingers on my right hand and I'm numb to the sensation. I can't feel a single thing. "Oh, fuck! Lea! Lea, please put the knife down! LEA!"

The cling of metal taunts me as the knife crashes down on the floor. Lea's eyes stay parallel to my bleeding hand, devilishly darkening in appearance when I take a step back, hitting my back against the wall. It feels like a full minute passes of our soft pants and deadly stare. It's only when she sucks in a deep breath and her face crumbles to pure distress that she parts her lips and says, "You want to leave, Santo? Go!"

"Lea—"

"GO! LEAVE ME ALONE!"

Swallowing thickly, I wince at the pain in my hand and glance at her pained light eyes before stepping out the door and slamming it shut behind me. I can't let go of my clenched jaw or my heavy heart as the cool California air tickles my spine, shaking me to the core. My entire body is pressed against the door, waiting for the unknown, because I don't have it in me to move.

I know I was the one who said I was leaving. I know I need to go to the ER. *But my heart's not in it.*

Shutting my eyes, I grit against the agony in my hand as I slowly count to fifty and return to normal breaths.

Everything's going to be okay, Lisconti.

Everything's going to be okay.

Okay.

Okay.

Oka—*BANG! BANG! BANG!*

What the fuck? My eyes slam open. *What the fuck was that?* My heart stops at the loud sounds from inside the house. *It sounded like a... like a...*

Everything inside me stops. *No. No, it couldn't be. It's impossible.*

I bolt through the door, desperately wanting to prove myself wrong, but I'm too late.

Crimson.

Crimson.

Crimson.

It's all I see.

Oh, God.

Lea is on her knees, gun slipping from her grip as she clutches her chest as it oozes blood all through the swimsuit fabric, all over the floor, all over my heart. My eyes widen in horror. *Oh, Dio. She shot herself. Lea shot herself. This is all my fault. All my fault for stepping out.*

"No. No, God, no, Lea," I cry, my vision blurring as I fall to my knees in front of her, desperate to help compress the wounds, but it's no use. Red soaks my hands. "Why? Why would you do that? Baby, baby, stay with me. Please stay with me. I'm going to call nine-one-one."

Where the hell did she get the gun?

Fuck. Fuck. Fuck.

"This is all your fault, Santo. I hate you," Lea whispers, her voice a raw strain as tears swim in her dim eyes. "I'll hate you forever. Remember that."

This is your fault, Santo.

I'll hate you forever.

Her words haunt me as I pull out my phone from my back pocket and frantically dial the number. The screen turns into a bloody mess. *Shit. She's losing too much blood.* Lea cries out my name in haunting screams I'll remember forever. *Santo, Santo, SANTO...* over and over and over again, until it all fades into a sea of nothingness. It all happens in seconds as Lea's face crunches up. She inhales her last sharp breath and lifelessly collapses to the hardwood floors, the story of us becoming swallowed in a wave of cruel fate I never knew existed...

Not when the operator's voice floods through the speaker, but it's all too late. *Especially* not when I look up and see Alexis at the bottom of the staircase, gripping onto her plush giraffe toy. It feels as though my heart is bleeding out too and I can't take all the guilt that ruptures through it, plaguing me.

Not now as my breaths slow to a rate that feels almost unsurvivable.

Not as Alexis begins to cry hysterically and stares at me as if I'm her lifeline.

Not when her mommy just darkened the light in our world... all because of me...

All because of *Santo...*

Chapter
TWENTY-THREE

Paisley

A SHAKY BREATH ESCAPES SAINT AS HE FINISHES HIS STORY AND I FEEL it right inside my beating heart. It aches for Saint. Completely aches for everything he's been through, for Lea, for Alexis, for himself, because I know it isn't easy for him to open up like this. Saint isn't the type of man to let it all out, so the fact that he's allowing me into his life tonight more than he ever has means the world to me.

His past explains why he was so cold and closed up from the world when I first met him three years ago. Explains why he never wanted me to call him *Santo*.

He proposed.

He was cheated on and Lea was expecting a baby that wasn't his.

He was severely stabbed and witnessed Lea dying right in front of him...

Holy shit.

I feel so bad for all Saint's been through. Despite the guilt that plagues him, I'm proud of him for being able to grow into the man he is today as a result of Lea's actions. Wherever she may be tonight in the heavens above watching down on us, I just pray she finally lets him be.

"I'm so sorry, Saint. So sorry that this all happened to you. It must have been so painful," I murmur, squeezing his hand before kissing the scarred white line softly. The one I now know some of the story behind. "Did you ever find out how she got the gun?"

"Yes, I later found out it was hers. Police found she had a permit for it, but I didn't know a single thing about it. The more I've thought about it over the years, the more I've realized I didn't really know who Lea truly was. It's as if she had all these secrets... a whole other life. I still don't understand why. I knew she was in a dark place. I just never thought it would reach where it did. All I wanted to do was help her and make her happy again. I didn't know she was at the breaking point. I didn't know I was only making it worse."

"I'm so sorry. Just know you didn't make it worse, Saint, you did everything you could for her. So that explains the scar too, hmm?"

"Mmhmm. I eventually got to the ER and the stab was so deep that I had to undergo surgery. Unfortunately, a nerve was too damaged to completely repair, so now whenever I'm stressed or nervous my hand shakes a little... just like you've seen before. Professionally boxing probably made it worse, but it is what it is."

"Our scars make us even more beautiful. They tell our stories without saying a word."

"I like that." The second I lift my gaze to his piercing blue eyes, I'm happy to see a glimmer of warmth despite the misery. "Did you think of that right now, babydoll?"

"Something like that, yeah." I cup his stubbled jaw and rest my forehead against his, a habit I love. "Sometimes, life throws us moments we don't deserve and at the time all it seems to do is strip us down. Make us vulnerable. Guilty."

384 | VANESSA LUISA

"Yes, vulnerable, and I hate that feeling. I hate the feeling of being completely out of control of my emotions."

"I understand, but I think what I've learned is vulnerability isn't a bad thing. It makes us human. You once told me to never hide what I truly feel or my emotions, and the same applies to you. You're allowed to feel broken down and bruised, you're allowed to search for your healing, it's our birthright." I squeeze my eyes shut and breathe in his scent mixed with the ocean. "I thought you went through some type of trauma but never imagined something like this. It must have been so scary, not knowing how to navigate it all... to see Lea like that... having to console Alexis."

"It was." Saint nods, pulling me closer into his chest. I straddle his waist. The warm touch his hand provides while slowly rubbing up and down my spine under the Harley T-shirt means something even more special tonight. "I felt as though I had nothing left. Like I was stripped of the type of man I was."

"Do you have any pictures of Lea or Alexis?"

"Not Lea. She hated photos and I never wanted to push it. I have a couple of Alexis and me together. I used to keep one in my wallet a few years ago. Took it out a couple months later because it hurt to look at her."

A memory comes back to me. "*Oh*, I remember that one! Was that Alexis, the one I saw two years ago when you gave me money to plant my flowers? The one where a little girl is kissing your cheek?"

"Yeah, that's Alexis."

"Aww, she was adorable. Have you seen her since?"

"No, and that's what hurts me the most. After Lea passed away, Michael won a court order to take legal guardianship of his daughter, Alexis. It's been thirteen years and I haven't seen her since."

"How did you ease all the pain?"

"Truthfully, I turned to late night drives when I wasn't even in the present, burning myself out at work, drinking, different women every night, boxing to ease the pain, smoking... they were all such fucking bad habits, but they helped numb the stress for a little while. It's just so much guilt, you know. I keep on thinking. *I could have stopped Lea,* even though I know she was too far gone, and I couldn't have saved her. I don't think what she did was selfish. She just was in such a dark place that she couldn't pull herself back up. I wish she'd talked to me before it escalated. It's fucked up, I know. Lea cheated on me and was pregnant with a child that wasn't even mine, but I… I still have this guilt."

"I can imagine, but we can't be the controllers of our destiny, Saint. You know what happened with Lea is not your fault, right?"

After a long moment, Saint gulps down and nods. "I know. I'm learning to start to believe that too. I haven't been to a professional, like a therapist, haven't had the courage to, but part of me thinks I should. I think it's going to be the only way I can move on, you know?"

"I think you should too. Not because you're incapable of getting through this on your own, but because you need somebody to help you at a level neither of us can. Somebody to guide you and support you professionally. If you like, when we go back to Sacramento and you set something up, I can wait outside the building for moral support during your sessions. Anything for you to know you're not going through this alone. Because you're not alone in this, Saint. Not anymore."

Our eyes flutter open and I can't begin to describe the warmth in my chest when the most beautiful smile works up his lips. The same one that rises on mine too.

Saint kisses my forehead.

Home. Home is all I feel when I look at him.

"All these years I've been searching for an angel to come save me from hell. Now I know that angel is you. I've never met a woman so beautiful and selfless. Never met a woman who cares this deep." Saint cups my face, brushes my hair behind my ears, and glances lovingly between my eyes. "Never met a woman like you, Paisley Reign, my forever girl."

If I thought making love with Saint before was incredible, this time it's so poetically beautiful it takes all my breath away. I'm laid out on his bed with him on top of me and my legs wrapped around his waist, wrapped inside a world of him.

Saint can't stop kissing me. Touching me. Devouring every inch of me, just like I can't stop worshiping him. His blue eyes roam across my face, the beautiful smile carved on his lips never dropping as he pumps into me with his hard cock. He feels so good inside me. We feel so good *together*. In a few hours I've gone from virgin to completely being lovesick and addicted to the warm sensation across my entire body as Saint drives me deeper and deeper into a type of pleasure I never want to escape. I love that this isn't just fucking, that it is deep... raw... intimate... slow... emotional. Honestly, I love that this feels like we're making love all over again.

Moaning, I tip my head back against the mattress, right on the pillow as he grinds into me so intimately I can barely take it. "Oh, yes. *Fuck*."

Saint's chuckle has me glancing back up at him.

"What?"

"Nothing," he murmurs, his lips tracing mine. "It's just that ever since we've been closer, you're swearing like there's no tomorrow."

I smirk. "Because you're a bad influence, Mr. Lisconti."

My response has him smoldering. "Ohhh, am I now?"

"Mhmmm."

"Interesting. We'll see about that." Saint winks, and then his lips are on mine, hard.

I moan into his mouth in complete ecstasy, feeling my pussy throb faster and faster as his hard cock fills me up over and over and over. I'm on the verge of losing control but want to hold on longer because I want this moment to last forever.

The pitter-patter in my chest hasn't stopped racing wildly all night. It feels as though it's bleeding the type of passion I never knew existed with Saint. Because he trusted me with his tragic past, we're closer than ever before, and as those warm blue eyes glance down at me now, all I see and all I feel is pure adoration. The more our hot stare extends, the deeper I'm falling in love with this man and I swear he can feel it too.

"Paisley... oh, *fuuuuck*," Saint pants, burying his head into my shoulder, and sexily biting it with a groan as my hips rock harder to meet his grinds. "Keep. Doing. That."

His spiky stubble grazes against my skin, and I love it, love the perspiration tracing our bodies and the smell of aromatic flowers, the ocean and sex mixed together, creating an *us*. The moody pendant light above each nightstand casts such a romantic glow around Saint's bedroom and projects a perfect darkened shadow on the wall of our bodies together—my long legs wrapped around his waist and locked at the heels, digging into his beautifully toned ass with every passion-filled thrust as he moves in and out of me. *Such an erotic visual.*

My heart warms with every single moment that passes with us going crazy wild.

Oh, God. This is what heaven must feel like.

Saint always says he isn't the romantic type, but after spending the past twelve hours with him here on the west coast of California, I beg to differ. He's a true romantic. So wise and masculine. So strong yet vulnerable. So genuine but kind.

My hands roam across his broad muscles and down his back, knowing I'm tracing over his tattoos and what they represent. My nails seep into his skin and I whisper out his name as he brings a firm hand to my thigh and pumps into me deeper, the headboard continuously hitting the wall behind the bed. Heat rushes across my entire body, continuously, pooling at my sex every time as I clench around him, so close to losing control... so much pleasure. So much *Saint*.

There's so much depth between us, so many words within the

silence as I cup his stubbled jaw and murmur breathlessly, "You're such a beautiful man, Saint."

I hope Saint knows what I mean is much more than just skin-deep. I'm referring to the beauty of his soul, his courage, everything he's not, everything he is, his past, his present, the man underneath all the tangled rose thorns and vines.

My heart is beating so fast, desperate to tell him how I really feel. This moment couldn't be more perfect. I owe it to myself and to him to be honest.

Saint and I share such a loving, tender grin. The pleasure builds as he glides in and out of me faster and faster, his forearms and biceps tensing tighter on each side of my head on the pillow.

"I love it when you smile," Saint whispers darkly. "I love it when you're happy."

"Saint?"

"Mhmmm?"

Nerves fizzle away as he increases the pace even more and the urgency to come undone ripples through me. *I'm so close.* My hands wrap around Saint's neck to pull him closer and ease my bouncing breasts as they press up against his hard, glistening chest.

"What is it you want to tell me, *tesoro?*"

"Something that may change everything..."

Saint glances between my eyes. "Tell me, *wildflower.*"

"I'm..." I part my lips and feel my heart swell at the next words that fall. "I'm so in love with you, Saint. I don't expect you to say it back. I know this may only be for the summer, but I need you to know I'm so completely and utterly in love with you. With *all* of you."

Saint's lips fall on mine and we come undone together in the same breath, at the exact same moment, swallowing each other's groans and moans. We give in to that overwhelming urge to fall into desire and my body moves in rhythm with his as we completely get lost in each other as I come hard around him, my body quivering in pure pleasure. Saint's cock pulses deep inside me, filling me good with his warmth as he continues to pump hard. Right now, I don't know where I end and he begins. All I know is I have never felt this completely sated in my life and I've never loved somebody more.

Our lips detach and Saint's blue eyes find mine, a darkening desire pooling in them as the thrusts slow until they stop. He smiles in admiration, but I see beyond it. I see the shadowed and silvery patterns of the moon outside cast over his beautifully structured face...

I hear the soft hush of the ocean waves outside...

I feel the first tear string my warm cheeks...

But it isn't from me... it's *him*.

I don't have enough time to realize that Saint's crying before he rolls us over and slides us inside the bed. Slipping out of me, Saint reaches to turn off the nightstand lights, only the silvery moonlight casting cut out shapes across the room now. As he lies down on his back against the mattress, I rest on top of him and love how he pulls the bedsheets higher and his arms remain wrapped around my waist, caressing my warm skin.

Definitely feels like home.

Cupping Saint's jaw, I furrow my brows at my beautiful man and kiss away his wet salty tears, which are so cold and fragile. I want to do everything there is in the world to make Saint feel better. It's so bittersweet... bittersweet because as much as it breaks my heart that he's crying, I'm relieved he's being this emotionally open with me.

"I tried to push you away." Saint's eyes shut as soft cries break through him and his voice cracks. "I tried to do everything I could to not fall for you, but I failed."

I press my lips against Saint's in comfort and when I pull back, my soul warms at the kiss he presses against my forehead. Gazing down at him, my right thumb traces small comforting circles on his face, just above his stubbled jaw, as I admire how the romantic lights illuminate his entire face.

It can't be any earlier than 2:30 a.m. and I love that we haven't stopped for one second since we got to Stinson Beach in Marin

County. It's almost as if sleep means nothing because I don't want to waste a second with him. Now, as I frown up at my blue-eyed boy, all I can think of is *maybe... maybe he doesn't want the same.*

Why else would he be crying?

Oh, shit.

"Tell me what you're thinking," I murmur, so low I barely hear the words myself.

It hurts to see Saint like this, but it brings a little solace that he's wrapped around me so tightly, destined to never let go. "It isn't really what I'm feeling, it's more of a realization."

So many possible scenarios are twirling in my head.

What if he regrets bringing me to Stinson Beach?

What if he's thinking about Lea?

What if he's crying because he wants to end this between us before the end of summer?

I inhale a deep breath, telling myself I'm not going to worry about the reason until it falls from his lips. Whatever it is Saint is going to tell me next, we'll face it together.

"And what is it you've realized?"

Saint reaches up his tattooed left arm and begins to slowly run his fingers through my hair, so calming and intimate.

So perfectly us.

"I have never felt like this before." Saint's deep ocean eyes flutter open, revealing a rim of tears, and my heart skips a beat at the look in his eyes... it's not regret, instead complete affection. "Paisley, I have never felt this complete. *Ever.* I'm emotional right now because I never thought I'd find something as beautiful as this, and here you are... saving me from the fire inside of me. The same fire that wouldn't stop raging for years, not until right now. Not until you."

I forget how to breathe. *Whoa.*

"Saint, that was so beautiful. I thought..." My cheeks burn with just how hard I'm grinning. "I thought you only wanted this for the summer, no?"

"Well..." Saint gives me a slow, sexy smirk. "Turns out I was right, rules *do* suck."

I can't help but break out into laughter and it brightens me to see him chuckling so hard too. His laughter is so damn sexy, so beautiful. I squeal mid-giggle as the sheets rustle around us when Saint turns us so we're lying down on our sides on the pillowcases, face to face. It brings a new definition to late night pillow talk. His touch revives me as he pulls me even closer, and I glide my hand over his warm shoulder blade. It feels so good feeling his every muscle, being so close to him as his sandalwood cologne mixed with me wraps me in a world of him.

We spend the longest time listening to each other's heartbeats, never letting go of our heated gaze and tracing each other's skin. Admiring each other in the moonlight with the ocean swaying outside the window. It feels like a dream. A gift. Such poetic fate that he's here with me, that it has me tracing his long dimples with my pointer finger. I murmur, "I didn't you know you felt this way too."

Saint's blue eyes sparkle in the moonlight. "To be honest, I've felt this way for a long time... since the day all the shit went down with Erik and I realized I cared about you more than I thought. I've just been afraid to admit it."

"Why were you afraid?"

"Aside from your father slaughtering me?"

"Yeah, aside from that."

"Well, I thought if we took things any further, like a relationship, I'd fuck it up."

"Why did you think that?"

Saint lets out a soft sigh, his hot breath hitting my skin. "Because fucking it up is all I seem to be good at."

My heart drops for Saint because straight away I know he's talking about his past.

"You know that's not true, blue-eyed boy." I smile warmly, our lips inches apart as I cup his face and hold him tight. "I wish you could see how special you are through my eyes. Wish you could see how beautiful life is because you're in it, Santo."

Santo.

I called him Santo.

I don't know what I was expecting next, but it certainly isn't the smile that curls up his full lips. It's so tender and intimately raw, filled with just the right amount of emotion and passion to make my heart thunder in my chest.

Saint brushes his thumb over my plump lips, slowly tracing the warm skin as we lie here in the early hours of the morning, just us... our thoughts... and our beating hearts. His eyes continue to flicker from my gaze to my lips, drinking up every second as I wait in anticipation of what comes next.

In the past Saint told me that calling him 'Santo' was off-limits, and I know it's because it scars him being the last word he heard come out of Lea's mouth, and only his mom and Nonna still call him that now. But seeing Saint so placid and content in this moment, it has me not afraid to admit that perhaps... perhaps I'm changing that.

Saint's touch is so gentle. So pure and delicate that it's as if he's strumming a rose with the pad of his fingertips, adamant not to break its velvety petals.

"Say it again," Saint whispers, all raspy and hot. "Say my name."

I smile, his finger smoothing my lips. "Santo."

"Again."

My heart skips a beat.

"Santo," I breathe. "I'm so deeply in love with you, Santo."

"I love the way you say my name. Love the way it slips from your tongue." Saint shuts his eyes for a moment, and when they reopen, tenderness is all I see. "I'm so in love with you, Paisley Reign. So fuckin' in love with everything about you. I fell in love, and I wasn't even trying. All I know is, if you let me, I... I don't only want one summer with you, *wildflower*, I want an entire lifetime."

Electricity pumps through my entire body and I literally forget how to breathe.

He wants this too, with me.

"I want that so badly too. I feel like the luckiest girl alive right now."

"No, *tesoro*." Saint grins. "It's me who's feeling lucky. Me who's thanking the heavens they sent me an angel. I know it isn't going to be easy with Alaric, but I so desperately want to try to be everything you need. I can't promise it'll be perfect, I can't promise there won't be times when I tell you that you deserve better than me, but what I can promise you is I'll never leave your side, not unless you want me to. I'll never regret the way I feel about you, no matter the costs. I'll never give up on us, no matter how hard it gets."

Us. I like the sound of that. *Love* the sound.

"I promise you this from the bottom of my heart, *wildflower*." Saint takes another breath as his fingers slip away from my lips as sparks inside me continue to erupt. "I want to be yours, Paisley Reign, so desperately yours. Only yours."

Everything inside me explodes into tiny rose petals of joy. I couldn't be any happier in this moment as my heart warms to pure bliss and I'm not afraid to show it. Grinning at him, I do the one thing I'm craving to do and kiss him wildly. Lovingly. Breathlessly. With everything I have. Saint kisses me back with so much meaning. So much desire. So much purpose. With one kiss alone, I'm able to communicate every single thing I'm feeling and thinking in this exact moment—*I want to be yours too, Saint Lisconti. So desperately yours. Only yours.*

Saint feels it. I know he does when we pull away and he looks at me with a passionate, darkened gaze that could inspire any poet.

"I want nothing more than to dive into a world full of you, Santo," I murmur against his lips. "Even if we have to hide it from my father, it's worth it. It's worth every second spent with you. I promise, from the bottom of my heart, to be everything you've ever deserved too. I promise to be me and let you be you. I promise to never let go because there's no me without us."

"That's so beautiful. *You* are beautiful."

My cheeks flush, aching from smiling so hard. "Stop it."

"Never." Saint smiles back. "Never going to stop telling you how beautiful you are. Ever."

"Aww."

"Got a question for you. What's your favorite flower? Can't believe I haven't asked you this before."

"Lilies. Blue tiger lilies."

"Ah, just like the ones I once destroyed, right? What's so special about them?"

"They were my nana's favorites and became mine too because they're extremely rare. They make me happy. It's just something about them, you know that feeling. What's your favorite flower?"

"Did you seriously just ask me that?" Saint chuckles, his fingers softly caressing my skin.

I smirk. "Aha."

"All right. Blue tiger lilies too."

"Ooo, what's so special about them?" I ask, impersonating him with a deeper voice.

The dimples on Saint's stubbled jaw deepen as he laughs hard, his rumbling laughter vibrating right through my body, prompting my own. "Because they remind me of a woman I know. A woman who means a lot to me. A woman who smells like jasmine, tastes like honey, and looks like a dream."

"Hmm, she must be a lucky woman."

"No, I'm the lucky one to have stepped on her flowers all those years ago."

"Aww." I smile, softly pecking his lips. "I'm the lucky one, baby."

"All right, we're both a little lucky then."

I part my lips to speak, but a wide yawn escapes instead.

Saint chuckles. "As much as I want to talk, we should probably get some rest. We have to get back to Sacramento early tomorrow ahead of your work shift, so sleep is probably a good idea."

"As much as I want to continue this conversation, you're right. We need some sleep, despite how thrilled I am that we're on the same page."

Saint rolls onto his back and pulls me close. Draping my leg over his naked frame, I rest my head and right hand on his solid chest, while his hands softly caress my hips, back, and ass.

"Good night, Santo. Thank you for everything."

He kisses my forehead, and I feel him smile against my warm skin. "*Buona notte, bella mia. Sognami.* Dream of me, *wildflower.*"

"Always do."

"God, I'm so fucking in love with you."

I grin into Saint's chest, completely exhilarated. "Ditto."

I've never fallen asleep in the arms of a man before. Especially not such a beautiful thirty-six-year-old man who means so much to me. Feeling his warm naked body against mine... it makes me so happy and proud of surviving everything we've been through to get to right now.

In the solace of Santo's strong arms, I know there's nowhere else I want to be than right here with my blue-eyed boy. Nowhere else but with his heart beating against mine. Nowhere else but so recklessly in love with a man so forbidden to others, but to me... he's everything I need.

Everything I've ever needed and more.

Much, *much* more.

The bright morning glow and a beautifully tattooed hand intertwined with mine on my pillow are all I see when I flutter my eyes open the next morning. The smile doesn't fall from my lips as I take in the heavenly sight of Saint sleeping so peacefully beside me. He's sleeping on his side, his face to me and the other wrapped around my waist so tightly. I don't think we let go of each other all night. Soft breaths escape him as the sun casts through the window, illuminating the dark whiskers of his stubble, his naturally lightly tanned olive skin against the tattoos, his long lashes I'm jealous of.

I'm so in love with you, Paisley Reign.

I love the way you say my name.

I don't only want one summer with you, wildflower, I want an entire lifetime.

The memories of last night have me so giddy and grateful. I can't believe this beautiful man beside me wants me too. It feels like a dream, like an absolute dream to know my love for him isn't a one-sided thing. That our love for each other will continue to bloom beyond last night and this morning. That it will thrive in a field of sunflowers, and as his favorite things become mine.

I softly brush my fingers across his defined, stubbled jaw, loving the distant sound of birds chirping, ocean waves crashing, and the world around us continuing to go on while it's just us in this bed, frozen in time. My fingers slowly rake through his tousled sex hair. It's so hot, seeing Saint so candid like this. Even though we fell right asleep after both confessing to being so in love with each other, remnants of our intimacy linger. Like our hair. Like the hickeys he made along my body. Like my rapidly beating heart as it screams in pure bliss.

Saint's dark, inky-colored hair is just long enough around to slip the sides behind the ears. I get a vision of his hair a little longer than this and tied up in a sexy man bun as he rides through California with such dominance in a muscle cut tank-top that softly flutters against his skin while his tattoos glisten in the summer sun. *Oh, yes, please.*

The heat between my thighs throbs in appreciation.

God, I love that thought of him.

Threading my fingers through Saint's hair now, the warmth of the day caresses our skin as soft ocean waves continue to crash in the distance. It's such a comforting sound, so calming and stunning. I've never woken up to the beach being my backyard. Never woken up beside a man. I'm savoring all my firsts and hope they become forevers.

The sun shining through the picture window hits Saint's striking blue eyes as he flutters them open. The moment he sees me, the longest grin rises on his lips as he lets out a satisfied hum and recloses his eyes. Then he buries his head into my bare breasts and begins to playfully rub his face against my cleavage. I literally burst out laughing.

"Well, apparently I'm dead because it seems like I'm still in heaven," Saint murmurs, his morning voice so sexily raspy, and I feel the smirk in it too. "Wanna stay here forever."

I giggle as he kisses each of my breasts and comes back up, so we're face to face. Saint leans his head against my pillow and has to squint against the sunshine. It almost looks like he's smoldering, which I love even more. He's so beautiful, always with that grin on his lips.

"What I meant to say is I want to stay with *you* forever, not against your breasts... although, thinking about it now... that'd be pretty nice too."

I can't help but giggle even harder. "So, you're sarcastic from the moment you wake up, huh?"

"I can be." Saint winks. "I can also be a lot of other things for you... like a gentleman."

"Oh yeah?"

"Mhmmm."

"Show me then, Mr. Lisconti."

Saint rolls us over in the bed so I'm underneath him and he's on top of me, holding up his weight with his forearms on the mattress on either side of my head. He smiles lovingly as he cups my face, and we share such a heated and intimate extended gaze. It's our strong emotional and physical connection merging into one. It's beautiful. It's us.

"Good morning, *wildflower*," he whispers.

"Morning, Santo."

"You take my breath away, so let me admit one thing before

I kiss the hell out of you..." Saint murmurs, glancing between my eyes and my heart melts. "I'm so fucking grateful you exist, Paisley."

Saint's words literally take my breath away too.

"I could say the same about you too, my blue-eyed boy."

We kiss passionately, such a tender morning kiss, and his hardening cock twitches against my lower stomach when our tongues begin to dance to a silent rhythm. *So good.*

Saint's eyes darken as we pull away and he lets out a sexy breath. "Hi, there."

I giggle, knowing exactly what he's alluding to as we softly grind our hips together and our breaths quicken. As much as I want it too, I'm conscious of the time seeing as I have work in a few hours and we still have to head back to Sacramento. "Do you know what time it is?"

Saint reaches over to the nightstand and taps on his phone. "Just past eight thirty. Why?"

My eyes widen. "Oh, shit! I have a shift at the florist at eleven! I can't even cancel because Maralyn will literally kill me!"

"So, we have to head back to Sacramento in thirty minutes?"

"If you don't want me six feet under, yes."

Saint groans and buries his head in my neck. "Fuck, that's one way to ruin a man. Maralyn doesn't even know how much of a cockblocker she is right now."

I laugh. "I know, I promise to make it up to you tonight."

"Pretty sure your father doesn't have a shift at the hospital tonight."

"Oh, true. Okay then. Thursday night. My father will be at work, so Thursday night I'm all yours."

"Perfect, it's date night then."

My eyes widen in awe. "What? Did Mr. *I'm-not-romantic* just say date night?"

Saint smirks. "Being in love changes a man, I guess. I just want you all to myself."

"You've got me."

"Good." A few seconds pass before he adds, "This is going to stay between us, yeah?"

"Of course. Look, you know my father as well as I do. You know he wouldn't be happy nor understand what's going on between us and say that it's wrong. He'll try to break us apart, attempt to tell you to walk away and tell me something along those lines too. I just know it. So, I think for now it's better we concentrate on starting this relationship and keeping it hidden between just us because I'd really prefer my boyfriend not to be annihilated."

Saint playfully arches his brow. *"Boyfriend, huh?"*

I bite my lip softly, doing such a shit job at hiding my grin. "Mmhmm."

Saint keeps going, teasing me with a smirk. "Did you just call me *your boyfriend?*"

"Maybe..." I giggle. "I know we haven't spoken labels or anything like that, but..."

"You don't mean maybe, you mean *yes.*" Saint grins and pecks my lips once more. "I have twelve hours with you at a time. You bet I'm not going to waste a single second by not calling you my girlfriend."

"Except for right now, because we're not going to have time to pass by home before the florist. You probably have to drop me off right there, so I should have a shower now. You could join me, save some water."

"But no sex?"

"No sex. You know if we do, we'll probably get carried away and then Maralyn will—"

"Kill you, yeah, I know, I know." Saint gets off me, jokily rolling his eyes as he sits up in the bed, the sheets slipping away from his body, and I drink up his glorious naked athletic frame... that raging erection that has me rubbing my thighs together to ease my throbbing pussy.

"All right, you're right, let's get ready, Paisley... However, we do have some time for me to make us a delicious smoothie."

I playfully narrow my eyes at Saint because he's looking at me so heated and what he just said definitely sounds like a sexual innuendo.

Saint stares back at me cluelessly before his eyes widen, and he throws his head back in laughter. "I know exactly what you're thinking and that's not what I meant at all. I meant *an actual smoothie*, you dirty freak. *Dio mio*. My God, Paisley, what am I going to do with you?"

"I don't know, draw me like one of your French girls."

"Did you literally just quote *Titanic*?"

I nod, scrunching up my nose in laughter, and accidentally snort. That has us laughing even harder and I go to cover my mouth with my hand, but Saint's too fast and takes my hands, using them to intertwine his fingers through mine as he hovers back on top of me. I've never felt this comfortable in my entire life as his dimples deepen and the laughter escaping us comes from a place so wholesome and with such utter affection and compassion.

"God, I'm so in love with you, Paisley." Saint smiles, resting his forehead against mine as we finally settle down. "So goddamn in love with you."

Chapter
TWENTY-FOUR

Paisley

I T'S SUCH A SCRAMBLE TO GET OUT OF THE BEACH HOUSE. WE HAVE A quick shower together and are fast to put on our clothes. I slip on my lacy panties and bra that I left on the bathroom floor last night before putting on my sundress and Converses, all while Saint voluntarily dries my dark wavy hair with a towel. Once we're both dressed and clean out all of the flowers from the bath, Saint heads downstairs to get a head start on making those smoothies he was talking about earlier, all while I make sure everything is packed inside my little duffle bag.

The strawberry, mango, and honey smoothies Saint made were mouthwatering. So deliciously sweet. I truly didn't want to leave this beach house, especially because of what it represents and how many memories Saint and I have made here in our sixteen-hour stay. I'll miss the fresh ocean breeze, the beach, the tranquility of it all… but Saint promises this won't be the last time we visit, and I believe him.

I so desperately want this to work between us. I know our relationship is not always going to be as easy as it is right now in Stinson Beach. Once we're back in Sacramento, everything is going to get a whole lot harder. There isn't the escape of the beach right in our backyards, the silence from all the loud voices, the escapism of it just being him and me. Hiding my relationship with Saint from my father is going to be the most challenging thing in my life, but for right now it's the right thing to do, and I'm so glad Saint feels the same way too.

Once we're all ready to go, we head toward the front door to exit the beach house and it doesn't get lost on me the reason Saint slows by the oak front door…

Lea. Right here was her final stance.

I expect Saint to be somber when I look up at him, expect him to be reminiscent of the past because he has every right to feel that way. Instead, when I glance up at him now, I see this bright smile on his face and it warms me the way he pulls me into a side embrace and brushes his lips against my damp hair, breathing in my jasmine scent from the body wash I convinced him to buy last night.

"It wasn't your fault, Saint. You didn't know she would do that. I bet nobody did. You saved Lea as much as you could, and sometimes that's all we can do."

He nods.

"There was nothing else you could have done, Saint. Nothing else because we can't control what people do. We can influence their decisions, but we can't control, because at the end it's all up to them," I murmur, feeling my heartbeat in my ears. "Please don't shy away from talking about her with me. You can confide in me about anything and everything. Whatever you need, just know that I'm here, unconditionally."

"You know what the crazy thing is?" Saint whispers.

I shake my head.

"That every time I used to pass this door, this heavy weight used to chain my entire body. These past two days… I haven't felt a thing. Not with you here. Acceptance is the hardest step, but with you now... I'm realizing guilt chained me for a long time, and that after all these years, I just needed the right person to come along to unchain me. I needed the right person to make me comprehend it isn't all my fault and that I'm not in this alone. That person is you, Paisley. *You* are my person, and nobody else on this earth or in the other could ever compare to that, understand?"

"Yes." I nod, tearing up at the beautiful words he spoke. "And I'll never betray you like Lea did by being unfaithful. I'll never hurt you, not intentionally anyway. I'll never leave you when you need me the most. *Ever.* You know that, right?"

"I know," Saint says, his voice riddled with raw emotion. "That's why I trust you more than I've ever trusted anybody else in my entire life before."

"I feel the same with you, Santo."

"God, I love hearing you say that."

We share a smile and I thread my fingers through his. "Come on, let's get out of here."

Saint nods and squeezes my hand tighter, his smile extending. "Let's."

After the thrilling Harley ride back to Sacramento, Saint parks his stunning motorcycle outside of my florist and dismounts it. The shiny onyx Harley is definitely a showstopper and attracts attention from both pedestrians on the sidewalk and motorists driving down the busy downtown street.

"Thanks for the ride, Saint." I grin, wrapping my arms around his neck as we embrace on the sidewalk. "Thank you for *everything*. I had the best time with you, the greatest time. I really did."

"So did I, babydoll. So much so. I'm looking forward to Thursday night. I'll text you the details later."

"Sounds good."

Saint tightens the embrace, and it feels so good to be in the solace of his strong arms. So good to be so close. For this all to mean so much. The wide grin never leaves my lips, not even as we step away and he hands me my small duffle bag.

I literally have five minutes until the start of my shift and although I should be inside the florist, I can't step away from Saint. Our stare extends and all I want to do is spend the rest of the day with him.

"What time do you finish?" he asks.

"In four hours, at three p.m. Why's that?"

"Well, I'm going to head home now and get ready to head to work too. I have a boot camp session just before midday until two thirty, so I can pick you up at the end of the shift if you like."

My heart flutters at the kind gesture.

"What happened to being discreet?" I tease.

Saint darkly smolders. "We agreed on being discreet around your father, not anywhere else."

"Hmmm." I smirk, playfully glancing up and down the busy street before returning to his piercing blue-eyed gaze. "I thought you were this big-time former professional boxer. No paparazzi?"

Crossing his arms over his solid chest, Saint lets out a beautiful chuckle. "My time's *finito*, babydoll. Up until a few years ago, I would have been concerned with the cameras, but now that I'm retired from the sport, there's no reason to chase me around and hound me. I've got no news. They're onto newer things, I promise."

"I'm only kidding. I trust you. It's so nice of you to offer to pick me up, but I think it's better if I walk home. It's only a half an hour walk, and besides"—grinning, I almost laugh at my next words—"there's no doubt my father will suspect something if I'm coming home *riding a Harley* with *his best friend*."

"Probably not the best idea then, huh?"

"Definitely not."

"Noted." Saint grins before kissing my cheek. "Have a lovely shift, beautiful."

I grin back. "I will, and once again thank you for everything."

"No, thank *you*. Catch you later, *wildflower*."

"See you then. Ride safe."

"Always do." With one last wink goodbye, Saint clips on his helmet, puts his leather gloves back on, and mounts his Harley. After revving the engine, Saint turns back to me and I blow him a kiss. He dramatically catches the kiss, blows one back, and gives me the 'rock and roll' hand gesture before taking off down the tree-lined street. The smile doesn't slip off my lips, not even once I step inside and say hello to a few customers on my way to the staff room.

It's only after I step inside the staff room and see Maralyn that I halt in my tracks. She stops making her tea and her eyes narrow playfully the second she sees me. "Well, well, well, look who finally decided to show."

I glance at her all confused. "Uh, what do you mean? My shift starts in a couple minutes."

"I know it does, but I've been calling for the past hour and a half and no answer."

"The past two hours? That's so strange because I would have heard…" My words fall to silence when I realize the logical explanation for all this. I was with Saint on his Harley riding back here an hour and a half ago. I haven't even checked my phone, but as I pull it out of my small duffle bag now, my jaw drops at the five missed calls from Maralyn *and* another three from my father.

"I'm so sorry Maralyn. It's been a… different kind of morning."

"I'll say it has." Maralyn takes three long strides until she's right in front of me. Crossing her arms over her chest, her eyes continue to narrow as she studies my face before traveling her gaze down my body. I hold my breath as she slows by my small duffle bag, knowing exactly what she's about to say…

Shit. Shit. Shit.

Play it cool, Paisley.

Don't stuff it up.

"Why the duffle bag?"

"I'm, uh… going to head to the gym after this." I smile weakly.

"You know, trying to continue my workout regime before… before… Seattle! *Yes*, that's right. I want to continue staying the fittest I can before I move to Seattle for college, you know."

Maralyn stares at me blankly, as if she knows something I don't. "So that's your story? Duffle bag because of the *gym?*"

Oh, shit. This is definitely not going well.

I gulp down thickly. "Yep."

"You sure?"

"Mmhmmm."

Maralyn's stare extends before she nods, and a sly smirk rises on her lips. "Okay, because that *totally* explains why your father came inside the florist a good half hour ago looking for you. He came in and asked if you were here, as he's been trying to get through to you and no avail. I told him you didn't start your shift until eleven, and he was starting to look so pissed off. Then I find out apparently *you* slept over at *my* house last night because we were *celebrating your graduation downtown.* GIRL! What the hell was that?"

My heart drops. *Oh no. No. No.*

"Oh shit. My *father* came *here?*"

"He sure did. You're lucky that I went along with the story he was giving me and convincingly told him that we had a big night last night, so you were curing your hangover at my house until it was time for your shift."

"Curing a *hangover?*" I panic. "Oh no. My father knows I don't drink. I'm not legal!"

Well, apart from that tequila with Saint yesterday.

"Well, according to your father you drank last night with me, woman! You drank the freaking house down because that's all I could come up with in literally two seconds. Damn, I've never seen a dad so damn protective about his daughter before. He was ready to go to my house to check you were really there, so I had to say he couldn't because you met this guy at one of the bars we went to and told him to come over in the middle of the night, so God knows what you were doing with him in the morning. I swear to God your father almost turned into Rambo."

My jaw drops to the floor. "MARALYN! Oh NO!"

"What? It's not like I said something a girl wouldn't do. I couldn't think of anything else but sex. I'm sorry!" She laughs, pressing a hand to her chest. "Calm down, Paisley, it's fine. It's a normal thing to do after graduation anyway. You're *celebrating*, for Christ's sake. But Jesus, next time give me a warning. I understand girl code, but girl code doesn't work unless you actually tell the girl in the first place."

"Maralyn, I'm so sorry. I was going to ask you to cover up, but I completely forgot. Thank you so much for covering for me, but now my father's going to think I hooked up with a stranger and had a one-night stand and he's never going to let this go. Oh God."

"No, he's not..." The smirk grows on Maralyn's lips. "Because that never happened. I only said that part to fire you up. What I *actually* told your father was after you and I went out to dinner last night, you fell slept at mine because I didn't want you to go home by yourself so late. I said you were sleeping in because we had a late night. Your father was convinced, said thank you, and walked out of the florist."

Relief ripples through me as my heartbeat returns to normal. *Holy shit, we actually pulled this off!!!*

I literally pull her into a big embrace, a grateful smile on my lips as I inhale sharply. "Maralyn, you're a lifesaver. Thank you so much. I love you! I really do owe you so much!"

"It's okay, it's what friends are for." She laughs, holding me tighter. "Just promise me you'll give me a heads-up if it ever happens again because I need some time to think of a convincing story that I can turn into a screenplay that will turn into a movie that wins an Oscar for plot and originality, which would lead me to the true husband I should have had all along. *Brad Pitt*. Promise?"

I laugh back. "Promise."

Maralyn's smirk only widens as we pull away. "Sooo, who's the real guy you're hiding from your dad?"

"Huh? No, there is no guy," I say fast, *too* fast.

"Really?" She arches a challenging brow. "Because I've been around for a little while, and to me the duffle bag probably has a change of clothes... the cover-up story... the grin on your lips the second you stepped inside this staff room and glowing complexion... it's all adding up to one thing—a hella good fuck."

And then just like that, the palpitations in my chest resume. Thump after thump after thump.

See! See, Paisley! See what happens when you celebrate before time. You didn't pull this off. You didn't pull this aspect off in the slightest.

My flushed cheeks feel as though they're burning. It's even worse when the damn smile on my lips doesn't disappear no matter how hard I attempt to keep a straight face. "I promise, Maralyn, there isn't a guy."

"Hmm, sure, sure," Maralyn says, the New York accent coming to play even more. "Because that *definitely* explains the hickeys. God, Paisley you're such a hot mess. Was the sex so good you literally forgot about the number one rule when it comes to being discreet? Rule number one... Be *discreet!*"

"OH MY GOD!" I gasp, slapping a hand on my neck, and let out a loud groan when I realize just how much I've fucked it all up. I'm a complete disaster, so completely defeated and frazzled. "You have my full permission to roast me. You're right. I'm such a hot mess right now, I literally am the girl who would be killed off first in a horror movie based upon my own indiscreetness."

Maralyn smiles and walks over to the other side of the room. Picking up her handbag from the kitchen counter, she rummages through it as I rub my hands over my face, wondering how I could be so clueless. I can't believe I didn't cover the hickeys. I've just been so giddy this morning that I didn't even realize I had to. Not even Saint picked up on it.

Maralyn walks back to me with a little zebra print makeup bag with the zipper forced three quarters of the way closed, looking as though it's going to explode any minute. She waves the makeup bag in my face and grins. "Never fear, your Fairy Godmother is here! I have a few concealers in here. Go to the bathroom and see the one that matches you more."

I take the bag from her and curtsey in gratitude. "Again, you're a lifesaver, Maralyn! Thank you so much. I literally am going to work double shifts for the rest of the time I'm in Sacramento before college!"

I'm already working four-hour shifts every day at the florist until I move to be more financially stable, but I'm more than happy to double my hours too if it means making it up to her after everything she did for me this morning.

"You said it. I didn't. What are you still doing here? Go get to work, girl!"

I smile, walking backward toward the restroom door on my left. "Thank you so much, Maralyn! I won't forget this!"

Her laugh echoes even as I step into the bathroom and get to work dabbing the concealer over Saint's love bites. Smiling to myself through the mirror, I breathe out a sigh of relief and tell myself I seriously need to up my game if Saint and I are going to continue to hide our relationship like this because I just gave out such a major giveaway, it's not even funny.

Don't stress. Everything is going to be all right.

I'm able to go the entire shift without Maralyn asking me anything else about *the guy*—Saint. But with my father it'll be different. Saint is his best friend. *He won't understand.* I just hope that after the terrible start to my shift, everything with my father will be smooth sailing because it can't be worse than the fool I made out of myself in front of Maralyn...

Or can it?

⁂

He won't suspect a thing.

I replay the words in my mind over and over again as I step inside my house. My father's sitting on the couch, flipping through television channels, and glances my way with a smile when he sees me. I smile back, my grip tightening on my small duffle bag straps as I walk past him into the kitchen, fill a glass of water, and when he's not looking, subtly pull out my birth control packet from the pantry. It's a few hours later than when I would usually take my pill daily, and I want to be careful seeing as Saint and I were intimate in Stinson Beach, but it will make no difference now. I pop a pill and down it so fast with water, quickly putting the packet back as my mind circles.

I summon the courage to join my father on the couch, shutting my eyes as he tugs me into a short embrace, and I pray to God he doesn't ask many questions about last night. As we pull away, thoughts of Saint have me grinning a little too hard and my father notices, his brows furrowing in amusement.

"You seem different," he says, a slight smile on his lips. "Happier."

"It's crazy what a decent night of sleep can do to you, right?" I laugh, cringing inside.

Okay, enthusiasm has to tone down to a zero right now, Paisley.

"Well, I take it you had a great time downtown last night with Maralyn."

"The best time! I heard you made a frantic rush down to the florist. Everything okay?"

"Yeah, all good." My dad nods. "It's just that I called you a few times and you weren't picking up, so I thought the worst considering you sent me a text saying you were going downtown. But then I saw Maralyn at the florist and she explained you were still at hers sleeping, which explains the missed calls."

"Yeah, it was a pretty long night. It was as if Maralyn wanted to show me every aspect of Sacramento's downtown, even though it's home. But that's Maralyn. You can't say no to her."

My father smiles. "I'm just happy you're okay and had a good time, sweetheart. You deserve it. Just wish you had a friend like Maralyn in Washington State. It'll have me less worried."

"There's no need to worry, Dad. Besides, I'm sure I'll find some like-minded people in college. I'll start applying for jobs at a florist or something like that as soon as I settle in Seattle and then at that stage, you'll probably get used to life without me per-fecting the garden twenty-four seven."

"I'll never get used to life without you here, sweetheart." My father sighs, shaking his head as he squeezes my shoulders in com-fort. "God, I seriously am going to miss you so much, Paisley. I know I don't say it much, but I really am so proud of you. Of ev-erything you are and everything you've become. I know we don't spend as much time together as we would like because of my job, but that doesn't take away from how much I love you."

Tears brim my eyes as I nod back, my heart clenching at my father's words. "I love you so much too, Dad. As I've said before, I know how important your work is. I'm going to miss you so much when I leave, but we're only a few states away. That's something."

"You're right, it is something. It's not like you're moving to Australia. But I'll fly you out here every summer. That way you can enjoy California and everything it has to offer. I promise I'll start taking some time off during the break, so you can tell me all about life in Seattle. You'll probably get so pissed that I've killed half of the flowers we have."

My father's last sentence brings some joy, and I can't help but laugh a little. "Oh, don't you worry, I'll leave you an entire list of exactly what to do with all the flowers. You can't be a doctor by occupation and then slaughter all my flowers at home. Doesn't work like that, Dad."

"Fair point." My dad chuckles. "Promise I'll be as attentive as I am with my patients. You have my word."

"Good, because I'm relying on you."

"Well, you're a genius when it comes to flowers, so I have some pretty big shoes to fill."

I smirk. "I'll take the compliment when I get it."

"You know you're amazing, Paisley. I'm so proud of you. I guess it's just hard for me to see you now as this beautiful, strong woman and not being able to protect you in Seattle."

"You know I can take care of myself, Dad."

"I know, but you'll always be my little girl." He smiles sadly, pulling me into his side. "I just don't want anybody to hurt you, that's all, especially when it comes to men. Good intentions and testosterone don't always see eye to eye. But don't you worry, from now on I'm going to step up my game and knock out any guy who looks at you for more than half a second. Not to mention, I'll have Saint knocking them out with me because it's always good to have a former Olympian professional boxer on your side, right?"

I smile back, but inside my heart is pumping so hard. It's ironic how my father said that Saint would be the one to protect me from gawking men, when Saint's the one I'm in love with. I know just how protective my father is and with how beautiful everything progressed with Saint at Stinson Beach, I'm nervous about how it will all unfold one day when the secret's out, but until then I want to cherish every moment I have with the two most important men in my life.

No matter what happens, I'm not letting go of Saint.

No matter what happens, I'm not letting go of my father.

I know you can't have your cake and eat it too, but in this case I'll keep hoping because I never want to let go of the happiness I'm feeling being so deeply in love with Santo Lisconti.

My father and I sit in silence for a few minutes before I find the words that have been on the tip of my tongue for all these years. "Is it hard for you to look at me and see my mom?"

He smiles softly. "From the day you were born, all I've ever seen in you is me. I know it's probably not what you want to hear. Your eyes... nose... smile, it's all mine. I don't love you any less because of it. Hell, I love you so much more. I think the constant reminders of seeing her in you would kill me. I prefer it this way. I like when I look at you, and I see a Reign staring back at me."

"Staring back at you like a deer in headlights, right?"

We share a laugh before settling down, and my dad shakes his head. "No, never like a deer in headlights. I don't think you're realizing how much you've changed in these past few months, even these past few weeks. It's like you're another version of you. A better version. Happier. Confident. You've gotten your spark back, Paisley. I don't know where it's coming from, but keep on thriving. Keep on making me proud, sweetheart."

I smile and feel the rhythms of my heart in my throat as my father finds the channel with *Seinfeld* reruns. It's a sitcom we used to watch together religiously when I was younger, but then between school and work it's been hard to keep up. But right now, we let go of all the past that's caged us and I lean my head on his shoulder as Kramer bursts through the door of Jerry's apartment, and my father and I erupt in laughter, just like we always do. It feels so nice to spend time with my father like this. So nice to connect with him like this before I leave at the end of next month.

But truthfully it kills me. Kills me that I have to lie to him, even though I know I have no other choice. He just told me how much he loves how in these past few months I've been changed into this better woman and finding my skin, and I know exactly why. I know I'm happier. More confident. Thriving. I'm all these things because of one man and one man only... Saint Lisconti. Santo. My blue-eyed boy.

Without even knowing it, Santo changed me for the better. He's *still* changing me, and now I'm finally living the best version of myself. All because he showed me that I'm worthy of blooming in a world I thought I was drowning in.

All because of his faith in me and influence to believe in myself and what I stand for.

All because of the way he stomped on my flowers all those years ago.

All because of him... fate... *us*.

Chapter
TWENTY-FIVE

Paisley

M Y HEART SKIPS A BEAT AT THE SIGHT OF SAINT STEPPING OUT OF HIS Maserati as I pull into the driveway of my house. From the passenger seat, my father glances over at Saint and waves. I don't miss the way those beautiful blue eyes flicker to mine a second after waving back. My father and I just got back from a nice dinner in urban Midtown Sacramento.

My father invited Saint and Nico along, but they declined as they were working late. I thought tonight would be smooth sailing as I didn't have to pretend I didn't have any feelings for Saint across the table when I did, but right now as my father and I step out of the Jeep, I almost lose my breath when I take a glance at the man I'm so in love with. We've been texting and calling ever since we returned from Stinson Beach, but nothing beats seeing this beautiful man face to face, especially considering our date night is Thursday night.

"Hey, man," My father grins, pulling Saint into a side hug

"Shit, I haven't seen you since you came back from Santa Rosa! How was it? Did you end up meeting up with your family?"

Santa Rosa?

And then I put two and two together. Saint told my father he was in Santa Rosa this past weekend with his family, when instead he was with me in Stinson Beach.

I smirk to myself. *Smart.*

"Yeah, so nice to see my mom and Nonna again." Saint smiles, raking a hand through his dark hair, his eyes flickering between my father and me. "It always feels like home when I'm there. My favorite place with my favorite people."

I muse my inner-actress and knit my brows. "Wait, *what?* You were in Santa Rosa?"

"Yeah, just for a short time. Most of Saturday, came back Sunday because of work," Saint chuckles warmly as he crosses his arms over his chest, his muscles unintentionally tensing in his perfectly fitted white T-shirt. "Don't tell me you didn't even notice I was gone, Paisley?"

"I literally didn't even realize! I guess I've been so busy with work…"

"You mean *celebrating.*" My father laughs, gesturing to me as he turns to his close friend. "This one goes downtown with her boss friend and then literally disappears off the face of the earth when I try to call her."

"I was sleeping!"

"Yeah, now I know, but I didn't know that when you didn't answer all three calls!"

"I was catching up on some beauty sleep." I grin, circling a hand around my face. *"See?"*

Saint throws his head back in laughter, all while my dad playfully rolls his eyes. "Dear God, help me."

"You're going to miss me when I'm in Seattle!"

My father nods and pulls me into a side hug. "I'm kidding. I know I am. I'm just protective of you, that's all. You're all I have, Paisley."

I swallow thickly. "I know."

I catch Saint's gaze and I can't help but notice the slight gloom in his piercing blue eyes as he watches us.

Seattle.

We haven't spoken about what's going to happen at the end of summer, only that we don't want this to end anytime soon. I'm so in love with him and I can only imagine how difficult long-distance must be, but when it comes to him... I'm willing to try anything.

Saint slips on his aviator sunglasses, despite it being just after 9:00 p.m., and it prevents me from seeing his eyes and I know it's because he doesn't want my father to see the emotion that was clouding them seconds ago.

"Anyway, did you two have a good time midtown?"

All while my father responds to Saint's question, I can't stop looking at Saint. The smile falls from my lips, and it feels as though I'm fizzling out at the seams because I hate playing this game of pretend with him now that my father's here. Saint and I need to talk about Seattle because I know me going off to college will change a few things. Distance creates distances, and I don't want that to happen to us.

I zone back in at my father's next words. "Want to come over for a drink, man?"

"Don't you have work?" Saint asks.

"Not until Thursday night... four p.m. for a twelve-hour shift, so I've got time now."

Four p.m. Thursday. Date night...

Saint looks everywhere but at me as he shakes his head and slips his hands into his black workout shorts. "Thanks for the offer, but work's been crazy, and I literally am going to go out like a light the second I step inside my house. So let's raincheck that drink, man, yeah?"

"Yeah, that works with me. All right, rest up easy and don't do any shit I wouldn't."

That makes Saint chuckle. "Literally am going to take a shower and fall into my bed."

Now that's a visual I'd love to join.

"All right, well, have a good one, man. Good night!"

"Night, Alaric." Saint nods before his head turns to me, and he slips off his Aviators. My father already begins walking back toward my house, the rattling of keys telling me he's about to open the front door any second now.

I turn back to Saint, smiling when I see that usual warmth in his eyes has returned. His gaze glances beyond me toward my father, then returns to me and winks when the coast is clear.

"Can I call you later?" he mouths.

I nod and mouth back, *"I'll tell you when."*

Saint smirks, those beautiful dimples deepening as he whispers, "You look beautiful, *wildflower.*"

I feel a blush rise on my cheeks as I glance down at my simple black cropped tank top and light denim frayed jeans and loafers. "It's the basics," I murmur back, "Nothing special."

"You still look beautiful to me."

My heart melts.

"Hey, mother's group over there! What are you two talking about?" my dad calls out from the porch and my entire body tenses up.

Oh shit.

Luckily, Saint is much more equipped than I am and replies within the same breath without even blinking. "Paisley wants to sign up for some boxing at the fitness studio. Was just telling her the different types of classes we have and availability."

I wait one second... *two* seconds... *three* seconds, and then I turn to my dad.

"Boxing?" he says, just as he opens the front door with a smile. "That's such a good idea, Paisley! That way you can punch any guy in the face that gets too close in college."

I breathe a little easier. *Oh, thank God he's buying the story.*

"Dad!" I laugh and turn to Saint with a warm smile. "We can talk more about it another time. Thanks for explaining all that to me, so useful. Good night!"

"Anytime at all," Saint says, his voice so gravelly and hot. "Good night, Paisley."

Once I'm inside my house, my father turns to me and claps his hands together with a grin. "Boxing lessons from a former professional boxer before you travel 761 miles away? YES! This is the greatest idea ever. I swear to God you're a genius, Paisley Reign. I mean, you kind of have to be one anyway. You *are* my daughter after all!"

I join in the laughter with him, but inside it's a whole other story. *Did Saint seriously just buy us more time to spend together without my father speculating a single thing?*

I grin to myself, mind blown.

Oh yes, he certainly did.

"Can you believe we actually pulled that off?" Saint chuckles through the phone as I slip into bed later on that night. "I literally had to pull that shit about the boxing out of nowhere."

"Well, you're officially my hero." I giggle softly, aware that my father is asleep across the hall, but still want to be quiet, even though he's softly snoring. "I just froze there and then there was you with a cover story in two-point-five seconds."

"Well, what can I say? I perform well under pressure."

"Mmhmmm."

"God, I miss you." A sharp sigh escapes Saint. "All I have been thinking about these past couple days is our time in Stinson Beach. How I wish we never left there. I liked when it was just us, when we didn't have to pretend that we don't feel what we do."

"I miss you so much too," I breathe through the phone. "And I couldn't agree more. I hate that we have to hide it from my father. It's almost as if we're lying to ourselves, you know?"

"I feel that, yeah. It's hard because we can't be our true selves around Alaric. He's super protective, and I completely understand, but I wanted nothing other than to kiss you when I saw you tonight. Wanted to whisk you away with me and have you lying right beside me in bed right now. I've been sleeping like shit without you here with me these past few nights. It may have been only one night sleeping next to you, but my body's grown accustomed to being with yours."

Aww.

"Stop being such a sweetheart." I smile, turning against my silk pillowcase.

Saint chuckles. "Why?"

"Because I'll have no control and tell you to sneak into my bedroom right now."

"*Dio mio,*" he growls. "Don't give me any ideas because you know I'll do it, babydoll."

Laughing softly, I feel my nipples harden through the thin emerald satin fabric of my camisole nightdress at the tone of his voice and what he said.

"What if I really wanted you to, though?" I purr through the phone. Temptation washes over me and I squeeze my heavy, ample breasts, rubbing my palm over my erect nipples through the fabric with a soft hum. "What would you say, Santo?"

"Fuck," he sexily groans. "I wouldn't say anything. I'd just be there with you in two seconds. *Dio.* You say my name like it was made for you because I'm certain it was. Wanna hear you say it forever now, *wildflower.*"

"In a heartbeat I would." I grin up at the ceiling and slip my hand through my wavy long hair over the pillow, scrunching up the ends. "Thank you for everything that came out in Stinson Beach. It means a lot to me that you trust me with so much, especially with your name, which I know is something big for you."

I can hear the smile in his voice. "You know I trust you with my life."

"Ditto," I say, just as something crosses my mind. "Earlier tonight when we were outside with my dad, I noticed something in your eyes changed when I mentioned Seattle. What were you thinking?"

I love how promptly Saint answers, with no hesitation. Love how open and honest he is.

"Part of me was wondering if we should tell Alaric about us before you leave for college. The other part craved running away with you to Seattle when the time comes, so we can play house."

My heart warms and the air crackles between the phone line. *Playing house. I want that too.*

"You mean us moving in together if you came to Seattle with me is an option?"

"Hell yeah. I mean, if you want that too… because you know that's what I want. Being neighbors, we practically already live together. Besides, I have connections to Giulio Giannotti at Notti Designs. Pretty sure he knows some good realtors for a property to suit our needs."

"As much as I love that idea, I literally only have just over ten grand to my name, Saint. I'll have more working until the end of July, but I've seen the properties Notti Designs makes and they're gorgeous, but far too expensive for my florist gig. I wouldn't be able to pay you back for at least the end of college, and everything I do make until then will go to my student loan. My dad offered, and I told him I wanted to do the apartment part on my own, and I will, but he's going to help with some college finances, so I don't want to be owing you too."

"Why would you expect that I'd want you to pay me back?"

"Because it's the courteous thing to do."

"Fuck courteous. I don't want anything out of you."

"Saint, I—"

"I mean it, Paisley," he cuts me off and there's some rustling on his end. "I'm with you because I want to be with *you*. That means taking care of you, not because I don't think you're capable of doing it on your own, but because whatever money you make, you should spend it on things you like. Leave everything else to me, and I mean it."

I shake my head, even though he can't see me. I don't want any advantages in this world. I want to know I earned something with my blood, sweat, and tears… so Saint buying me an apartment or property in Seattle… it just seems like too much too fast.

"I'm not letting you buy me an apartment, Saint."

"Then I'll move to Washington State with you, and it'll technically be *our* apartment. A shoebox studio apartment with popcorn ceiling and the only view is the parking lot? I don't want that for you. You're a poet at heart, you need stimulation, an apartment that inspires you. Come on, Pais, I literally have connections to an architect—Giulio. I'll call my cousin Enrico and try to set something up with Giulio. He'll know a good listing in Seattle and will take care of us. Unless… unless this isn't about the apartment and more about you not wanting us to move in together?"

"No, it's not that. Of course I want to move in with you… being with you is all I want."

"Then what is it, *wildflower*?"

"I don't know." I sigh, rubbing a hand over my face. "I just… Do you think we're moving too fast in terms of you coming to Seattle with me? I mean, an apartment is a huge step, no?" I shut my eyes and let the soft California breeze rush across my skin. There's still a warm tingle in the air. "I thought everything was perfect in Stinson Beach, but now being back home… reality is hitting me hard. The reality of the complexities of our relationship and how there are so many battles to come. And that even though I know our relationship is strong, sometimes it's scary to think of the outside noise… like my father… like what he's going to do when he finds out. Getting an apartment too on top of that is so exciting and beautiful, but it's also… look, I'm going to be honest, right now it's also a little daunting for me. I don't mean to place this hiccup between us, Saint, but I feel this needs to be addressed…"

Saint's silence taunts me for a few moments, and I let out a soft sigh.

Great, I unloaded too much.

And then just like that the weight lifts off me the second Saint murmurs through the phone, "I'm at your balcony. Is it okay if you open up?"

"My *balcony*?" My jaw drops as I open my eyes and slip out of the bed. "What? You're here? I didn't even hear anything!"

"It's called not wanting your father to hear me either."

"Mission accomplished then. Did you seriously just jump the fence?"

"Mmhmm." I can hear the smirk in his voice. "Something like that…"

I end the call and walk up to my balcony doors in shock. *I can't believe Saint's here.* My heart is pumping so hard as I pull the sheer drapes to the side and smile softly at Saint, who absolutely takes my breath away. He's standing on the opposite side of the sliding doors, phone in hand, smile on his soft lips, and only a pair of black boxers on.

Silvery moonlight shines through my bedroom as I unlock the door and slide it open, allowing Saint to step inside. The first thing he does is crash his lips on mine and it instantly soothes me, making me feel better about the deep conversation we were having over the phone seconds ago. The kiss is so addictive and intense, so thrilling like a passionate bliss to numb the nerves in my stomach.

I smile through it as his hands snake around my waist, settling by my satin-covered ass and pushing me closer to him. My hands can't stop roaming his smooth chest and neck, wanting to trace over every single inch of his warm Italian skin. Every inch of *him.*

Saint's the one to pull away and take my hand, warmth in his piercing gaze as he wordlessly leads me to my bed. We leave our phones on my nightstand. Saint and I slip inside the bedsheets, and I instantly cuddle up to his side, just like the other night, the only difference being my father is across the hall tonight. But the latter doesn't seem to bother either of us right now, no matter how risky it truly is having my father's hot best friend in my bed.

Shutting my eyes, I inhale a deep breath, taking in Saint's musky sandalwood scent, and focus on how much it calms me.

I think I've just been a little stressed tonight, so this right here, finding solace in his strong arms with his fingers caressing my skin, is exactly what I need.

"That's better." Saint kisses my cheek and I flutter my eyes open, loving the sweet blue of his as he glances down at me. He leans against one of my pillows with his left triceps, his head resting on his hand. His smile is so soft, so tender and *real* as he holds me tight and murmurs, "Talk to me, baby. Tell me exactly what's on your mind."

A breath escapes me because I'm opening my heart to him so much and appreciate the full extent to which he wants to explore every avenue with me, both so honest and open.

"Saint, I'm so in love with you," I start. "And now that I know you feel the same too… I just don't want to ruin things by moving too fast. I want everything to fall in place smoothly, naturally. I don't want either of us to regret anything, or our relationship to be the reason my dad doesn't speak to any of us. There's so much to juggle and… I know you can't have your cake and eat it too, so I'm not feeling overwhelmed, just a little nervous."

"Nervous?"

"Yes. As you know, I've never been in a relationship before, so I'm giving so much of myself, and I don't want to ruin it with major steps that may crumble us. Am I wrong to think that?"

"Not at all. I think that's fair that you're feeling this way. It's only normal to feel all these feelings, especially being nervous as these are all firsts for you. I hear what you're saying and agree. I'm sorry if I got a little too excited earlier and it put too much pressure on you. Paisley, you know I would never *ever* want to make you feel that kind of way. I want everything to fall into place naturally too. I don't want to rush a single thing and feel as though if we navigate a slower path to the other side of this, those nerves will start to flutter away."

All the built-up stress that has been rumbling inside me slowly fades at his words.

"That's exactly what I needed to hear." I smile, tracing a finger down his defined jaw. "You always know what to say to make me feel better. I'm just glad I let it all out now."

"So am I, *wildflower*. Thank you for being so honest and brave for me. I know it isn't easy, so I'm glad you allow yourself to be vulnerable and raw with me. Never be afraid of voicing your opinion to me, Pais. Even if you think it's something that'll piss me off, say it. As you know, I'm a direct kind of guy, so tell me whatever, whenever. I promise I won't crumble 'cause of it. Do you think living with you twenty-four seven is going to scare me away?"

I gulp down. "Maybe, yes."

"That doesn't scare me." Saint smiles brightly, his hand around my waist flushing me closer to his bare chest as he glances between my eyes in pure adoration. "I'm gonna need far more than that to run away, Pais. If you're worried that we're taking things too fast with the moving in together and apartment, then we'll slow it down. I just want you to know that I'm willing to move my life to Seattle for you. That's all I'm trying to say. We can do the distance thing with daily calls and seeing you summers and weekends. We can tell Alaric and move around more freely, no matter the consequence. We can play this out however you like, as long as it's what makes you the happiest and I still see you regularly. Whatever you're good with, I'm good with too. I have all my cards open on the table, and they all point to you."

Aww.

I can't stop smiling because his words touch my heart. Relief consumes my entire body, and I'm just so grateful for Saint because he always makes me feel heard.

"Thank you for that, truly," I say. "I always feel so comfortable around you. You let me be me and that means a lot. You're honestly so respectful. Many other men would have pushed me away for admitting that about the apartment."

"I'd never push you away, Paisley. Ever. Just want you to know there are options, that's all, whether you take them or not."

"That's what I love about you most. You respect my opinion, always."

"Of course I do. Mostly because it's logical." Saint grins before his eyes darken. "And mostly because I love when you tell me what you want."

"Well, I appreciate it. I just feel bad because I don't want to hinder your dreams because of mine, that's all."

"There's no need to feel bad. My career as a professional boxer ended three years ago, Paisley. That was my true calling and I'll never have it again, but it's okay because I've lived my dream. I lived it for ten good long years. Yes, I love co-owning a fitness studio now and bettering people's lives, but that job is adaptable and the rush I got every time I stepped in a ring, that was something else. There's nothing else I've wanted since, so let me help you with *your* dream now. Let me help you, Paisley, just like you always help me."

Saint smiles as a calmness settles between us and he cups my jaw and whispers, "I'm a jealous man, Paisley. So fucking jealous. Perhaps the world made me that way, but all I know is that I will protect you and keep you safe until my dying breath. Even if we don't turn out, I'm always going to take care of you. Those guys at college, your future work colleagues, everybody in Seattle… they see a beautiful girl like you, and I want to destroy them for thinking they're worthy of you."

"I'd never choose them. Besides, I'm pretty sure my boyfriend will knock them out cold in a second, so…"

"Damn right he will," Saint murmurs against my lips. "No Seattle, no moving in together, no apartment hunting, I get that now. I'm sorry, I just want to give you options."

"No need to apologize, baby. It's me who should have been clearer in the first place."

"It's clear now. That's all that matters."

I grin against his lips. "You're amazing. You know that, right?"

"It must be the Italian in me."

I scrunch my nose up in laughter before slapping a hand over my mouth with wide eyes. "Oh, crap, I forgot my dad is just across the hall."

Saint grins back, yet in my head the devil on my shoulder taunts me.

If Saint and I had our own place, we wouldn't have to worry about that...

"Okay, answer me this..." Maralyn says in her thick Brooklyn accent, crossing her arms over her chest behind the cashier counter of the florist. "It's my twenty-fifth wedding anniversary today and you wanna know what my *thoughtful* husband gave me this morning?"

Biting my lip to hide my grin, I glance away from the lilies I'm wrapping and turn to my boss, Maralyn. "I have no idea, but from that tone I can imagine it... wasn't what you expected?"

"Understatement," she huffs, chewing on her gum loudly. "He gave me *this week's trash* to put out on the street ahead of today's collection. But that's not all... he told me—get this—*don't buy a cheesecake this morning, you don't need it on the waistline.*"

My jaw drops. "Oh my... Do you think he just said that to throw you off but is actually planning a surprise?"

"A *surprise?*" Maralyn practically screeches. "That man forgot the words *surprise, anniversary, Saint Valentine's,* and *birthday* the second I said 'I do' twenty-five years ago." She shakes her head, raising a finger for each word she listed. "Don't get me wrong, I love him, but this morning I couldn't stand what he did. *So,* I showed him what I'm made of."

I grin, absolutely loving this story. Anytime Maralyn recounts something, it's bound to be good. Besides, anything else but talking about my apparent *mystery man* after the other day is great.

Saint... Gosh, I can't wait for our date night tomorrow night.

It's only after the customer pays for the lilies and I put through another two people that I turn back to Maralyn, who's rearranging the rose-gold-colored love-heart balloons we sell as add-ons. "So, what did you do?"

"Did what any other rational woman would have done, of

course. Got that trash bag and slammed it on the side of his head. That sure knocked some brain cells as he looked at me all funny looking with a banana peel at the side of his head. I didn't care. I was more riled up about the comment than the fact he forgot it's the second national day of l-o-v-e. *So*, I forgot about him, got in my car, stepped on the gas, and treated myself to a blueberry cheesecake across the street and ordered fifty to be delivered to his office at lunch. Don't feel bad about a damn thing. Sometimes you gotta do what you gotta do to show a man what he's dealing with."

I can't help but laugh as I look at her all wide-eyed. "You *actually* did that?"

Maralyn simply grins. "Sure did. I just lost it."

"I don't blame you. I can't believe he said that and never apologized!"

"Oh, he did." Maralyn taps the oak countertop with her pointer finger. "He called the second I opened the store this morning. Told me he was sorry and didn't mean to say what he did. I forgave him. Still didn't tell him about the cheesecakes, though. I'm sure he'll *love* me after that."

Smiling, I shake my head to myself. "I aspire to be more like you. I mean, the other day you gave a customer a manicure, last week you managed to make the parking inspector pay you, and the week before that, you were an extra in that new Brad Pitt blockbuster."

Maralyn blows out a huge bubble with her purple gum and lets it pop loudly. "It's called not giving a fuck, something a certain Paisley Reign needs to do more of, huh?"

"I'm getting there."

"Oh yeah?" She smirks, crossing her hands over her chest. "Okay. Tell me the boldest thing you've done in this past month, aside from your little getaway last week with Mr. *Mystery Man…*"

"This month?" Laughing, my mind circles as I try to not pick a memory that includes Saint, no matter how much I want to mention him because I've been so bold with him. "Well, I graduated college and have just been busy working, studying, and starting to think about an apartment in Seattle when I move there for college in a couple mont—"

"Excuses, Excuses. *Boldest* thing. *Go.*"

Think. Think. Think.

"Okay." I swallow down, running a hand through my loose waves. "Umm, I had my first tequila a few days ago when I'm not even legal yet. That counts, right?"

Maralyn shoots me a blank expression. "Jesus, Paisley, that can't be the boldest thing you've done this month. I've been drinking Cosmopolitans since the day I exited the womb all those yea—"

"Hey, Oprah and Drew Barrymore!" a man hisses nearby, having us avert our vision to a short man directly behind the counter. He snaps his fingers at us with an impatient scoff, a bouquet of roses in hand. "Should I just walk out without paying or are you both done with your *'boldness therapy'* chitchat?"

"Are *you* done with your attitude?" Maralyn grits while I slap a hand over my mouth, eyes wide and internally screaming at myself.

Oh my God! The line!

The line behind the man consists of another three men. All corporate with sleek suits. The man behind Mr. Smartass is on the phone, whisper-shouting to some man called 'Matteo' about dinner reservations. Behind him, a Ricky Martin doppelgänger is constantly glancing between a pink bouquet and a red bouquet of poinsettias he's holding with a clenched jaw as if it's a tennis match. The last man in line is indecisively glancing down at his gold watch.

Maralyn glances over at me with a warm smile. "I'll take over the register, babe. Work on the floor, but don't you worry. This conversation *isn't* over…"

I quickly apologize to the men before practically running to the first flower section I see—geraniums—and straighten up the area. I take in the sweet idyllic smell of the geraniums, a smile forming on my lips as a memory of Saint crosses my mind. The comment from a couple of years ago when he joked about these flowers being a pain in the ass still has me laughing.

Saint.

Saint's been so patient with me, respecting the fact that I want to take things one step at a time… *but could I be wrong in thinking him moving to Seattle isn't the best move?* Of course I'm scared of ruining everything by going too fast, but I don't know if I have it in me to be just under two hours away from Saint by plane. *What if I don't ruin things?*

Saint wants to be with me. He's willing to sacrifice moving to a whole other state because of me. Am I seeing it all wrong?

While my first encounter when Saint slaughtered my blue tiger lilies was one for the books, the years following have been the best ones of my life. To me, there isn't a life before Saint. My entire life up until this point… it's just *been* Saint. And I know, it's crazy how one person can only be in your life for three years and take up all the space in your heart, trust me I know, but when I'm with Saint, everything seems to fade away and it becomes us.

Us unraveling the world together.

Us so passionately in love.

Simply us.

Chapter
TWENTY-SIX

Saint

Thursday night can't come soon enough. After spending the day at work in between training members and working with both Nico and Leo, excitement thrills me when the clock strikes 4:15 p.m. and not only am I done for the day, but Alaric just stepped into a twelve-hour shift.

Twelve hours uninterrupted with my forever girl.

I was so quick to decline having drinks with Nico after work and practically sped home on my Harley. Once inside my house, I had a quick shower and slid on black jeans and a black button-down shirt. Which leads me to where I am right now, slipping on black leather cowboy boots with an embroidered paisley pattern. I bought them yesterday specifically for tonight, and because I liked the pattern... *paisley.*

I'm meeting Paisley at her front door in ten minutes—5:00 p.m.

Rubbing my dark stubble, I rake a hand through my slightly

wavy black hair and push back the longish sides behind my ears. The other night after I sneaked into Paisley's bedroom window and we had that intense chat, in conversation she mentioned how good I'd pull off a sexy man bun if I continued growing out my hair a little. I never thought about it until that night, and ever since I can't get the thought out of my mind…

Especially not after how good it felt when Paisley's fingers tugged on the ends of my hair as I fucked her so goddamn hard after. We fucked so recklessly, I had to keep my hand covered over her mouth to mute her loud moans from being heard by her father, Alaric, across the hall when we both came apart. I left a couple hours later in the middle of the night, despite her kisses to make me stay. As much as I wanted to, I knew that if I stayed with Paisley after sex I'd sleep beside her until the sun came up and didn't want to risk Alaric hearing me if I left at that hour.

Once I was in my own bed, I kept on running my fingers through my hair, feeling her taste on my tongue, and I caved and said to myself, *fuck it, I'm growing a man bun for her.* I'll be one of those tattooed guys riding around on a Harley with a man bun for her. I can already see my mom and Nonna laughing in my face because of it… But being in love with Paisley, it does crazy things to me, crazy things I so desperately need to survive.

Even now as I slip my wallet into my jeans back pocket, the memories return, filling me with desire. *I like Paisley's idea.* It's definitely worth a shot.

Grabbing my car keys, I begin typing Paisley a text as I step out of my bedroom and down the flight of stairs. Once I'm in the living room, I hit send and take a seat in my burgundy upholstered velvet armchair, my fingers continuously drumming over the dark shoebox on the coffee table beside me.

SAINT: You probably don't want to wear a sundress tonight…

Paisley's response comes in seconds.

PAISLEY: Sure, because going around naked on date night is ideal… What is it you're hiding, Mr. Lisconti? ;)

Just the thought of Paisley naked anywhere has my blood pumping hard in arousal.

I'm smirking as I type back.

SAINT: As much as I want you naked, I should clarify what I meant. Definitely wear clothes, baby, just perhaps not a sundress and jeans or shorts instead, or something of that kind... It'll all make sense when we get to where we're going.

PAISLEY: Ooo, got it. Do I get a clue as to where we're going?

SAINT: Hmm, okay. One clue.

Resting my feet on the coffee table, I lock my ankles and take a photo of my paisley leather cowboy boots. I send it to her and type...

SAINT: Hope you make a good Sherlock Holmes... This is all you're getting, babydoll. ;)

PAISLEY: Oh wow... Uh, a rodeo?

SAINT: We don't live in Montana, baby.

PAISLEY: True. Another clue?

SAINT: Okay... I've got your boots covered too, so I'll give you them when I come to your front door.

PAISLEY: No sundresses... No shoes... You sure you want me to walk out like this? ;)

I chuckle. That is until a photo comes through of Paisley in just a red lacy thong and my jaw hits the floor. *Holy fuck.* She looks so goddamn sexy with her hair in a French braid and that sultry lip bite. It's so suggestive and *fuck.*

Paisley knows exactly what she's doing to me in this picture. It must be taken in front of the large wall standing mirror in her bedroom, and my semi-hard cock twitches at the sight of her beautiful figure, crossed long legs, creamy ample breasts, and hard pink nipples, begging me to be sucked.

My mind goes crazy with all the positions I want to fuck her in right in front of that mirror. Paisley's becoming more and more confident as the days go by, and her boldness… I want to spank her for how much it turns me on.

I can't be quick enough to stand up, collect the shoebox in my hands, and reply to her.

> **SAINT: Fuck me, babydoll. You're so gorgeous I can't even take it. I'm coming over. Right. This. Second.**

> **PAISLEY: Looking forward, cowboy!**

> **SAINT: Say that again and I'll spank you.**

> **PAISLEY: As if that's even a punishment at this point… Cowboy!! ;)**

I'm at Paisley's front door in heartbeats, knocking only once before the door swings open in seconds, revealing the most beautiful woman I've ever known. Paisley grins over at me, so much desire pooling in her eyes as she assertively stands with her hands on either side of the doorframe, her confidence, pretty breasts, and lace red panties making my cock harder by the second.

Paisley's eyes drop to my leather cowboy boots and she smirks. The way she keeps her head low yet glances at me through her lashes is so sensual. Thick sexual darkness clouds them, making my heart skip a beat at how sexy she is.

Paisley bites her lip in pure seduction. "Are we going to be riding something, Mr.?"

I don't miss the way Paisley's gaze lands on my crotch through my jeans at the word 'riding'. I swear to God she sees just how strained my hard cock is against the denim fabric. It's throbbing, aching to be pulled out and stroked fast.

"Get inside so the neighbors don't see those gorgeous tits of yours," I growl, stepping forward as she takes one step back. I shut the front door behind me and am quick to drop the shoebox near her feet, between us. "Or else the only thing you'll be riding right now is my thick cock, babydoll."

"Hmmm, that's so hot…"

"I'll show you fucking hot."

Paisley grins, and I can already tell it is by how sexually frustrated I am right now. I want to begin date night so fucking badly, but seeing her like this tonight… it makes me want to take her right here in this hallway until she's screaming out my name like I'm the God she's praising.

I gulp down and cross my arms over my chest, telling myself I need to stop thinking about how addictive sex is with her. Nodding down toward the shoebox, I smile at the perfect deflection. "I bought you something for tonight. Why don't you try them on, baby?"

Cowboy boots won't turn me on.

It feels as though Paisley knows exactly what I'm doing by deflecting the conversation by the beautiful, smug smirk on her lips when she nods. Instead of leaning forward to pick up the shoebox, she steps around it until she's standing in the gap between it and me, her back facing me. There's not even an inch of room between us, and it all disappears as Paisley bends down. The view of her ass up in the air with that scrap of red lace sexily rushing down her hips and disappearing between her peachy cheeks as it presses up against my erection has me breathing harder.

Fuckkk.

Said it once, I'll say it again. This woman will be the death of me. The pure death.

Paisley slows for a second before circling her hips and grinding against me softly, rousing me up. I'm left to hiss out at just how much it aches with how hard I am. Paisley opens the shoebox and sets the lid down on the hardwood floor. I know the exact second she sees the glossy red thigh-high leather cowboy boots with thick tall heels and a striking floral pattern because she gasps and stands up, spinning around to face me just as I was about to spank her ass. She grins up at me, waving the boots in her hands as if I didn't just feel the warmth of her pussy through her lace panties against me seconds ago.

"I love them! They're gorgeous! Thank you for being thoughtful!"

"My pleasure. I thought you'd love them. Is the size all right?"

"Yes, eight. They seem perfect!"

"Good. Slip 'em on."

Paisley does and they look stunning on her. Seeing her with nothing else on but those tight glossy red floral thigh-high boots and lacy G-string… *Dio, cowboy boots just turned me on.*

Her gaze darkens, dripping in desire that I love as she backs up down the hallway before strutting to me as if she's on the runway in her new boots, her tits bouncing around. Paisley comes to a halt in front of me, smiling as she does a full spin and my eyes hungrily roam her body with a grin.

"So, how do I look?"

"Is that even a question?" I chuckle, pulling her flush to my chest with my hands by her lower back. "You look beautiful. So utterly beautiful. You know exactly what you're doing to me, *wildflower.*"

Paisley blushes. "So, you're saying we have some time before you whisk us away to that rodeo?"

I laugh. "It's not a rodeo."

"You know what I mean."

"I do, but I'll put you out of your misery and say we're going to a ranch just under thirty minutes away. It's a great escape with horse riding, scenic views, a campfire… the whole lot."

"Oh, that's incredible!"

"Also, the answer is *yes*…" I teasingly brush my lips over hers. "We have time before it."

"Time for you to fuck me hard."

My heart flutters in my chest, a little taken aback by what she just said. It turns me the fuck on because I never expected words so dirty to come out of the mouth of a woman so sweet.

I glance between her eyes. "Yeah?"

"Mmhmm. All you've got to do is tell me." Paisley stands on her tippy toes, her warm lips curling into a smirk before they press against my ear and she whispers so damn seductively, "Tell me how you want me, Santo."

Dear God.

I suck in a breath because Lord knows there's no saving my

soul from the beauty that is Paisley Reign. She's so damn special, like a piece of poetry I want to preserve forever. Like the one she wrote for me that I haven't stopped looking at and remembering since.

"I want you to sit your pretty ass on the edge of your bed. Legs spread. Eyes on me. Your vibrator in your hands waiting for my next instructions."

Her eyes widen. "My... my vibrator? How do you even remember I said I have one?"

"Because that's the type of thing a man's never bound to forget, babygirl. I want to see your vibrator, the one you come hard around when you think of me. Want to see it slipping in and out of you as I fuck you with it, as you moan out my name, as you beg me for my cock instead. I know you want to, baby. I know underneath you really are a sex freak, just like me." My fingers wrap around the lace of her panties and teasingly tug on them. "I want *these* off." Then I reach down and graze her thigh-high boots. "I want *these* to stay on at all times... *Hai capito*? Do you understand, *tesoro*?"

Paisley nods eagerly with a lip bite, her hard nipples rubbing over my dress shirt already driving me crazy. "How do you say 'I understand' in Italian?"

"*Ho capito.*"

"*Ho capito*, Santo."

I smile down at her in complete awe. "Good girl."

Paisley grins.

I love the way she threads her fingers through mine and doesn't let go of my hooded gaze once as she leads me down the hallway, through her living room, and upstairs. Once inside her bedroom, I close the door behind us and lean against it. I watch as Paisley slips off her panties and the red scrap of lace hits the hardwood floors in sync with my next heartbeat. She's quick to pull out the pink vibrator from her nightstand and sit on the edge of her queen-sized bed, setting the vibrator down on the covers as she spreads her legs out so I can see her glistening pussy just like I instructed her.

Oh God. So beautiful.

Warm afternoon sunshine floods through her bedroom, illuminating the white, dusty pink and rose gold accents in her bedroom and letting the sexy red thigh-high boots she has on really pop. I step closer to her and fall to my knees, positioned right between her spread thighs.

A growl escapes me when I cup Paisley's face, my thumb brushing extra slowly across her plump, pink-colored lips as they part, and her hot breath arouses me more. There's a scarlet blush across her cheeks and it has me smiling to see my *wildflower* so turned on, yet still the slightest bit bashful.

"Why are you blushing, baby?"

"Well, I never expected my vibrator to make a feature like this…"

I chuckle. "Why? You don't have any fantasies about it?"

Her eyes darken. "Quite the opposite…"

"Then let's make those fantasies come true."

Paisley bites her lip as I pick up her smooth vibrator and inhale a deep breath of it. "God, it smells like you," I moan. My tongue slowly runs the length of the toy with a satisfied groan as my cock twitches in my jeans. "It tastes like you too. So sweet. So *you*."

Paisley leans back on her forearms with a hum, but when she attempts to press her thighs together, I spread her legs apart farther, holding them down on the bed in possession.

"No taking the edge off yet, Paisley."

"Please, Saint," she pleads. "I need to feel you."

"Play with your tits for me first, baby."

Smiling, Paisley molds her ample breasts. The way her thumbs brush over her erect nipples makes me want to suck on them so badly. I grin back, my gaze hungrily lowering to where I know she needs me the most. It's so hot watching her so aroused.

"God. You're so goddamn wet for me, babydoll."

"Yesss, touch me," Paisley begs, her glistening pussy throbbing in appreciation, and I want nothing more than to have her clenched around me when she comes hard. Knowing I need to see her orgasm before that, I switch on the vibrator and the soft buzz echoes between us, mixing with my heartbeat and accompanying my cock's every pulse.

"You're driving me fucking crazy, Paisley. I'm so goddamn hard for you."

She moans as I press the toy over her clit before I lower it down her warm pussy and slide it inside of her. She gets wetter by the second as I begin to glide it in and out of her. The fact that I'm fucking her with her own toy and the constant vibration it gives drives me absolutely insane.

"Yes, keep doing that," Paisley pants, the beautiful blush on her cheeks deepening. She rakes a hand through my hair, tugging on the ends, and can barely hold herself up with just one forearm as I thrust the toy in and out of her faster and faster, her body shaking with every movement.

Hearing how wet she is… Her pretty pink pussy glistening… Watching her arousal drip down her sex and disappear through her ass cheeks… *fuck*.

"Look at us, Pais. Look at me fucking your pretty pussy with your vibrator. I swear to God I'll remember this for the rest of my life. So good. You're such a bad girl letting me play with you like this, aren't you?"

"Yes, so bad for you." She grins, a moan then taking over as she tips her head back and her mouth parts to shape a big O. I rub my free hand up her smooth inner thighs, the flash of her red boots making me so crazy as I lean forward toward her pussy. Still fucking her with the toy, I continuously flick my tongue fast up and down her swollen clit, spreading her arousal with every move. Her grip on my hair tightens when she cries out, "Yes! Yes! Yes! Keep doing that again and I'm going to come all over your face, Saint."

Damn right you are, baby.

I wickedly smirk against her pussy in appreciation, feeling my cock pulse hard as precum drips down my length in my boxer briefs at the way Paisley quivers under my touch. It's evident with how badly she's holding off coming by how hard she's breathing and the way she's clenching around the vibrator. She wants this to last, but I have other plans as my jaw tenses with just how fast my tongue is working her clit, and every inch of her body gives in to desire as she screams out my name and begins to orgasm intensely, her body convulsing around the toy and my tongue as she finishes.

Slipping out the vibrator, I replace the sensation and drive my tongue into her pussy, swirling it around and letting Paisley ride out her orgasm on it. She does until she settles down and her pants begin to soften, her sweet taste sending me to heaven.

I love her taste.

It's then when she wraps her legs around my neck, burying my face right between her legs, and it gives me so much pleasure the way I allow her to use me however she likes when my tongue starts moving like crazy inside her.

"Oh my God, Saint! Yes, yes, yesss!"

I slide my hands beneath her ass, squeezing her cheeks tight as Paisley rides my face and I passionately make love to her pussy with my mouth, edging her close to another orgasm just as electrifying. To see Paisley on her bed riddled up by pleasure because of the second climax I brought her to… it makes me want to reward her with my cock deep throating her mouth. But we have time, all the time in the world to explore each other sexually because right now I just need to feel my cock in her warm pussy, gripping it like a vice in nothing but pleasure.

I need her.

I need to reward her for being such a good girl. *Right. Now.*

"That was incredible." Paisley's legs slip from my neck as she lies on her bed completely spent with the biggest grin on her face. "You're something else, Santo Lisconti."

Smoldering, I throw her a wink. "Could say the same about you too, *wildflower*."

You're something else, Paisley Reign.

She smirks and eyes my clothes. "Uh, you're a little over-dressed, don't you think?"

I strip out of my clothes and boots in half a second. Paisley hungrily gazes at my raging erection when I slip off my boxer briefs last, the head beaded in precum and so damn ready for her. Paisley's sweet jasmine scent consumes me, making this even more real as I lick her sweet taste from my lips and climb up on the bed on top of her, adoring the way she's looking up at me with so much love as we share a grin.

"Better now?" I chuckle.

"Much better." Paisley giggles, caressing down my bare chest and then lower to trace my hard abs. A squeal escapes her when I grip her hips and spin her around to her stomach before she can reach my cock, knowing I'll explode the second she touches me. I need to be inside her when I come. I've never been this fucking close without a single stroke, suck, or thrust.

I spank her ass and murmur in her ear, "I want you on your hands and knees facing the mirror with your ass up, tits down, and eyes on your reflection. You have two seconds, baby."

"Gladly."

Paisley doesn't even take a second to submit to me as we re-adjust to face the large wall standing mirror on the right side of her bedroom. It reveals a perfect view of us on her bed.

A perfect view of Paisley beautifully bent over and me kneel-ing behind her, ready for it.

A perfect view of her lovely, flustered face, those perfect red thigh-high boots, and gorgeous ass, which I squeeze and spank before meeting her gaze in the mirror.

"You sent me that gorgeous picture of yourself by this mir-ror." I smirk. "You gave me an idea and now I can't get it out of my head."

"So don't. Give in to it instead." Paisley's already looking at me through the mirror with such allure, her honey browns darkening even deeper when we share the most beautiful grin as she purrs, "Ruin me, Santo."

Hearing her say my real name at a time like this has me gripping my thick cock and a moan escapes us both at the exact same time as I teasingly glide it over her warm sex, making it glisten more. *So hot.* Aroused heat flows through my veins and, knowing I can't tease this any longer, I hold Paisley's stare in the mirror and fully slip into her greedy pussy with three hard thrusts.

"I'll ruin you good, *wildflower*. Ruin you until you're mine."

"I already am yours."

"*Forever*," I growl. "I'm going to fuck you into *forever*. You want that too, babydoll?"

We've never fucked this way before, especially not in front of a mirror, so seeing Paisley bent over like this, those sexy boots on and her pussy already clenching around my cock... it has me giving in to every desire. Growling, I grip her ass and begin pounding into her so recklessly my every frantic heartbeat goes in rhythm with her relentless moans. "Oh, God, yes! I want that. I want forever with you. Fuck, Santo!"

"I love it when you say my name like that."

"Santo... Oh, *Santooo*!"

"Oh, yes. Just like that, babydoll. Scream it."

Paisley and I aren't only fucking so damn passionately, we're giving one another each other with no limits. And that's exactly what I do. I fuck her with every single thing I have and grind my hips, each pump in and out of her becoming deeper and faster with each grunt that escapes me.

So good.

I'm so fast her hands give way and slip. Her cheek presses against the bouncing bedcovers. It's so sexy the way Paisley turns her head and continues to watch us in the mirror, her eyes sparkling in desire as she leans up on her forearms instead and bites her clenched right fist to mute how loud she is, but her muffled noises only have me losing it more.

"Such a bad girl, watching a thirty-six-year-old man fuck

your eighteen-year-old pussy like this. So dirty." I spank her ass with a smirk and tell her how much of a good girl she is as I watch us in the mirror with hooded eyes. "You feel so good against my cock. Made for me, Paisley. Your pussy was fucking made for me."

"Yes, I want you to be my first and last. *Ohhh!*"

"I'll be anything you like, baby, any fucking thing." A couple of curse words slip from my mouth in Italian. "*Cazzo*, you're making me lose control, the way you're looking at me... *Dio*."

"I'm so close, Saint," she moans.

"Me too, *wildflower*, hold on for me."

I throw my head back and shut my eyes from the ecstasy I feel fucking her so hard into submission. Paisley's mine and my God how her body is letting me know it with how responsive she is to me. I reopen my eyes and glance at myself in the mirror. At my abs coated in perspiration, tensing tighter with every thrust. At Paisley's eyes, which almost roll back in pleasure. At my vaunted V-cut that slams against her ass again and again and again. And I know I'm so close to coming, so close to reaching the other side with her.

"*Mi stai facendo impazzire*," I moan out. "*Mi stai facendo impazzire e lo adoro. Adoro vederti così. Adoro vederci così insieme. Ti adoro.*"

The pleasure only intensifies between us as Paisley grinds her hips back to meet my thrusts and slide on my cock. My cock is pulsing like crazy, begging for me to fill her with everything I have.

"I love it when you speak Italian to me. Translate what you just said," Paisley pants.

She looks so sexy losing control beneath me like this. So sexy I trail her spine and take a hold of her French braid, wrapping the hair around my hand before I sexily tug it, and subsequently her head tips back too. I can't stop showing her the beast I am when I go wild, waves of passion fueling me.

"You're making me go crazy," I start with the translation.

"You're making me go so crazy and I adore it. Adore seeing you like this. Adore seeing us like this together." I roughly pull her hair again, this time real back until she's forced to look up at me from behind, upside-down, and I growl, "Adore *you*."

Then, I lean forward so she can see me better and I give her an intense upside-down kiss, still pumping into her fast while tugging her hair. My body continues to rock against hers and I feel her pussy start to clench around me as intense moans escape her throat mid-kiss. We kiss hard, breathlessly, so sensual and filthy with our tongues craving every single taste. I kiss her until my breaths become hers and hers mine.

Letting go of my grip on her hair, Paisley's face lowers so our gazes meet in the mirror again. Her face is so flustered from how crazy we're fucking, but that's what being in love with Paisley does to me. It ruins me whole, and I never want this feeling to grow old.

"I adore you too, Santo." She smiles through the moans. "I adore you. I adore you. I adore you."

Grinning, I lower on top of her more and my dark stubbled jaw grazes against her smooth cheek as our faces press together. Honey brown and ocean blue is all I see as I wrap my large hand around her throat and my other hand wraps around her waist, holding her body up as we watch ourselves seconds from losing control completely.

Breathing in her jasmine scent mixed with my masculine blend, desire grows insatiable. My heart warms because this moment couldn't be more perfect as I hold her close, kiss her cheek, and murmur something that I've been holding onto for a little while now. Something so meaningful and true. Something she needs to know because I can't live my life without her.

"I love you, Paisley," I murmur softly. "I love you so fucking much. More than I've ever loved anything else in my whole entire life. I love you to death. To the moon. To every ocean."

"I love you, Santo." I'll never forget the pure affection in Paisley's eyes as they glaze over in happy tears, and she grins so beautifully I melt. "To death. To the moon. To the oceans. *Forever.*"

"I love you more, my forever girl."

We're falling, falling, *fallen* and both begin moaning in pleasure as an earth-shattering orgasm ripples through Paisley, her entire body going wild in my hold as she comes so intensely around my pulsing cock. Her orgasm offsets my own and I explode, filling her hard with every drop of my warm cum while softly chanting a chorus of '*I love you, I love you, I love you*'.

As our pants return to normal breaths, I slowly pull out of her pussy and the second we collapse on the bed, I lie on my back and tenderly roll her to my side. Paisley's warm left hand rests on my chest, listening to the thumps of my heart as it beats wildly for her.

Her striking eyes meet mine and I hold her close with my arms around her waist, my fingers slowly caressing her skin. The grin we share never falls. There's so much warmth in my chest at the way Paisley's looking up at me with pure joy, pure admiration, pure trust. So beautifully poetic it heals every single one of my flaws and has me kissing away all of hers.

"Whoa," Paisley murmurs, that breathtaking grin turning to a giggle. "Your heart is beating so fast."

"Loving you makes it do that. Loving you is the reason I'm still breathing because now I know this is what it feels like to really be alive. To be crazy in love. To love a wildflower. *You* are my reason, Paisley Reign. You are the reason it's still beating. Only you."

When Paisley reaches up and crashes her lips on mine with a kiss so sensual and intimate, I feel her heartbeat against mine and know that our hearts have been racing so wildly in harmony this entire time.

Because this kiss tells me that I'm her *reason* too.

Because she and I are made for each other, and fate is real.

Because she's the only remedy to my skipped heartbeats, my dying breaths, my endless *I love yous*.

Paisley

"Out of all the places in the world, I never expected a date night at a ranch!" I smile as Saint accelerates up the Westside Freeway on Interstate 5. "You're very unexpected. You know that, Mr. Lisconti?"

Saint smirks over at me from the driver's seat, bringing our laced hands to his mouth to softly kiss my skin. "Well, what can I say… Expect the unexpected with me, baby."

"I'm starting to believe that. First Stanford, then a beach house, now cowboy boots… What's next? Are you going to tell me that you're actually reuniting your band with your cousin, Enrico, and are actually beginning the first leg of your sellout world tour soon?"

"You know I can arrange that, if you like." He winks.

I tip my head back in laughter against the leather headrest. "You totally would, though!"

"Anything for you, Pais."

"What was the name of your band? I can't believe I didn't ask you before!"

Saint chuckles as his eyes return to the highway. "Come to think of it, we didn't even have one."

"Well, there's always time."

We both burst out into laughter, and it just feels so nice to be this content. Like nothing can ever stop us. I smile to myself at the '90s chill rap playing on the speakers low, loving that it's so Saint.

According to the navigation on his Maserati's touch control screen, we're only thirteen minutes away from the ranch now. I've never been to a ranch before in my life and am thoroughly thrilled about what's to come. Saint's been so excited about it and honestly can't stop telling me how good I look in the beautiful red leather thigh-high cowboy boots he bought me, the same ones I'm still wearing. I'm beginning to think they're definitely a kink for him, especially considering Saint made me keep them on whilst we fucked.

Gosh, that sex... it was something else.

"Turns out my Italian professional boxer boyfriend is a sweetheart, huh?"

"Better add *former* to that title, baby."

"You're still a professional to me. You're very... *Ahem*, let's just say *athletic*."

Saint's blue eyes land on me for a moment and darken. *"Non dirmi queste cose mentre guido.* Don't tell me these things when I'm driving."

I smirk. "Want me to deflect the conversation?"

"Please do."

"Okay. When are you going to show me one of your fights?"

Saint's gaze returns to the highway with a smile. "You haven't searched one up? Not like your stunt with Stanford University or the Olympics, huh?"

"Nope." I giggle. "I'm waiting for the green light from you with this one. Will you show me a few of your boxing matches tonight when we come back from the ranch?"

He's silent for a moment before he lets out a soft sigh. "You really want to see me all roughed up and tough?"

"I want to see the Saint Lisconti the world saw before me, yes. I've seen everything that you are, every single piece. Your past life as a professional boxer is the only missing piece."

Saint glances over at me with one hand on the wheel and even after all this time, those warm eyes seep right into my soul. Eyes so blue I'm forced to do nothing else but drown in waves of him. Nothing else but him.

Our extended stare is so sweet and passionate, the most real thing I've ever felt in my entire life as Saint squeezes our intertwined hands and grins.

"Then, we'll watch a few of my boxing matches." His dimples are so deep and oh so beautifully carved. I just want to slowly trace them for a lifetime. "I love you, *wildflower*."

"Love you forever, my blue-eyed boy." I grin back. Squeezing his hand back tighter, I lean across the car's console and quickly peck his soft lips. "You know I always will. *Always.*"

Everything is perfect.

Every single little thing.

The brief kiss.

The sparkle in Saint's ocean blues.

Him.

Everything except the sudden deafening sound of a car horn, wheels screeching, and the bright white light that slaughters the music, our hope, and my greatest love with it too...

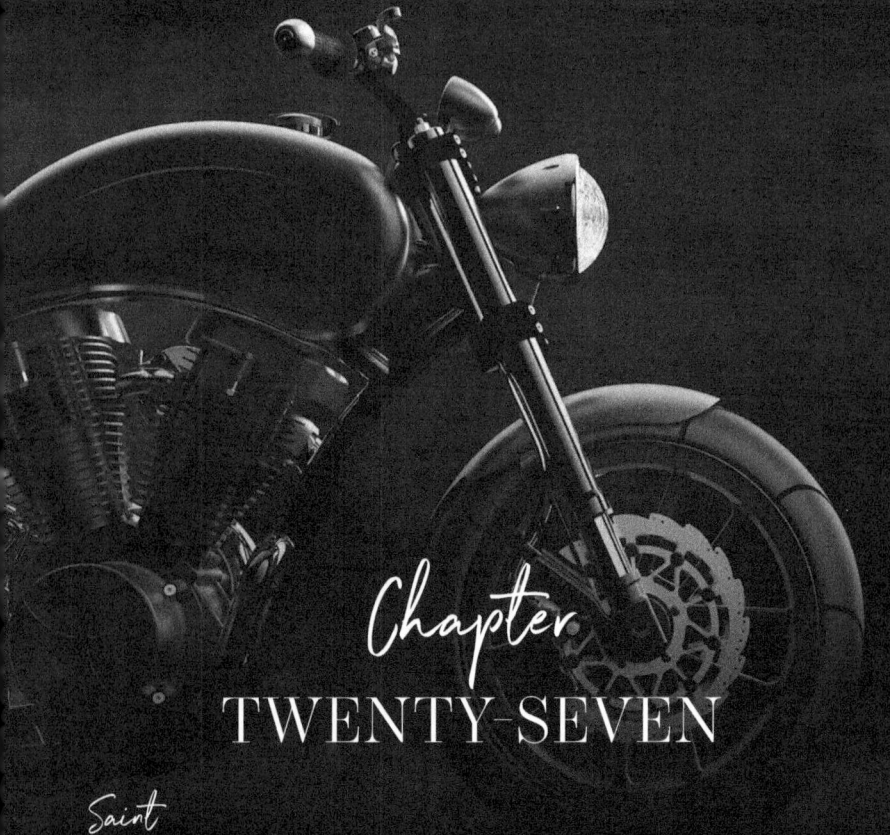

Chapter
TWENTY-SEVEN

Saint

NEVER IN A MILLION YEARS DID I EXPECT THE GREATEST DAY OF MY life to turn into the worst day like this. The deafening car horn. Her petrified scream before impact. The darkness. Everything felt as though it happened in slow motion. Every single little thing. It was as if the bow around my life was tightening, closing up as my entire life and everybody in it flashed before me.

Paisley's terrified gaze was all I saw before blacking out.

Fear.

Fear.

Fear.

"PAISLEY!" I scream out, intaking a huge gulp of air as my eyes snap open, instantly narrowing in confusion at the bright halogen lit room. *God, I feel like shit.* My head is throbbing and my entire body aches as I frantically sit up in the... *bed.* I'm on a bed. A *hospital bed.*

Paisley.

Where's Paisley?

Is she okay?

Groggily glancing around the hospital room, my eyes land on an older woman with rich dark curls. Smiling softly, she quickly walks over to the bed with a clipboard in hand. "Santo, dear, I'm Samantha, your nurse. You were in a high-speed car accident a couple of hours ago and—"

"Paisley," I choke out, gripping my neck at how ridiculously dry my throat is. "Where is…"

"Now, now, Santo, let's take it easy. One step at a time." The nurse takes a hold of the white plastic cup of water on the little table beside the bed and offers it to me. "Slow sips, okay? This will help you out."

My right hand is trembling as my fingers wrap around the freezing cold plastic cup.

High-speed crash. You were in a high-speed crash.

The cup jitters in my grip, becoming worse when I lift it to my lips and barely get a single drop of water in my mouth. Instead, the cold water brings chills to my chest, seeping right through my hospital gown.

"Fuck." I sigh under my breath, glancing down at the mess I've made with a frown. It's then I also see the IV drip I have and the couple of cuts and slight bruises on my arms, and a part of me breaks away. It's nothing I can't take as it brings me back to my boxing days, but the fact that I was in a serious crash… It concerns me so much. Especially since I know nothing about what exactly happened and if Paisley is… If she's okay.

"It's perfectly okay, Santo, I'll refill your cup. I just want you to relax for me, okay?"

I nod softly, even though my heart rate is beyond erratic. As the nurse walks out of the room with the plastic cup in hand, I glance over at the machine screens beside my bed. I swear to God if I hear one more *beep* out of it, I'll fucking go crazy. *Stop it. Just fucking stop it.*

I have no idea where my phone and wallet are, no idea if

Alaric, Nico, my mom or Nonna are even aware that I'm here. That there's a chance Paisley could be here too.

Shit.

I clench and unclench my right hand, mentally summoning all the strength inside me to stabilize the trembles. But it doesn't subside. I'm too nervous, too stressed to feel any sort of ease.

Where the hell is Paisley?

Before I can even gather my thoughts, the nurse is back. She smiles as she hands me the cup of water and this time I swallow it down fine. The refreshing water instantly replenishes me, so cold I feel it travel down my throat and chest. I finally summon the strength to set the cup back down on the table, the thoughts in my head eating away at me.

I need to know.

Need to know what happened to my forever girl.

"There are a few questions I have for you, Santo. Can you answer them for me?"

"Yes," I say, no matter how desperately I wish I had it in me to correct her on my name. I'm only Santo to Paisley. To my mom. To my nonna. Nobody else. It's Saint to the rest.

The nurse glances down at her clipboard, where my records must be. "Okay, can I have your full name?"

"Santo... Santo Lisconti."

"Do you remember the date?"

"Yes. It's Thursday the eighth of June, 2017."

"Perfect, and your place of birth?"

"Santa Rosa, California... America."

"Age and date of birth?"

"I was born on the third of June, 1981. I just turned thirty-six last week."

"Wonderful, it seems to me that you're all good. Very alert." The nurse nods. "Okay, now I just have one other question. Are you in any pain, Santo?"

I shake my head. "Just feel my head throbbing a bit. I see a couple of cuts and a few bruises coming along. I'm a former professional boxer, so it's nothing to me. I just want to know if… if something else is wrong? Am I going to be all right?"

The nurse, Samantha, smiles and nods. "Yes, Santo. You're going to be okay."

The slightest bit of relief fuels me.

Grazie a Dio.

"Fortunately, you only received very minor injuries as a result of the collision. Only a few treatable cuts and bruises, some shock of course too. Paracetamol will ease the head pain, but I'll also check your vitals." The nurse squeezes my shoulder in comfort, her emerald eyes boring into mine. "You are extremely lucky to be alive, Santo. Many people don't walk out of incidents like this. You must have had an angel watching over you. Truly."

I can't stop shaking my head. "The only angel I have is the woman I'm in love with. She's the golden part of me that keeps me going. What happened? Is Paisley okay? Paisley Reign, she was my passenger. Please, Samantha, please tell me she's okay."

"You don't remember anything?"

"Not all."

"Can you tell me what you *do* remember?"

I nod and clear my throat. "I was driving up Interstate 5 toward Willow Creek. Paisley and I were talking, happy, telling each other how much we love each other. Next thing I know, I hear this loud car horn and screeching. Paisley's scream. We must have been hit from behind, but I don't get it because I was going the speed limit and… the next thing I know it's as if my car's skidding. I lost control. There was a huge bang. That's when I blacked out. I don't remember anything else. Don't remember how I got to the hospital or in this room. I don't remember if Paisley's okay. I don't… I don't remember, Samantha."

"That's perfectly normal, dear." The nurse smiles. "Anterograde amnesia. Very common after a collision. At times, many people lose the ability to remember certain moments either leading up, during, or after an accident. It may come back in a few days, but shock tends to make us forget those moments too.

Everything seems to be okay, but you'll have an MRI scan soon to ensure the symptoms are nothing serious, which I'm sure they're not anyway. Oh, and the police will also be here shortly for your statement based on the events that happened."

"Okay…" My throat closes up at the prospect of the answer to my next words. My heartbeat is in my ears, beating so recklessly fast like the devil in me is winning the game. "Do you know who hit us? What happened after the incident? Are you able to check if Paisley Reign is okay?"

A tense silence surrounds the room and I fucking hate it. White noise and my heartbeat are all I hear as my vision blurs, my eyes all glassy 'cause I'm thinking the fucking worst. Never been this scared in my life. Never been this anxious for an answer that may destroy my entire soul. 'Cause it will. It will fucking destroy me if I don't hear what I want to hear. Paisley's my girl. I need her to be okay.

My entire body weakens in a second, because right now, in this moment, I realize how fragile of a man I am when I'm left to break into a million little pieces. How much Paisley is my only strength. How much more time I need with her 'cause she's the only thing that feels like home.

"Santo." The nurse frowns slightly, sitting up on the edge of the bed. She places her warm hands over my trembling ones, seeking to calm me. It doesn't help. I don't like the empathetic tone in her voice. Don't like it because I know what it means. "Unfortunately, as a result of the collision, there have been two fatalities…"

And just like that everything inside me stops. *Everything.*

My entire world comes to a crashing halt at the words the nurse just spoke. *No. No. No.*

My wildflower… My wildflower, she's…

My breaths burn my suffocating lungs. My heart… I don't even feel it anymore. *Fatalities. Two fatalities. It must be the driver of the other car and Paisley. It must be.*

I don't even wait for what the nurse says next before I begin shaking my head in disbelief, my entire body trembling in a violent sob as the tight knot in the back of my throat intensifies till I reach breaking point.

Paisley.

Paisley.

My Paisley.

I feel sick. Mentally, physically, emotionally sick. The nausea rises up in me, and I feel I'm either going to pass out or throw up any minute now. I just feel it. *My wildflower... She's...*

"NOOO!" I shout out, hot tears rushing down my cheeks like waves. "No, no, no. Paisley's not... She can't be. It can't end like this. Not like this. I need to see her, please, I need to see Paisley," I beg, frantically ripping off the bedsheet. My head continues to ache as I yank the IV drip from my arm and recklessly jump out of the bed. "Please, let me see her. Please, Samantha. I need her. I need her so much."

"Santo! Please sit—"

"Paisley, where are you?" I cry out to myself, my voice breaking as another wave of sobs drowns me in a world so lonely and cold. So scary without her as I fall to the white glossy hospital floor on my hands and knees, my face pressing up against it. "*Wildflower, wildflower,* my baby, come back to me. How could you..." Shutting my eyes, I struggle for my next breath as memories of her flash through my mind and how she won't be here to create any more. It hurts so much. It hurts because this was supposed to be the beginning of us, not the end. "How could you leave me like this, Paisley? I can't live without you. I can't live without my *wildflower...* This is... This is all my fault."

"Santo." The nurse sighs, and I can hear her footsteps nearing. "Santo, please look at me."

"I can't—"

"There were two passengers in the car that hit you." She cuts me off. "The police found evidence that established the driver was intoxicated and drug affected when he got behind the wheel. Speed was also a factor when he hit your car, resulting in the accident. The police stated while your car was severely damaged, it remained upright. The other driver's car didn't and rolled over multiple times. Sadly, he died upon impact... and *his* passenger, who has just been formally identified as his wife, passed a little while ago here in the hospital."

Oh, Christ. That's so fucking terrible.

My blood boils at the fact it was a drug and alcohol affected driver who shouldn't have been on the road driving to begin with... *This could have all been prevented.* I'd re-kill the fucker with my bare hands if I could.

But that also means... Paisley isn't...

"And Paisley?"

"Paisley Reign, the woman who was *your* passenger is alive. Dr. Reign informed me Paisley also sustained some injuries but nothing life-threatening. She's currently recovering a few rooms down. I can assure you that she's in good hands, Santo, so there's nothing to be distressed about. Paisley Reign is alive."

It takes a full moment for me to comprehend what the nurse, Samantha, said.

Paisley. Alive.

Some injuries. Nothing life-threatening.

Recovering. She's in good hands, Santo.

Paisley Reign is alive.

I reopen my eyes to the hospital's glossy floors, sniffling away my tears, but a few still glide down my cheeks, through my stubble and to the floor. My heart... I don't know how much it can take, but the flutter of hope and reassurance has me lifting my head to Samantha, well aware of how much of a mess I must look with my blue eyes still so glossy, my jaw dropped in shock.

"Paisley's alive?" I whisper as if the words should feel foreign to me after the scare. "Please tell me she's okay?"

The nurse's smile is a warm one as she crouches down in front of me and touches my shoulder. "Yes, Santo. Paisley's alive and doing well—"

"Oh, thank God." She doesn't even finish before I sit up and pull her into an unanticipated hug, just needing some type of support and somebody to thank aside from God right now. "Thank you. Thank you. Thank you."

An unexpected soft laugh escapes her as she pats my back. "I didn't do anything, dear."

Relief. Relief is all I feel. It's as if this weight has been lifted off my shoulders. Paisley's okay. She's here. She's right *here* in this beautiful world just where she belongs. Beside me.

The brightest grin rises on my lips as we pull away. I apologize about that whole IV drip episode, but the nurse says she understands completely and that makes me feel a whole lot fucking better.

It isn't until I stand up to my full height that I realize something she said, and as happy as I am right now, a part of me is still on edge...

"Did you say Dr. *Reign* before? As in Dr. Alaric Reign?"

The nurse nods. "Dr. Reign has been taking good care of Paisley. Being her father, he naturally put his hand up. Dr. Atkins is currently looking after you. However, Dr. Reign did come in to check on you a little while ago, but you were sleeping at the time. He seemed outraged... I can imagine it's all the shock of the accident, sadness for the other family's tragedy too, especially because it could have been prevented on the other driver's behalf."

Oh fuck.

Alaric's outraged... I just know it can't all be about the accident. He must have questions for both Paisley and me. *Of course he would.* The most obvious being what were Paisley and I doing out together. *There's no way Paisley and I can hide our love now. No way.*

"It isn't just about the accident," I murmur, wincing when I sit on the edge of the bed and my entire body aches, but I push on and admit something I've wanted to scream out loud to the entire world for a long while. "Dr. Reign and I are good friends... and I'm in love with his daughter, Paisley. I love her to death, but Alaric doesn't know... *didn't* know. It's all going to explode in my face now. He's going to finish off killing me because he won't

456 | VANESSA LUISA

understand how deeply I care for her and now with the crash, he's going to blame me. I just know it. I'm sorry. I don't know why I'm telling you about one of your colleagues and all these issues of mine. Just ignore everything I said."

"You're telling me because it means something to you…" The nurse reaches out and squeezes my hand, easing the trembling that's starting up. "Can I give you an unbiased opinion, dear?"

I nod, desperate to hear anything but my own circling thoughts right now.

Alaric is going to fucking destroy you, Lisconti.

Destroy you.

"Santo…?"

"Yes."

"I want you to know this isn't your fault, Santo. What happened is not your fault. Paisley isn't hurt because of you. She is hurt because an irresponsible driver decided to go behind the wheel when he shouldn't have and killed himself and his wife as a result of it. After today, you know firsthand how important life is, how important it is to live it right. If you love Dr. Reign's daughter, own it. Life is fragile, it's beautiful, but it's painful. I see it every day, believe me. I've been in situations with patients where miracles happen and other situations where lives fade away. An angel was watching over you today, watching over you both. I truly believe that, so summon that courage to fight for Paisley's love."

Samantha's words truly touch my heart.

What happened is not your fault.

After today, you know firsthand how important life is, how important it is to live it right.

Summon that courage to fight for Paisley's love.

I lift my gaze up from my hands and face Samantha. Everything becomes clearer. My perspective on how I've been looking at this wrong. Alaric is my best friend, and I love his daughter more than anything. He doesn't have to understand or accept it, he just needs to know that there's nothing in this world that I care more about than Paisley Reign.

Paisley's my *wildflower.*

The reason I'm still breathing.

Nothing makes sense without her... and I need him to know it too.

"Thank you," I whisper. "So you think I should tell him?"

"Yes. Tell Dr. Reign exactly what you feel. Even if you need to sacrifice his friendship for right now, I am sure with time it will be rebuilt. Trust will grow when he sees how much you adore her. I mean, I can see how much you love Paisley, and I haven't even seen the half of it. Just how much you broke down when you thought she was one of the fatalities showed me how much you care, but the way your eyes lit up when I told you that she was still alive... that's love. That's love on so many levels. Life can slip away, Santo, it can slip away just like that. So, don't spend a single second blaming yourself or hiding what you truly feel. It isn't worth it. Instead, spend those seconds loving her with all you've got. Because in the end, that's all that really matters. So..." The nurse grins, tears in her eyes. "Are you going to fight for her?"

"Yes." I smile back, my entire heart warming as I admit my greatest truth. "I'm going to fight for Paisley with everything I have, no matter the sacrifice, because we deserve it."

I mean every single word.

I'm going to fight for Paisley Reign with *everything* I have. Because there's no *me* without *her.* There isn't just a part of me that's her, it's *all* of me, it's all *her.*

Paisley and I, we're a forever kind of thing, because that's how long I'm gonna spend lovin' her...

Forever.

It's been five seconds since I've been discharged and I'm already racing to the nurse's desk, adamant to get information about which hospital room Paisley is in.

I need to see her so badly, it's killing me.

It's been a long three hours since I woke up in a hospital bed.

After the nurse checked my vitals, my MRI test came back all clear and the police came into my room to take my statement and clear up the missing pieces of the puzzle. I breathed in the biggest sigh of relief in my life. It meant being one step closer to seeing Paisley.

There's so much anger pent-up inside me for the fucker who caused this accident. The fact that my *wildflower* and I were caught in the crossfire, even though it could have been much worse for us. The fact he took the innocent life of his wife. Shit like that ruins me because now their family is grieving for something that should have never happened in the first place.

The second I'm given Paisley's hospital room number, I run down the sterile white corridor to her...

I don't care that my Maserati is a write-off.

I don't care that I probably look like an idiot running in my black button-up shirt, jeans, and... *cowboy boots*.

I don't care that Alaric is going to find out our secret.

All I care about is this feeling of complete and utter love circling my heart the second I step inside the hospital room and Paisley's emotion-filled eyes meet mine. The sleepy smile rises on her lips as she peacefully sits up in bed, all of me hurting at the sight of her in a hospital gown, the white cast on her left wrist, and faint bruises on her cheeks and arms. But it's nothing that won't heal in time, and that eases me.

Oh, thank God. Thank God Paisley's alive.

A miracle.

This is what this is—*a miracle*.

"Santo," she breathes as I bolt up to her and my strong arms wrap around her petite frame, giving her the tightest embrace of my life. "Santo! It's so good to see you!"

Pressing my lips to Paisley's warm forehead, I want to savor every piece of her and never let go. Her right hand laces up around my neck, pulling me in even closer, to the point we're crushing our lungs, but I don't give a fuck. *She's alive. Alive with me.* We hold each other tight, as if there's no tomorrow because a few hours ago I was convinced there wasn't.

It's only when we pull away that I bury my head into her neck, staying cautious of not rubbing my face against the bruises on her cheeks. Just intaking Paisley's sweet jasmine scent is enough to revive me. *I'm okay now.* I'm okay because I'm with her.

My heart continues to race as I tip my head back to see her. I'll never forget the brave smile on Paisley's face as I carefully cup her jaw, my thumbs smoothing over the pale purple bruises, wishing they'd just disappear under my touch. I smile back at my forever girl and replace my thumbs with my lips, brushing over her skin ever so slowly.

"I thought I lost you," I whisper, emotion still thick in my voice as I bring our foreheads together. "Thought I lost the remaining beats in my chest. I heard two fatalities and I thought... *Fuck*, I thought I'd never see you again. I can't comprehend a world without you, Paisley. You're my entire world and more."

Paisley's right hand reaches up to graze her fingers through my stubble, her soft voice without fear. "I'm here, Santo. I'm right here and I'm not going anywhere."

"Are you hurt?"

She shakes her head against mine. "Not really. I just woke up from a great sleep. My dad gave me some meds and it's easing the pain a little. I just feel a little beaten up, especially with some of the bruises, but the worst of it is a fractured wrist and the cast I have to keep on for about six weeks, but I can live with that."

"Mmhmmm, I'll take care of you good, baby." I gently run my fingers down the plaster cast Paisley has on her left wrist and I reach down and kiss it. For some reason, that has Paisley bursting out in giggles and the sound of her feminine laughter makes me lift my eyes to her, a smirk working its way on my lips against the cast as my heart warms at the smile that lines on her cheeks. "What's so funny?"

"The way you're kissing every part of me!"

My eyes darken as I take a seat on the edge of the bed and lean closer to her. Her eyes drink me up with so much intrigue and wonder as she stares back. "Thought you died tonight, *wildflower*.

You better believe I'm going to kiss every single inch of you to remind myself we're still alive. Don't know where I'd be without you. Just know that I never want to feel that way again, ever. I don't ever want to let you go or spend a second with you not by my side."

Somebody clearing their throat on the other side of the room has me turning my head in that direction. A nurse I didn't even see when I rushed in stands there, an awkward smile on her lips as she glances between us and gestures toward the door. "Okay, I'm going to step out for a few moments so you two have a little privacy. If you need anything, just buzz the assistance button that I showed you, Paisley."

"Thank you." Paisley smiles, while I just nod.

The second the nurse steps out of the room and leaves the door slightly ajar, I turn back to Paisley and for the billionth time I'm in awe of just how graceful she is, even sitting up in a hospital bed wearing a gown like she is tonight.

Paisley brings my face closer to her with the hand she has on my stubbled jaw. Her brows softly furrow as she studies my eyes and frowns. "My blue-eyed boy was crying... Eyes rimmed so red in a fear-like love, so poetic it could make the darkest devil turn into an angel's cry."

Exhaling a breath, I shut my eyes and they become glazed in tears when I reopen them. Paisley's eyes turn all glassy too as this unspoken emotion between us fills with so much adoration, vulnerability, and gratefulness. It's a silent prayer. A love letter written in the air between us. A thank you to both heaven and hell that we're still here, breathing together.

I blink through my blurry vision and quickly pull off my boots, slipping under the thin sheets with Paisley, and wrap my arms around her so we're chest to chest and I can feel her heart beating next to mine. We're so close. My head fills half of the pillow as we simply appreciate one another's existence, my hand cupping her face and fingers caressing her skin. Her fractured wrist rests on my narrowed waist, keeping it safe in the solace of my warmth.

"I love you, Pais. I love you so much it hurts," I whisper against her plump pink lips. "Wish there were a better word to express how much."

"I know how much, because I feel it too," Paisley murmurs back, glancing between my eyes before the brightest grin works up her lips. "Move to Seattle with me."

My heart clenches.

Aww, babydoll.

"Really?" I grin back in pure awe. "You want us to find an apartment in Seattle and move in together?"

The pillow flattens beneath our heads with how much Paisley is nodding against it. "Mmhmm, more than anything I want to live with you. Well…" She giggles. "That is if you aren't sick of me already…"

"I could never. Of course I want to live with you too, *wild-flower*. What changed your mind?"

"Well, I've been thinking about it for hours. Ever since I woke up in this bed. After the police came in and took my statement… I couldn't stop thinking about the guy who hit us. About his wife. We don't even know them, yet I felt so sick to my stomach knowing it could have easily been us. I've had all this time to think about it and realized the fear I had about moving too fast and me thinking you moving to Washington State with me and us moving in together isn't valid, because in life anything can happen…"

"It definitely can."

"Exactly," Paisley says. "So we need to take chances while we still have time, just like you were trying to say to me that night. I know we haven't been together long. I know this is so new for both of us. I know I'm still young and you're a little older, but I know what I feel for you is the most real thing I've ever felt. I know you love me too and there's a high chance we won't ruin what we have. I know what I want. I've known for a long time now. *You* are all I want, Santo, and I don't want to waste a second away from you or pretend I don't love you, not when I know how quickly life can slip away. I want to tell my dad about us. I want to tell the world about us. I want you all to myself in a Seattle apartment with your Harley, my flowers, and our cowboy boots."

"I'm already there, *amore mio*." I smile. "Already there."

I kiss her passionately, with everything I have. Every single part of me becomes hers as she kisses me back with so much possession and warmth, her wet tongue dancing with mine just how I like it. This insatiable kiss is like I was made for loving her, which right now I more than ever know I was. I was made for loving Paisley Reign so deeply in the way that I do.

My lips. Her touch. This love. Our kiss.

Irresistible, that's what she is to me.

With such heated urgency, I kiss Paisley into forever. Into blooming sunflower fields. Into Harley rides and sunsets. I want this kiss to last all night. But all of a sudden we're pulling away at the loud slam of the hospital door, and glance up toward it at the exact same moment, and... *fuck*.

Holding Paisley even tighter to me, my breaths slow as the person storms toward the edge of the bed with a reddened face, their vicious gaze narrowing in pure fury.

It's *him*.

Her father...

My best friend...

Doctor A. Reign...

ALARIC.

"What the... What the fuck, man? What the fuck do you think you're doing kissing my daughter?" Alaric roars at me, recklessly gripping the stethoscope around his neck and slamming it into the floor. "Get the hell off her before I call security, you piece of shit!"

Paisley's entire body tenses in my hold and that serenity I felt minutes ago... it all crashes away in tidal waves. My heart drops because I was right...

There isn't going to be anything reasonable about this.

It's obvious Alaric doesn't even need an explanation as to

what's going on between Paisley and me, because it was written in black and white the second he stepped into the hospital room and saw us kissing.

I sit up, ready to get up from the bed and approach him calmly, but Paisley halts me with a yank of my shirt. *Huh?* I glance over at Paisley, surprised to see the fire in her eyes as she fearlessly faces her father. With all these bursts of boldness over the years, it's as if she's now reached her breaking point and is nothing but a confident woman staring back at her father, who's standing there ready to explode.

Paisley remains poised and raises her head up high in determination, the tension in her shoulders seeming to leave just as quickly as it came. "Saint isn't going anywhere, Dad."

The anger in Alaric's eyes only intensifies. "What the hell is going on? I can't believe this. I can't believe you would both go behind my back like this. I don't even know what to say."

"Look, Alaric." I sigh. "I know what you're thinking but—"

"Oh, you *know what I'm fucking thinking,* do you?" her father spits, grinding his jaw as he stomps right around the bed, so he's face to face with me as I stand. "Tell me, Saint. What am I thinking, huh? Tell me exactly what you think I'm fucking thinking when I see my *thirty-six*-year-old *best friend* and my *eighteen*-year-old *daughter* in the same damn hospital bed telling each other how much they love each other and discussing moving to Seattle together, and then KISS AS IF IT'S NORMAL! Tell me, Saint. TELL ME! WHAT AM I THINKING?"

I gulp down. "You're thinking—"

"Let *me* tell *you* what I'm thinking," Alaric growls, cutting me off and completely exploding with a devilish gaze as he shoves me back. "I'm thinking you're supposed to be my best friend! The *only* one who knows all the shit I've been through! You're supposed to be somebody I trust. You're supposed to have my back, not your lips on my daughter, you sick fuck. I could kill you with my bare hands right now!" He roughly jabs his finger right over my heart. "Fucking *kill* you!"

"Dad, don't—"

"NO, PAISLEY! All the men in the world and you seduce a man double your age? My BEST FRIEND? Doesn't that seem psychotic to you? What the hell is wrong with you?"

"Please, Dad, stop screaming. They're going to call security in here!"

"Don't freaking tell me what to do, Paisley! You think I'm stupid, huh? I've seen the eyes you give him, but never thought you could be so irresponsible and go out of your way to make a complete fool out of yourself."

That's all I can take before I take a step closer to Alaric, towering over him in height. Clenching my jaw twice, my nose flares in outrage. "Don't you dare say Paisley's irresponsible or that she's making a fool out of herself! Have a little respect, man! Paisley's a beautiful, wise woman who is free to make her own choices and be with whoever she wants. That includes me."

"Don't freaking defend her or act like the hero here, Saint! Because when the day comes and you fuck it up with her, you're going to forget about her, but I know Paisley. She won't forget. She'll carry the baggage for the rest of her life because you don't know what love is!"

"You're wrong," I hiss, narrowing my gaze at my best friend. "I may not have known what love was once, but I do now. I have ever since I realized Paisley Reign is my lifeline. The only woman I can ever trust with my heart. The only woman I need. I know I betrayed you and went behind your back. And for that I'm sorry, but there is nothing else I regret. I want you to know that I will never *ever* hurt Paisley. I care about her too much to ever leave or forget about her. If we could turn back time, Paisley and I would have told you sooner, but—"

"Don't fucking test me with that *Paisley and I* shit!"

"Dad, please just listen to what I have to say—"

"How could you do this to me?"

"*Please*, Dad." Paisley sighs, slowly peeling off the bedsheets as I help her slip on the hospital slippers and then get out of the bed, beside me.

There's so much hope in her gaze, so much optimism despite the odds. She reaches out a hand to clasp with her father, but Alaric isn't having any of it and instead crosses his arms over his chest, on top of his crisp white lab coat.

He continues staring down at his daughter in malice. "Speak, Paisley, because I'm leaving in two seconds."

My hand traces soft circles over her hospital gown-covered hip as I pull her even closer to me, showing my support. My *wildflower* knows how to keep her emotion under wraps around her father and I respect that so much.

"Dad," Paisley begins, clearing her throat with a small smile. "I know this isn't how you should have found out, but I want you to understand that Saint means everything to me and make clear it all started after my eighteenth. I bet I know what you're thinking. That this is just some infatuation or puppy love, but it isn't. My relationship with Saint is *real*. I've been fighting the courage within me to tell Saint how I really feel for a long time because I know he's your close friend and I wanted to respect you. You mean so much to me, Dad, and I love you with all my heart, but there comes a time when I can't be your little girl anymore and that time is now. I know you want to protect me, but I don't need protecting from Saint... not from *Santo*."

My heart warms at every word. I can't stop gazing at Paisley in complete awe that she's opening up to her father and being so honest and vulnerable when it comes to us. Alaric may not want to hear anything that comes out of my mouth, but Paisley deserves so much more.

"Dad, I'm in *love* with Santo and I've understood more about myself than ever before along the way, thanks to him." Paisley takes in a deep breath and meets my eyes with so much tender emotion. "Thanks to *you*, my blue-eyed boy." She turns back to her father. "It was just the other day when you commented on how much more confident I am. That's because I'm *happier*. Happier than I've ever been. With myself. With my life. With Santo. He believed in me when I didn't even believe in myself. With him, I finally found the strength within me to believe in not only myself and what I'm truly capable of, but of seeing the light after the dark. And Santo is my light. He's a beautiful man inside and out who has the kindest heart and demons that render him misunderstood to others, the same demons he's setting free, just like I am with mine. I know we may seem like opposites, but we're more alike than I ever thought because we have the same outlook on life and our diverse morals complement us."

Damn right, wildflower.

"And I know we have a huge age gap. I know people will look at us and get the wrong idea, but I don't care about any of that. You want to know what I care about, Dad?"

Alaric grinds his jaw, no response at hand.

Paisley doesn't wait another heartbeat. "All I care about is the deep connection I have with him and the way he makes me feel so seen, so heard... So *me*. We started as two broken people with deeply shattered flaws, and piece by piece we helped put each other back together. Santo is nothing but a complete gentleman to me. He's my boyfriend and he's respectful. Loving. Vulnerable. Funny. Everything I could ever ask for and more and I love him so much, Dad. Whether you accept us or not, I love him, and I know in my heart of hearts that will never change. Not now when the man who began as the Devil of Sacramento turned out to truly be a Saint. *My* Saint. *Saint.*"

"Come on, Paisley. Don't you know people like Saint? They promise you the world and then crush it right there in your hands. Just like your mother did to me. Saint will destroy you. Why do you think he's never spoken to you about Lea?"

"He has."

Alaric's face scrunches.

I bet he wasn't expecting me to tell Paisley all about it.

"He's told me everything there is to know about Lea and Alexis—"

"Alexis?" Her father furrows his brows and turns to me. "Who's Alexis?"

"Lea's daughter," I explain, swallowing down thickly. "I never told you the full story that I told Paisley."

My heart continues to beat wildly for Paisley as Alaric turns to me, the same angered expression on his face, yet there's something in his eyes that dims, and I don't know if it's a good or a bad thing. It still hurts. Hurts because we were so close, and as guilty as I feel, he isn't accepting us, so I need to let go of our friendship because his daughter is my priority now.

"Saint won't destroy me," Paisley continues, "and I'm sorry that my mother caused you so much pain, but I'm not her, so please stop punishing me like I am. Saint has always been here for me, every step of the way, and there is nobody else I want to be with, Dad."

Silence greets us for a few seconds before her father whispers, "You *love him?*"

"Dearly."

Hearing Paisley admit her love for me makes me so happy. I can't resist kissing the side of her head and murmuring into her ear, "So proud of you, *wildflower*. Love you to death."

Alaric turns to me, distraught. "So, you're... you're intimate with my daughter?"

"Alaric..."

"Just answer the goddamn question, Saint," he hisses.

"Yes." I nod. "Paisley and I are intimate, but it isn't solely sexual. What we have is a very normal, a very genuine sexual *and* emotional relationship. One doesn't come before the other."

"Fucking hell. Were you really in Santa Rosa last weekend?"

"No," I admit. "I was in Marin County... Stinson Beach. With Paisley. I have a beach house there."

Alaric turns to his daughter. "So that whole *celebrating with Maralyn* was a lie?"

Paisley gulps down, tears in her eyes. "Yes. I'm sorry. I just didn't want to hurt you."

"And here I was worrying I was being a bad father for working so much. Little did I know you were fucking my best friend while I went to work! This type of shit is unforgivable. So goddamn heartless!"

There's a pang in my heart for her.

Shaking his head, Alaric turns to me as if it's a tennis match. "Are you seriously going to leave everything behind in Sacramento and move to Seattle to be with Paisley?"

"Yes. I want nothing more than to begin a new life with her in Seattle."

"So, you're choosing her over friendship?"

I respond in a heartbeat. "Yes, you're leaving me no choice to negotiate."

Alaric scoffs. "Do you love her?"

"I love your daughter with all my heart, more than I've ever loved before. Being so close to losing it all today, it made me realize how important it is to live life right. The only life I want to live is the one I have with her. I just wish you could see it, Alaric, wish you could see how I will never stop fighting for Paisley Reign for as long as I shall live."

The way her father looks at her with so much disappointment, it kills me inside because even though I knew he wouldn't understand, a part of me was still a little hopeful.

"I hope he makes you happy, Paisley," Alaric says, shaking his head to himself. "Don't come running to me when he burns you so deeply you don't even know yourself. Don't come running because I won't be here for you." He glances between us with a look of disgust, seconds before he begins walking backward toward the door. "Then you two have a *nice life* together. I don't ever want to speak to you ever fucking again, Saint. *Ever.* I mean it."

I shut my eyes for a brief moment and pinch the bridge of my nose. *Ouch.*

"Dad, please, don't do this," Paisley groans. "Can't you just accept that I'm happy? I don't want our bond to break because of this, Dad. *Please.* You know I love you so much."

"Love isn't going behind my back like this, Paisley. It's fucked up, that's what it is. I didn't know you could betray me like this—"

"BECAUSE SAINT WAS THERE FOR ME WHEN YOU WEREN'T!" Paisley screams, her chest heaving as her fists ball up by her sides. There's a wince in her throat as she clutches her cast, but that doesn't stop her determination. "I tried to talk to you logically, Dad, but now I understand that perhaps this is a blessing in disguise! If you are not able to respect *us*, you're not able to respect *me*!"

"Seriously, Paisley?"

She stands firm and nods, her jaw tensed. "*Seriously.* I'm not—"

The hospital door slamming shut slaughters Paisley's words.

I instantly glance over at her and kiss away the single tear that rolls down her cheek before cupping her face and slowly kissing her lips. "It's okay. I've got you, baby."

"We did all we could," she murmurs as we pull away. "He didn't want to hear it, but I feel at peace. I feel at peace knowing we told him everything we needed to."

"I'm so proud of you, *wildflower*. So proud of everythi—"

The door violently swings open and Alaric storms back in for a second time. With a death glare on us, he reaches down to collect his stethoscope from the floor before diving into one of the pockets of his lab coat. He pulls out a little square polaroid photograph and waves it around in the air.

"And *oh*," he huffs. "I found something I had buried in my desk drawer and was going to give it to you so you could cherish it, but that was before I walked in on you and your *boyfriend*. I really don't care what you do with it now, Paisley. So go on your damn rendezvous with Saint, *go*! Go because you're free to leave the hospital. You're discharged. Go because there's nothing else left for me to say. Go because I'm used to being abandoned, so freaking used to it. You want to live with Saint in Seattle? I'll give you something better. Move in with him here in Sacramento, because you've got until midday tomorrow to get out of *my* house! Period."

My jaw drops in disbelief that Alaric can be this fucking cold to his only daughter. Yes, we went behind his back, but you can't control who you love. Love is always love. Always.

Why can't Alaric understand that?

Paisley sniffles away her tears. "I didn't want it to be like this, Dad."

"Well, that's just too bad because love hurts. I know it first-hand." Alaric flings a photo toward us, and I automatically catch it. "It's a polaroid I found of your first Christmas with your mom, Paisley. Only picture I have of you two. It's yours now. Burn it for all I care."

I'm still left death staring Alaric with a tense jaw as I blindly hand Paisley the polaroid and I feel her glance down at it.

I thought I knew who my best friend was… turns out I don't know at all.

We've tried reasoning with him, but this… *this* is too far. I don't even care about the hurt in his eyes at this point. Paisley and I have tried our best to be on civil ground with him. He doesn't want to. End of story.

Paisley's jasmine scent calms my pumping blood down as I glance down at her. There's a trace of a smile on her lips, and that prompts my own as I pull her to my side and follow her eye line.

The polaroid.

It's a beautiful candid photo of Paisley and her mother on Christmas day. My cute little *wildflower* looking not even one year old with an oversized Santa hat on her head. She's sitting on the floor and grinning beyond the camera at who I anticipate would have been her father, Alaric. A few opened presents on the reddish carpet beside her the evident rush of Christmas morning. An average-sized Christmas tree with colorful lights glowing in the background. Then my eyes fixate on the woman sitting down beside her in the photograph and my entire body freezes up.

My eyes widen and it feels like I can't breathe anymore...

Oh.

My.

God.

What the fuck?

My voice betrays me with its brokenness. "That... that can't be your mom."

"What the hell do you mean?" Alaric roars. "You think I don't know what my former girlfriend who's the mother of my only child looks like? That's Faye, Paisley's mother!"

Paisley glances up at me, her brows knitting together. "Why did you say that, Santo?"

"Because..." I say, my throat swelling up as my heart begins to shatter into a billion pieces. "Because the woman in this picture... it's... it's *Lea.*"

Chapter
TWENTY-EIGHT

Paisley

OH. MY. GOD.

My jaw drops at the words Saint just spoke. *The woman in the picture… it's Lea.*

Lea… Lea is my mom? What the hell?

My mind is exploding with questions and thoughts that unravel inside me like lightning bolts. Those ocean eyes I love so much stay leveled with mine, filled with such dazed emotion as I attempt to come to terms with what this all means for me now. *But it's all too much.*

Lea—the woman Saint once was in love with—is my… mother.

Gosh, that feels so weird to even comprehend in my head.

"*What?*" I whisper in complete disbelief, searching his eyes to grasp if this is some kind of joke, even though I know Saint would never do that to me. Not with something this serious. "Lea is the woman in this polaroid with me? Are you sure? Are you sure it's really her?"

Saint glances down at the picture for an extended amount of time, and I gulp down thickly as my gaze follows his. The woman in the picture—my mother—looks nothing like me. Bright green eyes, while mine are a light honey brown. Thin dirty-blonde hair while mine is thick dark waves, just like my father's. My father was right in that conversation we had last week. I really do look all like him and nothing like the mother I never remembered.

Saint begins nodding without hesitation. "I'm positive. This is Lea." His eyes meet mine with such distraught sadness. "I swear to God I didn't know, *wildflower*. I didn't know she was your mother or that she even had another daughter before Alexis. You must believe me. I didn't know. This is just as great a shock to me as it is to you. I understand if... if this is too much."

"I... I honestly don't have any words. I'm... *Oh my God...*" I swallow down thickly, all speechless. I literally cannot even conjure up an entire sentence. My heart is beating like crazy in disbelief that this is even real life right now.

This is all too much to comprehend.

"Fuck this," my father growls, stepping forward and snatching the photo from my grip. He's fuming with a vein in his forehead almost popping out and eyes wide, riddled in outrage as he gestures toward Saint. "There is no way in hell we were in love with the same woman! This can't be Lea! It's Faye! Paisley's mother is named Faye. You telling me Faye changed her name and started another life after me? No. No. No. I'm not freaking buying it. It can't be true. Besides, it's virtually impossible. Faye told me she found a man in Spain and fucked off there. She went to Europe. I'm certain of it."

I watch helplessly as Saint rubs a hand over his face, smoothing out all of the tension-riddled lines. "When I met Lea in 2004, she had a three-year-old daughter named Alexis. Lea told me Alexis's father wanted nothing to do with her after finding out she was pregnant, so she returned to California. She told me the father was from Connecticut, but she could have been lying. It could have been Spain for all I know."

"But why would she attempt to fuck us all over by creating a new identity for herself over and over and over again? Faye left me months after this photo. If what you're saying is true, it means she then changed her name and found another guy, had Alexis, left him, and then found you all in a span of four years…" My father sighs, his jaw clenching in unease. "If she found you, why would she throw it all away just because you caught her out cheating on you with Alexis's *father*? Why would she go back to him? Because she wasn't happy *again*? It doesn't make sense. Doesn't make sense why she would block her old life and start something new, again and again. Why would she change her name?"

Silence fills the room until my mind settles from all the thoughts.

I glance between my father and Saint, who look as perplexed as I do.

"To not get caught," I whisper, because it's the most logical answer. "Dad, you always said my mom had a little darkness in her. You said the same, Saint. Perhaps she was constantly moving to escape the demons creeping inside. It appears to me she was a con woman. Used men for their money until she got bored and moved on to the next. It happened with you, Dad, it must have happened with Alexis's father… and then you, Saint."

My father can't stop shaking his head. "That can't fucking be true. Why would she leave me *and* you, Paisley, only to meet some other guy, get knocked up, and keep *that* child? Why cherish this goddamn Alexis and not you, huh?"

"I don't know."

"It doesn't make sense."

"I know it doesn't make sense," Saint agrees, rubbing his stubbled jaw slowly, his eyes glazed as he glances between us. "But to be honest… it does sound like something Lea would do. I saw her at her breaking point, and all she did was make impulse decisions, so maybe this was another one."

"You got the impulse decisions right," my father scoffs, shaking his head. "Faye always did the first thing that came to mind, even if it was at the expense of others. But I... I refuse to believe Faye and Lea are the same people. She... She had a beauty spot that looked like a butterfly on her arm. Very unique. Did Lea have—"

"Fuck." Saint nods. "Butterfly-like beauty spot on her left arm, yes. Always used to say she hated it."

"Yes, just like Faye... Oh God, I'm going to be fucking sick."

Every word caves in on me. It's as if I can't breathe because the history of everything I thought I was is crumbling away. My mom... *She's dead. She has been for the last thirteen years.*

Dead.

Saint was the last person to see her.

My head is spinning like I'm going to pass out any minute now. *This is all too much.* My vision blurs with all the hard truths that come with this unexpected twist.

I have a half-sister... Alexis.

Saint was in love with my mom.

She destroyed both my dad and Saint.

None of this is Saint's fault, he didn't know, but I still feel this guilt in the pit of my stomach because even though it's obvious in the end that Lea didn't give a shit about Saint. There was a point in time where Saint and my alleged mother were happy.

Would they have been okay if Lea didn't cheat on him or kill herself?

Would she have said yes to his marriage proposal?

Would they be happy now with a little family of their own?

Yes. The answers I feel are yes.

Saint would have never been in this hospital room with me right now. We would have never fallen in love and have this desire to want to spend the rest of our lives with one another. If my mom never let me go and I was right there beside Alexis all those thirteen years ago.

I would have had a mother.

I would have known my half-sister...

Saint would have been my stepfather...

Stepfather.

I don't even know what to think anymore because everything I do has my stomach churning in a way I've never felt before. It makes me stumble back and sit down on the edge of the bed to stabilize myself. Saint is quick to attempt to help me, clasping his hand in mine and ensuring I'm okay. He brings the cup of water to my lips. Rubs my lower back slowly. Tells me everything is going to be okay. *But...*

It hurts that I half expect to feel something different when I glance up at those ocean blue eyes that have held me tight and kept me sane for months now. I expect to feel as though my entire world is exploding around me. I expect to feel this unexplained jealously for something I shouldn't be jealous of rumbling inside me. But, instead I feel... I feel *exactly the same* as I did before about Saint. My love for him hasn't changed, and yet there's this heavy weight on my shoulders, this pendulum in my chest that begins swinging at the groundbreaking shock of it all.

For a split moment, I think I can survive this, think that *we* can survive *this. Together.* That perhaps this is the wake-up call my father needs to understand that we have no control over fate or our destiny, or who we love and the reasons why.

But that all breaks away the second he storms up to Saint, fury in his gaze. "You went after my *former girlfriend* and now you're going after my *daughter*, you mad fuck!" my father grits. "You may not have seen it moments ago, but now you have to! Paisley isn't the one for you. You're in a goddamn relationship with the daughter of the woman who ruined your life. If what we're alleging is true, you're devoting yourself to Lea's daughter. How fucked up is that!"

"Dad, stop! Saint didn't know!"

"I don't give a fuck about that, Paisley. I care about morals! You wouldn't be in a hospital bed with a fractured wrist if you weren't in the car with him! I told you he would destroy you. *This* is him destroying you."

That's all it takes for Saint to explode. He's been controlled this entire time, but now it seems like he's reached the breaking point. "I'm not destroying her, Alaric fucking Reign! You're the goddamn delusional one because you're treating Paisley as if she's a puppet on your strings! When the hell are you going to see Paisley for who she really is? Huh? WHEN?"

"I already see Paisley for who she is, thank you very much. Don't get it twisted! I look at my daughter and I see a confident, intelligent, loving woman. A very capable one who doesn't need your charm, Harley Davidson motorbike, and piece of shit vows dragging her along to Seattle."

Oh.

My.

God.

Is my father serious?

"Saint isn't doing any of the dragging, Dad!" I grit, standing to my full height with narrowed eyes because I am so sick of this damn conversation. "I'm with Saint because I love him! Because I want to spend the rest of my life with him! Sacrifice. Heartache. Joy. It's all that comes with love, but you should already know that!"

"So, you're *perfectly okay* with the fact that Saint *loved your mom* before he met *you*?"

I gulp down because what my father just said is the biggest pill to swallow out of all of this. My gaze lowers to my hands, and I stare down at the cast on my left wrist, hoping I'll feel some sense of resoluteness to answer him, but it all begins to fade away.

Am I okay with it?

I don't like how silent the room becomes, as if my father's right, as if Saint and I aren't worth fighting for because I can't get my shit together and give him a straight answer. But the truth is I don't know. It makes things a million times better that Saint had no idea, but still the *what-if* thoughts from earlier cloud my mind, and on top of that… I'm grieving the loss of somebody I barely even knew. A part of my blood that has ended up meaning more than I thought.

"It doesn't change the way I feel about Paisley." That sexy gravelly voice seems to revive me as Saint starts speaking words I'll cherish forever. "I thought I loved Lea. Thought I loved her with everything inside me. That was until I found out Lea was pregnant with another man's child. Still, the guilt of losing her ate me up inside to the point where I began my boxing career months later and let out all my pent-up anger every single match. It became my release to the shit I was feeling, but never my resolution to true peace. But then time passed, years rolled over, and I met Paisley and she made me realize that I wasn't the catalyst to Lea's pain. That I did everything I could for her and that in life we can't always be responsible for the decisions others make. I wish Lea sought out more help sooner. But ultimately, I couldn't get her out of the dark because it wasn't my place to. That's gotta come from somewhere inside her, you know."

Saint inhales a sharp breath and continues, "Ever since Paisley and I connected, she made me realize I was only a victim in Lea's story. Made me realize that it wasn't true love I felt with Lea. It was just a need inside me to keep Lea happy with a type of love that can turn toxic in every second. Lea manipulated me, ruined me, burned me to the fucking ground and I hate her for it. I will never, *ever* forgive her for it. With Paisley, the love is so real, so intense, so raw and intimate, the type of love that has entire fields of flowers blooming gold. What happened with Lea is in the past. I don't even want to think about her because, quite frankly I despise her more than you know. I despise her because thirteen years on she's still dragging me through shit when I should be enjoying life. When I should be enjoying it with Paisley."

"Saint—"

"No, listen to me, Alaric! Listen to me for once in your fucking life! Lea... Faye... Whatever the hell is her name, she conned us. She conned us both and I'm sorry she did this to you too, Alaric. I'm sorry she left, but we can't go back and change the past. All we can look forward to is the future, and the only future I want is with a woman I trust wholeheartedly. A woman I love more than the world itself. A woman I would never betray, and I know she would never betray me. Paisley is that woman to me. She's my poet. My reason. *My wildflower. Your daughter, Paisley Reign, is everything to me.*"

Aww, Santo...

My heart squeezes because the words Saint just spoke mean everything to me. It means that he's still committed. Still committed to us. I just wish I felt 100 percent the same way right now. Of course I'm committed to *him*, but all of these new surprises. *It's a lot to take in.*

Saint glances over at me and the beautiful smile he shoots me is just so genuinely real. Before my father can even respond, the nurse knocks on the door before stepping in. And the words she says next, well, just like that the missing piece to this puzzle connects.

"I'm extremely sorry to interrupt, but you have two visitors, Miss Reign. It's the family of the victims in the incident that occurred today. They requested to see you before you left the hospital, wanting to speak, and it seems perhaps to also find some peace following the tragic incident. Can I let the Goldberg family in?"

I don't even have to think about it, needing closure for what happened today. "Yes."

But it's a different story for Saint, who steps toward the nurse with pure shock written all over his face. "Excuse me, did you just say *Goldberg*?"

"Yes, that's the one."

"Oh God!" Saint steps back toward me with his head in his hands. "I can't fucking believe this."

"What?" Alaric snaps.

"Goldberg..." Saint murmurs slowly as the nurse steps out. "It's Alexis's last name..."

What?

My jaw drops, just as a girl with rich chocolate eyes and long dark hair, who seems a couple of years younger than me, steps in.

Our features are so different, with hers much more a sultry gorgeous Spanish mix, but the air in my lungs burns just the same.

"Alexis…" Saint whispers, pure emotion in both his voice and face as if he hasn't seen a friend in years.

Because he hasn't. Not since Alexis's father was given legal guardianship over her after Lea's passing… my *mom's* passing.

Alexis grins so beautifully through the tears rolling down her cheeks before her eyes flicker to me and they warm in this strange comfort, despite being so evidently red from crying. I'm staring back at my half-sister, at a girl I know nothing about, and yet this wave of emotion rushes over me.

This feeling of something missing in my life finally coming back to me…

It's been Alexis.

Having a half-sister.

Sharing the same blood.

Alexis is the missing piece. And yet… And yet it feels like I can't breathe.

I can't breathe. It's all too much.

"I'm sorry," I whisper, choking from the inside out as I glance over at Saint with a blurry vision. "I'm sorry. This is just too overwhelming for me. I just need… just need a minute to myself."

The words are out before I know as I scurry past everybody and into the private hospital bathroom, locking the door behind me. Saint's worried ocean blues are forever planted in my mind, the way it's as if he wanted to follow me in and make sure I'm okay. But quite honestly, I don't know if I am.

I've grown so much during these past months. Grown so much into the woman I've always wanted to be. It's why I don't understand why it feels like my entire world is caving in and I can't feel a thing. I should be stronger than this. I should be able to confront this situation head-on, grab it by the horns. I used to have this darkness in me. Just like my mother, but ever since I fell in love with Saint, all I see is the light.

I want to continue seeing that light.

I never want to let go of that light.

But sometimes in life there's no other choice than to let the greatest thing that ever happened to me slip away in exchange for my heart to continue to beat the same tomorrow.

Saint

No two fingers of whiskey can ease the shit I'm feeling right now. It's shock. Complete shock mixed with such disbelief that two worlds can collide so quickly like they just have. Since the day Paisley and I began to get close and understand each other on this deep connected level, I knew our souls must have intercepted in another life 'cause our conversations were just too fucking relatable to be real. My mom always says sometimes in life things are too good to be true, and right fuckin' now, I'm seeing the reasons why.

I had no idea. No fucking idea that Lea was Paisley's mother. I didn't know a single thing. Didn't even question it because I never had a reason to. Lea never told me much about her past life before she met me. She never wanted to reveal much, never wanted to meet my family. Always claimed she hated having her photo taken. Now I know *why*.

I can't believe it. Can't believe the name change. Can't believe how much she manipulated me and made me believe an illusion, even changing her hair color and probably made up all the shit she told me, including falafel being her favorite food. I feel… defeated.

Lea, the same woman I proposed to before learning she was cheating on me with her former partner, is a con. A con who till this day is fucking with my mind. She played me good with her charisma, her vulnerabilities, and pleas for help. Alexis was her hook. I became her anchor.

Fuck.

I feel sick to my stomach right now in this hospital room. Sick to my stomach because up until recently I've felt guilty for the past thirteen years with how Lea's life slipped away right in front of me. Paisley made me see things from a different perspective and realize I did my best to save Lea. So now... seeing Lea holding a little Paisley in that Polaroid, watching hopelessly as Paisley hurries into the private bathroom, turning back around and seeing Alexis in the flesh right in front of me. All I see is how much Lea lied to me. How she kept this secret life different. How she hid who she really was from me. She never loved me. She couldn't have.

Lea played me. Played with my heart. She ran away from Alaric. Ran away from me. Was going to run back to Michael. I swear to God I've never hated somebody more. Never hated somebody like I do right now as much as I do Lea. She fucked with me, and just may be the reason the greatest love of my life—my *wildflower*—slips away from me tonight.

And I never wanted that to happen. Never wanted to lose Paisley.

Not like this.

Not now.

Alaric has his head in his hands, pacing the glossy white floor with eyes shut so tight they seem glued. Paisley I'm sure is in such shock, at a complete loss for words. I saw how rigid she became before she ran to the bathroom. Saw how tense her shoulders were and how her breaths faded a little. I don't like it. Don't like that these shocking twists of events are causing so much bewilderment in her eyes. Because that's exactly what I felt when I looked back into those honey browns before she left... complete *perplexity*.

I never wanted to be the one to hurt Paisley, and now involuntarily... I may just be the one to ruin it all. *I was once in love with her... mom?*

Dio mio. Her *mom...* Alaric's *former girlfriend...* it's all connected and leads to me.

I didn't know. I swear to fucking God I didn't know any of it.

Paisley has a half-sister. And here she is standing right in front of me, thirteen years later. *Alexis. Alexis Goldberg—Lea's daughter.*

They look nothing alike. Paisley is all her father.

"Alexis," I say for the second time, in complete disbelief that this is actually real. The second she begins running up to me, I open my arms to her and Alexis crashes into my chest as I hold her tight. I don't care about the throbbing aches of the bruises that align my skin. All I care about is how good it feels knowing that the little girl I watched grow up is safe. The plush giraffe toy obsessed girl who loved playing dolls, eating apples, and all things pink is right here. She's *okay*, despite all the hell she must have endured growing up without Lea.

All the guilt I felt the day her father signed those legal guardianship papers and took her away from me washes away. All these years I've always kept Alexis close to my mind, praying that she was all right, so this right here is such a welcome relief from all the chaos my mind is in.

As we embrace, my gaze finds Alaric's, whose eyes darken in dismay. I'll never forget the way he grinds his jaw as his face scrunches up and he mouths, "*Fuck. You.*"

And then Alaric's gone, storming out the door with such speed he roughly slams shoulders with a dark-haired man dressed in a dark Henley top and black jeans who steps into the hospital room.

I know what Alaric's '*fuck you*' means. It signals everything is over. Our friendship. His relationship with his daughter. All because I'm in love with Paisley, a woman who's forbidden to me in his eyes.

"Oh my God," Alexis breathes, a bright smile on her lips as we pull away, yet I still see the grief twinkling in her dark eyes. "I'm so happy you're okay, Santo! I have all these photographs with you in them from when I was a kid. Found out who you were through my father, who let it slip one day. Been following your fights ever since. You were there for me when I needed it the most. It's impossible for me to remember you from when I was like three years old, but I see you in photos with me and this feeling of such comfort and warmth returns."

"God, I thought I'd never see you again, Alexis! I'm so happy to see you! I can't believe how fast you've grown up."

484 | VANESSA LUISA

"School and stress will do that to you." She giggles, and I can't help but softly laugh.

"What happened?" I ask. "The nurse said you were the family of the victims today... who were they, Lexi?"

Alexis shuts her eyes for a split moment, breathing out a brave breath before she focuses on me again with a broken frown. "My dad and my stepmom. They were killed. My father's been in and out of rehab for the longest time. If it wasn't alcohol, it was drugs. He was also borderline emotionally abusive toward my stepmom, who I absolutely adore. Ador*ed*. God, it hurts so much knowing that..."

She sniffs away a few tears, her voice a croaky mess as she continues, "He shouldn't have been driving today. His license was suspended. Police are saying witnesses stated my father lost control of the car and slammed into yours, causing all the carnage, and my father and stepmom ended up. *Shit*. It's just... I can't believe they're gone."

The dark-haired man who entered the room when Alaric stormed out walks up to us and pulls Alexis in a warm hug. He seems around the same age as me, perhaps a year or two older.

He whispers something to her in Spanish that I understand as I also speak it. *"Respira, hermosa. Respira, estoy aquí y todo va a estar bien. Tiene que ser."* It translates to, *Breathe, beautiful. Breathe, I'm right here and everything is going to be okay. It has to be.*

Alexis nods against his chest, her fists clutching his shirt in need as her body begins trembling through sobs. My heart aches from how much Alexis has lost today... *everything*. But I'm so desperately grateful she has this man by her side, whoever he may be.

Kissing her forehead, he squeezes her in comfort and lifts his gaze to me. He offers me a soft smile, emotion all over his face, and while he's still hugging her, offers me a handshake. "Hey, man. I'm Alejandro Sinato, Alexis's step-uncle."

"Saint Lisconti, I'm—"

"I've heard about you. Nice to finally meet you. You've meant a lot to Alexis."

485 | OF US

"She means a lot to me. Nice to meet you as well, Alejandro. Was it your sister who…?"

"Yes." Alejandro gulps down with a sigh, understanding exactly what I meant. "It was my older sister who was in the car with Alexis's father, Michael. She's been married to Michael for the past ten years, but in these recent years… their marriage has been pure hell. I told her for months to leave the piece of shit, tried to help her out of it, but… look where it got her."

Fuck.

"I'm so sorry, man. Truly am so sorry. It's such a terrible situation to be in."

"Hey." He shakes his head, a sad smile on his lips. "You were the victim in this, Saint. My crazy fucking brother-in-law could have killed you and your girl too, so don't apologize for something that isn't your fault."

A few moments pass as Alexis begins to settle down, wiping away her tears as she steps back beside Alejandro. She offers me a weak smile.

I shoot her one back, reaching out to squeeze her shoulder. "Grief takes a fuck load of a long time, Alexis. You've just got to follow the waves. Don't let anybody tell you where you should be on your grief journey. Feel what you need to feel. Don't keep it trapped inside."

"Thank you so much, Santo. I'll remember that for sure. I really appreciate it."

Santo. Alexis used to call me Santo too all those years ago before boxing and my fighter nickname was even in the picture. I thought the memories of the past and hearing her say my name like that would haunt me, just like it does every time I picture Lea, but for some reason it doesn't. I feel no tension, only ease. Just like when Paisley says my name.

Paisley.

Every part of me wants to excuse myself from Alexis and Alejandro and make sure Paisley's okay. I never meant to cause this pain. This carnage. And I know I'm only the victim in this all too, but fuck how bad I feel. It's as if I've been holding onto a rope for so long, all through the blood, sweat, and tears till my fingers redden with blisters, perspiration lacing my skin. And all of a sudden... the rope snaps, slipping from my grip, and I go falling. Falling into the unknown when I need stability the most. When I need my *wildflower* the most.

Never in a million years did I imagine this scenario for us. It's such an unexpected twist to my finally healing heart. The one that belongs to Paisley Reign, *only* her, and always will, because I know she'd never burn me down.

I trust her with all I've got.

Love her with all that I am.

Mean it with all I feel for her.

This revelation could break us. It could shatter us to pieces. Or, it could be the missing piece to our puzzle. The one that unites us forever, proving our love can truly withstand everything. I know for myself, my answer will always be the latter. Always.

This much I know is true.

Clearing my throat, I turn my gaze back to Alexis. "Did your dad, Michael, ever say anything about how your mom, Lea, was living... many different lives?"

"Yeah, he did mention something about it just a few months ago actually. He was drunk at the time, so I almost didn't believe him at first. It literally blew my mind that I have an older half-sister. The crazy thing is I was trying to stalk her on social media because I wanted to connect and invite her to the sixteen birthday I had a few weeks ago, but I couldn't find her anywhere. Doesn't help I don't know her name or what she looks like."

Alexis knows...

I gesture behind me to the door of the private bathroom, my heart racing out of my chest. "That was her. Your half-sister, Paisley." God, that feels so odd to say. "Paisley Reign."

"What? *Her?*" Alexis gasps, her eyes wide. "I thought she was just your girlfriend!"

"Oh, Paisley *is* my girlfriend." I smile, loving the way that statement sounds on my tongue. "Trust me, I'm just as confused and shocked as you are right now. I didn't know Lea had another daughter until just a few minutes ago either. I'm in love with Paisley, have been for a long while, so this is just all super over-whelming for her."

Alejandro seems to put two and two together as he asks, "And that was Paisley's father before? The *shoulder-slamming* doctor?"

I sigh. "Yeah, that's him, Alaric Reign. He wants to put me six feet under. He just found out Paisley and I have been hiding our relationship. He doesn't like me dating his daughter because we were close friends and I'm double her age. It's even worse now because it turns out our past girlfriends were the same people. Lea, or Faye, which apparently is her real name, left Alaric when Paisley was only one. Then, moved along to Michael, then me…"

"Don't worry about it, man. You don't owe anybody an expla-nation when it comes to love. It's dirty what Lea… Faye did to you all. He and you are the victims in all this. Just think of it that way." Alejandro shrugs. "Besides, you've got us now. Newfound family. I just lost my sister today. Alexis lost her parents. You lost a good friendship, and it seems Paisley's lost her relationship with her fa-ther. So, we'll all just have to be here for each other now, yeah?"

We'll all just have to be here for each other now…

Alejandro's words mean so much to me.

Never in my life did I think I'd be able to connect with such like-minded people following this tragedy. It means everything to me that Alejandro is acknowledging both Paisley and me for ev-erything that we are, choosing to accept our love. It's refreshing. So good. A type of reassured sensation Alaric refused to give us.

"Thank you." I smile widely. "You don't know how happy that makes me."

"That's Alejandro for you." Alexis smiles through the pain. Tenderly glances up at her step-uncle before reaching up and kiss-ing his stubbled cheek. "Always finding the positive out of the bad. Wish I could be more like you."

Alejandro chuckles. "Nah, you're perfect just the way you are, Lexi."

Just as she's about to reply, the sound of the bathroom door clicking open behind me has us all turning our heads there. There's so much warmth inside me as Paisley steps out, her eyes studying us, much calmer than before... and then it happens. Alexis starts running to her and Paisley smiles as they collide, embracing like two angels screaming out to hell.

"I actually do have a half-sister!" Alexis squeals, so goddamn happy.

Paisley buries her head into her sister's neck, and I hear her murmur, "I can't believe this."

My heart is aching as they sob through their tight holds, sisters finally coming back home to one another after their entire lives apart. It's such an emotional moment to witness. Such a beautiful moment for my beautiful girl. *I'm so proud of her. So in awe of her.*

Alejandro squeezes my shoulder and when I turn to him, I find his eyes already on mine. He smiles and it isn't fake. It's the most real thing I've seen. "You love Paisley, hmm?"

"So much, man. It hurts so much that I needed to sacrifice a friendship for it, but when it comes to love..."

"We don't choose it, it chooses you. I get it, man. We probably all need some time to comprehend all the shit that happened tonight. But let's stay in touch, okay? Alexis is all I have now, and after she and I organize the funerals. Let's all meet up when we have a clearer vision. This could be the start of something great, you get me?"

"I got you, Alejandro. I'd love that. We should definitely do that. Let's swap numbers."

I pull out my phone from my back pocket. The screen is a little cracked from the wreckage, but it's an easy fix. After we exchange numbers, we turn back to Paisley and Alexis, who are wiping away each other's tears with sad grins and haven't stopped talking since.

"I believe there's always a silver lining in life, even in the darkest of times. Seeing them both right now like *this*…" Alejandro nods toward the women and smiles. "It's the silver lining to everything, man."

Nodding, I smile back because I couldn't agree more. Seeing Paisley this happy brings some hope to my rapidly beating heart. Hope that everything is going to be all right.

But at the end of the day, it's Paisley's choice where we stand from here. There are so many things she needs to unravel now… the first being how comfortable she is with the situation, the second is the fact that her mother is no longer with us, and the third… the fact that she has a half-sister—Alexis.

I know a part of me wants to sway Paisley, wants to wrap her in my arms and kiss her with everything I have to prove to her more than ever that she's my entire world. That we can battle past this. That this is only a wedge in the way of our forever. But I'm much more of a man than that. Much more of a man than to give her these false illusions of perfection.

This news… it isn't perfect. It's fucked up and places a huge spanner in the way of something beautiful. I'm a thirty-six-year-old man. I've been through a hell of a lot in my life to know you can't hold onto somebody forever. Eventually there's a time when one needs to let go, and as much as it pains me… fate's giving me no other choice but to accept it.

If Paisley needs time to process this all… if she doesn't want to be with me after this… I'll accept it like a man, because I am not out here playing games. I told Paisley a long time ago our relationship wouldn't always be perfect. I just never expected *this* to be the ugly.

This may be a wave.

Or it may be a little hiccup.

Or it may be what breaks us… but whatever Paisley decides it is, I'll give it to her, even if that means stepping away from my everything. Because right now all I want is for her to be happy and if this is the cloud that rains over our glowing sunshine, I'll take it. I'll take it because…

Our lives...

Our love...

Our fate... it's all in Paisley's hands now. And all I want to do is lie beside her in a bed of roses and kiss those golden hands, no matter what she decides is best for us from here.

Ten minutes later, Alexis and Alexandro are stepping out of the hospital room after saying their goodbyes. It's crazy how fate has connected us all so deeply. They're such friendly people, so kind, understanding, and supportive, especially considering how tragedy has touched them today too.

Once they're gone, my eyes trail to Paisley, only to find her heated gaze already on mine. She's standing in the middle of the room, holding her right arm to her chest, and I swear to God I don't start breathing again until she flashes me a warm smile and my soul begins dancing in praise.

She's smiling. It's a start.

Internally, I'm pumping my fists and thrusting my hips at the little sign that we'll be okay. But externally it's a different story. I'm still so fuckin' scared. So scared she'll leave me tonight.

"You're not mad at me?" I ask.

"No, I could never be. You didn't know a thing, just like I didn't," Paisley murmurs after a few moments. "You don't have to be so nervous, Santo."

"Got no choice. I'm always nervous when shit gets in the way like this, *wildflower.*"

"Well, there's no need to be."

I swallow down thickly and sit on the edge of the bed, bringing Paisley closer to me as I clasp our left hands together and thread my fingers through hers. She stands in front of me, between my thighs, and just her warmth alone makes me so happy.

A slight smile lifts the corner of my lips as I kiss each of her knuckles ever so slowly. "There isn't?"

Paisley shakes her head sweetly.

There's still hope for us.

"I know there's a lot for you to take in… the first being Lea is your mom, the second discovering Alexis is your half-sister. So I understand if you need to take some time to reassess—"

"Reassess *what?*"

"I don't know." I sigh, carefully taking her injured right hand and bringing both hands to my chest, right over my heart. "If I'm still worthy of your love. Our relationship. *Us.*"

"Santo, look at me."

When I don't lift my chin, she does it for me. Slipping her left hand from my grip, Paisley rests her fingers on the stubble of my tense jaw, smoothing over the spikily dark hairs. I shut my eyes at the sparks igniting my body, at the sensation of her skin over mine.

When Paisley presses her fingers against my chin, it makes me tilt my head up at her, but I still don't open my eyes. With tightly squeezed shut eyes and a clenched jaw, I can't get rid of the distraught look on my face. I'm so fuckin' nervous, so fuckin' worried, and I've never felt this way before.

"Look at me, Santo," she murmurs softly. "Please open your eyes and look at me."

"Please don't leave me," I whisper so damn hopelessly into the space between us. "I'm so scared this is all just too much for you and that you need some space. If you need it, I'll give it to you. Fuck, you know I'll give you the entire world, Pais. But after seeing you with Alexis, seeing how happy you are that you have a half-sister… I don't want to be the man who ruins that happiness. I didn't know Lea was your mother. Didn't know she had a baby girl two years older than Alexis she left behind. Would have never gotten myself involved with her if I'd known she'd abandoned her baby like that. You would have had another younger half-sister or brother if that night didn't go the way it did. I robbed that from you, Pais."

"No, you didn't, Santo."

"Yes, I did, I robbed it from you because I was thinking about myself that night and thought leaving Lea was the best option.

When I heard the bangs of the gun from outside... when I heard Lea screaming out my name... all I could think about was her. Then I saw Alexis standing there by the stairs, and all I could think of was the little baby who died right there with Lea. Never thought I could feel sadder, but I do. It hurts me, hurts me right here, *wildflower*..." I continuously stab at my heart through the shirt to show her where. "Hurts me right here that I knew your mom and you didn't. I didn't need Lea. *You* needed Lea. I took her away from you without even knowing and I'm so sorry for that, Paisley. So sorry that it happened like this."

My breath staggers in my chest as her jasmine scent fills me everywhere.

Fuck, I love her so much.

"*You* didn't rob anything from me, Santo," Paisley murmurs to me. "*My mother* robbed it from me the day she decided to leave. She robbed it from me again when she pretended I never existed. She continued robbing it from me until she finally set herself free. Baby, look at me."

I flutter my glassy eyes open, a few tears rolling down my cheeks. Paisley's quick to collect them as she leans down and kisses away my salty tears. She smiles so lovingly at me, warming me with her touch as my hands move to her hips and I hold her even tighter to me.

"I'm having a good life, Santo," she whispers against my lips, smiling deeper as she glances between my eyes with so much assurance in her sugary voice. "A *wonderful* life with you in it. I don't care that my father hates us now. All I want to do is continue what we have. Find new purpose in our lives. Get closer to Alexis and Alejandro. We aren't weeks away from starting our new lives in Seattle. You want to know why? Because we're starting that life *tonight*. Right *here*. Right *now*. *You* and *me*. The *wildflower* and the blue-eyed man I love."

Paisley's words are so beautiful, so tender, the tears flow even harder. I've never cried as much as I am today because it's really hitting me how much she's changed my life.

It's all her. All Paisley.

"Yes, it would have been nice to have a mom," she continues, her own tears slipping now, but I can tell it's a mixture of pure emotion and also joy. "But my nana was my greatest inspiration, as well as my father. But now, all I need is you. A man who I know is going to love me no matter what. Through thick and thin. Every up and down. We're stronger than ever, Santo. We're stronger because we're *together* and nothing can hurt us anymore. Nothing. Let's promise from this day forward we're going to let go of our pasts and find that closure. Let's promise to not fear another thing. Let's promise to love each other forever and one day be the best parents to a little girl or a little boy or both and show our babies all the love we lacked in all the different stages of our lives."

Her words warm my heart so much as I sniffle away my tears and grin up at me.

God, yes.

"I promise. I promise with everything I have that we will be the best parents to little Harley and flower babies one day." Burying my head against her flat stomach, I wrap my arms around her waist tighter and whisper against her hospital gown, "God, I would give anything to be a daddy. I want to be the father of your children so badly, my *wildflower*."

Paisley grins down at me so poetically beautiful. "I want that too, Santo. Desperately."

Aww yeah, tesoro.

Music to my ears.

Paisley giggles as I gently tug her to me, and she's left to straddle my waist as I sit even farther back on the bed. She continues, "Let's love our babies with every single version of our love, every single ocean of us. Let's love our children so much they'll never ever breathe a breath without knowing we love them, and we'll accept whatever they want to do or be in life, or who they end up loving. We can't change the past, but we can change the future and make it the greatest thing that ever happened to us. Because I know that's what I feel whenever I'm with you. You're the greatest thing that ever happened to me, Santo Lisconti. The *greatest*... and I love you. I love you so much more than I ever thought possible because it feels like our souls have been connected this entire time. This entire time, your soul was screaming out in search of mine, and I'm just glad. Glad it finally found me. Glad you found me."

"Glad we found each other, *wildflower*." I grin, and then I crash my lips on hers, our warm kiss so intimately emotional, and suddenly the world is a beautiful place filled with color again.

Filled with forever.

Filled with *her*.

Chapter
TWENTY-NINE

Paisley

I T TAKES US A FEW HOURS TO MOVE ALL MY BELONGINGS OUT OF MY father's house the following day. Saint and I both took the end of the week off work while recovering, so he was adamant to help me move out and into his house instead. And when I say *adamant* I mean to not make me pick up a single thing because of my fractured wrist, so I'm playing supervisor.

We laugh over the ridiculous things we find in my closet, and he can't stop teasing me about all the floral sundresses I have. We joke how I'm like that girl in Seinfeld that Jerry once dated who every time he saw her she always wore the same black and white dress, even in photographs he picked up in her apartment. I love how Jerry was convinced she either had a daily wash cycle, a never-ending supply of those dresses or really was a female superman with strict attire. *At least my sundresses are of different colors and styles!*

Of course Saint winks over at me as he casually picks up my

nightstand as if it's nothing, his toned biceps tensing at the action. "You better believe I'm bringing this across with caution. It's got gold in it, remember?"

I throw my head back in laughter. "Don't tell me you're talking about my vibrator…"

"Oh, I'm *definitely* talking about that, baby. Not that you'll be needing it anymore because somehow I'm fortunate enough to wake up in bed beside you for the rest of my life."

"Aww." I smile, kissing his lips before he steps out of my bedroom. "Now, hurry! There are still a couple of things to move across before my dad comes back from his shift. Pretty sure he made it clear to me yesterday that he doesn't want to see my face when he comes back."

Saint says something under his breath in Italian and I can't help but giggle when all he does is smirk. We finish up clearing my room and all my possessions just after 11:00 a.m. The last thing we do is strip the sheets and leave my bed in the room, seeing as I don't have any use for it at Saint's.

The aftershocks of everything that happened yesterday are still circling my mind, but the tension isn't there like before. Now when I think of my dad's words and how he doesn't accept Saint and me as a couple, it doesn't even faze me. It brings me comfort to know Saint and I did everything we could to make my father understand how we feel for each other. Now it's up to him.

Of course I'm going to miss my dad. There's no doubt about that. He's my father after all and he brought me up all by himself alongside my nana until she passed. I love him to bits, but I need this happiness in my life to keep me going, and Saint makes me happy…

So damn happy.

It takes us under an hour to set up my items in Saint's house. I only have a huge wall mirror, my nightstand, bookshelf, desk, swivel chair, and then a countless number of books, clothes, and other possessions. What takes the most time is placing all my clothes in his closet in his bedroom, mainly because I'm a neat freak and want them in color order, which I love how much is driving him crazy considering he just put a white dress and a red dress together, as if there are no colors in-between them.

"I'm really enjoying playing house with you." I smile over at him as we walk down the stairs and to his open plan kitchen.

"We aren't just playing house. This *is* your *home*, babydoll. Always has been. Always will be. This is where you belong."

Aww.

My heart squeezes at the words. *This is where you belong.*

The look on Saint's face is priceless when I place my birth control in the kitchen pantry. "*Oh*, hi there." He winks.

"Oh my gosh! Shut up, Santooo!" I laugh, playfully shoving his chest with the hand that isn't in a cast. "Now that we live together, please don't tell me you're going to say that every morning when I take one."

"Of course not." He smirks, pulling me to his side as he brings his lips to my ear. "I won't say it when you're barefoot and pregnant and looking like a goddamn goddess."

"Yeah, that's only because I won't be needing them then!"

Saint winks at me for the third time this morning. "*Exactly.*"

"So, the entire world knows you're dating Mr. *Hot-and-sexy-former-professional-boxer* Saint Lisconti thanks to the news and TMZ, and I still don't know shit!" Maralyn picks up her coffee cup from the white oak café table and gestures it to me. "Speak now, woman," She smirks, holding it by her lips. "Or you shall forever *not* hold your peace."

Smiling, I take a sip of my delicious coffee before setting it down on the table. We're at the little bakery across the road from the florist that Maralyn's always raving about. It's a chic cozy place with exposed brick walls, white oak tables, and white Italian terrazzo tiled floors. It's simply *stunning*! The low chatter of diners and soft jazz music playing in the background is so therapeutic and warm.

Although I'm taking the rest of the week off work, Maralyn usually has a break in the afternoons on Friday, so it's been nice catching up for some coffee after setting up my things at Saint's this morning and making some nice lunch together in his kitchen for the first day of the rest of our lives together.

While I'm spending some time with Maralyn now, Saint had to stop by his Fitness Studio to talk to Nico. We had to take an Uber together considering we don't have a car between us anymore. I used to use my dad's car. Saint's Maserati was ruined beyond repair yesterday and going around with his Harley while we're still a little beaten up definitely isn't a good move. While the predicament we're in isn't ideal, we're trying to see the bright side of it. Saint knows a few guys at different car dealerships and called them up this morning, mentioning something about a few of the models they have available. So, Saint's going to head there after going to the Fitness Studio before picking me up from the café… hopefully in his new purchase!

"You're right. I definitely have some explaining to do. Okay, uh, where would you like me to start?"

Maralyn looks at me as if I'm crazy. "From the beginning, girl!"

I laugh and for the next half hour explain everything between Saint and me, from how we met, through all the hardships along the way, up until me moving in with him this morning. The only thing I do leave out is going too much into detail with everything to do with Lea/my mom. I know it's quite personal for Saint. He's never mentioned Lea to anybody other than the people closest to him, and while it turns out she's my mom, I still want to respect Saint and respect the rawness that we're still living in.

Maralyn goes from laughing at the fact he stepped on my flowers to gasping at the day I found him with a Swiss Army Knife close to hurting an employee in his backyard. She's crying when we get to the part where I tell her just how supportive Saint has been of me. Like the day at the cemetery where he eased my fears, where he told me to *forget everything you think you are because you are everything you think you are not.* She's swooning at the part where he not so anonymously bought me a cupcake for my eighteenth, and the day Saint caught me gawking at him at the beach, and then how things between us were never quite the same after I admitted I couldn't stop thinking about him.

I tell Maralyn about it all. The stolen glances. The deep emotional connection. The angsty physical attraction. The forbidden of being in love with an older man, who also happened to be my father's best friend. The confessions. The getaway to Stinson beach. The kisses. The passion. The mind-blowing sex. The Harley rides. The poetry I wrote him. The amount of openness and honesty in our relationship. The *love yous*. The cowboy boots. The crash. The talks of Saint moving to Seattle with me and our eagerness to live together there. The blow-out argument when my dad found out. The revelation of my true mother and my newfound half-sister, Alexis. The conversations about children and a family one day.

I wrap up telling Maralyn about how this morning I moved into his house, and she stares back at me with her arms crossed over her chest and the biggest smirk I've ever seen on her lips. "All I've got to say is, I need to be a bridesmaid at this wedding!"

"Maralyn!" I giggle, shaking my head to myself as her smirk grows. "Marriage is going to be a long time away, trust me. There's going to be some adjusting to do once we get to Seattle and between me starting college and finding a job, and Saint starting up his fitness studio there, we'll probably—"

She cuts me off before I can finish. "You know all I'm hearing right now?"

"What?"

"*Blah, blah, blah!* That's all I'm hearing! Girl, from everything you've just said I can tell how much Saint loves you, and you love him. And I mean *l-o-v-e*. It seems as though that hella sexy man of yours was a cold, closed-up beast and then he met you and became a better man. Now, he's romantic and sweet and so vulnerable, which is *amazing*. It's so rare for men to open up like Saint does to you."

"You really think it's that rare?"

"Uh, YESSS!" Maralyn squeals, diving her spoon into her blueberry cheesecake. "It shows just how great of a man he is and how he emotionally cares, alongside all the great sex. It's so, so rare to get the best of both worlds like you do. I mean, take my damn husband for example. Whenever he's got something to say he keeps it all pent-up inside and I hate it. Your relationship with Saint seems like it has so much transparency and trust and passion, and that's exactly what you need to make it work. That man adores you, Paisley. I wouldn't be surprised if he proposes like tomorrow. I mean it!"

Marriage. Marrying Santo.

Becoming Mrs. Santo Lisconti.

I can't help but smile. "As much as I love that idea, it's a little too soon, don't you think?"

"NO, GIRL! It's never too soon when you know you found the one! Men like him won't waste a second when they know what they want, and Saint? He definitely knows what he wants—*You*."

I grin across the table at Maralyn and take another sip of coffee. My heart is beating so crazily fast because hearing her say all these things makes me even more happy with how close Saint and I are. We're unstoppable.

"Maybe not tomorrow, but you're right… Saint's a pretty great guy. I'm lucky to have him."

"He's lucky to have you." She winks. "I mean, look at you, you're so beautiful."

Eyes wide, I gesture toward my face. "Oh please, I look like an extra in one of those cult zombie apocalypse movies. Still all bruised from the crash, my hair is like a bird's nest waiting to happen. I have no makeup and I'm still a little loopy from all the medication I was on at the hospital yesterday. Besides, this"—I raise up my fractured wrist and nod toward the cast on my lower arm and wrist—"definitely isn't *beautiful*."

"Surrre, I bet that's not what Saint said when you two were most likely going at it after you were both discharged from hospital last night. Or again early this morning before all the moving in."

Mid-laughter, my jaw drops. "Maralyn! Jesus!"

"What?" The smirk doesn't fall from her lips as she arches a suggestive brow. "I'm right, aren't I?"

I feel my cheeks heat, a dead giveaway that she's onto something. "I will neither confirm or deny... ANYWAY! Let's talk about you! How are you surviving without me at the florist?"

"Oh no, no, no. Deflection isn't going to work with me, honey. Today is all about you and your lover boy." Maralyn grins, reaching out her hand across the table, and clasps mine. "Also, I just wanted to say I'm so proud of you, Paisley. I know you've had a tough life, and it hasn't been perfect. You've been through a lot at eighteen and oftentimes, you're like the daughter I never had. I'm just so proud of how far you've come. When I first met you, you were so reserved and a shell of the woman you are today. You're confident. Fierce. Not afraid to get hurt when it comes to what you love, and your courage inspires me every day. It truly does."

"Maralyn," I breathe, a smile on my lips as emotion floods my throat. "Gosh, that's so sweet. Thank you so much. I really do appreciate you and during this year have really seen you as so much more than a boss. You're my friend. My mentor. My pseudo mom. I'm going to miss you so much when I leave for Seattle, but we'll stay in touch. I know we will."

"Oh God, Seattle. Why did you have to bring that up? Great, now I'm going to ruin my mascara for sure." Maralyn sniffles, her eyes glassing over. Squeezing our intertwined hands, she picks up her napkin with the other and dabs the corner of her eyes, trying to compose herself before the tears flow. Her nose becomes flushed as she shakes her head and glances back at me with a brave smile, sentiment written all over her face. "I'm going to miss you too, Paisley. You're such a lovely and inspiring friend. I'm so fortunate to see you really turn into a strong woman during these past few months. We definitely have to call every day, okay every week, and make a promise to catch up a few times a year. That has to happen."

"I've already scheduled it down." I giggle, sniffling away my own impending tears.

God, I'm going to miss her so much.

It's so bittersweet because as much as I love my life here in Sacramento, I crave searching for something new and I feel it in my gut that Seattle will provide that for me.

"Good! Besides, who else am I going to talk about my idiot husband to now?"

That brightens up the mood and we start laughing through our tears. It feels so nice being able to relate and spend time with somebody who understands you so much. I'm super introverted, while Maralyn's the biggest extrovert I know, but for some reason our friendship just works, and I value it so much.

"Well, I still have the rest of June and July working with you, so I look forward to all the stories for the next six weeks or so!"

"Thank God!" Maralyn breathes out a sigh of relief, and we laugh again after that.

Our hands slip away, and she reaches for her cup of coffee, her bold red lipstick staining the white cup when she sets it back down. She claps her hands together. "So, let's talk about everything to do with Lea actually being your mom! I bet that was the greatest shock of your life!"

"Very much so. I didn't expect that at all and neither did Saint, seeing as he didn't know a thing. I became super overwhelmed and basically trapped myself in the hospital bathroom. I kind of regret that I acted like that, but at the time I couldn't think of anything else. But when I was in there, I realized it was all fate and that I love Saint more than anything and we could battle through this too. Plus, in a way it gives me a little comfort knowing my mom trusted him too before she lost that piece of herself. I feel close to her when I'm with Saint, and that gives me some closure. All the questions I had have been answered, and that's all I really wanted."

"That's such a beautiful way to put it. I love that it didn't eat away at you completely. From what you said earlier, Saint thought you were going to leave him based on the discovery. It was brave of you to persevere, to explain to him how much you truly need him and how it doesn't change anything for you."

I smile into my coffee, the cocoa brown liquid swirling as I move the cup around. "Yeah, to be honest I'm proud of myself too. I'm just happy my head managed to not explode when it turns out the daughter of the man that hit Saint and me yesterday was my half-sister... Alexis."

"I know, right! I swear if that was me and I found out I had a half-sister on top of everything that happened to you yesterday, my head would have exploded and landed on Brad Pitt's front door... it's not necessarily classy, but I swear that's what would have happened..."

I cover my mouth to muffle the laughter that escapes. *Maralyn is something else!*

"I'm just so glad you're safe, hon," she continues. "What they're showing on the news is terrible. Feel sorry for the other family too, but that asshole shouldn't have been driving! Ugh! Things like that really hit a nerve. Anyway, what's Alexis like? How are you feeling about all that?"

Swallowing my last drop of coffee, I glance back up at Maralyn. "You want to know honestly what I feel?"

"Yes, no filters. Just say it."

"Happy." The biggest smile breaks out on my lips. "When Alexis and I embraced... it was as if I found that final piece of myself I always knew was missing. It just all made sense."

We spent the next two hours talking about anything and everything. Maralyn tells me about a few stories from her time living in New York and it feels so nice to unwind with her. We just get served our second cups of coffee when we're disturbed by the rumbling purr of a passing car. Seeing as Maralyn and I are sitting by the large exterior picture window, we casually glance out of it and a gasp escapes Maralyn at the gorgeous sleek black

Lamborghini that slows and pulls into the parking spot right in front of the café. The windows are tinted, and every feature is immaculate.

Wow.

"Holy smokes! I'd stop eating muffins for an entire month for that car!"

"Not just a month, a whole year!" My mouth waters at the Italian beauty. "It's stunning!"

"Yes, and *sexy*! Sexy is what that car is! I need to call my attorney and get divorced in the next two seconds because I'd happily remarry the person who steps out of that car."

As if on cue, the driver's side door opens upward and the moment dark leather biker boots hit the pavement, my jaw drops. *Oh. My. God. No, he didn't.* I slowly eye the beautiful man I know and love as he steps out of his Lamborghini. *Oh yes, he did!*

"Oh my God, it's Saint!"

Maralyn gasps and slams a hand to her heart. "Oh, shit. Lord forgive me. Sorry, Paisley, just ignore what I said before about that remarrying thing, you lucky bitch!"

I giggle as I turn back to the window, watching as Saint steps by his Lamborghini and rakes a hand through his longish dark hair. Dark gray T-shirt. Black denim jeans. Perfectly stubbled beard. Saint looks like a beautiful yet rough Italian wonderland. The gorgeous dark sleeve tattoo that runs down his left arm, complementing his naturally lightly tan olive skin.

Hmmm. My blue-eyed boy is definitely a looker.

Glancing up at the sign of the café, he leans back against his Lamborghini and pulls out his phone from his jeans pocket as the car door closes.

My phone buzzes on the table half a second later.

SAINT: I'm here, tesoro. x

A second text comes through.

SAINT: Can I come in or will Maralyn kill me?

Laughing, I show Maralyn the text. "Saint wants to know if you're playing nice?"

"I *always* play nice." She winks. "Tell him to come inside. My claws aren't sharpened."

PAISLEY: You're in luck, she says her claws aren't sharpened today. Come in! x

A smirk rises on those beautiful lips of his and he replies.

SAINT: Hmm, let's see about that... Coming in now, baby. xx

"Saint's coming in," I tell Maralyn as I set my phone back on the table and smile up at her. "For some reason he thinks you're going to bury him alive..."

"Of course I am. Going to give him the perfect grilling, just so I see him stress under pressure. I'm only joking!" Maralyn grins. "I'm not going to scare the poor guy. He's already proven himself to be good, and that's all I've ever wanted for you, honey."

"I'm glad to have you as a friend, babe, truly."

"I feel exactly the same way."

I turn my head toward the door as Saint steps inside the café, sexily slipping off his aviator sunglasses and folding them at the collar of his dark T-shirt. He's so tall and fit... *mine.* That's all I think as I smirk to myself as a group of women seated at one of the booths hungrily glance up at Saint and begin ogling him. He doesn't even notice them. *All mine.*

Those ocean blue eyes I love scan the room until they meet my gaze and instantly brighten, filling with such an abundance of passion as I wave him over with my good hand. Grinning, Saint's by our table in seconds, respectfully holding out his hand toward Maralyn as he slips into the seat beside me. "Hi, I'm Saint! Saint Lisconti. Paisley's boyfriend. You must be Maralyn! It's nice to meet you and finally put a name to the face!"

"Is *the face* better than you expected? Say yes because I need a compliment today."

Saint cutely glances over at me, almost for backup. "Uhm..."

I can't take how genuinely nervous he looks right now. My *bello*.

Snickering, I nod at him. "Just say yes, she loves playing games with people's heads."

Maralyn puts a hand to the side of her mouth as if she's telling a secret. "That's true. Husband would even say it's my specialty."

We all laugh, and Saint's mid-chuckle as he shakes hands with Maralyn and says, "Well, if you ask Paisley, she knows I don't generally stick to the rules. Sooo, I'm going to say *the face* is simply *meravigliosa*. Wonderful."

Maralyn's eyes almost turn heart-shaped as she puts a hand to her chest. "Dear Lord, as if you couldn't get any more perfect! That Italian is just *wow*..." She turns to me. "Um, excuse me, but how the hell are you not melted on the floor already, Paisley? The man has gorgeous dimples, speaks Italian, owns a Lamborghini. To be honest, I think *you* should be the one who proposes to *him*!"

Oh my God!

The laughter continues.

Saint sets my injured hand on his lap, his thumb brushing over the cast as he glances between us and says, "What I love about Paisley most is she overlooked all that. Whether it be on an emotional level or everything else in between... she just wants me for me, and that's all I care about."

Aww.

"Sooo..." Maralyn grins, leaning her head on her hand. "When's the proposal?"

Smiling, I nudge my boyfriend. "Don't mind her, she's been asking all day..."

But it doesn't bother Saint and he full-on smirks at us both with wiggly brows. "Sooner than you may think."

My breaths go crazy wild.

Sooner than you may think...

"What?" I grin, my jaw slightly dropping open in awe. "First time I'm hearing this."

"Then it definitely won't be the last." Saint winks and with that leans toward me. "Hi there, beautiful," he sexily murmurs, then his lips are on mine, kissing me softly with just enough sensuality to make me know he meant every word. We pull away, smiling. "Coffee. Now I want one too."

I feel my cheeks flush from the kiss as I swipe my tongue along my lower lip and catch Maralyn, who hasn't stopped smirking at us.

Her gaze says it all, '*Marry this man!*'

In seconds she slides her loyalty card across the white oak table to Saint. "Here, buy one with this. I'm up to the reward of having a free coffee, so you can get one for yourself."

Saint kindly slides it back. "Thanks, but I'll get one myself. Treat yourself when the time comes."

"Damn." She gasps. "It's like I'm looking into the reflection of the antonym of my husband. He would have claimed that free coffee so fast…"

Saint waves over the server in seconds.

The server smiles at us and pulls out a little notepad and pen from his beige apron. "Hey there, how can I help?"

"I'll have one double macchiato. Thanks, man." Saint then turns toward us. "Would you two like anything? It's on me."

"No, thanks." Maralyn smiles, standing up from her seat. "I'm just going to head to the ladies' room. Be back in a minute."

As she leaves, Saint continues gazing at me. "Want another coffee or something like that, baby?"

I shake my head softly and smile. "No, thanks, I'm onto my second."

Saint gestures to the server that *that's all* before turning back to me with dramatically widened eyes. "Only onto your *second*? I literally have five coffees a day. That can't be an excuse, baby."

"Oh God."

He grins and softly cups my face. "See what you're living with?"

"An Italian beast."

"Mhmmm, try again."

"A beautiful Italian beast."

"That's more like it," Saint whispers and pulls me closer before kissing me again. This time for much longer and much more intense, as if we were alone. I kiss him back hard, loving the groan that escapes his throat the second our tongues collide in steady, passionate rhythms. He pulls back with another satisfied groan. "Been waiting hours to do that. You like our new car?"

I raise a playful brow. "*Our?*"

"Mhmmm, what's mine is yours."

"Oh, is that how it is now?"

"Damn straight."

"I love it." I grin. "It's very sleek. Very sexy. Very *you*."

"Mmhmmm." Saint smirks. "Looking forward to taking you on a ride in it."

Picking up my coffee, I fail at hiding my smirk too as I speak over the cup. "Yeah, I'm definitely *not* walking into that double meaning."

Saint smugly winks.

Definitely walked into it already...

It's hard to believe that this time yesterday our lives were about to change forever. I'm just so happy he's right here beside me. Happy to be Saint's. Happy to call him *home*.

"So Maralyn's quite the character, huh?" he says.

"I thought you'd like her."

"I do. She's pretty cool. I can tell you'll miss her when we move to Seattle."

I frown just thinking about it. "Dearly."

"Well, it's a good thing I just bought a fucking fast car. We'll get from Seattle to Sacramento in no time!"

"Yeah, right, because the eleven-hour drive is *totally* a fast one!"

"Just like I said, *not* in no time..." Saint repeats, his smirk only deepening, and I burst out laughing as the solace of his arms pulls me closer to him. "Okay, maybe you're right, babydoll. But in other news," he murmurs in my ear, "I've got a little surprise to cheer you up..."

Oh *wow*.

"A surprise?"

"Mmhmmm."

"Not another pair of cowboy boots, is it?" I tease. "Even though you know how much I love them, it's just that they didn't bring us much luck considering the events of yesterday."

"*Dio*, I couldn't agree more." Saint starts chuckling and shakes his head. "As hot as you looked in them, and I mean *so hot I wanted to put you in every position*, I don't want to see another pair of cowboy boots in my life..."

"So, what's the surprise? Show me!" I beam.

"Patience, woman." He chuckles. "I want to show you later on tonight. After dinner."

"Oh no, Santo Lisconti, what did you do?"

Saint grins. "You'll see, my *wildflower*."

"Why are you so nervous?" Saint chuckles beside me on the couch, looking so cute with the rejuvenating face masks we both just applied while dinner is cooking. After coffee with Maralyn, Saint and I bought some groceries and started to prep dinner—Saint's apparent signature fettuccine with Alfredo sauce and roasted vegetables and seasoned roasted potatoes.

The only hiccup was when we arrived home, my father was stepping out of his front door and walking down the porch to his car. I stepped out of the brand-new Lamborghini, and we locked eyes. Motionlessly, he took one glance at the car, one glance at me, one glance at Saint before scoffing and jumping inside the car. He revved his Jeep out of the driveway and down Portola Way, creating skid marks around my heart. But as soon as the sadness came, it disappeared.

My father can't control my emotions.

He can't.

I was a rookie at the homemade pasta, but the way Saint taught me all the steps and we worked together around his kitchen as we danced to Bon Jovi blaring from his home music system. All I could imagine was one day years from today when we're married with children and we're all cooking together in a kitchen just like this. A little girl on Saint's hip helping him put the fettuccine pasta in the boiling water. A little newborn boy making a mess of all the vegetable scraps and us all laughing about it. Love. Love all around us.

I crave that. I crave a family desperately with Saint one day. I crave it all.

"Wildflower?"

I glance back at Saint a little dazed. "Sorry, what did you say?"

My blue-eyed boy simply smirks and gives me that knowing look. "Daydreaming about how good I look in this facemask, huh?" he teases.

I burst into a fit of laughter. "You wish!"

"Still nervous about this call, huh?"

"Nervous? Pfft, I'm not nervous."

I totally am.

Saint playfully rolls his eyes at me. "Okay, I'm just going to wait until that answer changes in three... two... o—"

I cut him off. "Okay, I *am* nervous, but just a little. I mean, I'm going to technically meet Enrico and he's one of your closest friends *and* cousin and that's big, you know?"

"It's only a phone call with my cousin to get in contact with Giulio Giannotti about purchasing a place in Seattle." Saint smiles. "Besides, he'll love you so much. I just know it. Trust me, baby, he will."

"All right." I giggle. "Let's do it!"

Saint chuckles and the butterflies in my stomach go wild as he picks up his phone from the coffee table. I scoot closer to him, grinning as he wraps an arm around my shoulders and scrolls through his contacts before tapping on Enrico's name. Excited bundles of nerves are jittering all along my entire body. *Saint's cousin. I'm going to meet Saint's family.*

The phone dials a few times and Saint dramatically rolls his eyes and glances at me with his smirk only growing. "You watch, he's going to answer with, *Enrico Martinez speaking*. He gets his work phone and personal phone mixed up all the time. You just have to laugh."

I giggle and snuggle into Saint's side, his cologne drifting me into worlds of him.

Enrico finally answers, his voice coming through the speaker. "Hi, Enrico Martinez speaking."

I smirk over at Saint, and he winks back at me as if to say, *'see, told you.'*

"Hi, Saint Lisconti answering."

Enrico's laughter brightens through me. It's infectious. "Oh shit, man, it's you! Hugo just woke up from a nightmare, so I was putting him back to bed and picked up the phone without even looking."

"All good, man. I know you're busy. How's Hugo doing?"

Saint's little nephew.

"He's good. Obsessed with *Toy Story* as always. Wouldn't go to bed without me singing him a lullaby in Italian, so bedtime went for a little longer tonight."

Saint smiles as he says, "He's lucky to have you, man."

"I'm lucky to have him," Enrico says through the phone. "I'm sorry I haven't really been in touch lately. Work has been crazy, and Hugo's needed me more than ever, so it's all been a little challenging. But I miss you, man, can't believe you're moving to Seattle and not here with me in New York! When you were in Santa Rosa, I moved to Seattle, then you moved to Sacramento when I was in New York, and now you're going to Seattle!"

"Damn, when you say it like that, we sound like we're scavengers."

"We are fucking scavengers, Saint."

They share a laugh and it makes me so happy seeing how content Saint is. I'm glad he has his true friends and family around when he needs it the most. *That's all that matters.*

"But don't you worry," Enrico adds. "In a little while I'm

thinking of heading back to Seattle, so we'll see each other every day. I'm sure of it. I still can't believe you bought a Lamborghini. I need to see that beauty in real life. Anyway, how's everything going with you?"

"Good, good, I'm happy." Saint's warm blue eyes hold mine as he says, "*Very* happy."

My heart clenches. *Aww.*

"I also just wanted to ask if you could talk with Giulio. Want to know if he has any of the houses he's designed currently on the market in Seattle, preferably in or near Madison Park so the University District and Downtown Seattle are both close by."

"Yeah, I can definitely organize that, man. How about I invite him on the call?"

Invite Giulio Giannotti, THE Giulio Giannotti aka. my dream future boss into this call?

Oh.

My.

God!

"Holy shit," I gasp, covering my mouth when the words are out.

The line crackles for a second before Enrico's confused voice asks, "Am I losing it, or did I just hear a woman's voice?"

"It's my girlfriend."

"Did you just *girlfriend*? Man, what the fuck? We don't talk for a little bit because life gets in the way, and you've got a girl? That's so good, man. What's her name?"

"Paisley. Paisley Reign."

"Is it serious?"

"Mhmmm, I love her to death. Never felt this way before."

To avoid kissing his facemask, I kiss Saint's neck instead and his chuckle has me giggling.

"Well, it seems like I definitely missed something." Enrico laughs. "Let's FaceTime! I want to meet the girl who stole your heart."

"*Now?* He wants to FaceTime right *now?*" I whisper-shout to Saint. "I look like shit!"

"Babydoll…" Saint throws his head back against the couch in laughter. "You know he can hear you, right?"

Oh, shit!

Enrico's soft chuckle comes through the phone. "Don't worry about it, Paisley, just ignore that lovesick boyfriend of yours. I'll pretend I didn't hear a word."

"That's very kind of you, but I literally have a facemask on… so does Santo."

"Santo in a facemask? God, I wish I were there to see that. All right, just wash it off and I'll call back in five. In the meantime, I'll text Giulio. Hopefully he's available to FaceTime too, okay?"

"Okay, bye!" Saint and I say in unison.

"Bye bye."

The second Saint ends the call my eyes widen in complete shock. "I'm going to meet your friends on FaceTime! What if they don't like me? What if… what if I stuff it up and make a complete fool out of myself in front of Giulio Giannotti, the *owner* of Notti Designs? It's such a renowned architecture and interior design company. What if I ruin my chances of ever working in their Seattle landscape architecture division in four years' time after college? I mean, do I call him Giulio or Mr. Giannotti? Or should I say his full name? What if I accidentally tell him something really awkward because I'm nervous and blow all of my chances with him?"

Saint can't stop laughing through my frantic slapstick panic. "You mean your *future boss*…"

"Santo! Don't jinx me!" I grin mid-gasp. "Let's get these facemasks off our faces before Enrico calls back!"

A few minutes later, we are back sitting on the couch, just in time as Enrico's FaceTime request lights up Saint's screen. Saint kisses me softly and murmurs everything is going to be okay while I'm patting down my dark waves. Then, he accepts the call and holds out the phone so we're both in the frame.

514 | VANESSA LUISA

A man with perfectly tousled dark hair and cocoa brown eyes grins at us through the screen and instantly all my fear fades away. *They're all going to like you. Calm down.* Enrico waves at us in a white dress shirt, a few buttons undone, and it seems as though he's in an office with a dark oak bookshelf behind him. "Aha, the facemasks are all gone, I see. Nice to meet you, Paisley. I'm Enrico, Saint's right-hand man. Or should I say left hand considering he's left-handed."

I giggle at the joke while Saint simply shakes his head with a bright grin.

"It's nice to meet you too, Enrico! Santo has said so many nice things about you. I'm really sorry if this inconveniences you in any way seeing as you were putting your son to sleep."

"Don't apologize, *wildflower*," Saint whispers in my ear before kissing my cheek. "You look beautiful."

"Ahh." Enrico grins. "Young love."

"I'm older than you, you idiot." Saint laughs, turning back to his cousin.

"I know, I know."

"Did Giulio get back to you?"

"No, radio silence. I'm just going to add him."

A ringing noise appears, and my heart is pounding in anticipation of this moment. I've been dreaming about the day I step into the Notti Designs office—my dream job—for years. I just never imagined I'd be meeting the CEO & founder, Giulio Giannotti like this!

I squeeze Saint's hand in mine, and a second passes before Enrico's video box lowers and Giulio appears in the video box on top. Giulio's in the middle of saying something in Italian when all of a sudden, his striking gray-blue eyes meet us, and he falls silent. He's shirtless and tangled in white bedsheets with a gorgeous woman by his side. It's evident they're naked under those covers. Giulio's dark hair is tousled and so visibly sex hair. The woman has the most beautiful hazel eyes, long lashes, and short, chestnut hair... graceful and a natural beauty.

"Holy fuck!" Giulio gasps. His eyes widen in horror, almost as if he has no idea he's even in this call. "Oh, *Dio*! I tapped the wrong thing!"

Ohmygod!

Saint and I look at each other and burst out in complete laughter.

This is the funniest thing ever!

"Oh, God!" Enrico chuckles, leaning closer to the screen. "Please don't tell me you guys were doing some post-sex kinky shit with your phone and accidentally picked up…"

"Well, sorry, buddy. You're in this on your own." The woman rolls away from Giulio and off the bed, bringing the sheets with her, and we all laugh even more. All except for Giulio, who's still in complete shock.

"Valencia! Lenciaaa!" Giulio groans, reaching out his hand to her off-camera. "Come back, *amore*. I pressed the wrong button. Forgive me, I'm old."

"You're thirty-three!" Valencia's sweet voice comes from afar.

He suggestively winks at her. "Well, you know what you say about being thirty-three…"

"There isn't even a comeback to that, man." Saint chuckles, shaking his head.

Giulio joins in the laughter, rubbing a hand along his dark stubbled jaw… that is until a pillow is slammed on his face and a smiling Valencia takes over his phone. "All right, I'm going to leave you all to it, but just so you know, we were literally watching a replay of when Italy won the World Cup."

Giulio appears behind her. He's wearing dark boxer briefs and wraps his arms around her waist from behind, resting his chin on her shoulder. "Don't lie to our friends. You know you like it when I…" he whispers something in Valencia's ear and her face turns red. She's giggling within seconds and playfully shoves his chest as she says, "Okay, I'm out of here! It's great to see you, Enrico and Saint. It's nice to meet you…"

"Paisley." I smile.

"Paisley." She grins back. "I'm sure we can chat more when my husband isn't being a complete pain in the ass."

"Don't give him any more ideas, Val." Enrico chuckles.

Giulio laughs, slapping her ass through the covers wrapped around her as she runs out of the room. Eventually, Giulio takes a seat on an emerald velvet chair that seems as though it's in the seating section in their stunning primary suite. "Hi, I'm so sorry about that. I honestly pressed the wrong button. Sorry, we haven't met before, Paisley...?"

"Paisley Reign." I can't help but grin. "And no, we haven't. It's nice to meet you, Mr. Giannotti."

"Call me Giulio, and the pleasure is all mine." He smiles. "I see you're with Saint... but if you were a possible client or employee, I'd probably hide under a rock for a very long time."

"Well, that's a little ironic because Saint and I are possible clients, and if I'm honest, I'm also an aspiring employee too."

"Jesus Christ!" The gasp Giulio lets out is hilarious as he rubs a hand over his defined stubbled jaw and groans. "I am so sorry you're seeing me like his, Paisley. I'm definitely giving you a raise the day you start working with me."

"You hear that, *wildflower*?" Saint laughs. "You've already got the job!"

"Oh perfect, no interview?" I joke.

"Yeah, literally no interview. You saw me gawk at my wife like I was in some porno. Don't worry, I'll remember your name and you can just walk into my building when the time comes. Want me to create the key card right now?"

"See, what were you stressing about? You got the job." Saint laughs.

"Great, I totally don't need to go to college now."

I half expect them to react to me admitting I'll be in *college* soon when I'm with a thirty-six-year-old man. Perhaps it's because we've received so much criticism and judgment from some people already that I think they're going to say something too, but Enrico and Giulio, they don't react badly to it. They *smile*. It's as if it isn't even a problem and that makes me so happy because I'm so sick of all the negative outside noise. This is a relationship between Saint and me. *Nobody else.*

"I love that you'll be the third person in this FaceTime call to go to college in Washington State!" Enrico grins. "Saint, you missed the fucking memo! What happened, man?"

"Sorry about that, man." Saint dramatically raises his hands with a smirk. "Guess I was too busy at Stanford to even notice."

"Yeah, yeah, smartass. How do you deal with him, Paisley?"

I grin over at Saint. "I think the question is how he deals with me."

"You're perfect for each other, trust me," Giulio says. "Tell me, what's your college and bachelor?"

"Landscape architecture at the University of Washington in Seattle."

"Aww, that's amazing. We'll practically be neighbors in Seattle! I went to WSU, which is a few hours away from that college. All right, I like you already. You say architecture, I say *Amennn!*"

"Oh no," Enrico groans. "Paisley, you've unlocked the volt. Giulio is the most professional guy I know, but I think he had a little too much vino and a little too much *ahem.*"

Giulio can't stop nodding to himself, his eyes glazing over a little. "Look, there comes a time when you have three children and there's still potential for your family to grow, so you just look at your beautiful wife and say, *I fucking love you so much, let's keep this going.*"

Enrico chuckles. "Oh shit! Are you *actually* freaking drunk, man?"

"No." Giulio shakes his head and hiccups so loud he bounces on the chair. "Date night with my wife just makes me this giddy. *Giddy*, isn't that a funny word?"

"Definitely had one too many glasses." Saint smirks. "I see the date nights at the Giannotti residence are something to envy, huh?"

"Lenciaaa?"

"Yeah?" Valencia's voice calls out from the distance.

Giulio grins and stands, jogging through his house. "Where did she go anyway?" he mumbles to himself, then all of a sudden he's in the primary bathroom and Valencia playfully rolls her eyes at him, tightening the sheets around her as she continues to wash her face at a marble vanity.

"Saint wants to know if the date nights at the Giannotti residence are something to envy."

"Holy hell! I'm so sorry to all of you." Valencia laughs, dabbing her face with a face towel as she reappears on the screen. "Giulio literally never gets drunk. Like *ever*. The one night he goes a little crazy, *this* is what happens."

"I'm not drunk, darling, I'm in loveeeee—*Oh shit!*" Giulio trips over something and the phone flies from his grip and goes sliding across the floor until it slams against something and the screen turns black. "Well, maybe just a little drunk…" he groans in the background, and then he reappears on the screen but upside-down and starts laughing. "Oops. Look, I don't want to make a fool out of myself, so whatever conversation you all wanted to have, let's have it tomorrow. That way we can talk when I'm not making an ass out of myself."

"Sounds good," Saint says. "We'll set that up. Have a good night everybody!"

Enrico nods. "*Buenas noches* to all, and great to meet you, Paisley."

"Nice to meet you too and also Giulio and Valencia as well. Night!"

Giulio smiles. "My pleasure. *Ciao, ciao!*"

"Sweet dreams!" Valencia's voice looms in the background, just before we all end the call.

Saint cuddles me to his side, and I laugh into his chest as he kisses my forehead with a smile. "Well, that was something else. See, you've got nothing to worry about, babydoll. We're all human at the end of the day, as I said, Giulio's the nicest guy you'll ever meet."

"He truly is! They all are such great people, I love them!"

Saint smirks. "Hope you still love me more..."

"Always." I grin against his lips, feeling such warmth inside me it's bursting at the seams. "Here's to Seattle, baby."

"Here's to the entire world and you."

※

After the romantic candlelight dinner Saint and I have at home, we move along to the living room and sit around the coffee table on the plush white rug. The lamps are on, giving a dimmed hue. Dinner was perfect and everything I love. Homemade. Alone. *With him.*

Now, as Saint pours us two tall glasses of water, a bowl of cherries on the coffee table between us, I smile at just how much of a beautiful man inside and out my Santo really is.

"That dinner was so mouthwateringly delicious!" I moan, leaning up against the couch as I cross my legs on the floor. "I didn't know you could cook like that."

"If I remember it right, you were right there cooking with me, *bella.*"

"I know, but you're the pro." I smile, sipping some refreshing water as he hands me the television remote control to his huge smart TV. "Can we watch one of your boxing fights?"

I don't know what I expected, but it definitely isn't the huge grin that works up his lips. "Yeah, what the hell, let's fucking do it."

I can't stop grinning and give him the TV remote back. "You know what to search up. Give me all the goods."

Saint chuckles as he goes to YouTube on his TV before typing up his name and one of his fights. For the next few hours, we watch a mash-up of his best fights and *my God* is it impressive watching the man you love dominating a ring with a single pair of fighting shorts, striking powerful boxing technique, and those fierce blue eyes screaming out victory.

Seeing his hard-working body glazed in perspiration... those abs tense with every jab... his endurance... the concentration...

the endless wins… his fury… the crowd chanting out his name as he delivers efficient hit after hit to his opponent, again and again and again, until he's crowned the champion.

"My boyfriend is a total badass."

"Yeah, my ass is pretty nice, isn't it?"

I laugh. "That's not what I said."

Saint playfully wiggles his brows. "But it's what you were thinking. Let's be honest."

As we continue watching his different fights, I rest my forehead against his shoulder and smile at the television. He wraps a hand around my waist, his thumb continuously caressing my skin through my dress. I breathe in his musky sandalwood scent and love all the versions of Santo Lisconti. The man fighting through the screen. The man beside me. *All* of him.

"Thank you so much for allowing me to see you like this," I murmur.

Saint kisses my hair and smiles. "Thank *you* for loving me through my every stage."

Chapter
THIRTY

Paisley

"YOU KNOW WHAT I'VE NOTICED?" I GLANCE OVER AT SAINT AS HIS fights continue to play in the background and smile. "It's nothing bad, I promise."

"What is it?" Saint asks, resting his hand on my right thigh. He slowly begins tracing circles on my upper thigh, warming my skin with a touch so *addictive*.

"Ever since we returned from Stinson Beach, you haven't been smoking a lot…"

He grins. "You noticed, huh?"

"Mmhmmm."

"I've been trying to stop the habit, yeah." He nods. "I want to be around, you know, want to be around for everything life has to offer with you. I thought back to those statistic numbers you told me about the day we first met three years ago. I don't want to be a statistic."

"I don't want you to be one either." My heart clenches. "So, you're stopping smoking?"

"Trying to ease out of it, yes."

"Why now?"

"Because I wanna have you for the rest of my life, *wildflower*. Don't want our future children to grow up in an environment filled with smoke and bad choices because of me, you know."

Not being able to resist, I peck his lips. "I'm proud of you, Santo, and just know I'm here to support you every step of the way."

"Thank you, baby. I also got in touch with my former counselor today, just asked him a couple of questions. He thought it best I perhaps see a therapist in Seattle, better to keep a solid therapist than keep changing, so I'm going to do that, I think. Don't want to book a session without you knowing, but I think it'll help with that closure. The door's closed and locked, but I wanna make sure it's *kick-the-door-open* proof and that the key is thrown the fuck away. What do you think?"

"I think that's the perfect choice. It makes me so happy you're doing these things now."

"Me too." Saint smiles and kisses my forehead. "Just wish I had the courage to do all this a long time ago. Wish I had the courage I do now back then. Thank you for encouraging me to do all this. It really sparked all these ideas in my mind that night at the beach house when I opened up about everything. You told me that seeking help isn't a bad thing, and it truly isn't. So, thank you."

"Anytime at all. You know I'll always be here to support you."

"Likewise."

I smile and we spend the next few moments wrapped in each other's touch as I straddle Saint's waist. I love that we simply stay like this, forehead to forehead, heartbeat to heartbeat, forever against forever.

"It takes a very strong man to admit to me everything you just did," I murmur against his lips. "Thank you for always being real with me."

I'm careful with my fractured wrist as I slip out of his hold.

It doesn't hurt me as much as it did yesterday and with the medication, it's slowly easing too. It's going to be a long six to eight weeks until it's off, but a summer I'll never forget nonetheless.

The bowl of glossy dark red cherries on the coffee table catches my eye and a memory crosses my mind. Grinning over at Saint, I gesture toward the bowl. "Last week you told me you can do that trick where you tie the stem with your tongue. Show me!"

Chuckling mid-groan, Saint throws his head back against the edge of the couch and shuts his eyes. "Oh God, nooo."

"Come on now, baby. Don't be shy. Damn, Maralyn's right. Is there anything you can't do?"

"Say no to you, apparently."

"Yeah, but you don't want to do that."

Saint flutters his eyes open and winks. "*Obviously.*"

"Come on," I purr, seductively biting my lip to make my point. "I'll show you how grateful I am if you do it."

He blindly takes ahold of the bowl of cherries and sets it down in the space between us on the rug. "Oh, really now?"

"Mhmmm."

Saint's eyes darken, pure dripping desire. "This better not just be some upscaled persuasion, babydoll, because my cock is getting harder by the second. *Ti guiro su Dio.* I swear to God."

My eyes flicker to his crotch through his jeans and then back up to those piercing ocean blues. "*Ti guiro su Dio, Santo.*"

"Fuckkk," he moans. "Don't do that, baby."

I giggle. "Do what?"

"Seduce me in Italian when I'm already turned on."

"But I don't even know Italian! I just said four words!"

"Trust me, that's enough." Saint smirks as he takes a cherry from the bowl with a long stem. "I definitely need deflection now, so let me show you this apparent *talent* of mine."

Saint's bedroom eyes never leave mine as he sexily tugs the stem off with his teeth and shuts his mouth, obviously moving the stem around inside.

Mmhmm.

This is easily the hottest thing I've ever witnessed in my life.

I stare at him in such fascination, pure awe as it only takes him a few seconds before he opens his mouth and holds out the knotted cherry stem with his teeth. *Whoa.*

Gasping, I take the knotted stem out of his mouth and the heat between my thighs intensifies as I cross my legs together on the floor, feeling my sex throbbing wildly. It's then I glance back up at Saint beneath my lashes and moan out in satisfaction, "Impressive."

The sexual tension between us is extremely high as our extended stare only becomes more heated. My nipples harden against my bra and I know exactly what Saint means with the way he's looking at me… the *quiet evening after dinner* plans we had are definitely not going to last. It's our first night living together, and I want to explore everything that comes with it. Sex can come a little later.

Yeah, right.

What a farfetched thought that is, Paisley.

"Sooo." I half laugh to myself. "You never told me how today went with Nico."

Well, that seemed to do the trick because at the sound of Nico's name Saint groans and rubs his face. We begin eating some of the cherries and Saint sighs. "It didn't."

It didn't? Huh?

My brows knit in confusion as my chewing slows. "What do you mean?"

"Well, apparently word around the city travels quickly. Didn't even realize at the time, but there are tabloids everywhere of the incident yesterday. There are a couple photos of you and me coming out of the hospital, but I don't give a fuck. Either Nico saw them or spoke with Alaric, but he practically told me to fuck off and laughed in my face when I mentioned expanding the fitness studio to Seattle. So I quit."

"You quit?" I gasp. "But you're the co-founder."

"I know I am," Saint says, leaning his head against the couch as his hand slips through mine. "But quite honestly, I'm at a stage in my life where I'm happy with what I have. Don't want to cause any drama, so I'm going to let him buy my portion and was thinking of opening another fitness studio in Seattle that's completely my own. But then that had me thinking about the early hours and late nights. Now, I start as early as four thirty some days, finish as late as eleven some nights. If I open my own place in Seattle, there won't be the flexibility I have with Nico here. I want to start a family with you one day, Pais. Want to be right there beside you for every step. Opening my own fitness center will be crazy wild, and while I'm capable, I just want to enjoy time with my family. I want to be there for the one a.m. wake-up calls when our baby can't sleep, the early morning school drop-offs, the date nights with you. So I thought about something that allowed all that."

My heart warms at the fact that he's not only thinking about himself, alongside *us*, but our future family too. *That truly says something about the type of man he is.*

"What's that?" I ask, loving to know more.

Saint's eyes sparkle. "Thinking about opening up a shelter for mental health sufferers, the homeless, and survivors of all types of violence. Volunteer work. Food runs. Accommodation. Listening to people's stories. Lifting them up. Providing them therapy and assisting them in getting back on their feet and working. Profits would come from myself and sponsors. Part of everything we make will go into the charity, Silent Hearts, which I created a few years back to assist sufferers of mental health, homelessness, and domestic violence to find themselves again. I've had the charity for so long, but it wasn't in my hands, you know... ain't afraid to face it anymore."

"Aww, that is such a beautiful idea, Santo. It's so touching and heartwarming. You're a great motivator and so very inspiring. A shelter is the perfect step forward. It'll help so many lives, save so many too. I think it's truly your calling."

"I think so too." Saint smiles the brightest, squeezing our hands together. "But if I really want to start something, I want to get the ball rolling now. Oversee a property to buy in Seattle and figure out all the logistics and finances. Thought also it could have a gardening section, some tips from yours truly. *You,* if you want to. Guess it's a form of therapy too. Giving something substance and watching it grow. I'm going to work at the fitness studio until we leave for Seattle, but already reduced my hours. Told Nico I want the mornings and evenings off. Need time to spend with my *wildflower* when she isn't brightening up the florist."

"You're so beautiful, inside and out, Santo." I kiss his cheek, feeling myself melt right here next to him. "I'd love to do that. Love that you're thinking about us as a family one day."

He smirks. "Let's allow you to enjoy college first, all right?"

"All right. But I've already got baby fever, so these four years are going to kill me."

"*Well,* we can still think about names now…" With his free hand, Saint brushes a strand of my hair behind my ear and smiles as his thumb brushes over my lips. "Look around for a house that'll suit a growing family… Write a list of all the sports our future children will play…"

"Yes!" I laugh, the funniest scenario conjuring in my head. "You're going to be such a coach, telling our son to do five push-ups every time he runs past you."

"Yes, and he'll just be like, '*Who the heck is my dad*'?"

"Bet you all those '*rules suck*' comments will bite you in the ass. I feel like our kids will be complete cyclones. I just hope stomping all over my flowers isn't in their blood."

Saint bursts out laughing. "Definitely in their blood. But don't you worry, baby, we'll put one of your crazy signs up and make our children stare at our garden like it's a museum. '*Look, but don't touch*'."

"They're going to hate us." I giggle.

"*Love* us," he murmurs against my lips. "They're going to love us to bits, just like we do."

I smile. "If you say so."

"I *know* so."

Saint sensually pecks my lips and we're grinning when we pull away. *I know so too.*

He slowly glances between my eyes, sentiments gushing through his gaze as he cups my jaw and whispers, "I want you to meet my family, Paisley. It's the last piece of us. When your wrist heals up real nice, come to Santa Rosa with me. My mom and Nonna have been calling like crazy ever since the news of the crash, so I wanted to visit soon... and I want you to come with me. I've never introduced a girl to my family before, *ever*, so they already know you're something special."

My eyes turn glassy with emotion. "You... you want me to meet your family?"

"More than anything in the world. I know they're going to adore you already."

"Yes." I smile, bringing him into a tight embrace that I never want to let go of. "I want nothing more than to meet the two women you love the most too. Nothing more, Santo."

"With you right here, it's three women I love. Always will be."

Moments pass in pure and utter comfortable silence filled with nothing but pure love. *Meeting Saint's family... that's huge for me, but something I so desperately would love too.*

"Okay," Saint says after a little while and stands up. "Let me get that surprise for you before I spend the rest of the night kissing you instead. Wait here, babydoll."

"Not going anywhere!" I grin back, as Saint disappears upstairs two steps at a time. Returning my gaze to the television, I pop a juicy sweet cherry in my mouth and feel my heart melt away.

Not going anywhere, my blue-eyed boy.

Saint's back moments later completely shirtless, holding a few pieces of paper, two gray led pencils, and an eraser. *Huh?*

My lips curve into a smug smirk as I eye his abs. *Well, I like this very much.* He chuckles when he sees the mixture of bewilderment and satisfaction on my face. "You're confused, right?"

528 | VANESSA LUISA

"Just a little."

"Well, it will all make sense in a minute."

Saint retakes his position beside me but doesn't sit down yet as he lowers the volume of the television. "So I kind of did something today after I bought the Lamborghini..."

"Seems like you did a lot today while Maralyn and I were talking our ears off."

"But I like it when you talk your ears off," he teases, and my heart skips a beat as he sets the pieces of paper on the coffee table and winks at me before turning around... and then I see it.

I gasp, staring at his lower back in complete awe. "Santo!"

"You like it? The tattoo artist who's a friend thought I was crazy for getting more ink after all the shit that happened yesterday, but I couldn't wait anymore. I wanted to do it, Pais."

Standing up, my finger grazes down his back where a few bruises from the incident are. I weave across the preexisting cross and angel wings he had there, but as my hand reaches his lower back and brushes over the plastic tattoo wrap, I completely lose my breath.

Wow.

I can feel the rapid beats in my chest at the pad of my fingers, those pitter-patters going wild as I trace over the plastic, over the tattoo by his lower back that he redid that previously read *Lea*. Now, the *Lea* is gone and instead the script writing reads, *Wildflower*, alongside all different types of roses, lilies, and daises surrounding the word in beautiful black and white shading, with a little tinge of blue over the lilies. It's a tribute. A tribute to me. Only me.

Saint remembered.

Saint remembered lilies were my favorite flower and the reasons behind it.

"Santo, it's so beautiful! I've never..." I get all teary-eyed seeing the breathtaking tattoo because it means the world to me. "I've never felt like this before... so happy."

I take it in a little longer, hot tears trailing down my cheeks as the warm smile continues to rise on my lips. The second Saint turns around, I jump into his arms and they wrap around me with so much security, holding me so close to him. I'm careful of my plaster cast as I wrap my arms around his neck, looking down at him lovingly.

I know Saint. I know what his tattoos mean to him. It's much more than just a tattoo or collection of tattoos together. Every brush of ink has a significant meaning and reasoning behind. To have me tattooed on his skin... it only confirms how much we're a forever thing.

Those ocean blues I'll always love warmly stare back at me, so much emotion in his gaze as my vision continues to blur. "You really did that for me? It's so stunning. I can't believe you got it done," I murmur against his lips, my voice breaking at the final words. "You went over Lea's name when you've had it for such a long time. What if you regret it?"

"I'll regret it more if I don't have you with me everywhere I go because I love you with every inch of my heart. Every inch, baby," Saint whispers. "My story with Lea... your mother... it's over. It has been since a long time ago, but yesterday really gave me a lot of closure when everything was revealed. My life isn't Lea, it never was. It's been you, Paisley Reign. I love you more than words exist. That's why I need to have my *wildflower* on me, every day, everywhere I go, because you remind me of home. Only you."

Because you remind me of home.

Only you.

Cupping Saint's jaw with my good hand, I rub my fingers over his stubble, tracing the deep dimples on his cheeks as he grins at me so damn beautifully. Everything inside me explodes as I grin back, my heart beating wildly. "You're the best thing that ever happened to me, Santo, the very best thing. I love you so much. Thank you. Thank you for turning my life around."

"You're not the only one who's feeling that way, babydoll."

"I'm glad."

"Surprise, *wildflower*." Saint smirks and then my lips are on his, kissing him with everything I have as his warmth becomes mine and I show him just how glad I am that I found him. He kisses me back fondly, addictively, as if nothing else matters... *because it doesn't.*

We continue kissing for what feels like forever, getting more urgent with tender moans by the second. So much love. So much resolution glossing over the people we once were and the ones we are together. We've grown together, mended our flaws, found love unexpectedly no matter how forbidden or bittersweet for people that don't expect love because all that matters is him and me...

Nobody else...

Nobody else but *us*...

I giggle as he spins us around before setting me down on my feet. It's then he picks up the sheets of paper from the coffee table and turns them around.

"Wow," I say, glancing over the first page, which is full of rendered and shaded designs of all different varieties of flowers. I see roses, irises, lilies, and so many others. A few different versions of veins, leaves, and thorns make a feature, as well as a beautifully drawn compass, which is so lifelike and 3D, almost as if it's popping out of the page with its detail and the *P&S* etched into the metal edge. All the other few pieces of paper are blank, ready to be drawn on.

"What's this all about, Santo?"

"I want to get my left arm tattooed in a complete sleeve too, but this time I want it filled with flowers, this stopwatch to show how time is the essence of all great things and everything that we are. So, I did a little mockup of some of the flowers and thorns, but I think we should design it together. Want to think of you every time I look at it. What do you say?"

There's this tang in my chest as Saint wipes away my tears. *I've never felt this complete in my life. So special.*

"I think that's the craziest idea in the world!" I lift my eyes to him in pure intrigue and awe. "And guess what? I LOVE it!"

"I'm so happy to hear that because I love it too." Saint grins, holding me tight in his strong arms as he pulls me even closer.

Strong arms that I know I'll be safe wrapped in forever. "Gotta get these flowers tattooed on me. Want to have you on me forever. A permanent reminder of exactly who we are from this moment forward. There's not going to be a day in my life where I'll regret it because I'll never regret loving you, my *wildflower.*"

Oh my… My heart.

I grin up at Saint, so crazy in love with my beautiful Italian blue-eyed boy. I adore him with more love than I ever knew existed as he continues his touching speech.

"I'm going to have your favorite flowers tattooed on my skin to remind me of you, Paisley Reign, and to represent the beauty of our love that's bloomed. Going to have thorns to represent all the hardships along the way that have all evidently led me back to you. Then, I want your name written in the flowers, in striking cursive, because I want every fucking person in this world to know you're mine. And next… next, I want the words in the piece of poetry that you wrote me etched on my skin. Want the title right there with it. Want to look at it every day, want to look at *you* every day, want to look at *us* every day and know we've made it. Going to have that piece of poetry written out across my back, beside the cross. Going to have it wrap around the left side of my chest, so it's script. Going to have it in a way you sign your signature by my heart, 'cause you're the only woman in it. My world is tattoos, yours is flowers… so, let me immortalize you with them both because that's how much I love you. I'll love you *forever*, my forever girl."

⁂

Six Weeks Later…

The conditions I've reduced Saint to in the last month and a half living together. I'm laughing in my head just thinking about some of them.

Late night self-care face masks.
Morning yoga to stabilize the mind.

Therapeutic bubble baths that always end in him devouring me.

It's a good thing he has the patience and really loves me... but this one right now tops the cake. It feels like we're less than a minute away from passing the *'Welcome to Santa Rosa'* sign on the highway when I tell Saint to come up with an impromptu song about Santa Rosa.

"No wayyy!" Saint's booms through my helmet in the Bluetooth intercom. "Nah ah!"

I'm riding on the back of his Harley, hands tight around his waist as we make our way to Saint's homeland. In just a few minutes I'm going to be meeting his mom and Nonna for the first time and I couldn't be more excited to finally be with the ones he loves the most.

"Oh, come on!" I giggle as his metal beast speeds closer and closer toward the city he grew up in. "Once it becomes catchy, I'll sing along too!"

"Why about *Santa Rosa*, though?"

"Because it represents who you are and is also iconic of everything we are... Santa is *Santo*.... Rosa is *Rose*. That's two of the things I love most in the world... *you* and flowers. It couldn't be more perfect!"

"All right, you got me," Saint sexily murmurs, and I can hear the smile in his voice. Bringing his left hand off the handlebar, his leather gloved hand moves to his waist, over my left hand, and threads our fingers together. I giggle as he brings my left hand to his lips, kissing my skin softly. "Anything for you, babydoll. Anything for you."

I was allowed to finally take off the cast at the start of the week and *gosh* how much better it feels. No more pain and no more not being able to do anything. It's such a relief. I grin at the sweet gesture, knowing how much this call means to us both. It's one step closer to Seattle. *One step closer to our future.*

Although there are still some slight nerves whenever we're on the road together after the car accident almost two months ago, I just keep on reminding myself that we weren't in the wrong and it gives me ease and confidence in our travels. Besides, Saint's such an attentive driver and rider... *even when he's riding the Harley with one hand.*

I can't stop the laughter that escapes me as Saint starts singing the best impromptu song about Santa Rosa just as we fly past the welcome sign and into the city. It's such a belly laughter that I feel it from the pit of my stomach and all up my body. Being with Saint makes me so happy. His quirky and hilarious side is such an added bonus.

Leaning my helmet against his shoulder, I grin at his beautiful voice. *Damn, this man can sing.* It's a sultry, sexy, gravely perfection... a perfect mixture between Ed Prosek and James Gillespie, and the soft compelling melody takes me to places beyond return. It's not his voice that I'm laughing at, but rather the lyrics as he sings about me and his nonna becoming best friends when we're in Santa Rosa because she'll bribe me with Italian food, him accidentally on purpose forgetting to pack facemasks for us while we're here, and loving falling in love with a forbidden kind of girl. The melody even turns a little country meets rock and I enjoy it so much.

We're laughing the rest of the ride and talk about anything and everything that we are.

It's the middle of July and we've had such a beautiful summer so far. Whenever we're not working, we're soaking up the last few weeks we have here in sunny Sacramento. From discovering new beaches, to decorating his home, to riding around on his Harley from dusk to dawn watching the surreal sunrises and sunsets, to weekend getaways to Stinson Beach, to flower shows and so much more... it's all been a dream. *An absolute dream.*

I'm going to miss the warm beaches and late-night swims, but the calming rain and possibilities in Seattle will be such a welcomed relief. Saint and I have passed the last six weeks simply enjoying one another and becoming lost in our little word. Saint's flower sleeve tattoo on his right arm and the poetry piece I wrote him is now tattooed on his left side, curling across to his chest, the signature I handwrote with the tattoo gun right by his heart.

It's such a beautiful tribute to everything that we are and so special to me. I love Saint so much, so seeing my words of poetry that I wrote specifically for him inked on his skin... it means so much to me. I fall asleep every night in his arms, my fingers tracing every word and his lips on mine.

I'd like to say the situation with my father has simmered, but it hasn't and is the complete same. He won't answer my calls, nor take one step into understanding, and while it hurts, I've learned to accept the things we cannot control. And as unfortunate as it is, my relationship with my father, or lack thereof should I say, is beyond my control.

Today was my last day working at the florist and between Maralyn and I both, we cried a river. We promised we would stay in touch and see each other regularly, even though I would be two states north soon. So, it was the perfect time to spend some time away in Santa Rosa.

We've also bought a house in Madison Park, Seattle, sight unseen. It was a gorgeous home that Giulio designed with a developer, and I was so in love with everything about it from the pictures and virtual tour the relator gave us via FaceTime. What I loved most about it is that it overlooks Lake Washington and the beautiful glimmering water will be our view forever.

A couple of weeks ago a huge blow-out between Nico and Saint saw the process of him giving Nico full rights of the fitness studio fast-tracked, so now it's completely out of his hands. It pains me a little that Saint had to sacrifice his friendship with both Nico and Leo (and my father) for our love, but it brings comfort knowing Saint wants this relationship more than anything. Both Nico and Leo have sided with Alaric, hating how Saint hid it all from them. Nico and Leo feel like they can't trust him anymore, and that hurts. A bittersweet hurt. I only hope with time these wounds will heal. If one day Nico, Leo, and my father turn around and accept us, then that will be beautiful, but if they don't, that's okay too. They'll just be missing out on knowing the greatest man to ever exist in this world.

✻

Saint

"WOW! You're beautiful!" My mother grins the second she sees Paisley, grinning as she pulls her into a tight hug right here in the driveway of my nonna's house. My mother's light blue eyes land on mine as they embrace, and I swear they haven't been any warmer... *prouder.*

Seeing two of the strongest women I've ever known together makes me so happy. I don't have a big family—it's only my mom, my nonna, auntie, and my cousin, Enrico—but I adore them more than life. Everything I do is for my family, and so it means the world to me that they're loving Paisley just as much as I do and are accepting of our love.

My mother throws me a thumbs-up and as she pulls away from Paisley, can't stop staring at her in awe. "It's so nice to finally put a face to the name. Santo's been talking about you nonstop. Now I see why!"

Paisley glances over at me and beams. "*Oh,* has he now?"

Oh yeah, they're definitely going to be best friends.

I feel my cheeks flush as my mother simply smirks at me. "Oh my God, Mom. Stop."

She snickers and leans toward Paisley. "You see that, honey? Look how red his cheeks are getting. He's totally into you, not that you needed the confirmation. I've never seen him like this before!"

"Mom, give Paisley some space." I laugh.

"She sees your face all day, let her see the face of the woman who made you!"

"Oh, *God.*"

My mom smiles devilishly and turns to her. "He's a sweetheart, isn't he?"

"A complete gentleman." Paisley grins back. "It's so nice to finally meet you too, Mrs. Lisconti. It's an honor."

"Oh, the honor is all mine, and please call me Cecilia."

The second I pull my mother in a tight embrace and her rose scent consumes me, life couldn't be more perfect. I haven't seen her in a long few months, so it feels so nice to see her so happy as she squeezes me hard and reaches up to her tippy toes to whisper in my ear, "She's beautiful, Santo. Inside and out. I can already tell she's the one for you."

I kiss her cheek. "I feel the same, Ma."

"I'm so glad you brought her home! I love you."

"Ti amo anch'io, mamma."

I love you too, mamma.

I'm grinning as I pull away and love that both my mother and my *wildflower* are too. Paisley is just about to say something when the front door swings open and my nonna comes rushing out with a wooden spoon with Italian sauce dripping from it. I can't help but run to her and embrace her so tightly. My nonna is my everything and I love her dearly. Her wisdom, her charisma, her humor… it's what makes home, *home.* And I'm just so happy Paisley's here with me too, because she's my home too.

"I missed you so much, Nonna!"

"Me too, Santo!" She grins, her eyes traveling down, and she lets out a dramatic gasp as she pauses at my legs. "Oh *Dio, Santino.* What happened to your jeans? Did you have a crash on your way here and ripped your jeans at the knee? Did you hurt yourself, *bello?"*

Throwing my head back in laugher, I glance down at my distressed ripped jeans and shake my head. "No, *Nonna,* I promise I'm okay. This is just the way these jeans are made."

Her eyes widen in horror. *"Gesù Cristo.* I was about to get out my sewing kit!"

Chuckling, I pull her into another warm hug and she sways us from side to side. *"Ti prometto che sto bene, nonna."*

I promise I'm okay, Nonna.

"*Bravo.*"

Good.

Before I can introduce her to Paisley, my nonna slips the wooden spoon laced in pasta sauce in my mouth. "Tell me if it's okay, Santo. I'm making your favorite meatballs because Nonna is the best."

Chuckling, I nod as I swallow down the delicious sauce and my eyes almost turn into hearts. "It's perfect, just like always, Nonna. There's somebody I want you to meet." I turn around to Paisley with the deepest grin on my face, my heart spasming at the huge smile on hers too. *So beautiful.* As Paisley steps to my side, I take her hand in mine and kiss her cheek. Then, I glance back at my nonna and say, "This is Paisley, *mia ragazza... La amo cosi tanto.*"

This is Paisley, my girl... I love her so much.

The love in both my nonna's and Paisley's eyes is so pure and tender. So much love as my nonna steps forward and cups her face, even though she's so much shorter than my girlfriend. A few seconds pass before my nonna whispers, "You love my grandson?"

Paisley smiles, her voice thick in emotion. "Very much so."

"Then I love you too, *gioia.*"

The second they embrace, my heart explodes and my vision blurs in such happy tears. Never been the type of man to cry, but ever since I met Paisley that changed. It all changed for the better. Seeing her with my nonna... with my mom... it has me praying heaven is just as good as this because I don't want to let her go into the next world. Want to hold onto her forever.

"Aww, baby." Paisley smiles beautifully when she pulls away from my nonna and turns to me. Wrapping my arms around her waist, I try to laugh a little to ease the knot in my throat, but it ain't any use because my forever girl notices. *I know she does.*

Cupping my stubbled jaw, Paisley glances at me with worry. "Everything okay, Santo?"

"Mhmmm, just glad you exist, that's all."

Paisley grins. The light freckles on her cheeks come out with the humid heat of Santa Rosa and the shining sun. "Ditto, my blue-eyed boy."

I have no mercy and crash my lips on hers, holding her tight as I kiss her like I mean it. I feel her smile against my lips at my mom and Nonna, who don't stop cheering, and it only makes the tears roll down my cheeks faster because Paisley Reign makes me feel this way. She makes me appreciate life so much, in a way I've never looked at it before. She makes me want to marry her. Have a family. Go to fucking Mars if she asked me to, because I would. I'd do anything for her.

We probably look like complete messes as we wipe away each other's tears while laughing because life is fragile and precious, but *God* how beautiful it can be too.

"You turned my son into a crier," my mom teases. "I love it. I love it when my son feels all these emotions. Makes me know his father and I have done a good job bringing him up."

"Your son has a heart of gold, Cecilia. A pure heart of gold." And then Paisley laughs. "It's funny because when we first met, I was just a kid and I hated him because he stepped on my flowers when he moved in next door to me."

My mom playfully shakes her head at me, while my nonna clasps her hands together with a gasp. "*Gesù Cristo, Santo!* How many flowers have you destroyed in your life?"

I furrow my brows in confusion. "What do you mean, Nonna?"

She glances at Paisley. "When Santo was a little boy, he helped me with gardening. One day, my friend Maria called, so I went inside the house for five minutes just to have a little talk. Then, when I finished, I stepped outside and my beautiful roses... all gone! This little *bastardo* cut them all out. They were the most beautiful flowers in the world."

I chuckle, remembering this story now. It's pure gold. Don't know how I forgot. "Kind of not the best thing you want to hear, right, Paisley?" I turn back to my nonna. "Tell her about what you did after."

"Well, I did what anybody else would have done. I chased him around the yard with a garden hose. I couldn't catch up to him. He has legs like a bloody frog, but the water got him."

Paisley can't stop laughing alongside all of us. My mom is wiping away happy tears from her eyes and I'm honestly doing the same. It's so nice to see the three women I love the most all here together.

My nonna claps her hands once more and turns to me. "So, when you gotta get married? They stopped making my favorite lipstick, so I gotta use it for the wedding before it finishes."

Paisley's cheeks heat and I chuckle, feeling mine do just the same. "I'm sure we can help you find another lipstick before, Nonna…"

"Nope." She shakes her head and grins. "You marry Paisley. I make the meatballs for the wedding. Deal?"

It's heaven being in my nonna's house again after so many months in Sacramento. It takes me back so many years… so much nostalgia of being a little kid and racing up and down the backyard I'm currently looking out at through the kitchen. The same backyard my mom and Paisley are walking around, talking, and laughing. This yard takes me back so much. Making the tomatoes with my grandparents during Pomodoro season. The sausages during the celebrations. Everything is so vivid and in exactly the same space it once was. It even smells the same, gorgeous, sweet citrus mixed with ripe peaches and zesty lemon.

I remember the races my father and I used to have from the fence and back, how he'd always let me win by accidentally tripping or creating some sort of disadvantage for myself. Now, I look around and while all the nature around me is the same, the people that made this place so vibrant and lived in have condensed to two. *Three with Paisley.* I've got everything to lose, and I used to hate that feeling. Now it's hope for me. Hope that with time

Paisley and I can start our own little family in a few years' time, and we can watch them run around this yard simply enjoying life.

Voluntarily helping Nonna with prepping the apple pie we're having later tonight, I peel the apples with a knife because that's as Italian as it gets, while my nonna cuts the apples into long, thin slices. Santa Rosa means a lot to me. I rediscovered my love of boxing here and put all of my dedication into training, working hard, and began playing at a professional level. From that moment, Santa Rosa wasn't just home to me—it was my happy place, as well as Marin County and Stinson Beach.

There are memories here.

A second chance.

Life is better... *much better*... just like it is today with Paisley by my side.

Paisley.

God... I love her so much.

"JESUS CROSS!"

Jesus Cross? Isn't it Jesus Christ?

"Huh?" I glance over at my nonna, whose eyes are practically bulging out of their sockets as she motions to my hands. "Look! Look what you're doing, Santo!"

I glance down to observe the mess I've made, laughing when I've peeled the apple down to the core. "Well, I guess I'm going to make a terrible husband, aren't I?"

Nonna smiles, playfully slapping my cheek with a hand towel. "No, *bello.* God will forgive you for that. But he won't for all the tattoos. Every time I see you, you have more!"

"What's wrong with my tattoos?" I ask, as if we haven't had this conversation since getting my first at sixteen. *Yeah, I wasn't going to wait another two years for it.*

"The devil will take you with those tattoos!"

That has me grinning.

"But I like the devil, *Nonna,*" I joke.

Nonna gasps and playfully hits me again with the towel. "*Cosa hai detto?*"

What did you say?
I smirk. *"Ho detto... Portami a chiesa."*
I said... Take me to church.
"FINALLY!"

Paisley can't shake the grin off her face as we slip into bed in my nonna's guest bedroom that night, and neither can I. The thrill of it all just feels so good... having Paisley in my heart like this feels *so good.*

"I didn't think I could love you more than I do," she whispers, tracing her fingers over the completed tattoo of her poetry piece and the completed left sleeve tattoo filled with flowers, a stopwatch and everything that we are. "But then I saw you with your mom and your nonna and I felt so alive... so happy to know you. It's been so beautiful seeing just how much you adore your family and how much you value it over everything else."

As Paisley falls asleep in my arms tonight, I can't wipe the smile off my face as I watch her so beautifully against me. I brush my knuckles over the soft skin on her cheek, feeling the action brushing over my heart. I may not have been a perfect man at the start of our relationship, I may have had falls, but lying with her tonight as the stars twinkle in the night skylight above, I feel my flaws flutter away and transform into scars of strength.

Everything is perfect.

Everything is perfect because I have her.

A soft knock at the bedroom door flickers my gaze there.

"Santo? You still up, dear?"

It's my mom.

Slowly slipping out of bed, I'm careful to not wake Paisley after the busy day we've had as I slip on my navy satin sleep pants. I greet my mom with a warm smile as I step out of the bedroom and softly shut the door behind me. She has her pink nightgown wrapped around her and her dark hair pulled back in a high bun, grinning at me.

"Hey, everything okay, Ma?"

"Yeah, perfectly okay. There's just something I wanted to say to you. It wouldn't get out of my mind all night, so I know I just need to say it to you before I head to bed."

I cross my arms over my bare chest and nod. "Go on."

"Well…" Her smile remains, but emotion clouds it as she swallows thickly and glances up at me. "I just wanted to say I know it hasn't been easy growing up without your dad. He was such a hero to us and I miss him dearly, but what I miss the most is seeing the awe in his eyes every time you excelled in life. Your father was so proud of you, Santo. Every single day he was. He still is. You know what he always used to say to me?"

I shake my head, afraid that if I speak my voice will break.

"He always used to say…"

I reach out and pull my mom to me as emotion takes over her voice. Rubbing her back softly, I kiss her cheek and whisper, "Breathe, *Mamma*. Take a breath and tell me."

She sniffles and nods with a sad smile as her blue eyes land on mine. "Your father always used to say he just wanted you to be happy and seeing you today with Paisley only reminded me of that. I'm so grateful you two found each other, Santo. She's an angel and I know how much she means to you because you've never brought home another woman. I know the revelations you uncovered a few weeks ago were shocking. I was shocked too that Lea is her mother, but that doesn't change anything. Lea didn't deserve you. She ruined you, Santo, and you were too good of a man to see it at first. But now you do, and I'm glad, because Paisley is the woman for you and I'm so happy you both worked past it. Life is so bittersweet, you know that already, *bello*, so I'm just so happy you're going to be sharing some of life's sweetness with her." My mom reaches out and softly cups my jaw while she glances between my eyes. "Your father would be so proud of you. So proud of the man you've become because of Paisley."

Gulping down the emotion in my throat, I nod and smile widely at my mom. "Thank you, Mom. I know he would be proud too, and not only of me, but of you too. I'm so happy you love Paisley as much as I do. She means everything to me. It just hurts a little that it all had to go south with her father. I wish Alaric could just understand that I love his daughter more than anything and will never do anything to hurt her."

"I know. It's such a tough thing. Do you see him ever changing his views?"

"I don't know," I say honestly. "But I really don't see us ever getting our friendship back. I miss him, you know. He was a good friend, but I can live without it. It's Paisley I feel worse for. He's her only family and I just want everything to be perfect for her."

My mom nods. "I understand but look at it this way. You told Alaric everything you could. Now, it's up to him. I know it was a shock, but love should be celebrated, all kinds of love. It shouldn't matter that Paisley's only eighteen or you were his close friend. He should see that and know he can trust you with her life. Your age gap with Paisley... who gives a shit about it. When you know, you know. I was eighteen when I had you and look how far your father and I made it. Age is only a number. It's what's in your heart that matters."

It's what's in your heart that matters.

I smile down at my mom as I pull her into another comforting embrace. "I couldn't agree more. Love should be celebrated, all kinds, no matter the risks. Which is why..." We pull away and I glance back into her glassy blue eyes. I clasp her hands in mine and admit to her something I've kept hidden in my heart for the past three weeks since I custom designed *it...*

Something I know we both so desperately crave...

Something Paisley has no idea about... *yet.*

My mom grins in curiosity. "Which is why *what?*"

544 | VANESSA LUISA

"Which is why tomorrow... I'm asking Paisley to spend the rest of her life with me."

Later that night as I lie in bed beside Paisley once more, I can't help but itch for my phone on the nightstand and pull up Alaric's contact. I know we haven't spoken since the day everything exploded in all our faces. I know it's just after midnight. I know he won't give a shit... But as much as I'm not in the slightest a traditional type of guy, I still feel in my heart of hearts this is the right thing to do. I won't be able to forgive myself if I don't at least try one last time.

> **SAINT: I'm not asking for your acceptance or understanding... I know I may never get that, Alaric. We've all been through a lot. I know it's a shock. I know it's tough. I know you're hurting, but I've learned time heals all wounds and I hope one day you can realize that too. All I want is a little closure, a little peace, a little resolution, if not for me, then for Paisley. She loves you. Always will. She's your daughter, your only child. Please don't lose sight of that in all of this. She deserves much more than this silence from you. I love your daughter, Alaric. I love her with all that I am. It's why I vow to always protect her. Always cherish her. Always support her, for however long I shall live. It's why I'll never stop loving her... Why I'm going to propose to Paisley tomorrow. I just want you to know all of this, because you still matter to us. To me. To her. No matter how much it seems as though she doesn't need you, she still does. Trust me. I know because I would do anything to spend another second with my father. I know because I feel Paisley deserves more than what you're giving her right now. And I know deep down in my heart of hearts... you feel the same way too.**

Sent.
Delivered.
Now it's the waiting game...

My heart is pounding as Paisley stirs by my side, and I bring my lips to her forehead until her soft breaths stabilize. Smiling, I turn back to my phone, a little stunned to see that the message doesn't have *'delivered'* down below anymore but *'read'* now.

Alaric's reading this... he's seeing it at least.

After a few minutes, those haunting three bubbles appear, notifying me that Paisley's father is typing. *Hope. This could be some hope.* And then, just like that, the typing bubble disappears and I feel my heart drop into my fucking stomach.

Completely restless, I stay wide awake until 1:00 a.m.

I wait, and wait, and wait for Alaric...

But that reply... It never comes.

Chapter
THIRTY-ONE

Paisley

AFTER TODAY, I'M PRETTY SURE BEACHES WILL ALWAYS BE SAINT'S AND my thing. Just feeling those ocean waves wrapped around our bodies as we swim out to sea, laughing so hard and kissing in slow motion underwater, is enough to make me feel like the luckiest girl in the world.

Saint and I spent the entire day exploring a couple of the stunning coastlines Santa Rosa has to offer, and now we're back at Saint's nonna's house and I'm getting dressed for the apparent date night Saint wants to have with me. It's a little odd considering we came all the way to Santa Rosa to spend time with his family, and not to whisk us away somewhere, but I'm not complaining because I want to spend every second of my life with this man.

After slipping on my panties and hooking up my bra, I sort through the clothes I brought with me to Santa Rosa and lay them all out flat on the guest bed. Since we're only staying for a few days, we didn't bring much, and even less considering we came here by motorcycle and only had space for a few items to put in Saint's Harley saddlebag, but I'll whip something up. Saint's getting dressed in another bedroom, so I can take my time.

Towel drying my hair, I pull it up into a sleek updo and just as I'm about to decide on which dress, my phone buzzes on the bed. The second I start reading the text a smile rises on my lips because it's so unexpected. Yet so sweet.

> **ALEXIS: Hey, girl! This is Alexis. Alexis Goldberg. How are you? I know it's been a little while since we ran into each other at the hospital… To be honest, it's been extremely hard to comprehend it all, but I feel like I'm ready to reach out now and admit that even though my world is spiraling, it's slowly starting to steady. I'm glad that out of all the hell that happened, this newfound sisterhood really has me hopeful… Hopeful of something new. I hope you have been well and your fracture has healed up all nice!**

Aww. She's so sweet.

We exchanged numbers at the hospital but haven't contacted each other yet… *not until now.* Alexis—my half-sister—lost everything in that crash… her father and stepmom. I can't even begin to comprehend the impact of losing such important people at the exact same time. It has me thinking of my father and all the bad blood there.

I feel terrible for Alexis, so saddened by all the news, but I'm always going to be here for support. I want her to know that. And hopefully day by day this could bloom into an actual relationship because I would love that. It's even better that she's sixteen and only two years younger. It means we can relate better.

> **PAISLEY: Alexis, it's so nice to hear from you! I've been pretty well, all healed up from that fracture gratefully. I've been thinking about you a lot lately, but didn't want to overstep by texting when grief is very much still fresh, so I'm glad you reached out and messaged. It means a lot to me. You're so strong and optimistic… It's honestly so inspiring. Know I'm always here whenever you need. I just pray that you get through this and am sending all my thoughts and love to you and your step-uncle, Alejandro.**

> **ALEXIS: Thank you, babe. That means a lot to me too. When you're ready and if you like, we should meet up! We don't need to force**

anything, but I think testing the waters of where this can go is exciting. Is that something you're open to? Please be honest and trust me, you won't hurt my feelings either way, I promise. Whatever you feel most comfortable with, we'll do! :)

I bite my lip and grin.

PAISLEY: Oh my God, how are you so sweet?!

ALEXIS: Oh, girl, you haven't seen me at my worst... ;)

PAISLEY: HAHA! Same, same. I would really love to meet up and see where this goes too! I'm currently in Santa Rosa with my boyfriend's family, but would love to organize something when I get back before I move to Seattle for college at the end of the month! I'll be in Seattle from the first weekend of August as I'm going to be spending some time there with Saint before college begins. Does that work for you?

ALEXIS: That works perfect! I look forward to it too. Text me when you're back in Sacramento then and we'll take it from there! Aww, that's so nice that you're spending time with Saint's family! I'm sure you're both enjoying that! ;) What are your plans tonight?

PAISLEY: Can't wait! Tonight is date night, so I'm getting ready for that... and by getting ready I mean staring at all of my options laid out on the bed. So indecisive.

ALEXIS: Oooo, date night!! Send me a few options of the dresses. More than happy to help!

Then another message comes in from her.

ALEXIS: Promise I won't add those pictures to my dating profile... not that I have one. Alejandro would kill me if I did... not that I wouldn't go behind his back... ;)

I burst out in laughter and type back.

PAISLEY: LOL. I love it. Here are the options.

I stand back and take a photo of the four dresses on the bed and send them through. She replies almost instantly. As new as this friendship is with Alexis... it feels so natural.

ALEXIS: The sexy red one! Go with that!

PAISLEY: You're amazing, thank you, lovely!

ALEXIS: Anytime, okay, now I'm going to let you go so you can get ready, but I can't wait to talk once you're back in Sacramento. Have a beautiful night and don't do anything I wouldn't do... Not that you'd know that, but you'll uncover that soon enough ;)

PAISLEY: Haha! I honestly am looking forward to uncovering it all. Talk soon and have a nice night, Alexis!

ALEXIS: Will do, and, Paisley?

PAISLEY: Mhmmm?

ALEXIS: I really feel like this could be the start of something beautiful! Xx

I smile with glassy eyes.

PAISLEY: You and me both! x

I'm quick to slip on the skintight red midi dress, feeling so complete inside that I texted with her. It's a satin delight with a daring thigh-high slit on both sides of my hips. Considering I didn't bring any heels, Saint's mom lent me a pair of classy nude heels earlier today *and they're stunning!*

For the first time in forever, I dive into my makeup bag and go for a striking look. Smokey eyes. A little blush and bronzer. Bold red lips. *Perfect.* Stepping back from the wall mirror to take a good look at myself, I rub my lips and grin at the woman in the mirror. *There she is, girl!*

Repacking all my other clothes, I sling my cream purse over my shoulder and it's just after 6:00 p.m. when I step out of the guest bedroom.

Saint's jaw drops the second I step into the mid-century living room and those ocean eyes meet mine and warm to so much passion. He looks so beautiful... so dreamy and Italian. Sexy slicked-back hair. Crisp white dress shirt with a few buttons undone and sleeves rolled up, exposing his gorgeous tattoos and lightly tanned skin. Sleek black slacks. Black paisley leather belt. Leather derby shoes. *I didn't even know he packed all of these!*

"Paisley... *Fuck*," Saint murmurs, striding up to me with the most beautiful dimpled smile. "You look so beautiful! *Dio*, I can't take my eyes off you…"

"So don't."

His eyes darken in desire. "You know I won't, *wildflower*."

Saint threads his fingers through mine and pulls me close. A satisfied moan escapes him as his hands roam down my hips and rush underneath the slits of my dress. I giggle as he squeezes my bare ass exposed by my lacy G-string.

"Dear God, Paisley, you're going to kill me." Smirking, his luxurious cologne consumes me whole as he brushes his lips against my ear and he sexily growls, "It's a good thing I booked a hotel for us later tonight, because I plan to fuck you so hard with this hot dress still on and panties to the side. Want to fuck you in this dress all night long, babydoll."

Ohmygod. Yes, please!

I want nothing more than to have him all to myself.

Grinning, I lock my ankles together and feel my sex throb in anticipation. "Mmhmmm."

"You want that, *wildflower?*" Saint whispers. "Want me to fuck you like a goddamn queen?"

"God, yes."

"*Guarda quanto sei bella.*" Saint lowers his lips down to my neck and tingles rush to where I need him the most with erotic kisses. I lose it when his hot tongue swirls over my sweet spot with every nibble, and I softly moan out his name, complete pleasure consuming every inch of me. His hands don't stop molding my peachy ass, and it turns me on so much.

Grinning, I can't help but shut my eyes in bliss and giggle as he has me completely losing my mind. My hands circle his shoulders, caressing his hair and tugging onto the ends as he devours my neck with so much need it's almost overpowering.

He's everything I need…

"Holy snakes!"

My eyes snap open and I gasp loudly at what I see in front of me, instantly pushing Saint away. His nonna has her eyes covered in the hallway of the living room, while his mother smirks at us as if she knows something I don't.

Tugging me to his side, Saint awkwardly chuckles and gestures toward the front door. "We're, uh… We're going to head out. See you both tomorrow. Love you, Ma and Nonna."

"Bye Cecilia and Nonna." I grin, feeling my cheeks so flustered and hot.

"Ciaooo!" his nonna says, running out of the living room while his mother, Cecilia, starts laughing.

"Don't worry, I'll pretend I didn't just see any of that." Her eyes flicker to her son and happiness floods them. "Take care of her, my boy."

Saint gets his stunning black blazer from over the couch and once he slides it on, slips his hand in mine. "Always will."

Saint and I are out of the house in seconds and we burst out laughing as we walk toward his Harley in the driveway. "I swear to God you're such trouble, Mr. Lisconti. Such trouble!"

Smoldering, he shoots me a wink. "But your kind of trouble, babydoll."

On the Harley trip to the secret location, Saint's hand occasionally returns to my thigh as we ride off into the pink and orange sunset. During the ride, I tell Saint of my texts with Alexis and it's just so comforting how happy he is for me. For *us*.

I'm thrilled about everything that tonight brings. We've had heaps of date nights during these six weeks and quite honestly, it's as if we're skipping all the steps considering we already live together and are about to move to Seattle, but I love it this way…

Love what it means.

Love that we're rewriting our own rules.

My jaw drops when after what feels like ten minutes Saint slows in front of a field of endless amounts of sunflowers. *Wow.* The sight of the field of bright yellow flowers is beyond breathtaking and I feel my heart beat out of my chest at all the beauty. The way the sun is glowing and stunning pinkish-orange skies paint the skies, the sunflowers are so vivid in their pigmentation, their holistic smell sending me to heaven.

"Wow." I gasp as Saint helps me dismount the Harley and we take off our helmets and he fixes them on his motorbike. "This is so beautiful, Santo! I can't believe we're freaking here!"

"You like it, *wildflower?*"

I grin and jump into his arms. "I *love* it! Thank you so much for remembering how much I love sunflower fields. I love you!"

Saint pecks my lips and grins back. "Love you more. Anything for you. Come on, let's go!"

The grins don't wipe off our faces as he leads me through the white fence and into the field. I literally lose my breath as we finally get to the middle of the tall sunflower field where there is a big, spacious oval-shaped section with no sunflowers. Instead, blue lily petals are scattered and lead to a romantic transparent canopy with bright fairy lights wrapped around the ceiling. A sleek table and two chairs are set up underneath it with romantic candles and two stainless steel cloche food covers.

This is so incredible!

But it doesn't stop there. Two cellists sit beside the canopy and begin playing to such an incredible instrumental tune that I quickly recognize as "With Or Without You" by U2. It's so meaningful and romantic that my eyes tear up... I can't believe Santo organized all of this. It's beyond my wildest dreams and my heart clenches in complete awe of everything in front of me.

This means everything to me.

Everything.

"Santo! This is so stunni—" The words slip from my mouth when I turn around and find Saint kneeling down on one knee in front of me. He's grinning so warmly, dimples so deep and in full sight as he holds a black velvet ring box in his hand and glances up at me with such desire sparkling in his gaze, the same desire I feel too.

It brings even more tears to my eyes.

Oh my gosh!

My heart is beating so wildly, I can hear it everywhere.

"Santo!" I gasp, placing a hand over my mouth in complete shock. "Oh my God!"

"*Wildflower…*" Saint chuckles, and I can hear he's just as nervously excited as I am in this moment. "I wrote a little something for you, a little piece of poetry you inspired. Of course it's not as good as yours, but it's everything I'm feeling right now. Everything I've been feeling for a long while, so…" Taking my right hand in his, Saint softly kisses my skin and sparks grow at his touch. "Can I read it to you, babydoll?"

"Of course." I grin, laughing to ease the bundle of nerves and set free the butterflies in my stomach all across my body, the same butterflies that are always there whenever I'm with my blue-eyed boy. Especially now surrounded in a field of sunflowers with his touch and the two cello players continuing to make this moment even more special. "I can't believe this."

Swallowing thickly, I can't get over the way Saint is looking at me with so much sincerity… like I'm his entire world. Ironic, because that's exactly how I feel. He's my everything. He's my everything and more.

"There were pieces of me I held onto. Hoping. Praying. Pleading, they would never come undone and ache. But they did. For you they bloomed. I find you in places only we know, because you once told me it's all it takes. In flowers. In poetry. In the ocean waves. In anything and everything that screams your name. When the water surrounds our bodies… when the sunset kisses our skin, all I want to do is thank you for loving me for all that I am, all that I'll be, and all that I have been." Saint sharply inhales and opens the ring box. "Baby, I'm so in love with us, so in love with all that we are. Some say it's wrong, but now I know, two hearts can merge into one."

My eyes flicker down at the gorgeous flower-inspired marquise cut diamond ring that glimmers brighter against the glowing sunset. *It's so beautiful… so me.* I've never seen anything like it!

The romantic tune of the cellos in the background... the poetry Saint speaks... *him*... it's all so perfect.

Oh my gosh. Wow!

"Spending the rest of my life with you is all I want to do," Saint murmurs, emotion heavy in his voice. "And I'll never stop loving you. Loving this new life you gave me. Loving all the different oceans of us..." My vision blurs as those beautiful ocean-blues meet mine and my heart skips a beat at his next words, "So, my *wildflower*... Will you dive into forever with me and marry me?"

I grin, nodding through happy tears. "Yes! Yes, I'll marry you, Santo!"

Grinning too, Saint frantically slips the stunning diamond ring on my left finger, and it fits me so perfectly. "I feel like the luckiest man in the world!"

The second Saint stands up, I practically jump into his arms and we're laughing in the middle of tears as I wrap my legs around his waist, and he spins us around in endless circles. When I lace my arms around his neck, nothing feels better than feeling Saint's warm lips on mine. We kiss so passionate, so wild, so breathless and it's such a beautiful sensation knowing he'll be mine forever.

There's no doubt Saint's changed me for the better in so many ways, but right now as we pull away from the kiss... *Tonight*... He's changed me in the best kind of way.

I'm *his*.

Unconditionally his.

I love how he wraps his arms around me from behind and lowers his chin to rest on my shoulder as we watch the cellists continue to play the heart of the beautiful instrumental U2 tune. It's beyond touching because each string is so passionately tender, and my tears continue to fall as Saint and I begin swaying from side to side and he softly begins singing the song to me. The lyrics are everything we are. It's such a beautiful rendition, so sensually slow and with his voice alongside the cellos... Purely *magical*.

"My fiancée..." Saint grins beautifully as he spins me around and his mesmerizing ocean blues meet mine again, filled with nothing but true love. "*Ti amo*," he breathes. "*Ti amerò per sempre, tesoro mio*. I love you. I'll love you forever, *tesoro mio*."

"*Ti amo*," I whisper back, meaning every single word. "Thank you for showing me life, Santo."

"Thank you for being in it, *wildflower*."

And just like that, I realize that sometimes it isn't about needing to be the boldest flower, sometimes it's just about finding the right person who sees you as their *wildflower*. Who never lets it go. Who allows it to live on forever...

Through every dark storm.

Through every bright spring.

Through every steady heartbeat.

Until it harmonizes to the rhythm of their own, floats across the deepest waters, and blooms wildly to fill the heart of two. Because that's exactly what happened to Santo and me.

My forever boy.

We love...

We're found...

We'll drown forever...

In all these oceans of us.

Epilogue

Saint

Four Years Later…
AUGUST 2021

My sweet girl's been waiting for the Tooth Fairy to come visit for the past six weeks. Ever since I told her that epic tale during bedtime and said the Fairy wears a frilly pink gown, glittery crown, and magical wand, my little girl's been trying to wiggle out her perfectly firm teeth, eats a bunch of raw carrots, and sleeps with her cute little hands under her pillow just so she can *'know when the Fairy is coming'*…

My sweet girl definitely got the attitude from her daddy.

Paisley and I have explained to our sweet girl numerous times that at three years old she's still a little too young to worry about that Fairy, but Lily Lisconti isn't taking in. She's adamant. Fierce. Unstoppable. *Just like her mommy and daddy.* Lily used to wake up sobbing that the Fairy didn't come… *so* my beautiful wife and I came up with an idea. Once every two weeks we secretly put a one-dollar bill under our daughter's pillow and tell her the Fairy must have heard her cries and felt bad, so she came as a way of saying she'll officially be visiting when Lily's older, but for now the one-dollar bills are just a lead-up.

There's nothing that makes me happier than seeing the bright grin on Lily's face whenever she wakes up early and skips to our bed with a one-dollar bill in hand. *Nothing.*

When my family's happy, *I'm* happy. And we've been happy. *Beyond happy.*

I love being the husband of the most beautiful woman in the entire world, Paisley.

Love being the daddy to our two children, Lily and a little boy, Harley, who's four months.

Love being the creator of my charity, Silent Hearts, and the owner of a shelter so close to my heart that assists sufferers of mental health, homelessness, and domestic violence.

Paisley and I got married four months after we moved to Seattle four years ago. It didn't matter that she was only eighteen. All she wanted was for us to officially be each other's worlds and fuck, how much I wanted that too. Lily came along a year later, while we welcomed Harley into our lives just over four months ago now. Life couldn't be any better for us right now.

It's been a dream.

It's crazy how much our lives have changed in four years, but it's been the best four years of my life. *Our lives.* The best years because *she* is in it.

In these past years, Paisley and I have become so close to her half-sister, Alexis, and Alexis's step-uncle, Alejandro. The distance between California and Washington State did nothing to our strong bond. We still meet up regularly and Paisley and Alexis chat daily, whether it be a text, phone call, or FaceTime video call. I love that even though we went through hell and back for years, Paisley gained a half-sister that she cherishes so much. Alexis is the missing piece. It brings me peace to see the girl I knew at three years old doesn't hold any grudges toward me and understands everything that happened with her mom, Lea. Alexis doesn't hold any resentment toward me, and that's all I've ever wanted—that giraffe obsessed little girl to still be there.

In these past years and with the help of therapy on both of our behalves, Paisley and I have also made peace with Lea's actions. It's finally closure. That chapter of our lives is over now. *Forever.* It's all in the past now, and damn how much I'm loving our future after the ruthless storm.

Paisley and Maralyn still speak almost every day, and I've just recently re-connected with Nico and Leo. It took a while and I was beginning to not give a shit about them as I've got a family I love, protect, and provide for now, but then they apologized, and I caved. They both said they overstepped and should have never taken it all so personally, because hurting them was never my intention. I appreciated it. With us being states away, I don't see them as much as before, but we always try to keep in touch.

I'm just glad I have my boys back.

As for Paisley's father, Alaric… we invited him to our wedding four years ago, but he never replied to the RSVP, and we didn't push it. That's when the trying stopped on our end. He's missed huge milestones in his daughter's life in these past years. Paisley beginning college, opening the wellness shelter, our marriage, our first little girl, birthdays, Paisley graduating college, our little boy, my fortieth earlier, Paisley starting her dream job at Notti Designs as a landscape architect a month ago.

A part of me still feels sadness on Paisley's behalf because she deserved more, but two weeks ago when we were in Sacramento for the weekend to visit Alexis and Alejandro, the wildest thing happened. We were at a park having a picnic, when a familiar man jogged by with a red-haired woman who seemed in her early forties.

Alaric.

It was *Alaric.*

The moment our eyes met, my breath halted in my throat. Then his eyes moved to Paisley, and he stopped jogging. The second he scanned our little kids his eyes started getting all glassy. Paisley stood up and within seconds they were running to each other and holding on to each other for dear life. It brought fuckin' tears to my eyes because I love seeing my *wildflower* happy, and I knew the distance with her father was really hurting her. It wasn't long before Alaric apologized for all the shit he caused us. He said he never reached out because he was ashamed of the way he acted and even apologized to me too. I think it made him smile knowing I'm taking care of his girl so well.

Alaric couldn't believe we had two little children—Lily and Harley—and said they looked like the perfect combination of us. I couldn't agree more. They're so beautifully cute. Now, Paisley and her father have been talking. It warms my soul because I know what it feels like to be beaten down, and fuck, how good it is to thrive now. There isn't a part of me that isn't thrilled that their relationship is getting better, as is mine with Alaric too. My former best friend and I don't talk daily like we used to, but something is better than nothing, I guess.

He's going to get remarried soon and asked me to be the best man and his fiancée asked Paisley to be one of the bridesmaids. We said yes because life isn't about holding grudges, it's about forgiveness, and I so desperately want to repatch what we had. I may not be able to get back my friendship with Nico and Leo, but Alaric, Alaric is the most important one because he's Paisley's father and my sweet girl and little boy's grandfather. *They deserve the best family in the universe.*

Now, as the glorious sun begins to rise outside the bedroom window, I smile to myself as I roll over in the bed, snuggling into Paisley. This is how I usually wake up, counting my blessings. Thanking God. Appreciating life. Mornings also usually consist of Lily sneaking into our bed as the sun comes up. It always happens around this time, and I can't help but chuckle every time she climbs into the bed and peacefully lies between Paisley and me.

I love Lily with all my heart, *but God, she's the biggest cockblocker to ever exist.*

It's rendered Paisley and me to devour each other late at night instead, whenever the kids are distracted with something, or date night when my cousin, Enrico, takes care of the kids for us. Nevertheless, Paisley and I can't go without having sex a few times a day. I just adore Paisley too much to not make love to her like she deserves.

Enrico recently returned to Seattle and it's so nice having him living in the same city as me for the first time since we were kids. It feels like the good old times again. Plus, I love that Lily and Harley have a cousin—Enrico's little son, Hugo, to play with.

I love seeing Paisley as a mom. Love how graceful and self-less she is. Always putting them first and making sure our kids are okay. Some of my favorite nights are when I'm working late doing some admin work at home and Paisley helps Lily fall asleep after a nightmare. Moments later when I step into Lily's bedroom to help, I always find Paisley dozed off in Lily's bed and still holding our daughter's hand; who's also fast asleep. It happens more times than I can count and it's the most beautiful snapshot of my beautiful family complete. *A family of my own.* I always find myself smiling at them peacefully sleeping like that, and cross arms and lean against the doorframe and watch on, because it brings so much warmth to my chest and feeds my soul seeing my *wildflower* and sweet little girl like that.

I love kissing Lily's forehead and whispering good night in Italian before carrying Paisley, my forever girl, in my arms and softly bringing her back to our bedroom to sleep. We're often not lying down in the bed for even an hour before Harley cries out, wanting to be fed by his momma.

My *wildflower* works so hard; just graduated college a couple of months ago when Harley was only six weeks old. Paisley's spent the past three months at home since he was born, but one month ago started working as a landscape architect at her dream job—the successful and award-winning architecture and interior design company, Notti Designs, after highly impressing the CEO & founder Giulio Giannotti with her knowledge and integrity.

Paisley even told me that Giulio joked about giving her the job the second she stepped into his office in regard to that hilarious FaceTime call we had with him years ago when he was slightly drunk and *really, really* loving his wife, Valencia, after date night.

Giulio's one of those humble kinds of bosses and allows her to bring Harley along whenever she needs to and even designated a private pump room for her. Her first day a month ago was super hectic for her. I was going to take care of the kids since I didn't need to go to the shelter that day. Paisley was so frazzled and nervous; kissing Lily's and Harley's foreheads a million times, kissing me a billion times, stressing as she rechecked her bag a trillion times to ensure she had everything. Just before she was about to leave for work, she couldn't find the keys to the Range Rover I bought her as a surprise for her twenty-second birthday. My *wildflower* was absolutely losing it. My poor *tesoro*.

She called me crying during her lunch break, saying it was all so overwhelming, how much she missed me and the kids. Then, she told me how during her first meeting with clients they were staring down at her breasts, and it wasn't until she glanced down and realized her nipples were leaking breastmilk through her silk blouse that she grasped she forgot to put on the nursing breast pads she uses to stop any possible leaks because she's breastfeeding Harley.

Thankfully, Enrico was able to swing by our Madison Park house and take care of the kids during a gap in his meetings. I met Paisley in her downtown office and kissed her better, told her how proud I was of her and how capable she is at this job before handing her a new box of nursing breast pads that she can keep in her office in case she forgets again. She couldn't stop grinning with teary eyes after that at how 'sweet' I was. *Anything for my beautiful wife*, I told her because I mean it from the bottom of my heart.

Paisley working at Notti Designs meant all the sleekest designs and gadgets around their offices. My *wildflower* was feeling a lot better after my pep talk and she frosted the glass in her office and I made love to her on her desk, making sure she knew just how much I loved her, how beautiful she is, and told her that whenever she feels frazzled at work again, to remember *this* moment. Ever since that day, she's been killing it at work, just like I always knew she would.

Right now, as I rake my fingers through Paisley's dark wavy hair as she sleeps beside me, I can't help but kiss her forehead. She's such a natural beauty. My hot twenty-two-year-old wife is the best thing that happened to me. My life changed forever the day I stepped on her rare blue tiger lilies. I may not have known it then, but I do now. Paisley made my black and white mind turn to color. Made me turn into a better man. I know perfection isn't real, but I'm trying to be the best husband...

Best father.

Best business owner.

Really trying from the bottom of my heart.

Whenever I'm at work at the shelter and find myself listening to people's heartbreaking stories, I always encourage them to continue the transformation to being their best selves. To never give up. To see that light at the end of the tunnel because as much as they don't believe it's there, I'm living proof that there is that light. And once you see it, fuck how much it shines...

Paisley's my light.

My savior.

My *everything*.

I wouldn't know where I'd be without her. Without our two cute little kids. Without this stunning house overlooking Lake Washington. Life in Seattle was a challenge for both of us to adapt to at first, but a challenge we gladly faced. I could handle the coldness and cloudiness of Seattle. The chilly, colder breeze. The emerald city. And now, we love calling this place home. I also love how Paisley and I still spend some of the summers between Sacramento, Santa Rosa, and Stinson Beach. My mom and nonna are always so thrilled when we visit. I ended up selling my house in Sacramento when we moved to Seattle, but still have the beach house near Stinson Beach. It's our oasis.

"Santo?"

I blink, and Paisley's bright grin is all I see.

"Good morning, *wildflower*," I murmur with a matching grin. *She's mine. Forever.*

"Morning, baby. What were you thinking about?"

I pull Paisley close, wrapping my arms around her warmth. Warmth I'll never get sick of. I glance into her pretty honey browns, adoring the devotion shining in them. "Life. Us. Everything that's happened in these past few years... Past few months. Just in awe of you really."

"Is my blue-eyed boy getting sentimental?" Paisley teases.

"Damn right he is." I wink and brush my lips against hers. "Just so glad you exist, *tesoro*. I love you so much."

"I love you more."

"I love you more *more*."

And then I press my lips on Paisley's and kiss her with everything I have. It's one of those slow kisses, as if I'm making love to her with such sensual passion and affection. She cups my jaw, running her fingers along my short dark beard, and moans against my lips with a smile as our tongues swirl in a dance, and I kiss her even more hungrily with possession as my cock stirs in my boxer briefs. The desire to fuck is so damn high, and I know she feels it too with the way her hand runs down my chest, toned abs, and then teasingly slowing at the band of my boxer briefs. *Mmhmmm, baby.*

I'll never get tired of loving Paisley Lisconti.

Of kissing her soft skin and worshiping every second she chooses to spend alongside me.

Of treating her like a queen 'cause that's exactly what she is to me—the queen of *my* heart.

We pull away, softly panting with bright grins.

Paisley lets out a giggle, smoothing the pad of her fingertips through my full man bun. "Gosh, I love your hair like this so much!"

I smirk. "Is this a '*compliment to the chef*' kind of morning, hmm, babydoll?"

I love how Paisley scrunches up her nose and begins laughing out of control. I can't help but chuckle too, feeling the warmth in my chest only expand across my entire body. Just like it always does whenever I'm with her. *Every day.* Every day I feel this way. It's my remedy. Seeing Paisley laugh is such a damn turn-on. But I'm just in awe of her and grateful. Grateful that this brave, strong woman with the most beautiful honey-brown eyes, light freckles on her cheeks, and most angelic smile is mine.

Always mine.

When we settle down, I take Paisley's left hand and kiss her diamond wedding ring. It's a habit I repeat every morning, thanking God her soul led me to her. Catch myself smiling down at my own wedding band countless times a day. This life with her... it's everything I've ever wanted and more.

"It's Saturday," Paisley says after a few seconds of us softly caressing each other's skin. "Lily has dance in a few hours, so we should get up."

"Five more minutes." I grin, and she dramatically rolls her eyes before kissing me hard, her tongue swiping through my lips. The kiss is so fuckin' electric.

Mid-kiss, I pull the sheets over us, my fingers rushing under her white satin and lace negligee, brushing over the tattoo on her left ribcage. It's a gorgeous flower stem with thorns that leads to four gorgeously shaded roses with a little red in them, one representing each of our family. It was the happiest day of my life when she surprised me with the outline of the tattoo she had drawn up. It's only a small tattoo, but something about my *wildflower* having a tattoo—especially considering it matches the sleeve tattoo I have for her filled with all different types of flowers and things that remind me of us—it makes me feel so special. Like I'm the luckiest man in the entire world.

"FAIRYYYYYY! MOMMY! DADDY! FAIRYYYYYY!"

Lily.

It's Lily.

Paisley and I pull away, and I glance at her with a playful groan as the bright sunlight floods through the white sheets, glowing Paisley's entire face and body... *and goddamn that negligee she has on.* It takes my breath away... *but now I've got to abort mission because I can hear our daughter's frantic footsteps thumping closer and closer to our bedroom suite.* It takes Paisley one good look at my devastated face for her to pull the sheets back down and throw her head into the pillow, laughing at me.

I smirk. "Yeah, keep laughing. You just wait until you're wearing that negligee tonight and what I'm going to do to you, Mrs. Lisconti."

"I look forward to it, Mr. Lisconti." Paisley smirks right back as she reaches toward the end of the bed and picks up her wine red satin nightgown and my silk navy sleep pants. Sitting up in the bed, I grin at the sight of her bent over, that stunning ass of hers aching to be revealed as the negligee rises higher up.

Fuckkk. I can't believe our daughter is cockblocking us AGAIN because of this FAIRY.

I shake my head to myself with a chuckle, crazy to admit I wouldn't want it any other way. Paisley quickly puts on her nightgown and ties the fabric belt around her petite frame. She's quick to throw me my pants and I catch them with one hand, my eyes still on her. It has us sharing a devilish smirk as I slip them on and she rejoins me in the bed, just in time for Lily to bolt through our bedroom door and climb up onto our kind-sized bed.

Our three-year-old daughter is so cute with her wavy dark hair in a high bun to match mine and those bright pink pajamas with llamas all over them. They're obviously her favorite pajamas. Without warning, she begins jumping up and down on the bed with the biggest dimpled grin, her piercing blue eyes meeting ours in excitement as she waves in the air the one-dollar bill that the *apparent Fairy* brought her.

"Look, Mommy! Daddy! I got one dollar! I got one dollar!" Lily squeals. "YAYYYYYY!"

Paisley and I can't stop laughing and grinning with her.

"That's amazing! You're going to fall off the bed, baby. Come here to Daddy."

"Noooo!" Our sweet little girl laughs, jumping higher and higher. "I WANT MOREEEE!"

"Baby, be careful." Paisley giggles as she sits up on the bed beside me. "No boo boos."

Lily continues jumping on our bed with a bright big grin, having the time of her life. My cheeks hurt from smiling so hard. I love seeing my baby girl happy. Lily begins jumping too high, missing our legs for inches and all of a sudden, she bounces a little too much to the right and I can already foresee she's going to fall off the bed when she comes down, so I dart up and out of the bed, catching her in my arms before she hits the floor. *Jesus.* My heart is in my throat. *Thank God, my sweet girl.*

"Oh, Lily, you scared Daddy so much. You should feel my heart." I smile down at her, feeling my heart rate racing out of control at the near miss. *She's going to be trouble when she's older. I just know it.*

Lily presses her adorable little hand to my bare chest, right on the tattoo Paisley wrote her name on four years ago, right under the 'Oceans of Us' poetry piece she wrote me. It's my favorite tattoo and after I surprised Paisley by buying and restoring an original 1940s olive-colored Olivetti typewriter I bought her on our first wedding anniversary, she retyped the poetry piece and blew it up and now we have it framed across from our bed, so we can wake up every morning to the words she wrote about us. I knew Paisley would love the typewriter as I remembered she once mentioned always wanting one. She's been using it religiously for writing poetry ever since while sitting on the porch and overlooking our pier and beautiful Lake Washington.

Still wrapped in my arms, Lily takes one look at me and starts giggling. It turns into squeals as I grin and begin tickling her sides. I playfully put her into bed right between her mama and me as I slip into the bed too and pull the sheets higher. All that's missing is Harley, who's sleeping in the nursery.

Lily's still giggling as she shoves the one-dollar bill in our faces, glancing between us as if it's a tennis match. "Look, Mommy! Look, Daddy! Fairy was here."

"She sure was, dear. And you know why?" Paisley smiles down at our daughter so lovingly.

"Tell me! Tell MEEEEEE!"

"Because you've been such a good girl and have been eating all of your vegetables!"

Lily gasps with a grin. "Tooth Fairy can see me? Like Santa?"

Smirking, I nod and cutely bop her nose. "That's right, sweet girl. That's why it's important you always listen to Mommy and me."

"Not *always*…" Paisley smirks over at me, and I know exactly what she's referring to. Her own father, *Alaric*. We wouldn't be here if we didn't rebel a little.

Touché, baby, touché.

I wink over at Paisley and glance down at Lily. "Mommy didn't mean that. All the time."

"Okayyy!" Lily shuts her eyes with a grin and then opens them up all wide as she starts moving around, dancing while still lying down on the bed between us. "I wanna llama!"

"Oh no, not this again!" Paisley groans with a giggle. "Baby, Daddy hired llamas for your birthday at the farm just a few months ago, remember?"

"Yes, but I want a llama FOREVERRR!"

Paisley smiles over at me and I know exactly what she's thinking… *We both love how her favorite animal has become our daughter's too.*

I press a kiss on Lily's forehead. "One day, baby, one day."

Lily hands the one-dollar bill over to me. "Here, buy with *this*!"

I smirk. "Pretty sure it's going to take more than one dollar, sweet girl."

Lily hums and scrunches her face up cutely as if she's deep in thought before she claps her hands and happily screams, "YOU BUY FOR ME!"

We all burst out in laughter and I agree that one day she'll get a pet llama like she always wanted. We're out of the bed in a few minutes and I join Lily out in our backyard and start playing outside with our adventurous Golden Retriever puppy, while Paisley heads to wake up little Harley in the nursery.

It's a warm sunny morning in Seattle. It's summer and my favorite season. The smile doesn't fall from my lips as I watch Lily happily running around our huge backyard with our puppy, Fruity.

Yes, Fruity...

Fruity Pebbles is one of Lily's favorite cereals, so when we got our puppy only a few weeks ago and allowed Lily to name it, she went for the obvious choice and called it *Fruity*. I'm chuckling just thinking about it because life couldn't be more perfect. I've been through so much shit but am so happy to finally have stability in my life. Stability, happiness, and purpose.

It gives me comfort that my father would be proud. *So proud of me. Of how I've turned my life around... How Paisley turned it around with me.*

I love our yard. Part of it overlooks Lake Washington and a private pier that leads to the stunning ocean water glistening in the sunshine every day and twinkling in stars every night. On the other side of the yard is a well-kept lawn and we have a firepit, swing set, and vegetable garden that the kids help us with (*well*, Harley will when he's older). The entire perimeter of the yard is full of all kinds of vivid flowers such as roses, germaniums, and infamous lilies, as well as lemon trees and fruit trees such as apple, apricot, and pear.

This holistic smell of flowers and sweet fruits makes my heart beat wildly. I love that flowers will forever remind me of Paisley. That now I plant and water them with her. That in the end they were the thing that brought us together. That our children's names—Lily and Harley—are the perfect combination of all that Paisley and I are.

The cute little coos behind me make me take my eyes off Lily and turn around to see my beautiful wife with our four-month-old son, Harley, in her arms and swaying from side to side. Pressed up against her chest, Harley cutely smiles, his adorable face stealing my heart as I rush up to them and press a kiss to his chubby cheeks.

"Ciao, bello." I grin, rubbing a hand on his little back, loving that he's wearing a white baby bodysuit with small black motorcycles and *'Daddy's Harley buddy'* printed all over it.

"Go over to Daddy!" Paisley smiles, handing me our son while blowing raspberries on his stomach that have him belly laughing so sweetly.

I hold Harley close to my bare chest with a hand behind his neck, unable to wipe the grin off my face and the best part is I don't want to. Harley is such a happy baby with my bright blue eyes and his mother's gorgeous nose and mouth. Our children are both such perfect blends of us.

I glance at Paisley in pure awe that all our past challenges of being together have resulted in our beautifully growing family. All the darkness was worth it, because now we're on the other side and our souls will forever be made for each other. We once were two broken souls attempting to fix each other's flaws, and now today, as I stand beside my wife and our children, I finally know we're healed. Our love will never fade because it's written in the stars above.

I'm so grateful *this* is my life.

That *they* are my life. *All mine.*

That nobody can take this away from me. *Ever.*

Paisley Lisconti is my forever girl. She always was and she always will be.

"I'm so proud of you, Pais," I murmur, stepping closer to her with Harley in my arms. "For giving me this entire world and more. For being my *forever girl.*"

Grinning, Paisley parts her lip and is about to say something when a loud squeal followed by loud laughter breaks our train

570 | VANESSA LUISA

of thought and has us glancing around toward the garden. It takes two seconds to observe what's happened before I burst out in laughter, but Paisley, on the other hand... she doesn't see the funny side at all at first.

"Oh, NO! OH MY GOD!" Paisley gasps beside me, brushing her hands through her long waves in pure shock. "NOOOO! MY LILIES!"

While running around and chasing after each other, Lily and our puppy, Fruity, must have crashed, because right now they're both lying right on top of the rare blue tiger lilies, crushing them all underneath them, and Lily can't stop laughing as the puppy licks her face, as if nothing happened.

Paisley simply stands beside me with her jaw dropped and eyes wide, so obviously distraught and in shock at what just happened. *Her lilies... they're crushed. Again!* It's history repeating itself all over again. I try to settle down, but I can't and continue laughing so hard that little Harley glances up at me in my arms and starts laughing and squealing too.

Paisley glances over at me frazzled and all I can do is laugh harder. *This is just too good.*

I shoot her a slow, sexy smirk. "Well, I guess it runs in the family..."

It's all Paisley needs to burst out into laughter with me. We laugh so hard and it's just too funny because there's so much irony in the fact that we met when I trampled all her lilies with my feet, and now years later we're beginning our forever with our daughter crushing lilies *again!*

When the laughter finally eases, Paisley wipes the happy tears from her eyes. "That's such a move *Santo Lisconti's* daughter would do..."

"*Our* daughter, *tesoro*," I say. "*Our* daughter."

Paisley grins. "I still can't believe she's our little girl, and Harley. Can you believe it?"

"Every time I look into your eyes, I believe it, *wildflower.*"

"*Awww*, Santo." She grins, and my entire body melts as we kiss so passionately wild.

It confirms everything I've known to be true. *Life is short.* Ever since the day I fell in love with Paisley, I've learned I need to make the most of life while I still can, when the ones closest to my heart are still on this earth. Because if we don't, we may just miss out on the best thing that could ever happen to us...

Just like Paisley, Lily, Harley, and Fruity are the best things that ever happened to me.

Preview of

Remember I'M YOURS

A PREQUEL TO DIESEL ROSE

Chapter
ONE

Rosalia

I THINK I HAVE A BOY CRUSH. OKAY, LET ME REPHRASE THAT, I *DO* HAVE a boy crush.

One of my favorite things to do at a quarter to midnight whenever I can't sleep is scrapbook. My mom is a hairdresser downtown and always brings home old magazines clients flick through so I can cut out whatever I like. At first, it gave me the heebie-jeebies touching magazines a dozen other women (and possibly men too) had touched, but now I guess I'm over it.

Tonight was supposed to be like any other night. Flip through the magazines, cut out aesthetically pleasing vintage pieces with my pink diamanté scissors, and slap them in my scrapbook. Except, tonight *isn't* like any other night, it's different, because my mom didn't only bring home old editions of *Vogue* and *Harper's Bazaar* in a white plastic bag that's laced with holes. There's also something else.

Rolling Stone magazine.

And the good thing is, it's the latest edition.

May.

She's never brought a *Rolling Stone* magazine home for me before, and I wonder if she accidentally got it from the barber section at her work. I wasn't going to look through it, but I did, and *God,* how grateful I am that I did.

It's the first page I randomly opened on.

Page twelve.

And I haven't dared look away since.

Dark-gray eyes, the lightest shade of onyx stare back at me. They're the kind of eyes that are so cold, they should scare you. Instead, they have a sense of sugary thrill flooding my body. They're devilish. Wolfish. Everything my parents warned me about. *And everything I crave.*

My heart skips a beat because he's the most beautiful man I've seen, in a dark and edgy kind of way. A deadly piercing gaze. Perfectly high cheekbones. Thin full lips that remind me of James Dean's.

Everything about the black-and-white picture of this man leaning against a barbed-wire fence intrigues me. His punk-inspired leather jacket with silvery spikes around his shoulders and safety pins by the edges. The destroyed white tee underneath. His distressed black jeans. Those unlaced black Doc Martens with a single white broken love heart on the side of the left one, almost as if it's been stitched.

It feels like there's a story behind those white Band-Aids wrapped around some of his fingers that he has looped above his head in the wire. I'm fascinated by the ink on his hands, the ones more visible like the skull, serpent, and roman numerals, and I instantly wonder if he has more.

Why is he making my heart go so funny?

I like the way he's looking at the camera with furrowed brows, a mixture between broody and motionless, making it seem like he just doesn't give a damn. Like life has done a number on him.

I stare a little too long at the thin black eyeliner around his eyes. I always thought eyeliner was for girls, but seeing it on him, I know I've been wrong... *wow, it's really hot.*

I brush the pad of my finger over his face, almost intimidated at first, as I wonder if his eyes are really that dark or are instead a dark cocoa brown. Maybe it's just the dark ink of the page tricking me? Maybe.

Beneath his photo, a white cursive font reads:

The true hatesick up-and-coming sinner of Manhattan; Elijah Diesel.

Elijah.

"Elijah," I murmur to myself, wanting to get used to the name on my tongue. "Elijah Diesel."

He seems a few years older than me, okay, *a lot* older. Ten years my senior at the least, and although I so desperately want to read all of the little text surrounding the picture, I kind of want to make my own impression of the guy.

After chewing my bottom lip for the longest time, I cut out his picture, being careful to make it perfect, and stick it on a new page in my scrapbook.

Elijah Diesel

I write in permanent marker as a title on the page, and then I draw four little black hearts.

A little lower down, toward the bottom of my page, I write all my feelings out with my heart beating a million miles per second.

Right now I'm looking at you for the first time, and I think I'm going to get addicted to you. I want to know everything about you, Elijah. Or should I call you Diesel?

Butterflies take over my stomach and I can't help just how deeply my cheeks burn. I roll over on my bed to my back and cover my mouth, softening my giddy giggles while New York's silvery moonlight merges with my warm yellow wall sconces.

"Stop being so foolish, Rosalia Philips," I whisper to myself. "He's just some hot rocker."

But I know he's much more than that.

He's the first person who's managed to make me crack a smile through my midnight blues.

The first man who makes me feel a funny type of way just staring at his picture.

The only one I think I'll get lost in forever, until he's staring right back at me.

Whoa.

I settle down and stare up at my ceiling, a seventeen-year-old girl trying to rebel from the world as she knows it, second by second.

Who are you, Elijah Diesel?

Exactly where can I find you?

And why does my heart beat so crazy for you?

It's been a month, and my mom hasn't brought home the next edition of *Rolling Stone* magazine for me.

I tried buying the latest edition before school this morning, but the damn newsagent had just sold out. I knew a couple more in the area, but I would have been late for the last day of eleventh grade before summer, so I promised myself I'd check out the other newsstands after school.

The anticipation has been killing me all day because as much as I know I can just search up Elijah Diesel on my phone, there's so much more thrill in turning a page and seeing him instead.

It's just after three o'clock when I step into the convenience store by my school.

The older guy behind the counter takes one look at my wavy blonde hair, my cropped white shirt, and pink-and-white plaid skirt and scoffs, "Kids these days."

With a clenched jaw, I ball my fists but continue walking to the section of the store I know all the hotshot magazines are, no matter how deeply the man's words hurt me.

I'm not even the worst of my generation. I swear, I'm not. First, I don't relate to my generation. At all. Second, I've never had a sip of alcohol. Never smoked. Done drugs in the bathroom. Hell, I've never even kissed a guy in my entire life.

I'm just a seventeen-year-old virgin who loves short plaid skirts and knee-high socks. I'm not hurting anybody, so to hell with this guy.

Why don't you fix your flickering lightbulbs, popcorn ceiling, and grossly stained carpet instead, dude?

I almost do a happy dance on the spot when the new edition of *Rolling Stone* stares back at me. It's the last one left. I grin and snatch it from the stand at record speed, then I actually start bouncing.

Yes. Yes. Yes.

Just as I begin flipping through it, wanting to see if I can see a glimpse of Elijah Diesel before I buy it, the man behind the counter clears his throat.

My breath slows and I don't like the glare he shoots my way. "Aye, blondie, this isn't a library. You want to read the magazine, you buy it and you get the hell out of my store."

Rude.

Narrowing my eyes, I slap a twenty-dollar bill on the counter and practically run out of the store, not caring about the change. My mom would kill me if she knew, but once won't make a difference, *right?*

Rushing down the street, I wait until I'm on the next block before I come to a slow by my bus stop. Even though I live in Brooklyn, I go to school in Manhattan. Don't ask me why, but my father—one of the most respected neurosurgeons in the city—wanted it that way. And that way it is.

Leaning against the bus shelter, I couldn't be more ecstatic as I slip my schoolbag between my feet and carefully turn each page of the magazine. New York's slightly warm breeze kisses my skin and blows my waves, giving me hope of a beautiful summer approaching.

But that hope slowly shrivels up when I go through the entire magazine, never seeing a photo of Elijah Diesel once.

My heart drops.

No.

No. No. No.

He has to be in here. *He's got to!*

I go over the magazine a second time, then a third, and by the fourth time I'm groaning. I seriously feel like slamming it right in the trash can, so devastated that I waited an entire month for nothing.

"It can't be." I sigh, shutting my eyes just as the bus pulls up. "How can he not be in it?"

It's just my luck. Something like this was bound to happen to me.

I just wasted twenty dollars. That idiot back in the store will probably wipe his mouth with it after devouring a greasy cheeseburger.

Ickkk.

For me, it isn't just false hope, it's giving in to the fantasy of Elijah Diesel slipping away from my very fingers. I so desperately craved another photo of him to put in my scrapbook. One I can stare at whenever I don't feel all right, just like I did for the past month, but now I feel like a fool for doing so.

You're the foolest of fools, Philips.

And yes, I'm hyperaware 'foolest' isn't even a word, but let's just pretend it is.

I flicker my eyes open, ready to take the bus all the way home with my head hung low, when something stops me. I don't know why, but my breath halts in my throat at the dark Doc Martens somebody stepping off the bus is wearing. I haven't glanced up yet, but those shoes look awfully familiar.

Doc Martens...

Unlaced...

A stitched white broken love heart on the side of the left one...

I swear I've seen them before but where?

Where? Where? Where?

And when it finally hits me, I internally gasp.

The picture! They were in that picture last month.

Wait, that would mean... No, no, it couldn't be. It can't.

As my gaze flickers higher, at the person descending the bus right in front of me, I slow by their studded leather jacket. And the moment those familiar melancholic onyx eyes bore into mine, I forget how to breathe.

Holy sweet Jesus, it's him.

Him.

Elijah Diesel.

And he's even more beautiful in person.

My mouth gets all dry and my hands become so sweaty holding *Rolling Stone* magazine that it slips from my grip. I cringe as it slides across the sidewalk like it's on skates. And I don't know if the timing could be any worse, but just as it slows, Elijah unintentionally stomps his feet right on the magazine.

Oops.

Almost on instinct, he picks up the magazine, stares at the cover, and then his eyes slowly flicker to the gap of sidewalk between us until they meet my pink platform sneakers.

Ever so slowly, his gaze rakes up my body with a sexily clenched jaw, and I'm happy to confirm his eyes are really that dark. It feels like a lifetime passes the way he's checking out my long, lean legs, my short skirt, and cropped white shirt with little floral-patterned peaches, some midriff exposed.

He stays there for a little while, and the longer his hot stare lingers, the more my chest heaves. My breaths are rushed and all frantic-like. I feel my nipples harden in arousal, stabbing through my lacy bra and outlining my shirt.

He does this to me.

He does this *all* to me.

And when those dreamy dark onyx eyes finally meet my face, my knees buckle.

The bus moves off behind him with a hiss, and it feels like we're in a slow-motion movie with the way his dark hair softly blows in the wind, the ends so wavy.

Arching a brow, Elijah gestures toward the magazine he's holding. "I think you dropped something, *Peaches*," he calls out to me, and *dear God*, his voice...

It's the perfect combination of a sexy raspiness and a murmur, as if he can disguise himself in them both, ready to pounce at any minute now.

Striding up to me, he extends the magazine out to me. Our fingers brush when I take it from him, and sizzling electricity shoots down my arm.

Gosh, this guy is a dream.

It feels so weird seeing Elijah up close after spending the past month looking at his picture all alone in my bedroom. *This is so much better.* I can't get over his musky, sandalwood scent with a hint of tobacco. It's a scent I've never smelled so up close before, and instantly I wish I could smell it forever.

Wow. He's so tall and I'm even wearing platform sneakers. He's easily six-two, six-three.

Wait a minute, did he just call me "Peaches?"

I nervously smile, an obvious blush crawling up my cheeks. "Umm, thank you."

Elijah nods, his broody gaze flickering between my eyes and my plump lips, which I can't help but softly bite.

He stares for a second longer, and just as his hot breath hits my lip, he steps back and begins walking away with such a swagger that his leather jacket sways from side to side.

Despite my fingers continuing to fizzle, a hollowness takes over my body and I don't know why. This was it, my chance to tell him whatever, and I just blew it. *Ugh!*

Chewing my lower lip, I watch as Elijah keeps on walking in the opposite direction of the convenience store. He must have lit up a cigarette in the seconds he walked away because now clouds of thick white smoke lace the air around him every so often.

He smokes.

Mama always tells me how bad smoking is. That neither me nor my older sister, Maya, should ever touch a cigarette. For the past years, I've believed her, thought it was such a dirty thing, but knowing *he* smokes changes everything.

He doesn't make it seem dirty as he looks both ways before jogging across the street, Elijah Diesel makes smoking look like it's heaven's cure to all the chaos here on earth. And perhaps it's that reason alone, (or the fact that I'm still astonished that he was right in front of me), but I do the unexpected.

Quickly stuffing the magazine in my schoolbag, I sling the backpack over my shoulder and wait for the lights before running across the Tribeca street.

Even though Elijah's several feet ahead of me, his studded leather jacket is still in view, and I use it as my guide while I weave through people, apologizing and jogging faster until I'm mere inches away.

The damn guy keeps on walking faster, and here I am treading along behind him, not even knowing what I'd say if he turns around. All I do know is that his scent makes me feel like home, and I could get used to the cigarette smoke hitting me from ahead.

"Hey, watch where you're going!" A lady pushing a stroller growls when I almost run into her as I turn a corner five feet behind Elijah.

I turn to her, mortified. "Oh my God, I'm so sorry, please forgive me, I'm just..."

She comes to a halt with a glare. "I don't care what you're '*just*' doing, be careful around corners!"

I feel bad right to my core, but she walks off with her stroller before I can say anything else.

Breathing out a strangled breath, I vow to forget it completely and focus on Elijah, but when I turn back around and there's no sign of him or any leather jacket, I begin to panic.

No. No. No.

I did not just lose him!

Where could he have gone?

He didn't cross the street again and there's no way he could have entered the cafés a little farther down unless he bolted, which is... highly unlikely.

Damn.

I glance around, frustrated with myself this too was all for nothing.

Stuff it, I'm going home.

Spinning on my heels, I'm adamant to call it a day when I unexpectedly slam into a solid chest and tumble back, almost losing my balance.

My schoolbag slips and falls to the ground with a thud.

What the hell...?

The second I crane my head up and glance at my victim, I'm pretty sure I'm about to piss my pants. It's Elijah, and unlike before, there's a deadly look in his steel-black-eyed stare.

"Are you following me?" Elijah growls ever so wickedly, stepping forward until we're only inches apart. "Because if you are, it ain't gonna be good for you, *Peaches*, believe me."

He continues to stare me down, awaiting my response, all while my mouth dries up and I wish I could just disappear. It doesn't matter how badly I've had a crush on him, right now if looks could kill... I'd be gone. Long gone.

Jerk.

I don't like the soullessness in his death glare or the way he clenches his jaw when I part my lips before closing them. I don't know this guy. At all. Which is why I do the only logical thing in my head during this current moment...

I take one last glance at my dark, edgy sinner, and then bolt in the other direction.

I run all the way home, (and yes, through the Brooklyn Bridge too) like I'm some sort of freak. It takes me over an hour, and by the end of it, I'm slow walking like I just won a marathon.

Or just came last.

But I keep on going until I lock myself in my bedroom, panting. And it's only then, as my breaths finally begin to stabilize, that I realize I no longer have my schoolbag. In fact, I don't think I ran home with it at all. It slipped from my shoulder when I slammed into Elijah's chest, and I never picked it up.

Oh. My. God.

He's with it. He has it.

And the worst part of all? I have a keyring on it with all of my information in case of an emergency.

My *name.*

My *number.*

My *home address.*

It's all at his fingertips.

Groaning, I dive onto my bed and bury my face into my silk pillow.

Ohhh no!

I'm so screwed.

Elijah Diesel is going to kill me!

Acknowledgements

I wrote *Oceans of Us* at a time where I lost somebody very close to me. I needed somebody. Somebody to come save me from the rising tides pulling me under. Then he appeared in my mind. A reckless, Italian, gorgeous, tattooed Harley lover... with the toughest exterior and most alpha male ways, but inside had the warmest heart of gold. He just needed somebody to unravel him and chip away the armor protecting his heart too. His name is Saint... Santo Lisconti... The hero of this book who invaded my mind and was there for me when I needed him the most.

Writing Saint's emotional, angsty, and sexy, forbidden love story with Paisley felt like coming back home. I will always be grateful of their raw, deep connection and opposites attract romance because they were with me during a time of grief—continued grief. Saint and Paisley were a fraction of light in the darkness... they still are. They will always be.

The Harley lover and his *wildflower* have a poetic brokenness to them, a brokenness that doesn't heal piece by piece unless they are together. And that's exactly how I felt writing them, and placing them into the world and my heart forever. It's why *Oceans of Us* and all my books, including *Merciful Vows*, will always have a poetic bittersweet melancholy to them, because I write from what's inside my heart... the darkness, the light, the ache, the angst, the emotion, the passion, the depth of both joy and fear. The emotions are embedded into Saint and Paisley and their beautiful forbidden love. These characters poured out of me. Saved me. Held me. Changed me. And I hope you felt it too!

Now, there are so many people I want to thank for all the love and support!

To Mamma, for everything. I couldn't do any of this without

you—my best friend, my greatest inspiration, my biggest cheer-leader. You mean everything and more to me. I love you!

To Nonna and Nonno, for teaching me a love beyond words. I will love you both forever. *Grazie per tutto.*

To Emily A. Lawrence, thank you for being an amazing editor and your beautiful editing/proofing to perfect *Oceans of Us* into the book it is today. I appreciate you very much!

To Gemma, for always being my cheerleader and loving Saint as much as I do! I really adored working with you again and appreciate all you do! Thank you for giving always giving me the kindest love and support. So super grateful to have you in my team!

To Stacey, thank you for the stunning formatting and kindness! I appreciate you and your work so much, and am so grateful of all that you do! Thank you for everything!

To Kim Bailey, for your gorgeous talent and beautiful cover! Couldn't have done this without you. Your kindness, love and support means the world to me. Thank you so very much!

To Tash, thank you for your stunning and breathtaking *Oceans of Us* teasers! I am always in such awe of your designs and appreciate you from the bottom of my heart! Thank you for your kindness, understanding, and always bringing to life such lovely designs.

To Clara, you are one of my biggest inspirations in keeping going. Thank you for always being so supporting and loving of my characters and all the worlds I bring to life! I appreciate your friendship and thank you for all of your gorgeous edits and graphics, but most importantly thank you for your endless love and support. It always touches me from the bottom of my heart. I also promise Enrico's book is coming, and hope you enjoyed the little snippet and taste of him in this book, *Oceans of Us*. It was the least I could do, haha! Love you, girl!

To all my author and blogger friends for always being by my side, my Instagram writing community for continuously showing my work so much love and my wonderful lovelies over in my Reader's Facebook Group: Vanessa Luisa's Lovelies. I love all of you. Thank you for everything! To all my other friends, I wish I could list you all—thank you so very much!

To the beautiful bloggers, ARC readers and PR, thank you. I appreciate you all!

And last but not least, I want to extend a big thank you to all of the readers because without you all this wouldn't be possible. Thank you for stepping into this journey with me.

Vanessa Luisa x

Also by
VANESSA LUISA

The Giannotti World:
An interconnected series of bittersweet romance standalones set in Seattle.

Merciful Vows (#1)

DIESEL ROSE:
The poetically tragic rock star and his muse...

Remember I'm Yours (#0.5)

Diesel Rose (#1)

STANDALONES:

Oceans of Us

Kisses in Heartache

Happy reading!
Vanessa Luisa xo

About the
AUTHOR

Vanessa Luisa is a contemporary romance author. She resides in Melbourne, Australia, with her army of current reads, sassy cat, and Tom Hardy…the latter is purely all in her mind, but shh don't tell her!

She loves writing angsty, emotionally gripping, sexy romance with passionate alphas and strong-willed women. Her love of reading and writing have always been with her, and while she has a background in certified personal styling, nowadays she's turning her dream of being an author into reality.

She adores all things from the Golden Age of Hollywood, Seinfeld and believes tea is a writing essential. When she isn't writing, she's busy running her own business and spending time with loved ones.

Vanessa loves interacting with readers so please feel free to reach out to her via socials, subscribe to her newsletter, and/or contact her at vanessaluisaauthor@gmail.com for any questions or comments.

Connect with

VANESSA LUISA

Join my Facebook Reader's Group:
www.facebook.com/groups/vanessaluisaslovelies

Subscribe to my MAILING LIST/NEWSLETTER to stay
up to date for all new releases, behind the scenes and receive
exclusive bonus material: www.vanessaluisa.com/contact

Instagram: @thevanessaluisa
www.instagram.com/thevanessaluisa

Facebook: www.facebook.com/vanessaluisaauthor/

Twitter: @thevanessaluisa
www.twitter.com/thevanessaluisa

Follow me on Goodreads:
www.goodreads.com/author/show/21142369.Vanessa_Luisa

Follow me on Amazon:
www.amazon.com/Vanessa-Luisa/e/B08W1V47PC

Follow me on Pinterest:
www.pinterest.com.au/thevanessaluisa

Follow me on Spotify:
open.spotify.com/user/itisnessa

Follow me on Bookbub:
www.bookbub.com/authors/vanessa-luisa

Website/Blog: vanessaluisa.com

www.ingramcontent.com/pod-product-compliance
Lightning Source LLC
Chambersburg PA
CBHW070148120726
47909CB00001B/24